DATE DUE	
OCT 3 0 2008		
APR 2 3 2012		
OCT 0 3 2016		
OCT 1 3 2016		
ILL		

WITHDRAWN

BATTLES OF DESTINY COLLECTION

VOL. TWO

BELOVED ENEMY

SHADOWED MEMORIES

AL LACY

Multnomah Publishers

BATTLES OF DESTINY, Volume 2
published by Multnomah Publishers
A division of Random House Inc.

© 2007 byALJO PRODUCTIONS, INC.
International Standard Book Number: 1-59052-946-4

Compilation of:
Beloved Enemy © 1994 by ALJO PRODUCTIONS, INC.
ISBN 0-88070-809-3
Shadowed Memories © 1994 by ALJO PRODUCTIONS, INC.
ISBN 0-88070-657-0

Cover Photography by Steve Gardner, www.shootpw.com

Multnomah is a trademark of Multnomah Publishers,
and is registered in the U.S. Patent and Trademark Office.
The colophon is a trademark of Multnomah Publishers.

Printed in the United States of America

For information:
MULTNOMAH PUBLISHERS
12265 Oracle Boulevard, Suite 200
Colorado Springs, Colorado 80921

07 08 09 10 11 12 13 14 — 10 9 8 7 6 5 4 3 2 1

Novels by Al Lacy

JOURNEYS OF THE STRANGER SERIES:

Legacy
Silent Abduction
Blizzard
Tears of the Sun
Circle of Fire
Quiet Thunder
Snow Ghost

ANGEL OF MERCY SERIES:

A Promise for Breanna
Faithful Heart
Captive Set Free
A Dream Fulfilled
Suffer the Little Children
Whither Thou Goest
Final Justice
Not by Might
Things Not Seen
Far Above Rubies

Novels by Al and JoAnna Lacy

HANNAH OF FORT BRIDGER SERIES:

Under the Distant Sky
Consider the Lilies
No Place for Fear
Pillow of Stone
The Perfect Gift
Touch of Compassion
Beyond the Valley
Damascus Journey

MAIL ORDER BRIDE SERIES:

Secrets of the Heart
A Time to Love
The Tender Flame
Blessed Are the Merciful
Ransom of Love
Until the Daybreak
Sincerely Yours
A Measure of Grace
So Little Time
Let There Be Light

SHADOW OF LIBERTY SERIES:

Let Freedom Ring
The Secret Place
A Prince Among Them
Undying Love

ORPHAN TRAINS SERIES:

The Little Sparrows
All My Tomorrows
Whispers in the Wind

FRONTIER DOCTOR SERIES:

One More Sunrise
Beloved Physician
The Heart Remembers

DREAMS OF GOLD SERIES:

Wings of Riches
The Forbidden Hills
The Golden Stairs

A PLACE TO CALL HOME SERIES:

Cherokee Rose
Bright Are the Stars
The Land of Promise

Book Three

Beloved Enemy

Battle of First Bull Run

To my precious daughters,
Connie and Kelli,
who will find the sweet and tender father-daughter
relationship in this story quite familiar.
I love you both…more than mortal words could ever express.

✳ ✳ ✳

PROLOGUE

In the wake of the Confederate assault against Fort Sumter on April 12, 1861, both the North and the South rushed to prepare for war. When President Abraham Lincoln called for volunteers to put down the "rebellion" on April 15, the act propelled the wavering Southern states of Virginia, North Carolina, and Tennessee into the new Confederacy.

A distinctive self-confidence inspired both sides as their hale and hearty citizens-turned-soldiers began their military training. In the South, the Rebels convinced themselves that the Yankees would never go to war. Having been soundly beaten at Fort Sumter, they would not have the courage for real battle. The Rebels believed that they were physically, mentally, and spiritually superior to the Northerners, and that success in establishing a new and free nation was foreordained for them by God Himself.

Meanwhile, north of the Mason-Dixon line, Yankee soldiers felt a keen resolve to avenge the attack on Fort Sumter, and at the same time an absolute conviction that the Rebels were nothing more than blustering, blundering "sod-buster" soldiers. With one swift campaign the Southern rebellion against the Union would be put down for good.

For fifty years the problems of states' rights and slavery had been fomenting sectional hostility between Northern and Southern states. At long last, the waiting was over. The war had finally come.

Yet the war that began with such impact at Charleston Harbor proceeded only by fits and starts during the weeks that followed. There were a couple of small engagements or skirmishes, mostly of a tentative nature. The first was at Philippi, Virginia (now West Virginia), on June 3, and the second was at Big Bethel, Virginia, on June 10. The first real battle took place at Rich Mountain in western Virginia, also now in West Virginia, on July 11 (see *A Promise Unbroken* from the "Battles of Destiny" series).

The Confederates had been put on the run at Philippi, and had been beaten at Rich Mountain, but having defeated the Yankees at Big Bethel, they were still confident they could drive the Northerners across the Mason-Dixon line for good if they engaged them in a full-scale battle.

The Yankees, however, exultant over their victories at Philippi and Rich Mountain, were gearing up to make a big thrust on the Confederate capital at Richmond, Virginia, and end the whole thing in a hurry. On Sunday, June 30, 1861, the *New York Daily Tribune* came out with bold headlines that screamed:

THE NATION'S WAR CRY!
Forward to Richmond! Forward to Richmond!
The Rebel Congress must not be allowed to meet there
on the 20th of July! BY THAT DATE THE PLACE
MUST BE HELD BY THE NATIONAL ARMY!

In response to this threat, President Jefferson Davis sent twenty thousand Confederate troops to Manassas Junction where the Orange and Alexandria Railroads met. To Davis, this appeared to be the best route for the Federal army to approach Richmond. The Confederates were commanded by their national hero, who had captured Fort Sumter in April. He was Brigadier General Pierre G.T.

Beauregard. The general and his troops were camped along a meandering stream known as Bull Run Creek.

Meanwhile, in Washington, D.C., the Federals made preparations for their Richmond offensive under Major General Irvin McDowell. President Lincoln would give him thirty-five thousand men to do the job. The rest of the Union army would camp around Washington to protect it in case of some sneak attack by the Rebels. Lincoln and McDowell, however, were unknowingly at a disadvantage. When the split came between the North and the South, certain individuals employed in strategic offices in the U.S. capitol building kept their jobs though secretly they were loyal to the South.

These spies became a crack intelligence unit, gathering classified military information that would prove invaluable to the Confederacy. The information was carried to the Confederates in Virginia by a network of young female spies under the direction of widow Rose O'Neal Greenhow, an attractive forty-year-old Washington socialite whose loyalty was with the Confederacy.

From the young women who charmed their way past Union lines on various pretenses for entering Virginia, General Beauregard learned the size of the Union army and on what date the assault was planned. Quickly he dispatched a message to President Jefferson in Richmond and received 12,500 additional troops prior to the Union attack.

Since the Union army had proven itself formidable over their enemies at Rich Mountain, the Northerners had no doubt that the battle at Bull Run Creek would result in victory over the Rebels. Certain that the men-in-blue would quickly vanquish the gray-clad Southerners, several Washington politicians took their families to the hills overlooking Manassas Junction to watch the show. Many other Washingtonians went along, taking their children and carrying picnic baskets. It was to be a day of rejoicing and celebration as General McDowell and his army vanquished what the civilians *and* the military thought was a much smaller army of "blundering plow-boys." The Civil War would be over almost before it got started.

There is nothing in military history quite like the story of the first conflict at Bull Run. It was the battle where some things went wrong for the Rebels and *everything* went wrong for the Yankees. The absolute rout of the Union army by the Southern "plow-boys" jolted Northerners into reality. The Northern dream of a short and glorious end to the war was shattered in one day. After Bull Run, the Federal government and its people knew the Civil War was going to be a long haul.

Here is my version of the Battle of First Bull Run.

The Battle of Bull Run

Map labels:

- CENTREVILLE
- To Washington
- 20 miles
- Union Mills
- Blackburn Ford
- Mitchell's Ford
- McDOWELL
- Bull Run
- BEAUREGARD
- JOHNSTON
- ORANGE & ALEXANDRIA R.R.
- MANASSAS JUNCTION
- Matthew's Hill
- Henry House Hill
- SUDLEY SPRINGS
- UNFINISHED RAILROAD
- WARRENTON TURNPIKE
- MANASSAS GAP R.R.

Scale:
0 ... 1 Mile

Legend:
- ▬▬▶ Union movements
- ▷ Union retreat
- ▬▬▶ Confederate movements
- ▷ Confederate retreat
- ▒ Confederate concentrations

ONE

A cool and quiet resolve filled him as he descended the stairs of Springfield's Illinois Hotel, shouldering into his overcoat. Feeling the weight of the two revolvers in his shoulder holsters, he approached the desk, hat-in-hand.

The slender, middle-aged clerk looked down at the small uniformed man, smiled and said, "Good morning, Colonel."

Laying his hat on the counter and pulling his wallet from his hip pocket, Colonel Elmer Ellsworth smiled in return. "Good morning."

"So this is the day, eh?" remarked the clerk.

Ellsworth's dark eyes ran to the calendar that hung on the wall behind the desk. Bold letters displayed the date: February 11, 1861.

Nodding, he said, "This is the day. If you'll tally up my bill, I'll be on my way."

"There's nothing to tally, Colonel."

"Pardon me?"

His smile broadening, the clerk replied, "You met our manager, Mr. Spalding, last week, I believe."

"Yes. Very cordial man, I might say."

"Well, Mr. Spalding left Springfield for Chicago on business yesterday, but before he left, he told me that your bill was on the house. There'll be no charge."

"But I've been here for nearly two weeks. It really isn't right that I should—"

"Mr. Spalding said to tell you that what you're doing to protect Mr. Lincoln is pay enough to more than cover your bill, Colonel. We love Congressman Lincoln—or I should say *President-elect* Lincoln. With all the threats that have been voiced against him, we are most grateful that he has someone like you looking out for him."

"I appreciate that, sir," smiled Ellsworth. "I assure you, and you can assure Mr. Spalding, that I am determined to get Mr. Lincoln to Washington safely. I've hired Allan Pinkerton and a host of his detectives to provide additional protection along the way, and I've laid out a plan in coalition with General Winfield Scott for military protection in addition to the Pinkerton men on Inauguration Day. We are not taking the Secessionists' threats of assassination lightly."

"I'm glad," nodded the clerk. "I understand, though, from what I've read in the newspapers, that Mr. Lincoln has not taken the threats seriously. Is this true?"

"I'm afraid so."

"Has he approved of all this protection you are providing?"

"He balked when I first told him what I had in mind, but Mrs. Lincoln put the pressure on him. That's all it took. When he saw the tears in her eyes, he gave in."

"God bless Mrs. Lincoln," said the clerk.

Ellsworth returned his wallet to its place and picked up his hat. "You be sure to thank Mr. Spalding for me."

"I will do that, Colonel. God speed. We need Mr. Lincoln in the White House to pull this nation together."

"Yes, we do," agreed Ellsworth. "I believe when the Secessionists hear his Inauguration Address and understand his intentions for this country's future, they just might take another look at the situation."

"I certainly hope so," said the clerk.

"And even if they don't, Mr. Lincoln is the man to lead us if civil war comes."

The clerk shook his head sadly. "Oh, I hope that doesn't happen, Colonel. I hope that doesn't happen."

"So do I. But if it does, I'm glad Mr. Lincoln will be at the helm."

Donning his hat, Ellsworth nodded toward the clerk and headed for the door. When he stepped outside, the cold wind knifed through his coat all the way to his bones. He pulled up his collar and walked toward the carriage that awaited him.

It was dawn, but the heavy gray clouds that covered the sky allowed little light. Snow was falling and the driving wind gusted it along the street. Bending his head against the wind, Ellsworth looked up at the driver, wrapped in a blanket, and asked, "You haven't been waiting long, have you, Charles?"

"No, sir. Just a few minutes."

"I assume the bell boy brought my luggage to you."

"Yes, sir. You'll find it inside."

Climbing in behind the driver's seat, Ellsworth said, "Let's go. I have to have the Lincolns at the depot by seven thirty."

As the carriage pulled away from the hotel and headed down the snow-covered street, Ellsworth brushed snow from his hat and coat and settled back for the ride across the city to the Lincoln home.

Colonel Elmer Ellsworth, who stood barely over five-feet-five and weighed 135 pounds, had earned his rank two years previously at the unheard-of age of twenty-two. His name was a synonym for patriotism to millions of Northerners. In a time when virtually every town in the northeast sponsored its own volunteer militia, the diminutive colonel was America's foremost parade-ground soldier and, in the popular imagination, the army's most promising military talent.

Stationed in Utica, New York, Ellsworth gained popularity as commander of the U.S. Zouave Cadets, whom he had transformed from a lackadaisical group of Northern soldiers into the national-champion drill team. He modeled his unit after the French Zouaves of Crimean War fame, dressing his men in bright-colored baggy-trousered uniforms. He developed his own variations of the Zouave drill, featuring hundreds of maneuvers with musket and bayonet.

In the summer of 1860—with the threat of civil war in the air—Ellsworth toured twenty cities in the northeast, challenging men to sign up in the U.S. army. He became a celebrity overnight. Newspaper and magazine writers lionized him, women idolized him, and politicians sought his friendship.

Ellsworth had followed Abe Lincoln's political career from a distance and became a great admirer. It was while demonstrating his drill team at Springfield in June of 1860 that they met. Lincoln took an instant liking to the brilliant young colonel and invited him to his home. Mrs. Lincoln and their two sons, Willie and Tad—ten and eight at that time—also were drawn to Ellsworth's warm and bright personality. When summer was over and the drilling demonstrations ceased, the youthful Zouave leader was invited back to the Lincoln home.

He returned on several occasions and was always welcomed, especially by the Lincoln boys because he would never fail to play "war" with them. Ellsworth was so close to Willie and Tad that he caught the measles from them. He was especially drawn to bright-eyed Tad, whom he called, "Mr. Personality."

Because of his love for Abraham Lincoln, Ellsworth campaigned for him in the 1860 election. Lincoln acknowledged that the "little colonel" had a great deal to do with his winning the election.

When the president-elect gave in to Ellsworth's protection plan, the young colonel also announced that he would be Lincoln's personal bodyguard on the trip from Springfield to Washington. Knowing that argument would be useless, Lincoln had quietly accepted.

The icy wind had eased some as the carriage pulled up in front of the huge two-story house, but snow was still falling. Two larger carriages were there, which would carry the six Pinkerton men and the Lincoln family's luggage to the depot.

It was a comfort to Ellsworth to see the grim-faced detectives huddled on the front porch. Heads turtled into their coat collars, they nodded at the young colonel as he mounted the snow-crusted steps. Even as Ellsworth, each man wore two revolvers in shoulder holsters.

"Good morning, gentlemen," Ellsworth said. "Are they about ready?"

"Yes, sir," answered the detective in charge. "Miss Winters just stuck her head out to say that it would be about ten minutes."

Before Ellsworth could knock, the door came open and a happy, childish voice exclaimed, "Uncle Elmer!"

"Hello, Tad!" laughed Ellsworth as the boy wrapped his arms around his neck.

Moving inside with the nine-year-old in his arms, Ellsworth closed the door just in time to brace himself for eleven-year-old Willie, who dashed up and hugged him.

Mary Todd Lincoln entered the vestibule, smiled and said, "Elmer, those boys will rub the hide off you."

The small man laughed. "Can't happen, ma'am. I'm a tough-hided Zouave, remember?"

Mrs. Lincoln laughed also, then said, "Boys, get your coats on."

Letting go of their adopted uncle, Willie and Tad hurried to a nearby closet.

The boys' governess, Patricia Winters, appeared at the top of the staircase, carrying her coat and hat. At twenty-two, Patricia was yet unattached. She liked the handsome colonel, but because she stood an inch taller, had never shown anything more than friendship. Leaning against the railing, she smiled, "Good morning, Colonel."

"And good morning to you," Ellsworth responded, sweeping off his hat and making a bow.

"Mrs. Lincoln, is there anything up here you were planning to take along?" Patricia asked.

Smiling up at the governess, Mary said, "No, honey. Everything I wanted to take is already in the suitcases and trunks."

"How about our toys?" Tad butted in while slipping into his coat.

"They're all packed," replied Mary.

"Don't worry about that, Tad," spoke up Ellsworth. "I brought something that'll keep you boys busy on the train."

"What is it?" Tad asked, eyes wide.

"You'll see," chuckled the colonel.

At the same time Patricia reached the bottom of the staircase, the president-elect appeared, carrying a valise, and started down the stairs.

"Good morning, sir," said Ellsworth.

A smile broke on Lincoln's craggy face. "Good morning, Elmer. I saw from my window that you've got your army here."

"That's right, sir. Can't be too careful with all the threats that have been made."

"Just political claptrap, my boy."

Lincoln had a warmth about him that made it a pleasure to be in his presence. His dark eyes glowed and sparkled, and though he was anything but handsome, the fire of his genius played on every feature. He had a keen sense of humor and a humble sincerity about him, yet he was obviously a man of rare power and magnetic influence. He was a man of deep moral convictions and possessed the backbone to stick by them. He had a deep resonant voice and eloquent command of the English language. His speech was edged with a slight Kentucky-Southern accent, and whether hearing him in personal conversation or from a speaker's platform, people found him captivating.

Ellsworth made no reply to Lincoln's "political claptrap" comment. They had been over the subject many times. Elmer was just glad Mrs. Lincoln had won out.

As the tall Kentuckian was putting on his overcoat and top hat, he said, "Patricia, I assume all the luggage is in the carriages."

"Yes, sir," replied the governess, tying a scarf around Tad's neck. "Everything is ready."

Mary had her hat on and her husband helped her into her coat. Bending down, he kissed her cheek and said, "Well, Mrs. Lincoln, I guess we're ready to go."

Mary ran her gaze over the house and, fighting tears, replied, "Yes, Mr. Lincoln, I guess we are."

Leaving her Springfield, Illinois, house was not easy for Mary Lincoln. She was a sentimental person and had a close attachment to the place. Her husband had hired a caretaker to watch over their home until the Lincoln family returned, whenever that might be. Mary was proud of her husband and looked forward to living in the White House. But she knew her stay there would not be permanent; she would keep a close attachment to her home in Springfield.

Patricia placed stockingcaps on both boys and pulled them down over their ears. Elmer helped her into her coat.

Tad moved close and said, "You got *two* guns on, don't you, Uncle Elmer. I felt 'em when we hugged."

"Yes, I do. I'm making sure your daddy gets to Washington safely."

When they stepped out onto the porch, both boys eyed the Pinkerton detectives. It was impetuous Tad who looked them over and said, "How many guns you guys carryin? Uncle Elmer's got two under his coat!"

"Tad!" came his father's sharp voice. "That's enough."

The boy knew when his father spoke, he was to obey. He looked up at Ellsworth and asked, "Can Willie and me ride with you, Uncle Elmer?"

"That's the way I planned it," grinned the colonel. "You and Willie head for that smaller carriage."

Snow was still falling as the train chugged out of Springfield at eight o'clock. Lincoln's private coach was furnished with overstuffed chairs and sofas, leaving an open area in the center. The six Pinkerton men placed themselves strategically with two by the doors at each end, and a man at the windows midway on both sides. When porters brought breakfast trays, they were not allowed inside. Pinkerton agents took the trays at the door.

When breakfast was over and the trays and dishes were stacked on a counter in one corner, Tad said to Ellsworth, "Uncle Elmer, you said you brought something with you to keep me and Willie busy on the train. It must be somethin' to play with. Can we see it, now?"

"Tad," came the level voice of the governess, who sat next to Ellsworth on a sofa. "It's *Willie* and *me*."

"I know," he sighed. "I jus' forgot. But I said it right on the porch this morning when I asked Uncle Elmer if Willie and me could ride with him in the carriage."

The Lincolns were sitting together on another sofa, looking on with pleasure. They appreciated the effort Patricia took to teach the boys correct English.

"Willie and *I*," said Patricia, trying to look stern.

"Huh?" said Tad, releasing an infectious smile. "*You* didn't ride with Uncle Elmer. Willie and *I* did!"

Patricia could hold it no longer. She broke into a laugh and said, "You little scamp! You know how to say it. You're just giving me a hard time, aren't you?"

"Me?" said Tad innocently, pointing to his chest.

The governess laughed again, left her seat, and threw her arms around the boy. While Tad hugged her back, he said, "I love you, Miss Patricia."

"I love you, too, you little scamp."

A Pinkerton agent seated at a window grinned at the Lincolns and said, "Quite a charmer, isn't he?"

The president-elect chuckled, rubbed his stubbled chin, and said, "Yes, he is. He could charm his way into Buckingham Palace and talk Queen Victoria out of her crown. He's especially successful with the ladies."

"It's because he's such a deceiver," spoke up Willie, who stood nearby. "Mom let's him get away with all kinds of things, and so does Miss Patricia."

"No, sir!" retorted Tad defensively. "I ain't no deceiver!"

"Tad!" cut in Patricia. "*Ain't* isn't in the dictionary."

"It will be when I write one."

"It'll be *dumb* if you write one," said Willie.

"Oh, yeah?" snapped the younger brother. "Well, if you wrote one—"

"Wait a minute!" blurted Ellsworth. "Before we get a fight started, let me show you what I brought."

Rising from the sofa, the colonel picked up a satchel he had carried aboard and opened it. He pulled out a cloth sack and handed it to Willie. "There you go, boys. Take a look inside."

Willie loosened the draw string on the sack's neck and said, "Oh, boy! Soldiers!"

As Willie spilled the wooden soldiers onto the floor, Tad said excitedly, "C'mon, Uncle Elmer! Play war with us!"

The hours passed as Abraham Lincoln worked on his inaugural speech at a small desk near the rear of the car. Mary and Patricia sat on a sofa together talking. The Pinkerton men stayed ready and alert for any sign of trouble. And Elmer Ellsworth played war on the floor of the rocking, swaying coach with his favorite "nephews."

When the train pulled in and rolled to a stop at the Philadelphia railroad station that evening, Allan Pinkerton himself boarded the train with twenty-two more of his men. Pinkerton chatted with Lincoln, explaining that he was leaving nothing to chance. He had planted agents along the rail bed all the way to Washington. He had arranged a series of lantern signals to be used by these agents against the possibility of track sabotage. There were more men waiting at the station in the nation's capital. In all, Pinkerton had employed over two hundred agents to see that the president-elect arrived safely in Washington.

Arriving without incident in Washington at six o'clock on the morning of February 12, the Lincolns, along with Patricia Winters and Colonel Elmer Ellsworth, were accompanied to the Willard Hotel by Allan Pinkerton and an army of his agents. Pinkerton and a number of his staff would stay in Washington and be a part of Lincoln's phalanx of protection until Inauguration Day was over.

At breakfast in the presidential suite, Lincoln eyed his boys with admiration, thinking how much they looked alike. Their facial features were very similar, as were their ears, which were overly large like his own. Both boys had mouse-brown hair and hazel eyes.

In personality, the brothers were vastly different. Where Willie was quiet, reserved, and laid back, Tad was high-spirited, boisterous, and aggressive. There was often a fun-loving devil-may-care look in Tad's eyes that had never appeared in those of his brother. Abraham Lincoln loved them both.

As Lincoln mopped gravy across his plate with a biscuit, he set his quiet eyes on Ellsworth and said, "Elmer, I want to thank you for everything you've done to see me safely here. It has taken valuable time from your work with the Zouaves. I really think you should return to New York, now, and catch up on lost time."

"I can't argue with you, sir. My work with the Zouaves is important in view of what's boiling in the South. We need to be ready for combat if war comes. I'd like to be here for the inauguration, but taking all things into consideration, I think I should get back to camp. As far as protection is concerned, you'll have plenty of that."

In view of the secession by the Southern states and the strong possibility of civil war, Ellsworth had gone to New York City a few weeks earlier and recruited a regiment of tough volunteers from the New York City Fire Department. He had set up a training camp near Utica, upstate some 250 miles. The colonel called his new regiment the New York Fire Zouaves.

"Thanks to you, I'll have plenty of protection," smiled Lincoln. He took a sip of steaming coffee, then said, "I'm going to work hard to avoid war, Elmer, and I hope I'll be successful. But just in case I'm not, the North must be prepared to fight. I appreciate what you're doing toward that most vital preparation."

After breakfast, Colonel Ellsworth hugged his "nephews," bid the Lincolns and Patricia good-bye, and took a carriage to the railroad station where he caught a train for New York.

Abraham Lincoln spent the next several days receiving an almost uninterrupted stream of visitors, newspaper reporters, and friends in his hotel suite. His most important visitor was President James Buchanan, who came by during the last week of February to work out plans for the day of inauguration.

In the precious private moments allotted him, Lincoln worked hard writing and revising his inaugural speech.

On the cloudy and brisk morning of March 4, the president-elect rode with President Buchanan in an open barouche from his hotel to the Capitol. Mary, the boys, and Patricia followed in a second carriage. Allan Pinkerton's agents and U.S. troops were everywhere along the route. Squads of sharpshooters were stationed on the roofs along Pennsylvania Avenue. Lincoln, his family, the governess, and Buchanan entered the Capitol through hedges of U.S. marines, alert and armed to the teeth.

A crowd, much larger than expected, was gathering on the east side of the Capitol where a platform had been built out from the steps to the eastern portico, with benches for distinguished guests on three sides.

At precisely one o'clock, Mrs. Lincoln, her sons, and their governess were ushered out of the Capitol onto the platform and seated on a bench near the lectern. U.S. Marines and Pinkerton men surrounded the platform, eyes scanning the crowd for would-be assassins.

Moments later, President James Buchanan appeared with the president-elect at his side. Buchanan, a large, heavy, awkward man, short compared to Lincoln, had to take two steps for one of Lincoln's to keep up.

Lincoln wore his black top hat, a three-piece black suit, and carried a huge ebony cane with a gold head the size of an egg. Cheers arose from the crowd as he reached the platform. He was a bit pale, but the only discomfort he showed was when he couldn't decide what to do with his hat and cane.

For a moment, he stood there holding cane in one hand and hat in the other, looking around. Finally, he stood the cane in a corner of the railing, but could not find a place for the hat. Senator Stephen A. Douglas, who had defeated Lincoln in his bid for a senate seat in 1858, was on the platform. Douglas stepped up and offered to take the hat. Lincoln smiled and handed it to him. Douglas returned to his seat and held the hat in his lap.

Chief Justice Roger B. Taney approached Lincoln, showed him a seat, then stepped to the lectern. Lincoln glanced at his family. Mary gave him a teary smile and the boys waved.

After a few introductory words, Taney called for the president-elect to come to the podium. Lincoln stood, nodded at Mary, and she hurried to him, taking his arm. When Lincoln moved onto the podium, Mary stayed close, lifting her adoring eyes to his craggy face.

While the crowd watched and listened intently, Abraham Lincoln laid his left hand on a large Bible, raised his right, and took the oath of office. After a prayer by the congressional chaplain, Mary Todd Lincoln returned to her seat. Chief Justice Taney introduced the country's new president to the crowd and sat down.

As Lincoln stepped up to the lectern and laid out his notes, there were loud cheers, mixed with a few boos and hisses. The eyes of the Marines and Pinkerton agents noted the areas of adversity and watched them carefully.

As the nation's sixteenth president began speaking, his nerves were taut and his voice slightly constricted. It took only a few minutes for him to overcome the tension, and soon he was waxing eloquent. In his moving address, Lincoln insisted that the Union was perpetual and that the secession by the Southern states was unconstitutional. He made it clear that the Federal government was determined to maintain its authority and would not bend to the whims or demands of the lawbreaking Confederacy. After pointing out the physical impossibility of separation between Americans who occupied the same land, he urged the Southern people to return to their place in the American household.

Pointedly addressing the people of the South, he said, "If it were admitted that you who are dissatisfied hold the right side in the dispute, there is still no single good reason for precipitate action. Intelligence, patriotism, Christianity, and a firm reliance on Him who has never yet forsaken this favored land, are still competent to adjust in the best way all our present difficulty."

Still directing his words to the Southerners, Lincoln said, "In your hands, my dissatisfied fellow countrymen, and not in mine, is the momentous issue of civil war. The government will not assail you. You can have no conflict without being yourselves the aggressors. You have no oath registered in heaven to destroy the government, while I have the most solemn one to preserve, protect, and defend it.

"I am loathe to close. We are not enemies, but friends. We must not be enemies. Though passion may have strained, it must not break our bonds of affection. The mystic cords of memory, stretching from every battlefield and patriot grave to every living heart and hearthstone all over this broad land, will yet swell the chorus of the Union when again touched, as surely they will be, by the better angels of our nature."

Lincoln picked up his notes and took two steps backward. There was some applause, but it lacked enthusiasm, and quickly faded.

Amid a few cheers and some well-wishers shouting encouragement to the new president, Abraham Lincoln, his family, and the governess were escorted from the Capitol grounds by James Buchanan and a host of bodyguards. A short while later, Buchanan led them into the White House, gave them a tour, then climbed in a private carriage and bid them a polite farewell.

The Lincoln family and governess stood on the front steps and watched Buchanan's carriage drive away. When it reached the street and disappeared, Tad ran his gaze over the White House lawn and said, "Look at all that yard! I hope Uncle Elmer will visit us soon so Willie and me can play war with him."

Silently the president wondered if it would not be long until instead of playing war, Colonel Ellsworth would actually be fighting in one.

Patricia broke the silence by saying, "Willie and *I*, Tad."

Little devils danced in the lad's eyes as he grinned and said, "You can play war with Willie and Uncle Elmer too if you want, Miss Patricia."

The president and Mrs. Lincoln laughed as Patricia seized their youngest son by the ear and led him giggling and squealing inside the White House.

That night Mary Todd Lincoln awakened somewhere in the wee hours to find that her husband had left their bed. Worried, she arose, slipped into her robe, and went into the hall. Lanterns burned at both ends of the hall and near the top of the stairs. Moving toward the staircase, she heard a voice coming from one of the bedrooms along the way.

She paused in front of the partially open door and peered inside. In the vague light, she could see her husband on his knees beside a chair. He was weeping as she heard him say, "Dear God, the people of this nation have elected me their president. They trust me to lead them and make the right decisions in this darkest of hours. Oh, I cannot do it without Thy guidance. We are teetering on the verge of what could be the bloodiest civil conflict ever seen on this earth, dear God. Please, hear my cry."

Mary suddenly felt that she was standing on holy ground and had no right to be there. She could hear her husband's voice continuing in agonizing prayer as she returned swiftly down the hall.

TWO

I n early February of 1861, the seven states that had seceded from the Union—South Carolina, Mississippi, Alabama, Georgia, Florida, Louisiana, and Texas—had held a convention at Montgomery, Alabama, and organized the government of the Confederacy. The convention drew up a provisional constitution (to be replaced in due time by a permanent document), chose Jefferson Davis of Mississippi as president and Alexander Stephens of Georgia as vice-president, and acted as a legislature pending the election of a regular Congress.

During March, both Lincoln and Davis chose their cabinets and set up their administrations under the gathering clouds of pending conflict. Lincoln clung tenaciously to the hope that war could be avoided. The Confederate nation had been born, but its creation might simply be a means of forcing concessions from the Union. No shots had been fired. The seven states that had left the Union might return if a compromise could be reached.

Leaders in Congress worked hard the last few days of March to perfect a last-minute compromise, and a committee led by Senator John Crittendon of Kentucky put one together. It would establish the old line of the Missouri Compromise, banning slavery in territories north of the line and protecting it south of the line. It would let future states enter the Union on a popular sovereignty basis, and it called for enforcement of the fugitive slave law, with Federal funds to compensate slave owners whose slaves got away. It also provided that the Constitution could never be amended in such a way as to give Congress power over slavery in any of the states.

Because of his conviction that slavery was wrong, Lincoln rejected the inclusion of slavery in the territories as provided by Crittendon's Compromise. His firm words were, "I refuse to entertain any proposition for a compromise in regard to the extension of slavery."

The Compromise collapsed.

Now Abraham Lincoln and Jefferson Davis faced each other across an ever-widening gulf. What happened in the minds of those two national leaders would determine whether a nation already divided by mutual hatred and antagonism would be torn apart by bloody conflict.

In his inaugural address, Lincoln had stated that the Federal government would not be the aggressor in a civil war; there would be no conflict unless the Confederates were the aggressors. Realizing the strong possibility of that aggression, Lincoln set up a Senate Military Committee on April 2. The Committee consisted of seven senators.

Meeting with the Committee on April 3 to set up a war strategy, the president and the senators soon realized they lacked a member with military experience. The seven senators agreed that the Committee was necessary—Congress had to have control over the Union's military leaders should war come. But the Committee that represented Congress would need advice from a qualified, well-experienced military man.

"How about General Winfield Scott?" spoke up one of the senators.

Lincoln rubbed his temples and replied slowly, "We can't spare him. His experience in the Mexican War is invaluable. He must be out there to lead the army."

"Then how about Major Irvin McDowell, Mr. President?" asked another. "He's a graduate of West Point and served under General Scott in the Mexican War…with distinction, I might add."

"I know," nodded Lincoln. "I already have him in mind for leading our forces if war comes. I must leave him available for that. We all know that General Scott cannot actually go on the battlefield. He's too old for that, and besides, he's not in good health."

There was a long silence, then Senator Henry Wilson, whom Lincoln had appointed chairman of the Committee, said, "Mr. President, I have just the man—Lieutenant Colonel Jeffrey Jordan."

The name brought nods from the rest of the Committee.

Continuing, Wilson said, "I know Colonel Jordan quite well, Mr. President. I believe you've heard of the widow Rose O'Neal Greenhow."

"Yes," smiled Lincoln. "The doyenne of Washington society."

"Well, my colleagues all know that my wife died three years ago, and for the past year or so, I have been seeing Mrs. Greenhow. She and Colonel Jordan are good friends. It was through Mrs. Greenhow that I met Colonel Jordan, and he and I have become good friends, ourselves."

"I assume you are well acquainted with his military record?"

"Yes, sir. Since I've come to know him, I have done some checking in the Mexican War records. As with Major McDowell, he also fought under General Scott in the Mexican War and proved himself time and again as a military leader. His military record is impeccable, and I'm sure General Scott and Major McDowell will both tell you that few army officers have more knowledge of military theory. He'd be the perfect man to serve as military adviser to this committee."

Lincoln was taking the suggestion in with interest when another committee member said, "I'm not against Colonel Jordan, gentlemen, but I should point out that he is a Southerner…Virginia born and bred. Will he stay with the Union if war comes?"

"Virginia is still in the Union, Senator," spoke up another member.

"But she is in sympathy with the new Confederacy," came the quick retort. "If war comes, Virginia will secede."

"I'm afraid you're right about Virginia," said Lincoln. "However, there are many leaders in our army who are Southerners, but I don't think we'll lose them all to the South if war comes. I know a little of Colonel Jordan's background in the Mexican War. He's recognized as a hero for courage on the battlefield. If none of you object, I will talk to him about becoming this committee's military adviser."

The senators agreed that the president should offer Colonel Jordan the position.

The next day President Lincoln was at his desk in his special capitol building office, pouring over some papers, when there was a tap on the door. Looking up, he said, "Yes?"

The door came open, showing the face of Lincoln's private secretary, twenty-seven-year-old John Hay.

"What is it, John?"

"Colonel Jeffrey Jordan is here for his appointment, sir. Should I have him wait, or—"

"Oh, no!" said Lincoln, rising to his feet. "Show him in."

Hay widened the opening, looked behind him, and said, "Mr. Lincoln will see you now, Colonel."

"Thank you," came a pleasant voice, and Lt. Colonel Jeffrey Jordan appeared, smiling at the president as he moved into the office.

Hay closed the door, leaving the two men alone. Lincoln reached across the desk, shook Jordan's hand, and said, "I'm honored to meet you, Colonel."

Amazed at the strength of the president's grip, Jordan said, "The honor is mine, sir."

Jeffrey Jordan was slender, straight-backed, and stood just under six feet tall. At forty-three, his ash-blond hair was thinning and his sideburns and thick mustache were flecked with gray. There was a kind of seasoned completeness about him that Lincoln liked immediately.

"Have a seat, Colonel," said the president, gesturing toward a chair that sat in front of the desk.

There was an inquisitive look in Jordan's eyes as he placed his hat on an adjacent chair and sat down. Lincoln eased into his own chair, laid his elbows on the desk top, and leaned forward. "I'll get right to the point, Colonel. I need a man of your caliber for an important job."

"Yes, sir?"

"I have known of your war record for some time. Before calling you here, I had my secretary bring me your file so I could learn some more details. Very impressive, I might say. I guess you know you're considered a hero."

Jordan's face tinted. "To some people, sir," he said, his words showing a slight Southern drawl.

"Certainly to Colonel George McClellan. From the report I read, you risked your life to save his in the Mexican War."

"Well, sir," said Jordan, clearing his throat, "it wasn't exactly like that. You see—"

Throwing up a palm, Lincoln cut in, "I know how you heroes are. You never like to take any credit for your deeds. Let's get down to business."

The president explained that he had formed the Senate Military Committee because of the threat of war, and that the Committee needed a competent, experienced military man as adviser. Senator Wilson had brought up Jordan's name, and the Committee had agreed that he was the man for the job.

The colonel was both pleased and flattered, and consented to take the job, adding that he thought there were men available more qualified than he.

Lincoln sat back in his chair, fixed his dark eyes on Jordan, and said, "There is one thing I have to ask you, Colonel."

"Yes, sir?"

"You're a native Virginian."

A slight smile curved the colonel's mouth. "And you're wondering where my loyalty will lie if civil war comes and Virginia secedes."

Lincoln nodded.

"I love my home state, Mr. President, but if Virginia secedes, my loyalty stays with the Union. Like you, I'm against slavery."

"Fine, Colonel," Lincoln said, rising to his feet. "We'll set you up an office here in the Capitol right away. I've set a meeting for the Committee and its new adviser for tomorrow morning at eight. My secretary, Mr. Hay, will show you where the conference room is…and he'll be the one to see that you have everything you need for your office. You will learn exactly what we want of you in the morning."

"Thank you, sir," smiled Jordan, who was now standing. Picking up his hat, he said, "It will be a pleasure to work with you and the Committee. I'll get with Mr. Hay, and I'll see you at eight tomorrow morning."

Rounding the desk, the president walked Jordan to the door. "One other thing, Colonel."

"Yes, sir?"

"Mrs. Lincoln and I are hosting a dinner party at the White House Saturday night for the Committee members and their wives. Since you are now part of the Committee, I'd like for you to come. I know you are a widower, but if you have a lady friend you'd like to bring along, she'd be more than welcome. Senator Wilson is bringing Mrs. Greenhow."

Jordan rubbed the back of his neck and said, "I'm really not seeing any ladies, sir, but I have a twenty-year-old daughter. Would it be all right if I bring her?"

"Of course. What's the young lady's name?"

"Jenny Marie, sir. Only she doesn't like the way Southerners call everybody by both names, so she's just Jenny."

"I'll try to remember that," grinned the president. "Dinner is at eight."

"Thank you. Jenny and I will look forward to it, Mr. President."

* * *

It was late in the afternoon on Saturday, April 6. Mary Todd Lincoln was overseeing the decorating of the table in the White House dining room. The servants found Mary a warm and congenial First Lady and enjoyed working with her.

After having changed the flower arrangement in the table's centerpiece for the third time, Mary stepped back to scrutinize it. Nodding, she said to the two maids who stood close by, "Yes, that's it! Perfect! Now, you young ladies can go ahead with the place settings. Be sure to fold the napkins like I showed you. I'll be back shortly."

Mary then had to look in on the male servants, who were rearranging the furniture in the nearby drawing room where her guests would gather both before and after dinner. As she turned about, she found her two sons standing at the dining room door. She knew by the look on their faces, they were wanting something. "Yes, boys?" she said, smiling.

"Mama," spoke up Willie. "Uh...Tad wants to ask you something."

Because of his younger brother's persuasive ways with adults, Willie knew their objective had a much better chance of being realized if the request came from Tad.

Mary's eyes settled on her youngest. "Yes?"

Tad grinned broadly, glanced at the centerpiece, and said, "You sure fixed those flowers pretty, Mama."

"Thank you," she replied dryly, folding her arms over her bosom. "Now, what is it that you want?"

"Well, uh, me an' Willie...I know you said we can't eat supper in here tonight because we're just kids, but...we'd really like to meet Lieutenant Colonel Jeffrey Jordan. He's a hero, Mama. A *real* hero! Miss Patricia has been teachin' us about the Mexican War, an' she read to us out of some old newspapers about some of the things he did in the war. Me an' Willie would really like to meet him. Could we sit by him at the table and ask him to tell us some war stories? Please?"

Shaking her head, Mary said firmly, "No, Tad. This is strictly an adult occasion. You and Willie will get the same food, but as I told you before, you will eat it in the kitchen with Miss Patricia. Now, that's final."

Tad had told his parents that he planned to go to West Point when he grew up. His only dream was to be a soldier. He thought about using that angle to point out to his mother how beneficial it would be to his military career if he could spend some time with a great war hero, but the look in her eyes told him he'd best drop the subject. He made no attempt to veil his disappointment as he said, "Yes, ma'am. C'mon, Willie."

Mary smiled to herself as she watched Tad lead his brother away.

By seven-thirty that evening, all the guests were collected in the drawing room, waiting only for Jeffrey Jordan and his daughter to arrive. President and Mrs. Lincoln were moving among the guests together, spending a few moments with each couple. Mary Lincoln had heard much of Rose Greenhow and had been eager to meet her. The young widow proved to be lovely and amiable.

At seven-forty, Lieutenant Colonel Jordan and his daughter were announced. When they entered the room with Jenny on her father's arm, all eyes went immediately to the strikingly beautiful young woman.

Jenny Jordan stood four inches over five feet. Her long, raven-black hair lay in graceful swirls on her shoulders. She wore a deep-crimson floor-length dress fitted tightly at the neck and waist. Her figure was the envy of every woman in the room. At the neck and at the ends of her sleeves, Jenny wore white lace. Two pearl eardrops danced when she turned her head, and a long triple-string of pearls adorned her neck.

Jenny's eyes were dark-brown and direct. Her skin was smooth and fair, and her face had strong and pleasant contours. She glowed with personality and her warmth attracted people to her…men and women alike.

The Lincolns moved quickly to greet the colonel and his daughter. When introductions had been completed, Jenny—who indicated no intimidation in the presence of the president and the First Lady— smiled at the president and said, "May I say, Mr. President, that I agree in total with the young lady who wrote and suggested that you grow the beard. It most certainly adds to your dignity."

"Why, thank you, Miss Jordan," said Lincoln, returning the smile.

"I mean it most sincerely, sir," she added.

"I'm sure you do, and I appreciate it."

"And I would like to express my deep gratitude, sir, for the honor you have bestowed on my father by making him military adviser to the Committee."

Charmed by her slight Southern accent and congeniality, Lincoln responded, "The honor is actually mine, Miss Jordan. Your father is the perfect man for the job."

Jeffrey Jordan was about to speak when his daughter unwittingly cut him off by saying, "Mr. President, you may call me Jenny if you wish."

Lincoln smiled, winked at the colonel, and replied, "Just so I don't call you Jenny Marie, right?"

Jenny blushed. Looking at her father, she said, "Daddy, did you have to tell him that?"

Jordan chuckled, "Yes. I did."

Jenny turned to the First Lady and said, "Mrs. Lincoln, I love your dress. And your brooch. It's beautiful."

"Thank you, dear," Mary smiled, herself captivated by Jenny's charm. "The brooch was my mother's. I had the dress made in Springfield right after my husband won the election."

Mary and Jenny chatted for another minute, then the colonel took his daughter around the room, introducing her to the senators and meeting their wives for the first time. When they came to

Senator Henry Wilson and Mrs. Greenhow, the senator greeted Jenny, saying he was happy to finally meet her. Then the Washington socialite embraced Jenny and said, "It's good to see you again, honey."

"You too, Rose," Jenny smiled, hugging her a second time.

"Isn't it just marvelous that your daddy will be working with the Committee?"

"Yes. I'm so proud of him."

"Let's just hope his job nor the Committee have to last very long," Senator Wilson interjected.

Rose turned to him and said, "None of us want a war, Henry, but as far as I can see, it looks inevitable."

"I know it does, but I'll hang onto the thread of hope until the Confederates jerk it out of my hand."

At that moment, the First Lady called her guests to the dining room. The Lincolns sat together at the head of the table. Mary was so taken with young Jenny that she arranged for her to sit at the corner to her left, automatically placing the colonel on the corner at the president's right.

As the meal progressed, Jenny was the spark of the evening. Committee members and their wives all along the table engaged her in conversation from time to time. Captured by her loveliness and fresh spirit, Abraham Lincoln looked at her at a quiet moment and joked, "Jenny, if I were tall, dark, handsome, young, and free, I'd be a-courtin' you."

Mary's eyes twinkled as she mildly retorted, "Abe, dear…tall, dark, and handsome you are. But young and free you're not. Jenny will just have to find herself another man!"

Everyone laughed, then one of the senators said, "I have an idea Colonel Jordan has already had to build a high fence and employ attack dogs to keep the young men away from Miss Jenny."

Jordan chuckled and said, "My daughter has many young hopefuls hanging around, but so far she hasn't been serious with any of them."

Mary took Jenny by the hand and said, "Don't you worry about it. When that right young man walks into your life, you'll know him…just like I did when this tall, handsome man walked into my life."

The president snickered, and the guests showed their amusement as Jenny quipped, "If I can do half as well as you did, Mrs. Lincoln, I will be very happy."

In the White House kitchen, the Lincoln boys and their governess ate their meal. Noting the sour look on Tad's face, Patricia said, "Tad, if your face gets any longer, it's going to be in your plate."

The boy gave her a pitiful look and said around his food, "All I wanted to do was meet a war hero."

"I know, dear," Patricia said softly, "but it just isn't possible this time."

One of Willie Lincoln's chief occupations was watching his little brother charm his way into just about anything he wanted. He observed as Tad said with a break in his voice, "I don't really care if me an' Willie can't eat in there, but wouldn't it be all right if we just went in an' *met* Colonel Jordan?"

"I'm afraid your father would consider your entrance a serious interruption, Tad. Those senators are very important men. It just isn't the time or place for children."

Willie knew his little brother had a special set of strings attached to the governess's heart. He smiled to himself as he watched Tad begin to tug on those strings. Willie had often thought Tad would make a better actor than a soldier.

Tad looked up at Patricia, showing misty disappointment in his eyes, his lower lip quivering. "But if that war starts, Colonel Jordan'll be too busy for me *ever* to meet him. I only want to see him for a minute, just so's I can say I met him. My daddy wouldn't get mad if *you* took us in and told him we just wanted to see Colonel Jordan for a minute."

Willie knew Patricia would give in. It was all over her face.

She held out a little longer by saying, "Tad, your father may not get angry at me, but I don't want even his slightest disfavor. Can't you see that—"

"He really likes you, Miss Patricia. He wouldn't even show—what'd you call it?"

"The slightest disfavor."

"Yeah, that."

Patricia looked at Willie, who pulled his mouth tight and shrugged his shoulders. With a long sigh, she said, "All right, Mr. Lincoln. I'll lay my neck on the chopping block and take you in there. But remember…it's only so you can meet Colonel Jordan, and that's all. It'll be real quick. Understand?"

Jumping from his chair, the nine-year-old charmer wrapped his arms around her neck, exclaiming, "Oh, thank you, Miss Patricia, thank you! I love you!"

In the dining room, the natural course for conversation was toward the threat of civil war. The senators expressed their fear that if war came, many of the good officers in the army who were Southerners would forsake the Union and join up with the Confederacy.

"We will no doubt lose some," conceded Lincoln, "but as I told you gentlemen before, I believe the majority of men from the Southern states will stay with the Union."

"There are a couple of officers that I'm concerned about, Mr. President," said Senator Wilson. Rose glanced furtively at Jeffrey Jordan, then looked intently at Wilson. "I speak of two well-known educators from Virginia—Colonel Robert E. Lee and Colonel Thomas Jackson."

Everyone there knew that for years Lee had been superintendent at West Point, and that Jackson was the best-loved instructor who had ever taught at Virginia Military Institute. Both were now active officers in the Regular Army.

Lincoln seemed a bit uncomfortable at the mention of their names. Adjusting himself on his chair, he said, "Since the subject has gone this far, we will take it a little further. But I will tell you ladies that what you hear at this table is to be kept under your hats unless and until Colonels Lee and Jackson abdicate their commissions in the Regular Army and join the Confederacy."

Each woman nodded her assent.

Continuing, Lincoln said to Wilson, "We have many officers who are Southerners, Senator. Why do you question the loyalty of these two men?"

"I question Colonel Jackson, sir, because he is so outspoken about being a Southerner. I find it hard to believe that if war comes, he could do anything *but* join the Confederacy."

"Even if Virginia should surprise us and stay with the Union?" queried one of the other senators.

Wilson grinned at him. "Once the first shot is fired, my friend, *everybody* will have to declare themselves. I'd lay my right arm down in a bet that Virginia will go Confederate the instant it happens, or shortly thereafter."

The rest of the Committee agreed.

"And as for Colonel Lee," proceeded Wilson, "we all know that General Scott has approached Lee about assuming principal command of all the Union forces in his place if war comes…and Lee keeps delaying giving him an answer. Why the delay unless Lee is figuring to join the Confederacy if Virginia secedes?"

"Good question," nodded Lincoln. He paused, drew in a deep breath, and said, "Only time will tell. If we go into war and Lee and Jackson stay with the Union, we'll owe them an apology."

"I go on record right here," said Wilson. "I'll be the first to apologize if I'm wrong."

One of the senators' wives looked at Jordan and asked, "What do you think, Colonel? You're a Virginian."

"I can't rightly speak for Lee and Jackson, ma'am," Jordan replied softly.

"But Colonel Jordan has spoken for himself," put in Lincoln. "He has pledged his loyalty to the Union."

"Amen!" laughed another senator. "If he hadn't, we wouldn't have made him military adviser of the Committee!"

While laughter made its rounds, Jenny stole a quick glance at her father. He met it, then looked away.

At that moment, the dining room door came open and governess Patricia Winters appeared. Everyone looked her direction as she smiled and said, "Excuse me, Mr. Lincoln. I have two young men here who have asked me to make a request for them."

When the president's eyes settled sternly on the governess, she spoke quickly. "Tad is very eager to meet Lieutenant Colonel Jordan, sir, and so is Willie. Just...just recently I was teaching the boys about the Mexican War, and we spent some time on Colonel Jordan's heroic deeds in battle. As you know, sir, Tad plans on one day being a soldier. He...he asked me if he and Willie could come in and meet the colonel. I told them we would have to make it very quick...just a minute or so."

There was pleading in Patricia's eyes as she spoke. Mary looked at her husband, who was rubbing his chin.

Abraham Lincoln was fully aware of Patricia's soft spot for Tad, and how very persuasive the lad could be. A smile parted his lips. "All right, Patricia. Bring the boys in."

The governess opened the door wider, allowing the Lincoln brothers to move past her into the dining room. The president left his chair, put an arm around the shoulder of each son, and said, "Well, boys, since you're in here, I think it would be appropriate for you to meet all these ladies and gentlemen."

Lincoln took his sons around the table, introducing them to the senators and their wives, purposely saving Lieutenant Colonel Jordan and his daughter till last. Willie and Tad politely shook hands with the men and did a slight bow before the ladies.

While the introductions were in progress, Patricia found Mrs. Lincoln looking at her. The nervous governess smiled weakly. Mary was too kind to show anger for what Patricia had done. Tad had worked his mother in the same way more times than she cared to think about. When Mary smiled back, Patricia felt relief. She opened her hands at waist level and mouthed, "I couldn't turn him down."

Mary mouthed back, "I understand."

Finally, Lincoln brought his sons to the beautiful lady in the deep-red dress and said, "Boys, this is Miss Jenny Jordan. She is the colonel's daughter."

Jenny warmed them with a smile and said, "Hello, Willie. Hello, Tad."

The Lincoln brothers were struck with the warmth Jenny showed toward them. They bowed extra low and said almost in unison, "Glad to meet you, Miss Jordan."

"You are fine looking young men," she responded. "Maybe someday one of you will be president like your father."

"That'll be Willie, ma'am," said Tad. "I'm gonna be a soldier like *your* father."

Everyone laughed. The president then turned his sons to the colonel and introduced them to him. Jordan shook hands with Willie first, then Tad. As soon as he let go of Tad's hand, the bright-eyed boy held the hand up and exclaimed, "Willie! I ain't never gonna wash this hand again!"

There was another round of laughter, then the colonel chatted with the Lincoln brothers for several minutes, answering questions they had about certain incidents in the Mexican War they remembered from Patricia's lessons.

"Colonel Jordan," Tad said, "tell me what it's really like on the battlefield. You know…what it's like to be out there with cannons firing an' muskets shooting an'…an' smoke all around, an' soldiers bein' shot."

Jordan looked to Mary for any signal to hold back. When she only smiled, he proceeded to answer Tad's inquiry. Tad's eyes danced with excitement as he heard first-hand from a veteran soldier about battlefield experience.

"All right, boys, it's bedtime," Mary said when Jordan was done. The president instructed his sons to tell everyone goodnight.

They thanked Colonel Jordan for talking to them, and told him goodnight first. Next they went to Jenny. She smiled and asked if she could have a hug. Everyone looked on with pleasure as the boys gladly embraced her. It took them only moments to tell the rest of the group goodnight.

When the governess and her charges were gone, the guests commented to the Lincolns about what fine boys they had. They noted especially Tad's forwardness and his interest in military matters.

The Lincolns and their guests moved to the drawing room where they were served coffee and sat down to chat. After a while, the president turned to Jenny and asked if she was working.

"Yes, sir. In addition to keeping house for my father, I work as a seamstress three days a week for Manley's Clothiers downtown."

"Oh, yes," Lincoln nodded. "I've seen their store." He paused a moment, then asked, "Do you work the same three days every week?"

"Usually Monday, Wednesday, and Friday, but sometimes I switch it around. Mr. Manley gives me a great deal of leeway."

"The reason I ask is that I am looking for a part-time receptionist for the Senate Chamber at the Capitol. I like the way you handle yourself with people, and I believe you'd make an excellent receptionist. The young lady who has been working at it full-time, wants to drop back to two days a week. I could give you a Monday-Wednesday-Friday job if you want it. And if once in a while you wanted to switch days, I'm sure that can be worked out. The starting salary would be twenty-five dollars a week."

Jenny's eyes widened. "Twenty-five dollars a week for *three days*?"

"Yes."

Turning to her father, she said, "Daddy, that's twice what I make at Manley's!"

"Sounds like Mr. Lincoln is making you a generous proposition, honey," Jordan smiled.

Looking back at the president, Jenny said, "I'll take it, sir!"

THREE

When South Carolina seceded from the Union in late December, 1860, Major Robert Anderson, commander of the Federal forces in Charleston Harbor, secretly moved his garrison of less than seventy men from Fort Moultrie across the harbor to Fort Sumter. He knew Sumter would be easier to defend than Moultrie if war came.

The question whether Anderson's small force should be withdrawn from the South Carolina harbor, or reinforced, agitated the closing weeks of the Buchanan administration and the opening weeks of the Lincoln administration. Before he had set up the Senate Military Committee, Lincoln discussed the problem with his cabinet over a period of several days.

While the fate of Fort Sumter was under lengthy discussion in Washington, Confederate president Jefferson Davis contacted the flamboyant General Pierre G.T. Beauregard, who was commander of Rebel forces at Charleston. Orders were given to Beauregard to lay siege on Fort Sumter.

Finally, against the advice of some of his cabinet members, Lincoln had decided not to reinforce Sumter but to merely send provisions. He was still clinging to a faint hope that war could be averted.

To send reinforcements would invite hostilities. For many long weeks, Major Anderson and his tiny garrison had waited behind Sumter's walls, facing the silent, menacing guns of the Confederates.

At 8:20 A.M. on Friday, April 12, Jenny Jordan was at her desk in the lobby just outside the door of the Senate Chamber. She observed the members of the Senate Military Committee as they topped the stairs at the end of the hall two and three at a time and moved down the hall toward her.

As they passed her desk and entered the Chamber door that led to their meeting room, Jenny picked up their words. The discussion was about the standoff between Anderson and Beauregard at Charleston Harbor.

It was 8:25 when the receptionist saw President Lincoln's tall, lanky form top the stairs, sided by her father. They talked as they came down the hall. When they arrived at Jenny's desk, they stopped to greet her.

The president's features were drawn and his dark eyes looked weary. She wondered if he had slept at all in the past few days. Mr. Lincoln had repeatedly sent supply boats into Charleston Harbor, knowing that Major Anderson and his men were running low on provisions, but the boats were turned back by the Confederates.

Lincoln set his tired eyes on Jenny, released a half-smile, and said, "Good morning."

"Good morning, Mr. President," she responded softly.

Lincoln proceeded into the Senate Chamber. Jeffrey Jordan leaned over, kissed his daughter on the cheek, and said, "Things are pretty tight, honey. The president and the Committee are at their wits' end over this Fort Sumter situation. I think things are about to pop in Charleston Harbor."

Jenny watched her father vanish through the door, then turned to her paper work. At ten minutes before nine, Jenny looked up to see a White House aide hit the top of the stairs and run down the hall toward her. He stopped at her desk, his face pallid. The troubled look in his eyes told her that something bad had happened.

The thirty-ish aide looked down at Jenny's name plate and gasped, "Miss Jordan...I must see the president...immediately."

Jenny wanted to ask what the emergency was about, but refrained. Rising, she said, "This way."

The breathless aide followed as Jenny led him into the Senate Chamber and down a narrow corridor. Stopping at a pair of closed double doors, she rapped loudly. Seconds later, one of the senators opened a door and said, "Yes, Jenny."

"One of Mr. Lincoln's aides is here, sir. He needs to see him immediately."

The aide was taken into the meeting room and Jenny returned to her desk. No more than two minutes had passed when the president came out with the aide at his side. They passed the desk talking rapidly back and forth, but Jenny was able to pick up that something dreadful had happened earlier that morning at Charleston Harbor.

Jenny bit her lower lip. Had the war begun?

Suddenly the Senate Military Committee came bowling through the Chamber door. Their voices were strained as they talked among themselves. Jenny was picking up bits and pieces when her father appeared and drew up. "The war's on," he said with emotion. "General Beauregard fired on Fort Sumter at dawn this morning. Major Anderson and his men are fighting back. Charleston Harbor will turn into a blood bath unless Anderson surrenders quickly."

Jenny's hands were trembling. "Daddy, what are you going to do, now? The very thing we dreaded has become a reality."

"I don't have time to talk about it now. The president is going to call an emergency meeting of Congress immediately. As military adviser to the Committee, I'm expected to be there. We'll talk this evening."

With that, he was gone.

Jenny's stomach was jittery. She returned to her work but had a hard time concentrating. April 12, 1861, was going to be a long day...and a black day on the calendar of American history.

That evening, Lieutenant Jordan entered his house and smelled the mouth-watering aroma of food cooking. Hanging his hat on a hook in the parlor, he moved into the kitchen to find his daughter adding a log to the cookstove. Replacing the circular lid to its place, she turned and said with a faint smile, "Hello, Daddy."

"Hi, sweetheart," he responded, and moved across the room toward her. Planting a kiss on her cheek, he asked, "What's for supper? Sure smells good."

"Your favorite," Jenny replied softly.

"Chicken and dumplings?"

"Mm-hmm."

"You really are a sweetheart!"

Turning back to the stove, Jenny said, "Better get washed up. Supper will be on the table in about five minutes."

Jenny set the food on the table while the colonel washed at a nearby basin. While moving back and forth between the cupboard and the table, she asked, "So can you tell me what happened in Congress's emergency meeting?"

"Sure. They agreed unanimously to declare war on the Confederacy. Mr. Lincoln is very angry at Jefferson Davis for giving the order for Beauregard to fire on Sumter. There will be retaliation. It'll take a little time, but Confederate blood will be shed."

"Neither side is really ready for war, are they?"

Drying his hands on a small towel, Jordan shook his head. "No. It will be a while before either side can wage full-scale war."

Jenny's face was pale. "Let's sit down," she said with a tremor in her voice.

They took their places at each end of the kitchen table. Jordan thanked the Lord for their food, but did not mention the war in his prayer.

As they began to eat, Jenny said, "Daddy, Virginia will secede, won't she?"

"I'm sure of it."

Jenny had been raised by her parents to love her native state of Virginia, and she felt a strong compulsion to remain true to it. President Lincoln's words at the White House dinner on Saturday night came back to her. "Daddy, Mr. Lincoln said the other night at the dinner that you had spoken for yourself...that you had pledged your loyalty to the Union."

"I noticed you looked at me when he said it. I had to assure him of my loyalty to the Union in order to get the military adviser position."

Cocking her head, she asked, "Am I understanding you correctly? You took the position with an ulterior motive?"

"I'm really not ready to discuss it with you, okay? Let's see what happens in the next few days."

"I hate the thought of civil war, Daddy. What a horrible thing...Americans killing Americans."

"Yes, it's horrible, all right. But you and I can't control what's coming. All we can do is react accordingly when it happens."

News came to Washington late Sunday afternoon, April 14, that Major Anderson and his small garrison had surrendered Fort Sumter to General Beauregard. Miraculously, with all the shelling that had gone on for nearly two full days, not one man had been killed on either side. Nonetheless, the divided nation was in the grip of civil war.

After meeting with his Senate Military Committee for a special session on Sunday evening, Abraham Lincoln issued a strong proclamation. Because the seven seceded states had opposed and obstructed the laws of the United States, Lincoln was calling for seventy-five thousand militiamen to follow his leadership in punishing them for their lawlessness.

The next day headlines on all the Northern newspapers announced Lincoln's proclamation in bold letters. Later in the day, the news reached President Davis in Montgomery. Davis bristled at the naked threat of Lincoln's call to arms against the South and, through a large number of Southern newspapers, asked for every loyal, able-bodied son of the South to prepare to meet the Union's militia head-on.

On Tuesday morning, Jenny had just arrived at her desk when John F. Calhoun, a native of South Carolina who worked as a recording and vital statistics secretary in the Senate Chamber, emerged from the inner offices and said, "Good morning, Jenny. I thought you didn't work on Tuesday."

"Ordinarily I don't, but Nelda sent word yesterday that she's not feeling well and asked if I'd fill in for her today."

"I see. Well…have you heard the latest news?"

Jenny placed her purse in a lower drawer. "Probably not, John. Has it something to do with the extra-early meeting my father is attending with the Committee at this very moment?"

"Yes. As you probably know, the president is in there with them."

"I assumed he would be," she said, shoving the drawer shut. "So what is it?"

"General Winfield Scott is in there, too. Seems when the president's proclamation hit the newspapers yesterday, several army officers from the South turned in their resignations and headed for home. Most notable among them was Colonel Thomas J. Jackson!"

Easing into her chair, Jenny said, "That probably didn't surprise anyone. Colonel Jackson is known to be an outspoken Southerner."

"Somebody said once that Jackson is such a strong Southerner that the blood in his body flows south. He's a good friend of your father's, isn't he?"

"Yes. Daddy attended VMI before going to West Point. Colonel Jackson was a professor there at the time. He and Daddy became very good friends." Jenny paused a few seconds, then asked, "What about Colonel Lee? Was he one of them?"

"No. At least he's not among the first bunch to go. The men

on the Committee are calling them *traitors*. It's pretty hot in that meeting room right now."

"What about you, John? You're a real beans-and-sow-belly son of the South, yourself. What are you going to do?"

At that instant, the Chamber doors burst open and Committee members poured out, heading quickly down the corridor toward the stairs. Behind them came Jeffrey Jordan, the portly General Winfield Scott, and President Lincoln.

Jordan halted at Jenny's desk. Lincoln said, "See you as soon as you get back, Colonel."

"Yes, sir," nodded Jordan.

Lincoln and Scott moved away. When they were out of earshot, Jenny said to her father, "I didn't know you were going somewhere."

"Well, something came up," he replied, looking around to make sure no one was around.

Jenny noted that Calhoun had disappeared.

"I'm going to Lexington," said Jordan. "Be back as soon as I can."

"Lexington, *Virginia?*"

"Yes. I'm leaving right now. I told Mr. Lincoln your Uncle Elbert has become suddenly ill, and that I need to go to him."

"But Uncle Elbert's healthy as a plow horse, Daddy," she reasoned. "Besides…he lives in Leesburg."

"I know," the colonel said hurriedly and kissed her on the forehead. As he hastened away, he said over his shoulder, "Tell you all about it when I get back."

Jenny stared after him. Who was he going to see at Lexington? Some old friend from his VMI days? Then she remembered…Colonel Jackson still maintained his home at Lexington. Jenny had heard her father say so not too long ago. What had Calhoun just said? *Several army officers from the South turned in their resignations and headed for home.* Jenny's father was going to see Colonel Jackson!

On Wednesday morning, April 17, Colonel Thomas J. Jackson stepped off the back porch of his house in Lexington, patting his stomach. His wife stood at the kitchen door, smiling. She had just fed him a good breakfast. He was home so little, she loved to pamper and spoil him good when she had the opportunity. She watched him enter the small barn behind the house, then turned away to clean up the table.

Jackson moved into the deep shadows of the barn, took a curry comb and a brush from hooks on the wall, and exited from a rear door into the small corral. His bay gelding was drinking at the water trough. As the colonel approached, the horse nickered and bobbed its head.

"Good mornin', ol' boy," grinned Jackson. "How'd you like a good brushin'?" The gelding stood still as its master brushed its coat and combed out the mane and tail. "Well, ol' boy," Jackson said as he brushed the sleek coat, "it looks like you and I are gonna be goin' to war."

The gelding stomped a hoof and nickered as if it understood. Then it swung its head around and nickered again. Jackson looked up to see a lone rider trotting into the yard. The rider had spotted him and was heading for the corral. Leaving the gelding, Jackson walked toward the corral gate, raising the curry comb to wave a welcome. "Jeff, what brings you here?" Jackson asked as Colonel Jordan hauled up and slid from his saddle.

Pushing his hat off his forehead, Jordan stuck a hand over the gate, and as the two old friends shook hands, he said, "I need to talk to you, Tom."

"Sure. Let's go in the house."

Jordan greeted Mrs. Jackson, who asked if he had eaten breakfast. Jordan explained that he had stayed at a country inn the night before and had eaten just before dawn.

Jackson led his former student into his den where they sat in overstuffed chairs, facing each other. "I'll get right to the point, Tom," said Jordan. "I learned yesterday morning that you had resigned from the Regular Army and gone home. I assume you're signing up with the Confederate Army."

"Already have. I'll be assigned a regiment to lead shortly. No doubt it'll be with a Virginia military unit."

"I guess you know you've been labeled a traitor."

"Yes," sighed Jackson. Picking up a well-worn Bible from a small table next to his chair, he opened it and began flipping pages, saying, "Have you ever read the book of Exodus, Jeff?"

"Yes."

"You will remember, then, that when the book opens, the Israelites are in Egypt under the thumb of Pharaoh."

"Yes."

"In chapter one, Pharaoh tells the Hebrew midwives that when they deliver babies for Hebrew women, they are to kill all the males."

"I remember that."

"Okay, now listen to verse seventeen, 'But the midwives feared God, and did not as the king of Egypt commanded them, but saved the men children alive.' You will notice, they disobeyed the king because they feared God. What God said came first with them."

"That's as it should be."

Flipping back to the New Testament, Jackson said, "In the days of the apostles, the government told them not to preach the doctrine of Jesus Christ to the people. But the apostles refused to obey the government. Acts chapter five. Listen to this in verse twenty-nine. 'Then Peter and the other apostles answered and said, We ought to obey God rather than men.'"

"I know where you're headed," smiled Jordan.

"Of course, the apostles' battle with the government of their day was the most vital and valorous battle men could ever wage…but ours is still very important. Paul wrote in Romans thirteen about obeying your government. He said to render to everyone their dues. Tribute to whom tribute is due, custom to whom custom is due, fear to whom fear is due, and honor to whom honor is due. Jeff, I can't honor a government that steps on the rights of plantation owners, telling them they cannot own slaves. I'm not particularly fond of slavery, but I'm for states' rights, and it is my conviction that God is, too. So, on that premise and the fact that I'm a Southerner to the core, I had to resign. I'm going to fight for the South and for dear ol' Virginia. Being called a traitor by Northerners doesn't bother me one bit."

Jordan's mouth pulled into a thin line. "That's what I want to talk about, Tom. I'm battling this loyalty thing myself."

"You're a Virginian, Jeff. That ought to settle it. I guess you know what's going on over at Richmond as we talk."

"Yeah. I heard about it at the inn last night. An emergency state convention to pass an ordinance of secession."

"It's as good as done," said Jackson, laying the Bible back on the table. "After hearing of Lincoln's call to arms, Virginians are more than happy to get out of the Union. On the way home, I heard that our esteemed governor spoke yesterday of Lincoln's call for militiamen to punish the Confederates for breaking the laws of the United States. He said Virginians will not stand for such 'crass, arrogant threats' and will gladly fight with the other seceded states against the Union."

Jordan was quiet for a moment. He bent his head, rubbed the back of his neck, and said, "Tom, I've got to take my stand with the Confederacy."

"Good! I'll see that you get a commission as colonel in the Rebel army."

Easing back into his chair, Jordan said, "I've been doing a lot of thinking, and I've got something else in mind."

"Oh?"

"I'm in a perfect position to get my hands on all kinds of classified military information. Have you heard about my being appointed military adviser to the Senate Military Committee?"

"No. I knew about Lincoln setting up the Committee, but I

didn't know about you being made military adviser. Your talking about being a spy?"

"Yes."

"Do you know what it means if you're caught?"

"Immediate execution, if the old spy rule holds firm with Lincoln and Winfield Scott."

"I'm sure it will. It's a real risk."

"Is it really any more risk than if I was out there on a battlefield with bullets and shrapnel flying around?"

"I guess not. How will you get the classified information into the hands of Confederate military leaders?"

"I have two close friends in key places in Washington who are loyal to the Confederacy. One is a secretary in the Senate Chamber. His name is John F. Calhoun, and he's from South Carolina."

"So as secretary in the Senate Chamber, you figure Calhoun can lay hold on information that might not be available to you?"

"Right. I haven't approached John on it yet, but I'm quite certain he'll go along with it."

"So who's going to carry the information to the Confederate military leaders for you?"

"Well, I haven't got it all worked out yet, but the second friend I mentioned is Rose O'Neal Greenhow."

"Ah, yes. The Washington socialite. Quite attractive, I understand—a widow and very wealthy. That's about all I know. I assume her husband left her a great deal of money?"

"That's right. He was Dr. Robert Greenhow, a successful attorney and State Department official. Dr. Greenhow left her quite a sizable sum. She'll never want for anything. She continually hosts parties and invites all the important people in Washington."

"So I understand."

"Rose has already declared her loyalty to the Confederacy to me, so I know I can depend on her for help. She has contact with many young socialite women. Many are Southerners, and Rose will know how to pick them. My idea is for the young women to carry the information to Confederate military leaders in Virginia. They'll be able to get past Union lines that will no doubt be set up. Men would be suspect. The girls can give all kinds of reasons as to why they're going back and forth between D.C. and Virginia."

Colonel Jackson pulled at his beard, nodding slowly. "That will work, Jeff. You've got a brain in your head."

"Rose is also my prime choice for this venture because she is romantically involved with Senator Henry Wilson of Massachusetts. Wilson is chairman of the Senate Committee. Her relationship with him will help keep her above suspicion."

Jackson's eyebrows arched. "You mean she'll stay romantically involved with Wilson and work as a spy right under his nose?"

"I feel confident she will. I know Rose's devotion to the Southern cause. The romance between her and the senator isn't that serious. At least on her part."

"You must know her well."

"Not romantically, professor," grinned Jordan. "She's not my type. But we are close friends."

"Well, like I said, this spy stuff is risky, Jeff. But if you can get this spy ring set up, let me know immediately. No doubt because of its proximity to Washington, Virginia will become the first theater of war. Whoever Jefferson Davis sets up as top commander of the Confederate forces will no doubt be situated in Virginia."

"Any idea who that might be?"

"I think it'll be Beauregard."

"He's certainly the big hero in Southern eyes since he captured Fort Sumter." Jordan paused, then asked, "What do you know about Colonel Robert E. Lee?"

A wide grin spread over Jackson's face. "He'll come over to our side. Mark my word. It'll happen real quick, now that Virginia is seceding. The man has Southern blood in his veins just like yours and mine."

"I'm sure you're right. With his reputation, he'll no doubt become a leader in the Confederate army."

"No doubt about it," agreed Jackson.

Jordan rose to his feet. "Well, I'd better be heading back for Washington, Tom. I just felt if I could talk to you, it'd give me the impetus to make my move. I'll get word to you as soon as possible so you'll know about the spy ring. You'll have to let me know where to send information once we get rolling."

Jackson clapped a hand on Jordan's shoulder and said, "Fine. I can't tell you right now when I'll get my assignment, or where I'll be stationed, but if you'll send the message here, my wife will see that it gets to me right away."

"Will do."

Colonel Jordan said good-bye to Mrs. Jackson and was escorted to his horse. As Jordan mounted, Jackson smiled up at him and said, "Jeff, if you make this spy ring work, it'll have a devastating effect on the Union's military progress and success in the war."

"That's what I'm counting on."

As he trotted away, Jackson called after him, "God bless you, Jeff!"

Word of Virginia's secession from the Union spread fast. While President Lincoln and General Scott were in serious discussion at the White House on April 17, a Virginia military unit under orders from General Beauregard moved swiftly to take the Federal arsenal at Harper's Ferry. The small Union garrison there found themselves hopelessly outnumbered and made a hasty retreat across the Potomac River to Hagerstown, Maryland, leaving behind some five thousand rifles and a large supply of ammunition.

At 10:00 A.M. the same day, Lieutenant Jordan arrived at the Capitol. Climbing the stairs that led from the rotunda to the second floor, he moved down the hall to find three Military Committee members in discussion with his daughter at her desk. Jenny greeted him as he drew near. Jordan excused himself to the Committee members while he bent down and kissed his daughter's cheek.

"How's uncle Elbert?" Jenny asked for the benefit of the others.

"He's a sick man right now, but with proper care, he'll be all right. Said to give you his love."

"He's such a sweetie," she smiled.

"We're glad you're back, Colonel," said one of the senators. "Mr. Lincoln has called for a big meeting with the Committee, the Cabinet, and General Scott first thing in the morning."

"I'll be there with bells on," replied Jordan.

"I don't suppose you've heard about Colonel Robert E. Lee," spoke up another.

"No."

"Resigned his commission at four o'clock yesterday afternoon. Announced proudly that he was joining the Confederate army. I figured he'd turn traitor, too."

The word *traitor* went all the way to Jordan's spine. Covering it, he remarked, "Didn't we all know he would?" Then turning to Jenny, he asked, "Is John Calhoun in?"

"Yes. He's back in his cubbyhole."

Jordan spent an hour with Calhoun. When the Chamber secretary heard Jordan's plan, he was immediately interest and volunteered to do his part. He was elated to know the plan had Colonel Jackson's approval and did not flinch when Jordan warned him of the consequences if he was caught as a Confederate spy. Calhoun's loyalty to the South was as strong as his love of life itself.

Late that afternoon, Jordan and Calhoun paid a visit to Rose Greenhow at her fashionable home on Washington's 16th Street. She welcomed them warmly and granted Jordan's request for a private talk. They went to the library, and the servants were told not to interrupt them for any reason.

When Jordan explained his plan, which had Colonel Jackson's approval and Calhoun's cooperation, she flashed her winsome smile and wholeheartedly agreed to become the go-between in the spy ring. She assured both men that she could produce young ladies loyal to the Southern cause who would find it adventuresome and patriotic to carry vital messages to the Confederate military authorities.

Then Rose looked at Jordan and asked, "Does Jenny know about all this?"

"No. I'm going to have to tell her, though. Jenny thinks a lot of Mr. Lincoln, and she loves her job…but her heart belongs to the South. She'll understand what I'm doing and keep mum about it, of course. The hardest part for her will be the risk I'm taking. She knows what happens to spies when they're caught."

"Well, that's part of war," sighed Rose. "She'll handle it all right, the same as she'd handle it if you were fighting on battlefields. I can't say that I cherish the thought of facing a firing squad myself, but if my contribution as a spy can bring a quick victory for the South, I'll be happy."

"What about your relationship with Senator Wilson?" queried Calhoun.

"I'll keep it intact, of course," smiled Rose. "What better way to cover my tracks? My loyalty to the Southern cause is stronger than my infatuation with Henry. Have I stated my position clearly?"

"Yes, quite," replied Calhoun, looking at Jordan. "Wouldn't you say so, Colonel?"

"Quite clearly," agreed Jordan.

FOUR

On Saturday afternoon, April 13, eleven hundred Fire Zouaves marched in perfect ranks on the training field just outside of Utica, New York. Leading the drill was Sergeant Casper Lynch, a tough, thick-bodied man with a gravelly voice.

Several hundred Utica residents looked on with pride from the surrounding hills as the Eleventh New York Fire Zouaves went through their paces under the brilliant glare of sunlight. The sound of a dozen snare drums echoed across the grassy field while the well-disciplined soldiers moved with precision as if all were part of one body.

The Zouaves were a striking sight to behold in their bright-colored uniforms. Styled after the famous French Zouaves of Crimean War days, Colonel Elmer Ellsworth's troops wore bright-red fezzes, white shirts, short blue coats, baggy red breeches, black boots, and yellow sashes about their waists.

Marching just behind Sergeant Lynch, in front of the line of drummers, were two Zouaves who carried flag staffs. Whipping in the breeze was a black-and-white regimental flag on one staff, and the red-white-and-blue of Old Glory on the other.

The sun was lowering toward the west when Colonel Ellsworth

came riding at a gallop across the rolling hills from Utica, where he had been since late morning. Though the marching Zouaves saw their leader thundering toward them, they did not break rank nor even turn their heads. When Sergeant Lynch saw Ellsworth excitedly waving his hat, he called for the marchers to halt.

The colonel skidded his mount to a stop in front of the neatly formed ranks, and said to Lynch, "I've got news from Washington."

"Is it what we've been expecting, sir?"

"Yes." Because of his lack of height, Ellsworth remained in the saddle to address his men. Sitting as tall as he could, he lifted his voice and said, "Men, I have news from Washington! While I was in town this morning to send some telegrams, a message came to me from President Lincoln's secretary, John Hay. Yesterday morning at dawn, under orders from Jefferson Davis, General Beauregard opened fire on our garrison at Fort Sumter. The Confederates have started the war! Right now, they are battling it out with Major Anderson and his men. Sumter is surrounded. There is little hope for survival of Major Anderson and his garrison aside from surrender."

There was a stirring amongst the Zouaves, and one of them near the rear of the ranks raised a hand. Ellsworth acknowledged him. "What is it, Private Zeller?"

"When do we get to retaliate, Colonel?"

"I can't tell you when yet, but I *can* tell you that you will get your chance!"

Suddenly the Zouaves went into a wild uproar, shouting fiery words of indignation and defiance against the Confederates. The colonel let them blow off steam for a few minutes, then raised his hand for silence.

"When I received Mr. Hay's wire," Ellsworth explained with raised voice, "I sent a message back right away, asking for orders from President Lincoln concerning us. Mr. Hay answered back that Mr. Lincoln was busy, but would get a message to us within two or three days. In the meantime, we will continue to drill, target practice, and work on our combat training."

"Yes, sir!" shouted a Zouave. "But with more exuberance, Colonel!" Muskets were raised in the air and men shouted their agreement.

Ellsworth called for silence again, and when it came, he shouted, "Let's knock off for the rest of the day, men. Get yourselves a good rest. We'll hit the training field at sunup in the morning!"

Sergeant Lynch formally dismissed the brightly clad soldiers. They broke ranks quickly and headed for their barracks. Vengeance against the Confederates was their only topic of discussion.

Colonel Ellsworth saw the civilians coming toward him, banded together. They had heard enough to know that Fort Sumter had been fired upon, and they wanted the details. Ellsworth took the time to tell them all he knew about it, adding that their local newspapers would no doubt have more information by morning.

The next morning at sunrise, eleven hundred Fire Zouaves charged onto the training field, adrenaline pumping. They were eager for battle. It showed in the vigor and intensity of their training exercises. While half of the Zouaves were doing target practice under the guidance of Sergeant Lynch, the rest were working on their hand-to-hand combat skills.

Colonel Ellsworth stood by the crowd of 550 men at the south end of the field and observed as his training specialist, Corporal Francis E. "Buck" Brownell, lectured them on physical fitness. Brownell, a native of Saratoga County, New York, was considered the most tenacious of the Eleventh Zouaves, and had the respect of the entire regiment.

Buck Brownell stood an even six feet in height and weighed 175 pounds. At twenty-six, he was intelligent, well-conditioned, agile, and rawboned. Handsome in a rugged way, he was dark complected and had lively black eyes that could warm a person or send an icy chill down their backbone. He wore a well-trimmed mustache that matched his thick crop of jet-black hair.

Brownell finished his lecture. "All right, gentlemen, we're going to take some more lessons at bayonet fighting. After a couple of you do a demonstration for us, I will point out the good moves and bad ones. As I have told you before, when you go up against an enemy in a face-to-face bayonet fight, one of the two combatants is going to die. You must have the proper mental attitude about it, or you're whipped before you start. You must have absolute confidence in yourself when you face the enemy. The only way you can have that confidence is by proving yourself here on the practice field. Once you have been successful in combat, your confidence will grow."

Running his gaze over the young and eager faces, Brownell said, "All right, I'm going to pick one man who has little experience and put him up against a man who is well-experienced. The newer man will learn quickly that way."

His black eyes settled on a young recruit who showed real promise. "Private Phil Harrison," he said crisply, "you come."

While Harrison was threading his way amongst the men, Brownell was trying to decide which experienced man to choose. Suddenly the little colonel stepped forward and said, "Corporal Brownell, let me go up against Harrison."

Buck's brow furrowed. "You, sir?"

"Sure," grinned Ellsworth. "Why not?"

"Well…you're our leader, sir. You're a colonel."

"So? I'm well experienced. Let's see what I can teach Harrison."

A soldier stepped up and offered Ellsworth his rifle. It was already fixed with a bayonet. The colonel thanked him, and under the eyes of every man in the crowd, he squared off with Private Harrison.

Though Harrison was a much larger man, he was intimidated by the little colonel. They parried with each other for several minutes, with Ellsworth giving verbal instructions at the same time. Harrison kept leaving himself vulnerable to the colonel's feinting thrusts. Ellsworth warned him of it, pointing out that such mistakes would cost him his life in actual battle.

Harrison also was leaving himself open for a rifle butt against his jaw. Ellsworth explained what the young recruit was doing, making sure he understood that if he was caught with a rifle butt, he would go down, and his enemy would drive his bayonet into his heart.

Private Harrison did better at countering Ellsworth's bayonet thrusts, but once again left his jaw unprotected. Ellsworth decided it was time to give Harrison a lesson. The rifle butt came swiftly against young Harrison's jaw, and he went down, dazed. Standing over him, the colonel raised his weapon, pointing the bayonet at Harrison's heart, and brought it down. Harrison's eyes bulged. Ellsworth drove the steel blade into the ground inches from the young recruit's arm. He then offered a hand and helped him up.

"I want all of you to think about what you just saw," Ellsworth said. "One wrong move in a bayonet fight, and it's over. You don't get a second chance. So you all can see exactly how it should be done—Corporal Brownell, grab your rifle. Let's show them."

Brownell had never done a demonstration with his superior officer, and would rather not, but he had to obey him. Picking up his rifle, he moved close to Ellsworth. Taking his stance, with bayonet ready to thrust, the colonel said, "All right, Corporal, come and get me."

Brownell held his weapon at ready and moved in. Ellsworth adeptly dodged his mock thrust and parried, but the quick-footed Brownell turned speedily and swung his rifle butt dangerously close to Ellsworth's chin. The heads of the bright-uniformed spectators bobbed at the close call.

Ellsworth laughed and said to the Zouaves, "See, men? I made an error. I should have prevented him from making that move." Then to Brownell, "Congratulations, Corporal. For playing around, that was perfect. All right, let's go again. This time, you won't out-maneuver me."

As the two men danced about and parried with each other, Ellsworth was quickly out-foxed again. Brownell had the opportunity to connect with the colonel's jaw once more, but purposely missed. This time, Ellsworth took advantage of it and cracked Buck's jaw hard, knocking him down. The colonel raised his bayonet as if to stab him, and said, "You made a mistake, Corporal! If I was the enemy, I would have killed you."

Rising, Brownell shook his head. "No, sir. You wouldn't have killed me. If you had been an enemy, I would've connected with your jaw and put you down. *You'd* be the dead man."

Ellsworth squinted at his opponent. "Are you saying, Corporal, that you missed me *that* time on purpose?"

"Yes, sir."

Disbelief showed in Ellsworth's eyes. "I don't think so. If you honestly had the advantage of me, you should have put me down. It appeared to me that you just flat missed."

"I didn't put you down, sir, because you're my commanding officer."

Ellsworth grinned at him, and in a cocky manner, took a fighting stance. "Forget my rank, Brownell. I'm coming after you."

Far be it from Corporal Francis E. Brownell to disobey his commanding officer. When Ellsworth came at him, the corporal sidestepped swiftly and cracked him solidly with his rifle butt. Ellsworth sprawled on the ground and lay still. He was out cold.

The Zouaves looked on wide-eyed and open-mouthed as Corporal Brownell called for a canteen of water and knelt beside Ellsworth. Quickly the canteen was supplied. Brownell uncorked it and splashed water in the colonel's face. The colonel slowly came around. Blinking his eyes, he looked up at Brownell and shook his head to clear it.

"Here sir," said Brownell, placing a hand at the back of Ellsworth's head, "let me help you sit up." Buck eased him into a sitting position.

"I'm sorry, Colonel," said Buck. "I—"

"Don't be sorry, Corporal. I told you to do it. You did. And yours truly found out he needs to sharpen up on his bayonet practice."

Brownell helped the colonel to his feet, then said to the Zouaves, "All right, men. Let's pair off. I want you more experienced men to choose partners with less experience. Time is of the essence, now. We'll be going into battle soon. While you practice, I'll move amongst you and give pointers where they're needed."

As Zouaves prepared to follow Brownell's instructions, Colonel Ellsworth said, "Corporal, I like your style. When we leave here and go to war, I want you as my personal aide. You will stay close to me at all times."

"Yes, sir. It will be my pleasure."

On Monday, Colonel Ellsworth received a special wire from President Lincoln, announcing his call to arms of seventy-five thousand militiamen and ordering the colonel to bring his Eleventh New York Zouaves regiment to Washington. War was being declared on the Confederacy, and Lincoln wanted the Zouaves in Washington, ready for battle. The wire also informed Ellsworth that the New York Central Railroad—by the president's order—would add several cars to bring the Zouaves to Washington. Other militia units from New York and New England would also be heading for the nation's capital.

When Ellsworth made the announcement to his men, they shouted with joy. They were eager to punish the Rebels for their insurrection against the U.S. government.

When Colonel Ellsworth presented his regiment at the Utica depot, on Wednesday morning, April 17, railroad officials explained that they would change trains in New York City and be on their way to Baltimore on Thursday. A third train would take them the thirty miles to Washington from there.

The Zouaves boarded the special cars, carrying what luggage was necessary, along with their weapons and ammunition. When the train rolled into the depot in New York, the Zouaves found that eight hundred men of the Sixth Massachusetts Infantry were there, also going to Washington. The Sixth Massachusetts was under the command of Colonel Edward F. Jones. They would be on the same train to Baltimore, along with a small regiment of soldiers from the

Seventh New York Militia, led by Captain Alex Frame.

Word spread throughout New York City that Federal troops would be changing trains in New York on their way to Washington. On Thursday morning, thousands of New Yorkers gathered to see them off and wish them well. A band played and people waved American flags.

Colonel Ellsworth was standing on the platform, observing his Zouaves as they boarded their special cars, when he saw Colonel Jones and Captain Frame coming toward him in a hurry, threading their way through the enthusiastic crowd. As they drew up, Edwards shouted above the din while waving a telegram, "This message just came to me through the telegraph office here. It's from John Hay, Mr. Lincoln's secretary. Mr. Lincoln wants us to know that there was serious trouble yesterday in Baltimore. A militia unit from Pennsylvania was passing through there on their way to Washington and was assaulted by a jeering mob of pro-Confederate civilians! They pelted the soldiers with rocks and bricks."

"So we need to prepare ourselves, is that it?" said Ellsworth.

"Exactly. We'll need to distribute ammunition to our men and have them load their weapons."

Captain Frame asked, "Are we supposed to fire at will if we are threatened, Colonel?"

"Tell your men to hold fire if at all possible, but if they judge that their lives are in danger, they have the president's permission to use their weapons to protect themselves."

Once on the train, the three regiments were given the president's instructions by their officers. Ammunition was distributed, and the troops loaded their guns.

The train reached Baltimore's President Street station at noon on Friday, April 19. Arrangements had been made for horses to pull the military cars over a track through the city to the Camden Street station, where the Baltimore and Ohio Railroad line to Washington commenced.

As the cars were detached from the train and horses harnessed to them, a railroad official entered Colonel Jones's car and warned him that an angry pro-Confederate mob was waiting in the streets. The Baltimore police estimated there were over ten thousand in the mob, and it was still growing. There were too few policemen to even begin to control them.

Jones called Ellsworth and Frame out of their cars and passed the warning on to them. As they discussed the situation, Ellsworth said, "Colonel, we'll be sitting ducks in these cars. Shouldn't we put the men in close ranks and just march them over to the other station?"

"Then we have no protection at all," argued Jones. "At least inside the cars, we have some protection."

"I think we'd be better off outside, sir," said Ellsworth. "I'm afraid our men will be hampered by the close quarters of the cars. They'll have a hard time wielding their weapons. If they're outside, they'll have freedom of movement."

"But they'll also be clear targets," objected Jones. "I say we stay in the cars."

Ellsworth knew army regulations quite well. When there are two officers of the same rank, and a decision has to be made, the officer with seniority is automatically in charge. Jones was nine years older than Ellsworth and had been in the army that much longer.

"All right, Colonel," said the younger man. "My men and I will do as you say. However, if we see that our cramped situation puts us in mortal danger, I will give them orders to move outside and fight."

"If that becomes the case and I see that my judgment was wrong, we'll join you," said Jones.

"Same for us," put in Frame.

"All right, gentlemen," said Jones, "let's get aboard. They're about ready to move out."

Colonel Ellsworth passed the word to his men to be prepared to move out and fight if he gave the order. The Zouaves trusted their leader explicitly, and would follow his orders without question. As Ellsworth had requested, Corporal Brownell rode in his car and sat beside him.

As the horses began to pull the cars out of the depot, Buck said, "Colonel, if this thing turns ugly, I'd like for you to get down on the floor."

Ellsworth shook his head. "Can't do that, Corporal. I'm the leader, here. I can't expect these men to have respect for me if I duck out of the fight."

"But you're our commander, sir. We can't afford to lose you."

"Only when I become a general will I remain aloof from the action. Until then, I'll fight right along with my men."

"I respect that, sir, but you've asked me to be your personal aide. At least let me do what I can to protect you."

"I want you as my aide to help me get things done when I need them. I didn't mean you had to risk your life to protect mine."

Buck grinned. "Okay, but since you want me as your aide, I'm sticking as close as the hide on a cow."

As the car moved slowly out of the station, they heard the roar of the angry mob. They could hear the sound of breaking glass in the cars ahead, and the soldiers in them were shouting amongst themselves. Buck moved to the front of the car, opened the door, and moved out onto the platform. Turning back quickly, he said so that every man in the coach could hear, "Colonel, the mob has blockaded the track. There's no way we can get the cars through. They're throwing bricks and stones…and they're looking plenty mean."

Suddenly the windows of the car began to shatter as rocks and bricks crashed through them. The wild throng was shouting and swearing at the Union soldiers. One man was heard to scream, "Welcome to Southern graves, Yankee swine!"

Colonel Ellsworth raised an elbow to protect his face from flying glass and shouted, "Let's get out of here, men! Use your guns. Maybe if a few of them go down, the rest will back off."

All along the line, soldiers poured from the cars and began firing into the mob. The first volley brought screams and curses, and for a moment it appeared that the Southern sympathizers would withdraw. But they quickly regrouped and attacked the soldiers, brandishing clubs and makeshift weapons. They also found more bricks and rocks to throw.

Colonel Jones was leading his troops toward the Camden Street station. Their progress was slow because the street had become a virtual battleground. Soldiers and civilians were going down and being trampled underfoot as rifles barked and the mob swung clubs, crowbars, hammers, and fists. When soldiers fell, their comrades dragged them along while fighting off the crazed citizens of Baltimore. Soon pistols and muskets were being fired at the uniformed men from windows, doors, and roofs of stores and houses. Most of the bullets, however, were hitting rioters.

The Union troops were sorely outnumbered, but fought back gallantly. Rioters wrestled with many of them, wrenching the muskets from their hands and using the bayonets on them. One Zouave took dead aim at a rioter who had just stabbed a soldier with his own bayonet and pulled the trigger. The musket did not fire. Five wild-eyed citizens leaped on the Zouave, yanked the bayoneted musket from his hands, and ran him through.

A few feet away, Colonel Ellsworth and Corporal Brownell were fighting side by side. Ellsworth had just shot a rioter through the heart and Brownell dropped one with his bayonet When they saw the Zouave go down, they turned on his killers. The colonel blasted two of them with his revolver and swung the gun on another, but the hammer came down on a spent shell.

Buck stabbed one of them with his bayonet, cracked another on the jaw, then pivoted to stab the one Ellsworth was facing. However, the little colonel had slammed the man on the temple with his gun barrel, putting him down. Another rioter came up behind Brownell, wielding a knife. Ellsworth saw him and shouted, "Buck! Behind you!"

Buck pivoted, but not in time to dodge the deadly blade. It slashed across his face, burning like a red-hot iron. Reacting quickly, Buck seized the man's arm and brought it down on a raised knee. Bone snapped, the man howled, and the knife clattered to the street.

Blood streamed down Brownell's cheek as he continued to fight alongside his commanding officer. The Union troops stayed in close ranks as much as possible as they battled the mob and worked their way toward the railroad station.

Finally they reached the station, but the frenzied throng tried to block them from boarding the train. The Union officers braced their men for a final push and commanded those who had reloaded to fire point-blank into the mob. The fusillade cut a path, leaving bleeding bodies in its wake, and the soldiers boarded the train, carrying and aiding their wounded. The train pulled out with members of the mob shouting obscenities, throwing missiles, and firing through the windows with muskets they had wrested from the soldiers' hands.

As the train left Baltimore behind, the troops began tending to their wounded. Colonel Ellsworth tended to Brownell's slashed cheek, doing what he could to stop the bleeding.

At Fort Sumter, no one had been killed. The riot in Baltimore left a dozen citizens dead and scores wounded. Four soldiers had died and over a hundred were seriously wounded.

Baltimore's bloody riot was an accurate omen of what was coming. America had tasted civil war on its own streets. No person would be guaranteed shelter from its effects, whether in uniform or out of it.

FIVE

Government authorities in Washington learned of the riot in Baltimore long before the train arrived with the soldiers. Baltimore's mayor had sent a wire, advising them that some of the soldiers had been killed in the clash with the pro-Southern civilians, and that a large number had been wounded. The wounded ones would need immediate medical attention when the train arrived in Washington.

The nation's capital city had only one small hospital, which was not equipped well enough to care for the number of soldiers who had been wounded. A vivacious and civic-minded young woman named Clara Barton—an employee at the U.S. Patent Office—quickly organized a makeshift hospital in the rotunda of the Capitol. Using congressional messenger boys, Clara called for doctors to come with medicine and equipment, and to bring as many nurses with them as pos-sible. Realizing she would still be short on help, Clara sent word through the Capitol and across the city, asking for volunteers to help care for the wounded soldiers.

When the train arrived at the Washington depot at five o'clock in the afternoon, President Abraham Lincoln was there to meet it. He met with the three commanding officers, and was relieved that his friend Colonel Elmer Ellsworth was unscathed.

Wagons, carriages, and surreys were provided by concerned citizens to carry the wounded soldiers to the Capitol. They were amazed to find the makeshift hospital ready for them. Most of the troops went directly from the depot to an army camp just outside the city. The commanding officers and a few unharmed soldiers accompanied the wounded to the Capitol.

Among the volunteers who had answered Clara Barton's call were Jenny Jordan and Patricia Winters. Mary Lincoln had encouraged Patricia to go, saying she would tutor the boys herself. Jenny, who was at her desk when the call for help came, responded immediately, since she was already in the capitol building.

Soon soldiers with blood-soaked uniforms were lying in rows on the floor of the rotunda. There were twenty wounded men for each doctor, and almost as many for each nurse. Those most seriously wounded were tended to first, while Clara directed her volunteers to make the other soldiers as comfortable as possible while they waited. Others were still being brought in .

Colonels Jones and Ellsworth, along with Captain Frame, moved amongst their wounded men. The smell of salves and antiseptics was strong in the place. President Lincoln and some of his Cabinet members stood on the stairs that led to the Capitol's second floor and observed with grave interest.

Corporal Brownell came through the large doors at the front of the rotunda, carrying a wounded Zouave in his arms like a man would carry a child. The Zouave had taken a bayonet in the upper thigh, and his bright-colored, baggy trousers were soaked with blood.

Clara was helping a soldier lay a wounded comrade on the floor when she spotted Buck coming in. Hurrying to him, she said, "Right over here, Corporal."

As Clara led the way, she looked over her shoulder and said, "He seems to be losing a lot of blood. Was anything done for him during the train ride?"

"Yes'm," replied Buck. "We wrapped it as best as we could, but the gash is pretty deep. He'll need a doctor to stitch him up as quick as possible."

Clara nodded, showed Buck where to lay him, and glanced toward Jenny, who was just finishing up a temporary bandage on the broken, bleeding hand of a soldier nearby.

Clara called, "Jenny, as soon as you're finished there, I need you to come and cut away this soldier's pantleg."

"Be right there," Jenny answered.

Clara knelt beside Buck, looked down at the wounded man, and said, "I'll have a doctor here as quickly as possible, soldier. In the meantime, Miss Jordan will tend to you."

The Zouave, a private named Wally Springer, tried to smile. "Thank you ma'am. I appreciate your wonderful help."

"We all do," Buck said, giving Miss Barton an amiable smile. "They told us on the train that you headed this operation up, ma'am. You *are* Clara Barton?"

"Yes."

"You're not a nurse?"

"No, Corporal—"

"Brownell, ma'am. Buck Brownell."

"No, Corporal Brownell, I'm not a nurse. I've never been able to afford the cost for schooling. I work in the U.S. Patent Office, but I've volunteered my services here in the city when there've been disasters of one kind or another."

"That's very kind of you, ma'am."

Clara smiled. "Thank you. I see some more men being brought in. Miss Jordan will be here in a moment, and I'll see that a doctor is sent over as soon as one is available."

As Clara walked away, Buck said, "Wally, you'll be okay. It looks like the bleeding has eased off." Just then Buck looked up to see Jenny Jordan drop to her knees on the other side of Wally Springer. She had a pair of scissors in her hand.

For a brief, magical moment, the eyes of Jenny and Buck locked and held. Corporal Brownell, roughneck Zouave and tough trainer of soldiers, was spellbound. His heart seemed to stop dead in his chest, yet his temples were pounding.

Jenny managed a sweet smile and said, "I'm Jenny Jordan."

Buck was so stricken that his brain seemed to go flat on him. For a moment he couldn't think of his name.

The wounded private saw the corporal's predicament and spoke up. "His name is Corporal Francis Brownell, ma'am. Mine's Wally Springer."

Jenny broke the spell by pulling her gaze from Buck and looking down at the wounded man. "Are you in pain, Wally?" she asked.

"A little bit, Miss Jenny, but it's not bad."

Leaning over him and tugging at the bloody pantleg, she aimed the scissors a few inches above the gash and said, "I'll try not to hurt you, but I have to cut this pantleg off so the doctor can get to the wound."

"That's all right, ma'am," said Springer, also taken by Jenny. "It'll be worth it just to have such a pretty lady taking care of me."

"Aren't you the flatterer?" she said lightly as she began to cut.

Buck watched Jenny work the scissors through the blood-soaked cloth and said, "I assume because you're not in a nurse's uniform that you're not a nurse, ma'am."

"You're right," she replied, concentrating on her work.

"You sure handle those scissors like you've done it before."

"Up until a short time ago I was a seamstress, Corporal Brownell," she replied without looking up.

"That answers it. So what do you do now?" He had noticed that she wore no wedding ring, so he wasn't afraid she would tell him she was now a housewife.

"I work for the government. I am a receptionist here in the Capitol for the Senate Military Committee."

"Sounds like an interesting job," Buck said.

Jenny finished cutting the pantleg and said, "It has its moments." Then looking up at Buck, she asked, "Would you help me, Corporal? He'll have less pain if the two of us slip this pantleg off together."

"Sure, just tell me how you want it done."

Suddenly Jenny caught sight of the gash on Buck's cheek. "Oh, Corporal!" she gasped. "You're wounded too…and it looks pretty bad. We'll get one of the doctors to check on it."

Buck's fingertips found the gash. "Oh, it's all right, ma'am. It's starting to scab over. It hasn't bled since this morning."

"But it looks swollen," she said, studying the wound. "I'll clean it in a moment, then we'll get a doctor to look at it. I think there might be some infection."

"Whatever you say," Buck grinned.

Jenny instructed Buck on how to help her slide the severed pantleg downward and over Springer's boot. Carefully, they worked together and had it done within a minute. Then she said to the private, "I'll get some alcohol and clean around your wound, Mr. Springer. Be back in just a minute."

While she was gone, Springer asked, "Corporal, you ever see a woman as pretty as her?"

"Not that I can remember."

"Kinda took your breath away, didn't she?"

"You might say that."

"*Might*, nothing. She had you so mesmerized, you couldn't even think of your own name."

Before Buck could comment, Jenny returned, carrying cloths and a bottle of alcohol. On her heels came a doctor and his nurse. The doctor did a quick examination of Buck's wound and told him he would have to take stitches. He asked Jenny to clean the wound while he and the nurse took care of Springer. Jenny took Buck a few steps away to a straight-backed wooden chair and sat him down.

While she worked, trying her best not to hurt him, Jenny said, "It's awful what happened to you and the other soldiers in Baltimore. I understand some of our men were killed."

"Yes, ma'am."

"I'm afraid what happened there is just a small foreshadowing of what lies ahead. I wish there wasn't going to be a civil war."

"I do, too, Miss Jenny, but I don't think there's anything that can be done to stop it." He paused, then asked, "Do I detect a slight Southern accent in your speech?"

"Mm-hmm. I'm from Virginia."

"I see. Your parents still live there?"

"No. My mother is dead. Daddy and I live here in Washington. You may have heard of him—Lieutenant Colonel Jeffrey Jordan?"

"*Colonel Jeffrey Jordan!*" Buck exclaimed. "The Mexican War hero?"

"One in the same," she said proudly. "He's now military adviser to the Senate Committee on military affairs."

"Do you suppose I could meet him sometime? I've heard a lot about what he did in the war."

"I suppose that could be arranged. Now, hold still, Corporal. I've got to clean very close to the gash."

Buck winced as the alcohol touched its fire to the open wound.

"I'm sorry," Jenny said quietly, "but this has to be done."

"I know. Sorry I jumped."

Jenny soaked the cloth from the bottle, then leaned close to apply the alcohol. Buck's heart was doing strange things with Jenny so close to him. He found her invigorating. Never had a woman so stirred him.

On the other side of the rotunda, Patricia Winters found herself wrapping a broken forefinger on the right hand of Lieutenant John Hammond of the Sixth Massachusetts. One of the doctors had set the finger, explained to Patricia how to splint it and wrap it correctly, then moved on to another patient.

While Patricia worked at getting the finger wrapped just right, the lieutenant looked at her admiringly and said, "The doctor called you Patricia, Miss. May I ask your last name?"

"You may," she smiled. "It's Winters. You know…like the cold time of year."

Hammond smiled. "And where are you from, Miss Patricia Winters?"

"Springfield, Illinois."

"Springfield, Illinois? Are you acquainted with our president?"

Patricia smiled, took a second to brush a lock of dark-brown hair from her forehead, and replied, "You might say I am."

"Now, what does that mean?"

She giggled. "I work for Mr. Lincoln."

"Really?"

"Mm-hmm. *And* Mrs. Lincoln."

"Doing what? Don't tell me you're a maid in the White House."

"No. I'm governess to their two sons, Willie and Tad. Have been for nearly six years."

"Governess, eh?" he said pleasantly surprised.

"Mm-hmm."

"Are the boys really like the papers make them out to be? I mean, Willie quiet and reserved and Tad a regular pistol?"

"Exactly," Patricia laughed. "I love them both, of course, but that Tad is the charmer. I have to be careful. He can turn on that personality of his and talk me into all kinds of things."

"So you like your job."

"Very much so."

"Not planning on nuptials, then, I take it."

"Oh, I wouldn't say that," she said, tying a small knot to finish the wrapping. "When Mr. Right comes along, I'll marry him and give up my governess job."

"Any prospects for a groom at the moment?"

"No. There wasn't anyone I felt serious about in Springfield…and I've been so busy since moving to Washington that I haven't had time to meet any single young men here."

"Don't the Lincolns ever give you any time for yourself?"

"Oh, yes. I mean…they do if I ask for it." Patricia could tell

Lieutenant Hammond was attracted to her.

"Well, then, what would you say if I asked you to spend a little free time with *me*?" asked Hammond.

Patricia cleared her throat nervously. "Well...well I'd say...*yes!*"

"Good! How soon can you get some time off?"

"I can have Sunday. I was going to ask the Lincolns for Sunday morning off, at least, so I can attend church. There's a Congregational church not far from the White House. I thought I'd try it."

"Would you mind some company?" he asked quickly.

"Not at all," she smiled.

"What about *after* church? I mean...maybe a picnic and a walk through the park?"

"All right. I'll make us a picnic lunch."

"How...ah...how do I get my buggy through the gates at the White House so I can pick you up?"

"That'll be easy. I'll be waiting at the gate on the east side at ten-thirty."

"Okay, Miss Patricia. I'll be there at ten-thirty sharp!"

When the doctor had finished stitching and bandaging Buck's face, he told Buck to come to his office in a week so he could examine the wound. If it was healing properly by that time, he would take the stitches out.

Jenny had gone to help Clara Barton with another patient while the doctor was working on Buck. Just as the doctor walked away, Jenny returned, smiling, and said, "Well, Corporal, it looks like you're all fixed up."

"Guess so," said Buck, who was still seated on the chair.

Jenny pulled up another chair and sat down. "We've got all the wounded men taken care of now. I have to get back to work upstairs shortly, but I thought I'd come back and see how you're doing."

"I'm fine, ma'am," said Buck.

"So…where are you from, Corporal? I know you're in the Eleventh New York Fire Zouaves, but if I understand correctly, that doesn't mean you have to be a native New Yorker."

"That's right. We have men in the Eleventh who are from Illinois and Pennsylvania, as well as New York. Myself, I'm from Saratoga Springs, New York."

"Your parents live there?"

"They're both dead, ma'am."

"Oh, I'm sorry."

"That's all right. How could you know? I have a sister who lives in California, and a brother who lives right here in Washington."

"Oh? Older or younger than you?"

"Both older. I'm twenty-six. Sis is thirty and has two children. Robert is twenty-eight. Married, but no children yet."

"I'm interested in what caused you to join the Zouaves. I mean…they are just a bit different than your usual state militia."

"Well, let me explain that."

Just then Colonel Ellsworth drew up and said, "Well, Corporal, I see you've been patched up. Did this young lady do that for you?"

"No, sir," said Buck, rising to his feet. "She prepared the wound, but a doctor actually did the bandaging after he'd taken several stitches."

"So it'll be okay?"

"Doctor says I'll have a scar, but it'll be all right, yes," replied Buck. Then gesturing toward Jenny, he said, "Colonel Elmer Ellsworth, I would like you to meet Miss Jenny Jordan."

Ellsworth clicked his heels, bowed, and said, "Miss Jordan, it is a pleasure to make your acquaintance."

"Likewise, I'm sure," Jenny said warmly, smiling. "I've heard much about you, Colonel. Your exploits with the Zouave Drill Team are quite well known and very much discussed in our family. My father is Lieutenant Colonel Jeffrey Jordan. Perhaps you've heard of him?"

"Well, I certainly have. Talk about exploits! Your father is what I call a genuine hero."

"Why, thank you. I'll tell Daddy I met you, and relay your kind words about him."

Buck felt a tinge of jealousy over Jenny's warmth toward the colonel, and quickly reprimanded himself. He had no claim on her.

"Please do, ma'am," said Ellsworth. "And tell your father I would like to meet him some time."

While Jenny and the colonel discussed her father's valor on the battlefield, Buck wondered if she had a man in her life. He told himself that no woman as charming and beautiful as Jenny would find herself short of attention from men.

The conversation about Lieutenant Jordan trailed off, then Ellsworth turned to Buck and said, "It's almost eight. We need to be getting out to the camp soon. I'll do a quick check on the rest of our Zouaves, then we'll go."

"Fine, sir," nodded Buck. "I'll wait right here." Ellsworth spoke a few departing words to Jenny and walked away.

Jenny rose to her feet and said, "Well, Corporal, I need to head for home. It's past my dinner time."

Buck had to satisfy his curiosity. "Miss Jenny," he said, "may I ask you a personal question?"

"Of course," she smiled.

"Is there a...a special man in your life? I mean...do you have a steady beau?"

"No, Corporal," she answered softly.

Surprised but pleased, Buck said, "Well, in that case, since you haven't eaten this evening, and neither have I...could I take you to dinner?"

"Well, I..."

Seeing her hesitation, Buck said, "Oh, you have to get home to prepare dinner for your father, don't you?"

"No. No, I don't. Daddy's eating dinner with friends."

"Then you can let me take you to dinner. There must be a good restaurant somewhere close by, isn't there?"

"Well, yes, but..."

"You said you wanted to know why I joined the Zouaves."

Jenny was feeling a magnetic pull toward the rugged Zouave, but was careful to mask it. "Oh, I do, but you heard the colonel. He wants you to go to the camp with him."

"I can talk him into letting me come to the camp after I take you to dinner."

A bit off balance at Buck's forwardness, Jenny laughed hollowly and said, "I doubt that, Corporal."

Patting her shoulder, he said, "You wait right here. I'll be back in a moment."

Jenny smiled to herself and watched as Buck hurried across the rotunda and approached Colonel Ellsworth. It took the colonel only seconds to glance across the wide room at Jenny, then nod his head. Buck whirled and hastened back to Jenny.

"Ready to go?"

Shaking her head in amazement, Jenny laughed, "Corporal, you're a real dazzler, you are!"

The restaurant was busy and full of chatter as Buck and Jenny sat at their candlelit table. "I'll walk you home after we've eaten, Miss Jenny," said Buck. "I hope your father will be home so I can meet him."

"He won't be. The friends he's visiting will keep him at their house past midnight. You'll have to meet him some other time. Now, Corporal, I want to hear why you joined the Zouaves."

Buck grinned in spite of the pain it caused. "Tell you what, Miss Jenny. I'd like it better if you would just call me by my name. You don't have to call me Corporal."

"All right, Francis," she said warmly.

"Not by that name, please. I don't know why my parents did such a thing to me. I guess they just didn't think about it."

Grinning broadly, Jenny said, "Sort of hurt your male ego?"

"Yes. Got me into lots of fights as a kid, too. When I was twelve, I started calling myself Buck."

"I see. Well, Buck does sound a lot more masculine than Francis, I'll admit. Okay, I'll call you Buck if you'll call me Jenny."

"It's a deal, ma'am," he said, reaching across the table to shake her hand.

"Not *ma'am*, Buck," she corrected him. "*Jenny.*"

"Jenny."

She shook his hand, then said, "Now, tell me about joining the Zouaves."

Pleased that Jenny was interested, Buck told her of his boyhood fascination with the military and that he had joined the Regular Army immediately after graduating from high school. When the rough-and-ready Zouaves captured his interest, he asked for a transfer and got it. That was a year and a half ago. He enjoyed being a part of the famous drill team and liked working for the colorful Colonel Ellsworth.

As he walked Jenny home after dinner, Buck said cautiously, "Jenny…"

"Yes, Buck?"

"I'm…going to pay a visit to my brother Robert and his wife tomorrow evening. Would…would you like to go with me?"

"Oh, I'd like to, Buck, but I have so much to do at home tomorrow night. With my mother gone, I have to keep the house in good order and see to Daddy's needs. Tomorrow I have to get the washing and ironing done."

"I understand," he said, feeling disappointed. "Then how about Sunday?"

"Well, Daddy and I always go to church on Sunday. You'd certainly be welcome to come along. You could have Sunday dinner with us, then the two of us could take a stroll through Stanton Park in the afternoon. We go to Penn Avenue Methodist. Our pastor is a fire-eater. You'll hear some hell-fire and brimstone preaching."

"I'm used to that," chuckled Buck. "I was brought up in a Baptist church in Saratoga Springs. And even if I wasn't used to it, I'd gladly endure it for the pleasure of that stroll with you in the park."

SIX

Corporal Buck Brownell stood on the porch of his brother's house in the light of the setting sun and knocked for the third time. He waited for the sound of footsteps from within, then sighed and turned from the door. He would look in the back yard. Maybe Robert and Kady were back there.

He had just stepped off the porch when he saw an elderly man looking at him from the front porch of the house next door. The silver-haired neighbor smiled and said, "You're one of them New York Zouaves, aint'cha?"

Buck knew his uniform was a dead giveaway. "Yes, sir. You wouldn't know where the Brownells are, would you?"

"Yep. I'll bet you're Robert's brother, Buck."

"Yes, sir," nodded Buck, walking toward him.

"They're lookin' for you, son. They been visitin' some of Kady's relations down in Richmond, and just got back this afternoon. I'd heard about all them soldiers what got kilt and banged up in Baltimore, an' I heard that some of 'em was New York Zouaves. So when Robert an' Kady come home a while ago, I tol' 'em 'bout it. They got all upset, 'fraid that you mighta been kilt or wounded, so they lit out like bats out of a burnin' belfry. I s'pose they headed for the Capitol buildin', 'cause that's where I tol' 'em the wounded was bein' took care of."

"How long ago did they leave?"

The old man scratched his hoary head. "Well, I reckon it was at least a hour ago. Mebbe more like a hour an' a half."

"All right, sir. I'll head toward the Capitol. Maybe I can—" Buck's attention was drawn to a buggy bounding down the street, throwing up a cloud of dust.

"Looks like that's them a-comin' now," said the neighbor.

Buck watched the buggy slow and turn into the yard, then moved toward it as Robert jerked the reins and brought it to a halt.

"Oh, Buck!" gasped Kady, leaping from the buggy and running toward him. "I'm so glad you're okay!" Kady was weeping as she threw her arms around her brother-in-law and held him tight.

Patting her back with both hands, Buck said, "Hey, Kady, don't cry. I'm all right."

Robert drew up and said, "We were really scared when we learned that your outfit was in that riot, Buck." He moved in to throw an arm around his brother's neck, but stopped short when he saw the bandage. "What happened to your face?"

Kady pulled back and eyed the bandage through her tears.

"Just a scratch," chuckled Buck. "Fella was coming at me from behind with a knife. My commander, Colonel Ellsworth, saw him and hollered at me. I turned around and took the tip of the knife in my cheek. Better than taking the whole blade in my back."

"It was Colonel Ellsworth who told us you were coming to our house," Kady said. "First we went to the Capitol. They told us you'd be at the army camp, so we hurried out there. A sentry told us you were the colonel's aide, and when we found him, we'd find you. I'm glad the colonel knew where you were headed."

Buck patted his stomach and said, "Well, I was hoping I'd be in time for supper. There's just no cooking as good as my sister-in-law's."

"Well, I'll see what I can whip up," Kady said, smiling.

During the meal, Robert and Kady asked about the New York Fire Zouaves and the famous Colonel Ellsworth. It had been a thrill for them to meet the national hero.

"Speaking of national heroes," Buck said, "guess who I'm going to get to meet tomorrow!"

"President Lincoln?" queried Kady.

"I saw him at the depot and at the Capitol, but I didn't get to meet him. I hope I'll get to do that, also...but tomorrow morning I'm going to attend the Penn Avenue Methodist church with none other than Lieutenant Colonel Jeffrey Jordan himself!"

"How'd this come about, little brother?" asked Robert.

"I met his daughter, Jenny, at the Capitol yesterday. She helped one of the doctors take care of this gash on my face."

"She a nurse?" asked Robert.

"No, she works in the Capitol building as a receptionist in the Senate Chamber...the Military Committee on Foreign Affairs, particularly. You know Clara Barton?"

"Everybody in Washington knows who she is," said Kady. "Always helping people in trouble."

"Well, she had put out a call for women to come and help the doctors with the wounded soldiers, and Jenny was one of the volunteers."

Robert grinned. "So my little brother turned on his charm with Jordan's daughter and wrangled himself a meeting with the famous Mexican War hero!"

Kady laughed. "Well, I know a little bit about how the Brownell men can turn on the charm!"

Robert reached across the table, took her hand, and said, "Yes, and you love it."

"You're right. And I bet Miss Jordan did too!"

Looking at Buck, Robert said, "Maybe if you get in good with Jenny and her famous father, we can meet him too."

Waggling his head, Buck said, "Well, I'll see what I can do."

The three of them laughed together, then the conversation

turned to the civil war hanging like a black cloud over their heads. Each hoped it would not last long. Buck said that Union military experts were confident that one good bloody battle would crumple the Confederate army, and it would all be over.

Sunday morning brought a clear sky, a soft breeze, and the sweet smell of cherry blossoms along Maryland Avenue, where the Jordan home stood a half-block from Stanton Park.

Jenny was in her bedroom, applying extra powder to her face in an attempt to disguise the dark circles under her eyes. She had not slept well for two nights, ever since her father had told her of his spy ring activities. She feared he would be caught and executed.

A shadow fell across the open door behind her. Jenny looked at her father reflected in the mirror, and said, "I'll be ready in a moment, Daddy."

"Honey, I'm sorry this thing has upset you so, but you know it's the patriotic thing for me to do. You and I are Southerners. We must be loyal to the Confederacy."

"It's not the loyalty part that bothers me, Daddy," she said, dabbing the powder puff under her eyes, "it's the risk you're taking. I'm a Virginian, and proud of it. If I was a man, I'm sure I'd be in a Confederate uniform by now. It's just that…well, unless somehow they take a different attitude toward spies in this war, you'll face a firing squad if you're caught. Not only do I fear it first and foremost for you, but also for Rose and her girls, and for John Calhoun."

"But, honey, like I told you…I'd be in danger of getting killed if I were a soldier. Colonel Jackson agreed that what I'm doing is no more of a risk than I'd be taking in battle. John Calhoun loves the South as much as I do, and he's willing to take the risk. And as for Rose and her girls, I doubt seriously that any of these Northerners would execute women."

Jenny placed the powder puff in its box, turned, and said, "Daddy, I think they would. Men do strange things in war time.

Women spies were executed on both sides in the Revolutionary War…and it happened in the Crimean War, too. Why should military leaders in this war be any different?"

"I just can't feature it, that's all. Anyway, I'm in the thick of it. If my espionage can help shorten the war and give the South the victory, it'll be worth whatever risk is involved."

A knock was heard at the front door.

"That'll be Buck," Jenny said excitedly, turning back to the mirror and smoothing the hair at her temples.

"I'll go to the door," Jordan volunteered.

"It's all right, Daddy," breathed Jenny, rushing past him. "Just be nice to him, won't you?"

Jeffrey Jordan followed slowly. He would allow his daughter to greet her guest before he arrived on the scene. He had not voiced it to Jenny, but he hoped she would not get too interested in this young Zouave. He was a Northerner. He felt the same way about Captain Jack Egan, who had been showing up on the doorstep too often lately. Egan was also a Northerner. Jordan wished Jenny would date only Southern men.

Jenny approached the door, took a second or two to smooth her hoop-skirted Sunday dress, then took a deep breath and opened the door. Corporal Brownell stood there in his well-pressed Zouave uniform, red tasseled fez in hand.

"Good morning, Jenny," Buck said, smiling broadly.

"And good morning to you, Buck," Jenny responded, showing him a warm smile. "Please come in."

As Buck moved past Jenny into the entry way, Lieutenant Jordan put in his appearance. His face was grim.

"Corporal Buck Brownell," said Jenny, stepping up beside him, "this is my father, Lieutenant Colonel Jeffrey Jordan"

"Colonel, sir, I am proud and pleased to meet you," smiled Buck, offering his hand.

"I'm glad to meet you," Jordan said, shaking Buck's hand with a touch of cool reserve. Jordan caught Jenny's apprising gaze on him and smiled in return. Putting a little more warmth in his voice, he said, "So you are in the same outfit as Colonel Elmer Ellsworth."

"Yes, sir. He's my commanding officer."

"I admire the young man."

"All of us who serve under him do too, sir. So does President Lincoln, as you probably know."

"Yes," said Jordan. Then he turned to Jenny. "Well, daughter, I guess we'd better head for church."

The Penn Avenue Methodist church was only a couple of blocks past Stanton Park. During the few minutes it took to walk it, Buck asked about Lieutenant Jordan's exploits in the Mexican War. Jordan was pleased with Buck's interest and warmed up to him even more.

That afternoon, Buck and Jenny took their planned stroll in Stanton Park, enjoying the warm sunshine and the allurement of the cherry blossoms that bedecked the trees that lined the paths. Buck wanted to hold Jenny's hand, but would not let himself be that bold. They both smiled and greeted other people they met along the way. Many were young couples holding hands. Some of the men were in uniform, but there were no other Zouaves.

When Jenny stopped to admire a bed of bright-colored flowers, Buck cleared his throat and said, "Jenny…I asked you Friday evening if you had a steady beau—"

"And I told you I don't. There are just three or four men that I see once in a while."

"Any one of them more than the others?"

Jenny was pleased that Buck was so interested. "I guess I probably spend more time with Jack Egan. He's an army captain, serving under Colonel William T. Sherman. Jack comes around more often than any of the others."

Buck felt a cold ball settle in his stomach. Being courted by a captain would give Jenny more social prestige than being courted by a lowly corporal. But Jenny seemed to like him. He would do all he could to make her like him even more. Somehow he would have to outshine this Captain Egan in her eyes.

* * *

On Tuesday, Jeffrey Jordan arrived home and entered the house to the smell of food cooking. Leaving his hat on a small table in the parlor, he moved into the kitchen. This had been one of Jenny's off-days from her job at the Capitol, and she had worked hard to prepare her father a special meal.

Jenny was at the stove, stirring gravy in a pan. Jordan approached her, kissed a cheek, and said, "Guess what news came to the president today."

"I haven't the slightest idea, Daddy," she said, concentrating on her task. "Why don't you just tell me?"

"You know we've been wondering about Colonel Robert E. Lee?"

"You mean if he'd go over to the Confederate army?"

"Yes. Well, he did."

"That's good!" she said with enthusiasm. "He'll become a leader with the Confederacy in no time."

"You're right," nodded Jordan. "He just signed up with the Confederates this morning, and Jefferson Davis made him a general before noon. There's talk that he'll be made commander-in-chief within a day or two."

"They couldn't have picked a better man," smiled Jenny.

Jordan moved to the counter that held the wash basin and began washing his hands. "I sent word to Colonel Tom Jackson today and let him know that the spy ring is taking shape. John Calhoun and I are ready to collect classified information and pass it on to Rose, and she's already enlisted a couple of young women for her team."

Jenny poured hot gravy into a bowl and set it on the table. "Daddy, I just keep thinking of what will happen to you if you're caught. I just can't bear the thought of you...dying at the end of a rope or in front of a firing squad."

Jordan dried his hands on a towel, moved toward his daughter, and said, "Honey, we've been over this already. Let's don't belabor it. I'm willing to take my chances, as are John, Rose, and her girls. This is war, and war has its risks." He was about to take the towel back to its rack when he noticed there was only one place setting on the table. "Aren't you eating?" he asked.

"Yes, but not with you this evening," Jenny replied softly. "Buck is taking me out to dinner."

"Buck, again? You just spent most of Sunday with him. Jenny, listen…with this war about to blast open, I don't think it's wise to get attached to any young man, but especially a Northerner. Just go easy, okay? With Egan, too."

"Daddy, I really don't care that much about Jack. But Buck…well, he's different. I've never met anyone quite like him. He's—"

"Jenny, I am your father. I don't want you getting hurt. Right now is not the time to fall in love."

"Daddy, you can't lock me up in a cage just because there's a war on. I am human, you know."

Taking hold of her shoulders, Jordan looked into her eyes and said, "I'm your father, Jenny. I care what happens to my little girl. Just ease up with Buck…and keep a close watch on your heart, okay?"

"I'll be fine, Daddy," she said, hugging him. "Now, you sit down and eat your supper. I have to go get ready."

Buck Brownell picked Jenny up while her father was finishing his meal. The two men exchanged greetings only briefly, but Jordan was kind to the young Zouave for his daughter's sake.

Buck and Jenny enjoyed dinner at a fancy restaurant, then he took her to a concert. When he brought her home in the rented buggy at ten-thirty, they sat in front of the house and talked for some time.

Jenny was reluctant to go inside, but she knew she had to get up early for work the next morning. She looked at Buck in the light of the street lamp that burned nearby and said, "Buck, it's been a very nice evening. Thank you so much the wonderful dinner and the concert."

Hopping from the buggy, Buck hastily rounded its back side and took Jenny's hand to help her down. When she was on her feet, he kept her hand in his, and said, "Thank you for honoring me with your company, Jenny. I've never enjoyed an evening this much."

Buck let go of her hand and walked her to the porch, then guided her up the steps. Jenny put her hand on the doorknob, then turned and looked up into Buck's shadowed face. Jenny had never felt toward any man like she was feeling toward Buck. For a brief moment, they looked into each other's eyes. Buck's heart beat his rib cage unmercifully.

Buck hesitated, then touched his hat, smiled, and said, "Well, I know you need to get inside...and I need to get back to camp. So I'd better say goodnight. Could I take you to dinner Saturday night?"

"You certainly may," she replied warmly.

"Seven o'clock?"

"That'll be fine," she said, and turned the knob.

Buck waited till she closed the door, then made it back to the buggy in five bounds. As he drove away, his heart was still pounding. Francis Eady "Buck" Brownell was sure he was falling in love with Jenny Jordan.

At the army camp the next morning, Buck was teaching the newest Zouaves how to become better marksmen. Colonel Ellsworth stood nearby, looking on. Buck was a crack shot and the envy of the rest of the regiment. When the training session was over and the Zouaves were scattering different directions, Brownell sat down on a tree stump and began cleaning his musket.

Ellsworth drew up and said, "Good session, Corporal. You have a real knack at teaching others what you know."

"Thank you, sir."

"Corporal, since you're my aide, I really care about anything that might happen to you."

Buck stopped what he was doing, looked up at Ellsworth, and

said, "Yes, sir? Am I in some danger I don't know about?"

"Well, I don't think you would call it danger…but I think you're in a precarious situation that you ought to know about."

"Yes, sir?"

"You've been seeing Jenny Jordan quite a bit lately."

"That's right."

"It just so happens that I was talking to a couple of men from General Sherman's outfit a little earlier this morning. It seems there's a captain in their outfit who's sweet on Jenny and has dated her a number of times."

"Yes, sir. Jenny told me about him. His name's Jack Egan. Has he something to do with this precarious situation you mentioned?"

"These two men told me that Egan has been away for a couple of weeks. He just returned, and someone informed him that some Zouave has been seeing Jenny. Apparently he was irate when he heard it."

Buck shrugged his wide shoulders. "He doesn't own her."

"Well, I just thought I'd tell you that Egan has vowed to make mince meat of this Zouave when he finds out who he is. I thought I'd let you know that Egan is on your trail."

"Thank you, sir. I appreciate the warning, but I'll tell you right now…the only person who can keep me from seeing Jenny Jordan is Jenny Jordan."

"I thought you'd respond that way," grinned the colonel. "Just watch yourself."

"You can count on it," nodded Buck.

On Thursday, Corporal Brownell was sitting under a shade tree after a good workout with a small unit of the Zouaves, drinking from a canteen. A number of the men of the Eleventh New York were doing a marching drill on the grassy field nearby. Buck's attention was on the marching Zouaves when a shadow fell over him. He looked up to see a lantern-jawed captain eyeing him coldly.

"I'm Captain Jack Egan. You *Corporal* Brownell?"

Buck noted the emphasis on his rank, and stood up in respect for Eagan's captain's insignia. "I am," nodded Buck. "How'd you know who I am?"

"Asked a couple of those sweaty Zouaves over there. I understand you've been seeing Jenny Jordan," Egan said, clipping his words short.

"That's right," Buck replied.

"I want to talk to you about it."

"Talk."

Egan clinched his jaw. "I'm here to warn you to stay away from her."

"You have no claim on Jenny. She can see anybody she wants to!"

"Well, you're not to see her anymore!"

"Did Jenny say that?" demanded Buck.

"*I* said that!" boomed Egan, scowling. "I'm telling you to stay away from her!"

"I'll quit seeing Jenny when *she* tells me to stay away, and not before!"

"That attitude will only get you hurt, Brownell. I'm going to marry Jenny, do you understand?"

"Funny. Jenny hasn't mentioned such a thing at all. Maybe you'd better go check on that. And while you're checking, tell her I'm still planning on picking her up at seven Saturday night."

Egan stared hard at Brownell, then whirled and walked away. He had taken about a dozen steps when he turned and pointed a finger at the corporal. "You stay away from her, you hear?"

Buck did not reply. He simply stared back with wintry eyes.

SEVEN

The sun was shining through a thin layer of clouds at mid-morning on Friday, April 26. The Federal army campground just outside of Washington to the northeast was patrolled by sentries at all times, and the only place allotted for an entrance was at the southeast corner, near a small creek. Soldiers were moving amongst their tents, washing clothes in the creek and clustering here and there in small groups. They had all taken part in marching drill and calisthenics earlier and were relaxing in different ways.

Guarding the entrance were privates Les Turner and Harold Byers. They were discussing the news that ex-U.S. army colonel Robert E. Lee had officially been appointed commander-in-chief of the Confederate military forces.

Byers spat angrily and said, "Dirty traitor! We oughtta put together a special unit and go kidnap him. He needs to be brought back so he can face a firin' squad!"

"I'm having a hard time about that, Harold," Turner said quietly.

"What do you mean, you're havin' a hard time about Lee's desertion?"

"Well think about it. Where you from?"

"You know I'm from Cumberland, Maryland."

"All right. Let's say that Maryland had seceded and joined the Confederacy. Which army would you belong to now?" When his partner did not reply after several moments, Turner said, "See what I mean? Isn't so easy to give an answer, is it?"

Byers gave him a grim look, then turned his attention to a rider who was trotting toward them aboard a bay gelding. The horse had a white blaze with four even white stockings to match, but neither of the guards noticed the beauty of the horse. Their eyes were glued to the woman on its back.

She drew up and flashed an engaging smile. "Good morning, gentlemen. My name is Jenny Jordan. You may have heard of my father, Lieutenant Colonel Jeffrey Jordan?"

The privates exchanged glances, then looked back up at Jenny. "Yes, ma'am," they said in perfect unison.

"I would like to see Corporal Buck Brownell. He's with the Eleventh New York Zouaves."

Byers grinned wolfishly, looked at Turner, and said, "I've never minded my name all these twenty-two years, Les, but right now, I wish my name was Buck Brownell!"

Turner chuckled, then looked up at Jenny and said, "I'm sorry, ma'am, but civilians aren't allowed in the camp unless they have a written order from a proper authority."

"Well," said Jenny, "how about one of you fine gentlemen finding Corporal Brownell for me while I wait here?"

"Sorry, ma'am," said Byers, "but we can't leave our post. And that's probably best, 'cause there'd be a bloody fight between Les and me as to which one got to stay here with you. However, maybe I can holler at somebody and—"

"Oh!" gasped Jenny, suddenly noticing an army wagon rattling up from her left. "Here's Corporal Brownell now!"

A smile spread across Buck's face as he pulled rein and hauled the wagon to a halt, the horses blowing. "Hello, Jenny!"

Jenny's mount bobbed its head at the wagon team and nickered, dancing about a bit. Steadying the animal, Jenny returned the smile and said, "Hello, yourself."

The two guards looked on with envy as Buck asked Jenny, "Aren't you working today?"

"No. Sometimes I switch off with my alternate. She owed me a day for a time I filled in for her, so I decided to take today off. I just rode over to see how you are. I see the doctor removed your stitches."

"Yes," nodded Buck, touching the reddened scar gingerly. "I just came from there." A flood of warmth washed through Buck. Jenny cared enough about him to ride to the camp and see about his wound.

"Does the doctor think the scar will be permanent?" Jenny asked.

"He says there'll be a tiny white ridge, and with my dark skin, it'll show some."

"Well, as far as I'm concerned," she said sweetly, "the scar won't hurt your looks at all."

Turner and Byers snickered. Buck's face tinted.

Jenny took a deep breath, let it out with the word, "Well..." and added, "I guess I'll be getting back home."

Buck hopped from the wagon, stepped up beside the bay, and looking up at Jenny, said, "I sure appreciate you coming out here to check on me."

Smiling down at him, she responded softly, "You mean a lot to me, Buck. I hope you know that."

The rugged Zouave's pulse throbbed. Struggling for breath, he said, "You mean a lot to me, too."

Tugging the rein to turn her mount, Jenny said, "I'll see you tomorrow night."

"You sure will," he replied.

Buck could hear the two guards laughing to themselves as he watched Jenny ride away. When she disappeared into a deep-shaded stand of trees, he wheeled to face his fun-loving tormentors.

Byers was elbowing Turner and still snickering as he said in a mocking falsetto, "You mean a lot to me, Buck. I hope you know that."

Turner grinned and said, "You mean a lot to me, too."

Buck showed them a mock-grimace and clipped, "You two are just green with envy."

Both guards burst into laughter, slapping each other on the back. Buck shook his head, climbed into the wagon seat, and snapped the reins. As the wagon rolled away, he heard Turner say, "As far as I'm concerned, the scar won't hurt your looks at all!"

Buck was grinning to himself and shaking his head again, but did not look back.

Saturday night came, and while Buck and Jenny sat eating in the Capital City Restaurant, they discussed the reports of skirmishes between Union and Confederate soldiers in various parts of northern Virginia. They talked of the military buildup on both sides and discussed their views on when and where a major battle would take place.

"The way I see it," Jenny was saying, "it'll probably happen somewhere along the banks of the Potomac."

"Could be," nodded Buck. "The river could very well be a point of contention…probably at one of the main bridges."

"That's what I'm hearing in the Capitol."

"On the other hand, the big battle just might be fought over the railroad. Maybe at one of the junctions. Talk at camp among the big brass is that to cripple the Confederate forces, the Union army will have to take control of the railroads."

Jenny sipped a cup of hot tea then set it in its saucer. "You said *the* big battle, Buck. Are you thinking the same thing I'm hearing from the Senate Military Committee…that one big battle will settle the war?"

"Yes. That's the consensus around the camps. Among the officers, I mean."

"Well, that agrees with the opinions I'm picking up at work from the men on the Senate Military Committee. They feel that once there's a full-scale battle, the Confederates will find out they're up against a military force much better equipped and much better trained. They'll fold the first time they face the Union army."

"You're a Southerner, Jenny. Do you think the Committee is right?"

A pained expression claimed Jenny's features. Giving her shoulders a listless shrug, she replied, "I don't know. I've given it a lot of thought. The Union has some good military leaders, that's for sure—General Scott, Colonel McDowell, Colonel McClellan, and the like. But since Colonel Lee has become commander-in-chief of the Confederate forces and we—*they*—also have such men as General Beauregard and Colonel Jackson, the South may not be the pushover the Committee and the Union military leaders have imagined."

Noting the slip of Jenny's tongue, Buck leaned forward, laid his arms on the table, and said, "You're having a hard time with this, aren't you?"

"You mean being born a Southerner but living in the North and working for the Federal government?"

"Yes."

Her lower lip quivered slightly. "Yes, Buck. I am having a hard time with it. I...I feel a loyalty to Virginia. It's my home state. Since Virginia is part of the Confederacy, now, I can't help but feel torn."

"I understand. I'm sure I would have the same sentiments if New York had seceded."

"Thank you," she said, smiling weakly.

"Of course, I'm plenty glad you're on my side. I sure wouldn't want you to be my enemy."

Jenny wondered how Buck would feel toward her if he knew her father was the key man in a planned Confederate spy ring. She took a nervous sip at her tea and said softly, "I wouldn't want that, either."

Buck decided to get Jenny's mind off the North-South

problem. Leaning back in his chair, he said, "Guess I ought to tell you about your friend, Captain Jack Egan."

Jenny raised her eyebrows. "Oh? Jack? What about him?"

"He paid me a little visit Thursday."

"Oh? You didn't say anything about it yesterday."

"I didn't think about it yesterday. I had my mind on the beautiful lady who rode all the way out to the camp to see about my face."

Jenny's features flushed. After a moment, she said, "Jack's been away from Washington for a short while. He came to see me Wednesday night. Someone informed him that I've been seeing a Zouave while he's been gone. He asked who it was, and I told him." Pausing briefly again, she squinted, cocked her head, and asked, "What was his little visit about?"

"He wanted to warn me to stay away from you."

Jenny's mouth dropped open. Her dark eyes went wide, and displeasure lay tightly across her face. "He *what*? What right has Jack Egan to warn you to stay away from me?"

"That's what I asked him. And I told him he had no claim on you, and that you could see anybody you wanted to."

"Good for you!" Jenny blurted. "Of all the nerve! So what did he say to that?"

"Well, I also told him that I'd quit seeing you when you told me to stay away. He said that attitude would get me hurt."

Jenny's back straightened. "He threatened you with bodily harm? Why, that impudent cad!"

"That's not all. He also told me he's going to marry you."

Jenny's jaw slacked and her eyes became even wider. Drawing a sharp breath, she blared, "If he was here, I'd slap his lying mouth! Marriage has never even been mentioned between us...and if he had brought it up, I would have told him I'm not interested in marrying the likes of him!"

Jenny's outburst drew the attention of people around them. When she saw it, she blushed brightly and slid down a little in her chair.

"I figured you'd be a little upset at the captain's announcement of your engagement," Buck said, smiling. "I'm glad you are. I assume it's all right, then, for me to ask you for another date?"

"Yes, it is."

"Okay. How about church tomorrow morning?"

"It's a date," she smiled.

Buck paid the waiter, and when they stood to leave, Jenny felt the eyes of the patrons around them fastened on her. She was glad when they were outside and in the buggy.

Buck and Jenny talked for a few moments in the buggy after it was parked in front of her house, then she said, "Well, Corporal Brownell, it's time for this girl to hit the hay."

Buck helped her from the buggy and walked her to the door. He looked into her eyes in the dim light of a nearby street lamp and said, "I'm looking forward to our time together tomorrow."

"So am I."

The night, dark and still around them, was silent except for the faint sound of countless crickets giving their nocturnal concert. Suddenly words were unnecessary. Buck slipped his arms around Jenny, drawing her close to him. She tilted her face upward and her two hands came flat against his chest. She felt his hands on her back, pulling her closer. This is the way she stood when he kissed her, long, sweet, and tender.

Releasing her, Buck whispered, "Goodnight, Jenny."

"Goodnight," she sighed, then turned and entered the house, softly closing the door.

Buck Brownell's heart was hammering his ribs as he stepped off the porch and headed down the walk toward the buggy. He was almost to the street when movement in the dark shadows slightly behind him caught his eye. He jerked his head around and slowed his pace.

A dark form glided into the soft ring of light cast by the street lamp. Buck stopped when he recognized Captain Jack Egan, though he was out of uniform.

"I saw what you did, Brownell!" Egan shouted in a strangled voice.

Buck felt the hair on the back of his neck bristle. "It's none of your business what I did. What are you skulking around here for?"

Egan moved within arm's reach. "I told you to stay away from Jenny!"

"You're not my commander, Captain," countered Buck.

"I gave you fair warning. You're going to wish you'd heeded me, Brownell!"

"Need I remind you that it's a serious offense for an officer to strike an enlisted man? It could get you in serious trouble."

"Don't you threaten me with army regulations, Brownell."

"There's another problem here, Captain—if you swing at me, I'll have to swing back. And if I strike an officer, I can be court-martialed."

"You won't have to worry about that, Brownell. I'm not in uniform, so you won't be swinging at an officer. I'll be the civilian. You be the soldier. We'll settle this man to man!" Even as he spoke, Egan's fist flashed toward Buck.

Buck dodged and countered with a hard right to Egan's jaw. The captain went down. Cursing, he scrambled to his feet and swung at Buck's head. Buck jerked his head to the side, and Egan's fist grazed his temple. Buck lashed back. Egan raised both forearms, blocking Buck's blows. Egan gave ground, then swung a haymaker that caught Buck flush on the jaw and sent him reeling. Thinking he could finish Buck off, Egan moved in quickly. Buck countered with a blow to the captain's stomach, doubling him over, then landed a solid uppercut to Egan's jaw that sent him to the ground once again.

Unaware that neighbors across the street had heard the ruckus and were standing on their porches, Brownell stood puffing over Egan and said, "I don't want to take...this any farther...than you force me to, Captain. When you're ready to stay down...I'll get in the buggy and...drive away."

Jack Egan was amazed at how hard the lighter man could

punch, but he was determined to teach Buck a lesson. Rising to his feet and shaking his head to clear it, he growled, "You will stay away from Jenny, Brownell…and it'll be me who makes you."

Egan grunted and sprang at Buck, eyes wild and jaw set, his fists swinging wildly. Buck dodged one fist, took the second one on his shoulder, and lashed back, striking Egan on the nose. The punch stunned Egan, sending him backpedaling and blinking against the water that flooded his eyes.

Brownell was after him. Egan took a blow on the jaw, which propelled him backward against the light pole. His head hit the pole and rebounded. Buck cracked him again, and sent him sliding down the pole to a sitting position. Egan sat there groaning, his head rolling. Blood was bubbling from both nostrils.

Buck stood over him for a few seconds and decided the captain had had enough. He wheeled toward the buggy and the nervous horse, and looked back toward the Jordan house. The windows on the first floor were dark, and only one window on the second floor showed light through gauzy curtains.

Still oblivious to the gaping neighbors, Buck untied the reins from the hitching post and lifted the long leathers over the horse's head. Speaking softly to calm the animal, he started to climb aboard the buggy. Suddenly, without warning, Egan's full weight slammed him into the buggy.

Buck yelped with pain as the side of the vehicle punched his ribs. He took a wild blow that put him on the ground. The frightened horse nickered and trotted down the street some twenty yards, pulling the buggy, then came to a halt, snorting.

While Brownell was on the ground, Egan—still somewhat dizzy but determined—sent a savage kick to Buck's stomach. Somehow Buck managed to roll away from the next kick that was aimed toward his face. He sprang to his feet. This time, he would put Egan out cold before turning his back on him.

Buck braced himself as the heavier man, his nose spurting blood, came at him. Brownell bobbed and weaved as he avoided two, three, four swings, then caught Egan flush on the nose again. The blow drove Egan backward. Buck hustled after him, unleashing two blows to his jaw. Egan's head whipped hard both ways and his knees buckled. They were under the street lamp, and Buck could see Egan's eyes glaze.

Two more rapid punches and Egan fell flat, unconscious. Brownell stood over his vanquished foe, sucking hard for air, making sure the captain was out cold. When Egan made no move to get up, Buck stepped around him and walked down the street to the buggy.

Inside the dark parlor of the Jordan house, Jenny peered past the edge of the curtain she had barely pulled aside and watched Buck climb into the buggy and drive away. She stared at Captain Egan, who was beginning to stir, then dropped the curtain and headed up the stairs.

When Jenny reached the landing and started down the hall toward her room, she saw her father come through his door and wait for her in the vague light of a lantern that burned low on a small table in the hall. Standing there in his robe, his hands on his hips, Jordan spoke in a level tone as she drew near. "I saw the fight, Jenny. This kind of thing must not happen again. I want you to tell both of those men you want nothing more to do with them."

Jenny's face registered her disbelief. "You can't do this to me, Daddy...you can't make me send Buck away. He fought Jack because Jack thinks he has some kind of hold on me. I like Buck, Daddy. I like him a lot. I...I've never met anyone quite like him. He—"

"Jenny, with circumstances as they are—I mean with this war building, and all—you mustn't get romantically involved with *any* man...especially a soldier. Just about the time you fall in love with one, he'll get killed. You can't put yourself in that position. Do you understand what I'm saying? I'm trying to save you some heartache."

Jenny's countenance fell. "Yes, Daddy, but—"

Gripping her shoulders firmly, Jordan said, "Honey, listen to me. This war won't last for long. Please...no more thoughts of romance until this thing is settled and our lives can get back to normal."

Jeffrey Jordan chose not to voice it, but he did not want his daughter hooking up with *any* Northerner. They were Southerners, and the family would stay Southern if he had anything to do with it. He must especially not allow Jenny to become close to a Union soldier now that he was a Confederate spy. Buck Brownell may be different than any man his daughter had ever met, *but he was the enemy*. Jenny must not cohort with the enemy.

Anguish showed in Jenny's eyes. "But, Daddy, I can't just send Buck away. I can't—"

"I'll handle it, Jenny," Jordan cut sharply across her words, increasing the pressure on her shoulders. "I know what's best for you."

"But, Daddy—"

"You're still not of age, Jenny. Until you turn twenty-one, you're under my authority and under my roof. I don't want you involved with a soldier with this war building up, and I already told you why. Now, the next time Buck shows up here, I'll talk to him."

Jenny had no desire to rebel against her father's authority. Neither did she want his displeasure. She understood the risk of falling in love with Buck, only to see him killed. But strong feelings for the handsome young Zouave had already taken root within her. How could she stand the pain of suddenly not seeing him anymore? And what would it do to Buck? He would be hurt, too. Tears filmed Jenny's eyes and her lower lip began to quiver.

"Now, honey," said Jordan, "don't turn on the water works. Haven't I always done right by you?"

"Yes," she nodded, as the tears started to flow.

Releasing her shoulders and wrapping his arms around her, Jordan held her close and said, "Jenny, you're young. You've got plenty of time to fall in and out of love over and over again. Just remember that my seemingly hard hand, here, is for your own good."

When Jenny sniffled but did not reply, Jordan asked, "Do you and Buck have another date set?"

Jenny nodded against his chest. "Tomorrow morning. Church."

"All right, then. You stay up in your room, and I'll meet Buck at the door when he comes."

Jenny knew better than to argue with her father. She would not be allowed to talk to Buck herself. She could only cling to the hope that Buck felt the same toward her as she did toward him, and that when the war was over, he would once again show up on her doorstep.

"Daddy," she said with a quiver in her voice as she looked up at him, "will you tell Buck why you're doing this?"

"Yes, of course. Now, you get to bed. It's late."

Corporal Buck Brownell's heart was aflutter on Sunday morning as he left the buggy and made his way up the walk toward the porch. Had he raised his line of sight, he might have seen the curtain pulled slightly aside at Jenny's window on the second floor. Instead, he bounded up the steps and rapped the brass knocker.

Heavy footsteps from inside greeted his ears, followed by the rattle of metal hardware and the door swinging open. Smiling broadly at Jenny's father, Buck said, "Good morning, Colonel Jordan. Jenny ready?"

A solemn look settled over Jordan's face. "No, she's not. She won't be going to church with you."

Surprise registered in Buck's dark eyes. "Oh? Is she—"

"Today, or any other Sunday," clipped the colonel. "In fact, she won't be seeing you any more at all."

The hard look on Jordan's face and the sharp, clipped words caught Buck off guard. For a moment, he was unable to speak. While he struggled for words, the thickening silence between colonel and corporal ran forward.

"You may leave now," Jordan said huskily.

"Don't I get a reason for this…this sudden end to my seeing your daughter, Colonel? If it's because of what happened here in front of your house last night, sir, it—"

"It's not that."

"Well, then…could I at least talk to Jenny, sir?"

"You may not," the colonel responded coldly. "But if it'll set your mind at ease, the termination of your relationship with my daughter is *my* doing, not Jenny's."

"May I ask, sir, what I've done that would cause you to stop me from seeing Jenny?"

Jordan decided to nip the situation in the bud and keep it from ever rising again. "It's not what you've *done*, Brownell, it's what you *are*."

"And what am I, sir?"

"As Jenny's father, I have set my sights much higher for her than a common soldier. She must move in high social circles and eventually marry a man of means. I mean to see to it that her life bends in that direction, and I am starting right now."

Buck felt as if he had been hit with a battering ram. "But, sir, what if this is not Jenny's desire?"

"That makes no difference. She is not of age, and she still lives under my roof. She will do as I say. She may not like it or even understand it right now, but one day she'll thank me for it." Backing into the house, he added, "Good day, Corporal. And good-bye."

The door closed in Buck's face. He turned and stood there a moment. He wondered why Jenny's father had waited until now to stop her from seeing any man not on the social level he wanted for his daughter. As he descended the porch steps, Buck told himself there was more to it than Colonel Jordan was revealing.

Not wanting to cause trouble for Jenny, he moved quietly toward the waiting buggy, feeling sick at heart. As he drove slowly away, tears flowed at a window on the second floor.

EIGHT

After the attack on Fort Sumter on April 12 and the passage of the ordinance of secession by the Virginia legislature on April 17, both the North and the South marked time. Neither was prepared to assume the offensive.

Conscious that they could never hope to match the military strength of the Union, the Confederacy chose to exploit the advantages of defensive operations and the use of spies to counteract the offensive of the enemy. President Jefferson Davis and his advisers agreed that there was little to gain by invading the North. The Confederacy was merely asking to be let alone. If President Abraham Lincoln and the Union military leaders were not willing to back off and let the Confederacy go its way in peace, it was willing to fight. The Confederate offensive at Fort Sumter was meant to demonstrate that fact.

The Federal government's military task was fixed and unavoidable. The Union must move into the South and conquer it. This required a more elaborate military organization than was possible to create in a few weeks. It meant training soldiers, building up immense quantities of weapons and ammunition, developing and maintaining long lines of communication, imposing blockades on the South, and wresting major ports and rivers from Southern control.

Union military strategists wanted to launch a major offensive as soon as possible down the Mississippi River, but circumstances at hand made it inadvisable. The proximity of the first armies that were being organized dictated that Virginia must be the first theater of war.

As the days came and went, the enlistment of great numbers of soldiers, the training of troops, and the buildup of war matériel continued.

On Saturday afternoon, May 4, 1861, a large crowd of Washington, D.C., residents gathered in an open field twenty miles due west of the capital city on the west bank of Bull Run Creek, some five miles northwest of Manassas Junction.

The field belonged to Frank Lewis, a Union sympathizer who was enthralled by Colonel Elmer Ellsworth and his Eleventh New York Zouaves drill team, which he had seen perform once outside of Gettysburg. Lewis had invited the Zouaves to perform on his place, and the citizens of Washington were turning out in droves.

About a mile and a half west of the Lewis farm, John Henry, the thirty-one-year-old son of Mrs. Judith Henry, an invalid widow who owned the large house on Henry House Hill, stood in the yard with neighbor Mike Durbin. As they looked across the fields toward the Lewis place, Durbin patted his big black Newfoundland dog and said, "John, Frank told me he invited the Eleventh New York Zouaves to give a drill team show in his field this afternoon."

"I've heard about those Zouaves," John nodded. "I'd sure like to get a gander at 'em in action, but...wouldn't we be sort of traitors to go and watch 'em?"

"Not like Frank is for inviting 'em out here. He told me even ol' Honest Abe might show up."

John watched the movement of vehicles and riders. "'Course,

ol' Frank is from the North—Pennsylvania. We ain't. Can't blame a fella for havin' an attachment for his home state."

"Yeah, I know." After a long pause, Durbin said, "I'm plannin' to join up with the Confederate army next week. What you gonna do?"

"Can't," replied John. "With Pa dead, I have to take care of the place for Ma. I guess you know Louise and I moved in with Ma a couple weeks ago so's my sister Mary Sue's husband could join up."

"Yeah. Carl's already done it?"

"He's in trainin' over by Richmond. Mary Sue's livin' in Ma's house, too. I ain't got no choice. I gotta stay."

The Newfoundland pawed at his master and whined for attention. Durbin leaned over and patted the dog's head and neck, and said, "Pal, I declare, do you think all I have to do in life is pet you?"

While the dog wagged his tail and whined in reply, John looked at him and said, "I thought the thing he likes best is ridin' in the hay wagon with you."

"It is. But if he ain't ridin', he wants pettin'. I can't go anywhere without him taggin' along."

"So, when you go into the army, who's gonna look after Jo-Beth and the place?"

"Jo-Beth's kid brother is comin' to stay with her and do the chores."

"I almost forgot Jo-Beth had a little brother. What's his name again?"

"Orville."

"Oh, yeah, Orville….So what do you think? Should we sneak over to the Lewis place and watch those Zouaves from the ditch bank?"

"Why not?" grinned Mike. Then looking down at his dog, he said, "Can't take Pal over there. He'd probably give us away."

"You can leave him in the barn. I'll go and tell the women where we're goin'. Be right back."

While John was in the house, Mike tricked Pal into the barn, then shut the door. The Newfoundland began to whine and scratch at the door. When John returned, he and Mike started across the sweeping green pasture toward the Lewis farm.

They were about a mile from Henry House Hill when John happened to look over his shoulder. He stopped, laughed, and said, "Lookee there, Mike."

Mike turned to see an ebony streak on the grassy field. Pal was running after him, his ears flying and his long black fur waving in the wind.

John shook his head. "How do you reckon he got out?"

"Well, knowing him, he either squeezed through a knothole or knocked your barn door off its hinges. I tend to lean toward the latter."

"So now what?"

"I'll have to forego the show. If I took Pal over there, he'd probably run right into the middle of the marching ranks."

Old Glory and the New York state flag flapped in the breeze at the head of the long, even lines of colorful Zouaves as all eleven hundred marched in front of the crowd some ten thousand strong. A military band played intermittently between announcements by Colonel Ellsworth.

In the audience was President Lincoln, his family, governess Patricia Winters, and Lincoln's secretary John Hay. Seated next to the president was the stout and stalwart Major Irvin McDowell. Lincoln was considering promoting the forty-two-year-old Mexican War veteran to brigadier general and making him field commander over the army of thirty thousand men gathered in camps around Washington.

In Lincoln's mind, the field commander would carry on his shoulders the onerous duty of invading Virginia to put down the Confederate rebellion. The president had been informed that just a few miles from where he sat—at Manassas Junction—General Pierre G.T. Beauregard was collecting troops.

Also in attendance were several units of fighting men, including the Sixth Massachusetts under command of Colonel Edward F. Jones, and the large Third Brigade of the Union army's First Division, under the command of Colonel William T. Sherman. Sitting astride his mount next to Sherman was Brigadier General Daniel Tyler, commander of First Division.

Lieutenant John Hammond of the Sixth Massachusetts—who had dated Patricia Winters four times since meeting her—found a spot next to her on a grassy slope where she was seated with the Lincoln boys. While the crowd thrilled at Ellsworth's drill team, Patricia thrilled at Hammond's touch when he took her hand in his.

Not far from the president and Mrs. Lincoln sat Lieutenant Jeffrey Jordan and Jenny. Also in the crowd were Senator Henry Wilson and Rose O'Neal Greenhow. Next to Rose were four pretty young ladies she had secretly engaged to do spy work.

Sitting on the grass next to her father, Jenny kept her eye on Corporal Buck Brownell, who was performing amid the Zouaves on the field. Suddenly Jack Egan eased down beside her. Jenny glanced at him, then said quietly, "Please find a seat somewhere else, Jack."

"Now, wait a minute. What'd I do wrong?"

"Well, for starters, you took it upon yourself to tell Buck he couldn't see me any more. You had no right to do such a thing."

Egan opened his mouth to speak, but Jenny cut him off. "And what's more, where'd you get the brass to tell Buck you were going to marry me!"

"Well, I—"

"Well, you're wrong, Captain Egan! Now leave me alone."

"But Jenny, I—"

Jeffrey Jordan eyed Egan with disdain. "Are you deaf, Captain?"

Ignoring Jordan, Egan hissed at Jenny, "Why'd you two-time me for that scum-bucket corporal? What do you see in him?"

Jordan leaped to his feet and stood over Egan as spectators in the area looked on. "On your way, Captain!"

"Okay, Colonel, I'll go. But I don't think I'm being treated right."

"Until this war is over and done with, Jenny isn't going to get involved with *any* man…especially a soldier. So the best thing for you to do, Captain, is find another girl."

Egan pulled his gaze from the stubborn eyes of Jordan and looked at Jenny. He found the same stubbornness there. Cursing under his breath, he stomped away.

The crowd cheered as Colonel Ellsworth led his brightly clad soldiers in snappy acrobatic maneuvers with musket and bayonet, all done in time to the music of the band. After a while, Ellsworth stood his brigade at attention and introduced Corporal Brownell, who would now demonstrate his skill at speedily loading and firing his musket at a stationary target, then a moving target.

Jenny bit her lower lip to keep from crying. Her heart seemed ready to burst with sorrow. She had fallen in love with the rugged Zouave corporal, and she would never forget him.

A few feet away, young Tad Lincoln looked on with awe as Buck continued his demonstration. Pressing close to his governess, who still held hands with Lieutenant Hammond, he told her he couldn't wait to grow up. He wanted to be a Zouave.

At the close of the performance, the crowd leaped to its feet and gave the Zouaves a five-minute ovation. Colonel Ellsworth then introduced Abraham Lincoln, and the crowd cheered and applauded some more as the president moved to the forefront. When it was finally quiet enough for him to be heard, Lincoln praised Colonel Ellsworth and his military achievements and Corporal Brownell for his expertise with firearms. Again the people cheered.

Lincoln stroked his beard and told the crowd that the Confederates better watch out. With rough-and-ready men like the Zouaves fighting for the Union, the Rebels didn't have a chance. Those words brought the loudest ovation. The people of Washington were certain the Confederates would be brought to their knees in the first major battle.

Colonel Ellsworth thanked the enthusiastic throng for coming, and dismissed them. Lincoln and those in his party rode away, with Colonel Ellsworth riding in the presidential carriage.

As the crowd was dispersing, Jeffrey Jordan leaned close to his daughter, and said, "Wait here, honey. I need to see Rose for a minute." Jenny nodded and let her gaze scan the milling crowd. She was trying to find a particular handsome face.

Rose O'Neal Greenhow was watching her four girls climb into her private carriage when she saw Jeffrey Jordan coming her way. She said to the young women, "I'll be with you in a moment," then moved out to greet her fellow spy, extending a hand.

"Hello, Colonel," she smiled, as Jordan took her hand.

Jordan felt the slip of paper press his palm as he greeted her in return. "Nice to see you, lovely lady. Did you enjoy the demonstration?"

"Very much so!"—then in a half-whisper, "Here are the names of the two new girls. We're ready to start carrying messages as soon as you're in a position to give them to us."

"It'll be a few more weeks, I think," Jordan whispered back. "It all depends on how fast Lincoln moves. By ready, I assume you mean you've made contact with Generals Lee and Beauregard, and they're expecting your girls to deliver the messages."

"Yes. Their military leaders have also been informed."

"Good. Then we're ready to roll."

"Definitely…and Henry doesn't suspect a thing."

"You're a doll, Rose," grinned Jordan. Casting an eye toward the carriage, he asked, "Will four girls be enough?"

"Not once we get under way. I'll have to recruit more when we're rolling, if the war lasts that long."

"Let's hope the experts are right, and it'll be a short one—only it's the Union that gets whipped in that big battle, and not our side."

"Amen," Rose whispered. "We'd better break it off. We'll meet again at the time and place we agreed on. Maybe by then, you'll know more than you do now."

Senator Wilson, who had been amid the dispersing crowd speaking to friends, drew up just as Jordan was turning to leave. "Hello, Colonel," Wilson said amiably. "Nice to see you."

Jordan shook his hand. "Nice to see you, Senator. What did you think of the demonstration?"

"Great! It was just great! I'm sure glad we've got those Zouaves on our side."

"Me too." Jordan smiled at Rose, told her he would see her soon, and headed for his surrey.

Threading his way through the crowd, Jordan spoke to several people who greeted him. As he drew near the surrey, Jenny was standing beside it, talking to Corporal Brownell. Jordan shot his undimmed hostility at the corporal as he drew up. "I thought I made it clear you are to stay away from my daughter!"

Jenny's face paled.

Buck said calmly, "I wasn't trying to get a date with her, Colonel Jordan. I was just greeting her and asking how she is doing."

"I don't want you coming around her at all, Corporal."

Buck and Jenny looked at each other. He could see the hurt in her eyes, and at that moment, he knew she was in love with him.

To Jordan, Buck said, "I apologize, Colonel. I didn't mean to rile you. But a man has to do what he has to do." Turning back to Jenny, he spoke softly, but loud enough for her father to hear. "I'm sorry, Jenny. I didn't mean to cause trouble. I only wanted to say hello…and…and that I love you."

The joy Jenny felt at Buck's words was marred by her father's outburst. "How dare you speak to my daughter in such a way when I just told you I want you out of her life!" To Jenny, he said, "Get in the surrey!"

While Jenny climbed into the surrey, Buck said, "It is not my intention to anger you, Colonel, but when a man loves a woman, he wants her to know it. I must tell you, sir, with all due respect…I am in love with Jenny, and I always will be."

A young Zouave soldier was showing his musket to a group of

teenage boys nearby. One of the boys asked if he could hold the weapon just for a minute. The Zouave told him to be very careful, advising him that the gun was loaded. The youth assured him he would be, and took the weapon in his hands with delight. The Zouave's attention was drawn to Colonel Ellsworth, who was coming his direction, surrounded by another group of youths.

The boy with the musket decided to show his friends how well he could handle a gun. He would cock the hammer, then ease it back down. "Hey, guys," he said, earing the hammer back into firing position, "look at this!" Before he got the hammer locked, his thumb slipped and the hammer came down on the powder charge.

The shot ripped across the rump of Jeffrey Jordan's horse. Jenny was just settling on the seat when the frightened animal bolted. The abrupt movement of the surrey threw Jenny off the seat, to the back of the vehicle, and left her dangling partway over the right side. She screamed and held on for dear life as the surrey bounded over the open field, swaying dangerously. The terror-blinded horse was headed for the bank of Bull Run Creek.

While everyone else stood slack-jawed and wide-eyed, Buck dashed to a horse a few yards away, leaped into the saddle, and put the animal into an instant gallop. Colonel Ellsworth watched Brownell thunder away, and stomped to the Zouave who had let the teenager handle his musket. The Zouave looked sheepish as Ellsworth dressed him down for his foolish move. The boy with the musket was weeping and apologizing.

Buck's hat sailed from his head as he rode across the field in pursuit of the surrey. Somehow Jenny had been able to get herself back inside the bounding, careening vehicle and was gripping the seat to keep from being thrown out. The terrified horse raced blindly toward the grassy bank of Bull Run.

The creek was no more than a hundred yards away when Buck pulled alongside the surrey and shouted, "We'll only get one chance, Jenny! Do what I tell you! Get ready to jump." The frightened woman nodded, then let go of the seat and with difficulty, crawled to the side. Drawing as close as possible, Buck leaned from the saddle, held out his right arm, and yelled, "Jump, Jenny! Quick!" Jenny took a deep breath and leaped into the curve of Buck's strong arm.

Buck drew her to himself and held her tight as he skidded his horse to a halt. Jenny wrapped her trembling arms around his neck and said with shuddering words, "Thank you, darling! Thank you! You saved my life!"

Both watched the bounding surrey as the wild-eyed horse scudded toward the bank of Bull Run Creek, then made a sudden turn to the left. The surrey careened, overturned, came loose from the harness, and rolled into the creek. The horse thundered along the bank with the singletree dragging behind, then bounded over a hill and disappeared.

Buck's horse danced about a little while Buck held Jenny close and kissed her.

"Sorry," he said, "but I had to do that—despite what your father says."

"Don't be sorry. I let you, didn't I?"

Buck grinned. "Here. Let me slide you behind me. Wrap your arms around me and hang on. I'll take you back to your father."

Moments later, Buck and Jenny rode up to a cheering crowd. Buck smiled at them, slid from the saddle, then helped Jenny down. Jenny's father moved up and with reluctance, said, "Thank you, Corporal. You no doubt saved Jenny from serious harm…maybe even saved her life."

"I'd do it again in a minute, sir."

Jordan took Jenny into one arm, leaned close to Buck and said, "I saw you kiss her, too. That I didn't like."

"I love her, sir. I told you…I'll always love her."

"I love you too, Buck," Jenny said boldly, avoiding her father's hard eyes.

Jordan turned quickly to Rose Greenhow and asked, "Can Jenny and I ride back to town with you?"

"Of course."

Jordan hastily ushered his daughter away from Buck toward Rose's vehicle. Jenny looked back with sadness and love in her eyes.

Buck stood with Colonel Ellsworth and watched the Greenhow party boarded the carriage. As it rolled across the field toward Washington, Jenny ventured a backward look over her shoulder at the man she loved. Tears glistened on her cheeks, reflecting the light of the lowering sun.

NINE

Extensive training continued at the Union army camps around Washington, D.C. As more new recruits arrived, Colonel Elmer Ellsworth went to General Winfield Scott, chief of the Federal army, and offered to let Corporal Buck Brownell move about the camps and give extensive training in the use of firearms and bayonets. Brownell's reputation had earned him a great deal of respect amongst Union military leaders. General Scott appreciated Ellsworth's offer and took him up on it.

Early in the second week of May 1861, General Scott began visiting each camp to inspect the troops and speak to them. He happened upon the camp where Buck was doing his training. General Scott, along with his accompanying officers, approached the training site and observed with keen interest for over two hours. When the training session was done, General Scott stepped up to Brownell and extended his hand. "Young man," he said with exuberance, "I like the way you work. I'm General Winfield Scott."

Meeting Scott's grip, Buck smiled broadly. "I know who you are, sir. I've admired you from a distance for a long time. Your record in the Mexican War has more than impressed me."

Scott was aging and showed it. His health had been poor for

the past few years, and he had put on a great deal of weight. He introduced his aides to Brownell, then excused himself to meet with the camp's officers before addressing the troops.

Twenty minutes later, a bugle called the troops together, where they stood at attention in perfect ranks while General Scott made his inspection. When that was done, the men were told to sit on the ground in a huge semicircle so the army chief could address them from the bed of a wagon.

Scott stood before them while the morning breeze toyed with Old Glory on a flag pole nearby. He took about ten minutes to give them a pep talk about the upcoming confrontation with the Confederate army, which no doubt would come before the end of summer.

When he had them eager to take on the enemy, Scott took a drink of water from a canteen handed him by an officer, then swept the faces of the troops with tired old eyes, and said, "Now, in order to build an efficient fighting force, there have to be rules, and there has to be discipline to enforce those rules. I'm from what they call the old school, men, and we're going to run this army the old-fashioned way."

There were some light-hearted chuckles, and the men exchanged mirthful glances.

Clearing his throat, the general proceeded. "Let me now give you some details concerning rules and discipline. Drunkenness, gambling, profanity, and absence without leave will be punished without exception. I emphasize the words, *without exception*. God is not a respecter of persons, and neither is General Winfield Scott. Neither are your commanding officers. Such conduct as I have just listed will result in punishment at the discretion of the commanding officers. The severity of the punishment will coincide with the degree of the infraction, running anywhere from extra duties to solitary confinement."

The mirth felt moments earlier among the troops began to subside.

Scott went on. "Blacklists of persistent offenders will be kept, and their names will appear on duty rosters for the purpose of digging latrines, burying dead mules and horses, and other such disagreeable tasks. Continued misconduct will result in actual physical punishment, employed to make examples of the offending soldiers…that others may fear.

"Physical punishment will be on the rack, or a lashing with a leather strap on a bare posterior while your fellow-soldiers watch. If that does not square the habitual offender around, the next step is court-martial. And believe me, gentlemen, you do not want to face a court-martial!

"Next, let's consider the most serious crime a Union soldier can commit—desertion. Deserters are the scum of the earth. They will be hunted down and shot by a firing squad. Let every ear hear this good. There will be no leniency. Deserters will die for their crime. Better to take a bullet from the enemy than face a firing squad made up of your comrades. During the Mexican War, I had thirty-four deserters shot, and after number thirty-four, there were no more desertions from the U.S. army in that war.

"This may seem like a harsh punishment, but it is the only sentence that equals the crime. Besides, I found out in the Mexican War that hard-line punishment resulted in overall fewer discipline problems, and without a doubt saved the lives of many soldiers in the remainder of that conflict. Thus, it will be done the same in this war."

The general's solemn words laid a sober atmosphere over the men in the camp.

"Now, let me deal with one other subject. All of you need to know Union army policy on this subject so if and when it happens, you will understand. I speak of spies. What I am about to tell you has been military policy for centuries around the world. President Lincoln has put his stamp of approval on it, and it holds firm.

"Any and all Confederate spies will be executed by firing squad within twenty-four hours of their capture. Spy executions will be overseen and conducted by the highest-ranking officer in command at the scene of the apprehension. That officer will not need to contact his superiors. The deadline holds. His duty is to see to it that the execution is carried out as ordered."

General Scott wished the men well, and turned the assembly over to the officer in charge. Announcement was made that immediately after the noon meal, Corporal Brownell would conduct a class on bayonet fighting. The men were dismissed and headed for the cook tents.

In early May, the South decided that Richmond, Virginia, would become the capital of the Confederacy. The capital had been in Montgomery, Alabama, but that was proving to be quite inconvenient since the war was shaping up to begin in Virginia.

While the Union was building up its army around Washington, the Confederates, under the capable leadership of General Robert E. Lee, were doing the same at two strategic places in Virginia. At the heart of Lee's defense was his twenty-thousand-man force positioned at Manassas Junction near Bull Run Creek, some twenty-five miles southwest of Washington. Virginia's two mainline railroads intersected there. This unit was under the command of Brigadier General Pierre G.T. Beauregard, hailed by Southerners as the Confederacy's first national hero for his leadership in the victory at Charleston Harbor.

Lee's other army was the twelve-thousand-man force stationed at Harper's Ferry under the command of General Joseph E. Johnston. Lee's thinking was that his two armies were strategically positioned so that no matter which spot the Yankees attacked, Beauregard and Johnston could use the railroad to join up quickly and defeat one section of the Union army before another could march to its aid.

At Harper's Ferry with General Johnston was Colonel Thomas J. Jackson, who—like General Lee—was Virginia born and bred.

Hand-picked by Johnston, Jackson was his man for training troops. The colonel, famous for his teaching years at Virginia Military Institute, believed that regardless of the patriotic spirit in a man or his will to fight, he was useless on the battlefield until he was well trained and knew how to carry out orders. Colonel Jackson's training program was rough and rigid, but his men loved him for it. Given enough time, Jackson assured General Johnston he would develop a crack fighting force.

On May 14, Major Irvin McDowell was made a brigadier general and, as President Lincoln had planned, assigned top field commander. On May 23, Virginia's popular vote ratified the ordinance of secession that had been passed by the legislature on April 17. Virginia was now officially enemy territory.

An immediate offensive was planned by General Scott in the Senate Military Committee chambers, with President Lincoln present. Scott explained that his objective would be to seize and hold a buffer zone between Richmond and Washington to protect the Union capital. Scott's "buffer zone" was a large area just south of Washington that included one town—Alexandria, Virginia.

Scott knew Alexandria was guarded by seven hundred Confederate troops. He told Lincoln and the Committee that he would send Colonel Orlando B. Willcox and his First Michigan Regiment to capture Alexandria. The Rebel garrison there was to be captured, run off, or shot down, whichever was necessary to lay hold on the town. Scott had great confidence in the Eleventh New York Fire Zouaves, under the leadership of Colonel Ellsworth. He would assign the Zouaves to help Willcox accomplish his mission.

The assault would be at dawn the next morning. Willcox's regiment would enter Alexandria by land and Ellsworth's Zouaves would approach from the Potomac River on three steamers with the sloop of war, *Pawnee*, as their escort.

President Lincoln and the senators liked Scott's plan and voiced their approval. Secretly, Lieutenant Colonel Jeffrey Jordan was upset. The planned assault was too soon for any of Rose O'Neal Greenhow's girls to carry a message to the Confederate military authorities. Alexandria was open prey for the Union forces.

Just before the break of dawn on May 24, 1861, Colonel Willcox and his First Michigan Regiment crossed the Potomac over Long Bridge north of Alexandria, while Colonel Ellsworth and his Zouaves drifted downstream toward the Alexandria wharf on three river steamers, escorted by the *Pawnee*.

Colonel George Terrett, commander of the small garrison at Alexandria, learned that Willcox's troops were marching toward the town from the north. He attempted to assemble his soldiers in the center of town to brace for a battle, but was unsuccessful. The Rebels were billeted all over Alexandria in their own homes.

They had another problem. Terrett's force was low on ammunition. It had no more than two bullets per man.

Willcox's regiment entered town on King Street, the main north-south thoroughfare, some fifteen minutes before Ellsworth's Zouaves arrived. It was several blocks from the river to Alexandria's business district.

When the Zouaves neared the center of town, Corporal Brownell—in keeping with Colonel Ellsworth's instructions—was shoulder-to-shoulder with his commander. Buck's bayonet was fixed, and he carried his rifle at the ready.

When they heard shots in the direction of the railroad station, Ellsworth shouted to his men, "Spread out! We'll work our way toward the station. Keep your eyes open!" The sun was peeping over the eastern horizon by the time the Zouaves reached the depot of the Orange & Alexandria Railroad and found Willcox and his men with thirty-five Rebel prisoners. A dozen other Confederate soldiers lay dead, scattered about.

"What happened, Colonel?" Ellsworth asked.

"Seems they had a bit of a warning," replied Willcox. "Most of the seven hundred got aboard a train that was about to leave town and took off. Their commander went with them. I guess the rest of these boys were rousted out of their beds too late to catch the train."

Brownell chuckled and said, "Well, Colonel Willcox, you did all three things General Scott had written in our orders. Didn't he say to capture them, run them off, or shoot them down?"

"I guess he did, at that."

"So what now, Colonel?" queried Ellsworth, who stood a head shorter than Willcox.

"Let's secure the town. I'll have some of my men take these prisoners to the local jail. The rest will take positions in the residential areas. You take your Zouaves and secure the business district."

"Fine," nodded Ellsworth. "You and I can get together once we've made sure the citizens are under control. Let's have a cup of coffee at one of the cafés."

"That's a deal, Colonel. Coffee it is."

Turning to his men, Ellsworth divided them up, assigning a detail to stay and occupy the depot. Another detail would move onto the town's main thoroughfare and watch over the shops and stores. Two other details would guard the north and south entrances to the town. Leaving himself a unit of eight men, the colonel said to them, "All right, men, you and I will take over the telegraph office. Let's go."

Alexandria was swarming with Union soldiers as the towns people looked on from their windows and porches. They seemed numb with shock.

When Ellsworth and his small detachment reached the edge of the business district on King Street, the colonel's attention was drawn to a large flag flying atop the Marshal House Inn. He slowed, then halted. His unit stopped with him and studied the unfamiliar design.

"That's the new Confederate flag, isn't it, sir?" said one of the Zouaves.

"Looks like it. I heard a couple of weeks ago that they had adopted a new one." Running his gaze over the faces of his men, he said, "Alexandria is now occupied by Union forces. It is no longer a Confederate town. That flag has to come down. We'll put the Stars and Stripes up there later, but that Rebel flag is coming down now."

"I'll get it, sir," Buck volunteered.

"Sorry, my friend," Ellsworth grinned, "but yours truly is going to handle that little chore himself."

"Whatever you say, sir."

Looking around at the others, Ellsworth said, "Halstead, Schmidt, Grover, and Elkins. Go occupy the telegraph office. I'll take these four with me. We'll meet you over there shortly."

While the designated four hurried up the street toward the telegraph office, Ellsworth led his four men into the plush lobby of the Marshal House hotel. The eyes of the elderly man behind the desk bulged at the enemy soldiers crowding through the door. There was no one else in sight.

Ellsworth had dressed himself for the assault in a resplendent new uniform. Pinned on his chest was a gold medal attached to a bright red ribbon. The medal was inscribed with words in Latin: *Not For Ourselves Alone, but for Our Country.*

As Ellsworth approached the desk, the clerk stammered, "Wh-what do you want?"

"Only that you don't try to give us any trouble, Mr.—What's your name, sir?"

"Ollie Evans," gulped the old man.

"Well, Mr. Evans, we'll not harm you if you stay right here and remain quiet. All we want is to take down that abominable Confederate flag you're flying on the roof. Alexandria is now under Union authority. The Confederate flag must be removed from the roof."

Evans said no more. His wrinkled face was sheet-white.

Turning to his men, Ellsworth said, "Frye and Manley, you stay here and guard the door. If anyone comes in, hold them at gunpoint until Lynch, Brownell, and I return."

"Yes, sir."

Frye and Manley watched the three Zouaves mount the stairs and disappear. Then Manley moved to the door and looked out on the street. Two male citizens were in a heated argument with five Zouaves across the street and down a few doors.

"Stan, come here," said Manley. "Looks like a couple of hot-headed yokels are about to tie into some of our boys."

Frye hurried to the door and eyed the scene. "Hope they're not foolish enough to try to take on our guys."

While the two Zouaves concentrated on the street trouble, Ollie Evans ducked through a door behind the desk and hobbled as fast as he could through the office. Reaching a side door, he moved into the rear of the lobby and cast a glance at the two Union soldiers. They were intent on the action down the street and had not missed him.

Gritting his teeth against the arthritis pain in his legs, he quietly moved up the stairs. He was puffing hard when he reached the third floor and limped down the hall to the manager's private apartment. Tapping on the door, he called in a subdued voice, "Mr. Jackson! Mr. Jackson!"

Light footsteps sounded inside the apartment, the doorknob rattled, and the door opened slightly. "What is it, Ollie?" came a young feminine voice.

"Mrs. Jackson, I need to talk to your husband, quick!"

"He's watching the trouble down on the street," said the manager's wife, "and he's very upset. Can I give him the message?"

"Miss Lily, there's trouble right here in the hotel! I gotta tell him about it."

Still in a robe, Lily Jackson widened the door, turned and called, "James! It's Ollie. He says we've got trouble right here in the hotel."

Thirty-two-year-old James Jackson appeared, his face pale, and asked, "What kind of trouble, Ollie?"

When the three Zouaves reached the fourth floor landing, Colonel Ellsworth quickly found the dark, narrow staircase that led to the roof. Buck was on his heels as he hurried up the stairs, with Jim Lynch right behind him. It took the colonel a few seconds to find the bolt latch in the gloom and slide it free. Sunlight flooded the dark space when the door came open.

"You two wait here," said Ellsworth. "I'll be right back."

Buck and Jim pressed into the doorway together and watched as their leader left the small platform and began to climb the steep slope of the roof toward the flagpole. The colonel's leather-soled boots slipped a few times, but he soon reached the peak. When he stood up, gripping the flagpole, a rousing cheer came from King Street below. Several Zouaves stood over two crumpled forms and cheered their colonel's appearance atop the hotel. Colonel Ellsworth detached the Confederate flag and wadded it up, then turned and carefully made his way back to the platform.

When Ellsworth was back inside, Lynch said, "Go ahead, sir. I'll close and lock the door." Ellsworth thanked him and descended the stairs behind Brownell to the fourth floor landing.

Buck paused on the landing in front of the colonel, waiting for Lynch to catch up. He eyed the Confederate flag, grinned at the colonel, and said, "You going to hang onto that for a keepsake?"

"Might do that. Spoils of war, they call it."

Lynch drew up behind them, and they headed on down the stairs. There were windows at each landing, allowing the bright sunlight to flood the hallways. Just as Buck reached the landing on the third floor, he saw a man with a double-barreled shotgun standing in an open doorway a few feet away.

Buck tensed. Instinctively he lunged forward and swung his rifle, batting the shotgun with the bayonet. One barrel of the shotgun roared. Colonel Ellsworth, who was still on the staircase with

Lynch behind him, took the blast square in the chest. The impact slammed him against the wall.

The man snapped back the hammer of the second barrel and aimed it at Buck, but too late. A slug from Buck's rifle entered the man's forehead, whipping his head back and throwing the double muzzle of the shotgun sideways. The gun roared, missing Brownell, but ripping a huge hole in the wall.

While the civilian assailant lay dead, flat on his back, Buck whirled to see Lynch grasp for Ellsworth. The little colonel was dead on his feet. His body slid partway down the wall, then pitched forward with a heavy, headlong weight. He hit the landing with a thud.

Buck's heart pounded his chest. He dropped to his knees beside Ellsworth's lifeless form. Lynch was instantly beside him. Neither man said anything. They only stared at their leader who still clutched the Confederate flag. It lay partially under him and was spattered with his blood. Ellsworth's gold medal had been driven into his chest by the shotgun blast.

The dreadful, silent moment was shattered by the scream of Lily Jackson, who stood on the stairs, beholding with horror the body of her slain husband. Directly behind her, Frye and Manley came bounding upward. The grief-stricken woman dropped to the floor beside her fallen mate. A chilling wail escaped her lips.

Only a brief glance at Ellsworth told Frye and Manley that their beloved champion was dead. The New York Fire Zouaves' grief and anger was violent. Some of them had to be deterred by their comrades from setting fire to the town.

The popular young colonel's death plunged the North into mourning. Bells tolled in church belfries and flags flew at half-staff. President Lincoln was grief-stricken. In honor of his fallen friend, he ordered the funeral ceremony to be held in the East Room at the White House. There would be a procession to the White House from the funeral home in Washington where the body was quickly embalmed. Upon viewing the body at the funeral home, Lincoln sobbed, "Oh, my boy! My boy! Was it necessary this sacrifice should be made?"

At nine o'clock on the morning of May 25, Corporal Brownell rode in the presidential coach with the president and Mrs. Lincoln as the funeral procession began at the undertaker's parlor. Buck was given this honor by Lincoln because he had slain Colonel Ellsworth's killer. Mary Lincoln carried a laurel wreath that she would place on the coffin when it arrived in the East Room at the White House.

Mourners turned out by the thousands. Double lines of grieving spectators filled the streets. Companies and regiments of soldiers from the Washington camps marched slowly to the beat of muffled drums beneath furled flags and banners.

The president's carriage led the procession, with the hearse next in line, pulled by four white horses. Ellsworth's pall was the country's flag. Six Zouave bearers walked beside the hearse, followed by a small band of Zouaves. Only a few could be spared, for the Eleventh New York was occupying Alexandria along with the First Michigan.

The small band of Zouaves was weaponless, walking with heads bowed in grief, eyes fixed on the hearse, and tears staining their cheeks. Behind them came a riderless horse, its back draped with the blood-stained Confederate flag Ellsworth had taken down from the flagpole of the Marshall House Inn. Following the riderless horse came the president's Cabinet, the Senate Military Committee, and the army's military leaders and their wives in carriages and buggies.

An honor guard was positioned at the White House, ready to carry the coffin to the East Room. Once it was in place, the lid was opened, and the body lay in state for several hours. At precisely three o'clock in the afternoon, a closed-coffin ceremony was conducted. The president sat near the coffin with his wife by his side. Head in hand, Lincoln shed silent tears. On his other side was Buck Brownell.

With the Senate Military Committee were Lieutenant Colonel Jeffrey Jordan and his daughter, Jenny. While listening to the minister, Jenny set her soft gaze on Buck. Several times, Buck let his line of sight drift to Jenny to find her looking at him. The occasion would not allow him to give her a smile, but he hoped she could read in his eyes his love for her.

Buck made a silent vow to himself. *When the war was over, he would find a way to make Jenny his bride.*

When the ceremony was completed, Lincoln turned to Buck and requested that he leave with him and Mrs. Lincoln. While everyone else waited, Buck filed out with the Lincolns. He managed to glance tenderly at Jenny. The glance did not escape Jeffrey Jordan's notice. Jenny saw her father's scowl and felt the pain of it in her heart. A tinge of despair washed over her. Why should two people in love never be able to have a life together?

Colonel Ellsworth's body was taken by train to City Hall in New York the next day, where thousands filed past the coffin to pay their last respects. Two days later, another train bore Ellsworth's body home to Mechanicville, New York, for burial by his family in a grave overlooking the lazy Hudson River.

TEN

The tragic death of Colonel Elmer Ellsworth had varied results in the North. Sermons, newspaper editorials, songs, and poems lamented his loss and proclaimed his heroism.

But in the midst of the mourning over Ellsworth's death, another hero was proclaimed—Corporal Buck Brownell. His shooting of the little colonel's killer catapulted Brownell to fame.

On Wednesday, May 29, a special ceremony was held on the steps of the Capitol, and President Abraham Lincoln presented Brownell with a medal for his heroism. The sudden thrust into eminence was a bit embarrassing to Buck, but he handled it well. Given the opportunity to say a few words to the crowd, he averred that any of the Zouaves would have done the same thing he did. After a round of applause, President Lincoln introduced General Winfield Scott, who stepped to the podium and surprised Buck with a promotion to lieutenant. This honor left the young Zouave nonplused.

Buck had noticed that Jenny Jordan was in the crowd. At the end of the ceremony, she stood for a long moment, watching, but because of the press of well-wishers around Buck, she did not attempt to approach him. While Buck greeted those who swarmed him, he let his eyes roam the crowd for Jenny. By the time the crowd was gone, so was she.

The next morning, the Senate Military Committee was assembled in its meeting room with General Scott and Brigadier General Irvin McDowell. Jeffrey Jordan was also present, sitting next to Senator Henry Wilson. Though Jordan was official adviser to the Committee, he was outranked in the assembly by Generals Scott and McDowell. Scott, however, had requested his presence in case he should have something to add to the plan that was about to be presented.

Scott, beefy and tired-looking, stood at a large Virginia map on the wall with wooden pointer in hand. At a small table, aloof from the committeemen, sat General McDowell.

General Scott held the pointer in both hands across his ample midsection and brought the meeting to order. "Gentlemen," he said in his customary authoritative tone, "you all know that under my direction, the Union army is planning for a large-scale confrontation with the enemy in northern Virginia. As I have pointed out to you and to the president, northern Virginia is the natural place for this major battle. At the moment, I'd say we're looking at such a battle in about a month. It will probably take place just about where General Pierre Beauregard is gathering his troops…at Manassas Junction, some twenty-five miles west-southwest of here. But don't quote me on it, yet. These plans are still in the making."

Clearing his throat, the general proceeded. "At the moment— because of the upcoming northern Virginia battle—I am quite concerned about *southern* Virginia." Turning toward the map and using his pointer to draw attention to the southern tip of the Virginia Peninsula, Scott said, "Right here is our Fort Monroe, under the command of General Benjamin Butler. Monroe needs to be better fortified." Looking toward McDowell, he asked, "Would you agree to that, General?"

"Indeed I would, sir," nodded McDowell. "Fort Monroe, because of its position, is strategic to the Union."

"Do you concur, Colonel Jordan?"

"Absolutely, sir. It is not only a threat to the Confederates with the prospect of Union land thrusts toward Richmond, but it is also a constant obstacle to Confederate boat and ship traffic on the James and York Rivers. It most assuredly needs to be bolstered up with men and guns."

"Exactly," smiled Scott.

Jordan felt a twinge of excitement. Before this meeting was over, he would have information for Rose Greenhow to pass on to General Robert E. Lee.

General Scott continued. Running the tip of the pointer upward along the west shore of the peninsula, he said, "I also want to make a military move up the peninsula from Fort Monroe and establish Union fortifications. We must be in control of the entire waterway once the large battle in northern Virginia is over. We are confident that one good, hard punch will knock the Confederacy down for good, but just in case there's any fight left in them, we must be prepared. We dare not allow them to control the waters of the peninsula."

There was a glass of water on the table where General McDowell sat. Scott moved to it, took a short drink, and returned to the map. Using the pointer again, he said, "In the path of my proposed military move from Fort Monroe northward—as you can see—is the village of Big Bethel. Big Bethel is the nearest outpost of the Confederate forces in that part of the state, which are headquartered up here ten miles further north at Yorktown on the York River. In command of the Rebel forces there is Colonel John B. Magruder. He fought under me in the Mexican War. Tough as harness leather. He won three commendations for bravery."

Scott called for any questions that the men might have. There were none. The Committee was waiting to hear the time and details of the attack.

"I am going to assign Brigadier General Ebenezer Pierce of the Fourth Massachusetts Infantry to lead the attack," said Scott. "There will be three other regiments—the First Vermont, the Third New York, and the Fifth New York Zouaves." He gestured toward the Union field commander, who sat at the small table. "General McDowell and I have already discussed these units. He is in full agreement with me that these units are the most ready for combat that we have."

McDowell nodded. One of the senators raised his hand.

"General, since you're sending in Zouaves, why not send the Eleventh New York? Certainly they have to be among the very best. Is it because they haven't yet been assigned a new leader since Colonel Ellsworth was killed?"

Scott looked toward McDowell and asked, "Would you like to reply to that, General?"

"Of course," nodded McDowell, standing up. "We *are* sending the Fire Zouaves, Senator McGivens. There is a report being printed now for the Committee. Just yesterday, I merged the Eleventh New York Fire Zouaves with Colonel Abram Duryee's Fifth Zouaves. This move, of course, was with the approval of the president and General Scott. My reasoning is that there is just no one among the Fire Zouaves who can fill Colonel Ellsworth's boots. Since Colonel Duryee is matured and experienced in battle from the Mexican War, I felt it would be best that the Fire Zouaves be placed under his command."

"Good move!" called out one of the other senators. The rest of the Committee agreed.

With the Fire Zouaves brought to mind, Jordan thought of Lieutenant Buck Brownell. He hoped Jenny would soon get the man out of her thoughts.

Laying the pointer on a slender shelf beneath the map, General Scott ran his weary gaze over the interested faces and said, "Our scheduled time to launch the surprise attack on the garrison at Big Bethel is at dawn on Monday, June 10. With the Confederate outpost there in Union hands, it will be removed as an obstacle."

A few other minor questions were presented and answered to the satisfaction of the Committee, and the meeting was closed. The men filed out of the Senate Chamber past Jenny Jordan's desk.

After everyone had gone, Jenny's father finally appeared and said, "I've been looking for John Calhoun. He's not in his office or any of the other offices within the Chamber. Do you happen to know where he is?"

"Yes, Daddy. He's downstairs posting some mail. He should be back shortly."

"Okay. I'll wait."

"If you're busy, I can give him a message for you."

"No, that's okay. I have to talk to John myself."

Jenny looked around to see if anyone was within earshot. Seeing no one, she said, "Daddy, did you learn something significant in the meeting?"

Bending over Jenny's desk, Jordan said in a low tone, "Did I ever! Four regiments of the Union army are going to pull a surprise attack on the Confederate garrison down at Big Bethel. I've got to get the message to General Lee. The safest way is for John to carry it to Rose Greenhow. She'll take it from there."

"I guess Rose's girls are champing at the bit to do their spy work," said Jenny. "They'll get their chance now."

Jenny's mind went to the man she loved. The question was out of her mouth almost before she had formed the words in her mind. "Daddy, do you know what regiments are going on this attack?"

"Yes. The Fourth Massachusetts, the First Vermont, the Third New York, and the Fifth New York Zouaves."

Jordan saw the relief come over Jenny's face and knew why she had asked. Sitting down in one of the two chairs in front of her desk, he leaned close, subduing his voice so it didn't carry down the hall, and said, "Jenny, you've got to get Buck Brownell out of your system."

"Daddy, I only asked—"

"You asked because you thought the Eleventh might be in on the mission, and you're concerned about Buck." Looking her straight in the eye, he said levelly, "Tell me I'm wrong."

Jenny's face flushed. "You…you're not wrong. Daddy, you can't legislate what goes on in my heart. I'm very fond of Buck. He's a good man and a gentleman, and he's—"

"He's the enemy, Jenny! You're a Rebel and he's a Yankee. You've got to forget him, do you understand?"

"But, Daddy, I can't just erase Buck from my mind! I can't snatch him from my heart like he never existed. Surely you can understand that."

"Look, honey, it was your Buck Brownell who shot and killed that innkeeper over in Alexandria. James Jackson was a Southerner, Jenny! Do you understand? James Jackson was merely trying to protect his nation's flag when he threw that shotgun on Ellsworth. He died for the Confederate flag, daughter, and he was your fellow-Virginian! This…this man you're so fond of put a bullet through his head and made a widow of his wife!"

"Buck didn't start this war, Daddy! He was with Colonel Ellsworth inside the hotel by orders. When he shot Mr. Jackson, it was because he fired first. What was Buck to do…just stand there and let the man kill him, too?"

John Calhoun drew up, cleared his throat, and said, "Excuse me. Am I getting into a family squabble here?"

"No squabble," Jordan replied, standing up and giving Calhoun a smile. "Jenny and I were just having a friendly discussion. I've been waiting to talk to you, John. Got some very important information for you."

"Good. Come on into the cubbyhole I call my office."

As Calhoun headed for the Chamber door, Jordan leaned close to his daughter and said, "You're right, Jenny. Buck didn't start the war. But he's a Northerner, and don't forget it!" He took two steps toward the door, then came back and said, "And just so you know, the Eleventh New York Zouaves have been merged with the Fifth New

York Zouaves because of Ellsworth's death. Your Lieutenant Brownell *is* going to be in on the sneak attack at Big Bethel."

Tears welled up in Jenny's dark eyes as her father followed after Calhoun. Her lower lip quivered as she stared after him and whispered, "I can't help it, Daddy. I *love* him. I do."

On the morning of June 4, Colonel John B. Magruder was in a meeting with his subordinate officers at the Confederate stronghold near Yorktown on the Virginia Peninsula. They were seated around a large table. Bright sunlight was shining through the open windows of the meeting room, and a warm breeze fluttered the sheer curtains. The discussion centered around how soon the skirmishes in Virginia would turn into major battles.

The door was standing open, allowing the morning breeze to cool the room. The discussion was interrupted by a light tap on the door frame. Seated at the head of the table, Magruder swung his gaze to the door to see a young corporal, who said, "Pardon me, Colonel. I'm sorry to disturb you, sir, but I believe you will agree that what I have to tell you is of utmost importance."

"That's fine, Corporal. What is it?"

"I have two young ladies out here, sir, who insist on seeing you. They say they have a message of vital importance. They were sent by a Mrs. Greenhow of Washington and have classified information about a Union attack on Big Bethel."

"Oh, yes!" Magruder exclaimed, rising to his feet. "A wire came from General Lee informing me that a couple of Confederate spies were on their way. I…ah…didn't realize they would be women."

The corporal grinned and winked. "They are definitely that, sir."

"Well, don't keep the young ladies waiting, Corporal. Show them in."

"Yes, sir."

The corporal stepped outside and ushered the two young

women through the door. Instantly the officers were on their feet.

Rose Greenhow's spies were in their early twenties. They wore fancy hoop-skirted dresses with wide-brimmed hats and carried parasols. Moving to them, Magruder smiled and said, "Ladies, I am Colonel John Magruder."

"Hello, Colonel Magruder," one of them said. "I am Bettie Duval, and this is Susan Rand."

Magruder told them he was delighted to meet them, and introduced his officers with the sweep of his hand. He then asked the young ladies to be seated at the table.

When all were seated, Magruder said, "I received a wire yesterday from General Lee, informing me that two spies sent by Mrs. Greenhow would be coming with some vital information. He didn't say exactly when, nor did he tell me the spies would be lovely young ladies."

"Was there anything else in General Lee's message, Colonel?" asked Bettie.

"Yes," nodded Magruder. "I was puzzled by it, but I assume you can clear it up for me. It simply said, 'Look for the circled R.' "

The ladies exchanged glances, smiling at each other.

Bettie said, "Two things we had to know before we proceeded any further, Colonel, was that you fit the description we were given, and that you would be able to tell us about the circled R. General Lee sent the message in a secret code, did he not?"

"He did."

"So when we show you a message with a circled R on it, you will know it is authentic."

"I assume the R stands for Rose."

"Yes, that's right." Then turning to her companion, Bettie said, "All right, Susan." Susan scooted her chair back and rose to her feet. Immediately the group of officers stood up.

Susan smiled and said, "Please be seated, gentlemen."

As the men were easing into their chairs, Bettie helped Susan remove the lengthy hatpin and took the hat from her head. Susan then unpinned her long, upswept hair and let it begin to fall. From its folds, she took a well-concealed paper and handed it to Colonel Magruder. "Here you are, sir. Bettie and I hope this will save the lives of many Confederate soldiers."

Allowing her hair to remain in graceful curls on her shoulders, Susan sat down, and Bettie did the same, laying the hat on the table.

Magruder's face went grim as he read the message. When he was finished, he lifted his gaze to the men around the table, and said, "The Yankees are going to attack our garrison at Big Bethel next Monday, June 10, at dawn. They're coming with forty-four hundred troops."

"Forty-four hundred!" echoed a captain. "Sir, we've only got twenty-five hundred in the whole peninsula!"

"I know," said Magruder, "but because of this message, we've got six days to get ready…and the Yankees won't have any idea that we know they're coming. Even if we can't match their numbers, we'll have the edge with the element of surprise. We can't pull all of our troops from the peninsula down to Big Bethel, but with this much of a forewarning, we'll be ready for them."

"Who obtained this information for us, Colonel?" asked a lieutenant. "It had to be someone on the inside in Washington."

"It doesn't say, and I understand why. If these young ladies had been caught and the message found, the Yankees would know who to put before a firing squad in Washington."

Another lieutenant, Burl Newman, looked at Bettie and said, "You ladies are aware that if you had been caught, you would no doubt have faced a firing squad. It's just about a universal law anywhere in the world that spies are executed when they're caught."

"Yes, Lieutenant," nodded Bettie. "We know the risks involved. So does Rose, and so do the spies who obtained this information. We are all loyal Southerners and feel honored—just as you soldiers—to serve the Confederacy."

"God bless you and the spies in Washington," said Magruder.

"Ladies," spoke up Lieutenant Newman again, "how did you

get past the Union soldiers…and how did you get down here?"

Bettie and Susan smiled at each other, then Bettie said, "We got past the Union soldiers by being a bit flirtatious and telling them we were going south to visit someone very special to us. That's you, Colonel Magruder."

Magruder blushed.

"You see, gentlemen," interjected Susan, "we figure men spies wouldn't have a chance getting past the Union lines. The Yankees would be too quick to suspect men. They'd search them…maybe even follow them if they found nothing on them. But Mrs. Greenhow came up with the idea of using female spies, and as you can see, it worked. She's already recruited two more girls to bring messages if the war lasts very long. And I'm sure if more are needed, she'll get them. Men are such pushovers for batting eyelashes and co quettish smiles."

There was a round of laughter. Magruder shook his head in wonderment. "I hope someday I can meet this Rose Greenhow. She must be some kind of woman."

"That she is, sir," Susan said.

"We hired a boat to bring us down here," said Bettie, answering Newman's second question. "Mrs. Greenhow paid for it."

"Bless her heart," breathed Magruder. "And you'll be going back the same way?"

"Yes, sir. The boat is waiting at the dock, and we must be heading back shortly."

"How about some good ol' army coffee and maybe a little something to eat before you go?" asked Magruder.

The ladies accepted the coffee, but politely turned down the offer of food. When they finished their coffee, they were escorted to the dock by Colonel Magruder. He thanked them and assured them their efforts would save Confederate lives. They climbed aboard the small boat and sailed northward.

Magruder went right to work. He left what troops he felt were necessary to slow any enemy advance on Yorktown and moved the rest of them to Big Bethel. He also sent for one of his best regiments, the First North Carolina Infantry under the command of his close friend, Colonel Daniel H. Hill, who had also fought with distinction in the Mexican War.

Hill and his men had to march to Big Bethel from inland Virginia. They reached the small town on June 7, and along with the men already there, spent the rest of that day and all the next erecting formidable earthworks and felling trees to build defenses on both sides of the Back River.

Colonel Magruder joined the troops at Big Bethel on the morning of June 9. He approved of the work that had been done to fortify the place, then studied the Back River for a few minutes. He suggested to Colonel Hill that if the Yankees from Fort Monroe chose not to come across the bridge, they might ford the river east of the bridge. To guard against this, Hill led the men to build more earthworks. The troops were stretched to the limit to finish the work, but the construction was finished by sundown on Sunday, June 9.

The thirty-three hundred Confederate troops at Big Bethel had their cannons in place by nightfall and were ready for the attack which reportedly would come at dawn. They laughed among themselves, saying the Yankees thought they were going to surprise the Rebels. Instead—thanks to efficient Confederate spy work—the Rebels would have a bigger surprise for the Yankees.

At 4:00 A.M. on June 10, 1861, the forty-four hundred Union troops drew near Big Bethel. There was a three-quarter moon, but it was continually obscured by low, drifting clouds.

Brigadier General Ebenezer Pierce of the Fourth Massachusetts Infantry was in command of the attack force. Taking advantage of what moonlight he had, General Pierce stood near the bridge that spanned the Back River, studied the situation, and called the other unit commanders to him for a consultation. When Colonel Edward Fitzpatrick of the First Vermont, Colonel H.G. Smalley of the Third

New York, and Colonel Abram Duryee of the Fifth New York Zouaves huddled with him to view the massive Confederate bulwarks, they were stunned.

"We weren't told about any fortifications like these, General," said Fitzpatrick.

Pierce rubbed his chin. "This is odd. Why would this little town have such ramparts? It's almost as if they were expecting us."

"But how could that be?" put in Smalley. "There's no way the Rebels could have known we were coming."

"Maybe they built these right after the incident at Fort Sumter back in April," suggested Colonel Duryee. "You know…figuring war would come."

"That must be it," nodded Pierce. "All right, gentlemen. We'll go in as planned…over the bridge. It'll be faster than fording the river just for the sake of moving in a little less conspicuously."

"I agree," said Smalley. "They won't be looking for us, anyway. Time we open fire, they'll still be sleeping."

The commanders returned to their units and prepared to cross the bridge. Lieutenant Buck Brownell was in charge of a company of two hundred Zouaves. When the colonel approached him, Brownell said, "Colonel Duryee, I'm concerned about those fortifications. Big Bethel isn't supposed to look like a fort."

"We were just talking about that with General Pierce. We believe they built all that earthwork right after the assault on Fort Sumter. They probably wanted to be in better shape against a Union offensive, if it should come."

"Could be. It makes sense, anyway."

The Union troops fell into rank and made their crossing of the bridge. Each regiment knew to fan out and to wait until General Pierce's signal at dawn to swarm the town.

Under Colonel Duryee's directions, Lieutenant Brownell led his company across a marshy area about a hundred yards from the eastern bulwarks. From there, they were to do as the other companies and rush the earthworks at General Pierce's prearranged signal.

In the dark moments just before the break of dawn, Buck could make out the rest of the Zouaves off to the north. He was thankful to be among many of the men he had trained for combat.

One of Brownell's corporals brushed up beside him and said, "Lieutenant, unless my eyes are deceiving me, I just saw the outline of a Howitzer being rolled atop that rampart right over th—"

Before the corporal could finish his sentence, the roar of cannons shook the entire area, and cannonballs whistled through the gloom. The flash of rifle muzzles from the ramparts joined with the roar and orange flare of cannon fire and there was instant bedlam. Cannonballs exploded and drove the Union troops behind anything they could find for cover.

"They knew we were coming!" one of Brownell's men shouted at him as they dived into a shallow ditch together. It was mushy and wet.

"No doubt about it," Buck agreed, then looked to see if the rest of his company was finding cover. They had been trained well and knew how to improvise. They were flopping into marshy ditches all over the open area.

While the Confederate howitzers thundered and muskets barked, the Yankees gallantly returned fire. The Union forces were finding it difficult to retaliate effectively because of the Rebel artillery. The enemy was well-prepared for them and had them where they had not planned to be...on the defensive. After some twenty minutes of ear-splitting gunfire, the Yankees were hard-pressed to make a dent in the Confederate bastions.

Buck Brownell carried a bayoneted rifle as well as wearing the customary sidearm of an officer. While he loaded and fired the rifle, he noted in the dawn's early light that Colonel Duryee and the company of Zouaves he was with were pinned down directly beneath three relentless Confederate howitzers. The big guns were in a grove of trees on a rise a few yards to the north of one of the giant man-made earthworks. Duryee and his men were helplessly trapped and would all die if the howitzers were not soon put out of commission.

Buck looked up and down the line of the ditch where he lay in the muck and spotted three of his best men. Shouting above the thunder of battle, Buck called to Sergeant Eric Barnes and Corporals Willie Smith and Theo Watkins. Within seconds, they were huddled beside him.

Buck pointed out the desperate position of Colonel Duryee and his men and explained that they needed to take out the three howitzers. The chosen Zouaves were eager to help their lieutenant accomplish the mission. Rifles loaded and bayonets fixed, they listened as Brownell laid out his plan.

Buck told his men around him to lay a barrage of rifle fire toward the three howitzers so as to keep the crews' attention away from their rear flank. Each of the howitzers' crews had three men—one to pack powder in the magazine, one to ramrod the cannonball, and the other to fire the fuse. Barnes, Smith, and Watkins knew their task was a dangerous one, but they had absolute confidence in their leader. They would follow Lieutenant Buck Brownell anywhere.

Amid the deafening roar of cannonade and the rattle of musketry, Buck led his three men across the marshy field in a wide circle, working his way to the tree-studded rise where the howitzers stood.

Prone on the grassy, open slope, Colonel Duryee and another Zouave were working on a young private whose left hand had nearly been blown off. The private had passed out from the pain. "Tie it off as best you can," Duryee said. "Get Worthington over there to help you."

Another Zouave crawled close and was ready to speak when a shell screamed in close by. Heads down, the Zouaves waited until the shrapnel hissed away and the dirt rained down around them, then looked up.

"What is it, soldier?" Duryee asked.

Rolling onto his side, the Zouave pointed toward the mound where the howitzers stood and said, "Look, sir—it's Brownell and three of his men. They're going after those Rebel cannons!"

"Good for them!" shouted Duryee. "Pass the word along. Tell

the men to fire as much as possible toward the howitzers. Even if they don't hit anything, it'll help distract them."

While the battle raged, Colonel Duryee and the Zouaves unleashed their guns on the howitzer crews. They watched with keen interest as Buck and his men rushed the first gun crew from behind and killed them. Even having one cannon silenced was a great relief.

The second crew was knocked out a few minutes later. The third crew was grabbing for their rifles when they realized the Zouaves were coming for them. But it was too late. All three were cut down before they could fire a shot.

There was a rousing cheer from the Zouaves on the slope when the last howitzer was silenced. Buck and his men packed the muzzles of the cannons with sod. When they were firmly packed, they loaded the magazines with powder, lit the fuses, and hit the ground. All three howitzers were destroyed beyond repair.

The battle continued for over three hours. The Confederates had the advantage, and soon the Yankees had to pull out and retreat to Fort Monroe. They had no choice but to leave their dead behind. When the Confederates saw them leaving with their wounded, they ceased fire and did not pursue them.

At Fort Monroe, General Pierce had the wounded soldiers treated as much as possible, then sent them up the peninsula on boats to Washington, where they could get better care under the watchful eye of Clara Barton. He sent Colonel Duryee and Lieutenant Brownell's company of Zouaves along to protect the boats. Duryee would also make a report to Generals Scott and McDowell.

When they arrived at the main Washington camp, Clara sent out word to the women who had helped her after the Baltimore riot, asking them to meet her at the camp as soon as possible. A few went with her immediately, and the work of patching up some sixty-five wounded men began.

Colonel Duryee left Brownell and his company at the makeshift hospital to do what they could to help, and headed for

General Winfield Scott's tent to make his report. General McDowell was called to hear the report also, and the three Union officers met in Scott's tent.

Duryee gave the details of the Confederate ambush, and reported that eighteen Union soldiers had been killed and sixty-five seriously wounded. He shared his conviction with Scott and McDowell that the Confederates had received details of the planned attack several days in advance. Someone in high places—or maybe more than one person—was a Confederate spy. The two generals agreed. There could be no other explanation. Scott would discuss it with the president as soon as he could get an appointment.

Duryee told the generals there was something else they needed to know. He then told them of Lieutenant Buck Brownell's daring and courage in taking out the three howitzers. He also named the three Zouaves who assisted Brownell, suggesting that all four should receive commendations. When the generals agreed, Duryee said that one of his captains had been killed in the battle and that he needed to fill his spot. He suggested that the new captain be Buck Brownell.

ELEVEN

Word spread quickly through Washington of the battle at Big Bethel, of the Union's defeat, and that the wounded men had been brought to the main military camp just outside the city. Jenny Jordan had been between work and home when Clara Barton sent messengers to round up volunteers. She was not aware of what was going on until she arrived home and was told by a neighbor. Jenny hurriedly saddled her horse and rode for the camp. She had to find out if Buck was all right.

Along the way, Jenny encountered one of Miss Barton's messengers, who informed her of the need for volunteers to help with the wounded soldiers. As she rode on, Jenny told herself she would be glad to help Clara, once she knew about Buck.

The sun was lowering as Jenny rode up to the camp's entrance. Two guards stepped up to greet her, blocking her way. One of them said, "Good evening, ma'am. What can we do for you?"

Knowing she would be allowed in only if she was there to answer Clara's call, Jenny smiled and said, "I'm here to help Miss Barton."

The guards relaxed and took Jenny's horse for her. She hastened to where the wounded soldiers were being tended to and approached Clara Barton, who was giving orders to two women who had arrived a short time earlier. Clara smiled at Jenny and finished her instructions to the two women. When they moved away, she turned to Jenny and said, "Hello, Jenny. I appreciate your coming."

"Glad to do what I can to help."

Clara quickly put Jenny to work making sure the wounded men had water. Carrying a jug and some tin cups, she weaved her way amid the cots. Fear filled her heart when she didn't find Buck. She hoped he was not among those eighteen men reported killed. Returning to the water barrel to refill the jug, Jenny spotted a small group of wounded Zouaves clustered together. Pouring cups of water as she went, she finally reached the Zouaves. Two of them were being treated by nurses, but the rest were already bandaged.

Standing over the cots, Jenny smiled and said, "I have some cool water, here. Anybody interested?"

One of them, a youth of eighteen, grinned and said, "Only if you put the cup to my lips, Miss. I...uh...I have a broken arm."

Jenny knew flirtation when she saw it. "You can't use your other arm?"

"Oh, no, ma'am," grinned the youth. "It became paralyzed the moment I laid eyes on you."

"Thank you, soldier, but I'm afraid you'll just have to make that good arm work. I have too many other soldiers to tend to."

The youth's friends kidded him as Jenny passed out cups to each of them. As she was finishing, she steeled herself for the worst and asked, "Do you men know Lieutenant Buck Brownell?" There were six affirmative answers. "Is he all right? I...I mean did he make it through the battle?"

"Oh, yes, ma'am," spoke up the one with the broken arm. "Lieutenant Brownell came with us from Fort Monroe."

Feeling sweet relief and breathing a prayer of thanks, Jenny asked, "Do you know where he is?"

"Yes, ma'am," spoke up another. "He's in General Scott's tent. But when he comes out of there, he won't be *Lieutenant* Brownell anymore."

"What do you mean?"

"Well, ma'am, he was here with us when General Scott's adjutant came and told him he was wanted at General Scott's tent. After Lieutenant Brownell hurried away, the adjutant told us Lieutenant Brownell was being promoted to captain. That's what's going on right now in General Scott's tent."

Jenny smiled and said, "That's wonderful."

"Do you know the lieutenant…the captain well, ma'am?" asked another Zouave.

"Yes, quite well," Jenny smiled. "Well…I must get going. There are many more soldiers who need water."

As Jenny turned to leave, the soldier with the broken arm said, "Ma'am?"

Jenny set her dark eyes on him. "Yes?"

"Are you Lieut—I mean Captain Brownell's girl?"

Jenny felt an icy wave wash over her heart. Buck loved her. She knew that. But she couldn't let herself be Buck's girl. Choking on the lump that had lodged in her throat, she replied, "Sort of."

The Zouave grinned and said, "If I had a girl as beautiful as you, I'd have the courage to charge three blazing howitzers, too!"

Jenny knew what howitzers were. She could only imagine what kind of courageous deed Buck must have done. Eager to find General Scott's tent, she excused herself and headed again for the water barrel. A carriage load of women pulled up as Jenny filled her jug and replenished her supply of cups. She kept an eye on the new women until she saw them approach Clara Barton for instructions.

Hastening to the spot where Clara was giving orders, Jenny pressed in and said, "Clara, could you have one of these young ladies relieve me? I have to meet someone at General Scott's tent."

Clara agreed, and Jenny showed her replacement where she had left off. Jenny then hurried to the guards at the gate and asked the location of General Scott's tent. Moments later, she approached it and was met by a young corporal. "May I be of help to you, ma'am?"

"Well, I don't know. I'm looking for Lieutenant Buck Brownell."

"I'm General Scott's adjutant, ma'am," said the corporal. "Lieutenant Brownell is with the general and some other officers at the moment. Are you with the Barton crew?"

"Yes. I…I've been working among the wounded. Some of the Zouaves told me I could find Lieutenant Brownell over here."

"Well, ma'am, you can either sit on that wooden chair over there and wait until the lieutenant comes out, or you can return to your job with the wounded men. I'll come fetch you when he's available."

Before Jenny could reply, the tent flap came open and Buck Brownell emerged, followed by a Zouave colonel Jenny did not recognize. The instant Buck saw Jenny, a smiled spread over his face. Turning to the man who flanked him, Buck said, "I want you to meet somebody."

The adjutant entered the tent while Buck was introducing Jenny to Colonel Abram Duryee. The colonel told Jenny he was glad to meet her, then courteously excused himself and walked away.

In the light of the setting sun, Jenny set her eyes on the captain's bars that graced Buck's shoulders and said, "Congratulations, Captain."

"Somebody told you."

"Yes, some of your wounded Zouave admirers over there. I think it's wonderful, and I'm sure you deserve it."

"You must have answered Miss Barton's call for help."

"Well, not exactly. Daddy told me a few days ago that your Fire Zouaves were going to take part in an upcoming battle. I didn't learn what had happened until I arrived home from work this afternoon. I was…concerned about you. I had to come and see if I could find out how you were." Moving close and laying a hand on his arm, Jenny said, "I'm so glad you're all right."

The newly made captain looked at the ground, then back at Jenny. "Thank you. I'm glad you care what happens to me."

"I…I have to go now. It'll be dark soon. I didn't leave a note for Daddy and he'll be worried about me."

"I'll walk you to your horse," said Buck, gripping her hand.

When they reached the camp entrance, Buck led Jenny to her horse. It was tied to a bush, along with several others. He raised the reins over the animal's head and dropped them in front of the saddle. He opened his hand, palm up, to help her aboard. When she took the hand, he squeezed it and pulled her close. "Jenny, I love you."

"And I love you, Buck," she said, her eyes misting.

Buck looked around to see if anyone was watching. When he saw that the coast was clear, he lowered his head and kissed her. Tears were visible on Jenny's cheeks when they parted. Fighting to keep her composure, she turned toward the horse.

Buck reached for her. "Jenny…"

Without turning around, she said, "Please, Buck. I must get home."

He carefully hoisted her into the saddle. When she settled in, she looked down at him through a wall of tears and said, "Thank you."

"When this war is over—"

"We can never have each other, Buck," she said, drawing a shuddering breath.

Buck reached up and grasped her hand. "Jenny, you can't let your father control you all your life."

"You don't understand."

"Jenny, your father will probably marry again someday. Then he won't even want you around the house. You have your own life to live. We love each other, Jenny, and we could be happy together. This war won't last forever. Please tell me that when it's over, we can be together."

Jenny's throat was constricted and she was crying so hard, her chest was heaving. Choking out the words, she said, "I'll always love you, Buck." Then she slipped her hand from his grasp and goaded the horse into a trot.

When she knew she was out of sight of the camp, Jenny pulled the horse off the road into a stand of willows and wept her heart out. Tears flowing, Jenny caught her breath convulsively, giving vent to the emotions tearing at her soul. She felt like a liar and a hypocrite before Buck, knowing her father was pretending loyalty to the Union while engaged in espionage for the Confederacy.

Jenny loved Buck desperately, yet what could she do? She was a daughter of the South and owed it her loyalty. She owed her father her loyalty too, and she knew how he felt about her keeping company with Buck.

Bent over in the saddle, Jenny sobbed and prayed, "Dear God in heaven...what am I to do? Please help me! I could ask You to take away the love I have for Buck, but I want to love him. I want to be his wife and to bear his children. But I also love my Daddy...and I love the South. Oh, God, I don't know what to do. I don't know what to do." Her words trailed off into groans of despair.

In the days that followed, a heavy-hearted Buck Brownell plunged into his work of training the new recruits as they arrived daily. Jenny was hardly out of his thoughts. Often he prayed that one day, in spite of Jeffrey Jordan, Jenny would be his.

As the Confederates continued to gather troops at Manassas Junction, the North fumed and fretted over the presence of Rebel troops at the very doorstep of the nation's capital. President Lincoln felt the pressure of it, and after the embarrassment at Big Bethel, he determined to take action. In a private meeting with Generals Winfield Scott and Irvin McDowell, the president directed them to proceed immediately with their proposal to launch a gigantic assault on General Pierre G.T. Beauregard's force at Manassas Junction.

Scott and McDowell went to work. Since the scheme was already in the embryonic stage, it didn't take them long to come up with a well-contrived plan. On Friday, June 14, the plan was presented to the president, his Cabinet, and the Senate Military Committee. Jeffrey Jordan sat in the meeting and smiled inwardly. He would send every word of the plan directly to General Beauregard through Rose O'Neal Greenhow's girls.

In the plan, the Federal army would divide into three columns to increase its pace and mobility, and advance west-southwestward on roughly parallel routes. It would seize the Confederate outposts at Fairfax Court House sixteen miles from Washington and at Centreville, five miles beyond. Two of the columns would then push ahead and make a diversionary attack on the center of the Confederate line at Bull Run Creek.

The third column would skirt the Rebels' right flank and strike southward, cutting off the railroad to Richmond and threatening the Confederate rear. The Rebels would then be forced to abandon Manassas Junction and retreat some fifteen miles to the next defensible line, at the banks of the Rappahannock River. The Northerners, and especially the citizens of Washington, could then breath easier, and the morale of the Confederacy would be severely damaged. Even beyond that, Generals Scott and McDowell were confident that the Rebel forces would be so completely overwhelmed that the whole war would come to an end and a Union victory proclaimed.

The president, the Cabinet, and the Committee agreed on the plan, giving Jeffrey Jordan, as the Committee's military adviser, opportunity to voice his opinion. When Jordan said he could not improve on the plan, it was finalized and the generals were given authority to proceed.

General McDowell, as field commander, was responsible to set the date for the campaign to begin. He told the gathering he already had a date in mind—Monday, July 8. He figured it would take five days to march the men to the point of attack, meaning the actual battle would occur on Saturday, July 13.

Chairman Henry Wilson ran his gaze over the faces of the group, and said, "I agree with Generals Scott and McDowell. This offensive will spell the end of the Confederacy. This ridiculous civil conflict will no doubt be history by July fourteenth."

Jeffrey Jordan laughed to himself. How shocked Senator Wilson would be if he knew that the woman he was courting was a Rebel spy and that General Beauregard would receive all the information on the Union plan through her hands. As with the other men in attendance, Jordan had been taking notes. He had it all down in his notebook. The papers he would pass through John Calhoun to Rose Greenhow would explain the plan in every detail, including a list—as given by McDowell—of every Union regiment that would be involved in the attack. Like at Big Bethel, the Confederates would have a big surprise for the Yankees on the morning of July 13.

It was just past midday on Thursday, June 20, when Bettie Duval and Lola Morrow drew up at a wagon blockade in the road as they were headed west out of Washington. A U.S. flag flapped in the breeze from a pole affixed to one of the wagons. The horse pulling their buggy snorted and blew, bobbing its head when two men in blue—one a private, the other a corporal—stepped up and smiled.

"Good afternoon, ladies," said the corporal. "May I ask where you're headed?"

"Nowhere in particular, Corporal," replied Bettie, who held the reins. "We're just out for a little ride…getting away from the city to breathe a little fresh country air."

As Bettie spoke, she and Lola flashed flirtatious smiles. Both wore hats that shaded their faces.

"You live in Washington, then, I take it," said the private.

"Yes," nodded Bettie.

"Maybe you should ride north out of town. You're heading into Confederate territory going this way."

"Could be dangerous, ladies," added the private.

Lola rolled her big blue eyes at them and said, "We appreciate your concern for us, gentlemen, but we're really not afraid the Rebels will harm us. There isn't any real country north of Washington for several miles. We like it out this way."

"But, ma'am," countered the private, "with things heating up between us and the Confederates, you don't know what might happen if you run into a Rebel patrol."

"We're not afraid, Private. The Southern gentlemen are known for being just that."

"But, ma'am—"

"Is there a law that says we can't drive into Southern country, Private?"

"Well, no ma'am, but—"

"Then we'll proceed," Lola smiled.

Both soldiers tipped their hats and watched as the buggy moved past the blockade.

A little over an hour later, the buggy rolled to a halt at a Confederate road block. Bettie and Lola could see the small depot at Manassas Junction from where they sat. To the south and east were thousands of Rebel soldiers milling about among hundreds of small white tents. In a field to the north were scores of soldiers in training.

Three Rebel privates moved up beside the buggy. The one who seemed to be the oldest, greeted them warmly and said, "The road is closed from here on, ladies. I don't know where you're headed, but you'll have to find another route."

"Actually we were headed straight for this camp," smiled Bettie. "We have a message for General Beauregard."

"Well, now, pretty little filly, what kind of message could sweet young things like you have for the general?"

Bettie fixed him with a steady gaze and asked, "Private, did you hear about the battle over at Big Bethel?"

"Sure did, ma'am!" he grinned. "We sent those blue-bellies a-skeedaddlin' for cover. They got the surprise of their lives!"

"And why was that?"

"Well, our guys got word ahead of time that the blue-bellies was comin'!"

"And just how did Colonel Magruder get that word?"

"Why, it was a couple of female spi…"

"Spies?"

"Yeah. That…that's what you are, ain't it!"

"Yes," Bettie replied, lifting her graceful chin. "Now, may we please proceed so we can deliver our message to General Beauregard?"

"I could save you the trouble, ma'am," spoke up a second private, "if you'll let me take it to the general for you."

"Doesn't work that way," said Bettie, shaking her head. "We have orders to deliver it to the general personally. Otherwise, we are to return to Washington immediately."

The trio exchanged glances, then the older one said, "Mind if I jump on the side of the buggy, ma'am? I'll guide you to general Beauregard's tent and let him know you're here."

"Fine," smiled Bettie, snapping the reins.

The private hopped onto the buggy's lower step and rode to the camp, pointing the way to General Beauregard's spacious tent. When the buggy stopped, Bettie and Lola were aware of many soldiers looking their direction. The private left the buggy, halted at the flap, and called, "General, sir, it's Private Donnie Lee Cowper. I have two young ladies out here who wish to see you."

"I'll be right with you."

Cowper glanced back toward the buggy, then the tent flap parted and a tall, slender man with coal-black hair and mustache appeared in a double-breasted uniform with parallel lines of gold-plated buttons running from the shoulders downward to the bottom of his knee-length coat. He wore no hat.

"That's him," Bettie whispered to Lola. "I've seen pictures of him. He's forty-three and dyes his hair so the gray in his temples won't show."

Beauregard's Creole ancestry gave him strikingly handsome features with marble-black eyes and dark, smooth skin. He dismissed Cowper and moved toward the buggy with squared shoulders and back ramrod straight. A smile parted his lips as he halted beside the vehicle. For lack of a hat to tip, he bowed his head politely and said, "Good afternoon, ladies. General Beauregard at your service. And to what do I owe the pleasure of your visit?"

"If I said 'Circled R,' General would it mean anything to you?" Bettie asked.

"Yes," he replied quickly. "It would mean you ladies have a message for me from Mrs. Rose O'Neal Greenhow."

"You are so right," Bettie smiled. "May we step down?"

"By all means," nodded the general, stepping up and offering Bettie his hand.

When Beauregard had helped both women from the buggy, he invited them to sit at a table in the shade of a large oak tree, saying that the tent was a bit stuffy at that time of the day.

As they moved to the table under the watchful eyes of an innumerable company of gray-clad soldiers, the general asked, "Am I permitted to know your names?"

Halting beside the table, Bettie said, "Of course, sir. I am Bettie Duval, and this is Lola Morrow."

"I am happy and honored to make your acquaintance," smiled Beauregard. "Please sit down."

"Before we do, General," Bettie said, "we may just as well give you the message."

Lola wore her long, silken-black hair in an upsweep. Bettie removed Lola's hat and helped her drop the thick, shiny waves. Producing a folded set of papers, Lola handed them to the general, then she and Bettie sat down. Beauregard eased down onto a straight-backed chair, unfolded the papers, and laid them out on the table. The women remained quiet while he read them through silently.

When he finished, he shook his head and said, "Ladies, the Confederacy is forever indebted to you and Mrs. Greenhow…and, of course, to whomever garnered this vital information in

Washington. Are you the two who carried the classified information to Colonel Magruder at Yorktown?"

"I am one of them sir," offered Bettie. "Another young lady was my partner in that venture."

"I see," he nodded. Then running his gaze between them, he asked, "Are you aware of the penalty if you're ever caught?"

"Yes, sir," spoke up Lola, "but since they won't let us put on a uniform and go into battle, we find great satisfaction in doing this job. We are honored to risk our lives for the Cause."

"Well, I'm very proud to serve the Confederacy with soldiers such as you. Together, we're going to give the Federals more than they can handle. Thank you."

"Our pleasure," smiled Bettie. "Now, sir, we must head back."

As the general walked them to the buggy, he lamented, "It really grieves me about this coming attack. You see, General Irvin McDowell was a classmate of mine at West Point, and I fought under General Winfield Scott in the Mexican War. This is a hard thing…to have them now as opponents."

"I'm sure it is, sir," Bettie said. "Didn't I also read that Major Anderson, whom you were ordered to fire upon at Fort Sumter, was one of your instructors at West Point, and that you had also been close friends?"

Beauregard bit down hard on his lower lip. "Yes, ma'am. Major Anderson and I are still very close friends. It just so happens that the way things are at the moment, we cannot pursue our friendship. I am hoping that when this awful ordeal is over, we can enjoy each other's company once again."

Leaving a sad-eyed Creole behind, Bettie Duval and Lola Morrow drove away.

TWELVE

By Sunday morning, July 7, General Irvin McDowell was aware that his projected date for launching the offensive against the Confederates was unrealistic. It would take eight more days to be properly prepared. He would march his men toward Manassas Junction on July 16. The attack would be launched on Sunday, July 21.

McDowell explained the situation and announced the new dates in a brief meeting at the Capitol with the president, the Cabinet, and the Senate Military Committee early on Monday morning. Jenny was at her desk when the meeting broke up, and was chatting with three of the senators when her father appeared. Jeffrey Jordan waited till the senators were gone and the hall was clear, then sat down in front of Jenny's desk and said quietly, "I've been meaning to talk to you about something very important, but I wasn't in any rush because I thought there was plenty of time. This meeting I was just in has changed that. We need to talk before this evening."

Jenny studied her father's concerned features. "All right, Daddy. Talk."

"No, honey. Not here. How about during your lunch hour?"

"Of course."

"I'll be back a little before noon. We can grab a bite at a nearby restaurant, then go for a walk around the capitol grounds."

"Okay, Daddy."

Jordan returned later, as promised. They were seated quickly and were done eating by twelve-thirty. Then they headed out into the hot afternoon sun and began their walk.

"Jenny, I told you about the upcoming assault on the Confederate army at Manassas Junction."

"Yes. Next Saturday." Jenny felt a pang in her heart. Buck would be in on that offensive.

"Well, that's changed. It's going to be a week from Sunday. The twenty-first."

"What has that got to do with me, Daddy?"

Jordan paused while they met another couple on the walk. When the couple was past and out of earshot, he said, "Rose Greenhow has been after me for several days to see if I'd talk to you about becoming one of her girls."

"You mean me be a spy?"

"Yes."

"Oh, Daddy, I couldn't do it."

"Yes, you could. I was at Rose's house yesterday afternoon, and she's having trouble getting volunteers. She can't let those who are working with her be seen too often at the Union blockades or the Yankees will get suspicious. She needs more girls. She thought at first she wouldn't have any trouble getting young women with Southern loyalties to join her, but when the Washington newspapers printed the president's policy on Confederate spies a couple of weeks ago, it put a crimp in things."

"Yes, I read it," Jenny said tightly. "And I don't mind telling you as I did when you first started this spy business…it worries me, Daddy. Immediate execution. No quarter."

"We've already been over this, Jenny. You wouldn't worry about me if I were on the battlefield?"

Jenny was quiet for a moment. A pair of Orioles was chirping in a tree just ahead, but she didn't hear them. Jenny's mind was intent on the discussion at hand. "Of course, I would worry about you if you were on the battlefield. But since you won't be in combat, I have to worry about you getting caught as a spy."

Jordan reached down, took his daughter's hand, raised it to his lips, and kissed it. "I'm glad that you care enough to worry about me, honey."

"Care enough? You're my Daddy! I love you with all my heart!"

He kissed the hand again and said, "And I love you with all my heart, too."

They continued along the shady path, Jenny pondering what her father had asked her to do. Finally, he broke into her thoughts. "Honey, are you asking yourself how I could love you as I do and ask you to put yourself in the dangerous position of a spy?"

"Not really," she responded softly. "I realize I'm already in a risky spot. I know what you're doing as a spy, and I'm aware of John Calhoun's involvement…and I know what Rose and her girls are doing. I am already a conspirator because I haven't turned all of you in. If any of you get caught, it won't take the authorities long before they come after me. I could perjure myself in court and say I knew nothing about it—that you were able to carry on your espionage activities right under my nose without my ever suspecting anything—but you and I both know I would never be able to do it. If they didn't execute me, they'd surely lock me up in prison. No, Daddy, I'm not questioning your love for me because you want me to become one of Rose's girls. When I said I couldn't do it, I didn't mean because I fear getting caught. I'm just as much a Southerner as you are. But…but…"

Jenny's throat went tight and tears filmed her eyes.

Jordan stopped and looked at her. Gripping her shoulders, he said, "Jenny, you've got to forget Buck Brownell. How many times do I have to say it? He's the enemy."

"But Daddy—"

Gripping her harder, Jordan caught her eyes square with his

own, held them there, and said emphatically, "Listen to me, honey! Your loyalty to the South must come first. When our Southern men and boys go into battle, they leave sweethearts, wives, children, and families for the sake of the Confederacy. On that battlefield, nothing else matters. The South comes first. The same principle applies to those of us who work as spies."

Jenny continued to weep, but she did not attempt to break the stare between them.

"This is war, Jenny. Our personal feelings must be put aside. Do you understand what I am saying?"

Jenny blinked against the hot tears and sniffed. "Yes."

"All right, then," Jordan said, releasing his hold on her shoulders. "I went to Rose's house this morning after we talked at your desk. I had to let her know of the change in plans for the assault on our forces at Manassas Junction. While I was there, Rose asked me about you. I explained that I would be talking to you about becoming one of her girls during your lunch break. And..."

"Yes, Daddy?"

"Well, I told her I know what my daughter is made of. I told her you would say yes."

"Oh."

"Was I right?"

Jenny swallowed hard. She knew she had no options.

Jordan could read his daughter's eyes and knew she was resigning herself to it. "Good!" he breathed. "I knew I could count on my little girl. Rose asked if you could be at her house right after supper tonight. I told her I'd bring you over myself. I can pick you up and bring you home later."

Later that afternoon, Jenny was busy at her desk, trying to bury herself in her work, when she suddenly became aware of a form standing over her. Looking up, she saw a young Zouave private, holding a small brown envelope and smiling at her.

"Yes?" she said, returning the smile.

"Miss Jenny Jordan?"

"Yes."

Extending the envelope, the Zouave said, "Captain Buck Brownell sent me to deliver this to you, ma'am."

Jenny took the envelope, noting that it was sealed, and thanked him. He saluted her and quickly walked away. Jenny's hands trembled slightly as she used a letter opener to break the seal. Looking around, she saw people milling up and down the hallway. She reached into a drawer, drew out a small wooden sign that read: "Back in Ten Minutes," and placed it on the desk top. Then she moved into the Senate Chamber and entered the file room. Finding it unoccupied, she pulled out the folded slip of paper and read it.

> *Darling Jenny:*
>
> *I love you more each day, and more than words could ever express. The only way my love for you can ever change is to grow stronger.*
>
> *Please don't forget me.*
>
> *Though I am still not high on the social scale demanded by your father, it should impress him some that I am now a captain. If you will wait for me until the war is over, I will approach your father and try to convince him that I am worthy of becoming his son-in-law.*
>
> > *Always,*
> > *Buck*

Jenny leaned against a file cabinet and had a good cry. When she was able to dry her tears, she touched up her makeup and returned to her desk, clutching the letter close to her heart.

At five o'clock, Jenny emerged heavy-hearted from the Capitol and started down the long, wide stairs toward the street. Other employees were leaving, and several people were moving about on the Capitol steps. Suddenly Jenny recognized Captain Jack Egan threading his way toward her. When Egan reached her, Jenny did not stop.

Moving in beside her as she continued down the steps, Egan said, "Hey, Jenny, it's me, Jack. Hold up a minute!"

Jenny's pace remained the same. Egan caught up to her and leaped in front of her, blocking her way. "I want to talk to you."

Jenny faced him head-on. Her stare was like the insistence of a knife point. "Please get out of my way."

Holding his ground, Egan said, "Come on now. What about us?"

"There is no us. Please move."

"Look, Jenny, don't let your father's attitude get in your way of happiness. You and I can still see each other—"

Jenny's eyes flashed fire. "I'm not interested in seeing you any more, Jack. I lost all respect for you when you took it upon yourself to tell Buck he couldn't see me, and that you and I were planning marriage. Now…out of my way!"

"It's Brownell, isn't it? No matter how your old man feels about you getting involved with soldiers, you're still seeing that egotistical, backwoods corporal, aren't you?"

Jenny's shoulders shook and her nostrils flared. "Buck is not backwoods, and he's not egotistical. And what's more, he's not a corporal!"

"Yeah, I heard that he wrangled himself a lieutenant's bar for shooting that helpless civilian."

Jenny slapped Egan's face. The impact resounded across the Capitol steps like a gunshot. People stopped and looked. Surprised and stung, Egan hunched his shoulders as if he might strike her in return, but restrained himself.

"Buck didn't shoot a helpless civilian! And he's not a lieutenant anymore, either—he's a captain!"

Just then a huge, muscular man bumped Egan's shoulder and growled, "This soldier givin' you trouble, ma'am?" Egan saw two more just like him standing by. His eyes bulged.

"Yes," replied Jenny, "but he was just leaving. Weren't you, Jack?"

Egan licked his lips. "Yes. Yes…I was just leaving."

"Before you go," Jenny said tartly, "I want to make it clear that I don't want to see you again. Find some other woman, Jack. My heart belongs to Buck."

Egan took a deep breath, looked at the three men, and walked away without another word.

"Thank you," Jenny said, smiling at the big man with the bear-like voice.

"My pleasure, ma'am," he grinned, showing two broken teeth. And, uh…ma'am?"

"Yes?"

"If you and this Buck fella should ever break it off…look me up. My name's Garth Heegan. I work at the Fair Oaks Farm just west of town."

Jenny managed to keep a straight face as she said, "All right, Mr. Heegan. I'll keep you in mind."

That evening, Jenny rapped Rose Greenhow's brass knocker and waited for her to open the door. Rose greeted her with a warm smile, and Jenny turned and waved at her father, who sat in his buggy at the curb. Jeffrey Jordan waved back and drove off.

Rose put an arm around Jenny and ushered her into the parlor. Sitting on a fancy overstuffed love seat next to a small table that held a glowing lantern was Bettie Duval.

"You remember Bettie, don't you, Jenny?"

"Of course," smiled Jenny. "We rode back from the Zouave demonstration together in your carriage, Rose. How are you, Bettie?"

"Just fine. Nice to see you again."

"Nice to see you, too."

"How about some tea, Jenny?" asked Rose.

"Maybe a little later, thank you. Right now, I'm too full. Daddy and I just had dinner."

Rose seated Jenny next to Bettie, then sat on a couch facing them a few feet away. Wasting no time, Rose reminded Jenny that her father had been there earlier in the day with information about the Union attack at Manassas Junction. When Jenny nodded, Rose said, "Your father told me you had agreed to become one of my messenger girls."

Jenny gave her a weak, "Yes."

"Well, honey, I've got a job for you immediately. You worked today, so you're off tomorrow, right?"

"Yes."

"I want you to go with Bettie and carry the message of the change in date to General Beauregard. Sometime in the future, I might send a girl on a mission alone, but not yet. We're finding it works quite well getting two girls past the Union lines. So, you and Bettie will go to Manassas Junction tomorrow."

Bettie felt Jenny tense up, and Rose saw it in her face.

Rose raised her painted eyebrows. "Is something wrong, honey?"

Jenny's hand went to her mouth. There was consternation in her eyes. "I…I didn't realize you would send me out so soon, Rose. I guess I thought there would be some training or schooling or something."

"You'll get your training by going with Bettie," smiled Rose. "Bettie has already delivered two messages for me. She and Susan Rand carried the message to Colonel Magruder at Yorktown." She chuckled. "We all know what happened there."

Jenny's features paled. She thought of Buck…and of the Union men who were killed and wounded in that fiasco.

When Jenny did not comment, Rose said, "Bettie and Lola took the message to General Beauregard about the upcoming Union assault on our army over there. Now that McDowell has changed the date, we want General Beauregard to know it as soon as possible. That's why it has to go tomorrow."

"I understand," said Jenny.

Rose chuckled and said, "Big Bethel was one thing, but this is going to be one to really set the Union back on its heels. I'm sure by now Lincoln and his boys are wondering how they were outfoxed at Big Bethel. On this Manassas thing, we'll give them a whole lot more to wonder about. Because of our espionage, we'll make those blue-bellies eat dirt on this one!"

Bettie looked at Jenny and said excitedly, "This is great, isn't it? What a thrill to know it couldn't be done without us. This'll be written down in history. Someday we can tell our children and grandchildren about it!"

Rose was concerned over Jenny's lack of enthusiasm. Trying to put a spark under her, she said, "Jenny, if General Beauregard can counter this Union assault with enough strength, this may be the first and last big battle. Wouldn't it be great for you to look back on it and say that you helped bring this war to an abrupt end? And even if this isn't the last battle, it will still help bring the war to an end much quicker than otherwise. The Union has more men and weapons than the Confederacy, but by our espionage, we can offset that advantage. You are willing to help, aren't you?"

The web of apprehension that was closing in on Jenny's mind became quite evident on her face.

Rose studied her for a few seconds, then said, "Honey, are you afraid? Do you have some reservations about joining us that your daddy doesn't know about?"

There was a tremor in Jenny's voice. "No, Rose. My father is aware of anything and everything about me. As for being afraid…I'm not afraid as you might think. I have no fear for myself. It's just that…"

Rose left the couch and knelt in front of Jenny. "What is it, honey? What's bothering you?"

"You were there at the Zouave demonstration. So was Bettie."

Before Jenny could proceed, Rose stood, clapped her hands together, and exclaimed, "Ah—it's that handsome young Zouave who rescued you from the runaway buggy! Yes…I remember now. I even heard you tell him you loved him right in front of your daddy."

"Yes, I did. And I meant it."

Rose bent over and looked Jenny in the eye. "What does your father think of your being in love with a Union soldier?"

"He…he doesn't like it at all. But that doesn't change a thing. I love my daddy, but even he can't control my heart. I'm in love with Buck, and I can't help it. I don't want to help it."

Rose turned and took two steps, then wheeled about. "I assume you didn't know Buck before the war started."

"No, I met him the day I was helping Clara Barton when they brought in all those wounded men from the Baltimore riot. Buck had been stabbed in the face, and I helped patch him up. I didn't realize it at the time, but looking back, I know that's when I fell in love with him. I'm sure it was the same time Buck fell in love with me, too."

Rose sighed and said, "Jenny, honey, I don't mean to sound like a know-it-all, but you should have kept a guard on your heart. Falling in love in wartime is always risky…but falling in love with a Union soldier, you've really done it."

Jenny looked at Rose and said, "If the war goes beyond this Manassas Junction battle, and I can carry messages that don't affect battles Buck will be in, I'll be glad to help you, Rose. Can't you get one of your other girls to go with Bettie tomorrow? Buck's going to be in the thick of this one. I…I just can't do it."

Rose was quiet for a moment, then she said, "The reason I wanted you for this job, Jenny, is that I don't want the faces of any of my girls becoming too familiar. I've chosen Bettie for this one because she has the most experience and is the best one to break you in. If the war goes on, it'll be quite a while before I send her again. I need a new face to go with her, and I need one that will captivate those Union soldiers at the road block. You're just so perfect for the job."

Jenny rose from the love seat, drew close to Rose and said, "Rose, I appreciate that, but please put yourself in my place. Buck was in that battle at Big Bethel. Thank the Lord in heaven, he wasn't killed…but he could have been. Do you realize if he had been killed, and if instead of Susan it had been me who went with Bettie to carry that message to Colonel Magruder...I would have been responsible for Buck's death! Please don't ask me to go with Bettie on this job to-morrow."

Rose and Bettie exchanged glances. Speaking to Bettie, Rose said, "Susan will go with you, I'm sure."

"Of course," Bettie smiled.

Jenny rushed to Rose, threw her arms around her, and said, "Oh, thank you!"

Rose hugged her tight, then held her at arm's length. Smiling, she said, "Your father didn't know that I had you in mind for this Manassas Junction job. We'll just tell him that you've agreed to work for me, and that if the war goes further, you'll go on whatever missions I ask you to. You and I will work those out by mutual agreement."

"Thank you, Rose," Jenny breathed a heavy sigh. "Thank you for understanding."

Bettie left the love seat, stepped up close, and said, "Jenny, what if the war goes on and you do work with us on espionage missions...then somehow things work out so you and Buck get together? How would he feel if you told him you've been a Confederate spy? You know...working underhandedly as his enemy?"

The thought was a new one to Jenny. Blinking, she paused, then said slowly, "I...I don't know. I couldn't marry him without confessing it. There shouldn't be any secrets between a husband and wife. I...I guess if by some miracle it came down to that, it would be a true test of his love."

"Well, honey," said Bettie, "I'm pulling for you. Sounds like you and Buck have got the real thing between you. I hope with all my heart it works out...and that Buck's love will be put to the test."

"Me too, honey," spoke up Rose.

Jenny managed a smile. "Just imagine," she sighed, clasping her hands under her chin, "a life together with my beloved enemy!"

THIRTEEN

On Tuesday July 9, Bettie Duval and Susan Rand delivered to General Pierre G.T. Beauregard the message containing the new date for the Union assault at Manassas Junction. Beauregard expressed his deep appreciation; they were going to have a big part in the Confederate victory because he had been forewarned of the attack.

In Washington, however, where neither military nor civilians were aware of the espionage going on under their very noses, there was a growing confidence that the pending battle at Manassas Junction would be a total rout for the North. When word hit Washington of the Union victory in the battle at Rich Mountain, Virginia, on July 11, Northerners found even more reason for their confidence to build.

On Tuesday, July 16, General Irvin McDowell led his troops out of the Washington camps toward Manassas Junction. Word spread through the city and into surrounding towns, and soon the populace knew the assault against the Confederates was going to take place on the following Sunday. A great number of people, including politicians and their families, made plans to take picnic lunches and watch the rout from the high hills on the north side of Bull Run Creek, near the railroad junction.

One unit of men-in-blue marched directly through Washington and down Pennsylvania Avenue past the White House on their way to the battle site. Citizens along the streets cheered when they saw the Yankee soldiers carrying a Confederate flag that had been captured in the battle at Rich Mountain. The city was buzzing with excitement.

At the Robert Brownell house, Kady told her husband at the supper table that she was going to pack a splendid picnic lunch for Sunday.

"That'll be nice," Robert said. "From what I hear, we'd better get an early start. Sounds like half of Washington is going out there."

"I can't wait to see the show. I guess that's how just about everybody around here feels. They all want to get a look at the Rebels on the run."

"That *will* be a good show!" laughed Robert.

Kady set down her fried chicken and said, "Do you think we'll be able to see Buck during the battle?"

"You mean Captain Buck Brownell, the famous war hero? The one who took us to dinner last week?"

"That's the one."

"I sure hope so. I'm taking my binoculars. He shouldn't be hard to pick out amid the colorful Zouaves."

"Let's take our flag, too. We can wave it over our heads to celebrate the victory."

"Sounds good to me, Mrs. Brownell," grinned Robert.

On Saturday, at the Jordan home, Lieutenant Jeffrey Jordan had been in his library reading since shortly after breakfast. It suddenly dawned on him that it had been nearly three hours since he had heard Jenny moving about the house.

Laying his book down, he left the library and went through the house. When he had covered the first floor without finding her, he mounted the stairs and headed for her room. The door was closed. Tapping lightly, he said, "Jenny? You in there?"

A few seconds lapsed before he heard a weak voice say, "Yes. Did you want something, Daddy?"

"Just missed you flitting about the house as usual. You all right?"

Again, there was a silent moment before the answer came. "Yes. I'm fine."

"You don't sound fine, honey. May I come in?"

"Of course."

Jordan opened the door and found his daughter sitting on the bed with an open Bible in her hands. Her eyes were puffy, and he knew she had been crying.

Moving closer, he asked, "What is it, sweetheart?"

"I'm just doing some praying and laying hold on some of God's promises. He says if we love Him, all things will work together for our good. And He says the effectual fervent prayer of a righteous man availeth much. So I was just asking Him to give me the faith to believe Him for some very important things I have on my heart right now."

"Things like the safety of a certain Yankee captain?"

Jenny swallowed with difficulty. "Yes," she replied, blinking.

Jordan rubbed the back of his neck and said, "Honey, I'm telling you for your own good—you must forget him. Even when the shooting stops and an armistice is signed, there are going to be hard feelings between the North and the South for generations to come. I want my little girl to marry a Southerner. It'll save her a lot of problems."

Closing her Bible, Jenny laid it on the bed and stood up. Deep lines creased her brow as she said, "But, Daddy, I'm in love with Buck. I can never love another man."

Jordan folded his daughter into his arms, held her close, and said, "That's the way it seems, right now, but it'll change one day. You'll see."

Jenny clung to her father, hugging him tight, but thought, *You're wrong, Daddy. It will never change.* After clinging to him for a long moment, she eased free of his arms and said, "I guess you know there's going to be a big gathering on the hills overlooking Manassas Junction tomorrow."

"Yes."

"I'm planning to go with Rose and her other girls. Rose wants to see first-hand the results of her spy work. I want to see it, too."

"I'd like to see it, myself, but I have to be at the Capitol with the president, the Cabinet, and the Senate Military Committee. Lincoln wants us all to wait there together for the news of the Union's victory." He paused, then chuckled, "I'm really looking forward to seeing their faces when it turns out the other way."

At the White House, Mary Todd Lincoln was seated on a cream brocaded Queen Anne chair, watching her maid, Myrtle Wetherby, stretch a new Battenburg lace cloth over the dining room table. When they heard the parlor door open and close, and young Tad's chatter, Mary said, "Sounds like Patricia and the boys are back from their walk."

Myrtle laughed, "What was your first clue?"

Seconds later, the boys charged into the dining room with their pretty governess following.

"Mom!" exclaimed Tad, eyes dancing with excitement. "Guess what we found out!"

"I haven't the slightest idea," smiled Mary.

"A million people are goin' out to watch the war tomorrow mornin'! Not only grown-ups, but kids, too. Can we go, Mom? Willie an' me want to see the battle!"

"Willie and *I*," corrected Patricia, tapping Tad's shoulder.

Lifting his eyes to the governess, the boy grinned mischievously, looked back at his mother, and said, "See? Miss Patricia wants to see it, too! You want to go, too, don't you, Mom? Can we go? Please?"

Mary set her loving gaze on the lad and said, "I'm not feeling very well, honey. I think I'm coming down with something. I doubt if I will feel well enough by tomorrow to venture out."

"How about Papa? Can he take us?"

"He can't, Tad. He told me he'll have to be at the Capitol while the battle is going on tomorrow. There's no way he can take you. Besides, it might be dangerous with all that gunfire going on."

"It won't be dangerous, Mom. Else all those other kids' parents wouldn't be takin' 'em. One man we talked to said everybody'll be up on top of a high hill so no bullets or cannonballs can get to 'em."

Mary looked at Patricia.

The governess said, "That's the way I understand it, too, ma'am."

"Well, it really doesn't make any difference," Mary said. "There's no one to take them. If I'm feeling better tomorrow, we'll see about it then."

"Is there anything I can do to help you feel better, Mom?" asked Tad. "I'll do anything." Turning to his brother, he said, "Won't we, Willie?"

"Sure," nodded Willie.

Mary smiled weakly. "No, boys, there isn't anything you can do. We'll just have to see how I feel in the morning."

The boys, disappointed that the venture was doubtful, were led from the room by Patricia.

Early that same day at Manassas Junction, General Beauregard welcomed brigades led by Brigadier Generals Joseph E. Johnston and Thomas J. Jackson. The brigades arrived by rail from where they had been stationed in the Shenandoah Valley near Winchester. As soon as the Shenandoah troops jumped from the train, it pulled out to head for the Piedmont Station to pick up the Georgia Brigade commanded by Colonel Francis Bartow.

Many other brigades arrived before sundown, including the

rugged South Carolina Third Brigade, led by hard-nosed Brigadier General Barnard Bee. By the time darkness had fallen, the forewarned General Beauregard had amassed an army of 32,500 men, ready and eager to fight.

On the other side of Bull Run Creek, General Irvin McDowell called his final council of war just after 8:00 P.M. at Union headquarters near the small village of Centerville. Present in McDowell's tent were seventeen officers representing five divisions, which ranged from two to four brigades apiece, plus a cavalry brigade under the command of Major I.N. Palmer. In total, the Union force was 35,000 strong.

McDowell spread an elaborate map on the floor of his tent. By lantern light, he made the battle assignments to his commanders. Outside the tent, beneath an ebony sky bedecked with countless twinkling stars, the Union soldiers sat around campfires watching the flames cast flickering shadows into the fields and woods that surrounded them. Those who felt like talking did so in hushed tones, allowing the reflective ones to hear the cattle lowing in the nearby meadows and the sound of the night breeze rustling through the trees. From somewhere in the camp, a lone harmonica played a mournful tune.

Hundreds of the Yankee soldiers were writing letters by firelight to their loved ones at home, expressing hopes for survival, yet acknowledging the possibility that tomorrow they could die.

After the assignments were made and battle-related questions were answered inside General McDowell's tent, Colonel Erasmus D. Keyes said, "General McDowell, there is something that concerns me, sir…and I feel no doubt concerns the others here. May I address the subject?"

"Of course," nodded McDowell.

"My concern, General, is the defeat our forces met at Big Bethel, and the evidence that Confederate spies had fed classified information to Colonel Magruder. Can you tell us what has been done to ferret out the spies?"

McDowell cleared his throat. "The president, General Scott, and I discussed this at length. Mr. Lincoln then broached the subject while we were in a joint meeting of the Cabinet and the Senate Military Committee. The Committee was assigned by Mr. Lincoln to conduct an investigation. This investigation is still in progress, but at the last report a few days ago, they had been unable to turn up a clue as to who the spy or spies might be. The general consensus is that it has to be someone in the Cabinet, on the Committee, or possibly a clerk or secretary who works in the offices of these two groups."

For a moment there was dead silence. Then Brigadier General Daniel Tyler looked around at his fellow-commanders and said with feeling, "It's bad enough to think it could be a clerk or a secretary…but to think it could actually be someone in the Cabinet or on the Committee!"

"General McDowell, I hope Beauregard wasn't fed information like Magruder was," interjected Colonel William T. Sherman.

"What we're hoping," said McDowell, "is that since everyone within the Senate Chamber offices knows the investigation is underway, the guilty party or parties have pulled their heads in. That he, she, or they have been scared off."

"Even if Beauregard *has* been given information on our assault," put in Colonel Ambrose E. Burnside, "it won't make that much difference this time. Their army is scattered all the way up the Shenandoah Valley. We probably outnumber them two-to-one."

General McDowell asked if there were any more pertinent questions. There were none, and he dismissed them.

By ten o'clock the brigade commanders had collected their men and passed General McDowell's instructions on to them. There was nothing to do now but try to sleep.

Most of the Union soldiers found sleep impossible. Many sat and stared into the fires. Others lay quietly surveying the starlit sky. Some spent their time praying, while still others wrote down their thoughts, reflecting on the situation at hand. One young private wrote, "This is one of the most beautiful nights imagination can conceive. The sky is perfectly clear, the moon is bright, and the air is still as if it were not in a few hours to be disturbed by the roar of cannon and the shouts and cries of fighting and dying men."

Colonel Abram Duryee's Fifth New York Zouaves had been placed in First Division under Brigadier General Tyler, and assigned as part of First Brigade under Colonel Keyes.

At the section of the camp where the Zouaves were positioned, Captain Buck Brownell lay on his back near a fire and gazed into the heavens. Jenny Jordan was on his mind. The cattle had settled down for the night, and whoever had been playing the harmonica had stopped. There was only the low murmur of a few men in the area who preferred to talk. Above their subdued voices could be heard the music of innumerable crickets.

Buck looked by faith beyond the stars and whispered, "Lord, when the battle is fought tomorrow, no matter how it goes for either side…a lot of us are going to be killed. Only You know if there'll be a bullet out there with my name on it, or a hunk of shrapnel, or even a bayonet. I settled things with You back there in that Baptist church as a boy, and I'm not afraid to die. You know my heart. And since You do, You also know that I want to live. I've talked to You about Jenny and me many a time. You're probably tired of hearing me ask for some kind of miracle that would change her father's mind, but here I am again. If You see fit to let me live through this war, please make it possible for Jenny and me to be married. And Lord, if in Your wisdom You choose to take me out of this world in tomorrow's battle, or another one…I ask that You take care of Jenny and give her a happy life."

Buck's prayer was interrupted by a hoarse whisper, "Captain Brownell?"

Looking up, Buck recognized the face of Corporal Derek Flanders, one of the men in his company. Sitting up, he whispered back, "Yes, Flanders?"

"We've got a young Zouave over here in another company

who's so all-fired scared, he's shaking all over. Colonel Duryee asked me to come and get you. He seems to feel you can help this kid."

"I'll try," replied Buck, rising to his feet.

While the captain and the corporal made their way among the campfires and men, Buck asked, "What's this boy's name, Flanders? Do I know him?"

"He's a fairly new recruit, sir—name's Danny Forbes. He told Colonel Duryee you taught his unit hand-to-hand fighting, but that the two of you hadn't actually met personally. He admires you a lot."

Colonel Duryee was standing over the frightened young private as Brownell and Flanders drew up. There was a fire close by. In order not to embarrass Forbes, the other Zouaves had withdrawn from the immediate area.

Danny Forbes was sitting on the ground, knees pulled up to his chin, and trembling like a leaf in the autumn wind. He was so frightened, his teeth were chattering. Brownell met Duryee's gaze and nodded. The colonel moved away, taking Corporal Flanders with him.

Buck laid a steady hand on the frightened soldier's shoulder, knelt beside him, and said, "Danny. Captain Brownell."

Danny's head came up, his face a mask of terror in the moonlight and glow of the nearby fire. "Y-yes, s-sir."

"Colonel Duryee told you he had sent for me, right?"

"Uh-huh."

"Got the jitters, eh?"

"M-more than th-that, sir. I'm just…just plain scared out of my wits! I…I'm ashamed of myself. I'm a…a coward. I was sittin' over there by the fire w-with some of the other fellas, and they were talkin' about f-facin' those Rebel guns in the mornin'…and I plumb fell to pieces. I mean, C-Cap'n, I started cryin' like a baby. I…I can't face those fellas ever again!"

"Hey, my friend," said Buck, squeezing the shoulder tightly, "you're only human. Your fellow-soldiers know that. If the truth were known, they're just as scared as you are."

Forbes blinked and drew a shuddering breath. "Then how come th-*they* haven't fallen apart?"

"We're all made different, kid," said Buck, hunkering down to look him in the eye. "You want to know something? I'm just as scared as you are."

Young Danny eyed him incredulously. "*You?*"

"Mm-hmm. And I can guarantee you, there isn't a man here who isn't scared. And over there at the Junction, every one of those Rebels is scared, too."

The truth was sinking in. Danny shook his head and said, "It's funny, Cap'n. When I signed up to be a Zouave, I was so eager to be a soldier and get into the fight. I never dreamed I'd have a moment like this."

"It's the same way with all of us, kid. How old are you?"

"Eighteen."

"Well, there are a lot of men your age and older going into battle for the first time in the morning. And there are some out here—on both sides—who fought in the Mexican War who've got the jitters, too. It's just a normal part of war, Danny."

Young Forbes sniffed, palmed tears from his face, and said, "So I'm not a coward?"

"No. You could've taken off through the woods and over the hills, couldn't you?"

"Yes."

"Did you?"

"No."

"Why not?"

"Well, because…even though I'm scared, I…I'm going to be here…to fight…in the morning."

"That proves you're not a coward. Being scared doesn't make you a coward. It's what you do when you're scared that shows what you're made of. You're made of the real thing, Danny. You've got what it takes to be a soldier. You're going to pick up that gun of yours and charge the enemy at dawn *because* you're a soldier."

Danny Forbes sniffed again and thumbed tears from the corners of his eyes. A smile worked its way over his face. He stood up, took a deep breath, and looked Buck—who rose with him—in the eye. "Thank you, Cap'n. I'm going to be all right."

Colonel Duryee had been waiting in the shadows. Both men heard the swish of his baggy trousers as he approached.

"Corporal Forbes will do just fine, Colonel," Buck told him. "He'll be ready to do his part in the battle tomorrow."

"That's right, Colonel Duryee," spoke up Danny. "Captain Brownell helped me get a grip on myself. I'm ready to face those Rebels and help whip 'em!"

"Atta boy!" gusted Duryee, placing a hand on Danny's shoulder. "I was sure you had it in you…and I knew Captain Brownell could bring it to the surface."

Duryee thanked the captain for his help, and Buck headed back toward his company, struggling with the butterflies in his own stomach, and thinking of Jenny Jordan.

General Irvin McDowell roused his army very early on Sunday morning, July 21, 1861, and had them marching toward a designated site east of Manassas Junction by 2:30 A.M. The adrenaline was flowing, and excitement was running through the men like an electric current as they prepared for battle.

Federal artillery batteries placed at strategic points along Bull Run Creek the day before opened fire at exactly 5:00 A.M., lobbing whistling shells toward Confederate lines.

The Rebels were ready. Return fire came immediately, and the Battle of Bull Run was under way.

FOURTEEN

he field of battle pivoted around the intersection of Warrenton Turnpike—which led straight to Washington—and Sudley Road. Bull Run was a meandering stream flowing south along the east side of the field. Warrenton Turnpike crossed Bull Run over Stone Bridge. There were also two fords where major roads crossed the creek: one was Blackburn Ford, which was on the main road from the north to Manassas Junction, and the other was Island Ford, crossed by a well-traveled road that led southwest to Sudley at New Market. Sudley Road was a direct thoroughfare southeast to Manassas Junction. In anticipation of a mass attack prior to the first message he received from Rose Greenhow's girls, General Pierre G.T. Beauregard had begun digging entrenchments along Bull Run from Warrenton Turnpike where it crossed Stone Bridge all the way to Union Mills, some six or seven miles to the southwest.

A small creek, known as Young's Branch, wound around the base of a high hill on which stood two farm houses. One was owned by an elderly invalid widow, Judith Henry, and stood atop the hill. The other, at a lower elevation, was owned by a free Negro named James Robinson. Warrenton Turnpike ran along the north base of the hill, which was called Henry House Hill by people of the area.

Dozens of other farm houses dotted the area, but the Henry house and the Robinson house—because of their locations—were destined to play vital parts in the battle.

As the dull light of dawn gave way to the pink and yellow streamers of the rising sun, deep-throated cannons—Union and Confederate alike—roared like a thunderstorm. Trees and brush on both banks of Bull Run Creek were aflame. The musketry sounded like an endless string of firecrackers. The constant bellowing of the big guns, punctuated with the sharp sound of rifled cannons and the crack of Minié rifles, left no question that Death was riding his pale horse along the banks of Bull Run and over the brightening fields.

When there was a brief, intermittent pause in the roar, the screams and cries of wounded and dying men could be heard resounding over the rolling hills.

President Lincoln had been in the Senate Chamber conference room at the Capitol, along with his Cabinet and the Senate Military Committee since an hour before dawn. He was seated at the head of the table listening to the group of men chatting happily as sunlight struck the room's several east windows. Confidence of a quick and easy victory at Manassas Junction was running high.

Servants wheeled breakfast in on trays. During the meal, the almost festive atmosphere began to grate on the president. He held his peace until the meal was over and the dishes had been taken away. Most of the men were sipping coffee, laughing and joking about the certain defeat of the "hillbilly army." Lincoln rose to his feet and cleared his throat. It took only seconds for him to gain the attention of every man. The sudden quiet was welcome relief to Lieutenant Colonel Jeffrey Jordan.

"Gentlemen," said the tall, gaunt-looking man at the head of the table, "I don't mean to speak to you in a scolding manner, nor would I for a moment throw cold water on your enthusiasm. But I feel the tone being set here is a bit out of line. Possibly I should remind you that even if the battle that is now underway goes as we all anticipate, a high price is going to be paid for victory. This is not some sporting event taking place out there. The Confederates do have artillery, rifles, bayonets…and the will to fight. Many Union soldiers will die today and will not be around tomorrow to share with us in the victory celebration. Others will be crippled or maimed or blinded for life. It seems to me we should be thinking of them."

For a long moment the room was quiet as a tomb.

Taking a deep breath, Lincoln spoke again. "Gentlemen, within an hour or so, our first messenger from the battle scene will be coming in here to give his report. I propose that we have a time of silent meditation concerning our fighting men, and a time of prayer. We need to hold before God our brave soldiers who are even now suffering and dying at Bull Run."

Senator Henry Wilson, chairman of the Military Committee, rose to his feet and said solemnly, "Mr. President, I believe we are all in agreement with what you have just said. We understand your feelings and deeply appreciate them." Running his gaze over the faces all around the table, he added, "As we have this time of prayer, I will also ask that as Cabinet and Committee, we hold our president before God. His load is heavy, and this is the best way we can help him."

Lincoln gave Wilson a tight smile and said, "Thank you, Senator."

As the men in the group bowed their heads, Jordan silently prayed for the Confederate troops and President Jefferson Davis.

As usual, breakfast was quite early at the White House. The Lincoln boys and their governess were eating in the small dining room in the family's private quarters. Mary Lincoln was feeling worse than the day before and had not put in an appearance. Myrtle was skipping breakfast in order to attend to the First Lady.

Speaking around a mouthful of scrambled eggs, young Tad looked across the table at the governess and said, "Miss Patricia, even if Mom isn't up to takin' us out to see the battle, you could take us."

Patricia Winters was sipping coffee from a steaming cup. She swallowed it carefully and said, "Tad, how many times have I told you not to talk with your mouth full?"

The bright-eyed boy grinned and closed his mouth to finish chewing his eggs.

"Well?" said Patricia, raising one eyebrow.

Pointing to his mouth, Tad mumbled, "Mm-mm-mm-m."

Patricia laughed. "Sorry! I didn't mean to make you do it again."

In a tone of disgust, Willie said, "He'll do it again anyhow."

Tad swallowed and said, "I don't know."

Patricia raised both eyebrows this time. "You don't know what?"

"How many times you've told me not to talk with my mouth full. I don't count 'em."

Patricia looked at Willie, who said, "He's really dumb."

"I ain't neither!" spat the younger brother. "I'm smarter'n you!"

"Hah!" laughed Willie. "That'll be the day!"

"I can prove it."

"You can prove you're smarter than me?"

"Yep."

"Okay. Go ahead."

"Bet I can make you say *black*."

"No you can't."

"Oh, yes I can."

"No, you can't."

"What color is the American flag?" challenged Tad.

Willie got a smug look on his face. "Red, white, and blue."

Tad laughed. "See there? I told you I could make you say *blue!*"

"You didn't either! You said you'd make me say *black!*"

Tad threw his head back and cackled. "You just said it! See, I told you I'm smarter than you."

While Willie disgustedly returned to his breakfast, Patricia giggled and asked, "Tad, where'd you get that one?"

"From Uncle Elmer. He pulled it on me one day when we were alone…before…before he was killed."

Patricia saw the sadness that filled the eyes of both boys at the mention of Colonel Elmer Ellsworth. "You both miss Uncle Elmer, don't you?"

The boys nodded, then Tad said, "If Uncle Elmer was still alive, he'd be fightin' out there at Manssas—Manssas…out there at Bull Run Crick. He'd show them Rebels, wouldn't he, Miss Patricia?"

The governess nodded. "He sure would."

"Would you take us, Miss Patricia?" begged Tad. "Ple-e-ease?"

"Ple-e-ease, Miss Patricia?" chimed in Willie.

Patricia Winters wanted to oblige the boys. She also was concerned about Lieutenant John Hammond and wanted to be on hand where he was fighting. Thinking on it a moment, she said, "Tell you what. I'll go talk to your mother and see if she'll give me permission."

While the Lincoln brothers raised a cheer, the governess left the dining room and made her way to Mrs. Lincoln's bedroom. Myrtle was just coming out the door as Patricia approached.

"I need to talk to Mrs. Lincoln for a moment, Myrtle," said Patricia.

The maid thrust a forefinger to her lips. "Sh-h-h! She's asleep. You mustn't disturb her."

Patricia nodded and returned to the dining room. Willie and Tad were waiting with eager eyes. Disappointment showed quickly when the governess said, "I'm sorry, boys, but your mother is asleep and mustn't be disturbed. I couldn't talk to her."

Their voices blended together as the boys begged Patricia to take them anyhow.

"I can't take you that far without her permission. I'm sorry, boys, but we just can't go."

Young Tad—who knew he held Patricia's heartstrings in his hand—left his chair and hugged her, saying, "I sure do love you, Miss Patricia."

Looking down at him and ruffling his hair, she smiled and said, "I love you too, Tad. But my loving you can't get me permission from your mother to take you to Manassas Junction."

Still holding onto her, but pulling back far enough to look up into her face, Tad said, "It really would be all right if you took us. Neither of our parents showed any objection to the idea when we talked about it the other day."

"That's right," put in Willie. "Neither one. It'd be all right, Miss Patricia."

The governess wrestled with whether she should make such a move on her own. She did so want to please the boys—and to be there with John when victory was won. Tad continued to beg. After a few more moments, Patricia squeezed the delightful boy who held onto her and said, "Oh, all right! I'll take you."

"Yahoo!" bellowed Tad and hugged her hard. Standing on his tiptoes, he planted a thankful kiss on her cheek. Willie kissed her on the other cheek and thanked her, too.

A White House carriage and driver were always at the disposal of the young governess. The White House kitchen prepared a quick lunch, and soon Patricia and the Lincoln boys were on their way.

As early as daybreak, hundreds of Washingtonians were arriving on the hills overlooking the Bull Run battlefield from the north. They thrilled to the sound of artillery, muskets, and exploding shells. They could hear the shouts and cries of men in battle and were mesmerized at the sight of Union and Confederate troops in fierce, bloody conflict. All over the valley, puffy blue-white clouds of smoke drifted on the morning breeze. When the sun peeked over the eastern horizon and spread its yellow light over the battlefield, the scene became even more graphic. There were repeated flashes along the creek, on the rolling hills, and amongst the trees as the rays of the sun hit bayonets and brass cannon barrels.

The attitude of the excited civilians was that Sunday, July 21,

1861 would be a banner day for the North. The Southerners were going to be conquered handily, and their exhilarating outing would be topped off with happy celebrations. The vanquished Confederates who were fortunate enough to live through the battle would be sent home like whipped dogs with their tails between their legs. And the Civil War would be over!

Amongst the gathering crowd were many government leaders. One of the most popular was Senator Charles Sumner of Massachusetts. Sumner, a fiery man of deep conviction, had shown more anger at the audacious Confederate attack on Fort Sumter than any other man in Congress. He stood on the hilltop in the midst of his peers and loudly proclaimed his confidence that Richmond, the Rebel capital, would be in the hands of the Union "sometime early this week."

Sumner's boundless confidence affected his colleagues. Congressman Albert Riddle of Ohio announced his plans to "meet our brave men on the field in order to rejoice with them." Senator Alfred Ely of New York said he would be down there "hopping over Rebel corpses to congratulate the New York brigades for their part in the victory."

Several Washington ministers and their families were there with their gigs, buggies, surreys, and carriages collected in a group. The louder-spoken of the clergymen were in agreement that "the Lord would deliver the Philistines" into the hands of the Union "Joshua," General Irvin McDowell.

Jenny Jordan was there, seated in a surrey with Rose O'Neal Greenhow and three other young women: Bettie Duval, Lola Morrow, and Susan Rand. Jenny was studying the battle, trying to catch a glimpse of the man she loved, but the distance was too great. Even if she could make out the Zouaves, it would be next to impossible to know which one was Buck. From time to time her lips moved silently as she prayed for his safety.

Just after nine o'clock, Jenny's attention was drawn to the White House carriage as it topped the hill off to the east. She waved at Patricia, and saw the governess speak to the driver and point in her direction. The carriage soon pulled up alongside, and Jenny and Rose greeted Patricia and the boys. The White House driver told Patricia he was going to join some friends he had noticed in the crowd.

Patricia and the Lincoln boys were introduced to Bettie, Lola, and Susan, then turned their attention to the battle below. Soon Tad tugged at the governess's sleeve and said, "Miss Patricia, could me an' Willie get out of the carriage and watch the battle from that big rock over there?"

"Willie and *I*," corrected Patricia.

Grinning mischievously, Tad responded, "I really think you would be happier here with these ladies."

Patricia laughed. The little scamp had bested her at it again. "Okay. *You* and Willie can go sit on that rock, but don't stray off somewhere else. Stay right there, you hear?"

"Yes, ma'am," nodded Tad.

"Yes, ma'am," echoed the other brother.

Robert and Kady Brownell were not far from the White House carriage, standing with friends. Robert was busy with his binoculars, searching the landscape for some sign of the bright-colored uniforms of the Zouaves. A captivating scene spread before Robert as he took it all in through his binoculars. Looking south and sweeping the valley east and west, he saw densely wooded country, dotted at intervals with green fields, plowed sections, and farm houses under large shade trees, flanked by barns and various other outbuildings.

The wooded country, fields, and farms in the valley were bounded by a line of blue and purple ridges, terminating abruptly in escarpments toward the east front and swelling gradually toward the west into the lower spines of an offshoot from the Blue Ridge Mountains. On the east, the view was circumscribed by a forest that clothed the side of the ridge where the crowd had gathered and covered its shoulder far down onto the open fields.

A gap in the nearest chain of the distant hills directly south was known as Manassas Pass, by which the railway from the west was carried into the valley floor. Still nearer to the south was the junction of that line with the line from Alexandria and with the railway leading due south to Richmond. Robert marveled at the golden ribbons of rail glistening in the sunlight.

All across the breathtaking valley, undulating lines of forest marked the course of Bull Run Creek and its tributaries. Robert thought what he beheld through the glasses presented the most pleasant display of pastoral woodland scenery that the God of heaven had ever made. But the thunderous sounds that came on the breeze and the exhibition of battle no more than a mile away were in terrible variance to the tranquil landscape.

The woods far and near echoed with the roar of cannon, and tiny clouds of blue-white smoke marked the spots from whence came the sharp sounds of rolling musketry. Larger puffs of smoke floated high above the treetops, shading the rippling waters of Bull Run, and the boom of howitzers marked the lines of artillery. Clouds of dust shifted and moved through the forests, mingling with the smoky mists, and thicker dust-clouds marked the presence of shuffling feet and pounding hooves.

Robert removed the glasses, looked back at his wife, and saw that she was shading her eyes with her bonnet. "I think I just saw some Zouaves!" she shouted. "Maybe one of them is Buck!"

"Where?" Robert asked.

Pointing, Kady said, "Down there along the creek bank where it bends at that cluster of trees. There! See them?"

Robert brought the binoculars up and peered in the direction Kady was pointing. For a brief instant, he caught a glimpse of the bright-colored uniforms of a handful of Zouaves wading across Bull Run, then they disappeared behind the thick foliage. "It's Zouaves all right, but that's all I can tell. No way to know if Buck is among them. They're out of sight again."

It seemed that more cannons had arrived at the battle scene, for the deep-throated roars came more often. The spectators on the hillside became more excited. One portly woman who carried an opera glass stood near the Brownells and their friends. When the unusually heavy discharge of cannons rolled across the fields and over the hills, she grabbed the arm of the skinny little man next to her.

"Oh, Ralph!" she shouted. "This is splendid. Oh, my! Isn't that first-rate?"

"Yes, dear," said Ralph, who was not so impressed.

Peering through her opera glasses, she gasped, "Oh, isn't this a sight to see, Ralph? We'll be in Richmond by this time tomorrow!"

"Yes, dear," nodded the little man.

Loud cheers suddenly burst from the spectators as a Union officer came riding at breakneck speed up the grassy slope, waving his campaign hat. Dodging large rocks that lay scattered on the hillside, and threading his way amid the few trees and bushes, he drew near the crest and shouted, "We're whipping them good! It'll be over before long!" With the cheers of the crowd in his ears, he thundered back down the hill and soon disappeared in the woods.

"Bully for our side!" shouted Senator Sumner as the congressmen began shaking hands all around. "Bravo! Didn't I tell you so?"

Sitting quietly with Rose Greenhow and the other girls, Jenny listened to the cheering crowd, clenched her hands into fists, and prayed in a whisper, "Dear Lord, let this awful thing be over quickly. And please...please protect Buck."

On the battlefield, Captain Buck Brownell hunkered with his two-hundred-man company along the north bank of Bull Run Creek about three hundred yards northwest of Stone Bridge. Next to Buck was Colonel Keyes, his commander.

The sun was nearly halfway in the morning sky, shining a dull yellow through columns of smoke, as Keyes pointed across the creek at a two-story farm house and said, "Captain, take as many men as you think necessary and capture that house. We're going to need it for a hospital before this thing is over. We're beating the Rebels back now, but it's way too early to say we have them under control. Once you've secured the house, leave some men there to protect it and come back here. I'll leave further orders with one of your lieutenants."

"Yes, sir," nodded Brownell.

Quickly choosing a dozen men, Buck led them along the bank. They bent low, trying to keep from being seen by enemy artillery dug in on the other bank. Soon they came upon several dead Union soldiers and two dead horses where Confederate cannon balls had taken their toll earlier. The Zouaves tried not to look at their dead comrades, but found it difficult to tear their gaze away from the bulging eyes and gaping mouths of men who died so suddenly.

Leading them on, Buck thought of Jenny, wondering where she was and what she was doing. It was just about church time. That's probably where she was…sitting in her favorite pew, lifting her voice with the rest of the congregation in a rousing hymn.

Bullets suddenly began to chop into the brush all around them. Instinctively, the Zouaves flopped on their bellies, looking around to see where the barrage was coming from.

"Straight ahead of us, Captain!" shouted a Zouave sergeant just before a bullet struck him between the eyes.

Buck saw a half-dozen men-in-gray squatting behind a heavy bush on the creek bank twenty yards ahead. "Let 'em have it!" he shouted as he raised his revolver and began to blaze away.

Zouave rifles barked, cutting brush and finding flesh and blood targets. When the volley was over, the Zouaves left the dead sergeant behind and followed their captain as he ran to the spot, gun ready. All six of the Rebels lay dead.

"C'mon," breathed Brownell. "We've got a house to capture."

General Beauregard had set up his headquarters in a large tent near Mitchell Ford on Bull Run Creek, which was located on a seldom-traveled road between Centreville and Manassas Junction about a mile west of Blackburn Ford. Beauregard had expected the main enemy blow to fall at a spot about a mile-and-a-half north of Mitchell Ford where the main road that ran between Centreville and Manassas Junction—which crossed Bull Run at Blackburn Ford—intersected with the less-traveled road. He was perplexed and alarmed when he heard no firing from the area of the intersection where he had concentrated several brigades and three artillery batteries. He heard only a little firing to the east, where five of his brigades were supposed to be crossing Bull Run to make a circular sweep and attack the Federal camps around Centreville.

Instead, fierce sounds of battle grew steadily in the west, his lightly defended left flank. The Yankees had surprised him by attacking where he had least expected. This confused him, and for some time he made no countermove. Finally, he sent the brigades of Thomas J. Jackson, Bernard E. Bee, and Francis S. Bartow to reinforce his threatened left.

As the sun rose higher, the July heat and humidity began to take its toll. Canteens were running low on both sides, and men were leaving the battle lines to fill canteens at Bull Run and other smaller streams.

As the battle raged, General Joseph E. Johnston, second in command under Beauregard, became concerned as he saw the left flank beaten back in spite of the three brigades sent to bolster it. Riding to the headquarters tent, Johnston confronted Beauregard and asked why more help had not been sent to that vital part of the battle. Angrily, Johnston blared, "General, don't you realize the Yankees are having a heyday on our left flank? Their officers are riding around waving their hats and shouting that the Rebels are about to give up!"

Beauregard mopped sweat as he paced back and forth in front of the tent. "I...I just got confused for awhile, General. The Yankees did the unexpected. If they'd centered the attack where I thought they would, we'd have them on the run by now."

"We can still have them on the run," said Johnston. "All we

have to do is shift more of our forces to the left. We've already surprised McDowell with the number of men we've got here."

"I know. I've already sent word for Ewell, Jones, Longstreet, and Holmes to come back on the south side of Bull Run. We'll have to forget hitting the Union camps at Centreville for now."

"I know it's important to hit those camps because of the reserves McDowell's got stashed there. Maybe we ought to pull Early and Bonham's brigades from the right and send them to the left. Let Holmes go with them, and send Jones, Longstreet, and Ewell on to Centreville."

"Sounds like a good idea," nodded Beauregard, who seemed to be settling down. "I'll just do it."

"Fine," grinned Johnston, who was two years younger than his commander. "I'm going out to the left flank right now."

It was a frustrating day for the brigades that Beauregard kept moving back and forth across Bull Run. The men never quite got their socks dry.

With substantial reinforcements sent to his threatened left flank, and his confidence rising, Beauregard mounted up and rode after Johnston to watch the battle.

FIFTEEN

A t the extreme northwest end of what had become the Bull Run battlefield was the small farm community of Sudley Springs, approximately two-and-a-half miles northwest of the Warrenton Turnpike at Stone Bridge where the fighting had become quite heavy by nine-thirty that morning. This was the left flank that concerned Generals Beauregard and Johnston, causing them to send several brigades to bolster.

Noting the Confederate buildup around Stone Bridge, General Irvin McDowell brought in reserves from the camps at Centreville, giving the Confederates more to handle. Meanwhile, McDowell decided to strengthen his right flank farther to the west in case the Rebels tried to send troops in a sweep around by Sudley Springs and move in on them from behind. McDowell was already finding out that Robert E. Lee and P.G.T. Beauregard had brought in thousands of troops to meet the Union assault. McDowell and his commanders were amazed and wondered how the Confederacy had learned of the very time and place they had so carefully planned the attack.

While the battle progressed, General McDowell sent for Colonel Ambrose Burnside and told him to dispatch a company of two hundred men westward toward Sudley Springs to counter any Confederate move in that direction. Burnside, in turn, sent his B Company, under the command of Captain Elrod Dunwaite, with instructions to call for help if he saw more Rebels coming than he thought he and his men could handle.

On a wooded hill above Sudley Springs was Sudley Church. The pastor, Reverend Clyde Walters, was at the door of the church at nine-forty, ready to greet his people if any chose to attend the services in spite of the fighting less than three miles away. His wife and two teenage children stood just inside.

While the sounds of battle met his ears, Walters was pleased to see a few buggies and carriages, along with some riders on horseback, turn onto the path that led up to the church. By ten o'clock, forty-nine adults and teenagers and eighteen children were gathered in the building as the song service began. The pastor counted only four families who were not present. Before it was time for him to preach, two more families had arrived.

Walters was not surprised to see every man of his congregation—young and old—carrying rifles and handguns. The people feared the worst from the Yankee soldiers, and the men were prepared to defend their families if the need should arise. Though Walters had objections to firearms inside the church house, he did not voice them. He was just glad to have his people there on such a frightful day.

General Beauregard caught up with General Johnston at Island Ford, where Johnston was in conversation with Brigadier General Thomas J. Jackson, commander of First Brigade, Army of the Shenandoah. Two of Jackson's officers stood beside him. As he dismounted, Beauregard recognized them as Captains Duane Gibson and James Black. Jackson had his hat off and was mopping sweat from his receding hairline and forehead. All four men greeted the field commander as he drew up.

"So how is it looking here, General?" Beauregard asked Jackson.

"We've got a hot scrap going on upstream at Bull's Ford, sir. And we're strung out on the bank all the way to Stone Bridge, where, as you know, it's hot and heavy. They sent in some reserves a while ago, so I brought up a few more companies to counter them. It's toe-to-toe, but we're doing more damage at the moment than they are."

Johnston interjected, "General Jackson was just explaining to me what he's about to do with a couple of companies."

"According to one of my scouts, sir," said Jackson, "there's some light Union activity going on over there toward Sudley Springs. I was just telling General Johnston that I'm sending Captain Gibson's company of 200 and Captain Black's company of 250 over there to head them off."

"Sounds good," nodded the field commander. "If you have instructions for the captains, please proceed. You and General Johnston and I will have a meeting of the minds once they're on their way."

It was ten-thirty when Captain Elrod Dunwaite and his company were hastening along the bed of an unfinished railway, heading south toward Sudley Springs. Suddenly a sergeant named Clifford Mayer pointed down the ridge where the tracks were meant to be laid and said, "Captain! Rebels!"

Dunwaite gave a quick command for his men to jump behind the ridge. His lieutenant, Boris Wyman, peered at the cluster of Confederate troops who were skirting a section of woods and heading directly toward them. Dunwaite was beside him.

"Looks like we're outnumbered, sir," said Wyman. "Shall we retreat back to that patch of woods we passed through a few minutes ago? We'll stand a better chance of holding them off."

Dunwaite shook his head. "No. We'll not retreat before any

backwoods hillbilly squirrel hunters. We're more than a match for them right here. Since they haven't broken rank, it's apparent they didn't see us before we jumped off the ridge. Pass the word along. We'll hold our fire till we can count the freckles on their ugly faces. When they're close enough, I'll give the signal to open fire by firing the first shot. Go!"

Captains Gibson and Black led their companies shoulder-to-shoulder in ranks of sixteen. The morning sun was bearing down with the promise of more heat to come as the day wore on. Warm water sloshed in half-empty canteens on their belts and sweat streaked their faces. Gibson and Black were marching in the forefront, side by side.

"Your idea ought to fake them out, Captain," Black said. "Sure enough, they'll think we didn't see them."

"I'm counting on it," Gibson drawled. "If that Yankee leader up there can count, he knows he's outnumbered. But these cocky Yankees think we're a bunch of dumb country yokels who'll fold up the first time we meet in battle. If McDowell's had a chance to teach that Yankee leader up there any tactics, the man will wait till we're within spitting distance before they open fire. Well, we won't give them the opportunity. We'll split our companies just outside of musket range and swing a wide circle. If they try to turn around and high-tail it the other way, they'll have to cross Bull Run. That'll slow them good, and they'll be sitting ducks."

"I'll ease back and pass the word," Black said. "I'll tell them you will give the command to spread out."

Wyman and Mayer flanked their captain as the fiery rays of the sun lanced down from the cloudless Virginia sky.

"Exactly what point are you going to allow them to reach before we open fire, sir?" Wyman asked.

Dunwaite ignored the question for the moment. He was intent

on the approach of the enemy. Dust rose around the marching columns. The metal of their weapons flashed bright against the relentless sunlight. Then with his voice hard, precise, and biting in the dead-hot humid air, he said, "When the first lines reach that clump of berry bushes, we'll unleash on them. All it'll take is a taste of hot Yankee lead to put them on the run—that is, the ones who are still alive. And while they're running, the—"

The captain's words were cut off when he saw the tight ranks suddenly break, and the Confederate soldiers began to spread out outside of musket range, ejecting wild Rebel yells.

"Captain!" gasped Mayer. "What are they doing?"

Dunwaite studied the movements of the enemy for a few seconds. "They're fitting a phalanx together to tie us up in a noose. We're spread too thin against that many men. We've got to retreat before they get us locked in. We'll have to get across the creek quick!"

Captain Dunwaite gave the command for his men to head across the weed-infested terrain that stood between them and Bull Run. By the time they were within fifty yards of the meandering stream, the Confederates were on the railway ridge, firing their muskets.

Men in blue began to drop, while others whirled around to make a stand. A few kept running toward the creek. Whooping like Indians, the Rebels charged. Within a few seconds, it was an all-out battle. Muskets cracked and bullets cut the hot morning air.

Lieutenant Wyman soon found himself flattened on the bank of Bull Run in the shade of an old oak tree. Bullets were thwacking into the tree and the bush that sided it. Within a few seconds, Wyman was flanked by a half-dozen other men who had sought the same refuge.

Bill Quinn rolled next to Wyman and said above the battle's roar, "Lieutenant, I don't know about you, but I'm heading across the creek while the going's good!"

"So am I!" said Darrell Bateman.

On the other side of Bateman were identical twin brothers,

Privates Eddie and Freddie Spangler. Straw-haired and blue-eyed, they said almost in unison, "Me, too!"

Corporal Arland White gasped, "Lieutenant, I just saw Captain Dunwaite get it! Bullet through the head. Let's get outta here!"

"Let's go!" shouted Wyman, and plunged into the two-foot depth of water. Quickly the others followed, including the sixth man, Thaddeus Pauley.

Bull Run was forty feet wide at that spot. It took the seven men about a minute to cross it fighting the current. As they ran up a gentle slope with the sounds of battle behind them, they soon came to a double-rail fence, supported by X-framed poles. Carrying only his handgun, Lieutenant Wyman vaulted the fence with ease. The others, each carrying a bayoneted musket, found it more difficult to get over. Hanging onto their weapons, they slowly worked their way over the double rails. Wyman shouted at them to hurry.

Freddie Spangler watched his twin make it to the other side, but found the task cumbersome with the musket in his hand. Seeing that he was the last to get over, Freddie swung his musket over the fence and stood it against the top inside rail. The shiny bayonet glistened in the mid-morning sun.

Freddie hopped onto the first rail, gripping one of the X-framed poles to steady himself. He shifted his right foot to the second rail, but when he let go of the pole to drop to the other side, he slipped.

The rest of them were talking to Wyman about which way to go when they heard Freddie's high-pitched scream. Their heads whipped around in time to see the yellow-haired youth plunge downward. Eddie, eyes bulging, wailed his twin's name as Freddie impaled himself on the bayonet.

The men in blue stood paralyzed as Freddie kicked and screamed. First to find his legs was Eddie, but by the time he reached the fence, Freddie had stopped flailing. There were no more screams.

Captain Wyman laid a hand on Eddie's shoulder and said,

"C'mon, kid. There's nothing you can do for him now. We've got to get out of here."

Eddie broke into uncontrollable sobs. "No, Lieutenant! No! I can't leave him here!"

"We're going, kid," sighed Wyman. "You can stay if you want." With that, he hastened up the slope telling the others to follow.

Eddie Spangler looked back across Bull Run Creek at the smoke of the battle. Swallowing hard, he glanced down at his twin's lifeless form. Then he turned quickly and followed the others, not allowing himself to look back.

As the Confederates began to overpower the Yankees at the creek bank, many of the men in blue tried to get away across the stream. Bullets cut them down mid-stream, and the normally clear water was crimson with blood.

Smoke hung like a pall over the area, but when a sudden breeze rushed over the landscape, it cleared a wide spot. At that instant, Captain Duane Gibson's attention was drawn to the crest of the slope beyond Bull Run where he saw Lieutenant Wyman and his five men running along the ridge.

Gibson sent a man to tell Captain Black that he was taking a dozen men to run down some escaping Yankees. When he had picked his squad, they hastened downstream some fifty yards, then splashed across, ran to the double-railed fence, clambered over it, and charged up the slope.

As Lieutenant Wyman led his men along the ridge, Sergeant Quinn looked back over his shoulder just in time to see thirteen Rebels wading across Bull Run, headed in their direction.

"Lieutenant!" shouted Quinn. "They're coming after us!"

Puffing as he ran, Wyman looked back and saw Gibson and his squad in pursuit. Quickly, he led his men off the ridge and down a steep slope into a mulberry thicket. They threaded their way through the mulberry bushes, the stiff branches clawing at their uniforms.

The thicket was about a hundred feet from one side to the other. When they emerged, they found a small tributary of Bull Run snaking its way through the grassy, daisy-strewn dell that lay before them. The small valley was about a hundred yards wide. Beyond its natural border on the other side was a gentle slope that lifted to a height of thirty feet and was topped by a road. Above the road, on a rounded hilltop amid a stand of tall trees, stood a stone church building. Parked in front and along one side were several buggies and carriages. Three or four saddled horses were tied to hitching posts.

Wyman shot a glance to the ridge behind them. So far there was no sign of the pursuing Rebels. Swinging his gaze back to Sudley Church, he said, "We're going to be all right, boys. We'll just attend us a little Sunday service. When those stinking Rebels get here, we'll tell 'em to go back where they came from or we'll kill us a bunch of Southern worshippers. Let's go."

Wading through the small stream and scurrying over the dell, the six Yankees huffed and puffed their way up the slope and across the road. The church door was open, as were all the windows, and they could hear the preacher delivering his sermon. They decided to stay hidden until they caught their breath. Wyman looked behind him and swore when he saw the dozen Rebels running along the ridge where they had been five minutes before.

Wyman cocked his revolver and said, "Okay, I'll go in first. Have your weapons ready. If any of the men in there are man enough to stand up to us, kill them."

Wyman charged for the open door and bolted inside with the others on his heels. "Everybody stay right where you are!" he bellowed, waving his revolver.

Women screamed, frightening babies, who began to cry. Children, eyes bulging, moved close to their parents. The people sat stunned. The soldiers stood poised with their bayoneted muskets cocked and ready to fire. Throwing his gun on the preacher, who stood behind the pulpit, Bible in hand, Wyman roared, "Put the Bible down, holy man, and take a seat down here with your congregation!"

The threat of violence hung like a thick cloud over the room. Everyone waited and watched in breathless trepidation. Mothers with babies were attempting to quiet them. Terrified small children were beginning to cry.

Reverend Walters looked at Wyman and said in a level tone, "You have no cause to come in here like this, Lieutenant. There's no one in this house of God who represents a threat to you. I ask you politely to take your men and leave."

"I'm not asking you, holy man, I'm *telling* you—come out from behind that pulpit and take a pew. *Now!*"

Walters knew the enemy soldiers had not yet spotted the muskets that lay at the feet of the men in his congregation. He hoped they wouldn't. And even more, he hoped no one would attempt to shoot it out with them. As he laid his Bible on the pulpit and started off the platform, he said to Wyman, "What do you want from us?"

"I want you to sit still and shutup. We've got a little problem here to handle, and—"

At that instant, a man sitting by a window leaped to his feet with a cocked revolver aimed at Wyman and shouted, "Drop your gun, Yankee, or you're a dead man!"

There were more screams as Bill Quinn swung his musket on the man and fired. The man took the slug in his chest, but reflex squeezed his trigger. The shot struck Wyman in the forehead, snapping his head back as he bounced off the end of a pew and crumpled in the aisle. While the shocking echoes filled the room, the preacher yelled for everyone to get down. His command was not needed; they were dropping between the pews almost as one person.

But not all of them. Defiant men, indignant at the soldiers for barging into the house of God, brought their muskets and revolvers to bear on the intruders. There was an outburst of yells and shots, mingled with screams and childish wails, as guns roared and bullets struck flesh, chewed into wood, and shattered windows. For the next half-minute the church building was a scene of desperate fighting, the ferocious, joyless task of killing.

When the shooting stopped, five of the six Yankees lay dead on the floor. The sixth, Eddie Spangler, hung partially on a pew. His cap dangled from one ear, exposing a mop of yellow hair. Four slugs had taken his life.

There was a wild maelstrom of weeping and wailing. Two newly made widows knelt beside the lifeless forms of their husbands. One of the dead was the man who had thrown his gun on the Yankee lieutenant. One other man was wounded, but not seriously.

The dazed congregation looked up through the smoke cloud that hung in the room to see Captain Duane Gibson and his men filing through the door. The preacher left the wounded man with two of the women and met Gibson in the aisle.

"I'm Pastor Walters, Captain," the preacher said solemnly. "These Yankees burst in here a few minutes ago, barking orders, and waving their guns at us. One"—Walters choked on the word—"one of my men produced a revolver and commanded the leader to drop his gun. One of the other Yankees opened fire, and…and you see the results. I was hoping it wouldn't come to this."

Gibson raised his hat, sleeved sweat, and ran his gaze over the six corpses in blue. "Well, that's a half-dozen we won't have to fight again. How many of your people were hit?"

"Only three, thank the Lord. Two of my men are dead, and another wounded. It was only the hand of God that kept the women and children from being hit."

"I'll say 'Amen' to that, Reverend. This could have been a real disaster."

Walter's wife and children moved up beside him. Closing all three in an embrace, he said, "I pray the whole Yankee army will be vanquished today, Captain."

"Well, keep praying, Reverend," said Gibson as he turned to leave. "We've given the Federals plenty of resistance so far, but there's a long day ahead."

SIXTEEN

I n the thick of the battle at Stone Bridge was Confederate Colonel Nathan G. Evans, who was looked upon by Generals Lee and Beauregard as a "Rebel among Rebels." Evans, an insubordinate, hard-nosed, egotistical South Carolinian, swore like a sailor and always carried whiskey in a flask on his belt. Hot-headed, with a hair-trigger temper, he loved to fight.

Though Lee and Beauregard were not fond of the colonel's way, they admired him for his fighting spirit. The men who followed him had the same crusty mannerisms and the identical love for fighting. The "Evansites" were a breed of their own. It was for this reason that Lee made Colonel Evans commander of his own brigade, and rather than give it a number like the others, dubbed it "Evans's Demi-Brigade."

Also in the fire and smoke at Stone Bridge was the First Louisiana Special Battalion under the command of Major Roberdeau Wheat. Wheat and Evans were very much alike in their appetite for fighting. The Special Battalion was better known as "Wheat's Tigers," notable for wearing bright-red shirts, and more notable for their belligerence and the same rugged fighting spirit as Evans's Demi-Brigade. Wheat had recruited his unit from the wharves along the New Orleans waterfront.

About a mile-and-a-quarter west of Stone Bridge was a farm owned by the Matthews family. Like so many of the farms in the area, the house, barn, and outbuildings sat atop a hill, overlooking the rest of the property. Thus, the hill on Union army maps was called Matthews' Hill.

As the morning wore on and the fighting grew more intense, Union field commander General Irvin McDowell sent Brigadier General David Hunter's Second Division out of Centreville in a wide sweep north and westward. Second Division was made up of two brigades. First Brigade was commanded by Colonel Andrew Porter, and Second Brigade by Colonel Ambrose E. Burnside.

The twenty-eight hundred men of Second Division were to cut south at the unfinished railway about a half-mile east of Sudley Springs and swing around Matthews' Hill. This would bring them up on the Confederates' rear flank without being seen. From there they could surprise them with artillery bombardment, then launch a devastating infantry attack.

General Beauregard, however, had posted Captain E.P. Alexander—the engineer officer in charge of his signals unit—on a nearby lofty hill just before dawn. Colonel Evans had a signal corpsman stationed at the fringe of the Stone Bridge battle site to keep an eye on Captain Alexander for word of more Union reinforcements being brought in.

The blazing sun looked down at the carnage on the banks of Bull Run and the dust and smoke at Stone Bridge. Bodies were scattered about on the blood-soaked ground, while others bobbed lifelessly in the crimson waters of the creek. The wounded lay bleeding in the heat with no one to tend to them. Sometimes the men in the thick of the fight could hear their cries, which usually faded into moans, then into silence.

Evans's lookout man crawled to him near Stone Bridge and shouted above the din, "Colonel! Captain Alexander just sent a signal. He estimates there are about twenty-five hundred Union troops coming from the north just this side of Sudley Springs. Captain Alexander thinks they're going to circle Matthews' Hill and come in behind us!"

Evans had been told only minutes before that General Beauregard was now using a farmhouse about five hundred yards southeast of Stone Bridge as his headquarters. "All right," nodded Evans, pointing that direction. "I want you to make your way to that farmhouse out there by the road. See it?"

"Yes, sir."

"General Beauregard is in that house. Relate Captain Alexander's message to him. Tell him I don't have time to wait for his approval, but that I sent you so he'd know what I'm doing. Tell him I'm going to take my brigade and Major Wheat's, and head for Matthew's Hill to meet those Yankees. Got it?"

"Yes, sir," replied the corpsman, and hastened away.

Evans knew that even with the eleven hundred men in his brigade and the five hundred in Major Wheat's battalion, they would be greatly outnumbered by the oncoming Union force…but he dare not take any more troops from the present battle site. Within twenty minutes, he and Major Wheat were leading their men toward Matthews' hill. Wheat was bringing along four howitzers, and Evans had six.

The heat was becoming unbearable as Evans and Wheat led their men across the green fields. Evans was glad to have Wheat beside him. Rob Wheat was a veteran of the Mexican War; he had also been a much-publicized filibuster in Central America, and a bloody mercenary warrior for Guiseppe Garibaldi during the war for Italian unification. Standing six feet four inches in height and weighing three hundred pounds, Wheat was an imposing figure in the thick of a fight.

Crossing shallow Young's Branch with their men and equipment, Evans and Wheat soon deployed their infantrymen and howitzers from the top to about halfway down the side of Matthews' Hill under cover of dense woods. They had a clear view of the open fields and lower half of the hill that Hunter and his eager troops would have to cross.

While they were digging in and anchoring the howitzers, Colonel Evans had two of his men check to see if anyone was in the farmhouse or any of the outbuildings. He wanted to give the Matthews family an opportunity to vacate the premises before the Federals arrived. He was not surprised to learn that the family was already gone.

The Confederates had barely positioned themselves for the battle when the columns of Union troops appeared, coming across the fields like a swarm of ants. General David Hunter was leading them on horseback, and Colonels Porter and Burnside rode their mounts not far behind, each in front of his brigade.

In the shade of the dense woods on Matthews' Hill, Evans and Wheat waited. Their men were all in place, ready to unleash their fire power. While Wheat sipped water from a canteen, Evans took a snort of whiskey from his flask.

Smacking his lips, the colonel extended the flask toward Wheat and said, "Good stuff, Major. Want some?"

"Not right now. I want to go into this fight with a clear head."

Evans chuckled as he corked the flask and hooked it back on his belt. "That's exactly what it does for me, Major. Clears my head."

The oncoming swarm was now about two hundred yards from the base of the hill. Instructions had been given to the men with the howitzers to open fire at Colonel Evans's command. Evans was sure Captain Alexander was right. The blue-bellies were planning to circle the hill and attack the Confederates at Stone Bridge from behind. Once the howitzers opened fire, the Union commander would know he had lost the element of surprise. If he ordered his troops to take the hill, the Confederate muskets would cut loose.

Evans lifted his hat and wiped the perspiration from his forehead. "When that front line gets another fifty yards closer," he said to Wheat, "we'll blast them."

Wheat nodded and pulled his revolver. "I'm ready."

Evans drew his sidearm and moved to the edge of the trees. He let about fifteen seconds pass as he eyed the enemy's front line of soldiers, then moved into the sunlight where the howitzer operators could see him. Lifting his hat high over his head, he brought it down swiftly, shouting, "*Fi-i-r-r-e!*"

The howitzers boomed in a planned staccato. Shells whistled downward and Yankees—with a helpless look of horror—began to scatter as the shells struck and exploded. All six were aimed well, and plowed into the ranks, blowing bodies every direction. There were shouts and curses as the Yankees followed their leader's command and began to swarm up the side of the hill.

Rebel muskets opened fire while the howitzers were being reloaded. Waving his revolver and trying to keep his frightened horse in check, General David Hunter shouted at the top of his voice, encouraging his men as they hurried up the slope. As they climbed, they fired their muskets at the puffs of smoke that appeared against the dark shade of the trees.

The first Rebel howitzer was reloaded quickly and fired again, just ahead of the others. A shell exploded a few feet from Hunter's horse, blowing him out of the saddle. The horse screamed and fell over dead.

Instantly, Colonel Burnside was kneeling beside Hunter, who was seriously wounded in the neck and left cheek. Burnside quickly called for two soldiers to carry the wounded general from the field of fire. As they picked him up, Hunter grasped Burnside's sleeve and said, "You're in charge. I'm leaving the battle in your hands."

While the Matthews' Hill and Stone Bridge battles raged, Union General Daniel Tyler's First Division was fighting brigades three, four, and six of the Confederate army along Warrenton Turnpike about two miles northeast of Stone Bridge. Fighting in Tyler's First Brigade under Colonel Erasmus D. Keyes were the Fifth New York

Zouaves, led by Colonel Abram Duryee. Under Duryee, Captain Buck Brownell commanded a company of three hundred. General Tyler's Third Brigade was led by Colonel William Tecumseh Sherman.

It was almost eleven o'clock when Buck found himself in a gully some three hundred feet from the Turnpike, where the Confederates were dug in and fighting fiercely. The Yankees had found other gullies and low spots in the open field and were firing in return.

The gully Buck was in was about forty feet in length. Fighting right next to him was one of Colonel Keyes's captains, Kenneth Merritt. Beyond Merritt were several of his men, and on Brownell's left was a string of Zouaves. The rest of Brownell's men were in gullies and ditches all around him. Though Buck was not aware of it, some thirty yards to his right, in another long gully, was Captain Jack Egan, who had been in Sherman's brigade since the war began.

While muskets barked and bullets buzzed angrily in the air, Egan noted where Brownell was positioned. A boiling hatred seethed through Egan toward Brownell. He had dreamed of putting a bullet through the heart of the man who had stolen Jenny Jordan from him.

Buck was bent low, reloading his musket when he heard a bullet strike flesh next to him and saw Captain Merritt slump down. Buck turned him over and saw that the slug had shattered the clavicle on his right side and had ripped open an artery. Merritt was conscious, in a great deal of pain, and blood was pumping from the severed artery. Buck whipped a bandanna from his pocket, wadded it up, and pressed it to the bleeding wound.

Lieutenant Bradley Runyon of Sherman's Third Brigade eyed his captain, then looked at Brownell and asked, "What do you think, sir?"

"I think we need to get him out of here or else he'll bleed to death."

Buck had noted a farmhouse a short distance off the Turnpike, about three hundred yards from where they were positioned. "There's a farmhouse up the road a ways. If we could get him to that house, we could leave a man with him to keep the pressure on the artery. When this battle's over, we can get him to a doctor."

"Sounds good to me," nodded Runyon. "For sure we can't keep that compress on him here. Not if those Rebels decide to rush us."

Eyeing the distance to the farmhouse, Buck said, "We'll have to crawl about two hundred yards. One of us will have to drag him while the other holds the compress." Looking down at Merritt, he asked, "Think you can stand it, Captain? It's bound to be painful with that collarbone broken."

"I can take it," replied the wounded officer through his teeth.

"Okay," said Buck. "You just hold on. We'll get you to safety."

"I'll drag, if you'll hold, sir," Runyon said.

"Fine. You can stay with him once we get him to the house."

"Not me, sir. I need to be out here with my men. You can stay with him."

"Can't," said Buck. "I need to be here with my men, too. You have a man along the line you want to take along?"

Looking along the line to his right, Runyon called a young private, Lanny O'Dell, to him and explained the situation.

"Okay," Brownell said. "Let's go."

Passing the word both ways about what they were doing, Brownell, Runyon, and O'Dell began their difficult task.

Enemy bullets whirred over their heads and plowed sod around them as they made their way over the grassy field toward the farmhouse. Jack Egan observed them from his position not far away.

Sweltering in the humid heat, the three men soon had the wounded officer within a hundred yards of the farmhouse and past the line of fire.

As they paused to catch their breath, Buck said, "I'll pick him up and carry him if one of you will hold the compress."

"I'll do it, sir," volunteered O'Dell, handing his musket to Runyon.

The lieutenant had just pulled his revolver from its holster for safety's sake, contemplating their journey across the hundred yards of open field. Slipping the gun back into leather, he cocked the musket and said, "Let's move."

Buck handed the blood-soaked cloth to O'Dell, knelt down, and picked up Merritt. "Hard part is over, Captain. We'll have you in a safe place in a few minutes."

Once O'Dell had a firm hold on the artery, they hastened across the field to the two-story house. They were drawing near when they saw movement at an open window on the ground floor.

"Somebody's in there, all right," commented Runyon. "Shortest distance is to the back of the house around that shed."

They rounded the corner of the old unpainted shed and headed toward the back porch. The door was standing open. Suddenly a tall, slender elderly man stepped through the door onto the porch, wielding a double-barreled shotgun. Both hammers were eared back, and a long, shaky finger was on the triggers. "Hold it right there!" he snapped. "Get off my property, you filthy Yankees!"

"Sir," Buck said, "we've got a wounded man, here. He's—"

"I said get off my property! *Now!*"

"Sir," reasoned Brownell, "we mean you no harm. This man has a severed artery and a broken collarbone. I'm asking you to allow him a place to lie down while Private O'Dell, here, keeps a compress on the wound."

"I have a wife and granddaughter in the house, mister!" spat the old man. "Why should I trust any of you stinkin' Yankees not to harm *w*?"

"I give you my word, sir," said Buck. "The minute this wounded officer is comfortable, Captain Runyon and I will head back to the battle. Private O'Dell will not raise a finger toward the women."

"That's right, sir," put in O'Dell. "I won't even have a weapon, and even if I did, I wouldn't harm you or anyone else in the house. All I want to do is take care of my captain so he doesn't bleed to death. You can hold that scatter-gun on me the whole time if you want."

"We'll be back to pick them up once the battle is over, sir," said Runyon.

The old man still held the shotgun steadily on the Yankees. His jaw was stern, but it was evident he was giving it consideration. Suddenly a voice thundered from the corner of the shed, "Drop that gun, old man!"

Buck's head whipped around and he saw Jack Egan moving in with his revolver aimed at the farmer. A frightened woman whined just inside the door as the old man bristled. There was fire in his watery old eyes. Holding the shotgun steady, he rasped, "That does it! All of you get off my property this instant!"

"You can't get us all with that shotgun, you old fool!" blared Egan, staying clear of his line of fire. "You pull those triggers, you'll die where you stand. Now put the gun down! We're taking over this house whether you like it or not."

"Egan, get back where you belong," Buck shouted angrily. "This kind gentleman was about to let us use his house for Captain Merritt. You're interfering."

Egan regarded Brownell with a venomous glare, then looked back toward the porch just as the farmer bellowed, "Get off my property! All of you! Right now!"

Egan swore and fired his revolver. The old man took the slug dead-center in the stomach. He buckled from the impact, and the shotgun flipped forward in his hands. One barrel discharged, sending the blast into the floor of the porch. As he fell, the women in the house screamed.

Buck railed, "Egan, you fool! You didn't have to shoot him!"

"Don't tell me what I didn't have to do, Brownell. The old buzzard was gonna shoot us!"

The farmer's wife and nineteen-year-old granddaughter ignored what danger they might face and crossed the porch to the old man, who lay face-down, sprawled over the edge of the first step. Both were sobbing and wailing.

"You're under arrest for murder, Egan!" Buck hissed. "Lieutenant Runyon, take his gun!"

Egan took a step backward and aimed his revolver at Runyon.

"Nobody's taking my gun. Put the musket down, Lieutenant."

Runyon shifted his flustered gaze to Brownell, then back to Egan.

"Egan, you'll face a court-martial for this," warned Brownell.

"Not if I kill all three of you."

"Right," said Brownell. "Then it'll be a firing squad."

Private O'Dell was positioned on Brownell's right side at an angle that blocked Buck's holstered revolver from Egan's view.

Shaking his gun at Runyon, Egan spat, "I told you to put the musket down, Lieutenant! Do it!"

Buck felt the slight tug at his holster a split second before the loud report of his gun rocked the air. Egan died on his feet with a bullet through his heart. The gun in his hand slipped through lifeless fingers and clattered to the ground just before he fell on top of it.

With the smoking revolver in his hand, the young private said to Brownell, "I'm sorry, sir, but when he spoke of killing us, I didn't know what else to do."

"You did the right thing," Buck said, glancing at Egan's crumpled form. "Now, let's see about the old man and get Captain Merritt inside."

At Matthews' Hill, General Hunter was carried from the field of battle. Colonel Burnside took charge and rode his horse back and forth along the slope, shouting at the men to take the hill. Intense Rebel fire from the woods above them mauled the Yankees. Bullets and cannon shells were dropping them all across the broad sweep of the hillside. Suddenly Burnside's horse fell beneath him, a bullet in its head. The colonel was able to leap from the saddle before the animal flopped hard to the ground.

Colonel Andrew Porter was close by on foot. He dashed to Burnside and helped him to his feet. Together they urged their troops upward, adjusting the lines as they sought to make their way to the Confederate stronghold. Both Union officers were surprised when Rebel infantrymen suddenly burst from the protection of the trees and swarmed down the hill toward them.

Atop the hill, Colonel Evans peered through the heavy brush and watched his musketeers exact their toll. Yankees were dropping along the front line, but no matter how many fell, more came up behind them. Little by little, they were gaining ground.

Moving to Major Wheat, who stood a few feet away, Evans said, "Major, we're outnumbered. We need reinforcements, and it won't be long till we'll be low on ammunition. I'm going to send a runner to General Beauregard. He's got to give us more men and ammunition."

"I agree, sir, but that'll take time. The way those Yankees are comin', I'm not sure but what they'll be on us before we can get help."

Holding his voice above the roar of the battle, Evans said, "I'll send a man on my horse. He can go off the back side of the hill." Evans moved among the trees and called a corporal from the firing line.

Major Wheat watched as Evans gave instructions, then the corporal ran to the colonel's horse and rode away.

When Evans returned, Wheat said, "It's still gonna take time to get help, sir. I've got an idea that'll buy us some time. I'll take my five hundred Tigers and rush 'em."

Evans raised his eyebrows and frowned. "You mean, just go running at them?"

"Well, runnin' and shootin' at the same time. We've got bayonets on our muskets and Bowie knives on our hips. We can cut a big hole in 'em, Colonel."

"Who am I to argue with a tough old veteran like you, Major?" smiled Evans. "Just let me know when you're ready."

Ten minutes later the Yankees were shocked to see five hundred red-shirted Louisiana Tigers swarming down the hill, yelling their bloodcurdling Rebel yell.

SEVENTEEN

Two hours before dawn that same morning, Private Mike Durbin hurried by the Henry house and climbed the hill to his own house, a half-mile to the south. He couldn't pass the opportunity to spend a few minutes with his wife before going into battle with the Yankees. Durbin had been assigned to General Barnard E. Bee's Third Brigade in the Army of the Shenandoah, and had not seen Jo-Beth for over two months.

The stars were twinkling overhead like diamonds against a black velvet sky. The old two-story house Mike had bought when he married Jo-Beth two years previously was a welcome sight as he topped the hill. He could make out that the upstairs bedroom windows were open. It was a warm night.

Mike planned to move up just under Jo-Beth's window and call to her. He knew that Orville, her fifteen-year-old brother, would be asleep in a bedroom on the other side of the house. He hoped he could stir his wife without awaking Orville. Pal would no doubt be sleeping in Orville's bedroom. If both bedroom doors were shut, Mike might be able to get by without disturbing the big Newfoundland.

Mike was within fifty feet of the house when he heard the

deep-throated bark of his dog. His sensitive ears had picked up Mike's soft footfalls on the grass. It was only seconds until Pal's big broad head appeared at Jo-Beth's window above. The dog was barking and snarling as if to warn the intruder against coming any closer. Moving up under the window, Mike said, "Hey, boy! Don't you know me?" Pal's demeanor changed instantly. Releasing a whine, he yapped a note of recognition and hoisted himself onto the window sill. He was so excited to see his master, he was going to leap down to him.

"No, boy!" shouted Mike. "No! Not from up th—"

Pal's one-hundred-sixty-pound bulk landed on Mike, knocking him down. Neither master nor pet were hurt, but before Mike could get to a sitting position, Pal was drowning him with long-tongued kisses. Mike hugged him and said, "I'm glad to see you, too, boy!"

"Mike!" came Jo-Beth's shriek of joy from the upstairs window. She was holding a lantern out the window, letting its orange glow cast a circle of light on the scene below.

Still lying on the ground with Pal all over him, the Confederate soldier looked up and said, "Hi, honey!"

But the lantern's light was back inside the room, and Jo-Beth had disappeared. Mike worked his way out from under Pal and headed for the front porch as he heard the door come open. By the dim light of the stars overhead, husband and wife were in each other's arms on the porch steps.

Jo-Beth was in her robe, her long blond hair showering over her shoulders. She kissed Mike several times, then settled into one long, tender kiss. Pal's whines for attention were momentarily ignored.

Jo-Beth gripped her husband's upper arms, looked up into his face, and asked, "How did this happen? Why did you get to come home? Are you hurt?"

"No, honey, I'm not hurt. Did you get my letters?"

"I got five. The last I heard, you were at the camp near Winchester."

"Well, I wrote another one a few days ago, telling you that we were coming this way to fight the Yankees over at Manassas Junction. We arrived at the Junction at noon yesterday."

"Oh," said Jo-Beth, gripping him harder. "I heard rumors about a pending battle. I didn't realize you'd be in it."

"I wanted to come sooner, but General Bee said I had to stay with my company. No one could leave the camp. Well, since there's no question the battle's going to start this morning, and since the general saw that I wasn't asleep an hour ago, he told me to come see you real quick, but to be back before dawn."

Jo-Beth began to weep. Embracing him, she sobbed, "Oh, Mike! I don't want you to have to face those Yankee guns!"

"I know, honey, but I have to. It's my duty. We're thinking that if we whip up good on those smart-aleck Yankees today, maybe this whole thing will be over. Maybe they'll go back home and let us Southerners live our lives in peace. That's the way I see it, and that's what I'll be fighting for."

Orville stepped through the door onto the porch, rubbing his eyes. "Hello, Mike," he said sleepily. "I didn't know you'd be home so soon."

Letting go of Jo-Beth with one arm to embrace Orville with it, Mike said, "I didn't either. And I can't stay but just a couple minutes. I have to get back to camp. We're going to have it out with the Yankees over by Manassas Junction today."

The dim light showed Orville's eyes wide. "You're gonna shoot Yankees *today?*"

"Yep."

"Good. I hope you kill all of 'em."

"Maybe we won't have to do that. Maybe we can just kill enough of them to send them running. I want this war business over with so I can come home."

Pal wagged his big bushy tail and barked.

Mike bent over and patted the dog's head. "You too, eh?"

Pal barked again.

"I guess he's missed me, huh?" Mike said to Jo-Beth.

"Has he ever! Every morning he goes all over the house, searching every room. He lies right next to your chair during breakfast, lunch, and supper. I've seen him out at the barn and over at the tool shed a dozen times a day, scratching at the doors, thinking you're in there."

"Yeah," interjected Orville. "Several times I've gone out and let him in both buildings, so he could see you weren't."

Smiling down at the soft-eyed animal, Mike rubbed Pal's ears and said, "You were well-named, weren't you, boy?"

Pal whined and licked his master's hand.

"He hasn't missed you as much as *I* have," Jo-Beth said, leaning her head on Mike's shoulder.

"That's for sure!" spoke up Orville. "She's been doin' a lot of cryin'. I mean…morning, noon, and—"

"That's enough, little brother! You don't have to tell everything you know."

Orville laughed, then hugged his brother-in-law and said since Mike couldn't stay, he would go back to bed so Mike and Jo-Beth could have some time alone. When Orville was gone, Mike and Jo-Beth kissed again, then sat on the porch swing together, with Pal at their feet. They exchanged words of love and talked of the future for a few minutes. Then Mike said, reluctantly, "Well, sweetheart, I have to go."

When they had kissed good-bye on the steps for the third time, Mike said, "Take Pal inside with you and close the windows far enough that he can't get through them…or you know what he'll do."

Eyeing the massive black dog with tenderness, Jo-Beth nodded. "Yes. He'll be going along to fight Yankees with you."

Mike stepped back inside the house and petted his dog while Jo-Beth made sure all the windows were lowered sufficiently.

Jo-Beth was weeping again when she kissed Mike at the door, then stood on the porch and watched him walk away. Inside the house, Pal whined and scratched at the door. When the darkness swallowed Mike, Jo-Beth slipped inside and closed the door. Pal was rushing through the house, checking every window and door to find a way of escape.

Heavy-hearted, Jo-Beth walked into the parlor, dropped onto an overstuffed chair, and broke into heavy sobs. She could still hear Pal pacing the house when she awakened. The sun was up, and she heard a sound like thunder in the distance. Making her way out onto the porch, she looked northward. The fighting was underway, she thought, somewhere near Stone Bridge on Bull Run Creek. Thick clouds of blue-white smoke rose toward the morning sky.

After feeding Orville his breakfast, Jo-Beth warned the youth to be careful going in and out of the house. He must not let Pal get out. When she tried to feed the dog, he ignored the food. Pal had pined for his master for weeks while he was gone. Now that he had seen Mike again, there was only one thing on his mind. He wanted to go to wherever his master was and be at his side.

As the morning wore on, the battle sounds never let up. Pal ran up and down the stairs continually, stopping at each window for a moment, then scratching at a door. When he had made the rounds of the house, he started all over again. Jo-Beth occupied herself by cleaning and recleaning every room, the incessant thunder of cannons and the rattle of muskets assaulting her ears. Orville sat on an old wooden box in the yard, in the shade of a huge oak tree, his eyes never straying from drifting clouds of powder smoke to the north.

It was high noon when Orville heard Pal's whine, and turned to see the determined dog using his bulk and strength to force the dining room window upward on its track. Somehow Pal had been able to work the gap of the partially open window wider with his head until he could get his neck under it. He soon had the opening wide enough to slip through. Like a black streak, the Newfoundland bounded down the hill, heading north.

Orville ran to the house, calling loudly to his sister. When Jo-Beth appeared on the porch, Orville shouted, "Pal got out! Pal got out!"

"How?"

"He managed to get the dining room window open enough to get out," panted the youth. "He's gone! He headed right for where Mike's fighting the Yankees!"

Colonel Evans looked on electrified from his position atop Matthews' Hill as Major Wheat led his five hundred Louisiana Tigers into a violent clash with the Yankees. Although the Tigers were vastly outnumbered, their wild charge had the exact effect Major Wheat had intended. Such daring and hardy warfare threw the Federals into confusion, and that was what Evans desperately needed. The confusion would buy time for General Beauregard to dispatch reinforcements to Matthews' Hill.

The sun climbed toward its peak as the battle raged. While Confederate guns continued to blast away, Colonel Evans's runner returned with the news that General Beauregard was sending reinforcements. If he could do it, Beauregard would send more help later. Colonel Evans's momentary elation was dampened, though, when the runner also informed him that Captain Alexander had sent General Beauregard a flag message that another column of Yankees was coming south past Sudley Springs.

Evans told the runner to get back on the firing line, then smacked a fist into a palm and swore. He belted down a swig of whiskey, then turned back to the battle on the hillside below. The gallant Louisiana Tigers fought hard in the suppressing heat, and though many were falling, they showed no sign of retreat. Face to face with overwhelming odds, they battled on.

The Confederates atop Matthews' Hill continued to hold the Federals at bay. Muskets popped and howitzers roared. Colonel Evans moved amongst them, checking on their ammunition supply. It was running dangerously low. It was about twelve-thirty when he returned to his regular position at the edge of the trees. His heart quickened pace when he saw General Barnard Bee and his two companies come rushing up to his left, guns blazing. The surprised Yankees turned to meet them, which took pressure off Evans's troops atop the hill.

The colonel's elation grew when he saw Colonel F.S. Bartow and his two companies coming on directly behind Bee. They quickly waded into the battle alongside Major Wheat and his troops. Evans's elation grew even more when he spotted a Confederate ammunition wagon riding the wake of Bartow's troops. The wagon broke through the lines, and the driver popped the reins, bawling hoarsely at the team, sending them charging up the hill toward Evans.

Colonel Evans's mind then went to the new column of Yankees that were coming by way of Sudley Springs. The whole Southern contingent on the hill was still outnumbered by the enemy, and a new arrival of Union troops would make it worse. Evans appreciated that General Beauregard would send more help if possible. But Evans needed more than that. He had to have more reinforcements, and he had to have them soon. Returning to his runner on the firing line, he sent him hurrying back to Beauregard with the message, "Without sufficiently more help, our men at Matthews' Hill are doomed."

Down on the hillside, the battle was fierce. Bee's and Bartow's men had marched six miles in the broiling heat to get to Matthews' Hill. Their canteens were dry. They were thirsty and a bit weary. There had been no time to rest, nor to stop and refill their canteens. The thrill of battle made them forget their thirst, and the adrenaline that flowed through their bodies soon erased the weariness.

It was nearly one o'clock when Colonel Evans saw the column of Yankees coming at a trot out of the northwest. He estimated there were about two thousand men in the column. There was only one thing to do. Evans would have to send his troops down the slopes. His brigade could do more good down amongst the other Rebels, especially now that they had plenty of ammunition.

Within minutes Evans had his infantry charging down the

broad hillside. Some filled in among the ranks of Rebels firing across sixty or seventy yards of slope at the enemy. Others joined the Louisiana Tigers as they met the Yankees head-on with bayonets and Bowie knives.

The battle at Matthews' Hill had become larger and more fierce than any of the other battles along Bull Run Creek, even the one at Stone Bridge.

The column of Yankees that forged into the battle were led by Brigadier General S.P. Heintzelman. Bartow's troops were on the northwest side of the hill and took the brunt of their fire. They drew back into a thicket, and from the wooded protection, rained hot lead on the Yankees. When the Yankees dug in and returned fire, it was a hurricane of bullets going both directions.

While Bartow's companies were battling at the thicket, Bee's troops pushed up a bald slope leading to Burnside's position. The sound of battle was deafening. As Bee's A Company crawled toward Burnside's position, some sixty yards across the open slope, Private Mike Durbin inched his way alongside Ozzie Zeller, a boyhood friend. They had to weave amongst lifeless bodies strewn on the ground.

Pausing, Durbin took aim at a Yankee lieutenant who stood erect—as if to blatantly defy Rebel bullets—barking orders at his men. Ozzie, head low, was ramrodding a ball into the barrel of his musket and watching Mike line his weapon on the enemy officer.

"Betcha can't hit him," Ozzie said above the roar of the battle.

"Just watch," retorted Mike. Holding his breath, he squeezed the trigger. The musket barked and the Yankee lieutenant went down.

"Hey, you got him!"

"You expected something else?" asked Durbin, who still had his head high enough so he could see if the Yankee lieutenant stayed down. Suddenly his attention was drawn to a furry black object moving up behind the Yankee lines. His breath caught in his chest and his heart froze.

"Oh, no!" he gasped.

"What's the matter?" Ozzie asked.

"It's my dog! He followed me here, and he's looking for me."

Bullets were dropping Yankees and chewing up sod where the big Newfoundland was heading. If Pal stayed on the course he was traveling, he would soon be in the open space between the firing lines. Durbin's mind was racing. Uncertain what to do, he could only gape at the scene.

"Keep your head down, Mike!" Ozzie shouted. "Don't let him see you! If he starts across that open field, he'll get killed."

"He'll come this way anyhow. He's got an uncanny sense about things. His big ol' heart must be telling him where I am."

Pal was almost to the front edge of the Union line and headed straight for Mike.

The relationship Mike Durbin had with his dog had been a special one since Pal was just a puppy. He loved the animal deeply. The awful knowledge that Pal was in imminent danger clouded Durbin's reason. Concern for his own safety was lost. From somewhere deep within him there erupted a sudden surge of panic, impelling him to his feet.

"No, Mike!" wailed Ozzie. "Get down! Get down!"

Mike was deaf to Ozzie's voice, to the din of battle, and to the angry bullets flying all around him. Screaming at the top of his voice, he waved the dog away. "Pal! Get outta here! Get outta here! Go home!"

The Newfoundland's sharp eyes focused on his master. Unable to hear Mike's words, Pal barked and darted for him.

"No! Go back! Go back!"

Pal was a black streak on the body-strewn slope. He had come to find his master, and now had found him. The dog was halfway across the open field when a bullet struck him in a back leg. Ejecting a yelp, he hit the ground, rolling. He came up on all fours and started toward his master, but the wounded leg gave way. Gallantly he attempted to go forward. A bullet seared across his broad back, and he fell to his belly.

Mike was running toward him, his eyes wild. His cap flew off just before he reached Pal and fell to his knees. "You big, wonderful pup!" he gasped, reaching underneath him. "You should've stayed home!"

Pal whined and licked his master's face as Mike stood up, cradling him in his arms. Just as Mike wheeled around to carry his beloved friend to safety, a bullet struck him in the lower back, severing his spine. Man and dog fell to the earth. A bullet hissed past Pal's head and plowed sod a few feet in front of them.

Mike Durbin felt as though his lower body had just dropped off. There was no feeling below his waist. Another bullet tore across his left shoulder, burning like fire. With his legs immobile and Pal seriously wounded, Mike knew he and his dog would not make it. Pal whined as Mike hugged him close and said, "Well, old buddy, I guess you and I are gonna go out togeth—"

Two slugs hit Mike simultaneously. When he went limp, Pal wriggled himself loose from Mike's arms and crawled painfully on top of him in an attempt to provide protection from the awful objects buzzing all around them. He was licking his master's face when another Yankee bullet struck him in the side, ripping through his valorous heart. Pal breathed out his last breath and slumped against the body of the man he loved so faithfully.

General Bee had seen the touching drama played out on the grassy slope by Private Durbin and his dog, but his attention was quickly drawn away to the desperate situation he and his men were in. General Bartow's troops had been driven away from Bee's right flank, and Colonel Evans's Demi-Brigade had been forced from his left, leaving both of Bee's flanks exposed to enemy fire. And the Yankees were coming on strong.

Another half hour of fighting found more Union forces moving in. Colonel Evans faced the cold hard fact that Matthews' Hill had at last become untenable. He signaled the retreat to both Bee and Bartow and began a hurried withdrawal back over Matthews' Hill southward toward Young's Branch. Bartow soon followed.

General Bee's troops began their withdrawal under heavy fire and suffered fearful casualties. As they hastened down the south slope of Matthews' Hill, they saw a new swarm of Yankees coming toward them. The fresh troops were Colonel Sherman's Second Wisconsin Battalion.

The Wisconsin Battalion had been resting north of Stone Bridge for over two hours. When General McDowell learned of the vehement Confederate resistance at Matthews' Hill, he ordered the Second Wisconsin that direction and told Sherman to leave the rest of his Third Brigade with subordinate officers.

Bee and his men met the oncoming horde with stiff resistance, carefully working their way to Young's Branch, where they would rejoin Evans and Bartow. Within twenty minutes, they had done so, but found that even with the combined units, they were grossly outnumbered.

Together, the Confederate troops fell back over Young's Branch. As the Federals closed in on them, panic set in. Many Rebel soldiers abandoned the line and raced across the Warrenton Turnpike and up the north slope of Henry House Hill. Bee, Bartow, and Evans found it impossible to stop them, in spite of shouting threats that they would face a firing squad for desertion.

Thankful that the majority of their men stayed to fight, the three Confederate officers regrouped and continued to offer courageous resistance. However, it soon became evident that the Rebels were about to be engulfed by an overwhelming tide of Yankees. General Bee called for them to withdraw toward Henry House Hill. They must find protection and keep fighting until General Beauregard sent reinforcements.

As the Rebels retreated southward, Sherman joined Burnside and Porter near the Matthews house on the newly won hill. Field commander McDowell and Third Division leader Heintzelman also joined them, feeling confidence rising. Together they watched as the Confederates fell back in full-scale retreat.

General McDowell ordered Sherman's fresh troops, along with Heintzelman, Burnside, and Porter's battle-weary units, to pursue the retreating Confederates. Sitting astride his horse, McDowell watched the troops march toward Henry House Hill. He smiled to himself. Despite heavy casualties, McDowell's army had the enemy on the run.

Things were going well. Once the Federals captured Stone Bridge and wiped out or captured the Rebels along Bull Run and those on Henry House Hill, they had to push only a little over three miles south to reach the tracks of the Manassas Gap Railroad. There they would be in position to cut off Confederate reinforcements coming in by rail from the Shenandoah Valley and could advance unimpeded to Manassas Junction. From there it would be a simple matter of putting his troops on railroad cars and running them down the tracks of the Orange and Alexandria Railroad to Richmond. Capture Richmond, bring the Rebels to their knees, and the Civil War would be over. The name of General Irvin McDowell would be on the lips of Northerners and Southerners alike.

The success that was at his fingertips flushed McDowell with excitement. Gouging his horse's flanks with his heels, he put it into a gallop and soon caught up with his marching men. Riding jubilantly along the blue-clad columns, he stood in his stirrups, waved his hat, and shouted, "Victory! Victory! The day is ours!"

EIGHTEEN

John Henry stood on the porch of his mother's house and watched the frightened Confederate soldiers run up the side of the hill. When they neared the house, they were panting hard for breath. There were about forty in all, and terror showed on their faces.

They paused to catch their breath. One of them looked at John and gasped, "Better…better get outta here, mister! The Yankees are beatin' us down. They…they'll kill you! If you…you got any family in the house…better take 'em…and run!"

The terrified Rebel soldier did not wait to see if his words took effect on the farmer. He took off, and the others soon followed. John watched them disappear over the back side of the hill, then hurried into the house.

Mounting the stairs three at a time, John hastened down the hall and entered his mother's bedroom. His wife, Louise, and sister, Mary Sue, sat beside the bed. Judith Henry lay with just a sheet over her as she lifted her dull, sunken eyes to her son and said weakly, "John, the Yankees are comin', aren't they?"

"Yes, Mama," he replied, moving to the open window and parting the sheer curtains. "Those Rebels who just ran through the yard said they're coming."

"They wouldn't harm us, would they?"

"I can't say, Mama. One of the Rebels seemed to think so."

Fear was mirrored in Mary Sue's eyes. Looking at her brother's back, she asked with a tremor in her voice, "Why would Yankee soldiers want to hurt us? We're no threat to them."

"Maybe just because we're Southerners," Louise said, rising from her chair and moving beside her husband.

Mary Sue was holding her invalid mother's hand. "What should we do, Johnny?"

Louise followed John's gaze and saw the Negro neighbors near the bottom of the hill. James and Hattie Robinson had their four children in the family wagon and were pulling out of the yard. "I wish we could do what the Robinsons are doing," she said.

"I wonder where they'll go," John said, releasing the curtains to look at his mother and sister. "Seems to me the Yankees have taken over the whole valley. I hope they head south, at least."

The elderly woman looked at the others and said, "If there's really a threat of danger, why don't you youngins jump in the wagon and go? I'll be all right. Them Yankees wouldn't harm a crippled old woman."

Louise returned to the bed, patted her mother-in-law's wrinkled hand, and said softly, "Mama, John and Mary Sue and I wouldn't think of leaving you. We'll just stay here and pray to the Lord that the Yankees won't bother us."

"That's right, Mama," said John, turning back to the window. "We'll just stay here and let God watch over us. If it's time for us to leave this world, it's in His hands."

The younger women comforted aged Judith Henry as John studied the landscape to the north. After a few moments, he said, "Looks like we're gonna have company pretty soon."

"Yankees already?" asked Louise, rushing to the window.

"No, but there are thousands of Confederate soldiers coming this way. And the way they're hoofing it, I'd say the Yankees aren't far behind. Could be we're going to see what a battle looks like real close up."

Colonel Erasmus D. Keyes's First Brigade was still battling it out with Confederates along the Warrenton Turnpike some two miles north of Stone Bridge. The Yankees had lost ground, however, and had been forced to pull back some five hundred yards from their original position close to the road.

When General Irvin McDowell pulled William T. Sherman and the Second Wisconsin Battalion from the Turnpike battle to help reinforce the troops at Matthews' Hill, the Confederates took advantage of it and mounted a charge. There was a fierce hand-to-hand fight that lasted until General McDowell realized his mistake and sent four companies of cavalry under Major I.N. Palmer to the rescue. At the arrival of the cavalry, the Confederates had fallen back to their ditches and gullies near the road, and commenced musket fire and cannonade.

Captain Buck Brownell and his company of Zouaves were in a four-feet-deep ditch that ran across the field in almost a straight line for over two hundred yards. Rebel cannons had taken their toll on the Union cavalry horses, and Major Palmer finally had ordered his men to dismount and fight from the gullies and ditches. Some four hundred cavalrymen were strung out in the front-line ditch intermingled with Brownell and his Zouaves.

The afternoon's heat settled over the battlefield and sucked dry the men in the ditches and gullies. Trying to ignore his thirst, his canteen empty, Buck blasted away at the enemy and longed for beautiful Jenny. "Dear God," he prayed, "please let me live through this war and let us be husband and wife. She's all that matters, Lord, and—"

Buck's heartfelt prayer was cut off as he saw one of his Zouaves fall a few feet down the line. Shouting toward the men next to the fallen soldier, he said, "Heflin! Domire! Check on Spalding. See where he's hit."

"He isn't hit, Captain," Gifford Domire called back. "He

passed out from the heat…and the lack of water. We've got some other men up the line here who've passed out. If we don't get some water, it's gonna get worse!"

Buck knew there was a small branch off of Bull Run that trickled across the field some three hundred yards behind the line. Calling above the roar to Domire, he said, "Pass the word along! Tell the men to send their canteens this way. I'll take as many as I can carry and fill them."

"I'll go, Captain," Domire replied. "The men need you here."

"I'll help him, Captain!" volunteered Lyle Heflin. "That way, we can fill twice as many canteens."

Buck granted permission for both men to go. The morale of the men in the long ditch seemed to pick up with the promise of water. They gladly passed their canteens down the line. When Domire and Heflin had their arms full, they told Brownell they would do the same for the men up the line the other direction when they got back. Buck hoped the other Yankees would see what Domire and Heflin were doing and send men from their own ditches for water.

Some 150 yards from the front line of battle, Colonel Keyes and Major Palmer sat on their horses in the shade of a stand of trees and studied the fierce conflict before them. As they discussed what to do if the Confederates brought in more reinforcements, they spotted the two Zouaves bent low and zigzagging their way across the battlefield in their direction, carrying the empty canteens. As they drew near, Palmer dismounted and walked out to meet them. Keyes followed, hurrying along at Palmer's heels. Palmer was by far the younger of the two.

"Is everyone up there out of water?" queried Palmer.

"Can't speak for those in other lines, sir," replied Corporal Domire, "but they sure are in ours. We've got men passing out from the heat. We're about to rectify that."

Both officers commended the two for what they were doing and allowed them to proceed. From the shade of the trees, they watched them reach the branch, fill the canteens, and head back. Weighted down with their load, they hurried to deliver the water to their comrades.

Suddenly, one of them went down. The other frantically tried to help him, but was hit, too. Now both men were on the ground, and neither was moving.

Palmer sucked in his breath as if a shaft of pain had hit his vitals. "Oh, God bless 'em! Those two boys are hit!" Wheeling about, Palmer ran to his horse and leaped into the saddle.

"Wait a minute, Major!" gasped Keyes. "Where are you going?"

"I'm going after those canteens—to distribute them to our men."

"No you're not! It's too dangerous! Let some of the men out there take care of it."

"They're too busy, Colonel. Now, please excuse me."

"Major!" rasped Keyes. "Get down off that horse! That's an *order!*"

Palmer looked at the older man and said, "Don't do this to me, Colonel. My men need water and so do yours. They can't keep fighting in this heat without water. I must take it to them…even if you maintain that order."

Keyes had been in the military since he was eighteen years old. He knew a real soldier when he saw one. Wiping a palm across his face, he sighed, "I'm probably sending you to your death, Major, but I withdraw the order. Go do what you must."

Palmer lashed his horse with the reins and put it into an immediate gallop. They soon reached the rear lines and came into musket range. Palmer's horse managed to keep a steady canter as it threaded among the corpses on the battlefield. It skidded to a halt when Palmer jerked rein and vaulted from the saddle, and stood there, ears laid back and snorting, as bullets tore sod all around and cannonballs exploded close by.

The major found that both men were dead, and water was

bubbling out of three canteens that had been punctured with bullets. He wrapped the leather straps of the two dozen or more undamaged canteens around his neck, slung them over his arms and shoulders, and with effort, mounted his horse. Bending low over the animal's back, he prodded it forward toward the front line, then veered off to the right and headed for the end of the line. When he reached it, he rode along the ditch, dropping a canteen every few yards and shouting, "Drinks are on the house, boys!"

A Zouave fighting beside Captain Brownell elbowed him and pointed up the line at Palmer. "What's the major doing delivering water?" Buck gasped.

"Something must've happened to Domire and Heflin, sir."

Palmer was within a hundred feet of Buck when a cannon shell struck a few feet to his left. Shrapnel tore into the horse, and it dropped hard on its side, pinning Major Palmer's left leg. Another shell blew several men close by into eternity. Shrapnel ripped into the dead horse, which kept it from hitting the major.

Shouting for his men to keep firing, Buck leaped from the ditch and, bending low, darted along the line toward the trapped major. Buck reached the spot and slid on the grass to a prostrate position. Major Palmer had a couple of small bloody spots on his face, but otherwise was untouched. He looked at the Zouave officer levelly and said, "Captain, you have no business out here. Get back in that ditch!"

"I have as much business out here as you did, sir. Now, let's get you out from under your horse."

"It's too dangerous. The Rebel artillery has found the range. Another shell could hit right on this spot any second. I'm ordering you to get back in that ditch!"

"Sorry, sir, but all this noise has my ears ringing. I can't hear what you're saying. Just be ready to inch your way out when I heave on this horse."

Shells exploded on every side as Buck strained to free Major Palmer. Some twenty minutes of effort saw the major free and clear of his horse and in the ditch with Buck.

Water was distributed along the line, and Union soldiers were refreshed. While the battle continued, Major Palmer took a drink for himself, then handed the canteen to the Zouave officer who had insisted that the major drink first. While Buck was drinking, a cannonball whistled down and struck Palmer's horse.

The major shook his head, wiped sweat, and said, "Captain, I owe you my life. What's your name?"

"It really doesn't matter, sir. What's important is that our cavalry still has its leader."

"I appreciate that," smiled Palmer, "but I want to know your name."

Before Buck could speak, the Zouave next to him spoke up. "It's Brownell, Major Palmer. Captain Buck Brownell. Far as I'm concerned, it should be General Brownell."

Palmer smiled again. "I don't think I can pull that one off, soldier, but if I have anything to say about it, he'll soon be Major Brownell!"

General Bee and Colonels Bartow and Evans led their troops up the north slope of Henry House Hill with the Federals in pursuit. They were almost to the crest where the house stood when beyond the house, they saw a Confederate flag waving in the breeze. The flag could barely be seen above the top of the hill, but it was moving toward them.

Evans pointed to it and said, "That flag can only mean one thing. Reinforcements are coming!"

The Rebel soldiers who followed the officers ejected a wild whoop. Coming over the hill were five regiments of the First Brigade of the Army of the Shenandoah, led by Brigadier General Thomas J. Jackson. There was elation at the welcome sight, and the gallant men who had fought so hard on Matthews' Hill were ready to turn around and meet the oncoming Union troops head-on.

Leaving Bartow and Evans with the troops, Bee put his horse

to a gallop and raced to meet Jackson. As he drew up, he smiled, raised a hand in greeting, and said, "General Jackson! Am I ever glad to see you!"

Smiling in return, Jackson said, "General Beauregard thought you just might be." Looking past Bee and the Confederate soldiers, he focused on the massive force of Federals crossing Young's Branch in the distance. "We'd best get fortified. We're still outnumbered, and those blue-bellies will be here in twenty minutes."

While the Confederates joined forces and prepared to meet the oncoming enemy with artillery and infantry, Jackson, Bee, Bartow, and Evans held a quick strategy meeting.

They had not noticed the faces in the windows of the Henry house, and were surprised when they saw a man emerge from the back door and head toward them. Jackson left the others to meet him. "Good afternoon, sir. I'm Brigadier General Thomas Jackson. Are you Mr. Henry?"

"Probably not the one you have in mind, General. My father is dead. My mother still lives here. I'm taking care of the place, along with my wife and sister. I'm John Henry."

As the two men shook hands, Jackson asked, "The women are in the house now?"

"Yes, sir."

"That's not good. There's going to be some heavy fighting here real soon." Swinging his gaze toward the barn, he said, "I see you have horses and a wagon. Best thing for you to do is harness up the team as fast as you can, load the women in the wagon, and hightail it out of here."

John rubbed the back of his neck and replied, "Can't do that, General. My mother's an invalid. She can't be moved."

"Then get inside and keep the women away from the window."

"Do you think the Yankees will want to take the house, sir?"

"I don't know. But we're going to do our best to see to it that they don't even get near the house. Now, you get back inside." Jackson wheeled and headed back toward the other officers.

He had taken only a few steps when John called after him, "General Jackson…!"

Pausing, the stalwart Confederate officer made a half-turn. "Yes?"

"God bless you, sir."

Jackson smiled. "He does, Mr. Henry. In spite of all my shortcomings, He does."

John returned the smile and turned toward the house.

The Confederates made ready quickly, positioning howitzers on both sides of Henry house, aiming their deadly bores down the gentle green slope. Infantrymen flattened out on the crest, cocking the hammers of their muskets and waiting for the Union forces. When the Yankees drew within cannon range, the big Rebel guns cut loose. Within a half-minute, Union cannons were answering back while their footmen came on like a swarm of hornets.

On the hills overlooking the smoke-filled battlefield, the civilian spectators ate their picnic lunches and drank warm lemonade, tea, and water in the oppressive heat. Though it was difficult for them to tell just how the battle was going, they endured the discomfort because they were certain of a Union victory and wanted to be on hand to observe it.

Governess Patricia Winters sat on the ground in the shade of Rose Greenhow's surrey and chatted with Jenny Jordan. Both Jenny and Patricia had given up the idea of trying to spot the men they loved. The distance was too great, and there were so many men in the battle.

When Tad and Willie had finished their lunches—having taken them to the big rock to eat, along with some other boys—Tad approached his governess and asked, "Miss Patricia, could me and Willie go a little farther down the hill? There are some trees and bushes down there a little ways. We could see the battle better down there. Could we, please?"

Patricia started to correct Tad's grammar but decided to let it go. Rising to her feet, she said, "Show me what trees and bushes you're talking about. I don't want you getting much closer to the battle."

Tad took her hand, looked up with a winsome smile, and said, "C'mon."

Five minutes later, Patricia returned, sighed, and sat down once again beside Jenny.

Jenny dabbed at the perspiration on her face with a hanky and asked, "So did Mr. Tad Lincoln persuade you to let them go farther down the hill?"

"Mm-hmm," smiled Patricia. "It's still a long way from the bottom, and plenty of distance from the battle. They'll be all right there."

Letting her gaze drift back to the scene of the conflict in the valley below, Jenny bit down hard on her lower lip. Somewhere amid the fire and smoke was Captain Buck Brownell. Again, she breathed a prayer for his safety.

General McDowell was positioned at the Robinson house, where he observed his troops slowly making their way up the gentle slope toward Henry house where the Confederates had dug in to make their stand. He was short of artillery and had sent for two batteries under the command of Captains James B. Ricketts and Charles Griffin, who were waiting in reserve at Centreville. As he paced back and forth on the safe side of the Robinson house, he nervously looked up the Warrenton Turnpike to catch sight of them.

There was still heavy fighting at Stone Bridge and beyond the bridge along the Turnpike. McDowell hoped the captains would make a wide circle around the two hot spots so as to arrive intact at Robinson house. From the looks of things, he was going to need their cannons to insure the capture of Henry House Hill.

Along the Turnpike between Centreville and Stone Bridge, Colonel Duryee's Zouaves and Major Palmer's cavalrymen were still battling it out with General Beauregard's Rebel forces. Bodies—in blue and gray—lay scattered over the fields, in the ditches, and even on the Turnpike.

Situated in an abandoned farm house high on a hill a mile east of Henry House Hill, and about a mile-and-a-half south of Stone Bridge, Generals Beauregard and Johnston were in conference. Beauregard had anticipated that McDowell would send troops from Centreville due south to Mitchell's Ford and had placed brigades there to meet them. As the fighting centered farther north and west, Beauregard decided to pull these two brigades to the Turnpike. Johnston agreed, and the two brigades were now on their way.

To fortify the Confederate position on Henry House Hill, Beauregard sent three companies from Captain William Smith's Forty-ninth Virginia and Colonel Jeb Stuart's First Virginia Cavalry. The Confederates still faced a foe that greatly outnumbered them, and Beauregard knew it. Together, he and Johnston made further plans to shift troops as fast as possible to Henry House Hill.

NINETEEN

At the Turnpike where Colonel Duryee's Zouaves and Major Palmer's cavalrymen fought hard against the Confederates, Captain Brownell was bent low in the ditch, doing what he could to help a wounded Zouave captain. Shells were exploding all around, sending their death-dealing shrapnel in every direction. Suddenly Buck looked up to see Colonel Duryee roll into the ditch a few feet away, landing on a dead Zouave private.

Duryee crawled toward Buck. He had lost his hat, and his face was smeared and caked with grimy sweat. The colonel looked at the fallen captain, then eyed Buck and asked, "How bad is it?"

"He's dead, sir. Just breathed his last."

Duryee shook his head. "Captain, there are three cannons out there that we've got to dispose of. They're cutting us to pieces. I know about your expertise in handling such problems. Do you think you can take a few men and wipe out those cannon crews?"

"It won't be easy, sir, but I believe we can handle it."

"Good! The quicker, the better."

In less than five minutes, Brownell had six Zouaves crawling on their bellies behind him toward the enemy howitzers. Colonel Duryee peered over the edge of the ditch and watched with keen interest. Beside him now were Zouave captains Dane Saltzer and Howard Beery. Both had given word to their companies to give as much fire cover to Brownell and his small group as possible.

The din of the battle remained steady as Brownell and his men slowly made their way to the first howitzer. The crew was cut down as Union guns barked from a nearby cluster of bushes. Within twenty minutes, all three howitzer crews were dead, and the Rebels were scurrying about, trying to find others who could man them. Buck and his men were racing back to their ditch. Just as they arrived and were being congratulated for a job well done, Zouave lieutenant Dean Frizzell came running across the field and dived into the ditch where Duryee and Brownell were crouched.

"Colonel!" Frizzell gasped. "They're coming up behind us!"

Duryee jerked around and peered over the edge of the ditch toward the southeast. Bonham's and Early's brigades were coming in a huge wave of gray. The threat behind was greater than the one at the Turnpike. By this time, Major Palmer found his way to where Colonel Duryee and his three captains were assembled in the ditch.

Quickly the colonel and the major turned two-thirds of their men and cannons toward the oncoming horde. Within minutes, the new battle was in violent progress.

The Yankees fought back furiously, but General Beauregard's tactical move had a devastating effect. Zouaves and cavalrymen were dropping along the lines, filling the ditches with corpses and wounded men. Buck saw Captains Saltzer and Beery die within two minutes of each other. Lieutenant Frizzell took orders from Colonel Duryee and began crawling back to his men. Before he reached them, Rebel bullets took his life.

Colonel Duryee shouldered a musket next to Brownell and fired. He rolled onto his back to reload and shouted at Buck, "Captain, where'd all those Rebs come from?"

Buck fired his musket, dropped down, flipped onto his back, and began reloading. "Looks like the Frenchman had them hidden somewhere, sir," he replied.

"I don't understand it," said the colonel, packing his powder and ball tight. "You'd think the Rebels knew we were coming and when."

"I think they did, sir. They were just too well prepared."

"Spies?" suggested Duryee, rolling back onto his belly, ready for the next shot.

"What else?"

"Guess that's what it had to be," said the colonel, raising up to sight and fire.

Suddenly a bullet slammed the colonel, making him howl. He fell, cursing the Rebels.

Buck leaned over him and asked, "Where you hit, sir?"

"Right shoulder," replied Duryee through clenched teeth. "I…I think the slug went on through."

Buck scrutinized the wound and found that the slug had exited the back side. "You're right, Colonel. Let me see what I can do to stop the blood flow."

Buck ripped up the shirt of a dead Zouave in the ditch and used it as a compress and bandage on the wound.

In evident pain, the colonel looked up at Buck and said, "Captain Brownell, you're the only Zouave officer left in this whole line. You'll have to take charge."

"Yes, sir," nodded Buck. "You just stay right here and hold on, Colonel. I'll regroup the men and lead a counter charge."

"There's not an officer in this entire outfit more qualified to lead it, son. It's in your hands. Go to it!"

General Thomas Jackson studied the oncoming Federal troops from the crest of Henry House Hill. He saw the Ricketts and Griffin batteries come wheeling their cannons and driving their ammunition wagons across Young's Branch. He knew that General McDowell was sending the fresh artillery to try to blow him and his army off the hill.

Sending a runner to Beauregard, Jackson described the artillery that was on the way. He asked for more artillery to offset it. The messenger returned, telling Jackson that the general was sending in a South Carolina militia unit known as the Palmetto Guard. They had ten howitzers and were good with them.

Jackson smiled. The Palmetto Guard was indeed good. One of their cannoneers was the "Father of Secession," Edmund Ruffin. Ruffin had been the man to fire the first shot at Fort Sumter.

The units of General Bee, Colonel Bartow, and Colonel Evans were spread out over the crest of Henry House Hill on both sides of General Jackson and his brigade. While cannons roared and muskets barked, Jackson stood tall and erect, shouting commands. Periodically, he stole a glance over his shoulder to see if the Palmetto Guard was coming up the backside of the hill.

A half hour had passed since the runner had brought the encouraging message, and in his mind, Jackson was trying to hurry them. The Yankees were making progress up the hill in spite of all the Rebels were throwing at them. The two new Union artillery batteries were getting closer.

Bee's brigade was being torn apart along the hill's southwest side. McDowell's artillery was pounding them hard. Soon Bee ran up the side of the hill and approached Jackson, saying breathlessly, "General Jackson, they're giving my unit a terrible pounding! If they wipe us out, they'll charge right over our bodies and wipe out every unit on the hill!"

"We've got artillery reinforcements on the way," replied Jackson. "General Beauregard is sending the Palmetto Guard up here. I'm expecting them just any time. When they get here, I'll have them concentrate on the Yankee guns that are blasting you. That'll take the heat off."

"I appreciate that, General," said Bee. He paused a moment, then added, "Seems to me both sides will be running out of powder pretty soon."

"No doubt," nodded Jackson, keeping his gaze on the lusty

battle below. "When that happens, we'll give them the bayonet!"

General Bee hurried back down the hill to give his men the good news that the Palmetto Guard was on its way. Using a rifle himself, he shouted words of encouragement to his men.

The battle was fierce. At one point, General Bee looked up to see the rough and rugged Jackson repositioning some of his cannons to give Bee and his men relief from the artillery onslaught. The Palmetto Guard had not yet arrived, and Jackson was taking alternative action.

"God bless him!" shouted Bee, pointing up the hill for his men to see what was happening. General Jackson stood like a statue, barking orders, while enemy fire whistled all around him. His concern for Bee's unit made him oblivious to his own danger.

Bee waved his hat and shouted to his men, "There's Jackson, standing like a stone wall. Rally behind him, men! Rally behind him!"

One of Bee's men shouted, "That's what he is, General Bee. He's a stone wall—Stonewall Jackson!"

A Yankee shell whistled down shrilly and exploded, ripping General Bee's body with deadly shrapnel. When the smoke had cleared, the gallant general lay dead.

The day wore on and the tumultuous conflict continued. On Henry House Hill, in the woods, on the open fields, at Stone Bridge, and along the banks of Bull Run Creek was the constant thunderous roaring of the big guns, the sharp sound of the rifled cannons, the crack of Minie rifles and muskets, and the fiery burst of shells.

At the old farmhouse, Generals Beauregard and Johnston waited eagerly for the arrival of the eight-hundred-man Palmetto Guard under the command of Colonel Bertrand Waverly. Beauregard had them bivouacked some five miles south of Manassas Junction in reserve. They would be fresh and ready to fight.

Beauregard had called in two other units that had been held in reserve along Aquia Creek on the lower Potomac: a brigade of three hundred men led by Brigadier General Theophilus H. Holmes and the six-hundred-man Hampton Legion, commanded by Colonel Wade Hampton. The colonel was a dynamic, wealthy South Carolina plantation owner and politician, and had put together, fed, clothed, and armed the legion at his own expense. They had their own infantry, artillery, and cavalry.

At 3:15, the Palmetto Guard arrived and was sent immediately to Henry House Hill to bolster the troops there. It was just past 3:30 when Holmes and Hampton brought their units in from the east. Beauregard and Johnston mounted their horses and rode like the wind to greet the two units. Beauregard sent Johnston back to the old farmhouse to keep an eye on the rest of the conflict, and personally led Holmes and Hampton to Henry House Hill. General "Stonewall" Jackson was very happy to see the two fresh units, and immediately spread them out on the crest of the hill to counter the new strength added to the enemy lines by the arrival of the Ricketts and Griffin batteries.

The Confederate lines stabilized with the additional troops and guns. General Beauregard had salvaged a defense out of what had seemed to be certain disaster just an hour before. Now fully in command of the situation, he rode his horse along the lines on Henry House Hill, urging his men to fight on.

Inside the Henry house, John and the two younger women moved from window to window on the lower floor, watching General Beauregard. Above the roar of the battle, they could hear him shouting to the men, telling them that the fight was turning toward their favor and that they must contend harder than ever to see it through to victory.

John Henry embraced Louise joyfully, saying, "Honey, it sounds to me like the South is going to win this thing!" Tears filmed Louise's eyes.

Mary Sue hugged them both, then exclaimed, "Let's go upstairs and tell Mama!"

While John, his wife, and sister were heading for the stairs, disaster was brewing at the bottom of the hill. Captain James Ricketts and his artillery battery had taken a position some three hundred yards from the Confederate line at the top of the hill. While Ricketts was getting his guns ready for action, the Confederate reinforcements located near the house began a rain of lead on the battery.

Ricketts saw his men and horses falling all around him. He peered through the dust and smoke and concluded that the shots were coming from inside the Henry house. He commanded his gunners to turn their cannons on the house.

John, Louise, and Mary Sue were halfway up the stairs when they heard a shell hit on the second floor. They halted, gripping the banister. Another shell tore through the west wall and exploded in the kitchen on the bottom floor. The women wailed in terror. John hastily ushered them to the cellar, telling them to stay put while he ran to check on his mother. Clinging to each other while sitting on the cellar floor, they both sobbed and begged John to be careful.

Ricketts had stopped shelling the house by the time John was climbing over rubble in an effort to enter his mother's bedroom. There were two huge holes in the wall, and the room was a shambles. Mrs. Judith Henry lay on the mattress of her collapsed bed. Shrapnel had torn into her body. One large fragment had torn off her left foot.

To John's amazement, his mother was still breathing. He made a hasty tourniquet for her ankle, then hoisted her frail body into his arms, carried her to Mary Sue's bedroom, and laid her on the bed. He was about to call his wife and sister for help when the elderly woman stopped breathing. Weeping, John pressed his ear to his mother's breast to listen for a heartbeat. The roar of the conflict outside was too great.

When he couldn't find a pulse with his fingertips, John knew his mother was dead. Something seemed to explode inside him. Leaving his mother's lifeless form on the bed, he charged down the stairs and through the front door. Standing on the porch, he shook his fists at the Yankee forces and wailed, "You killed my mother! You foul beasts! You killed my poor, innocent mother!"

By four o'clock, the tide in the Bull Run battle began to swiftly go against the North. General Stonewall Jackson unleashed the newly arrived artillery on the batteries of Ricketts and Griffin, and soon wiped them out. Then the big guns were turned on the other Yankee units all over the hillside. Clouds of dust, mingled with puffs of gun smoke, floated on the hot breeze over the valley. The acrid smell of burnt gunpowder stung the eyes and nostrils of Yankees and Rebels alike. Lifeless bodies were everywhere, and among them were wounded and bleeding men.

When General McDowell saw the tide turning against him at Henry House Hill, he sent for the Zouaves, who had beaten back the Rebel troops along the Warrenton Turnpike. While Colonel Duryee lay wounded in a ditch, Buck Brownell led the Zouaves to Henry House Hill. At the same time, McDowell had also dispatched what was left of a U.S. Marine battalion to the hill.

The Zouaves charged in, blasting away, but Buck could tell it was useless. Too many men in blue were dead. Multitudes of others had collapsed from heat exhaustion and dehydration. Many were dead of sunstroke.

The feisty Rebels had known that McDowell's forces were coming; they had been ready for them. In spite of the heat and other adverse elements, General Beauregard's troops were showing real grit and determination.

The Union troops fought doggedly, but they were being whipped. From time to time, Buck saw General McDowell riding to and fro along the fighting front, rallying his men. It was all academic. All over the valley, Federal regiments were becoming a jumble of fragmented, confused soldiers. Whatever semblance of organization that remained was on the verge of disintegrating.

At 4:45, McDowell committed the last fresh reserves to the battle: three regiments from Maine and one from Vermont, commanded by Colonel Oliver Howard. Howard's troops were not truly fresh, though they had yet to see combat. They had made the long march from Centreville over sun-burned hills and through waterless, heat-packed valleys with heavy field packs and empty canteens. They were at the point of exhaustion.

Though they gave it their best effort to obey McDowell's order to deploy at a run, at least a third collapsed before they reached the firing lines. When the other two-thirds reached the point of battle, they were unnerved to see bloodied Union soldiers throwing down their muskets and fleeing in terror.

Howard's first line was badly mauled by blasts from atop Henry House Hill. With dead men lying all around him—many from other units—Colonel Howard shouted orders for his second line to move up. But when he turned to observe them, they were drawing back, eyes bulging with horror. Howard had no alternative but to order all his men to retreat. They broke and fled, dashing for Young's Branch. When they reached the shallow stream, they threw themselves flat and slaked their thirst. On their feet again, they ran to the Turnpike and headed northeast, noticing that their comrades had forsaken the battle at Stone Bridge and were sprinting toward Washington.

While thousands of Union soldiers continued to fight at Henry House Hill, still other thousands were heading for the hills where the civilians had been watching the battle. Cavalrymen goaded their horses into a gallop. Ammunition wagons threw up dust as their drivers snapped the reins and aimed them toward the capital city.

General McDowell and his officers were alarmed at the signs of panic. They rode back and forth, desperately trying to keep any more men from fleeing. When men did make a break for it, the Union officers did their best to re-form the frightened, scattering soldiers.

Union horsemen were the first to reach the hills to the north and east. Eyes wild, they shouted at the hundreds of civilian spectators to run. Dozens of Union wagons bounded over the fields toward the hills at top speed. More cavalrymen were coming in waves on galloping steeds toward the alarmed and frightened Washingtonians. Stunned at the sudden unexpected turn of events and shocked to see their men retreating like scared rabbits, the civilians hastened to load their families in the horse-drawn vehicles and escape the Rebels. From what the soldiers were saying, Beauregard's troops were coming, and would shoot everybody.

Children had been allowed to play together in small groups. Parents and guardians were scurrying about, trying to collect them so they could get away.

As Rose Greenhow and her girls were piling in the surrey behind the hired driver, Rose turned to Jenny and whispered, "Looks like our little espionage effort has paid off. However, I hope your Captain is all right."

"Yes," nodded Jenny, "so do I."

Patricia Winters was chatting with a couple she had known in Illinois when the first wave of horsemen rode up, yelling for everybody to get off the hill. Patricia began looking for Tad, who had been playing near a clump of bushes some distance down the slope. Earlier, Willie had abandoned his little brother and was playing "war" nearby with several boys. Willie came running up out of breath, and cried, "Miss Patricia! We gotta get Tad!"

Expecting that the youngest Lincoln son would now be nearly to the crest of the hill, the governess ran that direction. Willie stayed beside her. When Patricia reached the crest and could not see Tad anywhere, she gasped, "Willie, I don't see him, do you?"

"Yes, ma'am," replied the boy, pointing. "Tad wanted to get closer to the battle, so he went down to those trees. See him? He's running this way."

The governess stared in disbelief. Tad had been in the shade of the trees a moment before, but now she could see him running up the hill for all he was worth. He was more than a hundred yards away, and a swarm of bounding wagons and galloping horses was moving up behind him at a distance of no more than five hundred yards.

Patricia stood rooted to the spot, her heart hammering. Tad was in the open now, and there was no way he could outrun the charging wheels and hooves.

Suddenly Jenny was beside Patricia, whose terror had her unable to move. Following the eyes of the governess and Willie, Jenny spied Tad and quickly understood his predicament. Before anyone could speak, Jenny had her skirt hoisted calf-high and was bolting down the slope toward the frightened boy.

As Patricia stood transfixed, her eyes glued on the scene below, she felt a hand grip her shoulder. Turning, she recognized Senator Charles Sumner. The senator also had a hand on Willie's shoulder.

"I couldn't help but notice," said Sumner levelly. "Isn't that Colonel Jordan's daughter?"

"Yes," stammered Patricia. "I...I don't know why Tad went all the way down there without asking my permission."

"They'll both be trampled to death. Come on. Let's get in the safety of these trees."

The senator ushered Patricia and Willie to a stand of trees a few yards away, where the three of them watched the scene below with grim fascination. In the safety of their surreys, buggies, and carriages, many others observed, also.

While Jenny plunged down the hill, she noticed a deep cleft in the ground just ahead of Tad. If the two of them could drop down in the cleft, the hooves and wheels might possibly pass over them. But could they make it? The deathly swarm was closing in fast.

Tad's face was sheet-white as he ran up the slope, looking back every few seconds to check the progress of the oncoming horde. Unaware of the cleft ahead of him, he set his eyes on Jenny, raising his arms and reaching for her.

When Tad circled around the cleft, Jenny shouted, "Tad! Jump in the hole! Jump in the hole!"

But the roar was too loud; he couldn't hear her. Certain death was on his heels. Running like a frightened fox before a pack of vicious hounds, he wailed in terror, reaching…reaching…

The front line of horses and wagons was no more than fifty yards behind the boy. Jenny, with sharp, cold needles prickling her face and neck, was closing in. Only a few more steps…a few more steps…

When Jenny and Tad came together, the impact knocked them both off their feet. Gasping for breath, Jenny snatched the president's son in her arms and dashed to the cleft. Diving in, she covered Tad's body with her own. It sounded like the whole earth was caving in on them as the pounding hooves and spinning wheels passed over harmlessly.

It seemed like an eternity for the galloping escapees to pass, but finally they were gone. Covered with dirt, her hair disheveled, Jenny raised up and looked down at the terrified boy. "You all right, Tad?"

Trembling, he nodded. "Yes, ma'am."

Glancing to the fields below, Jenny saw some stragglers, but the initial swarm was gone. Standing, she helped the boy to his feet. "Come on, Tad. Let's get out of here."

They had barely begun to climb the gentle slope when they saw a cluster of people hurrying toward them from the crest. Senator Sumner was in the lead. Directly behind him were Willie and a weeping Patricia Winters.

TWENTY

By 5:30 dark clouds were moving across the sky from the west, adding to the gloom that General Irvin McDowell felt in his soul. The Confederates, without a doubt, had been fed information that put them on the alert and enabled them to prepare for this morning's attack. Now they were hammering the Union troops unmercifully and beating them back.

McDowell saw some of his men fall under heavy fire, while others were fleeing across the fields, discarding their gear as they went. Those who were running away seemed to infect those they came in contact with. There was nothing to do but command a retreat and get his army out of the valley before they were annihilated. The general signaled his officers to lead their men in retreat and head for Washington.

At the time the retreat was sounded, Buck Brownell and some seventy-five of his Zouaves had a handful of Rebels cornered in the woods at the eastern base of Henry House Hill. Knowing he had to obey the retreat order, Buck led his men to rush the Rebels, guns blazing. They would get in one last good punch before heading north.

Though the Rebels in the woods were outnumbered, they fought back gallantly as the Zouaves closed in. However, when they saw their comrades falling all around them, they realized it was surrender or die. A Rebel sergeant began waving his white handkerchief and shouting at the Zouaves to stop firing. When the guns went silent, thirteen Rebels were still alive in the woods. Captain Brownell took them captive and herded them at gunpoint as he and his men began their retreat.

All over the valley, the Union retreat became a rout, then degenerated into a full-scale panic. Yankees, crazed with fear, stampeded up the Warrenton Turnpike toward Centreville. Some who stumbled and fell from exhaustion were picked up and dragged by their fellow soldiers. The best McDowell could do was attempt to cover the hasty withdrawal against enemy pursuit. He sent a battalion of hard-bitten Regular Army infantry to protect the vulnerable rear ranks of the fleeing Yankees.

General Pierre G.T. Beauregard sent one unit after another in pursuit of the enemy. Hundreds of Yankees were collapsing. Having thrown down their guns, they were quickly taken captive by the shouting, whooping Rebels.

While several of his units were chasing Union troops across Young's Branch, General Beauregard heard a rumor that there were Yankee units heading southeastward for Union Mills. Fearing they might regroup and try another attack, he sent the bulk of his troops toward Union Mills. By the time they returned to tell him it was a false alarm, the Union troops heading north were out of sight. Beauregard looked at his weary, bedraggled men and decided they were too exhausted to chase the Yankees. He officially called off the pursuit shortly after seven o'clock. Heavy clouds were now filling the sky, and daylight was beginning to fade.

Beauregard collected his troops on the banks of Bull Run just south of Stone Bridge to congratulate them on their hard-fought victory and to check on the wounded. They would bury the dead tomorrow.

As the Rebels were patting each other on the back and joyfully kidding General Jackson about his new nickname, a soldier rushed up to Beauregard and said, "Sir, I don't know where it came from, but there's a Union wagon sneakin' across the bridge."

Beauregard looked toward the bridge, squinting against the gathering gloom. "Well, look at that, will you? There's a straggling Yankee ammunition wagon. We can't let that get away."

The general had noticed only moments earlier that a howitzer stood close by. Running his gaze over the multitude of dirty faces, he asked, "Who's cannon is this?"

Colonel Bertrand Waverly of the Palmetto Guard moved forward and said, "It's ours, sir. And it's loaded."

Looking back at the Union wagon, moving slowly across the bridge, Beauregard said, "Looks like they're overloaded, Colonel. Blast the stinking blue-bellies."

Waverly motioned to a wrinkle-faced man in Palmetto uniform. As the old man responded, threading his way amongst the Rebel soldiers, Waverly turned back to Beauregard and said, "Sir, you remember who fired the first shot at Fort Sumter, don't you?"

"Certainly. Who could forget Edmund Ruffin?"

"Well, sir, he's here. Since he fired the first shot at Sumter, how about letting him fire the last shot at the Battle of Bull Run?"

Beauregard made a sweeping motion toward the howitzer and said, "Quite fitting, I would say."

Seconds later, as the Union wagon was just about to leave Stone Bridge, Edmund Ruffin—his long, silver hair dangling on his shoulders—fired off the cannon. The shell struck the wagon dead-center. There was a horrendous explosion, followed by a series of others as the wagon became a huge ball of fire, killing team and crew. The Rebels lifted a rousing cheer for Ruffin's accuracy.

Darkness fell with the smell of rain in the air, and the Bull Run battle was over.

***

Driving in haste, most of the civilian spectators arrived back in Washington before dark. They were in a state of shock over the Union defeat, but thankful that the blood-hungry Confederates had not followed them.

Jenny alighted from Rose's surrey and headed up the walk toward the house. She glanced at the sky. Black, ominous clouds told her a storm was on the way. Biting her lip, she entered the unoccupied house, aware that her father was still at the Capitol. Because she did not know if the man she loved was dead or alive, she sank onto a parlor chair and wept.

Patricia Winters was in a terrible mental state when she and the Lincoln boys arrived at the White House. Anguish registered all the way to her marrow as they alighted from the carriage and crossed the portico. She dreaded having to face Mrs. Lincoln. She had no choice but to confess that her negligence at the battle site could have gotten young Tad killed. If she was fired from her job, it would be only just.

The maid met them at the door, and Patricia asked how Mrs. Lincoln was. Upon learning that she was better and was sitting up in a chair in her bedroom, the governess hastened through the mansion, taking Willie and Tad with her.

When they entered the room, Mary opened her arms to the boys and embraced them. The president had already sent a message to his wife, informing her of the Union defeat at Bull Run, and she was happy to see that her sons were unharmed.

While Mrs. Lincoln clung to the boys, Patricia admitted her mistake in taking the boys to the battle site, then told the story of her negligence and Tad's brush with death. She gave full credit to Jenny Jordan for saving Tad's life at the risk of her own. The governess asked Mrs. Lincoln to forgive her and begged not to be fired.

Leaving her chair, Mary embraced Patricia, telling her she was forgiven and that she still had her job. Willie and Tad jumped for joy, hugged their governess, and thanked their mother for not firing her.

Mary told Patricia she was too good a governess to lose, then said she wanted to tell the president about Jenny Jordan risking her life to save Tad. She was sure Mr. Lincoln would want to thank Jenny for her heroic and unselfish deed. But that would have to wait. His mind was wrapped up in the rout at Bull Run. He had been at the Capitol all day and had sent word that he would be there all night.

Mrs. Lincoln would decide when to tell her husband about Jenny's deed. In the meantime, she would send a note to Jenny, expressing her appreciation. She then gave Tad a good scolding for his part in the near-tragedy.

On a dreary Monday morning, July 22, 1861, a light but steady rain was falling on Washington. Down-hearted citizens were at their windows and on their porches to view the beleaguered Union troops as they moved without any semblance of order up Pennsylvania Avenue toward the Capitol. They were covered with mud, soaked through with rain, and inching their way along the street.

The line of wagons, riders, and groping foot-soldiers was strung out for over ten miles. Observers along the avenue could not believe the change that had come over their army since they had seen them marching along the same thoroughfare on Saturday. Then there had been a look of confidence on their faces as flags waved and bands played. Now there were no bands. There wasn't a flag but that clung, limp and ashamed, to its staff. The look of confidence had been replaced with consternation, uncertainty, helplessness, and disappointment. Fearfully worn, they were hungry, thirsty, and haggard.

One frustrated male citizen shouted at the soldiers, "Bull Run was *your* work! If you were one-tenth the men we thought you were, this wouldn't have happened!"

Others—men and women—joined with him, casting the shameful defeat in their teeth. Not one soldier even glanced at them. Other Washingtonians brought food and hot coffee from their homes and shops, showing compassion for their whipped army. When the soldiers received the refreshment with weak smiles and faint words of appreciation, many of their benefactors wept.

It was a bitter, bitter hour for the United States. The vaunted Union thought to be so strong, so impregnable, seemed crushed beyond repair.

By midmorning, the last of the dispirited soldiers joined their comrades in front of the Capitol. General McDowell moved among them, speaking words of comfort and encouragement. President Lincoln appeared on the Capitol steps, along with his Cabinet, the Senate Military Committee, and General Winfield Scott. Each man carried his own umbrella, except for the president. His secretary, John Hay, held the umbrella that protected him from the rain.

High up in the Capitol, Jenny observed the heartrending scene from a rain-splattered window near her desk. The sky seemed to be weeping along with the Washingtonians. The steady rain made it impossible for Lincoln to speak to the soldiers, but he lifted a hand and smiled to show he had not lost faith in them.

The president called for an aide and told him to carry a message to General McDowell, who had remained among his downtrodden men. The general was to send the troops on to their camps. Clara Barton was overseeing makeshift tent hospitals at each camp to care for the wounded. Lincoln wanted to meet with McDowell and his division leaders in the Senate Military Committee chambers at eleven A.M.

While Jenny studied the throng of drenched, muddy soldiers, Lola Morrow—a part-time file clerk at the U.S. Patent Office—drew up beside her. Jenny glanced at her, then focused once again on the scene below.

"Seen any Zouaves?" asked Lola, knowing what was on Jenny's mind.

"Just caught a glimpse of some. They're hard to distinguish from the others because they're all so mud-caked." Pointing with a forefinger, she showed Lola a patch of dirty-red and said, "Right down there. See them?"

"Mm-hmm. Are you going down?"

Jenny turned and set weary, sleepless eyes on Lola. "I have to. I'm so afraid, Lola…afraid that those Zouaves will tell me Buck was killed yesterday."

"I understand, honey. You stay here. I'll go down and see what I can find out."

"No! I have to go down myself. Thank you, but this is something I can't shirk off on you or anyone else. If…if Buck is dead, I want to hear it from his men."

"All right. But I'll go with you."

"Thank you," Jenny said, gripping Lola's hand.

The scattered units were attempting to cluster together for their short journey to the camps. Jenny and Lola reached the street and threaded their way amongst them toward the rain-drenched Zouaves.

A young Zouave sergeant blinked against the rain, moved up to them, and said, "May I help you, ladies?"

"I hope so," half-choked Jenny, the rain dripping off her nose. "I'm…looking for Captain Buck Brownell. Is he—?"

"He's somewhere over that way, ma'am," replied the sergeant, pointing, "talking to our commander, Colonel Keyes. If you'd like, I'll go tell the captain you're looking for him."

"I don't want to bother him if he's busy," said Jenny, feeling a wave of relief wash over her. Buck was alive and apparently unscathed. She silently breathed a prayer of thanks.

"I assume the captain knows you well, ma'am?"

"Yes. Quite well," Jenny said, brushing rain from her face.

"You stay here. I'll be right back." He started to turn away, then asked, "May I tell him your name, ma'am?"

"Just tell him it's Jenny."

"Be back in a minute," he said, and was gone.

Lola took hold of Jenny's hand. "He's alive, honey. I'm glad for you."

Squeezing hard on Lola's fingers, Jenny said with trembling lips, "Yes! Thank the Lord, he's alive."

Lola looked around to see if anyone was within earshot. Deciding the rumble of voices and the patter of the rain would keep their conversation private, she said, "Jenny, I guess we don't dare hope that this whipping our Rebels gave the Yankees will be enough to bring the war to a halt."

"I don't think so. From what I hear around the Senate chamber, Mr. Lincoln is going to regroup and go after the Rebels again."

"Well, for your sake, I wish it was over. You and Buck deserve to be together."

There was a note of despair in Jenny's voice. "Lola, I love Buck with all my heart, but...how can we ever have a life together even if he lives through this war? Buck's love would turn to bitter hatred the moment he learned my father and I were spying for the South."

"Not if it's the real thing," Lola said calmly.

"Even true love has its limits," Jenny said with a quiver in her voice. "There would be no way I could conceal from Buck what Daddy and I had been. And once he found out, he'd—" Jenny's words were cut off as she spotted the young sergeant coming with the rain-soaked captain beside him.

Buck's eyes met Jenny's, and he dashed toward her. Jenny breathed his name and met him, weeping. "Oh, darling," she cried. "I'm so glad you're all right!" They locked in a tight embrace and their lips blended in an urgent kiss.

Holding her close, Buck breathed into her ear, "I thought of you all during the battle, Jenny. Hoping...praying that I could live to hold you in my arms again."

"Oh, Buck, I wish Mr. Lincoln would call the war to a halt. Just...just let the Southerners have their own states and live life the way they want. He's going to pull the army together and invade the South again. I just know it."

Keeping her in a tight embrace, Buck said, "I'm sure the war's far from over, honey. We got royally whipped out there, but I know our president and military leaders are not about to quit. But…when this thing *is* finally over, I want us to be together."

Lola was standing close enough to hear. When Jenny did not reply to Buck's words, Lola understood why. Butting in, she said, "Jenny, you haven't introduced me to your handsome fella."

Buck smiled at Lola as Jenny eased back in his arms and said, "Darling, this is my good friend, Lola Morrow. Lola works in the Patent Office."

Lola extended her hand, and Buck let go of Jenny to shake it. "Happy to meet you, Miss—it is Miss Morrow?"

"Yes," sighed Lola. "Much to my dismay, I still haven't found a handsome, dashing man to marry."

Buck was hoping Jenny would say something like, "Well, Lola, you can't have this one. He's all mine." But the words did not come.

Lola sensed Buck's thoughts, and feeling the awkwardness of the moment, saved it by saying, "Captain, I think you should know something that Jenny did yesterday."

Before Jenny could stop her, Lola was telling Buck the story of her daring rescue of Tad Lincoln. When she finished, Buck squeezed Jenny's hand and said, "That was a very brave thing to do."

"I didn't think about it being a brave thing," Jenny said shyly. "I just saw that sweet little boy running for his life…and I knew he wasn't going to make it on his own."

"Does Mr. Lincoln know about it?" queried Buck.

Jenny shrugged. "I don't know."

Buck folded her in his arms once more. "Well, I'm sure when he finds out about it, you'll hear from him."

By this time, women were converging on the weary, battered troops, looking for husbands, sons, and sweethearts. There were tears of joy upon finding men alive…and tears of sorrow upon learning that the bodies of their loved ones were lying in the fields and on the hills surrounding Manassas Junction. Some women were offered hope when it could not be verified that their men were dead. Hundreds of Yankees had been taken as prisoners of war.

Buck was still holding Jenny in his arms when a Zouave corporal told him Colonel Duryee was about to be moved to the Zouave camp in an ambulance and wanted Buck to accompany him. Reluctantly Buck kissed Jenny good-bye, then left to rejoin his commander. His heart ached. Somehow he would show Lieutenant Colonel Jeffrey Jordan he was worthy to take Jenny for his wife.

At eleven o'clock, President Lincoln held his meeting in the Senate chambers. He did not upbraid General McDowell and the other officers present for losing the battle, but shared his conviction that Confederate spies had gained access to classified information and carried it to Lee and Beauregard. There was no other way they could have been so well prepared. McDowell and the other officers agreed.

After three hours of discussion, Lincoln adjourned the meeting, asking Generals Scott and McDowell to remain. In private, the president told the generals the leak had to be right there in the Capitol where the classified information was passed out and kept. He was going to hire Allan Pinkerton and his detective agency to ferret out the spy or spies. Lincoln wanted that information kept between himself and the two generals, and Scott and McDowell assured him they would keep his secret. They wanted the guilty party caught and executed as soon as possible.

Lincoln emerged from the meeting room and found John Hay chatting with Senator Charles Sumner of Massachusetts. Stepping away from the senator, Hay approached Lincoln and said, "Mr. President, I have three letters that you need to sign so I can post them…and Senator Sumner wants to see you for a moment."

Lincoln nodded, then looked at Sumner and said, "I'm headed for a meeting at the White House, Senator. What can I do for you?"

"I have an appointment to keep myself, sir," Sumner replied, extending an envelope. "I'd like for you to take this. It's a letter from me pertaining to a valiant and brave thing I saw a young woman do at Bull Run when our troops were fleeing from the Confederates. You no doubt already know of the incident, since it involves your son, but I wanted to make an official statement about it. I believe her deed is worthy of a presidential commendation."

Lincoln's heavy brows arched. "My son? I—"

"Mr. President!" cut in Senator Henry Wilson, chairman of the Senate Military Committee, hurrying down the hallway, "I need to see you before you go to the White House. It's very important!"

Lincoln looked toward Wilson, then back to Sumner. Accepting the envelope, he said, "I'll give it my attention later, Senator. Thank you."

Sumner nodded, smiled, and walked away. Lincoln shoved Sumner's envelope into his valise, then followed his secretary to a desk and sat down to sign the letters. Senator Wilson waited patiently for his moment with the chief executive.

Forty minutes later, Lincoln was in a private meeting in the Oval Office with Allan Pinkerton. The famous detective assured the president that his agency would catch the spy or spies. His plan was to have the president secretly hire a Pinkerton agent to be John F. Calhoun's assistant. The agent would go by the name of Chester White. Working in Calhoun's office, White would be in a perfect position to observe clerical workers and members of the Senate Military Committee. Lincoln was optimistic of success and happy to know that White would report for work the next morning.

On Wednesday, July 24, President Lincoln had a private meeting in the Oval Office with his general-in-chief, seventy-five-year-old Winfield Scott, to discuss the shameful defeat at Bull Run. The shattered Federal army had to be pieced back together as quickly as possible. Both men agreed that it must be done under a new field commander. Though the loss could not be blamed on General McDowell, it happened under his command; the men had lost faith in him. It would take fresh blood to raise the troops' morale and make them ready for war again. Lincoln was adamant that it be done quickly. The Secessionists *must* be punished for breaking federal law and forsaking the Union.

General Scott suggested to Lincoln that General George B. McClellan, who did a brilliant job in leading the Union to victory at Rich Mountain, be appointed in McDowell's place. The president was favorable to the suggestion. He ordered Scott to relieve McDowell of his command immediately and to appoint McClellan field commander of the Union forces at Washington.

On Friday morning, Lincoln, looking weary and haggard, returned to the Oval Office at ten-thirty. He had been in a meeting with Generals Scott and McClellan, along with the Senate Military Committee, since seven o'clock, discussing the next military moves to be made against the Confederacy. Before another major battle could be fought, the Union would have to establish military strongholds in several key places across the Potomac in Virginia. Lincoln left it to the Committee, Jeffrey Jordan, and Generals Scott and McClellan to plan the offensive moves.

As the chief executive sank into the chair behind his desk, John Hay entered through a side door, carrying some papers. Lincoln rubbed his eyes and massaged his temples as he said, "Good morning, John."

Taking a seat in front of the desk, Hay responded, "Good morning, Mr. President. Are you all right?"

Easing back in the chair, Lincoln said softly, "Just tired, John. I have hardly slept since Sunday. Haven't seen my boys since last Friday, I think, and I've barely had a word with Mrs. Lincoln." Rubbing his eyes again, and blinking, he looked at the papers his secretary held in his hands. "Something important?"

"Yes, sir. I wouldn't bother you at this time if it wasn't. I have two letters, here. One from Major I.N. Palmer of the Union Cavalry, and the other from Colonel Abram Duryee of the Fifth New York Zouaves. Both have written concerning Captain Buck Brownell."

The president's face relaxed and a smile tugged at the corners of his mouth. "Ah, yes. Brownell. The man who shot Colonel Ellsworth's killer. Fine man. What about him?"

"Well, sir, everything else in this morning's mail I have either already taken care of or passed on to someone else to handle. However, these two letters demand your personal attention." As he spoke, Hay laid the letters in front of Lincoln.

The weary president donned a pair of half-moon spectacles and began to read the letter from Major Palmer. The major told how Buck Brownell had rescued him from under his fallen horse while cannon shells were exploding all around. Palmer felt the young Zouave officer deserved a presidential commendation for his bravery, and he also suggested that Brownell be promoted to the rank of major.

Smiling as he laid aside the first letter, Lincoln took up the second. Colonel Duryee explained in his letter how Captain Brownell had taken charge of the Zouave regiment when Duryee was shot and put out of commission. Brownell had led the regiment gallantly and had taken an impressive toll on the enemy. He had also captured thirteen Rebels, which were now incarcerated at one of the Union army camps. Duryee had been in conversation with Major Palmer and was aware that Palmer was suggesting Brownell be promoted to major. Duryee felt that since Brownell had performed so well in the battle, taking the place of a colonel, he should be promoted to that rank.

As the president laid the letter down, Hay said, "Some kind of soldier, this Buck Brownell."

"That he is," nodded Lincoln. "And I'm going to take Colonel Duryee's suggestion. We're going to need sharp young colonels like Buck Brownell in the battles ahead."

TWENTY-ONE

On Monday, July 29, Buck Brownell was cleaning and oiling his revolver in his private tent when a corporal stuck his head past the flap and said, "Captain, sir. General Scott would like to see you at his tent in ten minutes."

Rising from the cot he was sitting on, Buck smiled, "Tell him I'll be there."

Buck wiped the excess oil from his gun, loaded it, and slipped it in his holster. After checking himself over and wiping dust from his boots, he stepped into the stark sunlight and headed down the long row of canvas shelters toward the general's tent. As he drew near, he noticed several officers gathered with General Scott, including Major I.N. Palmer.

The officers greeted Brownell warmly, then General Scott said, "Captain, I have been instructed by the president to make a presentation to you on his behalf, in the presence of these men. Colonel Duryee expressed his desire to be here for this occasion, but as you know, he is currently laid up."

"Yes, sir," nodded Brownell, running his curious gaze over the smiling faces of the officers.

Scott then explained to Brownell that the president had received letters from Major Palmer and Colonel Duryee recommending a presidential commendation for the courage he displayed on the Bull Run battlefield and recommending a promotion in rank. While the men applauded, Scott handed Brownell an official-looking paper. The formal commendation was written on White House stationery and signed by the president.

Scott then said, "Captain Brownell, it is my honor as general-in-chief to advise you that you have been promoted to the rank of colonel."

The officers—who also included newly appointed field commander, General George B. McClellan—applauded and voiced their approval.

Scott handed an overwhelmed Brownell a pair of colonel's insignias to go on his uniform, shook his hand, and said in a lusty tone, "Congratulations, Colonel Brownell!"

After each officer had shaken the new colonel's hand, General Scott informed Buck that he was being assigned to do special training of the troops in all the camps around Washington. It would be Brownell's job to help lift the spirits of the men during the training sessions and get them ready to do battle with the Confederate army.

Late that afternoon, after a particularly strenuous training session with the troops at the main camp, Colonel Brownell bathed in a nearby creek. He had finished dressing and was combing his hair before a crude mirror in his tent when a voice called from outside, "Colonel Brownell."

"Yes?" he replied, moving to the flap and pulling it open. He recognized one of the sentries.

"Excuse me, sir, but there's a young lady at the gate who is asking to see you. I told her you were about to go to supper. She said it would only take a minute or two."

Grinning, Buck asked, "Is this young lady devastatingly beautiful, with hair like midnight and sparkling dark-brown eyes?"

"I'd say that's a pretty good description of her, sir," chuckled the sentry.

"Well," sighed Buck, reaching for his hat, "I'd gladly miss supper for a minute or two with her!"

Moments later, Buck approached the gate to see a smiling Jenny waiting beside her horse. Moving past the sentries, he took both of her hands in his and asked, "To what do I owe this pleasure, lovely lady?"

Jenny eyed the colonel's insignias on his shoulders and collar and replied, "I heard about your promotion."

"Now, how'd you hear about that?" he asked, smiling broadly.

"I'll never tell," she giggled. "I...ah...just have some friends in high places, and they keep me informed about such things." She paused, then added, "I wanted to come out and congratulate you. I think it's wonderful."

Buck folded her in his arms. "Thank you, Jenny. Do you suppose maybe my being made a colonel will put me in a different light with your father? I mean...am I now high enough on the social scale that he might give his consent for me to marry his daughter?"

Buck felt Jenny tense up. "I...I don't know what will go through Daddy's mind when I tell him. I hope he'll be pleased. But...since there's still a war on...and your a soldier—"

Buck drew his lips into a thin line. "I guess it's just wait until the war's over, huh?"

There was a lump in Jenny's throat. When the war was over, what then? How would Buck feel toward her when he found out both she and her father had been enemy spies? All she could say was, "I hate this war."

Buck ignored the watching sentries and planted a brief kiss on Jenny's lips. "Okay, I'll wait. War time is a bad time to start a marriage, anyhow."

Jenny was fighting tears as she told Buck she must head for home and prepare supper for her father. He helped her into the saddle, and told her he loved her.

"I love you, too, Buck," she said softly, and put the horse to a trot.

Jenny looked over her shoulder twice before the camp passed from view. Both times, Buck was standing where she had left him, watching. Tears wet her cheeks as she aimed her horse toward Washington. Her heart was torn asunder. Her attachment to the South stood between her and Buck, and threatened to keep them from each other.

Her father was the very center of a Confederate spy ring, and she must protect him at all costs. She must never be in a position where one slip of the tongue to Buck could expose Jeffrey Jordan. And now, since the war would go on, Jenny would be called upon by Rose Greenhow to carry messages to Confederate military leaders.

If Jenny gave in and told Buck that one day she would marry him, she would be living a lie. She had no doubt he would despise her the day he found out she had deceived him. *Whenever* he found out about it—now or after the war was over—what Buck felt toward her would die. To give him hope for the future would be inexcusable. There was no way she could do it. Even now she was eaten up with guilt that she had allowed the relationship between them to develop thus far.

In the weeks that followed, there were no major battles between the North and South. There were skirmishes and minor battles, however, along the Potomac as the Union attempted to establish military strongholds just across the river in Virginia. Each attempt was met with failure; the Confederates knew the Federal plans ahead of time and were there to meet them with sufficient fire power.

This was a direct result of classified information being pipelined from John Calhoun and Jeffrey Jordan to Rose Greenhow, then carried to the Confederates by Rose's girls. Rose had not yet pressured Jenny to carry messages for fear that Buck might be involved in one of the skirmishes and be killed.

***

On Tuesday, August 13, John Hay ushered Allan Pinkerton into the Oval Office. President Lincoln rose from his desk, shook the detective's hand, and said to Hay, "John, I do not want to be disturbed. When Mr. Pinkerton and I are finished, I will advise you."

"Yes, sir," nodded Hay, moving through the door and closing it behind him.

Lincoln sat behind his desk and the beefy man settled into a chair in front of him. "So you have something important to tell me?" said Lincoln.

"Yes, sir," said Pinkerton, wiping a hand across his heavy mustache. "I don't have enough evidence to make an arrest yet, but we're on the trail of your spies."

"*Spies*...plural?"

"Yes. Two at this point, and you're going to be shocked at one of them. There are others involved, but all I have for you right now are two names—John Calhoun and Jeffrey Jordan."

Deep lines etched themselves in the president's brow and there was horrified amazement in his eyes. "Jordan! Why, it can't be!"

"I'm afraid it is, sir. The man we're calling Chester White began to pick up on subversive things going on between Calhoun and Jordan. When he overheard them plan a meeting in the office after hours, White hid in the closet. Thinking they were alone, Calhoun and Jordan discussed how their spy work had contributed to the Confederate victory at Bull Run."

Lincoln looked ill. His face was rigid and grim. "When was this?"

"Friday night. I didn't come to you when White told me about it Saturday because I wanted him to work another day. Yesterday White overheard Calhoun and Jordan talking about a woman who was helping them in their espionage, but they only said 'she.' No name. Apparently they're still at it. That's why your army is having such stiff opposition along the Potomac every time they try to set up an installation. The Rebs know they're coming before they get there. Like I said, there's not enough evidence to make an arrest yet, but once we can get our hands on something on paper, we'll move in. I knew you'd want to be filled in on at least this much, though."

"Yes," Lincoln nodded, staring vacantly. Then focusing on Pinkerton, he said, "I just can't believe it. Calhoun is shock enough, but Jordan. *Jordan.* I even questioned him about his loyalties before I made him military adviser. He convinced me his allegiance was to the Union." Tugging at his beard, he added, "I guess you can never know a person for sure, can you?"

"Well, at least not in every case, sir."

"Tell your man to keep a close watch on them. I want concrete evidence as soon as possible. Once we get it, Jordan, Calhoun, and the woman—whoever she is—will face a firing squad."

"I have an idea more people are in on it with them. Seems like they'd need more than just one woman to carry those messages past our lines. For sure Calhoun and Jordan aren't involved in that part of it."

"Whoever is involved, we've got to root out every last treacherous one of them."

Pinkerton lifted his bulk off the chair. "You can count on it, Mr. President. I'll be in touch."

On Thursday morning, Jeffrey Jordan entered the kitchen with his mouth watering. The sweet aroma of bacon and eggs had filled the house and stimulated his appetite. Jenny was at the stove with her back to him, filling his plate from a steaming skillet.

"Good morning," he said cheerfully, taking his place at the table. "What's Daddy's little girl going to do on her day off today?"

There was a hot cup of coffee at his place-setting. Lifting the cup to his lips, he blew on it and took a sip. Then he noticed there was no place-setting for Jenny and that she had not responded to his greeting. He looked her direction just as she turned with the plate of hot food in her hands. Her eyes were red and swollen.

Jordan frowned as his daughter set the plate before him. "What is it, honey? Aren't you going to eat any breakfast?"

"I'm not hungry, Daddy," she said softly, her voice quavering.

He took hold of her hand. "Jenny, what is it?"

Tears began to spill down her cheeks and her lower lip trembled.

Pushing his chair back and rising to his feet, Jordan cupped Jenny's face in his hands, looked deep into her tear-filled eyes, and said, "It's Buck, isn't it?"

Sniffing, she nodded.

"You told me you saw him Monday. Have you seen him again?"

"No, but I'd spend every day of my life with him if I could. Oh, Daddy, I love him so much!"

As she spoke, Jenny broke into uncontrollable sobs. Jordan took her into his arms and held her close, saying nothing for a long moment. When her sobbing subsided, she clung to him and drew tiny shuddering breaths. Finally, he said, "Honey, I've thought a lot about this situation. I...I can't put reins on your heart and tell you who you can or cannot love. Buck loves you as much as you love him, doesn't he?"

"Yes," she said, sniffling. "He wants me to marry him. When the war is over, I mean."

"And that's what you want, isn't it? To marry Buck?"

"Yes. More than anything in all the world, that's what I want."

Looking deep into her eyes, Jordan said, "Jenny, I'm sorry. I was wrong to stand between you and Buck. I didn't want you to fall in love with a soldier because I didn't want you to have your heart torn out if he got killed. But...what I did was wrong. Please forgive me for overstepping my bounds."

Jenny stood on her tiptoes, kissed her father's cheek, then hugged him tight. "There's really nothing to forgive, Daddy. You meant well. You were, in your own way, trying to protect me, and I love you for that." She sniffed, then said, "I didn't tell you what Buck said when I went out to the camp to congratulate him on his promotion. He asked if maybe you would look at him in a different light now that he is a colonel...if he might be high enough on the social scale that you would consent to his marrying your daughter."

Jordan was quiet for a moment, then said, "I did understand you correctly—that Buck wouldn't want the two of you to be married until after the war is over?"

"Yes. We both know that would be best."

"Good. Then this North and South thing won't be a point of contention. It'll be a thing of the past."

A sick feeling washed over Jenny. There was still the spy situation. She was living a lie before Buck, and the awful dread of the moment he learned of it was haunting her. It would help if she could talk to her father about it, but that would have to wait. He was due at the Capitol shortly. At least he had put his blessing on her marrying Buck when the war was over. She breathed a prayer of thanks for that.

Easing back in her father's arms, Jenny said, "Well, Lieutenant Colonel Jeffrey Jordan, you'd better eat your breakfast before it gets cold."

Kissing her forehead, he said, "You're right. I'll have to hustle. The Committee is meeting with Lincoln at seven-thirty."

Ten minutes later, Jordan donned his hat and headed for the front door with his valise in hand. Jenny was at the door and pulled it open, warming him with a smile. "Now, that's more like it," he said. "I'm glad to see that smile again."

"I love you, Daddy," she said, tiptoeing to kiss his cheek.

"I love you, too, sweetheart." He kissed her forehead again, and was gone.

At nine-thirty that morning, Pinkerton detective Chester White was at his desk across the room from John Calhoun when the sound of male voices came through the open office door, echoing down the hallway.

White glanced at Calhoun. "Sounds like the Committee meeting is over."

"I'm surprised," remarked Calhoun. "I figured it'd go on all morning."

Seconds later, Jeffrey Jordan appeared at the door, glanced at White, then said to Calhoun, "John, I need to talk to you in private for a moment."

White rose to his feet. "I can leave, if you wish," he said politely.

"That won't be necessary," spoke up Calhoun, pushing his chair back and standing up. "The colonel and I can take a little walk and have our talk. By the way, Colonel, have you met our newest employee?"

"Haven't had the pleasure," smiled Jordan.

Calhoun introduced the two men, then leaving White in the office, walked with Jordan down the hall. Neither man was aware that the new "employee" was at the office door, watching them.

When they were out of earshot from everyone else, Jordan pulled a slip of paper from his pocket. Looking around to make sure none of the senators milling about in the hall were looking, he handed it to Calhoun and said, "Get this to Rose right away. McClellan is sending cavalry out of Porter's brigade across the Potomac due west of Hagerstown. Once Hagerstown is secure, they'll send in the infantry to hold it. All the details are on that paper."

Slipping the paper into the pocket of his suit coat, Calhoun said, "Rose will have it within the hour."

"Good. I've got to get back to the meeting room. We're only on a fifteen-minute break. Additional plans for Union aggression will be made in our next session. I'll probably have more for you to send to Rose before the morning's over."

"If you do, I'll have Lola take it to Rose. I'll tell Chester I've got an errand to run, and carry this one to Rose, myself, right now."

"Good."

***

Jenny was mopping the kitchen floor when she heard the knock at the front door. Placing the mop in the bucket of hot soapy water and leaning the handle against the cupboard, she hurried to open the door.

Rose O'Neal Greenhow smiled and said, "Hello, Jenny. May I come in?"

"Of course," Jenny nodded, noticing Rose's carriage and driver on the street.

Closing the door, Jenny followed the socialite to the dining room. Halting at the table, Rose asked, "Can we sit down? I have something very urgent and important to discuss with you."

"Certainly." Jenny pulled a chair out for Rose to sit on.

Rose sat down and pulled Jeffrey Jordan's paper from her purse. Handing it to Jenny, she said, "You'll recognize your father's handwriting. I need you to deliver this to General Stonewall Jackson *today*. My other girls are becoming a bit too familiar along the Union lines. Read it, then we'll talk about it."

Jenny read it, then set her dark eyes on Rose. "Who will be going with me?"

"No one. I'll have to send you by yourself. Like I said, my other girls are becoming too well-known by the Union sentries. They're willing to take risks, but I thought you wouldn't mind carrying this one because it involves only the cavalry, and Buck wouldn't be in on it."

Jenny swallowed hard. "All right. I'm a little frightened, but...I'll do it. It's my duty."

"Good!" exclaimed Rose. "I knew I could count on you. Now the safest thing is for you to fix your hair in an upsweep, fold this paper as small as you can, and hide it in the folds of your hair. If for some reason you should be searched, they'll never think to look there."

Jenny nodded. "Okay."

"You'll note the circled 'R' in the corner. This will tell General Jackson that the message is genuine."

"And where do I find him?"

"You know the bridge over the Potomac that leads to Fairfax Courthouse?"

"Yes."

"You take Constitution Avenue out of town west. You're in the country for about three miles, then you come to the bridge. There's a Union army camp right there on the river, and they've got sentries on the bridge. Just charm them with your good looks, honey. Tell them you're going to Fairfax Courthouse to visit your sick aunt."

Jenny's mouth tightened. "I hate to lie, Rose."

"No choice. Our soldiers don't like to kill, either, but war's war. Spies have to lie."

Jenny nodded, thinking of how she was living a lie before Buck.

"You go straight west on that same road for about two miles," Rose continued. "You'll find the Rebel camp right there. Just tell them you have a message for General Jackson. When he sees the circled 'R' on this paper, he'll know it's from me. Don't give it to anyone but General Jackson. Understand?"

"Yes."

"All right, honey," said Rose, rising to her feet. "I'll be going. How soon can you ride?"

"It'll take me about a half-hour to fix my hair and change clothes."

"Good. That'll put you in Jackson's camp by three-thirty...maybe a little before."

Chester White watched Jordan and Calhoun move down the hall, but soon they vanished from his view. He had not seen anything pass between them. However, when Calhoun returned to say he was going on an errand, White wondered if he was carrying a message to a partner in the spy ring. The woman they had mentioned, possibly? He wanted to follow Calhoun, but the man had given him some work that required immediate attention. He could not risk detection by failing to have it done when Calhoun returned.

White was working at his desk when Calhoun came back. White looked at the old clock on the wall, noting that it was almost noon. Calhoun had returned to the office at about eleven-fifteen and seemed a bit on edge.

Or is it just my imagination? White asked himself. *He keeps looking toward the wall, like he's expecting someone. Jordan, maybe? Is the colonel gathering information now, in the Committee meeting, that he'll pass on to Calhoun?*

Suddenly the hall was alive with committeemen, and their voices filled the place. "Lunch break, eh, John?" White asked.

Calhoun looked at him. "Yes. They'll take about two hours. Since it's noon, why don't you go on down to the lunch room yourself, Chester?"

"That's all right. You go ahead. I'll eat when you get back."

"I've got some work here that's quite urgent. You go on."

"Okay," sighed White, standing and stretching. "See you in an hour."

Picking up his lunch box, the Pinkerton man moved into the hall and weaved his way among the committeemen who were knotted in small groups and talking excitedly. White went as far as he could down the hall and still keep Calhoun's office door in sight. He casually leaned against the wall as if waiting for someone. It wasn't long before he saw Jeffrey Jordan hasten from the meeting room and enter Calhoun's office.

Calhoun set his anxious gaze on Jordan as he came through the door. "More?" he asked.

"Yes," nodded Jordan, closing the door. "Where's the new man?"

"He just went to lunch."

"Good," said Jordan, sitting down in the chair in front of Calhoun's desk. "Here's an urgent one."

Calhoun looked at the paper in Jordan's hand. "How urgent?"

"Has to be delivered to Rose immediately. The Committee just approved a plan of McClellan's to make a quick move on Virginia at a spot south of Washington where the Potomac and Rappahannock draw close together. McClellan convinced the Committee that that piece of land will be strategic for the Union in the days to come. Those rivers could become quite vital, and he wants the Union to control who sails them."

"So when's this move to take place?"

"At dawn tomorrow."

Calhoun's eyebrows arched. "Whooee! We've got to move fast."

"Real fast."

"Wouldn't look good for me to leave the building again," said Calhoun. "I'll take it down to Lola like I said earlier. She can fake a headache or something and rush it to Rose."

"Perfect," smiled Jordan.

The lieutenant colonel had already disappeared from the hall when Calhoun left his office with the vital paper in his suit coat pocket. He hurried down the broad staircase to the ground floor and made his way down a long hall to the U.S. Patent Office. He approached the receptionist's desk and asked, "Shirley, is Lola busy?"

"She's back at her desk, but I think she's about to head for the lunch room."

"Thanks," he said with a weak smile and moved toward the back room where huge file cabinets lined the walls. He spotted Lola at her desk, talking to another young woman.

Lola saw him, smiled, and gave a little wave. She quickly finished the conversation, and when the other woman walked away, John drew up. Looking around to make sure no one was within earshot, he said in a subdued voice, "I've got an urgent message that must be in Rose's hands immediately. Can you come down with a headache?"

"Strange that you should ask that. It hasn't been more than an hour since I developed one. My supervisor saw me taking some powders and asked if I wasn't feeling well. I told him I had a headache. He's at lunch, so I'll just tell Shirley that the powders didn't help, and I'm going home. She can pass it on to him when he gets back. No problem."

"Good," said Calhoun, pulling the paper from his pocket. "Take it and run."

Both Calhoun and Lola were startled when they heard Chester White's sharp words, "Run where?"

Behind the detective stood Shirley, eyes bulging. White was holding a cocked revolver on the startled pair. "I'll take that paper, John," he said, reaching for it.

"This paper is official government business, Chester. What on earth are you doing with that gun?"

"I'm holding it on you and your accomplice. I want that paper."

"I told you this is official government business!" Calhoun blared, clutching the paper. "You have no right to take it from me."

"Oh, but I do," White chuckled, snatching the paper from Calhoun's fingers. "Tell him, Shirley."

The owl-eyed receptionist moved closer, gulped, and said, "His name is Leonard Mansfield, John. He showed me his credentials. He's a detective with the Allan Pinkerton Agency."

"Pinkerton!" gasped Calhoun. He and Lola exchanged fearful glances.

"The president hired us to ferret out the spies who've been feeding information to the Rebel army," said the detective, shaking the paper at the guilty duo. "And here's all the evidence we need. Shirley, send for the police."

As the receptionist hurried away, bitter bile welled up in John Calhoun's throat. He knew the penalty for being caught as an enemy spy. Lola was white with shock. Fully aware that she would face a Union firing squad, her hands quivered and her knees turned to jelly.

TWENTY-TWO

Just after breakfast on Thursday morning, August 15, Colonel Buck Brownell crossed the grounds of the main Union camp, speaking to soldiers as he went, and drew up to General George McClellan's tent. An adjutant lieutenant stood at the opening, smiled at Brownell, and said, "Good morning, Colonel."

Buck still had not adjusted to his new rank. *Colonel* sounded strange when applied to him. "Good morning," he replied, returning the smile. "I'm here at General McClellan's request."

"Yes, sir, he's expecting you," said the lieutenant, then turned and spoke into the tent, telling McClellan that Colonel Brownell had arrived.

"Send him in," came the general's reply.

McClellan shook Brownell's hand and invited him to sit in front of his desk. The general eased himself onto the straight-backed chair behind his desk and wasted no time getting down to business. "Colonel, I have sought permission from General Scott to transfer you from the Zouaves into the regular army. I might say that he enthusiastically granted the request."

"Yes, sir," nodded Buck, wondering what was coming next.

"You've done a marvelous job in training the men, Colonel,"

McClellan proceeded, "but I've got a new job for you, which will carry a great deal more responsibility. You will get a change of uniform immediately. I think you'll look good in regular blues." Leaning forward, he said, "To tell you the truth, I've never cared for those gaudy uniforms of the Zouaves. Especially those baggy pants."

"Yes, sir," nodded Brownell. He hadn't cared for the Zouave uniforms, either, but had never voiced it to anyone.

Leaning back again, McClellan said, "With General Scott's consent, I am putting you in charge of the First Brigade of First Division, Colonel. You will replace Colonel Erasmus Keyes. As you know, he was wounded at Bull Run and is getting a medical discharge."

"I didn't know about the discharge, sir. I'm sorry to hear that his career has to end this way."

"Me, too. But since it's happened, I'm glad that I've got a man of your caliber to put in his place. You know, then, that you'll be under the command of General Daniel Tyler, commander of First Division."

"Yes, sir. I've only met General Tyler on a couple of occasions, and I like him very much. We'll get along well together."

"I have no doubt of that. You also know that First Brigade is camped about a mile-and-a-half south of here where the bridge crosses the Potomac just east of Fairfax Courthouse?"

"Yes, sir."

"That bridge is First Brigade's responsibility. Your men know they are to screen any and all civilians who come and go across the bridge. As commander of First Brigade, you must see to it that they never become lax in their screening. We've got spy activity going on, and it must be stopped."

"That's for sure," agreed Brownell. "Aside from what happened at Bull Run, we've had too many experiences of late where we've tried to move into Virginia and found the Rebs waiting for us. Has to be Confederate espionage."

"Well, it's going to come to a halt. One of these days we're going to catch those Rebel spies red-handed. When we execute a few of them, maybe the rest will find something else to do. Anyway…you've been at First Brigade camp, so you know Major Donald Sparks. He's in charge over there at the moment and will be your right-hand man."

"That's fine with me. He and I get along real well."

"You are aware, also, that First Brigade camp has a guard house where Union soldiers on detention from all the camps are confined?"

"Yes, sir, I've seen it. It's a big old barn where compartments have been built to form cells."

"Right. At present, only two or three soldiers are confined there…for drunkenness. I assume, then, you also know about the two sheds where your thirteen Confederate prisoners are being kept."

"Yes, sir."

"Both the incarcerated Union soldiers and the Rebel prisoners are now your responsibility."

"I understand, sir."

"Good," nodded McClellan, reaching into a desk drawer and drawing out a folder. Handing it to Brownell, he said, "Should any of the soldiers in the guard house cause trouble, here's the manual with discipline regulations. Such discipline will be at your discretion within the lines drawn by the Senate Military Committee."

"I'll stick strictly to the book, sir."

"I'm sure you will," grinned McClellan. "Also in the manual are regulations concerning spies. You are to oversee the execution of any spies caught within ten miles either direction on the river from your camp. Study them, Colonel. I have a feeling we're going to catch some Rebel spies at their game."

"Yes, sir. I hope we do. And again…I'll stick strictly to the book."

"All right," said McClellan, rising. "Of course, if you have any questions later, take them to General Tyler. I understand you already have some training sessions lined up for this camp today, so I want you to proceed with them after you get into your new uniform. You can work with the men until late afternoon, then ride on down to your camp. Major Sparks knows to keep an eye on things until you arrive and assume command."

As Buck left McClellan's tent to claim his new uniform, he saw General Tyler riding toward him from the rope corral. As Tyler drew near, he smiled, leaned from the saddle, and extended his hand. "Haven't had the opportunity to congratulate you on the promotion, yet, Brownell," he said as they shook hands. "I'm glad for you. No one deserved it any more than you."

"Thank you, sir," smiled Buck.

"General McClellan told me you're training the men here the rest of the day, then heading for your new post this evening."

"That's right, sir."

"I'm riding into Washington right now. I'll probably be back before you head down river. Maybe we'll have a few minutes to talk about some plans I have in mind for your camp."

"Fine, sir. I'll see you then."

Buck hurried to the supply shack and was given his blue uniform. He took it to his tent and changed clothes. Emerging into the brilliant sunshine, he headed for the spot where the training sessions would take place. He liked his new uniform; it made him look more distinguished than the uniform he wore as a Zouave. He told himself that Jenny would like him in blue, too.

It was almost three o'clock that afternoon when a nervous Jenny Jordan rode along the edge of the Union camp and headed for the bridge that spanned the Potomac. A small group of soldiers huddled at the bridge. Jenny eyed the camp with its long rows of tents and noted the old barn and the two sheds that stood in their midst. She figured there once must have been a farmhouse on the site.

The sun danced on the rippling waters of the Potomac as Jenny approached the bridge. Soldiers who milled about stopped to look at her. She wore her black riding boots, a black split skirt, and a ruffled white blouse. On her head was a small black hat, topping off the up-sweep of her thick, dark hair. A sergeant left the group and strode toward her.

Jenny's heart skipped a beat as she drew rein. Struggling to mask her fear, she painted on a warm smile.

"Good afternoon, Miss," said the sergeant, touching his hat brim and smiling in return. "It isn't often we see a young lady travel-ing alone. Are you a Northerner or a Southerner?"

"Half-and-half," she replied, maintaining the forced smile. "I live in Washington, but I was born in Virginia. I'm on my way to visit an ailing aunt in Fairfax Courthouse."

"You'll be returning yet today, I assume, since you're carrying no luggage."

"That's right, Sergeant. I'm only planning to stay an hour or so."

"Well, ma'am, I hate to detain you, but with all the spy activity of late, you'll have to be searched."

Fear formed and settled in Jenny's stomach. "Searched? Do I look like a spy, Sergeant?"

Scratching at an ear, the sergeant replied, "Well, ma'am, I wouldn't take you for one, but I'm really not sure what a spy looks like. All I know is, somebody's been carrying classified information to the Confederate army. General McClellan has laid down strict orders to search everybody who crosses from the Union to the Confederate side. No exceptions."

Jenny's face blanched. She ran her gaze over the men who stood around and said loudly, "Well, just who is going to make this search, sergeant?"

The sergeant blushed. Shaking his head, he said, "Oh, I'm sorry, ma'am. We have a farmer's wife just over that hill behind you who searches the women for us."

Jenny saw an officer detach himself from the nearby group and move toward her and the sergeant. Running his gaze between the two, he asked, "Is there a problem, here, Wilkins? The lady sounds upset."

"It's my fault, sir," said Wilkins. "I told her she would have to be searched, but I forgot to explain that Mrs. Harrison would do the searching."

Smiling up at Jenny, the officer touched his hat brim and said, "I'm Major Donald Sparks, Miss—"

"Jenny Jordan. My father is Lieutenant Colonel Jeffrey Jordan." Jenny hoped possibly this would spare her the search.

"I've long been an admirer of your father, Miss Jordan," said Sparks. "He made quite a name for himself in the Mexican War. I was pleased when President Lincoln made him military adviser for the Senate Military Committee."

"Thank you, Major," she nodded. "May I be allowed to resume my journey now? As I told the sergeant, I'm on my way to visit my sick aunt in Fairfax Courthouse."

"As soon as Mrs. Harrison searches you, ma'am. I'm sorry for this delay, but I'm under strict orders. Everyone who crosses this bridge must be searched. General McClellan made it clear that there are to be no exceptions."

Jenny had no choice but to submit to the search. If she told them she had changed her mind about visiting her aunt, they would immediately suspect her. If she wheeled her horse and galloped away, she would not get far. There were horses in the camp. They would ride her down. Besides…they knew who she was now. If she ran for it, they would soon have her in custody. She could only hope that the farmer's wife would not think to look in her hair.

The farmer's wife was summoned. Jenny was taken into the old barn, and in a private cell, she allowed Mrs. Harrison to search beneath her skirt and blouse.

When nothing was found there, Mrs. Harrison said, "I'll have to ask you to remove your boots, honey."

When the boots were cleared, the woman asked Jenny to remove her hat. While Mrs. Harrison ran her nimble fingers beneath the brim on the inside of the hat, Jenny felt a trickle of cold sweat run down her back.

Mrs. Harrison smiled and handed the hat back. "Okay, honey, you're cleared. Sorry to put you through this, but you understand."

"Of course," nodded Jenny, inwardly breathing a sigh of relief. "We must do all we can to stop this Confederate espionage."

As Jenny raised the hat to her head, Mrs. Harrison gazed at the thick folds of carefully upswept hair. "Just a minute, Miss Jordan," she said. "I just realized I didn't do as thorough a job as I should have. I'll have to ask you to let your hair down."

Jenny's nerves were suddenly taut and screaming. She was caught.

With shaky hands, she unpinned her hair. When the folded slip of paper fell out, Mrs. Harrison grabbed it. Jenny let out a tiny whine of mounting dread as the woman quickly read it and called for the soldiers.

Sergeant Wilkins and Major Sparks entered the small cubicle to find Jenny with her hair undone and her hands covering her face. She whimpered fearfully as Sparks read the message intended for General Thomas J. Jackson, grunted disgustedly, and handed it to Wilkins to read. Sparks turned to Jenny and said, "If you are really Jeffrey Jordan's daughter, Miss, this is going to bring great shame to him. His own daughter a Confederate spy."

Jenny's heartbeats felt like club blows in her chest. She could hardly breathe. Her mind was racing. Would this lead to her father's capture? What would Buck think of her? Jenny knew the president's edict concerning spies. She would face a firing squad and die without ever knowing the answers to these questions.

Excusing Mrs. Harrison, Major Sparks said, "Young lady, according to Federal law you must be executed within twenty-four hours. Nothing can alter that, but you could at least die with a clear conscience. How about telling me who the other spies are?"

Jenny lifted her tear-stained face and looked Sparks in the eye. She thought not only of her father, but of John Calhoun, Rose Greenhow, and Rose's girls. There was no way she would turn the Yankees on them. Moving her head slowly back and forth, she released a shaky, "Never."

"I thought so," Sparks sighed. "You will be locked in this compartment, ma'am. I'll see that you have water. It's really a shame, you know, for a beautiful young woman like you to have to face a firing squad. I'm sure glad your execution won't be on my shoulders. Our new commander will be here about supper time, and it'll be up to him to set the exact time of your execution."

Sparks and Wilkins left the cubicle and secured the door with a steel bolt. Jenny sat on the small cot in the gloomy cell. The terror that gripped her seemed to steal her breath, which was coming in short, painful gasps. She feared for her father's life, wishing somehow she could let him know she had been caught. Her mind then turned to Buck. Breaking down completely, she buried her face in her hands and sobbed Buck's name.

Jenny's weeping was interrupted by a young soldier who brought her a bucket of water and a tin cup. She said nothing, but stared at him while he set the bucket on a crude table, placed the cup beside it, and moved back to the door. Pausing, he looked at her with compassion and said softly, "I wish Mr. Lincoln hadn't set such a hard-and-fast rule about Rebel spies. It ain't gonna be easy to find men in the camp who will want to be part of the firing squad."

Jenny continued to stare at him, but said nothing.

"Well," the soldier said, "my prayers will be with you, ma'am."

When the steel bolt was shot home and the place was quiet, Jenny clenched her fists and said in a shaky voice, "Lord, You know I've hated living deceitfully before Buck. I didn't want to. I didn't ask for this awful war, and I didn't ask to be a Southerner living in the North. I...I don't want to die, Lord. Please let me live! And please, please don't let Buck hate me! I want to live...and to be his wife. Oh, God, please don't let them kill me!" Jenny broke down again, sobbing.

Word spread quickly through the camp that a Confederate spy had been caught at the bridge, carrying classified military information to General Jackson, and that the spy was a beautiful young woman. Major Sparks had told Mrs. Harrison and Sergeant Wilkins not to tell anyone that the spy was Jeffrey Jordan's daughter. He wanted to keep that kind of information confidential until Colonel Brownell arrived and decided what to do about it.

Some of the men-in-blue gathered around Major Sparks, concerned that they were going to have to execute a woman. Sparks ran his gaze over their faces and said, "Gentlemen, I admit this has me mighty shaky, myself. But this is war. Nobody is forced into becoming a spy. The lady knew what she was doing when she rode in here carrying that message for Jackson. We all know the army regulations about the fate of spies. The responsibility for the execution lies on the shoulders of First Brigade's commander. And I don't mind telling you, I'm glad I'm not in Colonel Brownell's boots. Putting a woman to death—especially one as pretty as she is—will wrench his insides, I'll guarantee you."

"Major," said one of the soldiers, "how will the colonel choose his firing squad?"

"He won't get any volunteers, that's for sure. He'll have to choose them, making it an order."

"Is it true, sir," asked another, "that the execution has to be done within twenty-four hours of the time she was caught?"

"That's right. When the president sanctioned the rule, he meant for the execution to be swift and without mercy. The rule is known far and wide, even in the South. Mr. Lincoln made it so to discourage enemy personnel from becoming spies."

Another soldier spoke up. "Major, I guess if Colonel Brownell chose me for the firing squad and I refused, I'd be in trouble, wouldn't I?"

Every eye was on Sparks as he nodded slowly and said, "You sure would, Corporal. Then you might be facing a firing squad. Not a man of us would volunteer to kill this woman, but the law says it must be done. Some kind of welcome for our new commander, eh?"

Inside the large shed adjacent to the barn, nine of the thirteen Confederate prisoners were making plans to escape. They had been working on a plan previously, but when they heard about the female spy who was to be executed within twenty-four hours, they accelerated those plans. When supper was brought to them, they would overpower the guards, seize their weapons, and take them as hostages. They would demand the release of their four comrades in the other shed, and the release of the woman spy.

They would then head deep into Rebel country, taking the woman and the guards with them. The Yankees would be warned that if they pursued them, the guards would die. If there was no pursuit, the guards would be held as prisoners of war.

As the sun was lowering toward the western horizon, Buck Brownell saddled his horse for the ride down the river bank to his new command. From the corner of his eye, he saw General McClellan coming his way. Grinning to himself, he made as if he was having trouble with the cinch.

Drawing up, McClellan frowned and asked, "Got a problem, Colonel?"

"Yes, sir. It's this weird saddle. Whoever designed it must've been half-asleep at the time."

The general's brows knitted together and his mouth pulled tight. "I'll have you know, Colonel, I designed that saddle!"

Feigning ignorance, Buck said, "Oh, no! Is that why they call it a McClellan saddle, sir?"

The general saw that Buck was joshing him. He broke into a hearty laugh and said, "You just about had yourself a court-martial!"

The two officers laughed together, then McClellan said, "I want to thank you for a job well-done, Colonel. You've really sharpened up the troops with your training. Next time they face the Rebels, they'll be ready for them."

As the general spoke, he looked past Buck to see General Tyler riding in, accompanied by a pair of adjutant lieutenants. Spotting McClellan and Brownell, Tyler excused the lieutenants and beelined for them. "Gentleman, I've got some mighty good news!"

As Tyler was dismounting, McClellan said, "I'm sure we can use some of that kind of news, General. What is it?"

"Unbeknownst to everyone except Generals Scott and McDowell, the president hired Allan Pinkerton and his agency to hunt down the Rebel spies he suspected were working within the Capitol. It paid off. Three Rebel spies were caught and arrested today. One of them was a genuine shock to Mr. Lincoln."

"Someone in high places?" queried McClellan.

Tyler hitched up his pants by the belt. "You might say that. Lieutenant Colonel Jeffrey Jordan."

The name hit Buck Brownell like the kick of a mule. His scalp tingled, and his mouth went dry. "*Jordan?*" The word left his lips before he was aware he had spoken it. *"Jeffrey Jordan?"*

"I'm afraid so," said Tyler. "You sound like you might know him personally."

"I do, sir. It…it just doesn't seem possible. Jeffrey Jordan a Rebel spy. This is going to hit his daughter awfully hard."

"Who were the other ones?" asked McClellan.

"John Calhoun, a clerical worker in the Senate Chamber, and a woman named Lola Morrow who is employed in the U.S. Patent Office. Or I should say *was* employed there."

"How'd they catch them?"

"Lincoln hired a Pinkerton detective to work undercover as assistant to Calhoun. He saw Calhoun acting suspicious with Jordan, whom we all know was military adviser to the Committee. Following his suspicions, the detective caught Calhoun passing a slip of paper to the Morrow woman and confiscated it at gunpoint. It was a message to Confederate military leaders, divulging classified information about an upcoming Union move on Rebel territory. The handwriting was Jordan's."

Buck was feeling sick all over for Jenny.

"So," proceeded Tyler, "the three of them are to die the moment the sun goes down. General Scott is overseeing the execution, and he told me that Pinkerton says there are definitely more spies in the ring…but all three refuse to name them."

Buck's mind was racing. He wanted to be by Jenny's side, though it was too late to get to her before the execution. What an awful thing for her to have to endure alone.

Looking at his superior officers, Buck said, "General McClellan…General Tyler…I need to ask something of you. I said a moment ago that I know Jordan. Actually, I know his daughter better. The fact is, I'm in love with her, and she feels the same way about me. This has to be an awful ordeal for her. I would like permission to ride into Washington immediately and be there to comfort her."

Tyler looked at McClellan. The field commander shook his head. "I'm sorry, Colonel, but you must be at your post down river as scheduled. For the young lady's sake, I wish I could let you go, but you are in charge of the camp down there, and you must go immediately."

"Yes, sir," Buck replied, trying not to show his disappointment. "I'm on my way now."

Buck rode south along the bank of the Potomac and watched the sun go down. Jeffrey Jordan and his two espionage companions were now dead. Buck vowed to go to Jenny as soon as possible. She would understand why he could not come to her immediately. Another thought came to mind. At least one good thing could come of this dreadful situation. With Jenny's father gone, they could have each other. Once she was over her grief, he would propose. He had no doubt she would accept the proposal.

Twilight was hovering over the camp when Buck rode in. Major Sparks was there to meet him when he moved past the sentries.

"Good evening, Colonel," said Sparks as Buck dismounted. "I was getting a bit worried about you."

"Had a slight delay in getting away," Buck replied.

"I have your tent ready, sir. It is the same one that Colonel Keyes occupied."

"Fine. Have the men had their evening meal yet?"

"No, sir. Ordinarily we would have, but we had some excitement around here. We're about ready to eat now, though."

"I would like to meet with you and the rest of the officers right after supper, then," said Brownell. "What was the excitement?"

"You remember when you brought the thirteen Rebel prisoners in, we put nine of them in that larger shed over there, and the other four in the small one."

"Yes."

"Well, sir, the nine in the large shed made an escape attempt about a half hour ago. They grabbed a couple guards to use as hostages and demanded to take the other four with them, along with a woman spy we caught this afternoon. Our marksmen went into action and took out all nine. The guards didn't get a scratch."

Buck's eyebrows arched. "A *woman* spy?"

"Yes, sir. She was carrying classified information to General Jackson. I'm sure you know what the regulation manual says about spies."

Buck felt a hot spot in his stomach knowing he would have to oversee the execution of a woman. "Yes, Major, I am fully aware of my responsibility. Executions are to take place at sunrise or sunset, but within twenty-four hours of the time the spy is caught. Executing a woman—even an enemy spy—is a distasteful thing, but it must be done. The execution will be at sunrise in the morning."

"Yes, sir."

"Major, I want you to pick out seven of our best marksmen for the firing squad. I have some news to tell you about captured spies, too, but it'll wait until later this evening when I meet with you and the other officers. Right now, I want to talk to this woman and see if I can get her to tell me more about the spy ring."

"All right, sir. I'll take you to her."

Sparks led his commanding officer through the big barn door, past several cubicles, and halted at one in a corner. Lantern light glowed through the cracks between the boards. "We've already given her supper, sir. I didn't want her to have to sit in the dark, so we brought in a lantern."

"Good gesture," nodded Brownell.

Sliding the bolt, Sparks said, "She's a pretty one, Colonel. You'll see that for yourself."

Buck waited for the major to pull the door open and step in ahead of him. Sparks moved inside the cubicle with Buck on his heels. "Miss Jordan, this is our camp commander, Colonel Brownell."

Buck saw Jenny sitting on the cot at the same instant he heard Sparks call her "Miss Jordan."

Their eyes met.

Jenny was stunned, but the horror that slammed into Buck was so powerful, it knocked the breath from him. A roaring began in his ears, red spots danced madly before his eyes, his flesh crawled. The cubicle seemed to swirl and heave around him.

TWENTY-THREE

Buck Brownell felt like he was in a wild nightmare from which he could not escape. Jenny's misty eyes were riveted on Buck with ill-concealed shame rising in their depths. Major Sparks could tell the two of them knew each other.

Buck was finally able to find his voice and gasped, "Jenny! I...I can't believe this. What—? I—"

"You know this woman well, sir?" cut in Sparks.

Keeping his stunned gaze on Jenny, who remained on the cot, Buck replied, "Yes. I've...been in love with her for several months."

"Then you know she's Jeffrey Jordan's daughter?"

"Yes. I know." It had been hard enough for Buck to accept that Jordan was an enemy spy, but his shock at finding out the same thing about the woman he loved was like nothing he had ever experienced before. His flesh crawled as he faced the burning realization that he must direct her execution.

Buck's mouth was dry as sand as he said shakily, "Major, I'd like to talk to Jenny alone. You go ahead and do what I told you."

"Yes, sir."

When the major was gone and the door shut, Buck stood over Jenny, trembling. His chest rose and fell irregularly. His voice was strained and his words ran breathlessly together as he said, "Jenny, I don't care what you've done…I still love you as much as ever."

Jenny had lowered her eyes and was staring at the dirt floor. Buck's words sank in slowly. When they registered, she lifted her graceful chin and met his gaze. Her lower lip trembled. For a long, unbelieving moment, she explored his face, reading him with a careful scrutiny. Her eyes filled with tears.

"You…still love me? Even when you know I've lived a lie before you?"

Buck fought the lump in his throat. "You weren't lying when you told me you loved me. I know you weren't."

Jenny released a piteous wail and flew from the cot into his arms. He felt the tremor of her body as he held her tight. Jenny had her arms around him and her head against his chest. "Oh, Buck," she sobbed, "I'm so sorry for deceiving you! I was eaten up with guilt. But I wasn't lying when I said I loved you. I love you with all my heart!"

Their lips came together. The kiss was long and full of desperation.

Once again Jenny laid her head against Buck's chest. As they held each other, she wept and said, "Buck, I need to explain something to you."

"No, Jenny, you don't owe me any explana—"

"Please, darling, let me get it out." Jenny paused to compose herself, then continued. "I've been under such pressure to do this spy thing. I ask you not to make me divulge where the pressure was coming from—I just can't do that—but let me explain this…I have been under constant pressure to carry messages since just before the Bull Run battle. I refused, because I knew you would be involved, and I just couldn't do it."

Jenny's words touched Buck deeply. He remained silent as she continued.

"You've got to believe me, darling…this is the only one I've had anything to do with!"

Laying a palm next to her face and pressing her head tighter against his chest, Buck said softly, "If you say that's the way it was, Jenny, I believe you." Knowing it was going to fall on him to tell Jenny about her father's capture and execution, he took a deep breath, held it for a moment, then said, "Honey, I know where this pressure you speak of was coming from."

Jenny pulled her head up and looked him in the eye. "You do?"

"Yes. Your father."

Jenny had been thinking more of Rose Greenhow than her father, but she blinked and asked, "How did you know that?"

"I think you'd better sit down. I've got something to tell you."

Sitting beside Jenny on the cot, Buck held her hand and told her of the capture and execution of her father, John Calhoun, and Lola Morrow that very day. Overwhelmed with grief, Jenny clung to Buck and wept a long time. When she regained control of her emotions, she held onto his hand and said, "Buck, there's something more I need to explain to you. It was Daddy's role as a spy—and the fact that I was as responsible as he since I didn't turn him in—that kept me from making any promises to you about the future. Daddy's attitude toward you, I could have overcome because I love you so much. But I had no choice but to let you think it was his attitude that was keeping me from making any commitment as to our lives together after the war.

"I hated deceiving you, Buck. There never should be any deceit between two people who love each other, but I was between a rock and a hard place, as they say."

Buck kissed her tenderly. "I love you more than ever, Jenny. And now…now…"

Squeezing his hand, she said dolefully, "Now it's your duty to carry out my execution."

It was a moment of dismay. Stroking her cheeks lovingly with both hands, Buck said with tremulous voice, "I have an idea, honey. It's a long shot, but it's the only chance we've got to spare your life."

"Run away?" she asked, fear evident on her face.

"Wouldn't work," he said, shaking his head. "We could make a break for it, but they'd track us down. As I see it, there's only one chance, and that's what I'm going to do."

"What?"

"You risked your life to save Tad Lincoln, didn't you?"

"Yes," she said weakly.

"Tad's still alive because of you, isn't he?"

"Well...yes."

"Did you ever hear from Mr. Lincoln about it?"

"No. I received a letter from Mrs. Lincoln. She thanked me for it in a very nice way."

"Certainly the president knows by now. Maybe your brave deed will be enough to persuade him to give you a stay of execution."

"But...but I'm a spy," she said in a despairing tone.

"But you only carried one message, and that under pressure from your father. He's got to weigh that against the fact that you could have been killed trying to rescue Tad. It's all we've got, honey. If I can get him to reduce the sentence to imprisonment rather than execution, we can still be together. This war can't last too long. When it's over, all prisoners of war will be set free."

Jenny wrapped her arms around his neck and squeezed tight, "Oh, I asked the Lord to perform a miracle. I prayed that He would somehow spare my life and let us be married. Maybe this will be His way. I can take being locked up if it means that eventually I can be your wife."

Buck kissed her soundly and said, "Okay, sweetheart, the execution is due to take place at sunrise. I've got to ride to the White House immediately. You sit tight and keep praying. I'll be back as soon as I can."

They kissed again, and Buck pushed the door open. Major Sparks was coming in the barn with a lantern in his hand. Beside him was army chaplain Glenn Harding. Buck had met him on a few occasions.

The two men drew up, and Sparks said, "I thought with what

your lady was facing, Colonel, she might want to talk to Chaplain Harding."

"I appreciate that, and I thank you for coming, Chaplain. Let me explain something to both of you, then I've got to ride for town."

Quickly, Buck told Sparks and Harding what he was going to try to accomplish by going to the president. Both men understood and wished him their best. Jenny observed it all from the cubicle. She set loving eyes on Buck as he said to Harding, "Please stay with her, Chaplain. Her daddy was executed today. Do what you can to comfort her. Read to her from that Bible in your hand, and pray that Mr. Lincoln will give her a stay of execution."

Hurrying back to Jenny, Buck kissed her once more and dashed out of the barn with Major Sparks on his heels. "Colonel, what am I supposed to do if somehow you don't return by sunrise?"

"I will, Major," breathed Buck. *"I will."*

"But…but what if something unexpected happens and you don't?"

They reached Buck's horse. As he swung into the saddle, he said, "I'll stop at the main camp upriver and tell General McClellan what I'm doing. If I'm not back here by the break of dawn, you ride to the camp and get your orders from him."

"All right, sir," said Sparks. "Go with God."

Colonel Brownell galloped hard along the bank of the Potomac by the light of a half-moon rising in the eastern sky. Moments later he arrived at the main camp to find that General McClellan had gone into Washington for the night and would not return until noon tomorrow.

Buck explained the situation to General Tyler, who was in charge. Tyler understood but told Buck that if he was not back by dawn, it would be Tyler's duty to ride to the camp and see to it that the execution was carried out at sunrise. Army regulations must be obeyed to the letter. Buck told Tyler he understood, but assured him he would be back in time. With that, he spurred his horse into a gallop and rode toward Washington.

It was exactly nine o'clock when the desperate rider reached the White House. After being delayed by White House personnel for nearly an hour, he finally learned that President Lincoln was not at home. He had gone to Baltimore, where he had a meeting scheduled early in the morning with some wealthy men from Europe who wanted to talk to the president about giving financial aid to the Union cause. Fearful of possible Confederate attack on Washington, they had asked Lincoln to meet them in Baltimore.

Learning that Lincoln was at the Baltimore Arms Hotel, Buck rode hard across the Maryland countryside in the pale moonlight. It was nearly forty miles to Baltimore, and his horse was showing signs of fatigue when he dismounted in front of the hotel and tied it to a hitching post.

Buck entered the lobby and hastened to the desk where he found a young clerk asleep in a chair. The place was dimly lit with a couple of low-burning lanterns. When the clerk did not stir at Buck's approach, he circled the counter, gripped his shoulder, shook it lightly, and said, "Pardon me."

The clerk awakened with a start, snorted, and looked up at the colonel. Sleepily, he said, "Umm…what can I do for you, General?"

"I understand President Lincoln is staying here. I must see him immediately. It's an emergency. What room is he in?"

The clerk rubbed his eyes and focused on a clock that hung on the wall above him. "Sir, it's one o'clock in the morning. Can't you wait until the president awakens at his regular time?"

"No, I can't! I told you. It's an emergency!"

"All right, General. Mr. Lincoln is on the third floor, room 360."

Buck bolted for the fancy winding staircase that led upstairs. Reaching the third floor, he hurried down the dimly lit hall toward room 360. As he drew close, he saw two well-dressed men sitting on straight-backed chairs, one on either side of the door. Both men rose to their feet, noted his rank, and eyed him warily.

"I'm Colonel Buck Brownell, gentlemen," he said, a bit out of breath. "I need to see the president immediately. I realize it's the middle of the night, but this is an extreme emergency…a matter of life and death."

The men explained that they were Pinkerton detectives, and that they had strict orders to see that Mr. Lincoln was not disturbed. The colonel would have to wait till morning.

Buck was on the verge of panic. Speaking fast, he explained the situation, and the men agreed to awaken the president. One of them ushered the nervous colonel into the first room of the presidential suite and stayed with him, while the other went to the bedroom. Buck prayed silently, *Oh, Lord, please…move on Mr. Lincoln's heart. He must give Jenny a stay of execution. I beg of You, please spare her life.*

The detective returned from the bedroom after a few minutes and said, "The president is dressing, Colonel. When I told him your name, he did not hesitate to say he would see you. Please sit down. He will be with you shortly."

"Thank you," sighed Buck, but preferred to stay on his feet.

The detectives returned to the hall, closing the door. Buck paced the floor, praying. No more than four minutes had passed when Abraham Lincoln emerged from the bedroom. He had put on his slippers and trousers, but showed his long underwear from the waist up. Running his fingers through his coarse, tousled hair, he said sleepily, "Good morning, Colonel. I understand you have an emergency."

"Yes, sir," nodded Buck, his voice showing the strain he was under. "I'm sorry to disturb you like this, Mr. President, but it is a matter of extreme urgency."

Buck told Lincoln he was aware of Jeffrey Jordan's arrest and execution. He quickly explained Jenny's dire situation and reminded the president of her heroic deed. He explained that she had gone on only one spy mission for the Confederates, and that under duress.

Stunned that Jenny had also been in the spy ring, Lincoln scratched his head and said, "Colonel, I'm sorry, but I know nothing of your young lady saving Tad's life. I didn't even know he'd been at the Bull Run battle."

Buck's blood ran cold. "I don't understand why no one told you about it, sir. Mrs. Lincoln wrote a letter to Jenny, thanking her for what she had done. If nothing else, I'm surprised the governess hasn't told you."

Rubbing his tired eyes, Lincoln said, "Colonel, there's a reason I haven't heard it from them. I've been so busy ever since the Bull Run battle that I've barely seen them. And even when I've been home with them, my mind has been so preoccupied with this war, they probably didn't feel they could bring it up."

Buck could feel time slipping away like sand in an hourglass. "Believe me, sir," he said with urgency lining his voice, "what I've told you is the absolute truth."

"I'm not doubting you, Colonel, but as you well know, this spy problem is a big one. I've made a lot of it with my Cabinet, the Senate Military Committee, and even with the newspapers. Such a timely and important thing as this forces me to have someone else's word about Jenny saving Tad's life. With all due respect to you, if I don't handle this correctly, it could create some serious problems with handling enemy spies who are caught in the future."

Buck's hands were shaking. "Mr. President, could you at least write an order giving me the authority to delay the execution until you can hear testimony from the boys and their governess?"

Suddenly Lincoln's eyes lit up. Snapping his fingers, he said, "Wait a minute!" and crossed the room to a desk where his valise lay on top. Pawing through it, he found the sealed envelope that had been handed him by Senator Charles Sumner.

While the president was slitting the envelope open, Buck asked, "What is that, sir?"

"I just remembered that shortly after the Bull Run battle, Senator Sumner handed me an envelope and said something about a valiant young woman who had done a brave thing at Bull Run. It's sketchy, but seems like someone else made a passing remark about that same time concerning my son at Bull Run. It slipped my mind until now. Sumner also said something that day about the young woman being worthy of a presidential commendation."

While Buck looked on with bated breath, the president unfolded Sumner's letter and read in the senator's own handwriting how he had witnessed Jenny Jordan's brave deed at Bull Run. With no thought for her own life, she had saved the president's son from a sure and violent death under the hooves and wheels of charging horses and wagons.

The hand that held the letter trembled as Lincoln set his tear-filled eyes on Buck and said, "Colonel, only God knows how much I love that bright-eyed boy of mine. Senator Sumner saw the whole thing, and wrote it all down right here. If...if it weren't for your Jenny's courage and unselfishness, I couldn't go home and feel that dear boy's arms around my neck."

Buck's heart was in his throat.

"You feel confident that she is telling the truth when she says she went on only that one mission...the one that got her caught?"

"Absolutely, sir. Would a woman who so gallantly risked her life to save Tad be a liar?"

Lincoln shook his head. "Of course not. Forgive me for even asking. You understand, I'm a very tired man right now."

"Certainly, sir."

Pulling out the chair, the president sat down at the desk. Producing a slip of paper from a drawer, he picked up a pen, dipped it in the desk's inkwell, and said, "Colonel Brownell, I'm going to write Jenny Jordan a full pardon."

While the room was filled with the sounds of the pen scratching the paper, Buck brushed tears from his eyes and offered a silent prayer of gratitude to the Lord.

When the pardon was written, Lincoln hastened to the adjoining room and awakened his secretary. John Hay witnessed the president's signature on the document by signing his own. The pardon was now official and beyond alteration.

Placing the life-saving document in an envelope and handing it to Buck, Lincoln said, "Due to the nature of this situation, Colonel, it would be best for both you and Jenny to relocate immediately. After having three spies executed just yesterday—and one of them Jenny's father—it would be wise to remove her from the Washington area. Since you've been so deeply involved, it's best that you leave here, too. As you no doubt know, we have Union forces in Missouri, and it looks like there'll be fighting there soon. We need men like you on that front, Colonel. I'll put through an order tomorrow that you be transferred as soon as possible. Jenny's been a good receptionist at the Capitol. I hate to lose her. But take her and go to Missouri with my blessing."

Elation had Buck's heart drumming his ribs. "I will, sir. Jenny and I will get married before we head west."

"Wonderful. Congratulations."

With deep emotion, Buck thanked Lincoln for Jenny's pardon and soon was on his horse, galloping southward. It was just past two o'clock. The hour's rest had refreshed the animal, and it was running at full speed. Buck figured he could make it to the camp in a little over three hours if the horse could keep up the hard pace. It had to. Jenny's life depended on it. General Tyler had no choice but to go ahead with the execution if Buck was not back by sunrise.

Dawn came about five-thirty, and sunrise about six. All things going well, Buck would make it to the camp just at the break of dawn.

The gallant steed obeyed Buck's promptings and galloped hard. Saliva from its mouth flecked Buck's uniform and sometimes sprayed his face. It mattered not. The eager rider knew every rapid step took him closer to the camp…and closer to Jenny. Jenny, who was going to live and become his wife!

The moon had shifted to the west, but was still giving off enough light to illuminate the roads, hills, and fields as horse and rider flew like the wind. Recognizing certain landmarks along the way, Buck was just telling himself he was only about six miles from the camp when suddenly his horse stumbled and fell. Buck was thrown about twenty feet and hit the ground hard. He was in a grassy field when the horse went down, and a haystack stopped his roll. Buck was momentarily stunned, then he managed to struggle to his feet and stumble toward the fallen animal.

The horse's sides were heaving as it lay on its side, its eyes bulging. Then Buck saw the broken leg. The horse must have stepped in a hole. Buck knew he'd have to put the horse out of its misery. Standing over it, he wagged his head sadly. Just before he pulled the trigger, he said, "I'm sorry, boy. You did your best. You really did."

Looking past the haystack, Buck saw a farmhouse and outbuildings about three hundred yards to the south. Making sure he still had Lincoln's pardon in his pocket, he ran toward the farmhouse as fast as he could. He had to get another horse, and fast. The eastern horizon was showing a dull gray. It would soon be dawn, and he had six miles to go. Panic gripped him as he ran.

Buck's lungs felt like they would explode by the time he drew near the buildings. Three saddle horses and two Holstein cows stood together in the corral. He was headed for the house when he caught sight of a shadowy figure moving from the back porch toward the barn. The farmer was carrying a milk bucket. There was enough light from the sky for Buck to tell that the farmer was in his late thirties or early forties. The man hauled up, clutching the handle of the empty milk bucket, and eyed Buck's blue uniform in the gray gloom.

Gasping for breath, Buck said hoarsely, "There's no...time for an...explanation, sir...but I need to borrow...a horse...*fast.*"

The farmer eyed Buck with disdain. "I ain't interested in helpin' no Yankee. I may live in Maryland, but my heart's below the Mason-Dixon Line. You ain't gettin' no horse from me."

The farmer's rude refusal riled Buck. "Mister, a woman's life is at stake. She'll die if I don't get to her before sunrise!"

Squinting, the farmer said with a sneer, "What kind of poppycock you tryin' to feed me, Yankee? Get off my property!"

The wild fury of the desperate moment ripped through Buck. He lunged at the man, striking him on the jaw with his fist. The farmer went down and lay still.

Buck dashed to the barn. It took him a few seconds to locate a bridle in the dark interior, but once he had one in his hand, he hurried into the corral, picked the fastest-looking horse, and bridled it. He wouldn't take the time to put on a saddle. Every second counted.

Leading the horse to the corral gate, he opened it, brought the animal out, then closed the gate. He was about to hop on its back when he heard from the shadows, "Hold it right there, Yankee!"

The farmer stood beneath a huge oak tree some twenty feet away. He was a bit unsteady on his feet, but he had produced a musket from somewhere and had its black, ominous muzzle leveled at Buck.

Buck had a mental picture of the seven men of the firing squad rising from their cots.

"Get away from the horse, Yankee! I want you off my property *now!* I don't hanker to kill you, but if you don't make tracks real quick-like, I will!"

Desperation was a living thing in Buck Brownell. Turning from the horse, he moved cautiously toward the farmer, opening his hands and saying, "Sir, I tried to explain that a woman's life is at stake—a Southern woman, caught yesterday spying for the Confederacy. She is scheduled to be shot at sunrise, but I have a pardon in my pocket signed by President Lincoln."

Moving steadily toward the farmer, Buck continued. "As you can see, it won't be long till the sun comes up. I've got six miles to go to reach the camp. If I don't get there in time, they'll put her before a firing squad. You're in sympathy with the Confederacy; won't you even help save the life of a Southern woman?"

Buck was now eight or nine feet from the man. The muzzle was still trained on his chest.

Extending his free hand, the farmer said, "Let me see that there paper. I wanna know if you're tellin' the truth."

This was exactly what Buck was hoping the man would do. Stretching out his arm to place the envelope in the man's hand, Buck waited till it was almost there, then with the swiftness of a cougar, seized the barrel of the musket and thrust it upward. The hammer came down and the weapon discharged, sending the roar echoing across the surrounding fields. The envelope fluttered to the ground as Buck twisted the musket from the farmer's hand and used it as a club in one smooth motion. The stock cracked solidly against the Southern sympathizer's head, and he went down like a tree in a high wind.

Buck was aware of someone appearing on the front porch of the farmhouse as he vaulted onto the horse's back and galloped away. He didn't bother to look back and see who it was. The envelope was again safely in his coat pocket, and he was driving the animal as fast as it could go.

The eastern sky was coming alive with light. Buck's blood turned to ice as he pictured the men of the firing squad loading their guns. General Tyler would do his duty. He would see that Jenny was shot at sunrise if Buck was not there.

With the wind in his face, Buck pictured Jenny being led to the place of execution and Chaplain Harding flanking her. "Please, God," he prayed, "let me make it in time."

TWENTY-FOUR

At the First Brigade camp, Chaplain Glenn Harding stood over Jenny Jordan as she sat on the cot in her cubicle. She was holding his Bible. She had slept little, and her eyes showed it.

Gripping the big black Book until her fingers turned white, Jenny looked up at Harding and said, "The Lord is going to do it, Chaplain. I just know He is."

Harding glanced at the cracks in the barn wall that were showing increasing light. He wanted to say, *He's going to have to hurry*, but instead, he said, "Miracles are God's business, Jenny. He can perform one any time He wishes."

Footsteps were heard outside the door. Jenny jumped up, holding the Bible to her breast and said, "It's Buck, Chaplain! He's back!"

The door came open. Jenny's countenance fell as Major Donald Sparks, looking dismal, said, "Miss Jordan, I'm sorry. It's time."

Harding asked, "Can't you give it a few more minutes, Major? I'm sure Colonel Brownell has got to be on his way."

"I wish I could, Chaplain, but it's sunrise. General Tyler is here. He gave the order for me to come and get her."

Harding turned to Jenny, gripped her shoulders, and said, "Don't give up yet. Buck could come riding in here any minute."

Jenny bit her lip and nodded.

A corporal moved in with a short length of rope in his hand. There was a black cloth stuffed in his hip pocket.

Harding eyed the rope, looked at Sparks, and asked, "What's the rope for, Major?"

"We have to tie her hands. I don't like it, but it's army regulation."

"Look," Harding argued, "this ordeal is bad enough for her, certainly you don't have to—"

"It's all right, Chaplain," Jenny cut in. "I don't mind." Turning toward Harding, she handed him the Bible. "Thank you for letting me read it," she said softly. "It was a real comfort."

The corporal's hands were trembling as he tied Jenny's wrists together behind her back.

Noting the black cloth, Harding asked, "And what's the cloth for?"

"It's a hood," replied the corporal. "Miss Jordan has her choice whether she wants it on when she faces the…faces the firing squad."

Jenny stared at the hood but said nothing.

Taking her arm gently, Major Sparks said, "We have to go now."

Sparks led Jenny outside, with Harding and the corporal following. The sun's upper rim was peeking over the eastern horizon. Jenny's line of sight ran across the open fields to the edge of the forest westward; soldiers stood at attention in a straight line at the edge of an open area. Each one held a musket by its barrel with the butt resting next to his leg on the ground.

Major Sparks led Jenny to a spot some forty feet in front of the firing squad, then halted. The sight of the seven muskets sent an icy chill down her spine and her knees buckled. Sparks steadied her as the morning breeze blew a long wisp of hair across her eyes. She couldn't brush it away with her hands tied behind her back. The chaplain saw it and brushed it away for her.

"Thank you," she said.

Harding nodded, then ran his gaze in a panorama and said to Sparks, "Where are all the soldiers? Camp looks empty."

"They didn't want to watch this," replied the major. "They've all gone into the woods."

Jenny looked toward Washington, but again there was no movement…no rider coming that way. Where was Buck? Had something happened to him? From the corner of her eye, she saw a man emerge from a tent and move her direction. She did not recognize him.

Nobody moved. The stately officer drew up and said, "Miss Jordan, I'm General Daniel Tyler. We were expecting Colonel Brownell back by now, but since he has not returned, it is my duty to conduct this…this execution in his absence."

Jenny raised her eyes to meet Tyler's then dropped them and nodded.

Tyler looked to the corporal who now held the black hood in his hand. "Have you offered Miss Jordan the hood, Corporal?"

"Not yet, sir." The corporal stepped to Jenny and asked, "Would you like to have this over your head, ma'am? It…makes it easier when you can't see."

Jenny's heart thudded wildly. The horror of what was about to happen rose in her throat, choking her, making her incapable of speech. Her cheeks twitched as she bit her lip and gave a jerky little nod.

The corporal raised the hood toward Jenny's head, but Harding gently seized his wrist and said, "Just a moment, Corporal."

The corporal looked to General Tyler, who indicated it was all right. He lowered the hood, and Harding let go of his wrist.

Positioning himself directly in front of the condemned woman, the chaplain said, "Jenny, I'm sorry. There is no way to know what's happened to Colonel Brownell…and no time to try to find out. The Lord doesn't always do things the way we think He should. His will is often far different than ours."

Her features pale, Jenny nodded. Then finding her voice, she said, "Chaplain…please tell Buck I know he did his best…and that I died loving him with all my heart."

It was Harding's turn to choke on a lump in his throat. He nodded, bent down and kissed her cheek, and stepped back. The corporal's hands trembled as he carefully dropped the hood over Jenny's head.

General Tyler made a gesture toward Sparks, Harding, and the corporal, directing them to move aside. When they were far enough away, Tyler stepped out of the line of fire, backed up a few more steps, and set his eyes on the firing squad. Taking a deep breath, he barked, "Ready!"

Seven muskets were brought into firing position and the hammers cocked in a staccato of dry clicks. Tyler glanced at the victim. Her entire body was shaking like a leaf in the autumn wind. He took another deep breath and barked, "Aim!"

The unwanted sun shafted its yellow light on Buck as he thundered toward the camp. He gritted his teeth and prayed as the camp came into view. He could make out the long rows of tents in the open areas, but a stand of trees blocked his view of the spot where the execution would take place. Lashing the horse with the tips of the reins, he bellowed, "Hyah! Hyah!"

He was some fifty yards from the center of camp, the trees still blocking his view, when above the rumble of the horse's galloping hooves he heard the unmistakable sound of rifles being fired in a short, crisp series of shots.

Buck's heart seemed to burst in his chest as he cried, "No-o-o!"

Seconds later, horse and rider burst into the clearing, and Buck wailed again as he saw Jenny lying on the ground. Her hands were tied behind her back, and there was a black hood over her head. She lay motionless in a crumpled heap.

The horse skidded to a halt in a cloud of dust as Buck sailed from its back and landed beside her. Kneeling, he sobbed, "No! No! Jenny! No!"

His shaky hands tore at the hood and slipped several times before he got it off. Her eyes were closed and her face sheet-white. But she was still breathing!

Buck looked for blood and bullet holes, but there were none. Puzzled but ecstatic, he realized that Jenny had simply fainted. She moved her head slowly back and forth, and moaned. Buck quickly removed the rope from Jenny's wrists and gathered her into his arms. She moaned again.

It was then that Buck realized there was no firing squad to be seen. There were no soldiers in view at all. Where was everybody? Jenny's third moan brought his attention back to her. Elated and thankful that she was unharmed, he kissed her, then stroked her cheek tenderly and said, "Jenny...Jenny..."

Her eyes rolled beneath the lids, then fluttered and came open. It took only seconds for her to focus on the face of the man she loved. "Buck!" she gasped. "I...I'm alive!" She flung her arms around his neck and wept, sobbing out words of thanks to the Lord for performing His miracle.

Buck held her tight, doing some praising of his own. Suddenly both were aware of a shadow falling over them. They looked up to see General Tyler above them, sided by Major Sparks and Chaplain Harding. The chaplain was thumbing tears from his cheeks.

Buck helped Jenny to her feet and stood holding her as he saw the seven-man firing squad coming toward them from the woods to the east, followed by hundreds of men in blue.

Buck reached in his pocket and handed General Tyler the envelope. "President Lincoln gave Jenny a full pardon, General. It's all there, spelled out word for word."

"Thank God!" breathed Harding.

Buck gave a quick explanation of what had delayed him, then squinted against the morning sun and asked, "What happened here, General?"

Tyler scrubbed a hand over his handsome face and explained that just as the firing squad was ready to fire, the four remaining Confederate prisoners hit the door of their small shed and burst out. Apparently they had planned their escape carefully. Watching from a window in the shed, they had meant to time it with the firing of the guns, so the noise of the smashing door would not be heard.

General Tyler, feeling sick at heart for having to order Jenny's death, paused extra long before giving the order to fire. The nervous prisoners jumped too soon. When they came piling through the door, Tyler and the firing squad saw them. While the seven Union soldiers swung their guns around, Tyler shouted for the prisoners to halt. When they kept running, he gave the command to fire. All four of the Confederates were cut down. It was this volley of shots that Buck had heard.

Everyone had rushed to the fallen escapees, including Chaplain Harding, but all four were dead. Their bodies were carried into the woods for burial. Tyler, Sparks, and Harding went along, then it suddenly dawned on them that in all the excitement, no one had stayed with Jenny.

Looking at Jenny, who was still in Buck's arms, Tyler said, "I saw you collapse, but the prisoners were my first concern. I'm sorry we neglected you, Miss Jordan."

"That's all right, sir," Jenny smiled. "I really didn't know I was being neglected. When I heard you tell the firing squad to aim, my head began to spin. I guess I didn't hear your command for the fleeing prisoners to halt. The last thing I remember was the sound of the rifles firing. Naturally, I thought it was the moment of my death…and I must have fainted."

All the camp personnel gathered close, happy to see Jenny still alive. Taking advantage of the moment, General Tyler read President Lincoln's pardon so everyone could hear. While the soldiers cheered, Jenny clung to Buck, weeping with relief and thanking God in her heart.

Buck turned to Tyler and said, "General, I need a few minutes alone with Jenny, then I would like to talk to you and Chaplain Harding."

When Tyler agreed, Buck led Jenny into the tent that had belonged to Colonel Erasmus Keyes. He dropped the flap, took her in his arms, and kissed her soundly. Then he held her at arm's length and said, "Honey, President Lincoln is going to issue an order immediately, transferring me to a post in Missouri. You're aware that things are heating up out there."

"Yes," she nodded, a quizzical look in her eyes.

Grinning, Buck added, "Not only that, but the president feels with all that has happened—you know, all this spy business with you and your father—it would be best for you to leave the Washington area. So he has ordered me to take you to Missouri with me."

A smile tugged at the corners of Jenny's mouth. "He has?"

"We can't disobey the president of the United States, can we?"

Jenny knew what was coming. The smile broadened. "No, of course not. Not your Commander-in-Chief, darling."

"Well-l-l, it really wouldn't be proper for us to travel all that distance together without—"

"Yes, I'll marry you!"

"Wonderful!" Buck exclaimed, and kissed her again.

They held each other in a long embrace, and Jenny said aloud, "Thank You, dear Lord in heaven. Thank You for giving me the miracle I asked You for."

"Amen and amen," breathed Buck.

Holding his wife-to-be at arm's length again, Buck said, "This is what I wanted to talk to Chaplain Harding about. I'm going to ask him if he'll perform the ceremony."

"Wonderful," she said. "And just where and when will this ceremony take place?"

"At my brother's house…tomorrow. Robert and Kady have a big front yard. We can hold the ceremony right there."

"Buck," she said, looking at him askance, "we can't just show up at your brother's house and announce that we're going to use his yard for our wedding ceremony. Besides, isn't tomorrow a bit soon?"

"Mr. Lincoln is putting my orders through right now, honey. We'll probably be leaving tomorrow. You don't think you can be ready by then?"

"Well…if I can get into Washington real soon, so I can make some arrangements for Daddy's burial, and for his house and furniture. I'll have to pack my belongings in a couple of trunks."

"All right, we'll head for town immediately. We'll go to Robert and Kady's first. They'll be very happy to meet you, and I'm sure they'll be glad to let us use their yard. They live at Sixth Street and Florida Avenue, which is only a few blocks from the railroad station."

"That puts them pretty close to the White House, then, doesn't it?"

"It does. The station's about halfway between Robert's place and the White House."

"Well, my love," Jenny said smiling, "we have a lot to do. We'd best get started."

After another long, sweet kiss, the couple emerged from the tent. Buck explained his pending transfer to General Tyler, and told him he and Jenny were getting married the next day. He then asked Chaplain Harding if he would perform the ceremony. Harding was happy to oblige, and the wedding was set for eleven o'clock the next day at the house of Robert and Kady Brownell. General Tyler congratulated them and wished them his best.

Buck drove Jenny to Washington in an army wagon. Robert and Kady were delighted to meet her and were more than happy to hold the wedding in their front yard. From there Buck and Jenny went to the Capitol, where Jenny learned that her father had already been buried. With mixed emotions, she made arrangements for the Jordan house and furniture, then packed her belongings in two trunks from the attic. She would spend the night in the house, and Buck would pick her up for the wedding in the morning.

During the afternoon, the president's order of transfer was delivered to General Tyler. There was a letter enclosed, which explained that John Hay had made arrangements for Buck and Jenny to catch the 2:00 P.M. train from Washington to Kansas City the next day.

At 10:45 the next morning, a dozen soldiers of First Brigade—invited by Buck—stood in the Robert Brownell yard, waiting for the ceremony to begin. An army wagon bearing Jenny's trunks and Buck's luggage waited in the street to carry the newlyweds to the railroad station. Colonel Abram Duryee sat in a wheelchair nearby, attended by a First Brigade corporal. General Tyler and Major Sparks stood close, in conversation with Robert and Kady Brownell.

The situation did not allow Jenny to wear a wedding gown, but she wore her nicest Sunday dress, and Buck was pleased at how beautiful she looked. The happy couple stood with Chaplain Harding, waiting to begin the ceremony. As they chatted, Buck and Jenny noticed that Harding kept looking westward down the street.

"By the way, Chaplain," Buck said to Harding, "I haven't even thought to ask you how much your fee is."

Harding pulled out his pocket watch, glanced down the street again, then flashed a sly grin and asked, "How much is she worth to you?"

Buck grinned and said, "There's not that much money in the world."

Harding chuckled. "Well, in that case, I guess there won't be any fee." As he spoke, he let his eyes stray down the street once more. A wide smile spread over his face.

Buck and Jenny followed his gaze and noticed two important-looking carriages approaching, one behind the other.

"Darling," said Jenny, "who would this be?"

"I can't tell yet, but I think Chaplain Hardy knows."

Hardy kept his eyes on the carriages and said, "You just wait and see."

A moment later, Jenny gasped when she recognized the people in the first carriage. President Lincoln wore his stove-pipe hat. Mrs. Lincoln sat next to him. Behind them were Willie and Tad, crowded next to Patricia Winters and Lieutenant John Hammond, his arm in a sling.

"Oh, Buck, look!" Jenny exclaimed.

"I see," responded Buck, smiling broadly.

In the second carriage were several armed men from the Pinkerton Detective Agency, who had come along as bodyguards at Allan Pinkerton's insistence.

While watching the carriages draw near, Harding said, "I contacted the president yesterday afternoon and told him about your wedding. I felt sure he would want to attend if possible. He canceled a couple of appointments to be here."

While soldiers and civilians looked on, the Lincolns alighted from their carriage, along with the governess and the wounded lieutenant. President Lincoln spoke to his sons, and they waited beside Patricia a few steps from the carriage.

The president and the first lady approached the bride and groom. Chaplain Harding greeted them, then retreated a step or two.

The tall, rawboned man smiled at the couple and said, "Mary, you know Jenny."

"Yes," smiled Mary. "Nice to see you Jenny. And...congratulations."

Then looking at Buck, the president said, "Mary, this is Colonel Brownell."

"Nice to meet you, Colonel. And congratulations to *you*. Jenny is a wonderful young lady."

"My pleasure, Mrs. Lincoln," said Buck, doing a slight bow. "And I couldn't agree with you more."

Lincoln towered over Jenny and said, "Young lady, I want to express my gratitude to you for saving my son's life. Such courage is highly commendable." Reaching inside his coat, he produced a large white envelope. Holding it in his hand, he spoke with quivering voice. "This is a presidential commendation for your brave and unselfish deed. I'll see that you have it in your hands after the ceremony."

"Thank you, Mr. President," replied the beautiful bride. "I will treasure it."

Lincoln cleared his throat. "Jenny, there is a boy back here who wants very much to hug the bride. Is it all right?"

Jenny glanced toward Tad Lincoln where he stood beside his brother and governess. "Of course," she smiled.

Looking back, the president said, "Okay, Tad."

The bright-eyed boy broke into a run and didn't stop until his arms were wrapped around Jenny. She kissed the top of his head and said, "I'm honored that you would come to my wedding, Tad."

"Thank you, Miss Jenny," he replied, "I love you."

"I love you, too," she said softly.

Tad stepped back at his father's word, and Mrs. Lincoln embraced Jenny, followed by young Willie. When Willie backed away, the president looked at the bride with tired eyes and asked, "May I?"

"Of course," she smiled.

Buck looked on with pride as Abraham Lincoln discreetly embraced his bride.

The ceremony was performed, and after congratulations were offered all around, the president gave Jenny the envelope containing the presidential commendation.

Robert and Kady welcomed Jenny into the family with hugs and kisses, then said good-bye to the bride and groom. Buck and Jenny thanked them for the use of their yard. Good-byes were said to the other guests, then Colonel and Mrs. Francis E. Brownell boarded the army wagon and hurried off in the direction of the railroad station to catch the westbound train.

Standing with his arm around Mrs. Lincoln, the president watched with tears in his eyes as the wagon rolled up the street. When the bride and groom were seen kissing, the soldiers whooped and whistled. Abraham Lincoln leaned over and planted a kiss on Mary's forehead.

When the wagon turned a corner and passed from view, the great man sighed and said, "Well, Mrs. Lincoln, we must be on our way, too. I've got a country to run…and a war to win."

EPILOGUE

Though the Confederate army decisively routed the Federals in the first battle at Bull Run, it was done at a high cost. Of General Pierre G.T. Beauregard's 32,500 men, 387 were killed, 1,582 wounded, and 13 captured. Of General Irvin McDowell's 35,000 men, 460 were killed, 1,124 were wounded, and 1,312 came up missing. It is estimated that about a thousand of the "missing" were deserters who had experienced all the war they wanted under the Confederate guns at Bull Run.

In early fall of 1861, Allan Pinkerton's continual pursuit of enemy spies led him to the door of Rose O'Neal Greenhow. A search of her house produced proof of her espionage for the Confederacy. She was placed under arrest and jailed. The Union had quickly lost its taste for executing female spies. Rose was given a stiff prison sentence, but because there was no place for women in the Federal prisons, she was incarcerated in her own home under heavy guard. The house became known as "Fort Greenhow."

For the next few months, Rose was somehow able to communicate with the Confederacy, right under the noses of her guards. In

January 1862, Major General John E. Wool telegraphed the Senate Military Committee from a distant army post, advising them that someone in Washington was obtaining "all the information necessary for those who command the Rebel army. They know much better than I do what is going on in Washington."

Rose was then transferred to the Old Capitol Prison. Her fellow inmates were Rebel soldiers, Union deserters, and escaped slaves who had no means of supporting themselves. Because of squalor and disease in the prison, Rose was released on "parole" by the end of March 1862 and transported beyond the Union lines in Virginia with a solemn warning not to come back North for the duration of the War.

Rose O'Neal Greenhow never crossed the Mason-Dixon Line again. She drowned in a boating accident in the Cape Fear River near Fort Fisher, North Carolina, on September 1, 1862.

Clara Barton, a clerk in the U.S. Patent Office, had no formal nurse's training, but she labored unselfishly during the entire Civil War, soliciting and distributing medical supplies and caring for wounded Union soldiers. Oftentimes, she also found herself administering medicine and medical help to wounded and ailing Rebel prisoners.

In 1881, because of her love for helping others, Clara left her job at the Patent Office to become the first president of the American Red Cross. She spent herself caring for the injured, sick, and dying until her own health failed and she died in 1912 at the age of ninety-one.

BOOK FOUR

SHADOWED MEMORIES

BATTLE OF SHILOH

To Dick and Pete,

my very special sons-in-law.

The Lord has blessed me in many ways.

If you want to see two of my greatest blessings,

take a look in the nearest mirror.

I love you both more than you will ever know.

✳ ✳ ✳

PROLOGUE

J ust as the Potomac, the Shenandoah, the Rappahannock, and the York Rivers shaped the Civil War in the eastern theater, so it was with the Mississippi, the Ohio, the Cumberland, and the Tennessee Rivers in the west.

At the outset of the war, Major General Albert Sidney Johnston commanded the entire Confederate Department of the West, which took in all of Tennessee, Missouri, Arkansas, western Mississippi, and the Indian country farther west.

The Union command, however, was divided. Major General John C. Fremont, with his headquarters at St. Louis, Missouri, commanded the huge Department of the West, reaching from the Mississippi River to the Rocky Mountains, and on the east side of the Mississippi, southern Illinois and all of Kentucky west of the Cumberland River. Major General Robert Anderson of Fort Sumter fame commanded the Federal Department of the Cumberland, with central and eastern Kentucky and all of Tennessee as its potential maneuvering area.

Fremont gained fame in his early manhood as an explorer. Upon entering the U.S. Army, he became an officer in the Corps of Engineers. A controversial figure in the conquest of California and the Mexican War, he later became a politician, and in 1856 he was the first presidential candidate of the Republican Party. He owed his rank and command, not to his sketchy military experience, but to his political clout.

Of a different mold, Johnston was a West Pointer who had distinguished himself as a leader in the Texas War for Independence, and later in the Mexican War. He also had experience as an Indian fighter, and had commanded the U.S. Army expedition of 1857-58 against the rebellious Mormons in Utah.

Within a month after the Battle of First Bull Run in July 1861, both the Federals and the Confederates were massing large forces of militia on the borders of "neutral" Kentucky. By the end of August 1861, some sixty-five thousand Union troops were camped along the Ohio River in Illinois, Indiana, and Ohio while forty-five thousand Confederate troops were concentrated in northern Tennessee.

Newly promoted Brigadier General Ulysses S. Grant was appointed by President Abraham Lincoln on August 30 to command Federal forces in southern Illinois and southeastern Missouri, a part of Fremont's jurisdiction. Grant, an 1843 graduate of West Point, had distinguished himself for heroism in the Mexican War, and had then resigned from the army in 1854 to pursue a civilian career.

A respected merchant in Galena, Illinois, when the Civil War broke out, Grant immediately offered his services to the state. He was soon assigned command of an Illinois regiment with the rank of colonel.

Born Hyram Ulysses Grant, he received a congressional appointment to the West Point Military Academy and entered school in the fall of 1839. A clerical error on his appointment papers identified him as Ulysses Simpson Grant. The young cadet liked Ulysses Simpson better than Hyram Ulysses, so he left it alone. Later, at the battle of Fort Donelson (as depicted in this volume), the initials "U.S." proved to be a hook upon which to hang a new and admiring title: *U*nconditional *S*urrender Grant.

Wearing the new brigadier general insignias on his uniform,

Grant arrived at his command headquarters on the Mississippi River at Cairo, Illinois, on September 3, 1861. That same day Johnston ordered his subordinate, Major General Leonidas Polk, to seize key points in western Kentucky. On September 4, Grant learned of the movement of Polk's troops into Columbus, Kentucky, just eighteen miles south of Cairo on the east bank of the Mississippi. Grant realized that a major objective of both Union and Confederate forces was control of the Mississippi.

Cairo, at the southern tip of Illinois, was a critical point because it stood at the junction of the Ohio and Mississippi Rivers. It was also the place where Illinois met the key border states of Missouri and Kentucky. Cairo's significance as a base for future Union operations was further enhanced by two major geographical spots nearby.

Less than forty miles upriver, east of Cairo, the Tennessee River flowed into the Ohio at Paducah, Kentucky. The Tennessee, rising far to the east in the mountains of southwest Virginia, swept nearly a thousand miles on a wide arc through the heart of the Confederacy. It provided a natural water highway between the critically important points of the South and the great agricultural regions of the North.

Just as important was the Cumberland River, also flowing into the Ohio, and forming a snake-like concentric arc with that of the Tennessee, flowing through Nashville. At the town of Dover, in western Tennessee, the Cumberland and Tennessee Rivers were only twelve miles apart. From that point to the Ohio, they flowed in parallel, never less than three nor more than twelve miles separating them.

General Johnston recognized the strategic position of the two rivers and ordered two Confederate forts constructed—Fort Henry on the Tennessee, and twelve miles across the mucky lowlands to the east, Fort Donelson on the Cumberland.

While construction was under way during the next four months, there were skirmishes between the Yankees and the Rebels along the banks of the rivers. It soon became evident that major battles were in the offing. By New Year's Day, 1862, some five thousand

Confederate troops manned Forts Henry and Donelson under the command of Brigadier General Lloyd Tilghman.

Telegraph lines were strung between the two forts so there could be instant communication between General Tilghman—who headquartered at Fort Henry—and Brigadier General Simon Buckner, who was his officer-in-charge at Fort Donelson.

During those same four months, two major command changes occurred in the Union ranks. General Robert Anderson became seriously ill and was replaced by Brigadier General Don Carlos Buell, who had distinguished himself in both the Seminole War and the Mexican War. In Missouri, General John C. Fremont was proving to be incompetent. He was relieved of his command by President Lincoln and replaced by Major General Henry Halleck, a brilliant, tough-minded, abrasive veteran of the Mexican War.

Though January was bitter cold, there were more skirmishes between the two factions. General Grant concluded that sooner or later he was going to have to deal with the forces at Forts Henry and Donelson, since they served as watchdogs over the two strategic rivers. Grant consulted Flag Officer Andrew H. Foote, commander of the Union Navy flotilla of river gunboats in General Halleck's Department of the Missouri. As a result, on January 28, 1862, Halleck received similar telegraph messages from Grant and Foote. Grant's message said briefly, "With your permission, I will take my seventeen thousand troops and attack Fort Henry and establish a camp there for Union forces. When Fort Henry is secure, I will do the same with Fort Donelson."

Foote's message to Halleck endorsed Grant's proposal and expressed his readiness to support the move.

The next day, Halleck received a telegram from Washington, informing him that Confederate General P.G.T. Beauregard was leaving Manassas (where he had been since the Battle of Bull Run) and heading for Kentucky, taking fifteen regiments with him.

Halleck decided to strike a heavy blow against the Confederate strongholds before Beauregard and his regiments arrived. Unaware that the information about Beauregard was false, Halleck telegraphed Grant on January 30, telling him to make his move on Fort Henry as soon as possible. Halleck also began to seek reinforcements for Grant. At the same time, he commanded Buell to make demonstrations and diversions to keep Johnston from further reinforcing western Kentucky.

Grant informed Halleck of plans he and Foote had prepared for moving his Union troops down the Ohio, Cumberland, and Tennessee Rivers by steamboat. Grant and Foote agreed that they would have the troops at Fort Henry's door, ready to attack, by Wednesday morning, February 5. General Halleck wired back his consent, encouraging them to make quick work of it. When Fort Henry was secured, Halleck would decide when to attack Fort Donelson.

Little did the military leaders on both sides realize that the Fort Henry-Fort Donelson conflicts would become the prelude to one of the Civil War's bloodiest battles on April 6–7, 1862, at Shiloh, Tennessee. The Shiloh battle would end in a draw, with nearly twenty thousand casualties.

The Western Theater, Winter-Spring 1862

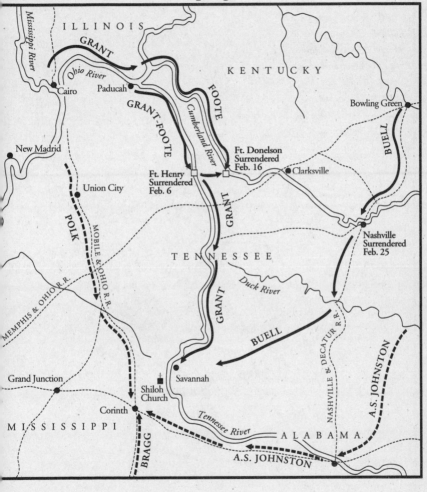

The Battle of Shiloh—April 6, 1862

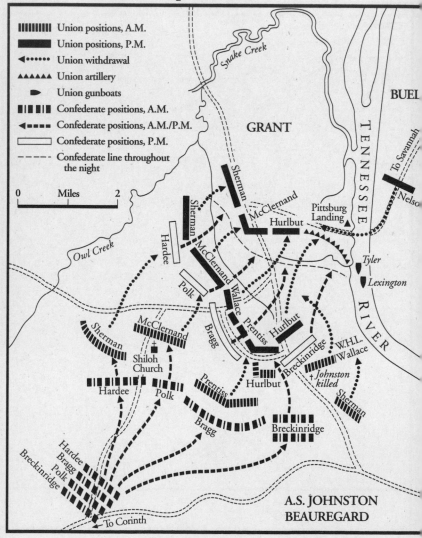

Union positions, A.M.

Union positions, P.M.

Union withdrawal

Union artillery

Union gunboats

Confederate positions, A.M.

Confederate positions, A.M./P.M.

Confederate positions, P.M.

Confederate line throughout the night

0   Miles   2

Snake Creek

GRANT

BUEL

TENNESSEE

To Savannah

Nelso

Sherman

Sherman

McClernand

Hurlbut

Pittsburg Landing

Hardee

McClernand

Owl Creek

Polk

Wallace

Prentiss

Hurlbut

Tyler

Lexington

RIVER

Bragg

McClernand

Sherman

Shiloh Church

Prentiss

Hurlbut

Breckinridge

W.H.L. Wallace

Johnston killed

Hardee

Polk

Sherman

Bragg

Breckinridge

Hardee
Bragg
Polk
Breckinridge

To Corinth

A.S. JOHNSTON
BEAUREGARD

The Battle of Shiloh—April 7, 1862

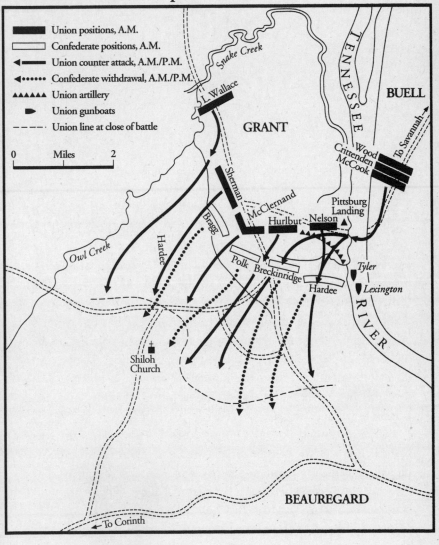

Union positions, A.M.
Confederate positions, A.M.
Union counter attack, A.M./P.M.
Confederate withdrawal, A.M./P.M.
Union artillery
Union gunboats
Union line at close of battle

0   Miles   2

Snake Creek
L. Wallace
GRANT
BUELL
TENNESSEE
Wood
Crittenden
McCook
To Savannah
Sherman
McClernand
Pittsburg Landing
Bragg
Hurlbut
Nelson
Hardee
Owl Creek
Polk
Breckinridge
Tyler
Hardee
Lexington
RIVER
Shiloh Church
BEAUREGARD
To Corinth

ONE

The light of the full moon lay like silver on the carpet of crusted snow and ice that covered the fields all around him. Lying on an icy knoll, rifle in hand, he turtled into his upturned collar and let a shudder crawl over his body. The night wind sliced through his gray wool overcoat like knives, sending chills all the way to the center of his bones.

There was a warmth within him, however, that the winter's cold could never quench. As a loyal Union soldier and marksman, he had been sent by the Federal Office of Intelligence in Washington to do a job. He was to kill as many Confederate officers as possible. The thrill of what his successful task could mean to the Union cause kept a flame burning in his soul.

His intended victim on this frigid Tennessee night was Confederate Colonel Nelson Parker, who was on his way from Fort Henry to Fort Donelson under cover of night to join Brigadier General Simon Buckner. Brigadier General Lloyd Tilghman, who commanded both forts from his headquarters at Fort Henry, had given in to Buckner's oft-repeated request for a colonel to serve under him, since his previous colonel had recently been sent to Nashville.

Since Tilghman had two colonels at Fort Henry, Buckner felt he deserved one of them.

The assassin chuckled to himself. Here he was, dressed in a gray uniform, neatly inserted into the ranks of the Rebels, and they didn't suspect a thing. He thought back to earlier in the day when he happened to be passing the telegraph room inside Fort Donelson as General Tilghman's wire was coming in. The corporal who manned the telegraph key at the time had just written down Tilghman's message when a wire from Major General Albert Sidney Johnston started coming through from Johnston's headquarters at Nashville.

While busily writing down the Johnston message, the corporal had handed the assassin the slip of paper and asked him to carry it at once to General Buckner. While moving toward the general's quarters, he had read the message:

31 January, 1862
Brigadier General Simon Bolivar Buckner
Fort Donelson
At your request am assigning Colonel Nelson Parker to your command. Because of daily skirmishes with Union forces, Parker and escorts will ride at night. Will arrive Fort Donelson app. 9:00 P.M. Escorts will return at once.
Brigadier General Lloyd Tilghman

The Yankee impostor delivered the telegram to Buckner and rejoiced at his good fortune. He was scheduled to be among the four hundred men going into town that evening. General Buckner was allowing his soldiers to spend an evening in Dover in rotations of four hundred per night. Most made the rounds between the town's six taverns. Though Buckner did not allow them to drink alcoholic beverages, they enjoyed the time away from the fort.

Dover, like Fort Donelson, was on the west bank of the Cumberland River, barely three-and-a-half miles south of the fort.

Twelve miles due west of Donelson stood Fort Henry on the east bank of the Tennessee River.

The assassin glanced in the direction of Fort Henry, then did a panorama of the wooded hills to the east and north, marked only by the spiderweb tracery of dark-shadowed, naked oaks and dogwoods, their skeletal shapes bent to the wind.

The Cumberland River was broad where it flowed beneath the towering fort, and its wind-ruffled waters reflected the silver hue of the moon. There was no sign of life in the woods or fields. Some three miles to the southeast lay Dover, where lantern light glistened from the windows of houses.

He had no idea how many men would make up Colonel Parker's escort, but with the weapon in his hands, he could knock Parker out of the saddle at eight hundred yards. If there were no more than four or five men in the group, he could take them all out before they knew what hit them. If there were more, and he had to make a run for it, there were plenty of places to hide. Besides, the soldiers in the convoy would think a bunch of Yankees had set up an ambush. Not knowing how many Yankees might be out here, they would high-tail it for Fort Donelson.

The assassin's rifle lay in the Y-shaped crotches of two small tree limbs he had positioned solidly in the ice. Parker and his escorts would have to ride across the fields north of him in order to cross the Cumberland at its lowest spot before beginning their climb up the steep, winding path to Fort Donelson. Their course would place them in the crosshairs of his new telescopic sight.

Not long after he had joined the Confederate army at Nashville, he was assigned to General Buckner's brigade. When it was known that Buckner and his men were being sent to the newly built fort, the Confederate army outfitted them with brand new .58 caliber Spencer repeater rifles. Buckner's men were the only Confederate soldiers to receive the Spencers, which had an accuracy range of eight hundred yards and a magazine that held eight rounds. By rapidly changing magazines, an expert rifleman could fire up to twenty-one rounds a minute. The Confederate army had fitted the Spencers with specially developed sights, but the assassin had replaced the government-issue sight for this occasion with his own German-built sight, a full-length brass tube that provided twenty-power vision. The challenge was to hold the rifle steady enough to cope with so much magnification. The assassin's Y-shaped tree limbs solved that problem.

Suddenly movement on the moonstruck land caught his eye. Riders coming from the northwest. Had to be Parker and his escorts. Shouldering the rifle, he peered through the sight. It was Parker, all right, and there were only five men with him. They didn't know it, but they had seen their last sunrise.

The killer estimated them to be about fifteen hundred yards out. They were in a trot, and would be within range soon. A thrill slithered down him, and suddenly his body felt warm. The only cold he could feel was in his hands, and he cupped them now close to his mouth. Putting his right eye to the scope again, he caressed the long barrel and whispered, "C'mon, you rotten Rebs. Just a little closer, and you'll be shaking hands with the devil."

The riders-in-gray seemed to be moving in slow-motion, but finally they were within the Spencer's range. He sighted in on the rider in the lead, following his movement. His finger rested comfortably on the trigger. The silvery fields lay in absolute stillness. A silence of death hovered over the snow-laden earth as the crosshairs locked on Colonel Nelson Parker's chest.

He squeezed the trigger. The cartridge exploded and the wooden stock kicked against his shoulder.

Some eight hundred yards across the wintry Tennessee landscape, the Confederate colonel was unaware that death was in flight. He would never hear the shot as it echoed over the frozen turf.

The assassin witnessed the impact through crystal-sharp German glass. He saw the fleeting amazement on Parker's moon-lit face as his hat flew off when the bullet tore through his chest. The colonel twisted in the saddle, then fell gracelessly from his horse's back.

Instant panic sent two escorts from their saddles to attend to the fallen officer. The other three brought up their rifles and fired in the direction the shot had come from. The killer knew he was safely out of their range and calmly returned fire as fast as he could. Within fifteen seconds, the three who had remained in their saddles were lying dead. The other two had flattened themselves on the cold ground, conversing excitedly.

The killer's elevated position gave him the advantage. Though the Rebel soldiers lay flat, he had no problem bringing them into focus through the scope. Taking careful aim, he put a bullet through the one on his left. The other one, realizing he was now alone, scrambled to his feet and dashed for his horse. He had his left foot in the stirrup and was swinging the other leg upward when the assassin's bullet plowed into his back. He arched in pain and fell backward to the ground, never to move again.

On his feet, rifle in hand, the killer ran toward Dover, leaning into the wind. When he reached the outskirts, he ducked into the shadow of a small barn and removed his telescope from the Spencer. From the lining of his overcoat, he took the government rifle sight and fitted it back in place. He then slipped the German sight into the lining and walked casually onto the main street toward the Cumberland Tavern.

The place was alive with piano music and Confederate soldiers laughing and joking as they sipped their coffee and sarsaparilla. Citizens of Dover drank and laughed with them. Unnoticed, the killer slipped off his coat, hung it on a wall peg, and leaned his rifle against the wall. He moved slowly through the place, studying faces, and decided to move on. He would find the men he had come to town with.

He checked out two other places before he spotted his friends in the Two Rivers Tavern. Had he found any greater excitement touring the other taverns? He said he had not, then ordered a sarsaparilla and sat down among the men-in-gray.

Some of the men of Dover were discussing the war situation

with the soldiers. The hated Yankees had set up camp just north of Fort Henry, and word was that General Ulysses S. Grant had left his headquarters eighty-five miles northeast of Cairo, Illinois, and was going to set up a temporary headquarters somewhere near Dover. The five thousand Confederate troops in Forts Henry and Donelson were bracing themselves for the assault they knew was coming. These visits to town would soon come to an end.

Among the civilians was a big farmer named Clarence Clubson. Twenty-two years of age, Clubson stood six-five and had bull-like shoulders, a pillar of a neck, deep chest, and arms like tree trunks. "Club" was known for his fighting prowess and hair-trigger temper. The men of Dover and the surrounding farming country feared him, and always gave him a wide berth.

Club had a booming voice to match his mountainous body. His face was blunt, with wide-set hazel eyes and a broad nose. He had a tangled mass of straw-colored hair that rarely saw a comb.

Club bore within him a vehement hatred for Yankees. When General Grant was mentioned, Club rose to his feet and began smacking a meaty fist into an open palm. Everyone in the place grew quiet. Club swore, then boomed, "I'd like to know just where that stinkin' Useless S. Grant plans on settin' up his headquarters! Just gimme three minutes with that bearded skunk, and I'll tear his head off!"

A young man with twisted legs sat in a chair holding a pair of crutches. "Club," he said, "if Linda Lee heard you swear like that, she'd drop you like a hot potato. You know she don't cotton to foul language."

"Yeah," spoke up an elderly man with no teeth, "and neither does the rest of her family. If you're gonna marry into the Claiborne family, Club, you're gonna have to clean up your mouth and start goin' to church."

Club ran his gaze between the two men and grunted, "What Linda Lee don't know ain't gonna hurt her none. I get mad, and when I do, I cuss. I just don't do it around her or her family. As for goin' to church, we'll see about that once't Linda Lee and me are hitched up."

"I'm not too sure you'll get hitched up," the young man said, "unless you make the family think you're a Christian. And you ain't gonna do that without bein' in church when the doors are open."

Everybody in and around Dover knew that Linda Lee Claiborne was not in love with Club. She had no intentions of marrying him, though she always treated him kindly. Linda Lee had even told Club in her gracious manner that she would not marry him, but he would not accept it. He was sure she loved him and would eventually marry him.

"Aw, Linda Lee wouldn't care so much about this church business if her ma and Hannah Rose weren't such hounddogs about it," Club said.

"Pardon me, Mr. Clubson, but could I ask you a question?" a young Rebel private asked.

"Sure, soldier."

"I don't mean any offense, mind you, but from the looks of you, I'd say you're about the biggest, strongest feller in these parts."

"Ain't no 'about' about it," Club growled. "I am the biggest and strongest. Ain't nobody gonna challenge that."

"Well, what's bothering me is how come you're not in a Confederate uniform?"

Club set steady eyes on him. "There's nothin' I'd like better, private. Nothin'. But my pa died just before the war started last year, and there's nobody to run the farm. The crops I raise are goin' to the Confederate army for food. I tried to enlist, but they told me I could best serve the Confederacy by raisin' corn and cabbage and such and sendin' 'em to the troops. So that's what I'm doin'. 'Sides that, I'm takin' care of the Claiborne place so's Linda Lee's brothers can fight."

"What's there to do at the Claiborne place, Club?" another man asked. "I mean, besides just keepin' the buildin's and fences in good repair? Other than their wagon team, they ain't got no animals."

"Well, you're right…that's about all there is to it. But somebody's got to do the stuff them women can't handle."

"I bet you wouldn't spend so much time at the Claiborne place if you weren't in love with Linda Lee," another man laughed. "When are you and Linda Lee gonna tie the knot, Club?"

The elderly man flashed a toothless grin at the others, winked, and said, "From what I've been hearin', there ain't gonna be no knot between that beautiful girl and Club. Seems she's been seein' a couple other fellas."

"Oh, no she ain't!" Club snarled. "I took care of Luke Smith and Harry Binder both! Beat 'em to a pulp. They wouldn't dare go near Linda Lee again. 'Sides, I happen to know that both of them are in the army somewhere in eastern Tennessee. Chattanooga, I think."

"I ain't talkin' about Luke and Harry. I'm talkin' about them two boys from Fort Donelson."

Club's neck turned red and the color rose to his face. "I don't know about any boys from the fort. Who are they? When have they been here?"

"You talkin' about those two young corporals, Abe?" asked Wally Speck, one of the Claiborne's neighbors.

"Yeah. Come to think of it, I did hear that they're both corporals."

"They've been visitin' Hannah Rose, not Linda Lee."

"You sure about that?"

"Positive. I was in the general store 'bout a month ago when those two came in. Hannah Rose was there, and they struck up a conversation. Taller one introduced himself as Jim Lynch, and the other one called himself Lanny Perkins. When Hannah Rose left the store, I heard both of 'em arguin' 'bout which one was gonna date her first. Since then I've seen her with Perkins four or five times. They ain't interested in Linda Lee, I can say that for sure."

A scowl rode Clubson's brow. "Well, they better not be. Any man shows interest in my gal will get hisself beat to a pulp." He went to a peg on the nearest wall and retrieved his coat and hat. "Milkin' time comes early, boys. See y'all later."

When Club was gone, Speck said, "I feel sorry for the big brute. He's so blinded with love, he cain't see that pretty little Linda Lee ain't never gonna marry him."

"Guess he'll figure it out someday," sighed one of the others.

Abe Smalley shook his head and said, "Tell you who I feel sorry for. That's the guy Linda Lee falls in love with. Club'll probably kill 'im."

No one said anything for some time after that. Then one of the sergeants glanced at the clock on the wall and said, "Well, my military comrades, it's gettin' late. Time we were makin' our way back to the fort."

"Colonel Parker oughtta be there by now," one of the soldiers said. "I'm sure glad General Tilghman is letting us have him."

The assassin felt a warmth spring up in his chest and spread pleasantly through his body. Other Rebel soldiers spoke of their admiration for Parker, and how pleased they were that he was becoming part of the command force at Fort Donelson. The man who had shot Parker only an hour before grinned to himself as he slipped into his coat, feeling the telescopic sight in its lining.

At Fort Donelson, General Buckner was sitting behind his desk in the rock-walled room he called his office. Seated in front of him were Captains Waldon McGuire, Eric Donaldson, and Britt Claiborne. Two lanterns burned overhead.

Buckner, in his early fifties, was a West Point graduate and a long-time friend of General Grant. A colonel in the regular U.S. Army before the Civil War, he had trained five thousand militiamen in Kentucky. Some of those men were now with him at Fort Donelson.

A stern-faced man with a thick head of salt-and-pepper hair, Buckner wore a droopy mustache and had a pair of wide-set, piercing gray eyes. At the moment, those eyes were resting on the pocketwatch in the palm of his hand. "This isn't like General Tilghman or Colonel Parker. It's almost ten-thirty. I don't like the smell of this."

There was a knock at the door.

"Come!" called Buckner.

The door squeaked open, and the face of Corporal Darrell Tomberlin appeared. "I'm sorry, General, but I can't get any response. They must have the telegraph key turned off at Fort Henry."

"All right. Thank you, Corporal."

"Anything else I can do, sir?"

"Not at the moment."

"Yes, sir." The door clicked shut, and Tomberlin was gone.

Worry etched itself on Buckner's face. Rising, he said, "Captain Claiborne, I want you to take a platoon of men and ride to Fort Henry. I must know what's going on."

All three captains stood up.

"Sir?" said Donaldson.

"Yes?"

"May I suggest that Captain McGuire and I go with Captain Claiborne, and that the platoon be at least fifty men? I just don't trust those blue-bellies. I hate to say it, but maybe…maybe they ambushed Colonel Parker and his escorts. If they did, and they're still hanging around out there, we'll need enough men to repel another ambush."

The lines in Buckner's brow deepened. Wiping a palm across his mouth, he replied, "An ambush doesn't make sense, Captain. It's colder than blue blazes out there. The Yankees would have no way of knowing that Colonel Parker was riding here tonight. It would be impossible for them to plan an ambush. I seriously doubt they'd be patrolling, just waiting for some gray uniforms to show up in the moonlight. The whole reason General Tilghman planned to send Parker at night was to eliminate any chance of him running into some Yankees."

"I agree, sir," Donaldson replied. "My first thought was ambush, but you're right, that isn't likely. But I see the concern in your eyes. What do you think may have happened to Parker?"

"We know that General Grant has plans to move his headquarters to somewhere in this area," Buckner said. "It crossed my mind that possibly he decided to make his move at night…and just maybe his troops and Colonel Parker's group stumbled onto each other."

"If anything has happened to Colonel Parker, sir," Claiborne said, "it would more than likely be just what you described. I hope not. I hope it'll turn out that for some reason, Parker and his escorts couldn't leave Fort Henry as scheduled, and that there's something wrong with the telegraph so General Tilghman can't get a message to us."

"I hope you're right," breathed Buckner. Turning to Donaldson, he said, "I appreciate your willingness to go with Captain Claiborne, and I'm sure Captain McGuire is just as willing, but I don't dare risk all three of my captains on one venture." Shifting his gaze to Claiborne, he proceeded. "Captain, take Lieutenant Benson, your brother William, and two other sergeants, along with fifty troops. Ride to Fort Henry as fast as you can. I've got to know if something has happened. Should you get there and find that everything's all right, and that their telegraph key was merely shut off, wire me immediately. I'll see that Corporal Tomberlin keeps our line open. Otherwise, I'll be anxiously waiting for your return with whatever news you can give me."

"I'm on my way, sir," Claiborne said as he hurried to the door.

TWO

Clouds were scudding in from the north and periodically covering the moon as Captain Britt Claiborne watched his men saddle their horses. Beside him were Lieutenant Blythe Benson and Sergeants William Claiborne, Cliff Nolan, and Jed Masters.

At twenty-eight, Britt Claiborne was the oldest of the Claiborne brothers, and stood the tallest. He was six-three and weighed a slender two hundred pounds. William was twenty-six, stood an even six feet, and weighed the same as his older brother. Their youngest brother Robert (who had recently been promoted to corporal) was twenty-three and of the same build as William. There was a strong family resemblance among the three brothers.

Wind gusts flung ice crystals in the faces of the men-in-gray as they made ready. Captain Claiborne tugged at his hatbrim and gave the command for the platoon to mount up. Sentries on the walls bent their heads into the wind and watched as the fifty-five men rode down the gentle slope and turned due west, leaving the fort and the river behind.

After riding for no more than a quarter-hour, Lieutenant

Benson raised a gloved hand and pointed directly in front of them. "Look, Captain! Horses! Looks like five or six of them huddled together out there."

The moon was shining without hindrance at the moment. Claiborne could make them out clearly. He also saw dark forms scattered about on the white, frozen turf. His heart quickened pace as he said, "Looks like bodies on the ground!"

"You're right, sir. I...I'm afraid it's Colonel Parker and his escort."

Captain Claiborne put his mount to a gallop, and the platoon followed his lead. As they drew up, hooves scattering snow and ice, the captain slid from his saddle and shouted, "Heads up, men! There's been an ambush here! Form a circle and keep a lookout! Lieutenant, you and Sergeant Claiborne dismount and come with me."

Sergeants Nolan and Masters took charge of the remaining troops and led them into a circle around the six bodies scattered on the snow. Kneeling beside Parker, the captain found the bullet hole in his coat. Shaking his head, he spoke above the wind and said, "Right through the heart. There's hardly any blood. He probably died instantly. Let's check the others."

As they checked on the last dead man, the captain said, "This was no ordinary ambush, gentlemen. If there had been even a squad of Yankees in on this, each man would have several bullets in him. All of these poor men took a single bullet. Looks like the work of a lone sharpshooter to me."

"Yeah," Benson said, "a sharpshooter with a repeater rifle."

"But why would a Yankee sharpshooter be out here in these fields at night?" William asked. "There's no way he could have known that Colonel Parker and these men were coming from Fort Henry. I mean...a man doesn't just load up his rifle and go for a ride in this kind of weather, hoping to run onto some enemy soldiers."

"You're right," Britt nodded, stomping circulation to his feet. "It's got me puzzled, too."

"Maybe if we can find where the sharpshooter was firing from, we can learn something," Benson said. "You know…maybe some footprints in the snow that'll tell us where he came from, or where he went."

"We need to do that all right, Lieutenant, but it'll have to wait till morning." Britt said, looking skyward.

The other two looked at the moon and saw that it was about to go behind a cloud bank that reached all the way to the northern horizon and was spreading south.

"You're right," Benson agreed. "Let's get these bodies back to the fort. General Buckner will be biting his nails if he doesn't hear from us soon."

Thirty minutes later, Captain Claiborne and Lieutenant Benson sat in General Buckner's office and reported what they had found. Stunned, Buckner sat back in his chair and sighed. "I hate this. It's tragic to lose those five escorts, but its double tragic to lose an excellent officer like Colonel Parker. We really needed him here."

"Would you like for me to ride to Fort Henry and inform General Tilghman of this, sir?" Claiborne asked. "I could take a few men for safety's sake and be back in less than three hours."

"No," Buckner replied, shaking his head. "We can send a wire to him in the morning. General Tilghman's learning about it tonight wouldn't change anything, except to rob him of a night's sleep."

"I'll have Captain McGuire see to the burial detail," Buckner said. "I want you gentlemen to take the same group you had tonight first thing in the morning and see what you can learn about the sharpshooter. Mystery to me why a man would be out there at that time of night in this kind of weather."

Morning came with dismal, low-hanging clouds that looked loaded with snow. The wind had died down some when Captain Claiborne led his platoon out of the fort. Returning to where they had found the bodies, they stayed close together in case of an ambush and rode in a wide circle, searching for clues.

After some two hours in the wintry cold, the captain decided it was of no use. The man who had cut down Colonel Parker and his escorts had managed to leave no trace of himself. Turning to Lieutenant Benson, Claiborne said, "We're wasting our time. This circle has us more than six hundred yards from where we found the dead men. I'm sure those Yankees don't have rifles or gunsights any better than ours. The sharpshooter had to have been inside this range, especially since he was shooting at night. We might as well get on back to the fort."

"We've seen a lot of hoofprints in the snow, Captain," Benson said. "Maybe the guy did his shooting from astride his horse. Maybe he never even touched ground."

"I thought of that, but no matter how good the man is with a rifle, I doubt he'd try to take out six men from the back of his horse. Doesn't allow for a steady aim."

"How else you going to explain it?"

"I can't, but I know enough about shooting a rifle that when you need precision, you find a way to brace yourself or your gun. We've found no footprints around any of the trees out here, and..."

Claiborne's attention was drawn to a wagon moving their direction from Dover. It was about a hundred yards away, but he recognized Louie Metcalf and his wife, Elsie. Their farm was some five miles north of town.

"Captain, sir, what's our next move?" Sergeant Nolan asked.

"Lieutenant Benson and I were just discussing that, Sergeant. We've made our search just about as far as is sensible. Even if the sharpshooter had a gun that could shoot from beyond this distance, the most up-to-date gunsight couldn't give him the kind of accuracy he had last night. Somehow he managed to kill six soldiers and get away without a trace."

"He'd have to be some kind of spook to do that, wouldn't he, sir?" asked one of the men. "Seems to me a mortal man, no matter how careful he was, would have to leave some signs that he was there."

"Well, if he was a spook, he sure was an accurate one," the captain said. "I hate to leave this thing a mystery, but we've done all we can do. Let's head back to the fort. General Buckner isn't going to be happy with my report, but I don't know any other option."

Claiborne saw that Metcalf and his wife were drawing near. They recognized him and drew their wagon to a halt. "Hello, Britt," Metcalf said. "You fellas on some kind of patrol?"

The captain touched his hat, smiled at Elsie, and said, "Good morning, Mrs. Metcalf. And good morning to you, Louie. No, this isn't a patrol, it's a search party."

"A search party? What are you searching for?"

"Long story. Six of our soldiers were riding from Fort Henry to Fort Donelson last night, and somebody gunned them down."

"Yankees ambush 'em?"

"More like one Yankee with a repeater rifle. General Buckner sent us out to see if we could find where he did the shooting from—maybe find some tracks that would tell us which direction he came from and where he headed once his killing was done. We've made a series of circles trying to come up with something, but with no luck. I figure by now we're past the point he could've done the shooting from."

"Wait a minute!" Louie exclaimed. "That's it, Elsie! That's what those two tree limbs were for!"

"What are you talking about?" Claiborne asked.

"Elsie and I noticed a couple of broken tree limbs stuck in the ice on top of a knoll back toward town as we were drivin' in earlier this mornin'. I'd bet my bottom dollar that's where your sharpshooter did his shootin'. The way those limbs are standin' there, they'd make a perfect cradle for a long-range rifle."

The captain cast a glance in that direction. "How far is the knoll from here?"

"Oh, couple hundred yards or so," said Louie, twisting around on the wagon seat and pointing. "Look over to the right of that clump of trees just north of the road. See it?"

Claiborne's gaze followed the farmer's finger and settled on the snow-covered mound. "Yes, but…that would make it some eight hundred yards. Man would have to have some kind of gunsight to shoot as accurately as he did from that distance, even if he had one of those new Spencer .58s we just got. The gunsights on those Spencers aren't that accurate."

"Seems to me it would take one of those new telescopic sights like they have over in Europe, Captain," Sergeant Masters said. "S'pose the Federals got their hands on some of those?"

"I hope not. If they have, we're going to have real sniper trouble. Let's take a look at the knoll."

The captain thanked Louie Metcalf and led his men at a gallop toward the knoll. When they hauled up at the base of the mound, every eye was fastened on the two Y-shaped tree limbs pointing toward the murky sky.

Before leaving his saddle, Captain Claiborne said, "Everybody stay mounted. Lieutenant Benson and I will investigate."

When Claiborne and Benson reached the top, they knew Louie Metcalf was right. Scattered in the snow were six spent .58 caliber shells.

Claiborne squatted down and looked northward, following the sharpshooter's sight line. "This is it, Lieutenant. Some Yankee marksman laid in wait right here and took out Parker and his men."

"Then he had to know they were coming, sir. But how?"

"Only one explanation. Somehow the Yankees have tapped into our telegraph lines."

"But why wouldn't they have sent at least a squad for the ambush? Seems to me that would be playing it safe. I mean…sending one man to take out six could have gotten him killed."

"Well, maybe it was gambling a little to send one man, but he must've been sure he could take out Parker and his group."

Sergeant William Claiborne's voice carried through the cold air. "So what did you find, Captain?"

The captain glanced at his brother, then said to Benson, "I

want to see if we can pick up some tracks around here. That killer was no spook—he came from somewhere and went somewhere."

Returning to his men, Britt Claiborne told them what they had found and showed them the spent cartridges. He also explained the conclusion he and Benson had drawn.

Puzzled and amazed, the Rebel soldiers dismounted and began the search for footprints. The wind had blown loose snow and ice crystals over the field, but it took only minutes for them to find the assassin's fading prints. They were amazed to discover that the man had come from the direction of Dover and had returned the same way.

Following slowly on horseback, they traced his steps all the way to a small barn, where they found evidence that he stood at least for a short time, then proceeded directly into town. As they neared the main street, they lost his trail. People on the street gawked at the cluster of mounted soldiers as they made a half-circle around their leader.

"Gentlemen, we've got a puzzling situation here," Captain Claiborne said. "Last night four hundred Fort Donelson men were in town at the same time this sharpshooter cut down Colonel Parker and his escorts. Now, we find that he came from Dover and returned to Dover. I can only draw one conclusion."

"It's a sickening conclusion, sir," Sergeant Masters said. "It looks like we've got a killer in our midst."

"My guess is that he was at least dressed in Confederate gray. That way, he could come into town along with all the others, then slip away unnoticed and do his killing. When he was finished, he came back, slipped in amongst the rest, and nobody was the wiser."

William Claiborne glanced northward and growled, "And the dirty rat is up there at the fort this minute."

"Sir," said Sergeant Nolan, "how are we going to catch this guy? He's either a Rebel turned traitor or a Yankee plant. Either way, he can kill again just about any time he wants to."

"Well, we can narrow the field," one of the men said, "by

finding out which men came to town last night."

"That wouldn't prove much," Captain Claiborne replied. "With twenty-five hundred men in the fort, it wouldn't have been hard for any one to slip out of the fort with the four hundred and come back with them, unnoticed. Our assassin wouldn't have to have been one of the four hundred given permission to come into town."

"Then it could be just about anybody in the fort," said Sergeant Claiborne.

"I can vouch for Captains McGuire and Donaldson," Britt said, "but that's about it. The four hundred were back in the fort before I assembled you men, so none of you are exempt from suspicion either unless you can verify that you were in the fort from immediately after supper until the time we rode out on our search. So you're right, it could be just about anybody."

General Buckner's features were completely drained of color. His mouth turned downward and his head slowly shook back and forth. "Captain," he said with constricted throat, "this is bad news…very bad news."

"I hate to be the bearer of it, sir," Britt Claiborne said as he sat across the desk from his commanding officer. "Even when we eliminate the men who can verify they were in the fort all evening, we'll still have quite a number who can't. As I see it, we could even have more than one enemy amongst us. If that's the case, they would lie for the assassin."

Buckner rubbed the back of his neck, staring vacantly at the desk top. "The ramifications of this are mind-boggling, Captain. As you said, this could be a case of treason or infiltration. There's no way at this point to know which it is, or how many are involved. We've got five captains, seventeen lieutenants, and well over twenty-four hundred enlisted men, and any one of them could be the killer."

"Well, I know it's not either one of my brothers, sir. They're not enemy agents, that's for sure. They're both good shots, but they couldn't have done what that assassin did without a telescopic sight like they've developed in Europe. I can tell you for sure, neither William nor Robert have a gunsight like that."

"I'm sure you're right, Captain, but whatever investigation is done here, everybody within these walls except you, Captains McGuire and Donaldson, and myself will be suspect until the killer is ferreted out."

"So what do you plan to do?"

"First thing is to wire General Tilghman and let him know about Colonel Parker. I haven't done that yet because I wanted to wait and see if you came back with any pertinent information about the ambush. General Tilghman will make the decision on what to do once he has all the information."

Rising, Captain Claiborne picked up his hat off the chair next to him and said, "Well, sir, I'll get out of your way so you can get the message sent to General Tilghman. I, uh, told the men who went with me to keep this under their hats until further notice. It's going to be difficult because the troops are already asking what we found. Do you want them to keep their lips sealed?"

Sighing, Buckner rose from his chair. "Tell you what, Captain. Let me get the message sent to General Tilghman, then we'll call assembly in the yard. I'll address all of them at that time. Why don't you go ahead and spread the word. We'll assemble at—" Buckner paused to look at his wall clock; it was nearly noon. "We'll assemble after lunch, at one-thirty."

"Yes, sir," Claiborne nodded, turning toward the door.

Suddenly they heard the sound of rapidly approaching footsteps, followed by a hard knock on the door. "General Buckner! It's Captain McGuire, sir! I need to see you immediately!"

Buckner motioned for Claiborne to open the door.

When the door was swung wide, Captain Waldon McGuire met Claiborne's curious gaze, then looked past him to Buckner and gasped, "General, sir, it's Captain Frank Sullivan! He's been stabbed to death!"

The words hit Buckner like a whip. Blood pounded in his head as he rounded the desk. "Where is he?"

"A couple of men found him down by the armory, sir. Just outside the door. There's a bayonet in his back."

A large crowd of soldiers gathered around the armory door as Buckner, McGuire, and Claiborne drew up on the run. Charging ahead, McGuire shouted, "Clear a path, men! General's here!"

Fort Donelson had no physician, but medical corpsman Dwight Murdock was kneeling over the lifeless form. Sullivan lay face down with the bayonet protruding from his back. Corporal Murdock looked up and said, "The bayonet went right through his heart, General Buckner. I didn't pull it out because I wanted you and the other officers to see him the way he was found."

"Who found him?" Buckner asked.

"Private Stine and myself, sir," said a young corporal. "My name is Hank Lynch. We were just passing by here when we saw him."

Buckner nodded, then looked at Murdock. "Any idea how long he's been dead?"

The killer stood in the tight crowd and thought, I could tell you, Buckner, if I wanted to. It's been exactly thirteen minutes.

"Not very long, sir. I'd say by his body temperature, not more than fifteen minutes."

Buckner looked around at his men and said grimly, "I want an assembly of all personnel in the yard in five minutes. The only men excluded are the watchmen. Those who aren't close enough to hear what I say will be given the message by the chief officer of their unit as soon as I'm through."

The sky was spitting snow as General Buckner stood in the bed of a wagon and addressed his men. Mincing no words, the rough-and-ready general told the fort personnel every detail of Captain Claiborne's report. A pall of gloom seemed to descend over the crowd as they realized that at least one man in their midst was a heartless killer. It was worse to think that the killer might also have accomplices.

Buckner explained that he would be wiring this information immediately to General Tilghman. He would await Tilghman's decision about what to do.

A soldier raised his hand. "General, sir?"

"Yes, Sergeant Weathers."

"What kind of precautions should we take until this thing is cleared up and the guilty man is caught?"

Buckner's mouth turned down and he stroked his droopy mustache. "All I can say is that no man should be anywhere in this fort alone. If we have more than one killer in our midst, even that might not be enough. But right now, there isn't anything else I can suggest. I hope we'll get government attention on this problem soon."

"What about yourself, sir?" asked Sergeant Ralph Ederly. "We all know that this killer is standing right here among us, listening. You're alone in your quarters and in your office a great deal of the time. Shouldn't you have a bodyguard?"

"I'm really not afraid, Sergeant."

"But sir, what's good for the goose is good for the gander, they say. You just said no man should be anywhere in this fort alone. I think we need to protect our commanding officer."

Many voiced their agreement with Ederly, urging Buckner to protect himself.

"And just whom would you appoint as my bodyguard, Sergeant Ederly? How many men in this fort are above suspicion?"

"Well, sir, if there is only one killer, you know he can't be Captains Claiborne, Donaldson, or McGuire or Corporal Tomberlin. By what you told us a few minutes ago, they were with you most of last evening. Couldn't one of these men stay with you?"

"Sergeant, I appreciate your concern for my welfare. But I would be safe only if there is only one killer. If he has accomplices, then who is to name them? As far as you or any of these other men know, even I could be a traitor. I assure you I will take necessary precautions."

When Ederly said no more, Buckner ran his gaze over the faces of the men and said, "If any of you see or hear anything suspicious, I want it reported to me immediately."

Buckner dismissed them and headed for the telegraph room. The men-in-gray moved about quietly, stunned by the news that at least one of them was a cold-blooded killer.

THREE

Brigadier General Ulysses S. Grant arrived at his command headquarters on the Mississippi River at Cairo, Illinois, in September 1861. Some five months before, the Senate Military Committee in Washington decided that the war in the western theater could well hinge on the control of the region's rivers. They would need to build a fleet of warships adapted to navigate the shallow, tricky waters.

The man who won the contract to produce the ships was James B. Eads, a veteran riverman, salvage expert, and hard-driving taskmaster. He would need to be a taskmaster, for the vessels had to be built quickly.

Eads and his associates faced enormous technical difficulties. The Confederates were actively constructing forts along the banks of critical rivers and equipping them with heavy guns. The Union ships would have to be strongly protected to withstand bombardment from the forts, and would have to carry cannon as heavy as the fixed artillery of the forts. Yet, the ships had to be capable of navigating in less than ten feet of water.

Eads's engineers and construction crews went to work. While one crew rebuilt a five-year-old ferry known as the *New Era* into an ironclad, the others built larger ironclads from scratch. The contract called for seven identical ships, distinguished by colored bands painted on their smokestacks.

Each of the ironclads was to be 175 feet long and 51 feet wide in the beam. The casemate, its walls slanted at 35 degrees to deflect enemy fire, would be protected with iron plate 2.5 inches thick on the bow and sides. Each vessel would be armed with 13 big guns and powered by two high-compression steam engines.

Eads's construction crews swelled to four thousand men who worked night and day. By the last week of January 1862, ironclads *St. Louis* and *Carondelet* were anchored at Cairo, along with the smaller *New Era* which had been renamed *Essex*.

On Friday morning, January 31, 1862, Grant stood on the Cairo dock overlooking the broad Mississippi. Flanking him were Brigadier General John A. McClernand, Captain Henry Walke of the *Carondelet*, Captain Leland Timmons of the *St. Louis*, and Captain Douglas Oliver of the *Essex*. All three captains were under Grant's command.

A lash of cold lanced them as they watched the small, innocent-looking steamer *Lexington* chugging up the river from the south. Aboard her was another subordinate of Grant's, Brigadier General Charles F. Smith.

"Well, sir, we'll soon hear General Smith's expert opinion about Fort Henry," Captain Timmons said.

Grant, who was soon to turn forty, was a beefy man, and at five feet nine inches, was shorter than the other men who stood about him. He wore a full but well-trimmed beard and mustache and chewed on an unlit Havana cigar.

"I can already tell you what he'll say. I know the man too well. No matter how well-fortified the place is, he'll say we ought to go take it."

The *Lexington* was now veering toward the dock, and General Smith emerged from the cabin. He stepped to the railing and raised a hand to greet his fellow-officers, who stood half-frozen but smiling on the dock.

Grant held deep respect for Smith. The tough old Regular Army general had been commandant of cadets at West Point when Grant was a cadet there, and Grant had grown to respect Smith more than any man he knew. He still did. Though Grant was Smith's senior officer, Grant was inordinately respectful of him and found it difficult to give him orders. A professional to the core, Smith always sought to put him at ease.

Grant moved to the edge of the dock as the boat floated close. A deck hand tossed a rope to Captain Oliver from the bow. While Oliver wrapped the rope around a post, the generals grasped hands and Smith hopped onto the dock.

"Let's move on Fort Henry immediately, sir," Smith said.

Grant turned and smiled at Timmons, then said to Smith, "If they had ten thousand men and a hundred cannons, you'd still say, 'Let's move on Fort Henry immediately.'"

Smith looked down at his commanding officer and grinned. "Well, may be, but it's nothing like that."

The other officers closed in to hear the general's words above the wind that lashed at them off the cold, choppy surface of the Mississippi.

"Gentlemen, let's get our half-frozen carcasses inside before we hear General Smith's comments," Grant said.

General Grant had set up his headquarters in an old vacant house, which stood some two hundred yards westward from the riverbank. The Union officers walked briskly to the house with hardly a word passing between them. There an adjutant corporal was stoking the fire in an old pot-bellied stove as they entered the parlor, now the general's office.

Grant removed his hat and gloves, handing them to the corporal. "You're a good man, Corporal Bates. Since they don't allow sergeants to be adjutants, I'll make sure you never get a promotion."

There was a low rumble of laughter among the officers as they removed their wraps.

Corporal Albert Bates grinned and said, "May I take your coat, sir?"

Grant let his coat slip into the hands of the adjutant, then moved the cigar to the opposite side of his mouth with his tongue. "I want you to keep an eye on the river. The instant you see the *Cincinnati* steaming in, let me know."

"Yes, sir," Bates nodded.

Grant gestured for the officers to sit down around a large table opposite his desk, and took a seat at the end. "All right, General Smith, tell us what you saw down there."

"Well, since the *Lexington* looks like just any old steamer, I was able to get close and appraise the situation quite thoroughly…uh, without inviting myself inside for a better look, you understand.

"The fort encloses about three acres of ground in a five-sided earthwork parapet about eight feet high. I counted seventeen guns. There's a 128-pounder, two 68-pounders, six 32-pounders, and eight 6-inch cannon rifles. This may sound like they're ready for us, but the Confederates have made a grave mistake, General. They've built the fort on land that is too low. Right now, the Tennessee River is rising rapidly because of the heavy rains east of here. I think in another week, Fort Henry will be fighting its worst enemy—the river. If we move on them by, say, Thursday the sixth, most of their guns will be under water. A couple of those ironclads we've got anchored out there will make short work of Fort Henry."

Grant threw his chewed-up cigar in a wastebasket and said, "Then all I have to do is wire General Halleck in St. Louis and get his permission to attack Fort Henry next Thursday. I know he holds great respect for your opinion, General Smith. It's as good as done. However, instead of a couple ironclads, we'll go with four. As you know, Foote is coming down the Mississippi with his spanking new flagship, *Cincinnati.* That'll give us three big ones and your smaller *Essex,* Captain Oliver. We've got seventeen thousand men camped here at Cairo. I've already made arrangements for enough steamboats to come down from St. Louis to transport them. All they need is a day's notice. We'll hit that Rebel stronghold and capture it all on the same day. Once we've done that, we'll make a quick move on Fort Donelson. We don't want to give them time to fortify Donelson any more than it already is."

The Union officers all agreed with Grant's plan. McClernand was adding some suggestions of his own when the voice of Corporal Bates came from the other side of the room. "Excuse me, gentlemen. The *Cincinnati* is here."

The arrival of Flag Officer Andrew Hull Foote was the final ingredient in Grant's potent gunboat fleet. Like Grant, Foote was a stocky man who wore a well-trimmed beard, only without a mustache. He was in his early fifties and was military in every aspect. His fellow-officers found him amiable, yet blunt when it came to military matters. A devout Presbyterian, he crusaded passionately against the use of liquor in the Union navy. When he was commander of the *USS Cumberland,* he regularly gathered his crews on deck and preached hell-fire-and-brimstone sermons to them.

General Grant and the other officers welcomed Foote to Cairo, and he joined them at the table. After Grant explained the plan of attack against Fort Henry, the fiery flag officer spoke of his eagerness to put to use the fighting abilities of his new ironclad.

The meeting adjourned, and the navy officers returned to their ships, and the army officers to their quarters at the camp. General Grant told them he would wire General Halleck immediately and let them know as soon as he received a reply.

Within three hours after sending his message, Grant had Halleck's response. Grant was to begin preparations immediately for an attack on Fort Henry at dawn on Thursday, February 6. He was to use the steamboats from St. Louis to transport his seventeen thousand men down the river, preceded by the four ironclads, which were to bombard the fort heavily. Once General Tilghman's forces were sufficiently reduced, Grant was to swarm the fort and capture it. Once the task was completed, Grant was to advise Halleck by wire. Halleck would then tell Grant when he should move on Fort Donelson.

General Grant sent word to the officers to reconvene at his headquarters. He relayed General Halleck's message, then worked with the officers on the details of the attack. When every part and particle had been discussed and was clearly understood, Grant told them he wanted to set up temporary headquarters nearer the forts. Preferably, he would locate a farmhouse north of Fort Donelson and as near the Cumberland River as possible. This way, he could board the ships whenever necessary and steam toward Fort Donelson, which would be much harder to conquer than the smaller and less protected Fort Henry.

The meeting broke up, with the Union officers eager to return to their men and prepare them for the assault.

At the break of dawn on Sunday morning, February 2, Myrtle Crisp awakened with a start. The second-story bedroom of the old farmhouse had two windows, one in each outside wall. The east window gave a view of the slow-moving Cumberland River some seventy yards away, and the north window overlooked the front yard.

Myrtle rubbed her eyes, wondering what had jerked her awake. She raised up on an elbow and looked around the room. The dim gray light coming through the windows left heavy shadows lurking in the corners.

She heard horses nickering and blowing and realized it was the sound that had awakened her. Sitting up, she threw back the covers and swung her feet over the side of the bed. She stood up, gathered her robe from the back of a nearby chair, and padded across the hardwood floor to the north window.

While slipping into her robe, she put her back to the wall and slowly inched her way to the edge of the window. She looked into the yard. What she saw brought a chill to her spine and caused her heart to quicken pace. "Yankees!"

There was enough light that she could clearly make out the

dark-blue uniforms of the dozen or more men who had dismounted and were gathering near the front porch.

The abrupt, heavy knock at the front door startled the old woman. Her mind was racing. What did Yankee soldiers want with her? She turned from the window and whispered, "Dear Lord, the enemy is at my door. Please help me!"

The pounding was repeated at the front door.

Myrtle knew if she didn't go down and open the door, the Yankees would break through it anyway. Shivering from the cold, she left the room and hurried down the stairs. Again she heard the pounding accompanied this time by a loud voice demanding whoever was inside to open up.

"I'm coming! I'm coming!" she half-screamed, hastening through the parlor, sliding the dead-bolt, and opening the door.

A husky sergeant filled the door frame. Myrtle could see three other soldiers directly behind him, and the rest clustered about the yard, looking on. "This is private Rebel property," she said stiffly. "There's nothing for you here. Please leave this instant."

The sergeant touched the bill of his cap and said, "Pardon me, ma'am, but General Ulysses S. Grant is here, and would like to talk to you."

The sergeant's courtesy gave Myrtle a little more courage. "I don't know any such man. And since he's in a blue uniform, I'm not interested in meeting him." She backed away and started to swing the door closed, saying, "Good day!"

The sergeant checked the door's motion with his boot. "General Grant is going to talk to you, ma'am."

General Grant pushed his way past and stood facing the elderly woman. Before he could say a word, Myrtle dashed to a corner of the parlor where an old flintlock musket leaned against the wall. Just as she brought it around, the sergeant was on her. Quickly but gently, he seized her wrists and said, "Please, ma'am. We don't want any trouble."

"Then you should go home and leave us Southerners alone!"

The sergeant slowly twisted the gun from her grasp. "It was the Southerners who fired the first shot, ma'am."

"Wouldn't have been any first shot if you blue-bellies hadn't been below the Mason-Dixon line at the time!"

The sergeant stepped back as his commander moved in to face the irate woman.

"I'm Brigadier General Ulysses S. Grant, ma'am," he said softly. "Neither I nor my men are here to do you any harm."

"Then what do you want?" she retorted, her bony jaw jutting.

"I need a house to set up temporary headquarters, and this one's perfect. My adjutant and I will be occupying it until further notice. I assume you have relatives or neighbors nearby who will take you in until we move on."

"And just what would you do if I said there's nobody who'll take me in?"

"I'd say you're not telling the truth, Mrs.—what is your name, ma'am?"

"Myrtle Crisp. I'm a widow."

"We'll be glad to transport you to wherever you'd like to go, Mrs. Crisp."

"I don't need your transportation. I can transport myself. But I shouldn't have to. You've no right to come busting in here and run me out of my own house."

"I understand that, ma'am, but this is war. Everybody's rights get stepped on in war."

Myrtle knew she was powerless to do anything about it. The hated Yankees were going to take over her house with or without her consent. Meeting Grant's level gaze, she said, "I suppose you'll eat up all my food and tear my place apart before you're through, won't you?"

"No, we won't. We have our own food, and I promise that no damage will be done to your property."

Myrtle threw her head back. "I could go to Fort Donelson and tell General Buckner you're here, y'know. How would you like to have a swarm of Rebels coming at you?"

"There's a reason you won't go to General Buckner and report our presence, ma'am," Grant said.

"Oh? And that is?"

"If those Rebels swarmed in here, before the battle was over this house would be nothing but a pile of broken glass and splintered wood."

Myrtle glared at him for a long moment. "You've got me no matter what, don't you?"

"Yes, ma'am."

"It'll take me a few minutes to get dressed and comb my hair," she sighed. "Am I allowed to do that?"

"Certainly. We'll wait right here."

Myrtle wheeled and started toward the staircase.

"Mrs. Crisp?"

"Yes?"

"I assume you live here alone. I mean, there isn't anyone else who calls this place home?"

"No. Just me."

"What about animals? Do you have some that will need feeding and watering?"

"Only one. My horse. When I'm through dressing, I'll hitch her to my wagon and be gone."

Twenty minutes later, Myrtle Crisp came downstairs to find that the Yankees had hitched her mare to the wagon and had it waiting at the front porch. Bundling up good, she moved toward the door and scowled at Grant, who stood with his hand on the knob. "If you Yankees have anything decent about you at all, you'll replenish my wood supply before you leave."

"That we'll do," the general assured her.

"And just how will you notify me when you're ready to go so I can occupy my home again?"

"Everyone in the area will know when we're gone, ma'am. When you hear that the Union has taken over Forts Henry and Donelson, I will have duty elsewhere."

Without another word, Myrtle moved outside. Her mare nickered at her as she stepped off the porch. A young corporal stood beside the wagon, ready to help her aboard, but as she approached she said curtly, "Don't you touch me."

The corporal looked at General Grant, shrugged, and stepped back. Myrtle hoisted her dress calf-high, climbed into the seat, and took the reins. "C'mon, Nellie. The air smells of blue-bellies around here. Let's go someplace where we can breathe." She drove away without looking back.

"I wish she was on our side, General," the sergeant said.

Grant grinned, ran a finger over his mustache, and said, "She's got spunk, I'll say that for her."

Though Clarence Clubson was busy running his own farm, he would drop by the Claiborne place whenever he could find the time and ask if anything needed attention. Everyone in the family knew his fascination for Linda Lee had a great deal to do with how often he came by.

At nineteen, Linda Lee was the youngest of the Claiborne children; Hannah Rose was twenty-one. Both sisters had long, thick chestnut hair and stood five-feet-five. Linda Lee's eyes were a soft blue, while Hannah Rose's were a vivacious emerald green.

The Claiborne sisters, however, were of a different makeup. Linda Lee was impetuous and sometimes made decisions on the spur of the moment. Hannah Rose was self-possessed and more careful about life in general.

The brothers—Britt, William, and Robert—loved their sisters dearly, but found Hannah Rose more approachable for sharing problems or heartaches.

Their father, Ewing Claiborne, had died suddenly of heart failure four years earlier. Their mother, Wilma Jean, was now bedridden most of the time from a long-term battle with tuberculosis. Dover's physician, Dr. Elmer Stutz, told the children their mother would probably live only another year or two at best.

Linda Lee did her part to care for her mother, though not with the level of compassion her sister showed. Often when both girls had offers for dates, Hannah Rose would decline and let Linda Lee go. She was not willing to let her mother stay home alone, though the ailing woman insisted she would be all right.

In mid-January, Britt's wife Donna Mae and William's wife Sally Marie gave up their apartments in Dover and moved to the six-bedroom farmhouse to help care for their mother-in-law. They were still close enough their husbands could visit them whenever they could get away from the fort. (The Claiborne farm was about two miles due south of Dover, putting it a little over five miles south of Fort Donelson.) Robert liked the arrangement because his sisters-in-law promised to cook him special meals whenever he could come home.

Three of the Claiborne women were sitting down to breakfast when they heard a wagon rattle into the yard and haul up at the back porch. Linda Lee started to rise from her chair, but Hannah Rose came into the kitchen carrying a tray— having just fed her mother breakfast upstairs— and said, "Don't bother, honey. I'll see who it is."

Hannah Rose laid the tray on the cupboard and hurried to the door. Parting the curtains, she peered through the window and said, "It's Aunt Myrtle. I wonder what she's doing here?"

Hannah Rose stepped out and met Myrtle at the edge of the porch. "Hello, Aunt Myrtle. What brings you here at this time of the morning?"

The elderly woman waved her hand toward the door and said, "Get yourself back in the house, child! You'll catch your death! I'll tell you inside. Go on…get in there!"

Myrtle greeted the women around the table, then took off her coat and hat and hung them on a peg next to the door. She moved near the welcome heat of the big kitchen stove and said, "First day we've seen the sun in awhile, but it's still colder'n a crock in a krauthouse out there." Her hands, opened palm out, almost touched the stove.

"Well, are you going to tell us why you're here and what the suitcase means?" Hannah Rose asked.

"If you've got an extra plate, I'll tell it while we're eating. If I can get these hands of mine thawed out enough to handle a fork, that is."

Moments later, the women were consuming bacon, eggs, grits, toast, and hot coffee as Myrtle told them about General Grant and his men forcing her from her home.

"Those Yankees think they own the world, don't they," Hannah Rose said. "Wish you'd had a houseful of Rebel soldiers waiting for them. That would've fixed General Grant's little red wagon."

"Sure would," Myrtle nodded. "But since I didn't, there was nothing I could do about it. I had to go. I told that buzzard I could go to Fort Donelson and tell General Buckner the Yankees were at my house, but he said if I did, and Buckner sent his soldiers to attack, my house would be destroyed in the battle. I figured he was right about that, so I gave up and came on over here."

"Well, you're perfectly welcome to stay here, Aunt Myrtle," smiled Hannah Rose. "You can take the room just east of Mother's."

"Thank you, dearie. Sure is wonderful to have family who care about me."

"Did you bring your Sunday clothes, Aunt Myrtle?" Sally Marie asked.

The elderly woman's hand went to her mouth. "Oh! I didn't even think of it! That…that General Grant had me so upset, I plain forgot." She gazed back and forth at the faces of the young women. "Who's turn is it to stay home with Wilma Jean?"

"It's my turn," Donna Mae said.

"Tell you what, honey"—Myrtle reached across the table to pat Donna Mae's hand—"you go ahead and go to church. I'll stay and look after Wilma Jean."

"You don't mind?"

"Of course not. It'll give us older girls a little time together.

Wiley and I always said she was our favorite niece. Is Britt going to be able to get loose from his duties to go to church with you?"

"No, and William can't either. Even Robert has duty."

Myrtle looked at Hannah Rose. "So which one of your boyfriends is escorting you to church today? Let's see…what are their names? Jim and—Jim and—"

"Lanny," Linda Lee said. "Jim Lynch and Lanny Perkins. Only things have changed since we saw you last Sunday."

"How's that?"

"Well, Lanny finally noticed me and decided to let Jim pursue things with big sister here. Both were by on Monday on their way to town, and Lanny asked Hannah Rose if it would hurt her feelings if he dated me."

"Really? And what did you say, Hannah Rose?"

"I told Lanny it wouldn't hurt my feelings at all. I would've said the same thing if it had been Jim, too."

"You would've?"

"Aunt Myrtle, I'm just not ready to get serious with any man right now. Jim is very nice, but we're only friends."

"At least that's the way Hannah Rose sees it," Sally Marie giggled. "I've seen the way Jim looks at her. It's more than friendship to him."

"Oh, Sally Marie, don't be silly," Hannah Rose said, waving her off.

"So are Jim and Lanny coming to escort you two to church?" Myrtle asked.

"Yes," Linda Lee nodded. "They were both able to get free for this morning. They'll be here about nine o'clock to pick us up."

The women finished breakfast and Donna Mae led Aunt Myrtle upstairs, carrying her suitcase for her. Myrtle would get settled in her room, then look in on Wilma Jean.

Donna Mae returned to the kitchen to help clean up. When the dishes were done and the kitchen was sparkling, they went to their rooms to get ready for church.

At 8:45, they were all ready and waiting in the parlor. Sally Marie was wearing her hair in an upsweep, and had discovered an unruly lock of hair on the nape of her neck. While the others were seated, she stood at a large mirror and worked on the stubborn lock. The mirror reflected a front window. Turning, she walked to the window and looked out to make sure she had seen correctly.

"Are they here?" Hannah Rose asked, rising from her chair.

"No," her sister-in-law replied in a dismal tone. "It's Club."

"Club!" Linda Lee gasped, jumping up and dashing to the window. "Oh, no. Lanny and Jim will be here any minute. When Club finds out Lanny's taking me to church, there's going to be trouble."

FOUR

Club Clubson swung his wagon around the house and noted the horse and wagon parked next to the back porch. Hauling his own vehicle up beside it, he eased his massive frame groundward and headed toward the porch, eyeing the other wagon with suspicion. The door came open and Hannah Rose appeared.

"Good morning, Club," she said, trying to cover her nervousness.

Touching the bill of his cap, Club showed his buck teeth in a wide grin. "Same to you, Miss Hannah Rose. Had a little time this mornin', so I thought I'd come by and replace that broken hinge on the barn door."

"Oh, I appreciate that, Club. You might check the door at the back of the barn, too. I think the top hinge may be coming loose."

"Will do. Whose wagon?" Club threw a meaty thumb over his shoulder.

"Oh, that's Aunt Myrtle's. Seems the Yankees took over her house this morning to use as headquarters for General Grant. She came over here to stay with us till they leave."

"Grant, huh? I'd like to get my hands on him for five minutes. That's all I'd need. Five minutes."

Club's eyes fell on a broken ax handle that leaned against the house near a pile of cut wood. A new handle stood next to it. He grinned at Hannah Rose and shook his head. "Oh, yeah, the ax handle. I'll fix that, too. You want me to cut some more wood?"

"That would be nice." Hannah Rose rubbed her arms against the cold. "We sure appreciate your help."

"Glad to do it, ma'am. Uh…before I start workin', could I come in and see Linda Lee?"

"Well, we're about to leave for church."

"Oh, that's right. It is Sunday, isn't it?" Club turned toward the barn and saw the Claiborne wagon parked near the corral gate and the team behind the pole fence. "You goin' to church in your Aunt's wagon?"

"Ah…no, but I'd sure appreciate it if you'd unhitch the mare from the wagon and put her in the corral."

"Be glad to."

"Just park her wagon over there by ours and hang the harness inside the barn, would you?"

"Sure. You want I should hitch up the team to your wagon so's you can drive it to church?"

"You won't need to do that. We…ah…we have a ride."

"Oh?"

"A couple of soldiers from the fort are stopping by to take us in their wagon. Aunt Myrtle is going to stay with Mother so all four of us can go to church."

"Coupla army guys, eh?"

"Yes. They…ah…well, I've dated both of them before. Nice young men. They're kind enough to come out of their way and take all four of us."

Club nodded and said, "Well, I'll get my tools from the wagon and go to work on those barn doors. Tell my girl I'll see her later."

Hannah Rose wheeled and headed back inside. Before closing the door, she saw Club at the side of his wagon, reaching into the bed. "Maybe you ought to put Aunt Myrtle's mare in the corral before you start on the barn doors, Club," she called.

"Oh, sure. I'll do that."

"Thank you again for your help," she said, smiling.

"Oh, sis, what am I going to do?" Linda Lee was standing in the kitchen where Club could not have seen her. "Club's like a leech. I've told him over and over that I have no romantic interest in him, but he won't let go."

"I know, honey," Hannah Rose responded. "None of us want to hurt the big lummox. Maybe you'll just have to find the man you're going to marry and let him deal with Club."

"Hey, girls!" Sally Marie called from the parlor. "They're here!"

Jim Lynch and Lanny Perkins were all smiles as they mounted the steps of the front porch to escort the women to the wagon. When Jim did not see Hannah Rose, he asked, "Where's Miss Beautiful?"

"I'm right here," Linda Lee giggled.

"That's for sure," Perkins said with conviction, giving her his arm to assist her down the porch steps.

Donna Mae spoke up. "Since I assume you are referring to Hannah Rose, Corporal Lynch, she's upstairs making sure Mother Claiborne is all right before we leave. Our aunt is staying with her."

"Oh, so that's it," Lynch grinned. "When I saw the three of you come out the door, I was afraid maybe plans had changed and Hannah Rose was going to stay home this time."

Just then Hannah Rose came through the door, buttoning her coat. She greeted Lynch, and he gave her his arm.

Nobody noticed the pair of wide-set hazel eyes watching from the corner of the house.

Donna Mae and Sally Marie reached the wagon first. Corporal Perkins hurried ahead and helped the married women up first so they could sit in the rear seat. For such occasions, two seats could be fitted in the wagon bed, allowing room for four extra people.

Corporal Lynch would be doing the driving, and planned for Hannah Rose to sit beside him. This left the middle seat for Corporal Perkins and Linda Lee. Lynch led Hannah Rose toward the front of the wagon to help her in, and Perkins took hold of Linda Lee's hand and led her toward the middle seat.

Linda Lee heard Perkins chuckling and asked, "What're you laughing about?"

"I just decided I'd put you into the wagon by picking you up instead of helping you in."

"Oh, you couldn't pick me up."

Even as she spoke, Perkins swept Linda Lee off her feet and cradled her in his arms. The others looked on with amusement.

Linda Lee giggled and clung to his neck. "Lanny, you're so strong!"

"Why, you're light as a feather. I just might carry you all the way into town!"

Hannah Rose was about to give her hand to Jim so he could help her into the wagon when she saw movement out of the corner of her eye. She looked and saw Clubson rounding the side of the house and coming on like an enraged bull.

Linda Lee saw the look on her sister's face and turned to see the oncoming Clubson. "Oh, no! Put me down, Lanny. Quick!"

By now, everyone was looking on as Club charged up, eyes blazing, and blared, "Put her down, soldier!"

Perkins took in Club's size and eased Linda Lee to the ground. "Who's this?" he asked her.

"He's a neighbor—Clarence Clubson, though everybody around here calls him Club."

"He have some kind of claim on you?"

"She's my girl," Club snapped, "and you ain't got no business holdin' her like you was!"

Perkins looked at Linda Lee. "Is this true? Are you his girl?"

"No, I am not! I've told you time and again, Club, I'm not your girl. You don't own me. You've been very kind to come over here and help us when we've needed things done, and I've tried to show you that I appreciate you, but when are you going to understand that it goes no further than that?"

Club's jaw was set. "I know you love me, Linda Lee. I've seen it in your eyes. You just don't want to admit it, yet. But you will. I'll treat you so good, you'll—"

"Club, you can't push yourself on her," cut in Hannah Rose. "She has a right to see any young man she cares to, and without interference from you."

"But she wasn't just seein' this soldier, Miss Hannah Rose. I saw him holdin' her."

Anger slashed through Perkins, reddening his face. "Since you have no claim on her, don't be telling me what I should have done! It's none of your business!"

Lynch saw a gathering fury in Clubson's face and stepped past Hannah Rose to confront him. "Best thing for you, Club, is to get back to whatever you were doing and let this incident die. We're about to take these ladies into town for church, and if we don't get going, we'll be late."

But Clubson was already blind with rage. His right fist lashed out, caught Lynch flush on the jaw, and flattened him.

Perkins rushed to his friend's defense. Club turned to face him, and Perkins landed a glancing blow to his jaw. Perkins's second punch landed solidly, but it hardly fazed the massive farmer. Club countered with a haymaker as a surprised Perkins backed away. The thick fist brushed past Lanny's chin. There was a sharp, popping sound as Perkins planted his feet and struck Club in the nose. Club roared like a grizzly and slammed home a punch to Perkins's ribs.

Club sensed Lynch coming and turned to meet him. Lynch lashed out with his right and caught Club square on the mouth, splitting his upper lip and staggering him backward. Lynch waded in, fists pumping. But Club grabbed him and threw him to the ground, knocking the wind out of him.

Perkins leaped on Club's back. Club roared like a wild beast and seized Perkins by the head. Bending forward, he flipped Perkins over his shoulder and slammed him to the ground.

Hannah Rose knew Club's reputation for whipping two or three men at a time. She moved up close and shouted, "Club, stop it! These are soldiers who fight for the Confederacy! You mustn't—" But her words fell on deaf ears.

Club spit blood, wiped the back of his hand across his cut lip, and sent a swift kick to Perkins's head. Club had both men down and was pounding and kicking them.

Hannah Rose realized there was no stopping Clarence Clubson. He was angry, and his size and strength were too much for the two soldiers. They were both going to be seriously hurt if something wasn't done. She darted away, intent on one thing. Reaching the rear of the house, she grabbed the new ax handle and ran back toward the front.

Perkins was stretched out on the ground, unconscious and bleeding from the mouth. Club had Lynch down, pounding his face with both fists as he straddled him on his knees.

The other women looked on wide-eyed as Hannah Rose moved up behind Club and swung the ax handle at his head. Wood met skull with a dull thud. Groaning, Club slumped on top of Lynch.

Lynch lay under Club's weight, gasping for breath, his strength spent. Helplessly he looked on through clouded eyes as Hannah Rose stood over Club, breathing in rapid, shallow breaths.

Club moaned, lifted himself to his knees, and turned and looked at Hannah Rose with blazing eyes. She bit down hard and swung again with all her might.

Club reeled and tried to fight off the effect of the blow, but his eyes rolled back in his head and he fell over backward. His legs lay across Lynch's waist.

The sisters-in-law scrambled out of the wagon, and Linda Lee hurried to Lanny Perkins, who was beginning to stir.

Dropping the ax handle, Hannah Rose lifted Club's legs by the ankles, allowing Lynch to roll free.

Sally Marie and Hannah Rose helped Lynch to his feet. He looked at Hannah Rose, blinked at a tiny trickle of blood flowing into his left eye, and said through swollen lips, "Remind me never to get on your bad side, lady! You really gave Goliath a couple of tough cracks on the head!"

"Well," Hannah Rose smiled, "I guess it's a good thing I didn't have my slingshot."

"I guess church is out for today," Sally Marie said. "We need to get you two into the house and tend to your wounds."

Holding a hand to his bleeding mouth, Perkins stood over Clarence Clubson and said, "What about him? He'll be coming around any minute. Maybe we ought to tie him up so he can't start this thing all over again."

"There's no need for that," Linda Lee said. "Y'all go into the house and see about those cuts. I'll talk to Club when he comes to."

Club's feet slowly moved, then he rolled his head from side to side and groaned.

"But what if he decides to take it out on you, Linda Lee?" Perkins asked.

"He won't. He would never hurt me. But you two better get in the house."

It took Club another three or four minutes to regain consciousness. Linda Lee helped him to a sitting position, and while he rubbed his aching head, she explained why Hannah Rose had been forced to hit him with the ax handle.

Club looked at her with glassy eyes and said, "I wouldn't have done what I did if that guy hadn't held you, Linda Lee. You're my girl, and no man should hold you like that."

Linda Lee sighed and looked toward the sky, shaking her head. What would it take to convince Club that she was not his girl? They had been over it so many times, she didn't know what else to say.

"Club, you're not mad at Hannah Rose for knocking you out, are you?"

"Them two guys had it comin', what I did to 'em. That shorter one had no business holdin' you like that."

"That isn't what I asked you. What I'm concerned about is you being angry at Hannah Rose and doing something rash to get back at her."

"Did you say a little while ago that she hit me because I wouldn't listen when she tried to get me to stop beatin' on those guys?"

"Yes, I did."

"I don't remember her sayin' anything to me about stoppin'." Club worked his way to a standing position and rubbed his head again.

"Well, she did. You were just so crazy with anger that you didn't hear her."

"Guess I was pretty mad."

"Club, if Hannah Rose hadn't knocked you out, you might have seriously hurt those soldiers, even killed them. If you had, the army would have come after you. My sister saved you from prison, maybe even execution, by knocking you out."

Clubson stared at her a long moment. "Yeah, I guess you're right. So I shouldn't be mad at her, huh."

"No, you shouldn't."

"Well, then, I ain't mad at her, okay?" A weak smile graced his thick lips.

"Okay," responded Linda Lee, relieved.

"So I better get to doin' the work I came here to do," Club said, looking toward the barn. As he spoke, he lifted both hands and massaged his temples.

"Club, maybe you'd better wait till you're feeling better."

"Yeah, I think you're right. Maybe I oughtta go home for awhile and come back later."

Linda Lee took hold of Club's muscular arm and guided him toward his wagon at the back of the house. He climbed up and settled on the seat. He released a weak grin and said, "G'bye. I'll be back later."

"Good-bye," she replied, and watched him drive away.

She entered the house through the back door and found the three women working on Corporals Lynch and Perkins. Their faces had been washed and now shone with salve smeared over the iodine spots that covered their cuts. Their bruises were beginning to turn purple.

"So what's he like now?" Hannah Rose asked.

"He's not mad at you. When I explained what kind of trouble he could have gotten into, he said he understood. He was going to go ahead and work, but I talked him into waiting. He's got a boomer of a headache, so he's heading for home."

"Well, I hope this'll be the end of it," Sally Marie sighed.

"I doubt it. Sure as he sees me with another man, he might go berserk again."

"Well, I'm not afraid to be seen with you again," Lanny said. "When I get a break from the fort, may I come see you again?"

Linda Lee smiled. "Of course."

"If we get a break," Jim said. "I think we'll be fighting the Yankees any day now. Our scouts tell us Grant is building up a fleet at Cairo. Who knows how long the battle will last when he brings those gunboats against us."

"Grant must be planning to come at you soon," Donna Mae said. "I didn't get a chance to explain why Aunt Myrtle is here. At dawn this morning, General Grant and a bunch of his soldiers rode up to her house and told her to leave. They're going to use her house as a headquarters. She lives only about a mile-and-a-half north of Fort Donelson on the Cumberland."

"Our scouts may know about it by now, but they may not. Lanny and I better head back and tell General Buckner."

"Yeah, he'd sure want to know if he doesn't already," Perkins said.

Lynch looked at Hannah Rose. "Could we talk in private before Lanny and I leave?"

"Of course. Let's go to the parlor."

When they reached the parlor, Hannah Rose guided him to a small couch. "Please, sit down."

"You first," he responded, smiling in spite of his battered face.

She sat down and followed Jim's face with her eyes as he eased down beside her.

"Hannah Rose, we've dated several times now and…well, I'd

like to know if you'd be my steady girl. I really have strong feelings for you, and—"

"Jim," she cut in, speaking softly, "please let me explain something. You know that my mother is quite ill."

"Yes."

"I told you the first time we met that she probably doesn't have more than a year or two to live."

"Yes. I'm very sorry."

"I appreciate that." She cleared her throat and proceeded. "My first responsibility right now is to Mother. Until she…until she dies, I must do all I can to make her comfortable. There just isn't any room in my life for a steady boyfriend. I like you a lot, Jim, and I enjoy your company, but I'm just not ready to fall in love."

Disappointment showed in the corporal's eyes. Nodding slowly, he said, "I understand, Hannah Rose. And I will abide by your wishes. I must tell you, though, while we have this moment alone, that I love you, and I want to be the one you fall in love with, whenever the time comes. I realize you're free to see other men. All I ask is that I still be allowed to see you often."

She reached out and touched his forearm. "Of course you may, Jim. I appreciate that you understand. The Lord has a plan for your life, as well as for mine. If in His wisdom, He has planned for us to have a life together, He will work it out. So let's remain as friends until such time as the Lord leads differently."

"We can't miss if He's guiding our lives, Hannah Rose. I just want you to know I'll be praying that you'll fall in love with me."

Hannah Rose smiled. "That's in His hands, Jim. We'll leave it there. You're a fine man, and you'll make a good husband to whomever He has chosen for your mate."

Hannah Rose surprised him with a discreet kiss on his cheek.

"God bless you, Jim," she said quietly. "I'll look forward to the next time we can be together."

"Me, too," he replied, touching the place on his bruised cheek where she had kissed him.

FIVE

It was nearly noon when Corporals Jim Lynch and Lanny Perkins pulled up to the gate at Fort Donelson. The two privates who manned the gate eyed them carefully. While one swung the gate open, the other stepped close to the wagon and said, "Looks like you two must've run into some Yankees."

"Wasn't Yankees," Lynch replied.

"Meet up with some wild animal?"

"You might say that."

Lynch drove the wagon to the stables, and they unhitched the team and put them in the corral. As they were heading toward General Simon Buckner's office within the fort, they came abreast of Lieutenant Larry Faires. "What happened to you two?" he asked.

"We ran into a huge madman who thought Lanny was trying to take his girl away from him," Lynch replied. "We'd planned on going to church, but of course we didn't make it. But we uncovered some important news for General Buckner, and we're on our way to see him."

"Can you tell me what it is?"

"We found out that General Grant is occupying the house of a widow about a mile-and-a-half north of here. We figured the

Yankees must be planning an assault mighty soon."

Faires frowned. "You're sure the information you have is reliable?"

"Absolutely," Perkins said. "The widow is staying with the women we were to take to church. She's their aunt."

"Sounds reliable enough to me. Don't let me detain you. I'm sure General Buckner will be eager to get your report."

Lieutenant Faires moved across the compound, greeting several men on the way. He was unaware that he was being followed.

Moments later, Faires entered the quarters he shared with Lieutenant Edgar Brinton. The room was vacant since Brinton was on the wall with the gunners, watching the river for any sign of an enemy approach.

Faires took off his coat, hung it on a peg, then took three steps back and tossed his hat at the peg next to it. He grinned when the hat settled on the peg. "Practice makes perfect, Larry ol' boy."

There was a knock at the door. "Come in!" he called across the room.

The soldier who stepped in was wearing a coat without insignia, so Faires could not tell his rank, though his face was familiar. "What is it, soldier?"

"Sir, I'd like to talk to you about the shooting of Colonel Parker and the escort, and the stabbing of Captain Sullivan."

Faires studied him with quizzical eyes. "Close the door."

"You know something about the killings?" Faires asked as the soldier stepped close to him.

"Yes, I do."

"Well, what is it?"

"I know who did the killin'."

Faires's eyebrows arched. "How long have you known this?"

"Since the killin's happened."

"Since they happened?"

"Yes, sir."

"Then why haven't you come forth with this information before now? You should have told General Buckner immediately!"

"I couldn't do that, sir."

"What do you mean? Why not?"

The soldier's hand suddenly came out of his coatpocket, wielding a knife with a nine-inch blade. Before Faires could react, the soldier plunged the knife into Faires's stomach and clamped his free hand over his mouth.

Faires's eyes bulged as the soldier yanked the knife out and stabbed him again, saying, "The reason I couldn't tell the general who the killer is, sir, is because it's me!"

Faires's knees gave way and a dark curtain descended over his brain. He felt the knife come out and strike his chest, piercing his heart. He was dead before the killer let him slump to the floor.

The assassin wiped the blade clean on Faires's shirt and put it back in his coatpocket. He did a quick check, making sure none of the lieutenant's blood had gotten on his coat.

He went to the nearest cot and pulled the covers down. Hoisting the body into his arms and being careful not to get any blood on him, he carried it to the cot. He laid Faires's body on its side and covered all but the top of his head with the blankets. It looked like Faires was sleeping.

"Won't they be surprised when they find you?" the assassin gloated. "Well, there'll be plenty more bodies before I get through." He stood a moment, admiring his work, then headed for the door.

He heard voices. Peeking out the small window, he saw Lieutenant Brinton coming his way, walking with Lieutenant Bruce Frye. The killer's heart quickened pace. As the two officers drew nearer, he flattened himself against the wall beside the door, knife at the ready. He cursed himself for not getting out of the room faster. This could end his deadly mission. If it didn't go right, he would be caught and executed.

Brinton and Frye paused outside the door. They were talking about the news General Buckner had just received about General Grant. While the killer waited, the officers discussed whether they thought Buckner should send a platoon upriver and try to capture or kill Grant.

The killer was relieved when Frye said, "Well, my friend, I'll see you in an hour or so."

"Okay," Brinton replied.

The man with the knife tensed as the door came open. Brinton stepped into the room, pushed the door shut behind him, and did a double-take when he saw his roommate on the cot.

"Hey, lazy bones! What're you doing in my cot?"

When Faires did not respond or even move, Brinton went to the cot, yanked the covers away, and saw the bloody shirt. Suddenly the killer drove his knife full haft into Brinton's lower back and clamped a strong hand over his mouth.

Brinton emitted a muffled cry and tried to break free. When the knife came out, he twisted around, trying to get a look at his assailant. He barely caught a glimpse of the man before he swung the knife over Brinton's shoulder and drove it into his heart. Brinton was dead when he hit the floor, the knife still in his chest.

Brinton's blood stained the front of the killer's coat. He dashed to the wall peg and found that Faires's coat was the same size as his. He quickly took his coat off, threw it on the floor, and slipped into Faires's. Nobody would ever know the difference; most of the men in Fort Donelson had identical government-issue coats without insignias, except for those worn by the generals and colonels.

He made his way to the small window and saw two soldiers walking by. When they were out of sight, he carefully opened the door, peered out, and found the coast clear. He looked back at the dead officers and whispered, "Well, at least you boys won't have to worry about General Grant and his gunboats." Moving outside, he closed the door and walked away humming a nameless tune.

It was just past one o'clock in the afternoon when General Buckner stood in the room where the two murders had taken place. Lieutenant Frye stood next to him, looking down at the bloody corpses. Captains Britt Claiborne, Ray Temple, and Nathan Willett were a few feet away, looking sick at heart, and a number of Rebel soldiers waited outside, trying to see through the half-open door and the small window.

Frye was pale as a ghost. He fought tears as he said, "The way the blood is drying, General, it had to have happened only minutes after I left Lieutenant Brinton. The killer must have either been in the room when he entered, or came in shortly afterward."

"Or killers," Temple said. "If Faires and Brinton were killed at the same time, they faced more than one man."

"I tend to believe it was one man," Claiborne said. "Looks to me like he killed Faires first, then when Brinton came in, he killed him."

"Why do you say that?"

"Well, for one thing, there's blood on this blanket where it touched Faires's back, but there's no hole in the blanket itself. The killer had to have stabbed him, placed him on the cot, and covered him up. But Brinton was left lying in a heap on the floor. If there were two or more killers, why did they bother to put Lieutenant Faires on the cot and cover him up, but just leave Lieutenant Brinton on the floor?"

"Good question," Temple admitted.

Turning to Frye, Claiborne said, "Lieutenant, you said when you came in the room, you found them exactly like we see them now. You didn't touch a thing, correct?"

"That's right."

"So Lieutenant Faires was not covered?"

"No, sir."

"Yet the evidence is quite clear—the blood on the bottom side of the blanket proves that he had been covered. So the way I see it, there was one killer. He was either waiting in the room when Faires entered or followed him in a little later. Either way, the killer took Faires by surprise and murdered him with the knife. For some reason—maybe a flare for the dramatic—he decided to place the lieutenant's body on the cot, cover it up, and make it look like he was simply asleep."

"Makes sense, Captain," Buckner said. "Proceed."

"Then maybe the killer heard Brinton coming and hid. When Brinton came in, his attention was on Faires. It's plain to see that Brinton was stabbed in the back first, which means he was most likely attacked from behind."

"I think you're right on the button, Captain," Buckner said. "So you think we're dealing with only one killer amongst us?"

"That's the way it looks to me, sir. But just because we proved that one sharpshooter took out Colonel Parker and his escort, and one assailant apparently killed Captain Sullivan, that doesn't mean they and the two lieutenants here were all killed by the same man. We could have two or three killers. I tend to think there is only one murderer, but we dare not assume it. We must remain alert and face the fact there could be more than one."

"Sir, we haven't heard from you about General Tilghman's reaction to your wire about the other killings," Temple said. "What's being done?"

"General Tilghman wired me back within an hour after I sent him the message. He said he would get through to General Lee about it as soon as possible. He's sure Lee will take necessary action to bring the killer—or killers, if there is more than one—to justice. I haven't heard any more from him. I will, however, wire him about these two deaths immediately."

"General?" said Captain Willett.

"Yes, Captain?"

"Have you decided what to do about blue-belly Grant's headquarters north of us in that farmhouse?"

"I wired General Tilghman about that, too. He said to sit tight until further notice, so we sit tight on it until further notice."

"Yes, sir."

"We've got to give these men a proper burial. Other than that, we need to ready ourselves for the assault that's definitely coming. I just wish I knew when."

On Monday afternoon, February 3, an armada of steamships moved down the Tennessee River from the north, carrying seventeen thousand Union troops. They were preceded a distance of five miles by Union gunboats *Essex, St. Louis, Carondolet,* and flag ship *Cincinnati* under the command of Andrew H. Foote. Drawing within six miles of Fort Henry, Foote anchored them for the night.

On Tuesday morning, General Grant rode across the marshy "land between the rivers" to a rendezvous point on the bank of the Tennessee and boarded the *Cincinnati.* From there they proceeded down the river to within several hundred yards of the fort and opened fire.

When the Confederate guns roared in retaliation, Foote's boat took a shell, then quickly scurried out of range. Grant noted where the Rebel shell struck the river. He would put his troops ashore just beyond that point the next morning.

Inside Fort Henry, General Tilghman stood beside Jesse Taylor, his artillery chief, as the cannons fired.

A large, husky man of fifty-five, Tilghman had a thick head of salt-and-pepper hair with a heavy mustache and goatee to match. A broad smile spread over his face when he saw the *Cincinnati* take the first shell. "Good shot, Captain!" he said with exuberance. "Give them another one!"

The walls of Fort Henry were lined with excited Rebels, and a rousing cheer erupted when they saw the Union flag ship take the hit. They continued to shout and shake their fists at the *Cincinnati* as it made a fast turn and retreated up the river.

Tilghman wired Buckner at Fort Donelson, informing him that the Union boat had fired on Fort Henry, and warning him to keep a sharp eye in case the Yankees decided to attack both forts simultaneously. He was expecting the Yankees to come full-force within a few hours.

At Fort Donelson, General Buckner was standing over the lifeless form of Captain Temple in the infirmary. Some soldiers had found Temple near the armory with a bayonet in his back, though still alive. Temple was quickly carried to the infirmary, where the fort's medical corpsman began working on him, but he died within minutes.

"This slaughter has got to be stopped!" Buckner said to Captain Claiborne.

"I agree, sir, but how?"

"That's the corker. I don't know how."

Several other officers had gathered in the infirmary. "General Buckner," Lieutenant Chet Nolan said, "we've got to come up with something. The way it looks to me, this maniac only has his eye on officers. I know those men with Colonel Parker weren't officers, but as I see it, they died only because they happened to be with him. There are plenty of enlisted men in this fort he could've murdered, but his other four victims have all been officers."

Just then Corporal Tomberlin came through the door. "General, a wire just came in from General Tilghman. Looks like the Yankees are about to launch their attack."

Buckner took the slip of paper from his telegraph operator and quickly read it. Lowering the paper, he looked around at the apprehensive faces of the men in the room and said, "The Yankees sent a gunboat down the Tennessee a few moments ago and fired on Fort Henry. General Tilghman is expecting them back with more gunboats for a full-force attack within a few hours. He thinks they might send armadas against both forts at the same time. Wants us to be on alert."

"I don't know what else we could do," Claiborne said. "Our lookout positions are all filled, and the artillerymen have been at their posts around the clock for weeks."

"Yes," Buckner nodded. "If those blue-bellies come steaming down here, we're ready for them."

Turning back to Temple's body , Claiborne sighed, "We can fortify against the Yankee army and navy, but how are we going to fortify against this?"

"Tough," Buckner replied. "He's either a deranged killer who has it in for officers, or he's a dirty Yankee murderer sent here to whittle down our staff."

"I assume, sir," spoke up Captain Leonard Billings, "that there's been no word from General Tilghman concerning his plea for help on this from General Lee."

"No. I'm sure if he'd heard anything, we'd know it."

"I suppose we should wire General Tilghman and advise him of Captain Temple's murder, sir," Captain Willett said.

"Not right now. General Tilghman's got his hands full with the pending Union attack. I'm going to wire directly to Richmond, advise them of the latest, and ask for at least one new captain, since we're down to six. I'll also remind them that we're waiting to hear from General Lee."

"Sir," Claiborne said, "may I suggest that you have another meeting with all the men? They're strung tight over these killings, and I think it would help if they heard from you that we're expecting some action soon."

"Good idea. I need to let them all know about what just happened at Fort Henry, anyhow, and alert them to the possibility that both forts may be attacked at the same time."

The meeting with all the fort's personnel was held thirty minutes later. General Buckner's words were relayed to those manning guns and lookout stations out of earshot. When the meeting was dismissed, Buckner was standing with his six captains and fifteen lieutenants near a wall of the enclosed yard, discussing the Union attack, when three sergeants approached, halted, and waited to be recognized.

"Were you men wanting to see me, Sergeant Weathers?" Buckner asked.

"Yes, sir. We've been talking, and we'd like to make a suggestion to you and the other officers."

Buckner smiled faintly and said, "I'm always open to suggestions. This is concerning what?"

"The officers being murdered in this fort, sir."

"Go on."

"First, sir, I'm sure not everyone here is acquainted with these two men and myself. This is Sergeant Ben Blanchard. This is Sergeant Ralph Ederly. And I'm Sergeant Randall Weathers."

There was a general nodding by the officers.

"So what do you men have to suggest?" queried Buckner.

"Well, sir, like everyone else in Fort Donelson, we're deeply concerned about our officers being murdered. We sort of put our heads together and came up with a way to possibly put a stop to it."

"We're listening," said the general.

"Well, sir, we would like to suggest that every officer be assigned a man to guard him."

Buckner looked down a moment, then looked at Weathers and said, "But one of those assigned men could be the killer, Sergeant. This would put the officer he's guarding in immediate jeopardy."

"Anticipating that you might say that, sir, we suggest then that there be two men assigned to each officer. And we suggest that the officers choose their own bodyguards."

"I appreciate this suggestion, gentlemen," Buckner said. "It will make things a little cumbersome and inconvenient at times, but it might just do the trick. I'm for anything feasible that'll keep another one of our officers from being murdered."

The other officers showed their agreement.

"We'll implement your plan right away, Sergeants," Buckner said. He paused briefly, then added, "However, such bodyguarding will be impossible in a time of combat."

"You're right about that, General," Ederly said, "but during combat, I'd think the killer would be too busy trying to save his own hide. Besides, it'd be pretty hard to murder an officer with men all around him in battle. Too easy to be seen doing it."

"Makes sense," Lieutenant Frye said. "I hope before too long, General Lee will do something so we won't have to worry about the killer anymore."

Buckner scrubbed a hand over his mouth. "I'll sure be glad when he's been caught and executed."

"So will the rest of us, sir," Lieutenant Boyd Diamond said. "And when he's buried, I'm going to dance on his grave!"

SIX

Late Monday afternoon, warm air flowed into northern Tennessee, and everyone welcomed the rise in temperature. By early evening, dark clouds rolled in, and by midnight the cloud-laden sky opened up. What would have been snow a few hours earlier came down in a torrent of rain.

It was still raining hard by morning, causing General Grant to postpone the assault on Fort Henry, including the landing of his seventeen thousand troops. They sat aboard their steamships some six miles north of the fort and watched the pounding rain drench the land.

The rain did not let up all day. It continued through the night, and rained hard until midafternoon on Wednesday, February 5. Though the rain eased up, it still did not stop. Fort Henry's greatest enemy, the Tennessee River, was rising fast. The swift current carried an immense quantity of driftwood, broken fences, tangled clumps of brush, trees large and small, and the bloated carcasses of cattle and horses.

General Tilghman stood on the highest ramparts of Fort Henry in the light spray from the low-hanging clouds and unhappily observed the floodwaters pouring inside the fort. He cursed the military engineers who had built the fort on such low ground. Already the water was over two feet deep.

Flanking Tilghman on either side were Colonel David Head and the fort's artillery chief, Captain Jesse Taylor.

"The way the water's coming in, General, those guns on the lowest level will be submerged in another couple of hours," Taylor said.

Movement on the choppy surface of the river northward caught Colonel Head's attention. "We've got more trouble, gentlemen," he said glumly, pointing that direction.

Four Union gunboats were dropping anchor just out of range of Fort Henry's guns.

"I'd say the Yankees are expecting the rain to stop soon," Taylor replied in a strained voice. "When it does, they'll come in, shooting."

"Even if it stops before dark, they won't come till morning," Tilghman said. "I doubt they want to start a fight with only a couple hours of daylight left. I'm sure this is a ploy of Grant's to make us nervous."

"You're right about that, sir," Head said. "As you know, I was a classmate of his at West Point. I know him well. He's a schemer for sure."

"I don't know about you gentlemen," Taylor said, "but if those gunboats are there to make us nervous, the ploy is working on me."

Tilghman grinned. "I don't like the looks of those gunboats, either, Captain. But if all they've got to throw at us are four ironclads, we can blow them out of the water, even if our lower guns are out of commission."

"But they have maneuverability, sir."

"Granted, but we've got more firepower than they have," Tilghman replied. "I'm going to wire General Johnston. Bowling Green isn't that far away. If he'll send us reinforcements just in case the Yankees have some land troops waiting to come at us from upriver, we can still win this fight."

Head and Taylor waited on the high wall and kept an eye on

the enemy boats while Tilghman went below and wired General Johnston. His message carried a tone of optimism: if reinforced quickly, he had a "glorious chance to overwhelm the enemy."

A return wire moments later, however, caused Tilghman's heart to sink. Johnston regretted that he had no reinforcements to send. He had been trying to get Richmond to send more troops to the western theater, but the eastern theater was getting more of Jefferson Davis's attention, and therefore more men. Tilghman and his nearly twenty-six hundred troops would have to meet Grant's forces—no matter how large—on their own.

Head and Taylor were looking upriver when the general climbed to their perch on the wall. They gave Tilghman a dismal look. "We're done for, sir," Head said.

Tilghman looked to the river northward. His mouth went dry when through the light mist he saw the great fleet of Union troop transports coming down the turbulent river to join the ironclads. As far as the three officers could see, the course of the swollen Tennessee could be traced by columns of smoke from enemy smokestacks.

General Tilghman, face pallid, looked at the colonel and said, "You're right. General Johnston has no reinforcements to send. Just the troop ships we can see are enough to carry ten thousand men. We haven't got a chance."

"What are you going to do, sir?" queried Head as he wiped rain from his face.

Tilghman stared at the gathering armada for a long moment. "There's no reason to subject all our men to the inevitable pounding that's coming." He turned to Taylor and asked, "How many artillery-men would it take to man the higher guns, Captain?"

"Well, let me see…about seventy."

"And how many qualified gunners do we have?"

"Ninety-six, and twenty-eight others who can fill in if needed. They're just not as well-trained or experienced."

"Okay. Let's hope we can get seventy out of the hundred and twenty-four to volunteer."

"Excuse me, sir," said Colonel Head, "but I'm not following your line of thought, here. At least I hope I'm not. You're not thinking of sending the troops out of the fort and leaving seventy men here to man what guns are not under water...are you?"

"Precisely," nodded Tilghman. "If I can get seventy men to volunteer to bombard these Yankees when they come within range, we can cripple their fleet and take a toll on their infantry."

"We, sir?" blurted Head. "You don't mean that you plan to stay."

"I most certainly do. I'm not about to ask for volunteers to stay and fight it out, then leave, myself. If I get my volunteers like I believe I will, that'll leave just about twenty-five hundred men for you to lead on a dash for Fort Donelson."

"But sir, let me be the one to stay, and you lead the troops to safety."

"Can't do it, Colonel," Tilghman grinned. "Let's call a meeting of the gunners, including those who can work as substitutes. No man will be ordered to stay. If fewer than seventy volunteer, I'll make do. We can't just let the Yankees come in here and take the fort without a fight."

"I agree, sir, and I'm your first volunteer," Taylor said. "After all, this fight can't be properly carried out without your chief artillery man."

Tilghman grinned again. "Why am I not surprised that you're volunteering, Captain? I mean...there are three or four men who could lead the artillery if you were out of commission."

"Well, I'm not out of commission, sir," Taylor grinned back. "So you've got your artillery leader. Let's go see who else will stay and fight."

"Before we go, General," said Colonel Head, "I'm volunteering to stay here with you. I don't have to tell you, it's going to be a tough situation. You'll need me."

Looking the colonel square in the eye, Tilghman said, "I need you to lead the troops to Fort Donelson, so that's what you'll do. And that's an order."

The colonel knew it was useless to argue. "Yes, sir," he replied without enthusiasm.

Moments later, while special lookouts kept an eye on the enemy boats, General Tilghman gathered his regular gunners and those who qualified as substitutes in the rock-walled dining hall. He explained the hopeless situation and laid out his plan to make the Yankees pay for daring to attack the Confederate bastion.

"In a moment, I'm going to ask for volunteers. But before I do, I want to be sure all of you understand what you're facing. The enemy has at least ten thousand men on those steamers. Maybe we'll all die, or maybe some of us will live to be captured. But the more we cripple his attack force here, the less trouble General Buckner will have when Grant moves on to attack Fort Donelson. With an extra twenty-five hundred troops to bolster his forces over there, Buckner just might be able to beat them back."

A youthful corporal raised his hand for recognition.

"Yes, Corporal," nodded Tilghman.

"Sir, I'm Corporal Timothy Redmond. I joined the Confederate army in Nashville, because that's been my home for the past seven years. But I was born in Texas, and I just want to say that what's happening here right now reminds me of a mighty important historical moment that took place in my home state almost exactly twenty-six years ago."

Tilghman let a tight grin curve his lips. "You speak of the Alamo, Corporal."

"Yes, sir," nodded Redmond. "There was a principle to be fought for at the Alamo, and there's one to be fought for here. I'm volunteering right now to stay and fight."

There was a sudden eruption of voices as every man among them volunteered to stay and do what they could to cripple Grant's forces.

Overwhelmed at the sight, though not surprised, Tilghman fought back tears and said, "You're a great bunch of men. Since I only want seventy to stay behind, I'll keep the ninety-six regulars here. The rest of you are dismissed. We'll draw straws among the regulars and eliminate twenty-six."

Disappointment showed on the faces of most of the substitutes as they filed from the room. Within twenty minutes, twenty-six regular gunners filed out the door, also deeply disappointed that they were not among the "sacrificial company." Among those who remained to fight was the young Texan.

With an hour of daylight left, Colonel Head led the twenty-five hundred Confederate troops out of Fort Henry, moving eastward for Fort Donelson. The seventy-two men—including General Tilghman and Captain Taylor—prepared themselves for battle.

It was cloudy at the break of dawn on Thursday, February 6, but the rain had stopped. General Grant stood on the bow of the *Cincinnati* with Andrew Foote, the captains of the other gunboats, and his infantry leaders, Charles Smith and John McClernand.

Glancing at Fort Henry's big guns, Grant said, "All right, gentlemen, here's how it will go. The troop ships will remain out of cannon range, but go ashore as soon as the gunboats begin to move toward the fort. General Smith, you and your column will go ashore on the west bank, mount and secure the high points directly across the river from the fort. I want that bastion well-covered from your position."

"Yes, sir," nodded Smith.

Grant turned to McClernand. "And you, General, will go ashore with your column, make a circle around to the rear, and cut their escape route on that side. This way, if they try to escape by river or land, we've got them boxed in."

"Sounds good to me, sir."

"All right, you two get to your men and have them ready."

When the generals were gone, Grant ran his gaze over the faces of the navy men and said, "You gentlemen know what to do. Blast the devil out of those Rebels. I want that fort in our hands before dark."

Foote set determined eyes on the other naval officers. "You men know the procedure. I'll take the *Cincinnati* in first. Captain Walke, you'll be at my starboard side and sixty yards behind me. Captain Timmons, you'll be at my port side, the same distance from my stern. Captain Oliver, you will bring the *Essex* straight behind me at a distance of a hundred yards. This will give the Rebels headaches trying to figure out who to shoot at. All of us must keep our guns firing as rapidly as possible."

"I assume you will signal us to start firing by unleashing your own guns, sir," Timmons said.

"Correct," Foote nodded. Turning to Grant, he said, "Well, sir, it's time for you to go ashore. Could we pray before you go?"

Grant was not an atheist, but there was no room for the Lord of heaven in his life. He respected Foote and his faith, however, and removed his hat and bowed his head. The others followed suit, and stood quietly as Flag Officer Foote prayed loud and clear, asking God to give the Union forces victory over Fort Henry that day.

General Grant went ashore, joined his adjutant, Corporal Albert Bates, and mounted his horse. Grant and Bates rode to a high point about five hundred yards north of the fort on the west bank where they could get a good view of the battle. They were accompanied by a dozen mounted men who remained close to Grant at all times, following a special order made by President Abraham Lincoln.

It was twenty minutes before seven o'clock when Foote steamed down the choppy waters of the Tennessee River, with the other three ironclads positioned as he had commanded. When the *Cincinnati* was within seventeen hundred yards of Fort Henry, Foote ordered his gunners to open fire. Immediately the other three gunboats cut loose with a roar. The fort's big guns belched fire and smoke, and the battle was on.

Inside the fort, General Tilghman looked on as his chief artillery officer shouted commands at the gunners. The lower guns, as expected, had been completely covered by the flood waters during the night. The higher guns, however, were manned by gunners eager to unleash a hail of cannonballs on the four enemy vessels. Taylor had assigned each gun a specific boat as target.

The boom of cannons was deafening as the boats steamed steadily forward, the *Cincinnati* closing to within three hundred yards of the fort. The other gunboats were in their places, blazing away. Fort Henry's big guns rained cannonballs on the small Union fleet. A rising wind blew along the river southward, carrying the giant billows of smoke rapidly away.

One of the Rebels' big shells struck the *Cincinnati* like a thunderbolt. It ripped at her side timbers, showering splinters all over the deck. Though shell after shell pounded the flag ship, she did not slow down nor slacken fire.

The *Essex* had taken fourteen shots before a big shell plowed through the port casemate and burst her center boiler. The explosion opened a chasm of scalding steam and water. Inside the hull, men screamed and dove overboard through the port. Others clung to the casemate outside.

Captain Oliver was scalded by a blast of steam and threw himself blindly from a port. As he went into the muddy, turbulent river, one of his men caught him about the waist and lifted him out. In horrible pain, Oliver screamed wildly while another sailor helped lift him onto the narrow platform outside the casemate.

The larger ironclads continued to blast away at the fort. For the most part, their armor was giving excellent protection from the heavy artillery raining upon them.

Within half an hour, Fort Henry's two biggest guns had been disabled. The six-inch rifle received a direct hit, exploding with a deafening roar, killing the gunners instantly and scattering them in every direction. Almost simultaneously, the 128-pounder somehow fouled itself and would no longer fire. A quick examination by the crew revealed that it could not be fired without extensive repair. The two most effective guns were silent.

Moments later, two of the 32-pounders were struck almost at the same instant. Flying gun fragments and shrapnel killed every man at the two guns. One of the men to die was Corporal Timothy Redmond.

The Union gunboats' maneuverability gave them a distinct advantage over the fort's stationary guns. Cannon after cannon and crew after crew were rapidly disposed of. After one hour and ten minutes of battle, only four of the Confederate's guns were still in action.

Those four, however, fought back with fury.

In the first seventy minutes of bombardment, the *Cincinnati* had taken thirty-one hits. Her after-cabin and lifeboats were riddled with gaping holes, and her smokestacks were badly damaged. The top half had been blown off one of them. Two of her guns were disabled. One was struck by a Rebel 68-pounder directly on the muzzle, blowing it apart. The other took a 32-pounder in its side, destroying its firing ability.

The *St. Louis* and the *Carondelet* remained the least damaged and pounded the fort relentlessly. The *Cincinnati* still fired away, but the smaller *Essex* drifted slowly downstream. Her captain was hanging on for dear life on the narrow platform outside the casemate, being attended to by the two men who had rescued him. A number of her officers and crew were dead at their posts, while many others on deck writhed in agony from their burns.

As soon as the scalding steam dissipated, uninjured men explored the forward gun-deck. Both pilots had been scalded to death in the pilot-house. A sailor who was shot-man to the number two gun was found frozen in death on his knees. He had been in a kneeling position, taking a shell from its box to be passed to the load-man. The sudden blast of steam had struck him square in the face.

The *St. Louis* and *Carondelet* continued to fire without letup on Fort Henry, and the *Cincinnati,* though crippled and missing most of its guns, sent cannonballs hissing over the walls.

When the fort was down to two guns, General Tilghman stood beside his artillery chief under a shattered doorway, looked at the bodies strewn about, and said, "Captain, it's time to surrender. If we don't, the rest of us will die needlessly. We've inflicted plenty of damage to the boats, especially the smaller one. We've also battered their flag ship pretty good. Our fire power is almost nil. Tell your men to cease fire."

Captain Taylor looked toward the two crews busy reloading their cannons and shouted for them to cease fire and take cover.

Tilghman's features were stiff as he looked toward the flagpole and said, "Haul the flag down, Captain."

From his protective cubicle aboard the *Cincinnati,* Flag Officer Foote observed the Confederate flag being lowered. He knew it meant the Rebels were surrendering. He called for his men to cease firing, and signaled same to the *St. Louis* and the *Carondelet.* Suddenly there was silence.

Men aboard the Union boats—including the *Essex,* which had dropped anchor—lifted a rousing cheer.

Foote stepped onto the deck of his battered vessel and ordered his men to lower the only lifeboat that had not been destroyed. He commanded four men to row the boat through the flooded main gate of Fort Henry and invite whoever was in command to come aboard the *Cincinnati* for a formal surrender. He was hoping Tilghman was still alive and in charge.

Foote was pleased when he stood on the bow of his boat and observed General Tilghman emerge from the fort and board the small boat. When the boat drew up to the *Cincinnati's* port side, Foote said, "Welcome aboard, General. I assume you wish to make a formal surrender."

Tilghman's face was grim as he stepped aboard the gunboat. "I don't want to, but I have no choice."

"Spoken like a true soldier," said Foote, extending his hand.

It galled Tilghman to shake the hand of his conqueror, but he did anyway.

When their hands parted, Foote said, "Come, General. You look hungry. Let's go into my cabin, and you can surrender while we have a bite to eat."

An hour later, General Grant wired General Henry W. Halleck in St. Louis, and Halleck wired Washington the same message: FORT HENRY IS OURS.

The meaning of the message was unmistakable. The Confederacy's Tennessee line had been breached, and the war in the western theater was starting to turn in the Union's favor.

SEVEN

On Thursday, February 6, Major General Henry Halleck wired Ulysses S. Grant that he was sending him ten thousand more troops. Grant was to wait until the troops arrived before moving across the twelve-mile neck of marshy land and launching his attack on Fort Donelson. The reinforcements were coming from a Union camp near St. Louis, and would arrive at Fort Henry by February 11.

Grant wired back that he would wait. Flag Officer Andrew Foote would need a few days, anyhow, to take his fleet upriver to Cairo for repairs. Both the *Cincinnati* and the *Essex* needed work before they would be ready for the assault on Fort Donelson.

Grant was eager to move against Fort Donelson. His handy victory over Fort Henry had put fire in his veins, and he was ready to do the same thing to Fort Donelson. The capture of these forts would not only clear two great rivers, but would cut the Confederate line of defense from Columbus to Bowling Green in Kentucky. This could force the Confederates to retreat to Tennessee.

On the same day, Major General Albert Sidney Johnston was joined at his Confederate headquarters in nearby Bowling Green by his newly arrived second-in-command, Brigadier General Pierre G.T. Beauregard. The handsome Creole had gained fame for his leadership in Confederate victories at Fort Sumter and at Bull Run.

Beauregard, a vain, touchy man, had quarreled with President Jefferson Davis over the conduct of the war, and Davis was only too glad to oblige Johnston, who had called for help, by sending the hotheaded general to be his second-in-command. The Louisiana Frenchman found General Johnston in a state of despair.

As they sat down at a table in Johnston's quarters, a puffy-eyed Johnston looked at Beauregard and said, "We're whipped in the western theater, General."

Beauregard stiffened. "I can't agree, sir. Just because you lost Fort Henry doesn't mean we're whipped. It looked like we were whipped at Manassas, too, but we just kept fighting with the determination that we were going to win. And it wasn't long till we had those Yankees splashing across Bull Run Creek and running for Washington. You mustn't allow the Fort Henry loss to defeat you, sir."

"I'm just being realistic," Johnston countered, rubbing his eyes.

Beauregard leaned on his elbows, stared at his commander across the table, and asked, "Are you not feeling well, General?"

"I'm all right," sighed Johnston. "Just tired. I haven't had a good night's sleep for a week. Got absolutely no sleep last night."

"I'm sorry, sir, but you mustn't let your weariness mar your judgment. We can still drive those blue-bellies out of Tennessee and Kentucky."

The older man shook his head. "There's no defense possible on those Tennessee rivers, General. When a Federal army can be landed, supplied, and reinforced against any position we might choose, we're whipped. After what happened at Fort Henry, it makes me think the Union gunboats can reduce Fort Donelson to rubble before Grant moves in with his land forces. He's got seventeen thousand at Fort Henry, I understand. We only have a little over five thousand to defend Donelson."

Beauregard ran his fingers through coal-black hair, which was dyed to cover the gray. "General Johnston...pardon me, sir, but if our men see you looking and acting defeated, it'll be like the measles. Your discouragement will spread throughout our ranks. If that happens, we're whipped for sure."

"Like I said, I'm just being realistic. When a man's got the chips down on him and refuses to admit it, he's a fool. Do you realize we only have forty-five thousand troops in Tennessee and Kentucky? I've begged Davis for more, but I can't seem to get his attention. Lee and Jackson can get all they ask for in Virginia, but it's like we don't exist here in the West."

"So we have forty-five thousand," said Beauregard. "How many's Grant got?"

"Well, I don't know exactly, but right here in Kentucky, Buell has about fifty thousand. Halleck has who-knows-how-many thousand in Missouri and Illinois. Probably forty, at least. And Grant's got seventeen thousand at Fort Henry. There's no question that the Federals have more than twice the troops we do."

"But, sir—"

"As soon as Grant has control of Fort Donelson, my position here and General Polk's position over at Columbus can be taken by the Yankees any time they choose. These are just the cold, hard facts."

Beauregard eased back in his chair. Clasping his hands together in a tight knot, he asked, "So what are we going to do?"

"The only thing there is to do—retreat."

Retreat was not in Brigadier General Beauregard's vocabulary. His irritation started with a frown, then as it grew in intensity, his face crimsoned. Rising to his feet, he banged the table with his fist and blared, "General Johnston, I didn't come all the way here from eastern Virginia to join in a retreat! I'll not be a part of turning tail and running from the enemy! If this is going to be your plan, then count me out! I'll head back for Virginia immediately."

Johnston fixed him with bloodshot eyes, now turned hot. "Don't speak to me that way, mister! Have you forgotten who's highest in rank here? Now, sit down and listen to me!"

Beauregard held his stiff posture before his senior officer, shoulders thrown back, and eased onto the chair.

Johnston leveled a steady look on Beauregard and said calmly, "Before Grant hits Fort Donelson, we'll abandon the fort, Polk's position at Columbus, and mine, here at Bowling Green. We'll move south into Mississippi."

"But, sir, you were sent here by General Lee with President Davis's sanction to rush to Nashville's defense if the Federals moved against it. With Nashville's important commerce and industry, it will fall into Union hands immediately if you pull out. There's got to be an answer, other than retreat."

"No," Johnston said. "In the long run, the retreat can teach Mr. Jefferson Davis a lesson. When Nashville falls, it'll get his attention. Davis has got to see the true peril here in the West. When he receives word that we've pulled out and that Nashville is in enemy hands, it'll force him to send men and arms where they're needed most."

"But, sir, the retreat you propose will demoralize our troops. They won't be worth their salt if that happens. They'll be no good as soldiers. Let me suggest that we mass our entire western army at Fort Donelson. We can smash Grant's seventeen thousand, then wheel back into Kentucky and take on Buell's army."

Johnston massaged his temples wearily. If Beauregard's words were not taking effect, his attitude was. He considered showing more fight by leaving a small garrison to hold Fort Donelson until he could withdraw the bulk of his army intact. It was either that or take Beauregard's suggestion and concentrate his forty-five thousand troops at the fort.

The Frenchman studied Johnston quietly, knowing his comments had produced a change in thinking. Just how much of a change he wouldn't know until the general came out with it.

After a lengthy silence, Johnston met Beauregard's steady gaze and said, "Tell you what, General."

"Yes, sir?"

"You angered me a little while ago, as I guess you could tell."

"Yes, sir."

"But sometimes a man has to be stirred up some to get his thinking gears turning."

"I'll agree to that."

"My mind tells me, General Beauregard, that the Fort Donelson situation is hopeless. But I have the heart of a soldier, and my heart—thanks to you—tells me to make a stand and fight."

"Yes, sir!" A broad smile spread across Beauregard's finely chiseled features.

Johnston sighed and scrubbed a shaky hand over his mouth. "We've got five thousand men at Donelson. I'll dispatch six thousand from here and six thousand from General Polk's camp over at Columbus."

"But, sir, that will only put seventeen thousand men at Donelson."

"Correct. I figure if we meet Grant's number evenly, we can still win the battle. Our men have more of a will to fight than the Yankees do. Look how you routed them at Bull Run."

"So what are you going to do with the other twenty-eight thousand?"

"Retreat to Corinth, Mississippi."

For a moment, rebellion and anger made a bleak battleground of the Creole's face. Johnston saw it, and fixed him with hard eyes.

"Don't say it, General," Johnston said, clipping his words short. "You wanted me to order a stand at Fort Donelson, and I will…with seventeen thousand men."

"But, sir—"

"That's final, General Beauregard. We'll take the remainder of our army and regroup at Corinth. Maybe, just maybe, President Davis will send us troops there, so we can make a full and proper stand. I'm sure I'll have his attention when Nashville is under the Union flag."

Johnston's words and the tone of his voice told Beauregard the issue was settled. "You're in charge, sir. As second-in-command, I assume you'll send me to work with General Buckner at Donelson?"

"No. You'll take charge of the camp at Columbus and lead General Polk and his troops to Corinth. I'll lead this camp."

"Me lead a retreat? Now wait a minute, General, I'm not cut out for leading retreats. My nature just won't let me. General Buckner will need leadership help at the fort."

"I'm aware of that," Johnston replied. "I'm sending General Pillow and General Floyd to bolster the leadership at the fort."

Brigadier General John B. Floyd, formerly governor of Virginia and secretary of war under President James Buchanan, was a politician, not a soldier. His political connections had landed him in uniform as a high-ranking general. Floyd lacked both training and talent in military affairs, shortages made worse by his vacillating nature. Before being assigned to the western theater, he had served long enough in Virginia to demonstrate his incompetence with stunning clarity.

Brigadier General Gideon J. Pillow was another politician who knew little or nothing about military matters. Pillow, a native of Tennessee, was a self-styled lawyer and public servant. He had served a short time in the Mexican War and received two minor wounds. Using his political clout, he convinced the powers that be that his brief military experience qualified him to be a premier soldier.

Floyd was higher in rank than Pillow, and both were higher than Buckner. Beauregard shivered at the thought of those two incompetents being in charge at Fort Donelson, but what could he say or do? General Johnston was his commanding officer, and Johnston's mind was made up. Though it galled him, Beauregard would have to lead the troops camped at Columbus, Kentucky, in a retreat to Corinth.

On Friday, February 7, 1862, General Buckner was seated behind his desk, discussing the fall of Fort Henry with Colonel David Head.

Buckner was glad to finally have a colonel under his command to relieve him of some of the administrative load.

"I wonder how many of them are left alive," Buckner said. "If there are wounded men, I'm not sure what kind of treatment they'll get."

"Not very good, sir," said Head. "Those who are seriously wounded will probably die. The Yankees have recently opened a prison camp just outside of Chicago. That's probably where they'll be taken."

"Yes, I've heard that, too. Sure hate to think of General Tilghman and those brave men having to ride out the war in a prison camp."

"Yeah, me too, but every one of them knew he was facing prison or death when he volunteered to stay. I tried to talk Tilghman into leading the men here and letting me stay, but he would have none of it."

"Good man," Buckner said with conviction.

"The best, sir."

General Buckner adjusted himself on his chair and laid an arm on his desktop. "Up until now, there's been no time to talk to you about the killer in our midst, Colonel."

"I know General Tilghman wired Richmond about the problem. As far as I know, there hasn't been any response."

"I knew there hadn't been as of late yesterday," Buckner replied. "I sent a wire directly to General Lee myself, but haven't heard anything yet. We just set up a plan where every officer in the fort is to choose two men to accompany him at all times. I'll call for a meeting of the other officers who came with you and get them to do the same."

"Too bad we have to contend with such a thing. Since you've taken me into your quarters, will I need bodyguards at night? While we're sleeping, I mean."

"It'll just be you and me in the room. Door has a dead bolt." A grin curved Buckner's mouth. "Of course, I could be the killer as far as you know, Colonel. Maybe you'd rather have a couple men of your choosing sleep on the floor."

Colonel Head chuckled. "I'll take my chances on you, sir. There'll be no need for any extra men in those crowded quarters."

There was a knock at the door.

"Come in!" Buckner called.

The door came open, revealing the youthful face of Corporal Darrell Tomberlin. Smiling, he said, "I have two telegrams and a letter for you, General. One telegram is from General Johnston in Bowling Green, sir. The other is from General James Longstreet in Richmond. The letter came only moments ago by a special rider. It's directly from the office of general Robert E. Lee."

"Ah," Buckner smiled, "this must be in response to my plea for help in catching the killer."

"Would you like me to stay until you read the telegrams, sir?" Tomberlin asked.

"Please. I may want you to send return messages."

Buckner silently read the telegram from General Johnston. When he had read it through twice, he looked at Colonel Head and said, "General Johnston is going to send us twelve thousand men immediately—six thousand from his camp, and six thousand from General Polk's camp."

"Good," smiled Head. "We can use them."

"Says he and General Beauregard are going to lead the rest of the troops in retreat down to Corinth, Mississippi."

"I hate to hear that. We could use the rest of them right here, especially if Grant comes with a larger bunch than he's got at Fort Henry."

"There's more. General Johnston is also sending Generals Floyd and Pillow. General Floyd will be first in command, General Pillow will be second, and I'll be third."

Tomberlin's face screwed up. Head noticed it and said to Buckner, "I know I'm not supposed to question the decisions of my superior officers, sir, but I think both the corporal and I are unhappy with this one. With all due respect to Generals Floyd and Pillow, you certainly are better qualified to command this fort, especially with a big battle coming. Floyd and Pillow are amateurs."

Buckner shrugged his shoulders. "Orders are orders, Colonel."

He unfolded the second telegram and read it silently. General James Longstreet was commander of Fourth Brigade, Confederate Army of Northern Virginia, presently stationed at Richmond.

Buckner was smiling when he finished reading the telegram. "I wired a request a few days ago for at least one new captain to be sent here. One is all I'm getting. I was down to six until you brought the eight with you, Colonel. I'll be glad to have this man from Fourth Brigade, too. Name's Wayne Gordon. General Longstreet says he'll be arriving on horseback in approximately a week."

"Would you like to dictate responses to the wires, sir?" queried Tomberlin.

"Briefly, yes."

Buckner took less than two minutes to give Tomberlin his return messages, then dismissed him. He picked up a letter opener and was about to open the letter from General Lee when Colonel Head rose to his feet, massaged the back of his neck, and said, "Sir, for some reason, I've developed a headache. Been having these quite a bit lately, and don't know why. I have some powders in my satchel at your quarters. Would you excuse me for a few minutes while I run over there and take them?"

"Of course," smiled Buckner. "However, Colonel, they are now our quarters."

"Thank you, sir," the colonel smiled back. "I won't be gone long. I'll be interested in hearing what General Lee has to say about catching the devil who's been killing your officers."

When the door closed behind Colonel Head, Buckner slit the envelope open, took out the folded sheet of paper, and read it carefully. A grim smile curved his lips as he opened a desk drawer, took a match from a small box, and struck it on the side of his chair. He let the flame flare up, then touched it to the bottom of the letter.

Colonel Head closed the door behind him and hurried along a narrow walkway toward the general's quarters. He was unaware of the man-in-gray who had been watching the office door and was now following him.

Head greeted several men along the way. He reached the door of the general's quarters, went inside, and closed it behind him. Crossing the room to his cot, he sat down and pulled a black satchel from underneath, and opened it. He took out a white envelope, went to the small table that stood against a windowless wall, and poured water from a pitcher into a tin cup.

Just as he set the pitcher down, there was a knock at the door. "Come in," he called.

A man entered the room and closed the door behind him. Finding the face unfamiliar, Head smiled and said, "You must be a Donelson man."

"That's right, sir," the man replied as he moved closer, one hand in the pocket of his heavy coat.

"Who are you, soldier?"

"Name's Woodley, sir. Jack Woodley. I'm a corporal."

"Well, what can I do for you, Corporal Woodley?"

"Die!" blurted the killer as he plunged the knife into Head's chest.

Shock showed on the colonel's face and his knees gave way. When he landed on the floor, the killer bent over, yanked the knife free, and stabbed him again. Head's body went limp and his eyes closed. The killer wiped the knife clean on the colonel's coat and headed for the door. Opening it a crack, he paused, then hastened away.

Colonel Head moaned and struggled to a sitting position. Gritting his teeth, he rolled to his knees and crawled toward the door. Twice he fell flat and had to force himself to a crawling position again. When he finally reached the door, his strength was nearly gone.

Try as he might, he could not lift himself high enough to reach the latch. Lying face-down, he attempted to cry out, but the sound wasn't loud enough to be heard. He was going to die, and he knew it. Rolling on his side, he used his forefinger to write a message in blood on the back of the door with shaky hand: CPL JACK WOODLEY.

The tail of the "Y" went all the way to the floor.

Colonel Head had been gone for nearly a half hour when General Buckner sent for Captain Britt Claiborne and told him to call a meeting of all the officers. He had received some important messages and wanted to tell the other officers about them.

A quarter-hour later, Buckner stood in the dining hall and watched as the officers filed in. When the last ones had entered, he scanned the faces of the group, looking for his new colonel, but didn't see him. Turning to Claiborne, he said, "Captain, I believe Colonel Head has been overlooked. He's aware of these messages, but he needs to be here for discussion. I forgot to tell you to stop by my quarters and advise him. He has a headache and may be lying down. Just stick your head out the door and send someone to fetch him."

"Since you won't want to start until he's here, sir, I'll go get him."

Britt made his way across the yard and turned down the stone-walled passageway that led to the officers' quarters. When he arrived at General Buckner's door, he tapped lightly and called, "Colonel Head…Colonel Head, are you in there, sir?"

There was no response. The captain thought possibly Head had fallen asleep, so he tripped the latch and opened the door a couple of inches. "Colonel Head. Meeting time for the officers, sir. General Buckner desires your presence."

When this did not bring a response, Claiborne pushed the door open further. The door struck something soft. Sticking his head and shoulders inside, he saw the body on the floor. "Colonel Head!" he gasped, turning sideways to slip inside.

As Captain Claiborne knelt beside the body, his eye caught the bloody scrawl on the back of the door. "Corporal Jack Woodley? Oh, dear Lord in heaven, he's identified the killer!"

Moments later, General Buckner stood in his own quarters and said to Britt Claiborne, "The name isn't familiar to me either, Captain, but it won't take long to find him, now. When Corporal Whiting gets back here with the roster, Jack Woodley is a dead man! I have power to execute spies or traitors. Whichever he turns out to be, he'll be dead before dark!"

While the other officers waited outside in the narrow corridor and dozens of curious enlisted men pressed close, Claiborne took a blanket off the dead colonel's cot and covered his body. He was just finishing when Whiting pushed his way past the press around the door and entered the room. Buckner wanted privacy for a moment, so he excused himself to the officers and closed the door.

Whiting carried the folder to the small table where the water pitcher sat. "This folder contains the list of corporals who were here before the Fort Henry troops came, sir," said Whiting, flipping pages. When he reached the Ws, he ran his finger down the list. There was no Jack Woodley.

Buckner and Claiborne were looking over his shoulder. Turning, he said, "I'm sorry, General, but we don't have any such corporal in the fort."

Buckner's face was livid. "Maybe he got the rank wrong. I want you to check every list in the place. Captain Claiborne and I will go to the records room with you."

Thirty minutes later, Buckner stood before the officers and told them about the name written in blood on the back of the door. There was no one named Jack Woodley in Fort Donelson, and none of the soldiers named Jack had a last name that sounded remotely close to Woodley.

Though greatly saddened by the violent death of his only colonel, Buckner went on to talk about the important messages he had received earlier in the day. There was already talk going around the fort about the letter delivered earlier that day by a Confederate rider on a puffing horse. Buckner told the officers that the letter was from General Lee advising him that Lee was taking steps to ferret out Fort Donelson's mysterious killer.

One of the lieutenants from Fort Henry raised his hand. When Buckner acknowledged him, he said, "Sir, I'm Lieutenant George Lamont, and I would like to ask what General Lee is doing to track down this murderer."

Officers all over the room voiced their agreement. They wanted to know exactly what was being done.

General Buckner quieted them and said, "Gentlemen, I'm sorry, but I am not at liberty to divulge General Lee's plan. It's possible that the killer could be an officer. We've had no reason to rule out that possibility. If he should be in this room at the moment, and I revealed how General Lee is planning to catch him, he would have opportunity to stay one step ahead of us. We must commence our bodyguard plan for you men from Fort Henry and keep it in effect for all officers until such time that the killer is caught and executed."

The officers from Fort Henry looked around at the Fort Donelson officers with wary eyes. Silence prevailed over the room.

"All right, gentlemen," Buckner said, "there's another enemy lurking about. We need to make plans for meeting Ulysses S. Grant's attack when it comes."

EIGHT

The sky was clear on Friday morning, February 7. Just as the sun was peeking over the eastern horizon, the two sentries at Fort Donelson's gate saw a wagon bounding their direction from the south. As it drew nearer, they could make out two young women on the seat.

Private Lester Dole turned to his partner and said, "Open the gate. I'll go out and see what they want."

Dole passed through the gate and the wagon team skidded to a halt. He smiled and said, "Good morning, ladies. How may I help you?"

The one holding the reins said, "I'm Donna Mae Claiborne, wife of Captain Britt Claiborne. This is my sister-in-law, Sally Marie, who is Sergeant William Claiborne's wife. There's been a death in the family. We need to see our husbands, please."

"I know them both, ma'am. You wait here. I'll bring them to you."

"There's a third Claiborne, Private," Sally Marie said. "Corporal Robert. Will you bring him too?"

"Sure will ma'am. Be back with them as soon as possible. Is...the deceased someone close?"

"Yes. Their mother."

"Oh, I'm so sorry."

Moments later, Britt, William, and Robert were at the gate, embracing Donna Mae and Sally Marie. They shed tears as Donna Mae told them how their mother had awakened Hannah Rose in the middle of the night, coughing and wheezing. Hannah Rose did her best to help her, but Wilma Jean died in her arms.

They had already contacted the family's pastor and the undertaker in Dover on their way to the fort. The funeral was scheduled at ten o'clock the next morning.

Leaving the others at the gate, Captain Claiborne went to General Buckner, asking for the rest of the day and all day Saturday to attend their mother's funeral and spend some time with the rest of the family. Buckner granted them three days, asking that they return on Monday morning.

There was a tearful meeting between brothers and sisters when the Claiborne wagon arrived at the house.

The funeral took place as scheduled, and members of the church brought food for the family. It was early afternoon when they sat down to eat, but no one had much of an appetite. They reminisced about their childhood and shared memories about their wonderful parents. The conversation then turned to the war and the brewing battle. They talked of Fort Henry's fall, and what the chances were that Fort Donelson could stand against the Union's attack, even with the additional twelve thousand men on their way from Kentucky.

The women wept out of fear for their men, who tried to comfort and encourage them. They were interrupted by a knock at the front door.

Robert jumped up and said, "I'll see who it is." Hurrying to the front of the house, he opened the door to find Club Clubson staring at him.

"Hello, Club. What can I do for you?"

"I'd like to see Linda Lee."

"She really isn't up to seeing you right now, Club."

"Yeah? Why not? I'm the guy who loves her. How come she ain't up to seein' me?"

"Our mother died yesterday, that's why! We just buried her."

Club blinked and his head bobbed. "Well, all the more reason she should see me. I can comfort her."

"All she needs right now is family, Club."

"I'll bet if that puny little soldier I caught holdin' her had knocked on the door, you'd let him in!"

"If I did, it wouldn't be any of your business! Listen, I appreciate what you've done to help my sisters here on the place, Club, but that doesn't give you the right to beat up on any man Linda Lee wants to see. You'd best get that into your head!"

Club stood like a post, boring holes in Robert with fierce, blazing eyes. "Ain't no man gonna have Linda Lee but me!" Club's voice carried all the way through the house to the kitchen.

Robert was a much smaller man, but when it came to defending one of his sisters, he would take on a dozen Club Clubsons. "My sister might have something to say about that! She has a right to choose who she spends her time with, and who she marries! If she doesn't choose you, then that's the way it is. Stay out of it!"

Club was about to make a sharp retort when Linda Lee moved up beside Robert. Britt and William were on her heels.

"That's enough, Club!" Britt said. "We've had a hard enough day without you coming around here making trouble. I heard the last few words between you and Robert, and I'm here to tell you right now that you don't have any claim on Linda Lee! I don't like at all what you did to Lanny Perkins and Jim Lynch."

"Perkins shouldn't have been holdin' Linda Lee!" Club boomed.

"Was she trying to get loose from him?" pressed Britt.

"No, and that made me mad, too!"

"Maybe she wanted Lanny to hold her. And if she did, that's none of your business."

"Well, I love her, and I don't want no other man anywhere near her. She's gonna marry me someday!"

William pushed his way to the front. "Is Linda Lee wearing your wedding ring, Club?"

The big man blinked. "No."

"Is she wearing your engagement ring?"

"No. But she's my girl."

"Has she told you she's your girl?"

Club looked at Linda Lee. "No, but she is."

"That's all in your head, Club," Britt said. "I don't want you putting that kind of pressure on my little sister. You embarrassed her something awful the way you acted with Lanny Perkins. She can't be living in your shadow, worried sick that the next time she has a caller, you're going to beat the daylights out of him. This business is going to stop here and now. Do you understand that?"

Club was growing angrier, and Linda Lee could see it. Laying a hand on Britt's shoulder, she said calmly, "Let me talk to Club alone, Britt."

The elder brother looked down at her, shaking his head. "I'm not about to leave you alone with him, the way he's acting. Who knows what he might do?"

"Then, at least step back so I can talk to him, please."

The three brothers retreated a few steps to find Hannah Rose, Donna Mae, and Sally Marie standing a few feet to the rear of the scene.

Moving closer, Linda Lee said, "Club, I don't want to hurt your feelings. You know that."

"Yes."

"Haven't I told you before that I'm fond of you, but I'm not in love with you?"

"Yeah."

"Do you understand what that means?"

"Sure, but it don't mean you won't one day fall in love with me."

Linda Lee sighed. "We've talked about that, too. Club, there's no future for us. There are many reasons for that. One of them is that you're not a Christian."

Club lifted his hat, ran splayed fingers through his tangled hair, and said, "I'll become a Christian if you want me to."

"No, Club, it doesn't work that way. It won't be real if you go through the motions just because you want to please me. I wish you'd become a Christian for your sake, not mine. But as I said, there are many reasons you and I cannot have a future together."

"But you'd learn to love me if you tried…and if your family would leave us alone."

"That's not true," Linda Lee said, stiffening at his mention of her family.

"It is, but you just don't know it."

Linda Lee was at her wits' end. She was trying to think of something to say that would make him understand, when suddenly Hannah Rose shouldered her way next to her and said, "Look, Club, I've listened to this conversation all I'm going to. Since you won't listen to reason, I now pronounce it over and done. You may leave now."

Club's tremendous body seemed to swell. His surly stare was a fixed and wicked pressure against the oldest and biggest of the Claiborne brothers. Barely moving his lips, he hissed, "If I'm of a mind to do it, Britt, I can beat you to a pulp."

Britt's jaw squared. "You might get yourself a meal, pal, but I'll get me a sandwich."

Club knew Britt was not afraid of him. Club was sure he could whip the smaller man, but the idea of Britt getting a "sandwich" in the scrap took away his will to fight. "I'll be goin' now," he grunted. "G'bye, Linda Lee. I'll be back to see you later."

The family watched as the huge man climbed into his wagon and drove away. As he snapped the reins and put the team into a gallop, Club looked back toward the Claiborne house with malice. "If you don't fall in love with me, Linda Lee, I'll kill the man you do fall in love with. And that's a promise."

Late in the afternoon on Wednesday, February 12, General Ulysses S. Grant left the Crisp house with his adjutant and private body-guards, and rode to Fort Henry. He was angry at General Henry Halleck because the ten thousand men Halleck had said would be there had not arrived. Eager to make his move on Fort Donelson, Grant decided to go without the reinforcements.

At Fort Henry, Grant assembled fifteen thousand troops and led them eastward toward the Cumberland River with Brigadier Generals Charles F. Smith and John A. McClernand flanking him. He had left two thousand men at Fort Henry under the command of Brigadier General Lew Wallace, just in case the Confederates sent in troops to recapture the fort.

The weather was mild, and the Union troops left their tents and overcoats at Fort Henry. With most of the fifteen thousand on foot, they crossed the marshy twelve-mile stretch and arrived within a thousand yards of Fort Donelson as darkness fell.

Grant told Smith and McClernand he would be back at sunrise to get a good look at the Rebel fortress. Andrew Foote's gunboat flotilla was in good repair and due to arrive at a designated spot on the Cumberland River. They would launch their attack once the ironclads were in place.

Grant set his troops in for the night and rode back to the Crisp house. He commented to his escorts how unseasonably warm it was. Corporal Albert Bates said it was too early for such warm weather. Certainly a cold front would soon be coming down from Canada.

At dawn on February 13, General Grant left the Crisp house and rode southwest, arriving where his troops were camped just as the sun's rays were spreading over the horizon.

Grant stood on a lofty knoll with Smith and McClernand and studied the fort in the light of the rising sun. From where he stood, the land rose quickly toward the river, topping out at the hundred-foot high bank. Fort Donelson frowned over the Cumberland River from that height, armed with powerful batteries. The land approaches were well-entrenched with rifle pits and protected by abatis, just as Grant's scouts had reported. Taking Fort Donelson would not be as easy as taking Fort Henry.

"It looks just as we had been told, gentlemen, so we'll proceed as in the briefing last night," Grant said.

General Smith's division was to fan out and cover any and all escape routes to the north of the fort, all the way to the river. General McClernand's division was to do the same on the south. Though Foote's flotilla had not yet come into view on the Cumberland, Grant told the generals to get their men ready.

From the knoll, General Grant observed the movement of the troops as they fanned out in a massive half-circle. He soon became troubled, however, when he saw that with both divisions stretched thin, General McClernand's unit did not reach the river bank on the south. This left the Confederates an escape route. He was anxious to close the gap, but knew he could not stretch the line any thinner. Since the ironclads had not yet arrived, he sent a rider to Fort Henry, ordering General Wallace and his troops to come immediately.

From their perch high atop the walls of Fort Donelson, the triumvirate of brigadiers observed the spread of Union troops. Nervously the garrison's gunners waited by their cannons and the bulk of the infantrymen lined the walls, standing by for action. Others were inside the fort being charged up for battle by their unit leaders, while still others were already outside the walls in the rifle pits, watching the Yankees fanning out around them just out of range.

The early morning wind stroked General Buckner's face as he scanned the river northward and said, "As sure as Monday follows Sunday, my friends, it won't be long till we see Union gunboats coming this way."

"You think they'll come with more than they brought against

Fort Henry?" queried General Floyd, who though first in charge, was the least experienced in warfare.

"If they have them available."

"From what I know," General Pillow said, "the four they brought against Fort Henry did a pretty devastating job."

"We have more firepower than Fort Henry did," Buckner said. "If they only send those four, maybe we can blow them clear out of the water."

Within the confines of the fort, Captain Britt Claiborne was preparing the five hundred men under his command. "General Buckner is expecting the naval assault to begin first, men," he said. "Depending on how quickly the Yankees send in their infantry, we'll go into action. General Floyd will be the one to give the order for us to storm out of the fort to meet them. And don't forget the Rebel yell. From what I've been told, it curdles Yankee blood."

There was a round of nervous laughter. Britt let his eyes roam to his brothers, who were in his division. He had also chosen them to be his special bodyguards.

"I won't pull any punches with you, men. It's going to be a fierce battle. If it goes on long enough that our ammunition runs out, it'll be bayonets, knives, fists, and fingernails."

There was another round of laughter, but this time more subdued.

"How about it? Are you ready to go out there and show those blue-bellies how to fight?"

Fists and rifles were raised as the unit lifted a rousing cheer. Just as the excited voices were growing quiet, there was a loud commotion over by the latrines. Captain Claiborne dashed that direction, followed by his unit.

Several soldiers were gathered around a lifeless form in a lieutenant's uniform. Shoving his way through the press, Claiborne saw the young lieutenant lying on his back with a long-bladed knife buried in his chest. Looking around, he asked, "Who found him?"

"I did, sir," spoke up a private. "I was going into this latrine right here. When I opened the door, the lieutenant fell out."

Claiborne called for someone to fetch the three generals, then asked, "Anybody know who he is?"

"Yes, sir," a sergeant said. "He's Lieutenant Blake Matson. Belongs—belonged to Colonel Nathan Forrest's cavalry division. One of our men has gone after the colonel."

"Colonel?" squinted Claiborne. "I didn't know we had any colonels here since Parker and Head were killed."

"Well, sir, we were sent to Fort Henry when it first opened up…from General Polk's command in Columbus. Before we left, the general told Captain Forrest he was being promoted right past major to lieutenant colonel. The papers never came through to him at Fort Henry, but we started calling him 'Colonel' anyway. I'm sure it's official, even though he hasn't actually been told so."

"I see. I met Captain Forrest at the officers' meeting a few days ago. Seems like a good man."

"He sure is, sir. He's tough as nails, but we love him."

Just then the three brigadiers appeared, and the collection of soldiers cleared them a path. Right behind them came Captain Forrest, eyes wild. He pushed his way past them and swore as he knelt beside the dead man. Breathing hard, he looked up at the three generals and said heatedly, "It's bad enough that we have to send these men into battle to die, but when they die like this, it's insane! Something's got to be done! This bloody barbarian has got to be caught!"

"Captain Forrest, had Lieutenant Matson chosen his two bodyguards like he was supposed to?" General Buckner asked.

"I don't know, sir," replied Forrest, rising to his feet. "But I'll find out. If he had, and those men failed to stay close to him, they're in deep trouble."

Voice low, General Floyd said, "Captain Forrest, I owe you an apology."

"What for sir?"

"When I passed through the camp at Columbus, I was given an envelope to be delivered to you. General Polk placed it in my hand, saying it was important. I didn't know who you were until now. I just plain forgot I had it. Please wait here; I'll go get it."

Four men carried Matson's body away while Forrest, some of his men, and several officers waited for General Floyd to return.

"I bet I know what it is, sir," one of Forrest's corporals said. "It's your promotion papers."

Nathan Bedford Forrest, a tough amateur horseman, had joined the Confederate army at the beginning of the war. Because of his expert horsemanship, he was placed in a cavalry unit in Virginia, and soon was rapidly making himself a professional soldier. His adept handling of himself in battle gained the attention of General Robert E. Lee. Forrest was made a lieutenant, and by the time the war was six months old, he was promoted to captain.

General Floyd returned, apologized for forgetting he had the envelope, and handed it to Forrest. Forrest opened the envelope and found official papers declaring his promotion to lieutenant colonel, along with a letter of congratulations from General Lee. The other men gathered there offered their congratulations also.

Lieutenant Colonel Forrest then said to General Buckner, "I know you can't reveal General Lee's plan for catching this killer, sir, but can you at least tell us if it's being put into action yet?"

"I can tell you that necessary wheels are rolling, Forrest. I will be interested to learn whether or not Lieutenant Matson had chosen his two bodyguards."

"I'll let you know as soon as I can look into it, sir."

Nerves drew taut as the men in Fort Donelson were reminded afresh there was a cold-blooded killer loose in their midst and as they observed the enemy at the edges of the forests and in the fields, preparing for battle.

The brigadiers climbed back to their high perch and looked to see if any Union gunboats were coming down the river. So far there were none.

A gun crew stood nearby, leaning on their cannon. "General Floyd," called the shot-man, "how about letting us turn this gun around and blast those blue-bellies out there in the fields?"

"Can't do it. We've got to save our cannonballs for the gunboats."

"Are you sure they're coming, sir?" the powder-man asked.

"Without a doubt."

"We know it because the Yankee infantrymen haven't come at us," General Buckner said. "I have no doubt that General Grant plans to lay the fort in a shambles, then finish us off with the infantry."

Forrest moved amongst his men, questioning them about Lieutenant Matson, but none of them could tell him who the murdered lieutenant had chosen as bodyguards. Forrest ran his gaze over the faces of his men as they stood waiting to go into battle. He swore and said, "I have a hard time believing Lieutenant Matson had not sought protection! He had a good head on his shoulders. I think some of you know who his bodyguards were, but you're covering for them! I can't prove it, so I guess the matter dies right here. But if I somehow ever find out who Matson's bodyguards were, those two are going to wish they'd never seen a gray uniform!"

The soldiers in nearby units heard Forrest's outburst. Sergeant Ralph Ederly detached himself from his group, approached Forrest, and said, "Colonel, I saw Lieutenant Matson heading for the latrine a few minutes before he was found dead, and no one was with him."

"You're sure?"

"Positive, sir. I just don't like to see a rift between you and your men, especially when we're about to go into battle."

"We'll handle it all right, Sergeant. Did you see anyone else around the latrines?"

"No, sir. Lieutenant Matson was alone."

"Not quite alone, Sergeant. The killer was there somewhere."

"Yes, of course, sir. But what I'm saying is that I saw no one else near the latrine when I noticed the lieutenant heading for them. Certainly if he had chosen his bodyguards, they would've been with him and waited at the door for him to come out. I really think, sir, that the lieutenant may not have taken the situation seriously. He just might not have picked himself any bodyguards."

Forrest rubbed his chin thoughtfully. "It's hard to believe, Sergeant, but you may be right. I'll make sure all my men know that I don't distrust a one of them."

As the morning passed, tension grew tighter inside the fort and in the rifle pits. The tension increased when the men of Fort Donelson caught sight of General Wallace and his men marching in from the west to join those already poised for attack.

NINE

Pacing back and forth atop his lofty mound, General Ulysses S. Grant muttered angrily, blowing smoke from his cigar. The gunboats had not yet arrived, and it was two o'clock in the afternoon. Heavy clouds now covered the sun, and a north wind swept down the Cumberland River, dropping the temperature quickly. To make matters worse, Grant and his army had just witnessed a large influx of Confederate troops march down the west bank of the Cumberland and enter Fort Donelson. Grant and his generals estimated their number to be somewhere between ten and twelve thousand.

Swearing, Grant threw his cigar down, stomped on it, and said to his generals, "If those ironclads had been here when they were supposed to be, we'd have had the fort under fiery siege, and those new troops wouldn't have been able to get inside. What in the world is keeping Foote?"

"There has to be something wrong, sir," General Wallace said. "It isn't like Commander Foote to be late."

"I know, that's part of what's worrying me. I'm thinking that Johnston has pulled one on me. Maybe he figured out a way to blockade the river and keep our boats from getting through."

"If that's the case, we'll have to attack the fort with our infantry, sir," spoke up General Smith.

"You're right, but I sure hope we don't have to. Some of those big guns can be turned this direction, and they'd take an awful toll on us. We'll give Foote some more time. He's just got to get here and soon."

By nightfall, the ironclads still had not arrived, and Grant was fit to be tied. It was too late to turn back now. If Foote and his flotilla didn't show up by sunrise, Grant would have to send his troops against the fort and its big guns. If that happened, this was going to be the bloodiest battle Grant had ever seen. He wished for the ten thousand men General Halleck had promised, and wondered where they were.

All over the fields, Union soldiers rubbed their cold bodies, wishing they had brought their tents and overcoats from Fort Henry.

A dismal dawn came on the morning of February 14. The cutting north wind whined over the land, and the iron-gray sky was spitting snow. General Grant, his adjutant, and his bodyguards left the Crisp house and headed toward the fields where the Union soldiers waited impatiently to launch the attack.

The Cumberland River was nearly out of sight behind Grant and his companions when Corporal Albert Bates happened to cast a glance to the rear and saw pillars of black smoke rising toward the gray overcast. Hipping around in the saddle, he saw six gunboats, each flying the Union flag as they steamed down the river. "General, look!"

Grant and his bodyguards cheered when they saw the flotilla. Then the general wheeled his mount around and put it to a gallop. The others followed, lashing their horses to catch up. Grant reached the bank of the river and looked the boats over. Only two, the *St. Louis* and the *Carondelet*, were familiar from the force that attacked Fort Henry. There were two new ironclads, the *Pittsburgh* and the *Louisville*. They were flanked by two unnamed wooden gunboats.

The flag ship of the fleet was now the *St. Louis*, and it drew up to a high spot on the bank where the water was deep enough to carry it. Flag Officer Foote appeared on the deck and raised a hand in greeting.

Agile for his age, Foote hopped off the boat onto the grassy bank and hastened to meet the general. "I'm sorry we're late, sir. We were slowed down and even stopped several times by debris on both rivers. Our worst problem was where the Tennessee and the Cumberland come together. It was blocked up real bad. Took us eight hours at that spot alone to maneuver the boats through."

Grant managed a weak smile. "I'm glad that's all it was. I was afraid the Rebels had waylaid you some way or the other. I see you have more boats."

"Yes, sir. My *Cincinnati* was battered up so bad, it's going to take a month to have it ready for service. The *Essex*…well, I'm not sure she'll ever be seaworthy again. They had the *Pittsburgh* and the *Louisville* ready at Cairo, so I asked for them. Thought I'd bring along the two wooden jobs, too. Gives us more firepower than we had going up against Fort Henry."

"Well, we're going to need it," sighed Grant.

"So what's the status?" The wind was whipping snow into their faces.

"We've been holding off the attack, waiting for you. I've got the troops fanned out around the land side of the fort, all the way to the river on both sides. There's no way they can escape."

"Good."

"I should tell you, though, the Rebs brought in an additional ten to twelve thousand troops yesterday. Even with the bombardment you're going to lay on them, we've got a tough scrap on our hands."

"I would say so," Foote nodded. "I assume you want us in attack formation."

"Correct. How soon can you be ready?"

"We've got some work to do first, but we should be ready by two o'clock."

"Two o'clock? Why so long?"

"Well, sir, we've needed every man on board to clear debris practically ever since we left Cairo. We need to fortify our decks against those Rebel shells."

Grant wanted to get the attack going—especially with snow falling—but he knew Foote wanted to be prepared before entering battle. "All right," he said with a sigh. "Just get ready as soon as possible. I want you to go in there with every gun on every boat blazing. I expect you to destroy Donelson's waterside batteries in short order. When those guns are silent, start lobbing shells behind the walls and blow the guts out of the place. Once I know all of their cannons are out of commission, I'll send the infantry in."

"We'll get the job done, General. I'll have men aboard the *St. Louis* keep an eye on shore, so if you send messengers, we'll see them."

"Good enough. Okay, Commander Foote, get going. I'll pass the word that you'll be ready to go at two o'clock."

"See you on the victory side," grinned the devout Presbyterian, and hopped aboard his flag ship.

Foote spent the morning getting the boats ready, piling the upper decks with heavy chains, lumber, and gunny sacks loaded with coal to protect them from bombardment. It took a little longer than he had anticipated. It was exactly 3:00 P.M. when the six Union gunboats steamed down the river in battle formation.

At 3:30, at a range of less than two thousand yards, the *St. Louis* opened fire, and immediately the *Louisville* followed suit. The gunners, high above the river in Fort Donelson's batteries, did not respond. They wanted the gunboats closer. Cannonballs exploded against the thick stone walls, showering the Rebels with bits and pieces of stone.

As the boats closed to about a thousand yards, the fort opened fire with its biggest guns, a 10-inch smoothbore Columbiad and a 32-pounder rifled cannon. The boats courageously came on until they were within four hundred yards. At that close range, all the

Confederate guns could reach them. The Confederates were using mostly solid shot, hoping to do extensive damage by penetrating armor and plowing gaping holes in the decks.

The gunners shouted at the tops of their voices as their targets rocked and reeled in the choppy waters from one direct hit after another. The river rang like a giant forge with the sound of metal striking metal.

Out in the fields, thousands of Union soldiers listened and shivered in the cold. Some had asked their commanders to let them return to Fort Henry for their coats and tents, but permission was denied. Every man would be needed when Grant gave the command to attack.

While the cannon battle raged, the snow fell harder and the icy wind grew colder.

The Rebel guns were doing tremendous damage to the Union gunboats. Commander Foote's men, however, pushed their vessels against the river's powerful current under heavy fire and sent shell after shell at the fort. The Rebels continued to blow off smokestacks, batter decks and hulls, and kill Yankee crewmen.

Aboard Captain Henry Walke's *Carondelet*, a 128-pounder shell struck the anchor, which lay on deck, and smashed it into countless flying chunks of metal, wounding and killing crewmen and taking away part of the smokestack. Another Rebel shell whistled down, ripped at the iron plating, and fell in the river. Another struck and went through the plating, lodging in the heavy casemate. Another tore into the pilot house, ripping the plating to shreds, and sent sharp, spinning fragments into both pilots. One was killed outright; the other fell to the wooden floor, mortally wounded.

No matter how hard the Union boatmen fought, the Confederate shells continued to come harder and faster, taking flagstaffs and smokestacks, and tearing off the side armor as lightning rends bark from a tree.

High up in the parapets, the Confederates were taking heart as they beheld the damage they were inflicting on the enemy boats. The booming of cannon on the walls and on boat decks was constant and deafening, so that commands had to be given by hand signals.

An hour after the assault began, the first wooden gunboat took two direct hits in the lower part of the hull and began to sink. The captain commanded his men to abandon the doomed vessel, and dove into the icy waters as soon as the last crewman was gone.

The second wooden vessel was hit so many times, it had no operating guns. The captain gave orders to head back upriver. Before they could get out of cannon range, a huge shell struck the powder magazine. The exploding gunpowder turned the boat into a huge fireball, and left the entire crew dead in the water.

In desperation, Foote brought his ironclads in to point-blank range. He must destroy the waterside guns, which were taking such a horrendous toll on his fleet. Not until they were in close did Foote realize his mistake. The close position beneath the lofty wall forced the Union guns to fire at maxim elevation, and the arcing trajectories tended to completely overshoot the fort.

The ironclads were in a vulnerable position and taking a vicious pounding.

Daylight began to wane, and Foote attempted to withdraw his battered flotilla to safer waters. But the *Louisville* took a 10-inch solid shot in the starboard bow-port that demolished a gun carriage, killed three men, and seriously wounded four others. Another shell came shrieking in behind it, plowing into the forward starboard deck, blowing the rudder chains apart, killing one man, and wounding two. With the rudder chain destroyed, the boat could not be steered. It began drifting helplessly downstream.

Foote was in the pilot house aboard the flag ship *St. Louis* when a shell struck. It tore into the flag officer's left foot, killed the pilot, and carried away the wheel. Out of control, the *St. Louis* washed downstream after the *Louisville*.

The *Pittsburgh* took a shell low in the bow on the port side, and began to sink. Only when her captain shifted the heavy guns to the stern did the bow lift high enough to keep water from flowing in.

Seeking to escape, the captain commanded the vessel to be turned sharply, but when it began the turn, it collided with the *Carondelet,* shearing her starboard rudder.

Captain Walke's boat was already heavily battered. This mishap dropped a cold blanket of discouragement over him. Frantically, he tried to rig emergency steering as the boat drifted downstream after the other ironclads. In the midst of the near-panic, Walke had enough presence of mind to keep his guns blazing away in hope that the heavy smoke would provide a screen from Donelson's relentless guns.

As darkness fell, the Rebels watched the boats drift helplessly downstream. During the entire battle, not one man in the fort had been killed, though a few had been wounded. A shout of exultation leaped from the lips of every man on the walls.

That night, General Grant, who had watched the debacle from the knoll, sent a wire to General Halleck in St. Louis. He told him of the Confederate victory over the gunboats and informed him that he was going in with the infantry the next day. He also complained that the ten thousand reinforcements had not arrived.

Inside the fort, the resounding Rebel victory did little to lighten the gloom that had settled over Generals Floyd, Pillow, and Buckner. During the afternoon's battle, they had agreed that the fort was a virtual trap and would cost them their army if they did not escape. Their pessimism had been bolstered by a somber telegraph message received late that morning advising them that General Albert Sidney Johnston had decided to take his troops to Nashville and fortify there. Johnston's message was: "If you lose the fort, bring your troops to Nashville if possible."

The three brigadiers were sure that with two of his boats sunk and the others severely damaged, General Grant would bring his infantry in full-force the next morning. They agreed on a plan. They would send their troops out of the fort like a flood at the crack of dawn, strike Grant's army with a sudden hammer blow of artillery and infantry, then make a fast break for Nashville, seventy-five miles to the east.

The Confederate commanders worked on their attack plan until nearly two o'clock in the morning, then went to their beds for a short sleep.

Snow continued to fall until about 4:00 A.M., then the sky began to clear. With the clearing came a howling, Arctic wind. Though the heartless wind knifed through their coats, the Confederates welcomed it because it covered their noise as they moved into attack position a few minutes before dawn. All was ready when dawn broke in a clear sky, showing the ground covered with fresh snow and skeletal tree limbs sheathed in ice.

Suddenly there was a crashing volley of cannon fire from the lofty parapets of the fort. At the same time, with a wild Rebel yell, over sixteen thousand infantrymen converged on the half-frozen, surprised Union troops.

Without overcoats or tents, the Yankees had spent the night huddled around small campfires and shivering against the cold. They fought back valiantly, but the surprise attack soon had those near the river bank retreating to the open fields to join their comrades.

The cannons roared on the walls for some time, then went silent as the battle spread across the fields and into the forests. Formal lines dissolved into separate skirmishes. Units on both sides quickly lost touch with each other, and soldiers waged countless individual fights, bitterly contesting each ditch, gully, mound, frozen bush, and ice-covered tree. Rifles barked and streaks of flame darted from the edges of the forest. Men ran from rock to rock and ditch to ditch on the open fields, threw themselves down, fired, and found shelter while they reloaded their guns.

Observing the battle from the walls, the three brigadiers realized things had not gone as planned. With the battle spreading out so much, there was no way the Confederate troops were going to be able to make a fast retreat. However, the battle seemed to be going in their favor, so the generals decided to let the fight take its natural course.

At the edge of a small forest, Corporal Jim Lynch was using a huge oak tree for cover while he shot it out with a Yankee soldier who was on his belly in a shallow draw. They had exchanged several shots, and both were reloading.

Unknown to Lynch, a second Yankee had noticed the contest and was working his way up behind him. Lynch finished reloading, dropped the ramrod, and cocked the hammer. Bracing the single-shot musket against the tree, he aimed it toward the draw and laid his finger against the trigger.

"C'mon, blue-belly," he whispered. "Just give me a little piece of target. C'mon."

Suddenly the Yankee's gun roared and the lead ball thwacked into the side of the tree, splattering bits of bark into Lynch's eyes. Blinking, Lynch fired directly at the spot where he had seen the powder flash. He pulled the trigger just as the enemy soldier raised up to see if he had hit his target. Lynch's bullet caught him at the base of the throat, and he fell back into the draw. It took him only seconds to die.

Lynch was thumbing bark from his eyes when a cold voice from the shadows behind him said, "Hey, Reb!"

He whirled around to find himself looking down the black muzzle of a .58 calibre musket. The Yankee squeezed the trigger, and Corporal Jim Lynch saw the flash an instant before the slug took his life.

In the fields and forests, the fighting continued. Late in the afternoon, ammunition began to run low on both sides. Soldiers took ammunition from the bodies of the dead to replenish their supply. By sundown, it was hand-to-hand fighting with bayonets, knives, rifle butts, and fists.

When darkness fell and a full moon began to rise, General

Floyd ordered his weary men to return to the fort. Bedraggled Rebels helped their wounded comrades back to the fort from the forests and the fields. The temperature was plunging as the battered and bloodied Rebels gathered inside the fort.

Corporal Lanny Perkins, stumbling on tired legs and assisting a wounded private, came upon the body of Jim Lynch. Tears filled his eyes as he paused to look at him in the moonlight. Perkins wished he could carry the body to the fort, but he had to help the wounded man who was leaning on him. They stumbled wearily away, tears staining Perkins's cheeks.

The Yankees were just as weary. They regrouped and began to build fires at the edge of the woods a half-mile west of the fort. Confederate and Union bodies were scattered in the woods and on the open fields, their blood staining the snow a deep crimson.

While watching the battle, General Floyd had changed his mind about retreating to Nashville. He kept it to himself, wanting Buckner and Pillow to learn of it when he told the other officers. Gathering the officers in the dining hall, he noted that some were wounded and patched up, while others were missing. Two captains and three lieutenants were dead. Captain Leonard Billings and Lieutenant Bruce Frye had been seriously wounded and were being tended to in the infirmary.

Floyd looked at the exhausted men and said, "Gentlemen, General Pillow, General Buckner, and I observed the marvelous way our men took the fight to the enemy today. It was evident early on that our plan to strike hard, then run for Nashville wasn't going to be realized. No one could help it, but the battle spread too fast for a clean pullout. However, Generals Pillow and Buckner are as pleased as I am the way the battle went today. Our men really put it to them.

"In view of what I saw today, I've changed my mind about retreating to Nashville at all. I'm convinced that one more day of that kind of fighting will give us the victory. We can whip those Yankees."

There was a loud, startling knock at the door, followed by an excited voice. "General Floyd! General Floyd!"

"Come in!" Floyd called as every eye in the room swerved to the door.

Sergeant Cliff Nolan bolted into the room, face pallid, and gasped, "Sir, we've got real trouble! There are a bunch of steamers pulling ashore upstream out of cannon range, and they're unloading thousands of Yankee troops!"

The officers left the room and dashed to the walls. Hearts sank as they observed thousands of men filing out of the boats onto the west bank of the Cumberland.

Somberly, they gathered back into the dining hall. General Floyd stood before them, face drawn, and said, "Gentlemen, this puts a whole new light on the situation. I'd estimate the Yankees have brought in easily eight thousand men…maybe more. We're vastly outnumbered now."

"We've only got one choice, sir," General Buckner said. "We've got to get out of this trap of a fort immediately. If we don't, they'll have us pinned in here and helpless by morning."

Colonel Forrest said, "I agree a hundred percent, General Buckner. This fort is nothing but a trap, and I say we'd better get out while the getting's good."

"But our men are too tired to strike out for Nashville," General Pillow argued. "Seventy-five miles is a long way in this weather. The bulk of us would never make it."

Pillow's words had a profound effect on most of the officers. General Floyd cleared his throat and said, "General Pillow is right. Our men are too fatigued to head out for Nashville tonight. I don't see that we have any choice but…to surrender."

"Surrender!" Forrest gusted. "You can't mean that!"

"None of us like the idea of surrender, Colonel, but General Pillow is right," General Buckner said. "We'd lose half of our men, or more, if we tried to make it to Nashville in this weather. All we can do is surrender."

"I hate the idea, too," Pillow said, "but there's no reasonable alternative."

Forrest swore, slammed his fist into his palm, and growled, "I can speak for my men. We would rather die attempting to make it to Nashville than be locked up in a stinking Yankee prison camp!" Stomping to the door, he opened it, looked back and said, "My men and I will be leaving in a couple of hours. Anybody who wants to go with us is welcome."

When the door slammed, the brigadiers exchanged somber glances. The room was silent as a tomb.

Captain Claiborne broke the silence. "I'd like to say something, General Floyd."

"The floor is yours."

"I think you generals ought to give the men an opportunity to choose between staying and surrendering, or trying to make it to Nashville. If they want to gamble the journey, they ought to have that option."

"I'll tell you right now, Captain," said General Buckner, "the bulk of them will choose to stay. A Yankee prison camp is better than dying in the wilderness. As fatigued as they are right now, to attempt the journey will be nothing but suicide."

"I'm sure you're right, sir," Claiborne replied, "but I think each man should be given the choice."

"Fine. We'll let them choose," Floyd said. Turning to Buckner, he asked, "Are you determined to stay here and surrender, even if the bulk of the men choose to head for Nashville?"

"They won't, I assure you. But even if all we have left here is a handful, I'll stay and surrender with them."

"All right," Floyd said, "since you've stated your mind on it, I'll go with Colonel Forrest. Since I didn't have to fight today, I'm not fatigued. I can make it to Nashville."

"I can too," Pillow said. "I'll go along with you and Colonel Forrest."

The officers were dismissed to go to their men and offer the choice of surrendering or braving the winter weather.

When only the three generals were left in the room, Buckner

said, "General Floyd, since you and General Pillow are leaving, I'll need both of you to formally pass the command of Fort Donelson to me…in writing."

"Okay. Let's go to the office."

When the necessary paper was written and signed, Floyd and Pillow left to make preparations for travel. General Buckner then sat down and wrote a proposal of surrender to be carried by messenger to General Grant.

On the battlefields and in the woods below, Union soldiers moved about in the clear light of the full moon, removing clothing from the bodies of dead soldiers—Union and Confederate alike—to help keep them from freezing during the night.

At the camp near the woods, General Grant welcomed his ten thousand new troops before retiring to the Crisp house for the night.

As midnight came, campfires winked against the silvery light that illuminated the countryside.

TEN

His first sensation when coming to was that of bitter cold. He could hear the wind wailing about him like a wounded, dying beast, and the ice crystals that stung his face stimulated his senses and tore at the fog that webbed his brain.

The solid surface beneath him seemed to whirl and undulate. Suddenly aware that he was spread-eagled on his back, he slowly raised up on his right elbow and shook his head. A flash of blinding pain stabbed his left temple, and lights glittered before his eyes like a shower of meteors. His head swam and he tried to open his eyes. The right one cooperated, but the left one refused to come open. He caught a glimpse of a frozen landscape of white and shadow just before dizziness claimed him and an inky black curtain descended over his brain.

He stirred to consciousness again. His body was numb with cold. He recalled coming to before, but had no idea how long it had been. With effort he opened his right eye again. Looking directly above him, he saw the full moon hovering in a black, starlit sky. He felt around him and realized he was lying on crusted ice and snow.

Pain lanced his throbbing temple as he forced himself to a sitting position. Though he could see fairly well with his right eye, the left one stubbornly remained shut. He raised his left hand to find out why, and his fingertips touched a mat of clotted blood. He clawed at the clot until it was gone and he could see with both eyes.

He found that he was in a low spot on an open field. There was a stand of trees nearby, their ragged, naked branches resembling skeletal hands in the moonlight.

The pain in his temple caused him to probe with his fingertips till he found a long, slender ridge that burrowed horizontally along his temple and into his scalp. It was sticky with blood.

What could have caused this?

He looked down and discovered that he was clad only in long underwear and socks. No wonder he was so cold! Working against the stiffness of his joints, he forced himself to his knees. The silver moonlight showed him bodies strewn everywhere! Some were prostrate on their faces, some lying face-up, others crumpled. They had all been stripped of their outer clothing—their *uniforms*.

Yes, their uniforms! He was on a battlefield!

Now he knew what had caused the bloody ridge along his temple. A bullet had creased his head. He had narrowly escaped death.

He was on a battlefield, all right, but what battlefield? What war? Wait…the war between the states. The Civil War! Abraham Lincoln. Jefferson Davis. But…but *who am I?*

He could recall the names of Lincoln and Davis, of Lee and Jackson, of McClellan and Grant. But why couldn't he remember his own name? And where he was from? He was a soldier. But which side was he on?

He searched his memory for answers, but found none. He could remember nothing about himself except that he had come to consciousness some time earlier, then passed out again.

He struggled to suppress the fear welling up inside. He tried to calm himself, telling himself that soon he would remember everything.

The wintry wind lashed him with snow and ice. His eyes fell on a pair of boots lying a few feet away. Quickly, he crawled to them, sat on the frozen crust of snow, and pulled the boots on his aching feet. They fit. They were likely his boots.

With extreme effort, he worked his way to his feet and took a deep breath. A gust of wind hit him like a fist, knocking him off balance. Steadying himself, he fought off a wave of dizziness. When it cleared, he looked at the corpses that surrounded him. He moved among the dead soldiers and studied their faces. None were familiar. He couldn't even remember what his own face looked like. Another dizzy spell halted him in his tracks, and he swayed with both hands to his head. His breath puffed out in cones of frost. Crossing his arms over his chest, he tucked his freezing hands into his armpits.

When his head cleared once more, he continued moving amongst the dead. If he could remember the names of Lincoln and Davis, and even recall what they looked like, why couldn't he recognize the men he fought beside? The evidence around him was clear—the battle had been fierce, and there were dead soldiers from both sides. There should be men here that he had known. There had to be. Yet there was not one familiar face.

He groped among the dead, hoping to find one man who had not been stripped so he could don his clothing. Whoever had stripped the bodies must have thought he was dead. Or did they? Maybe they were the enemy, and just left him to die.

Cold! Yes, it's so cold.

This clothing search was getting him nowhere. Every man in sight had been stripped. He must get to a warm place, or he would soon freeze to death.

But where?

He rubbed his arms vigorously and continued walking, though still unsteadily. Try as he might, he could not make any of the white, moon-struck land look familiar. The fear that had been rising within him now threatened to become panic. "Why can't I remember who I am?" he cried out. "Or where I am?"

Directly ahead of him, he saw a wide river, shining like a silver ribbon as it reflected the brilliant moon. Following its trail off to his left, he saw the land rise up and top out at the edge of the river in a complex of square roofs, surrounded by a dark, looming wall.

A fort!

Abruptly he recalled that the war between the states was being fought on Southern soil. Then he was looking at a *Confederate* fort, and it was occupied, for he could make out movement atop the walls. He caught sight of winking campfires farther up the riverbank. It had to be a Union camp. Both sides were no doubt waiting for morning so they could resume the battle.

His heart quickened pace. There would be *warmth* in either the camp or the fort.

But which one was the enemy?

The panic within him surged. With effort, he strove to suppress it while his mind raced. If he went to the wrong place, he could be executed as a spy. Anyone captured in a battle zone out of uniform could very well be taken for a spy. If they believed he was a spy, he would be shot. There was no way he could prove otherwise. And even if they believed he was a soldier, if he didn't know which side he was on, certainly they could not either. They would have no choice but to incarcerate him for the duration of the war.

The truth came home. *Either* place was the wrong place. Yankees or Confederates would have to deal with him the same— shoot him, or put him in a prison camp till the war was over. He could not go to the camp, and he could not go to the fort.

Pain lanced through his head. Dizziness followed, and waves of nausea washed over him. He dropped to his knees and braced his hands against the crusted snow to keep from falling on his face. The wind took his breath. Soon the nausea was gone, and the dizziness eased off. If he could just get to a warm place and rest...

He decided to see if he could find a farm. In a barn or a shed he could get out of the wind. He dare not approach a farmhouse. This was Southern soil, and if the farmer chose to believe he was a

Yankee, he could still be shot. A barn or shed would have to do for now, until he could thaw out and decide what to do.

He struggled back to his feet. Rubbing his hands together and whacking his upper torso with his arms, he headed back the way he came. There had to be a farm somewhere near. Threading amongst the dead, he moved as quickly as his legs would carry him. He recognized the stand of trees near the spot where he had first awakened, and another two hundred yards beyond them, he saw the beginnings of a forest. He would cut along the edge of the forest. Surely it would lead him to a farm…and warmth.

As he stumbled toward the woods, he noted for the first time that no weapons were in sight. Whoever stripped the bodies also took whatever guns, bayonets, and knives they could find. He was drawing nearer the edge of the forest when something off to the right caught his eye. He stopped, turning his head in that direction.

Something moved over there, didn't it?

Or was it a trick the wind and the shadows played on his confused mind?

He blinked against the wind, searching for further movement among the scattered corpses.

Then something else halted him. Was that a moan? It was hard to tell with the wind whining about him. He held his breath, straining, listening.

Then they came, both movement and sound at the same time. One of the men on the ground moaned and moved his legs, trying to raise his head.

The amnesiac breathed, "Oh, dear Lord in heaven, he's alive!" Even as he spoke, he stumbled toward the fallen soldier. "Lord, please let him know me! Please!"

He reached the wounded man and saw the broad spread of blood on the long underwear that covered his chest. Gripping the man's shoulder, he said, "Soldier, can you hear me?"

The moan stopped abruptly, the head quit rolling, and the bleeding man opened his eyes. Attempting to focus on the moonlit form above him, he gasped, "Who...who is it?"

"I'm a friend. Can you see me?"

"Yes."

"Do you know me?"

The soldier squinted, licked his lips, and replied shakily, "I...I can't...see you that good." He coughed, winced with pain, then said, "I'm hit bad. Can you...get me to the camp?"

The camp! He's a Yankee.

The amnesiac's thoughts jumbled, then cleared. If he took the wounded man to the camp, it would leave him in the fix he had pondered earlier. But this man was in bad shape. If there was a chance he could save his life, he must do it, no matter the risk to himself.

For a moment, he wondered at his willingness to sacrifice himself for a man he didn't even know, who might even be his enemy. Somehow it was a settled thing in his mind. He would carry the man to the camp.

"Sure, my friend," he breathed. "I'll get you to the camp. I assume there's a doctor there?"

"A medic," came the weak reply. A frown creased his brow. "But if you're a Yankee...you already know that."

No time to explain. He reached underneath the wounded man and surprised himself as he cradled him in his arms and stood up. Where had he gotten the strength to do this? The man had to weigh somewhere around two hundred pounds.

As they headed toward the camp, the wounded man looked at him with half-glazed eyes and said, "You're a Rebel, aren't you?"

"Yeah." No sense wasting breath.

"And you're willing...to carry me into the camp? You know they'll...take you prisoner."

"Yeah."

The wounded man was quiet for a long moment. Then he said weakly, "You're a Christian, aren't you."

"Yes, I am," he replied before he even pondered the question.

"I thought so. Only…only a man who…knows Jesus would do what you're doing."

His mind raced again. He couldn't remember who he was, where he came from, or even what army he belonged to, but he knew what a Christian was, and he knew he was one. His thoughts rushed to Calvary—the cross, the blood, the dying Redeemer with nails through His hands and feet. And he knew that this Jesus lived in his heart. This was not only a source of peace and comfort, it was also encouraging. Maybe his memory was already coming back!

The wounded Yankee coughed and spit up blood as they continued slowly across the battlefield. When he could speak again, he said with a voice that was growing even weaker, "I'm a Christian, too…my brother. I thought about it before we…attacked Fort Donelson. I wondered how many men…in that fort were my Christian brothers. Bad enough…bad enough for blood brothers…to fight each other, but even worse for…men in God's family…to be killing each other."

A sick feeling went through the amnesiac. He couldn't say if that awful thought had ever crossed his mind before, but he figured it was true.

His legs were growing weaker. They had traveled about a hundred and fifty yards when he said, breathing hard, "I'm going to have to put you down and rest a moment."

There was no response as he stopped and carefully lowered the Yankee soldier to the ground. The Yankee's eyes were closed and his mouth was sagging open. A quick check for a pulse revealed none. The man was dead.

There was a sudden piercing pain in his left temple, and with it came a rush of dizziness. His equilibrium gave way, and he found himself on the frozen ground next to the dead Yankee. The earth went into a spin and a black shroud began to overwhelm him. He was almost unconscious, but the sensation of spinning in a tight circle seemed to keep the shroud from blacking him out.

It took about three minutes for the spell to pass. When he felt he could stand once again, he struggled to his feet. The wind was easing some, though it still lashed his face enough to dispose of the sweat that beaded his brow.

He stood still for a moment waiting for his legs to quit shaking. Looking down at the dead man's face, he said softly, "I never asked your name, dear brother, and couldn't have told you mine. Well, now that you're in heaven, you can ask the Lord my name. He knows it, even if I don't."

He looked toward the hulking Confederate fort on the bank of the wide silver stream. "Fort Donelson, eh? Then that must be the Cumberland River." He paused, then said, "I can remember the name of the fort and the name of the river, but there's a fog bank when it comes to my own name."

He felt pain in his hands and looked at his fingers. They were deep purple. He feared frostbite. Breathing on his hands to warm them, he moved on unsteady legs toward the edge of the forest once again.

Turning slightly to follow the wooded rim, he felt another sharp pain in his temple. He staggered a few steps and fell. He clawed at his frozen surroundings, but was soon swallowed by a swirling black vortex.

When he came to, the moon had reached the western sky. He was chilled more than ever. His fingers were numb and so were his toes. Forcing himself to a sitting position, he pulled off his boots and rubbed his feet until some measure of warmth returned. When his boots were back on, he breathed on his hands and rubbed them together until the stiffness left them.

His knees felt watery as he rose once again, but he forced himself to keep moving. If he didn't get someplace warm soon, he was going to freeze to death. He had been plodding along the edge of the trees for about fifteen minutes, scouring the moonlit landscape for some sign of a farm, when from within the woods, he heard the distinct blow of a horse.

He looked into the deep shadows and listened. Above the rush of the wind through the treetops, he heard the sound again. There was a horse amongst the trees, and not very far away.

He plunged into the shadows, using the solid trunks to steady himself. It took only seconds for him to find the horse, a bay gelding standing beside the crumpled body of its rider.

A few other bodies lay amid the trees, and none of them had been stripped. They were all clad in Rebel gray.

The horse nickered at him as he moved about, studying the dead men. He would take the uniform and coat of the man nearest his own size. He was already anticipating the warmth the clothing would give his shivering body. He finally decided the rider of the horse was closest in size.

The man had been a Confederate captain, and a single slug had plowed into the left side of his forehead, killing him instantly. There was a little blood on his hat, which lay next to him, and a small sprinkling of crimson on the left shoulder of his overcoat.

He hastily removed the outer clothing from the dead officer and put it on. The uniform fit him perfectly, even the hat, which he had to wear cocked to the right side because of the bloody furrow on the left. He touched the furrow and found that it was oozing blood. He must have reopened it when he fell the last time.

Searching the dead captain's pockets, he found a bandanna and tied it around his head. He then picked up the captain's gunbelt and strapped it on. As he was buckling the belt, he noted how natural it felt, even the heft of the revolver's weight against his hip.

Was he an officer? The very thought seemed right. But of which army?

The horse seemed a bit nervous as he prepared to mount. It nickered and danced about. Stroking the side of its face, he said gently, "It's all right, boy. I'm friendly, even if I'm a Yankee."

The soothing strokes and the low tone of voice settled the animal down. The amnesiac put his left foot in the stirrup, and with effort, swung into the McClellan saddle. This, too, felt natural.

A sudden wash of dizziness came over him, and his stomach experienced waves of nausea. Bending low, he waited for the nausea to pass, then with his head still spinning slightly, he nudged the horse forward. Soon they were out of the trees and moving across the body-strewn field. By the position of the moon in the low western sky, he knew he was headed south.

He kept the animal to a walk because of the pain in his head. He'd ridden but a short distance when he felt a warm trickle of blood down the side of his face. Drawing rein, he removed the bandanna, wrung the blood out of it, and tied it around his head tighter than before. Though his body welcomed the warmth of the captain's uniform and overcoat, he knew he must find help. Now that he was in a Confederate uniform, he could at least approach a farmhouse. Surely they would help a man they believed to be one of their own.

"Thank You, Lord, for letting me find a gray uniform. Since I'm in Tennessee, I'd be in grave danger in a blue one."

Dizzy spells came and went as horse and rider moved across the fields southward. It struck him that he had used his voice several times since finding himself on the frozen battlefield, but even it did not sound familiar. "Lord," he said in a half-whisper, "how could the loss of my memory serve any good purpose?"

Suddenly his mind was filled with a verse of Scripture. *And we know that all things work together for good to them that love God, to them who are the called according to his purpose.*

"Romans 8:28," he heard himself say. "I do love You, Lord. Bad as my memory is, I know that. All things work together for good, You say. All right. I'll accept that. It's in Your Word, so I believe it. But I sure don't understand this situation. Why can I remember some things but not others? As soon as that poor man back there identified the fort as Donelson, I knew it was on the Cumberland River, and that I was in Tennessee. But why can't I remember my own name, or where I'm from…or which army I belong to?"

He stayed on a southern course, unaware that the town of Dover was less than two miles off to his right behind a low line of hills. Between dizzy spells and intermittent waves of nausea, he racked his brain, trying to stimulate his memory.

Many names came to mind, all military or political. He recalled Richmond and Washington and knew they were the Confederate and Federal capitals, but frustration came over him because he could not remember where his own home was or the name he had lived with all his life.

All his life? How old was he? By the looks of his hands, he guessed himself to be somewhere in his late twenties or early thirties. Maybe. Why would he remember that hands change with age, but not remember his own age? Still, he was sure he was yet a young man. His body seemed strong and firm. In spite of his wound and the freezing cold, he had been able to lift the wounded Yankee and carry him in his arms.

Soon the moon dropped out of sight in the west, and was replaced by the breaking dawn. The early gray light showed that he was passing by a cemetery. He knew there would be names and dates on the grave markers. Strange. He knew he was in the Civil War, but could not recall what year it was, or even the decade.

Turning into the cemetery, he dismounted and studied the names on the tombstones, thinking that looking at some names might possibly jar his memory and tell him his own. He noted that the stone of a fresh grave indicated the deceased had died on February 3, 1862. He estimated the grave to be two, not more than three weeks old.

So it was February 1862.

He tried to recall the year he was born, but there was nothing. Nothing but that horrendous blank wall in his brain.

Once again, he was aware of blood trickling down the side of his face. A dizzy spell came over him. He leaned against the horse and clung to the saddle until it began to pass. He was about to mount up when the faint sound of water met his ears. He looked over the horse's back, through the trees, and saw a small ice-edged brook on the far side of the cemetery.

He led the horse around the cemetery's perimeter to the gurgling stream. He removed his hat and the blood-stained bandanna, knelt on the bank, and tossed the icy water into his face. It refreshed him and helped clear the thin fog that remained in his brain.

He washed the bandanna in the stream, squeezing out the blood, then broke off a piece of ice along the bank. Pressing the ice to his wound, he held it there with the bandanna for several minutes, hoping to stay the flow of blood. When he checked it, the bleeding had slowed. He broke off another piece and held it there until it appeared the bleeding had stopped. Soaking the bandanna in the stream and wringing it out, he tied it around his head once again and replaced the hat.

He was just rising to his feet when he heard his horse nicker, and a cold voice from behind him snapped, "Get your hands up, Reb!"

ELEVEN

S tartled, the man in the Confederate captain's uniform whipped around to see two Union lieutenants on horseback, pointing their revolvers at him. Their faces were grim and full of determination.

The amnesiac's eyes bulged, and he recoiled as though he had been slapped in the face. Being in uniform would save him from a firing squad, but even the thought of the Yankee prison camp was repugnant. He thought of himself as a wild animal who had roamed free, suddenly cornered and about to be caged.

"I said get those hands in the air, Captain!" bawled the same man who had spoken before.

Slowly he lifted his hands, holding them at head level.

"Now, you just stay like that," the man said as he dismounted.

His partner kept his weapon trained on the man they believed to be a Rebel captain until the first man had both feet planted on the ground. Both Yankees were about the same age—late twenties—but the man on the ground was short and stocky, while the other was tall and thin. The stocky one held his gun on their captive while the thin one dismounted, then together, they moved toward him.

Halting about eight feet from him, the stocky one asked, "What brigade and division you belong to, Captain?"

"I…I don't know," he replied levelly.

"Don't play games with us, Reb!" the thin one snarled. "Answer Lieutenant Hovey's question!"

"I did. I have a head wound, as you can see. Bullet grazed me and I passed out. When I came to, I was lying up there on that battlefield near Fort Donelson. Somebody had stripped me of my uniform. I happened to find a dead Confederate captain, so I took his clothes."

"So what're you doing here?" Hovey demanded. "Why aren't you inside Donelson getting some medical attention?"

"Because I don't know whether I'm Rebel or Yankee."

The Union officers exchanged glances. Disbelief was in their eyes.

"That's the best cock-and-bull story I've heard in a long time," Hovey said. "Well, you're our prisoner now, Reb."

"But I might be a Yankee," protested the man-in-gray. "You wouldn't want to treat me as a prisoner if I'm one of your own."

"I'm sick of this claptrap," the thin one said. "Take his gun, Duane. I'll cover him." Lieutenant Hovey kept a wary eye on the prisoner as he moved up to take the gun from his holster.

Panic raced through the amnesia victim. He must not let them put him in a prison camp. Instinct took over. When Hovey was within arm's reach, the man-in-gray grabbed Hovey's revolver and wrested it from his grip. Surprised, Hovey swore and grappled with the prisoner for his weapon. The other Yankee raised his gun and took aim.

In one lightning-swift move, the amnesiac seized Hovey's coat collar with his free hand and used him as a shield just as the other Yankee fired. The bullet tore into Hovey's back. Still operating on instinct, the would-be prisoner lined Hovey's gun on the thin man's chest and fired. The slug went clear through him. Hovey, back arched, hit the ground barely two seconds before his partner did. Both men were dead.

The man-in-gray looked around to see if any other Union soldiers were in sight. He saw none, but thought there might be some close enough to have heard the shots. He dropped the gun, hurried to his horse, and leaped into the saddle. Sharp pain stabbed his left temple, but he tried to ignore it as he galloped out of the cemetery and once again headed south.

He kept the horse at a gallop for over a mile, while looking about him for blue uniforms. Soon he could ignore the pain no longer. He slowed the animal to a walk and pressed a palm against his pounding head. The sun was shafting a yellow fan of light on the eastern horizon when he caught sight of a farm up ahead.

For a brief moment, his mind went back to the two Yankee lieutenants he had just killed. His instincts were definitely honed for action. He had done that kind of thing before. What area of military work was he in? What kind of training would make him adept for a situation like the one he just faced?

Another question stabbed his mind. Had he killed foes or friends? The question faded from his thoughts as he drew nearer the farmhouse. It was a white, two-storied frame structure with a large porch. To the rear of the house, across a well-kept yard, stood a barn and several outbuildings.

The pain in his head was severe, and now a fresh fog was claiming his brain while the whole world seemed to go into a spin. Or was the horse dancing in tight circles? He had to grip the saddle to keep from falling off the horse as it carried him into the yard and up to the side of the house.

All the strength was leaving him. He was aware of a horse whinnying at the corral by the barn, and he heard his horse nicker back. He was bent low over the horse's neck and trying with everything that was in him to keep from passing out as the animal came to a halt.

He raised up to take a deep breath, and for a brief instant, his head cleared. He caught a glimpse of a female face at an upstairs window, then felt himself slipping from the saddle. He didn't even know when he hit the ground.

Some forty-five minutes earlier that morning, Hannah Rose Claiborne rose from her bed by the dull light of dawn and slipped into her robe. She lit the two lanterns that sat opposite each other on each side of the bed, then crossed the chilly room to the fireplace. Within a few minutes she had a blaze going, and stood before it, soaking up its pleasant warmth.

Soon there were soft footsteps in the hall, followed by a light tap on the door. Hannah Rose turned her back to the fire and called, "Come in, ladies."

The door opened, and Linda Lee entered first, carrying her Bible. Behind her came Donna Mae and Sally Marie, who also had their Bibles.

"You're early," Hannah Rose smiled. "I didn't get a chance to brush my hair."

"We'll forgive you this time," piped Sally Marie, "but don't let it happen again. You're so homely with unbrushed hair."

The others appreciated Sally Marie's attempt at a little humor. By their weary eyes, anyone could tell the four young women had not slept well. Immediately they began to discuss the battle that everyone in the area knew had taken place the day before at Fort Donelson.

Donna Mae's features were pale as she said with a tremor in her voice, "I hate this war. If those bullheaded Yankees had just kept their noses out of our business, there wouldn't have been any trouble at Fort Sumter. And the hundreds of our men and boys killed in these past ten months would still be alive."

"And we wouldn't be spending sleepless nights worrying over William, Britt, and Robert," Sally Marie added.

"And Lanny, too," Linda Lee said.

"Yes, honey," nodded Hannah Rose, patting her hand, "Lanny, too. You're becoming quite fond of him, aren't you?"

"Yes, I am," the younger sister said, apprehension showing in her eyes. "If God wills it, I believe Lanny and I will one day be married." Tears filmed her eyes, and her lower lip quivered. "That is, unless…"

"Unless what, honey?"

"Unless he was killed yesterday. Or he gets killed in some other horrible battle."

Hannah Rose moved to her little sister, put her arms around her, and said, "If God wills it, there's no *unless*. The Lord knows the end from the beginning. He won't plan for you to marry Lanny if He knows Lanny isn't going to make it through the war."

Linda Lee began to cry. Amid her sobs, she said, "The Lord just *has* to watch over Lanny, Hannah Rose. He knows I'm beyond being fond of him. I'm in love with him. Why would He let me fall in love with Lanny, then let him be killed?"

"Sometimes the Lord does things we don't always understand, honey. His thoughts are not our thoughts, and His ways are not our ways. Remember? And He tells us as the heavens are higher than the earth, so are His ways and His thoughts higher than ours. He often looks at things quite differently than we do.

"And that's where faith comes in. We not only must trust the Lord for our salvation by faith, but also for each day. And you know the Bible says without faith it is impossible to please Him. And we want to please Him above all things, don't we?"

"Yes."

"Well, that's why we're here right now—to read His Word and to pray for those men we love, trusting the Lord to answer our prayers and bring them back safely to us."

Linda Lee nodded, sniffed, and pulled gently away from her sister. While she went to Hannah Rose's dresser and picked up a handkerchief, she asked, "And what about you, sis? Are you falling for Jim?"

"Jim's a nice enough young man, and I like him very much…but no, I'm not falling for him."

"Now that Mother Claiborne is gone, Hannah Rose," Donna Mae said, "I think it's time you begin to think about yourself and your future for a change."

"I'll let the Lord take care of my future," smiled Hannah Rose. "And as for falling in love, that will happen when Mr. Right comes into my life. I'll let the Lord take care of that, too."

Hannah Rose now guided the Claiborne women to the Psalms, where they took turns reading aloud. They garnered strength for their hearts from the words of David, who trusted the God of Israel to deliver him out of all his troubles. When they finished reading, they knelt beside Hannah Rose's bed and prayed together, asking that God's hand of protection would be on Britt, William, Robert, and Lanny.

The sun's upper rim was about to peek over the eastern horizon as the four young women finished praying. They wiped tears, embraced each other, then returned to their rooms to dress for the day.

Hannah Rose quickly made up her bed, then changed from her robe and flannel nightgown into a simple cotton dress and topped it with a wool sweater for warmth. Sitting at her dressing table, she looked at her reflection in the mirror and began to brush her long, reddish-brown hair. She was almost finished when she heard the Claiborne family mare whinny three times in succession. When she heard a different horse softly nicker a reply, she knew someone was in the yard.

She hurried to the window. Pulling back the curtain, she saw a bay gelding with a Rebel officer slumped forward in the saddle. When the horse came to a halt below her window, the man in the saddle suddenly sat upright, looked toward her, then slumped over again. Slowly, he began to slide from the saddle, then fell to the ground and lay still.

Hannah Rose bolted through the door, ran down the hall, and bounded down the stairs. Her sister and sisters-in-law opened their doors just in time to catch a glimpse of her descending the stairs. All three stepped into the hall, exchanging puzzled glances. Sally Marie said, "Something's got her excited. We'd better go see what it is."

Hannah Rose burst through the front door of the house and dashed to where the man-in-gray lay crumpled on the ground. His horse nuzzled her as she knelt down beside him.

She knew by the insignias on his uniform that he was a captain. His hat had fallen from his head, and she saw the bloody bandanna that encircled his head. She made sure he was breathing, then rose to her feet and stretched out his legs and arms. She was checking him over for other wounds as the other three women arrived, out of breath.

"Oh!" exclaimed Linda Lee. "It's one of our soldiers!"

As all three pressed closer, Donna Mae asked, "How bad is he hurt?"

"Looks like the only wound is here on his head," answered Hannah Rose, pointing to the blood-soaked bandanna. "There's blood on the left side of his coat, and on the left side of his hat. Apparently the head wound has bled a lot. Let's get him in the house."

Together, the four young women carried the unconscious man inside the house and placed him on the bed in the first-floor guest room.

Working as a team, they removed the overcoat, then took off his uniform coat. Hannah Rose called for a pan of water, towels, washcloths, bandages, wood alcohol, iodine, and salve as she began removing the bloody bandanna.

The others scurried out of the room, and in a few minutes had placed everything she asked for on a small table beside the bed. Using two towels, she double-folded them and placed them under his head. As she began cleaning the wound, Hannah Rose spoke over her shoulder, "It would be a good idea if you ladies would fire up the kitchen stove and get breakfast started. Aunt Myrtle will be rising soon, and this young captain will probably be hungry when he comes to."

"Do you want one of us to stay here and help you?" Linda Lee asked.

"No, honey, I can manage. I would appreciate it, though, if you'd go put the captain's horse in the corral. Might as well remove the bridle and saddle, too. He's not going anywhere for a while."

"How bad is it?" Sally Marie asked, leaning close.

"Nothing life-threatening. A bullet creased his temple and cut a pretty good furrow, but I think he'll be all right. If that slug had been a half-inch to the right, it would've killed him. As it is, I'm sure he's got a concussion."

"You don't think he's lost so much blood that he might die?" Donna Mae asked.

"Well, there's no way to be sure, but his breathing is strong. I would think if he's exceptionally low on blood, his breathing would be more shallow."

"You should have been a doctor," Donna Mae said.

Hannah Rose took a moment to look up at her sister-in-law and smile. "I'm afraid it takes a lot more than having a little horse sense to be a doctor. Like being a *man*. You've never heard of a woman doctor, have you?"

"Well, there should be," Linda Lee said. "Who's to say that women can't be good doctors?"

"*Men*," chorused the other three together, then laughed.

"All right, ladies," said Hannah Rose, "get to work."

The room was quiet after the others had gone, and Hannah Rose proceeded with her task. First, she washed the left side of the wounded man's head with cold water, then she cleaned the wound with wood alcohol. Now she applied a liberal amount of iodine to kill any germs the alcohol might have missed. She knew the captain was deeply under when he did not even flinch. The wound began bleeding more freely when touched by the antiseptic, but Hannah Rose knew it was essential to kill the germs.

Working carefully and adeptly, she spread salve along the bloody furrow, then placed a thick bandage against it and wound white cloth around his head to hold it tightly in place.

That done, she removed the towels she had placed beneath his head earlier and replaced them with a pillow. She lay the towels on the table, went to the foot of the bed, and pulled off the captain's boots. Leaving him in his shirt and trousers, she drew the covers over him, then stood there looking down at him.

"Well, Captain," she said softly, "I wonder what your name is. Whoever you are, you appear to be in excellent physical condition. Everything's in your favor to come through this ordeal okay."

Hannah Rose found the man's angular features quite handsome. Complementing his good looks were his thick head of dark-brown wavy hair and neatly trimmed mustache. She told herself he had the polished look of an officer, and was probably a graduate of West Point. She speculated about the color of his eyes. "If I was a betting woman, Captain, I'd bet they're dark blue. Mmm, no, maybe dark-brown like your hair." Putting a forefinger to her cheek, she shook her head. "No, dark blue. That's it—I change my bet to dark blue."

Hannah Rose knew he had to have been in yesterday's battle at Fort Donelson. She wondered what part of the South he was from. Did he have a sweetheart waiting for him back home? Or maybe a wife? Children?

She sighed and half-whispered, "I hope you come out of it soon, Captain. I want to know who you are, and if you're acquainted with my brothers."

Presently, Aunt Myrtle appeared, and the women sat down at the breakfast table. They told Myrtle about their unexpected house guest, and she asked how he was doing. Hannah Rose showed concern in her eyes. "I think I've about got the bleeding stopped, but he's been unconscious for such a long time. I thought he would have come to by now. Maybe we ought to get Doc Stutz out here to look at him."

"I agree," Linda Lee said. "If someone will go with me, I'll drive into town and ask Doc to come."

"I'll go," Sally Marie volunteered.

"I'll go, too," Donna Mae said. "With all that's going on at Fort Donelson, it would be better if the three of us go together."

"Would you mind if I ride along?" asked the elderly aunt. "I just as well get something done while I'm staying here. I'd like to pick up some sewing materials and yard goods. Make me a new dress."

The four of them agreed to take the family wagon into town and return with Dr. Stutz, Dover's only physician. Hannah Rose would stay with her patient.

When breakfast was over, the kitchen cleaned up, and dishes done, it was only a short time until the wagon was on its way into town. Hannah Rose made a brief trip to the barn, then returned to the guest room. She sat in a chair beside the bed and watched the unconscious Confederate officer, praying that the Lord would bring him around soon.

Club Clubson was riding past the Claiborne place on his way to Dover. He eyed the house and wondered if he should stop and see Linda Lee for a few minutes. It was almost nine o'clock.

"Naw. They'll be cleanin' house about now. Linda Lee wouldn't have time to talk to me. I'll stop by on my way back."

His eye strayed to the corral behind the house and locked on the unfamiliar bay gelding standing with its head over the top rung of the split-rail fence. He drew rein and stared at the horse. Then he shrugged his bulky shoulders and concluded that one of the brothers had returned home.

Club nudged his mount forward, then drew rein again. Looking back at the horse, he shook his head. "Or," he said aloud, "that animal could belong to one of Linda Lee's suitors. If that's the case, he's here awful early in the day, and he's flirtin' with a broken neck."

Club rode into the Claiborne yard, breathing raggedly with the prospect of what he might find. No man—be he soldier or civilian—was going to stand between him and the woman he loved.

Reining in at the front porch, he left the saddle, mounted the steps, and knocked loudly on the door. When no answer came in what Club figured was a reasonable time, he banged on the door again, even harder. Presently he heard light footsteps, and the door came open.

"H'lo, Hannah Rose. I'd like to talk to Linda Lee."

"She's not here right now, Club," Hannah Rose responded quickly, annoyed that he was there.

"Well, where is she?"

"She's on her way into town."

"And who does that strange horse in your corral belong to?"

Hannah Rose looked him straight in the eye. "I don't like your tone, Club, and I don't like your attitude. It's really none of your business who that horse belongs to."

"Well, I just thought—"

"I know what you thought. You thought Linda Lee had a caller. She's not your property, Club. When are you going to understand that?"

He opened his mouth to speak, but she cut him off again.

"I don't have to explain anything to you, Club, but I will anyhow. That horse belongs to a Confederate captain who rode in here just before sunup. He was wounded in yesterday's battle at Fort Donelson. Passed out the instant he drew up to the house. Linda Lee and my sisters-in-law have gone to get Doc Stutz. Now, if you'll excuse me, I need to get back to my patient just in case he awakens before Doc Stutz gets here."

Club stared at her blankly for a moment, then asked, "Anything I can do to help?"

"No, thank you. The only help the captain needs now is the kind Dr. Stutz can give him."

"Oh…sure. Uh, in case I don't run onto Linda Lee while ridin' into town, tell her I was here to see her."

"I will," nodded Hannah Rose, stepping back to close the door.

"Tell her I love her."

"She already knows that, Club. I really must get back to my patient."

Hannah Rose moved briskly toward the rear of the house and entered the guest room. Her heart quickened when she saw the wounded man moaning and rolling his head.

He was regaining consciousness!

TWELVE

Hannah Rose rushed to the wounded man, whose eyes were fluttering as he rolled his head back and forth and licked his lips. She pushed the hair back from his forehead with one hand and dabbed at the perspiration there with a soft cloth in the other.

Finally, his fluttering eyes came all the way open. They were a bit glazed, but she congratulated herself when she saw them. They were dark blue.

As the brilliant sunlight struck his eyes, the amnesia victim felt a spasm of pain shoot through his head. Hannah Rose pulled her hands away and said quietly, "Don't open your eyes all at once, Captain. Go at it slowly."

He nodded and closed his eyes. After a few seconds, he opened them briefly, then closed them again. After he had repeated the action several times, his eyes began to adjust to the light and to lose their glaze. As his vision cleared, he saw that the woman standing over him had reddish-brown hair, and recalled seeing a female face in an upstairs window just before he passed out. This had to be her.

Hannah Rose smiled down at him. "Good morning, Captain. My name is Hannah Rose Claiborne, and I already know yours."

The man's hazy thoughts did not lay hold on her words at first. He noted instead her long chestnut hair, highlighted by the sunlight, which shone through a nearby window. He saw that her emerald-green eyes were warm and compassionate.

Suddenly her words sank in.

His heart pounded as he licked his dry lips and said excitedly, "You know me?"

Smiling, she replied, "Well, not really. But I know your name, and that you are a Captain in the Fourth Brigade, Confederate Army of Northern Virginia, temporarily assigned to Fort Donelson."

"I *am?*" he gasped. "H-how do you know this?"

"From this letter," Hannah Rose replied, turning toward the nightstand. She picked up an envelope and pulled a folded sheet of paper from inside it. "I found it in your saddlebags. I hope you'll forgive me for opening it and reading it, but I felt I should know the name of the man I had taken in and patched up."

"Patched up?" he echoed, placing fingertips to the bandage that encircled his head.

"Yes. My sister and sisters-in-law helped me carry you in here and laid you on the bed. I cleaned your wound and bandaged it up. I think the bleeding has just about stopped. My sister and the others have gone into town to bring the doctor."

"Doctor?"

"I was worried because you had been unconscious so long. I thought it best to have Dr. Stutz take a look at you. I'm so glad that you've come out of it, but it's good that he's coming, anyhow. I'll feel better if he checks you over."

Managing a smile, the wounded man said, "You are very kind, Miss Claiborne—it *is* Miss, isn't it?"

"Yes."

"I can never thank you enough for what you've done."

"Just doing my patriotic duty," she smiled. "Being a true daughter of the South, I must do all I can to help us win this war. I saw one of our fine officers wounded and in trouble, so I did my duty and helped him. I have three brothers in the army, all attached over here at Fort Donelson. Two of them are married, and their wives live here with my sister and me. All of us feel the same way toward the Confederacy. We only wish we could do more to help."

"God bless you," he breathed. "You...you say you know my name?"

"Yes, it's here in the letter. Captain Wayne Gordon. The letter was sealed, of course, and addressed to Brigadier General Simon B. Buckner, commander at Fort Donelson. It's from Brigadier General James Longstreet, commander of Fourth Brigade, Confederate Army of Northern Virginia in Richmond. It introduces Captain Wayne Gordon as the officer requested by General Buckner. I was hoping you were already part of Fort Donelson's forces so you could tell me about my brothers, but according to this, you were just arriving here from Richmond, so you wouldn't know them. We've heard there was quite a battle at the fort yesterday."

He thought of all the bodies strewn on the moonlit battlefield. "Yes, ma'am. Quite a battle."

Looking at the letter, Hannah Rose said, "General Longstreet gives some of your military background and accomplishments, Captain. Quite impressive, I might say. But it doesn't tell where you're from, or anything about a wife and family."

He did not reply.

Feeling that possibly the captain did not want to talk about that part of his life, she said, "How...ah...did you get the wound on your head? You came very close to being killed, you know."

"Yes, I know. But, Miss Claiborne, I am going to have to be honest with you."

"Pardon me?"

"I'm not Captain Wayne Gordon."

"But this letter says you're Captain Gordon."

"Let me explain, ma'am. I don't know *who* I am. I know I'm a soldier, but I don't even know which side I was fighting on...whether I'm a Rebel or a Yankee. You see—"

"Now, wait a minute, Captain. You're not making sense. This letter says you are Captain Wayne Gordon, attached to Fourth Brigade at Richmond, Confederate Army of Northern Virginia."

"Please, ma'am…let me explain."

Hannah Rose went to a straight-backed chair near the window and carried it to the bed. Sitting down, she said, "All right. I'm listening."

"Ma'am, not only can I not remember my name, I can't remember anything beyond last night. Apparently when I was struck by that slug, it took my memory."

Hannah Rose's hand went to her mouth. "You mean you don't know anything about yourself—where you're from or who your family is?"

"That's right, ma'am."

"But even though your memory's gone, you have this letter. You're in a Confederate uniform. All we have to do is contact General Longstreet and his staff. We can have you reunited with your family—"

"No, ma'am. You still don't understand. Let me tell you the whole story."

"All right."

The wounded man told Hannah Rose his story, going back to the night before when he awakened on the frozen battlefield.

When he finished, Hannah Rose was staring at the floor. She pressed fingertips to her temples, shook her head, and said, "This is all so incredible, Captain." Then she raised her head and met his gaze. "Sorry. I don't know what else to call you."

"I guess you could call me ol' Blank Brain," he grinned. He was amazed at how relaxed he was in her presence, in spite of his dilemma.

"I wouldn't call you that," she smiled. "You…ah, you might be a Yankee. You don't have a Southern accent."

"Strange that I can remember this, ma'am, but many Southerners never develop an accent. In fact, yours is barely noticeable."

"Really? I've had many Northerners comment on how strong my accent is. Do you suppose you *are* a Southerner, and that's why my accent seems only slight to you?"

Hannah Rose saw a shadow of anxiety and a hint of panic in his eyes as he took a deep breath and sighed shakily, "This is all so...so nerve racking. Here I am in your home under your care, and I might even be your enemy. I can't go to the Rebels, and I can't go to the Yankees. If I'm a Yankee, there are no doubt men who know me over at that Yankee camp. If I'm a Rebel, there'll be men at Fort Donelson who will know me. But the problem is...if I chose the wrong place to present myself, at best I'd be locked up in a prison camp for the duration of the war. They might even think I'm a spy and stand me before a firing squad."

"They wouldn't execute you if you were in uniform, would they?"

"Well, I'm not sure. No matter which side I presented myself to, they might not believe my story. They might think I'm trying to pull the wool over their eyes. But even if they did believe my story, they couldn't put a gun in my hand. My memory might come back all of a sudden, and if I found myself amongst the enemy, I might start putting bullets in them. This has to be how they would think. So, either way—Yankees or Rebels—they'd have no choice but to lock me up. No thanks. No filthy, disease-infested prison camp for me."

"I can't blame you for that," Hannah Rose said, rising and laying a firm hand on his shoulder. "I want you to know, though, that you're welcome to stay here as long as you wish. I don't know anything about amnesia, but Dr. Stutz no doubt does. He'll be here soon. Maybe he can help."

The touch of Hannah Rose's hand on his shoulder was pleasant. There was something about this young woman that caused a gentle peace to settle over him. He thought her name fit her perfectly. Before he realized it, he was voicing his thoughts. "You're name fits you perfectly, ma'am," he said softly.

"In what way?" she asked, gently removing her hand from his shoulder.

"You're wholesome, like Hannah in the Bible, Samuel's mother. And…and you're tender and beautiful like a rose."

His words left her short of breath. "Why, Captain. I…I don't know what to say."

"You don't have to say anything, ma'am. I wasn't speaking flattery. I meant what I said very sincerely."

"I'm sure you did. Thank you." She paused, then said, "Captain, I'm surprised that with your amnesia, you can remember Scripture. I mean, about Hannah and all."

"Well, ma'am, I can quote whole verses, and even tell you where they're found. *For I delivered unto you first of all that which I also received, how that Christ died for our sins according to the scriptures; and that he was buried, and that he rose again the third day according to the scriptures.* That's First Corinthians fifteen, verses three and four."

Hannah Rose clapped her hands together. "That's wonderful, Captain! Are…are you a Christian?"

"Yes, ma'am. Bad as my memory is, I know that for sure."

Hannah Rose told the captain she had become a Christian when she was seven years old, and her sister and brothers had come to know the Lord in their childhood. Her sisters-in-law were also Christians.

When she finished, the wounded man said, "You know, while you were talking, a powerful thought hit me. The concussion of that bullet affected my brain but not my heart, the center of my soul. Maybe that's why the amnesia doesn't affect what I know about my salvation and why I can remember Scripture. Christ is in my heart, and His Word is in my heart, not just my mind. So the amnesia doesn't affect that part of me."

Smiling and shaking her head in wonderment, Hannah Rose said, "I never thought of it like that, Captain. Maybe you were a preacher before you went into the war."

"I don't think so, ma'am. Not that the idea is repugnant to me, but somehow it just doesn't seem to fit. Of course, since I can't recall one little thing about my past, I could be wrong. But it seems to me that if I was a preacher, I would've gone into the army as a chaplain."

"Maybe you did. Since your clothing was gone when you came to, how would you know?"

He looked blankly at her for a moment. "Well...ah...I seem to recall that chaplains don't go into battle."

"Oh. Well, it was just a thought. Anyhow, you would make a fine-looking preacher."

"Well, thank you. I..." His eyes widened.

"What is it, Captain?"

"It just dawned on me. I don't know what I look like. Maybe if I saw my face in a mirror, it'd jar my memory. Might bring something back."

"It's worth a try. I have a hand mirror upstairs in my room. I'll go get it."

The wounded man had noticed the large mirror above the dresser on the other side of the room. "Wait a minute, Miss Hannah Rose. I can get a look at myself in that mirror over the dresser."

"I don't know about that, Captain. You've had quite a shock to your system, and you've lost a lot of blood. You shouldn't be trying to walk, yet."

"I can do it. Really."

"Are you sure?"

"Yes," he said, throwing back the covers. Sitting up, he twisted around on the bed and dangled his feet over the edge. His head went light, and the room started to spin.

Hannah Rose stepped close, touched his shoulder, and said, "You'd better lie down, Captain. Let me go get my hand mirror."

"No. No," he said, lifting a hand in protest. "I'll be all right. Just let me sit here a minute. Head's a little light, that's all. It'll clear up."

"Typical man," she said, placing a hand on her hip.

"What's that supposed to mean?" he asked, looking her straight in the eye.

"The male ego. My brothers have it. My father had it. My grandfathers had it. The old, 'I'm a rugged he-man, and don't you forget it' routine."

He gave her a crooked grin. "Think you're pretty smart, don't you?"

"Doesn't take much smarts to figure you men out. Any woman of average intelligence can stay ahead of the smartest man."

The wounded man liked Hannah Rose. Not only was she beautiful, but she had a keen sense of humor. Repeating the crooked grin, he said, "Who's to argue with such a woman?"

As he spoke, he planted his feet firmly on the floor and, using the nightstand to steady himself, stood up. When he swayed slightly, Hannah Rose gripped his arm.

"You going to be all right?" she asked.

"Sure. I'll be fine. Gotta get over there and see what kind of face I've been living with all of my life."

Hannah Rose let go of his arm and stayed at his side as he headed slowly toward the dresser. He had taken four short steps when both knees buckled. Her strong hands took hold of his arm, stabilizing him. Swaying again, he blinked and said, "Didn't realize I was so weak."

"Well, I hate to say I told you so but...I told you so."

He grinned, looked back toward the bed, then toward the dresser. "Well, since we're just about halfway, I'll humble my male ego and ask you to help me to the mirror."

"Aha! Mark one up for the female of the species!" She put an arm around him and gripped his waist, then held the arm closest to her and guided him toward the dresser. When they reached it, he braced himself on its top.

Slowly he turned his eyes to the mirror. Hannah Rose stood close, watching him.

He was quiet for nearly a minute as he eyed the man who

stared back at him, turning his head from side to side.

"Well?" she said.

"Don't know him. As far as I'm concerned, I've never seen him before in my life."

"I'm sorry," Hannah Rose said. "I was hoping you'd see something that would trigger a memory."

"I had guessed my age by looking at my hands. Judging by my face, I'd say I guessed pretty close."

"And what was that?"

"Late twenties or early thirties. Pretty close, wouldn't you say?"

"I was kinder than that. Before you awakened, I estimated twenty-eight or twenty-nine...but not yet in your thirties."

Still braced against the dresser, he awarded her another crooked grin and said, "Thank you. I hope you're right. And you're what? Nineteen?"

"I am not!" she said in mock indignation. "I'm twenty-one."

"That's what I really guessed, but I wanted to be as kind to you as you were to me."

"You're impossible, Captain," Hannah Rose retorted, laughing lightly. "I think we'd best get you back to the bed."

"I think I can do it on my own. I'm feeling a little stronger."

"Are we going to go through this again?"

Without replying, he let go of the dresser and took a step toward the bed. Suddenly his knees gave way, and he started to go down. Hannah Rose leaped in front of him and caught him in her arms. "Feeling stronger, huh?" she chided.

"Well, I thought I was."

She eased her hold on him and moved back slightly. He was eight or nine inches taller than she, but their eyes met and locked for one magical moment. There was dead silence between them. Both of them felt the magic, but neither one let on.

Hannah Rose broke the spell. "All right, Captain Whatever-your-name-is, get a good hold on me, and we'll have you back to bed in no time."

He marveled at her strength, and figured it came from doing her share of the work on the farm.

When they reached the bed, she helped him onto it. Working his way to the center and lying flat on his back, he heaved a big sigh and said, "Remind me to listen to you next time."

"I'll do that," she laughed, covering him up. "Are you hungry?"

"Yes, definitely."

"You look a little pale after your little walk. No nausea?"

"No, thank the Lord, but I sure feel weak. I think some food will help. I have no idea when I ate last."

Bending over him, Hannah Rose said, "Lift your head."

When he did, she picked up the pillow, fluffed it good, then placed it under his head. "There. Comfortable?"

"Yes, thank you," he replied, lifting a hand to the bandage.

"Pain?" she asked.

"A little."

Looking closely at the bandage, she said, "I think I see blood seeping. I hope your jaunt to the mirror hasn't started it bleeding again."

"I hope not, too. Guess I'd better take it easy till I'm feeling stronger."

"Now you're making sense, Captain," she smiled. "My sister and the others should be back shortly. Well, that is, unless Doc is extra busy. All we can do is wait. Whenever he gets here, I'm sure he'll work on that wound. You lie still and rest, now, and I'll be back with something to eat. Do you feel like breakfast, or are you in the mood for lunch? We're a little closer to lunch time, but I can make you either."

"Whatever's easiest, ma'am. Just don't go to a lot of trouble."

"Whatever I do won't be any trouble, Captain, I assure you. After all, the kind of sacrifice you soldiers make for us, we could never repay you."

"Even Union soldiers? I could be one, you know."

"I know," she said, moving toward the door. When she reached it, she stopped and said, "If all Union soldiers were like you, Captain, there wouldn't be any Civil War."

"And if all Confederate women were like you, ma'am, there wouldn't be any men in the North."

Hannah Rose batted her eyelashes coyly. "Why thank you, kind sir. That's the nicest compliment I've had all day. Or even yesterday and today put together."

She was almost out the door, when he called, "Miss Hannah Rose, I...don't know how I'm going to repay you. You didn't happen to find any money in those saddlebags, did you?"

"No, I didn't. But don't you fret about paying me back. It's not necessary, and besides, I wouldn't let you if you had money falling out your ears."

He watched her walk away, then laid an arm on his forehead and looked heavenward. "Dear Lord, whatever I may forget, please don't let me forget Hannah Rose Claiborne."

THIRTEEN

Hannah Rose returned with steaming food on a tray and found her patient lying flat on his back with both hands covering his face. He brought his hands away when he heard her light footsteps and the swish of her skirt.

"Are you all right?" she asked, moving toward the bed.

He squinted tightly, then opened his eyes wide. "Just having another dizzy spell. It's about gone now."

"I decided to fix you breakfast. I've got grits and gravy, scrambled eggs, bacon, and coffee. Are you having any nausea?"

"No. No nausea. Grits and gravy, eh? Now I must be a Southerner, Miss Hannah Rose. That sounds awfully good to me."

"Could be just because you haven't eaten for so long," she said, setting the tray on the nightstand. "Think you can sit up?"

"Yes, ma'am. Smells delicious. I'm so hungry I could eat an elephant."

Hannah Rose helped him to a sitting position. "Sorry, but I don't cook elephant. Too hard to get them in the oven."

He grinned. "Shucks, I was hoping to have baked elephant for supper."

"Supper? Don't they call it *dinner* up north? I'm beginning to believe you're a son of the South, Captain."

"The thought is not unpleasant to me, ma'am. You may be right. Trouble is, I don't know how to find out."

She picked up the tray and set it on his lap. "Well, for sure we're not going to find out in the next few minutes. Might as well go ahead and eat."

He bowed his head and audibly thanked the Lord for bringing him to the Claiborne house, and for the kindness and care shown him by Hannah Rose. Then he started eating.

"You'll probably choke on it."

He looked at her, chewing a mouthful of scrambled eggs, and raised his eyebrows. "Hmm?"

"You thanked the Lord for everything but the food."

He grinned and shook his head. "Guess I'm getting a little forgetful."

Hannah Rose enjoyed his sense of humor. She laughed and said, "I don't think this latest forgetfulness is from your head wound. I think you're just a bit over-appreciative of my services."

"Well, I appreciate what you're doing, ma'am. More than you'll ever know."

Hannah Rose sat in the chair beside the bed, and they talked while he ate. He was almost finished when the sounds of people entering the house met their ears.

"Oh, they're back," she said, jumping up and heading for the door. "I hope they have Dr. Stutz with them."

Hannah Rose disappeared for a moment, then returned with the women and Dr. Elmer Stutz, who had followed them from town in his one-horse buggy. The women were glad to see their house guest awake and alert, as was the physician. Introductions were made, then Hannah Rose stayed in the room while Dr. Stutz prepared to work on the patient. Laying him flat on his back, he lit a lantern and used its light to examine his eyes. Nodding, he handed the lantern to Hannah Rose and said, "Concussion, all right. That bullet really did a job on you, Captain."

"It would've done a bigger job if I had been standing a half-inch farther to the left."

"Might say that," grinned Stutz. "Let's get this bandage off, and let me see just how bad the wound is."

When the bandage was off, Dr. Stutz complimented Hannah Rose on the excellent job she did in cleaning and dressing the wound. It had bled some since she had bandaged it, but was not bleeding any longer.

When the wound was dressed once more and wrapped with fresh gauze, the physician said, "Now, Captain, I want to hear the story you told Hannah Rose after you came around. About all she told me in the parlor was that you can't remember anything about your past, where you are from, or even what your name is."

The women returned at Hannah Rose's call and stood by while the amnesia victim told the doctor his story. When he finished, the doctor said, "Captain—I guess it's all right to call you that—what you have is known as *selective amnesia*. While it leaves the victim with partial memory, it usually steals his identity, resulting in a blank concerning his name and anything about his past. It also leaves a blank in regard to his family and those he is close to. It doesn't change his personality or his values. A real mystery to say the least, but this is how it works nearly every time."

"Is there anything you can do that would help me get my memory back?"

Stutz shook his head slowly. "I'm sorry, but there isn't. Medical science is baffled by amnesia, especially the selective kind. There's just no medical cure for it." Pausing, he grinned and said, "Of course, experience with amnesia has taught us that sometimes a second jolt to the head will bring the entire memory back. But I don't recommend letting somebody whack you over the cranium with a club, or worse yet, having some crack-shot marksman zing another bullet along your temple."

"You don't have to worry about that," the patient chuckled. Then in a somber tone, he said, "I've got a real problem, Doctor. I know I'm a soldier, but as I mentioned in my story, I don't know of which army. The worst thing a soldier can do is run away. I don't want to be a deserter, but I can't report to either side. There's a 50 percent chance it would be the wrong side."

"You really are in a pickle, son. Tell you what. I know this Claiborne family well. The three brothers are fine men. Sooner or later, they'll show up here. Since Britt is a Confederate officer, he can give you proper advice on what to do."

"But what if it's weeks or even months till he comes home? I don't want to wear out my welcome here."

"You'd have a hard time doing that," Hannah Rose assured him. "Besides, once you're feeling up to it, we'll put you to work around here. We'll make you earn your keep."

"Besides, in the meantime your memory could come back," the doctor said.

"It could?"

"Yes. Quite often the memory will suddenly return all at once, for no apparent reason. And there have been a number of cases where the memory returned a little at a time."

"And probably a great number when it never came back at all," the patient said plaintively.

"Yes. That, too. There's really nothing you or I can do to make a difference. Only time will tell."

Dr. Stutz said he needed to get back to town, and closed up his medical bag. When the patient explained he had no money to pay him, Stutz told him there was no charge. The good doctor said he would be back to check on him in a few days and headed for the door. Linda Lee walked him to the front of the house and watched him drive away.

When she returned to the guest room, she found Hannah Rose doing what she could to make the patient comfortable. Sally Marie said, "Since this gentleman is going to be our guest for awhile, what are we going to call him? We can't just call him 'Captain'."

The guest chuckled. "Especially when you don't even know that I *am* a captain."

"Well, since the real Wayne Gordon is dead, we could call him by that name," Linda Lee said.

"Why not?" said Aunt Myrtle. "It's a nice enough name."

"I agree," said Donna Mae.

Hannah Rose turned toward the bed and asked, "How's that sound to you?"

"Well, it's better than Herman Schmohauser or Leonardo Finklestein."

"Well, then," Hannah Rose said, "until further notice, our guest's name is Wayne Gordon."

Wayne Gordon rested the remainder of the day and got up to eat the evening meal with the Claiborne women and Myrtle Crisp. His meal earlier in the day had definitely improved his strength. At one point during supper, a dizzy spell overtook him, but it lasted only a few seconds.

When the meal was over, Hannah Rose escorted Gordon to his room. When he was back in bed, but sitting up, she told him she would return after the dishes were done and the kitchen was cleaned up.

As she turned to leave, he asked, "Miss Hannah Rose, would you have a Bible I could borrow?"

"Yes, of course," she replied, opening the top drawer of the nightstand and pulling out an old black Bible. It was well-worn, and the lettering on the leather cover was faded. Its pages were frayed on the edges. "This was my father's. As you can see, it's had a lot of use. Daddy loved God's Word and taught us from this old Book every day."

"He must've been a great man."

Tears filmed her eyes. "Yes, he was. I still miss him terribly."

When Hannah Rose was gone, Gordon opened the Bible and angled it toward the lantern that glowed on the nightstand. In the flyleaf, he found that the Bible had been a gift to Hannah Rose's father from her mother on his fortieth birthday, January 9, 1844. Soon he was carefully leafing through it, noticing the underlined verses and notes in the wide margins.

Suddenly Romans 8:28 stared him in the face. It was under-lined in red, and Ewing Claiborne had written beside the verse, *It's still in here!*

Wayne Gordon smiled and laid his head back against the bed-stead. He looked up and half-whispered, "According to Your purpose, Lord. All things work together for good to them that love You, who are the called according to Your purpose. This amnesia. My coming to this house. Is this part of Your plan and purpose in my life? If that bullet hadn't stolen my memory, I would never have come here. I would never have met—"

"Are you comfortable, Captain Gordon?" Myrtle Crisp asked from the open door.

"Yes, ma'am," he replied with a smile, looking her direction. "Quite comfortable, thank you."

"May I talk to you for a moment?"

"Yes, of course. Please come in."

Myrtle was a pleasant little woman, and her wrinkled face dis-played the warmth of her personality. Sitting down in the chair beside the bed, she said, "When you were telling your story to Dr. Stutz, you mentioned that you could remember such names as Robert E. Lee and Ulysses S. Grant."

"Yes, ma'am."

"So you know that Grant is our enemy."

"Yes, ma'am."

"The dirty dog is living in *my* house."

Wayne Gordon wasn't sure whether to believe her. Certainly if Grant was commanding the Union forces battling it out with the Confederates in Fort Donelson, he would be housed somewhere near. He decided to test the waters. "I, ah, I thought you lived here with Hannah Rose and the others, ma'am."

"Oh, heavens no. I live several miles north of here. On the Cumberland River. Just north of Fort Donelson, in fact. That no-good Useless S. Grant just marched himself up to my front door one Sunday morning and ran me out of my house. Ornery skunk! I've had to stay here ever since. Whenever he's gone, and I can go home, who knows if I'll even have a home to go to?"

Just then Hannah Rose came through the door. Smiling, she said, "Oh! I see my dear, sweet aunt has taken a shine to you." She drew up to the bed and patted the elderly woman's shoulder. "Now Auntie, dear, Wayne is too young for you to be flirting with."

"Aw, Hannah Rose, I wasn't flirtin'. I was just tellin' this nice young man about General Useless Grant a-runnin' me out of my house."

Wayne looked to Hannah Rose for confirmation of Myrtle's claim. She understood and nodded.

"I sure hope General Grant doesn't harm your property, ma'am," he said.

"He'd better not, or I'll…".

"You'll what, Auntie dear?"

"I don't know," she replied, rising from the chair, "but I'll find some way to make him pay. Sure hope you don't turn out to be a Yankee, young feller. Sure would be a disappointment."

Nonplused, Gordon swung his gaze to Hannah Rose, who hunched her shoulders, then patted Myrtle's shoulder and said, "It's almost your bedtime, Auntie. Goodnight."

Myrtle nodded and said, "Goodnight, dear." Then to Gordon, "Goodnight to you, and pleasant dreams…unless you're a Yankee."

"Since I don't know whether I am or not, ma'am, I'll try not to dream at all."

"Well, if you ever find out that you are a Yankee, there's one thing you'd better do."

"What's that, ma'am?"

"Ask God to forgive you!" With that she wheeled and headed out the door.

Wayne Gordon looked at Hannah Rose and said, "She's a fireball."

"Quite," Hannah Rose said, easing onto the chair. "Rebel to the bone."

"Person ought to go whole-hog for what he or she believes in."

"I'll say amen to that."

There was a lengthy silence, then Hannah Rose said, "You commented earlier that you don't think you could've been a preacher. Said it just didn't seem to fit."

"Mm-hmm."

"Any hint at all about what you might have been before the war?"

He started to say no, then checked himself.

Hannah Rose caught it. "There *is* something. Tell me about it."

"I just remembered something," he said quietly, looking into her emerald eyes. "Early this morning—not long before I showed up here—I was at a small stream, washing the blood off my face and trying to slow the bleeding with ice. All of a sudden there were two Yankee lieutenants behind me, holding their guns on me. They were going to take me prisoner. I tried to explain my problem, but got nowhere. They thought I was lying."

"So what happened?"

Gordon scrubbed a hand over his face. "Well, Miss Hannah Rose, I figured I just couldn't let them take me and put me in a prison camp. So I…well, it was like…my natural instincts went to work. Before I knew it, I'd taken the gun from one of them, and a couple of seconds later, they were both dead. It was…well, it was like I'd done the same thing, or at least something akin to it, many times before."

"But it bothered you that you had to take their lives, didn't it?"

"Yes, ma'am. Especially when I thought there was a 50 percent chance I'd killed men from my own army."

"Well, if you're that good at hand-to-hand fighting, I'd say you're probably a veteran of some kind, maybe even an officer and a graduate of West Point. You've been trained to fight, so it's natural to do so."

Wayne thought about her suggestion for a moment, then said, "The West Point idea is possible, but to be a veteran, I would've had to fight in the Mexican War. I don't know if I'm old enough to have done that. When was that war?"

"I'm not sure. Let's see…I remember being about eight or nine years old then, so it must have been 1846, 1847. Let's say that you're thirty, though I think you're shy of that by a year or two. That would mean you were born in 1831 or 1832, so you would've been only fourteen or fifteen during the Mexican War. You're definitely not a veteran of that war."

"Maybe I've just been in enough hand-to-hand battles since this war began to develop some natural instincts. How long has this war been going on?"

"It'll be a year in April."

"That must be it. Maybe I'm part of one of those ranger groups in the Confederate army."

"My brothers haven't said anything about any rangers at Fort Donelson, but that doesn't mean there aren't any. Oh, I hope you are a Southerner."

Their eyes met, and before Hannah Rose looked away, he held her soft gaze and said, "I do too."

Hannah Rose met his eyes again and expressed another hope, this time only in her mind. *Oh, Wayne, I hope you don't have a wife and family.* She silently asked the Lord to forgive her selfish thoughts, and said as she rose from the chair, "Well, Captain, I think it's time for my patient to call it a day. Is there anything I can get you before you go to sleep?"

"No, thank you," he smiled. "I'm fine."

"All right, then I'll say goodnight." She extinguished the two lamps in the room and walked to the door.

"Goodnight, Miss Hannah," Wayne Gordon said warmly. "Thank you for taking in this wounded wayfarer."

"You are entirely welcome, Captain. I hope you rest well."

She closed the door, leaving him in almost total darkness. As he lay there, he marveled at the effect she had on him. He thought of that moment when their eyes locked, and wondered if she felt the same thing he did. Then he pondered the possibility that he might have a wife somewhere, maybe even children.

He tried hard to conjure up some scrap of memory, but there was only the familiar blank wall. Perspiring heavily, though the room was cool, he asked himself, *Am I married? Widowed? If I am married, what is she like? If I'm a father, what are my children like? If I have a family, will I ever see them again? Are they somewhere out there tonight, praying for my safety?*

His thoughts came back to Hannah Rose. There was no mistaking that though he had known her only a few hours, she stirred him in the depths of his heart. He lashed himself. If he had a wife, he had no business letting himself be attracted to another woman. He must keep his vows. He must keep himself only unto his wife, even in his thoughts. Especially as a Christian.

But was he married? For now, there was no way to know. Since there was a chance he was, he must not allow his heart to reach for Hannah Rose.

"Oh, dear Lord," he prayed, "You know all about me. You know who I am, where I'm from, whether or not I have a wife. Please…help me."

Lying in the darkness, he clenched his fists and held his breath, straining, trying to force his brain to reach back into the past, seize something—*anything*—and bring it to the fore. But it was like dipping a bucket into a dry well. He could recall nothing.

He lay there for a long time, weary but wide awake. His thoughts ran to Hannah Rose. He struggled to prevent it, but soon could resist it no longer. It was not until he let his mind return unhindered to her, picturing her beautiful face and remembering the tender touch of her hand, that he was able to relax and drop off to sleep.

FOURTEEN

At the same time the amnesiac was putting on the captain's uniform in the forest, Brigadier General Charles F. Smith rode up to the house owned by Myrtle Crisp and dismounted. The moon was slanting westward in the starlit sky, and the four sentries who guarded the house came off the porch, collars turned up and greeted him.

"A bit nippy tonight, isn't it?" said Smith.

"Quite, sir," nodded one of the sentries. "Unless you have something urgent for General Grant, we must ask you to come back at sunrise. Right now, he's asleep."

"What I have is *very* urgent, Corporal," responded Smith. "Believe me, if he's not awakened immediately to see what I have for him, he will have your hide."

"Yes, sir. Let me take you inside at once."

When they stepped into the house, Smith felt the warmth of the pot-bellied stove in the parlor. Lying on the couch under a blanket was General Grant's personal physician and friend, Dr. John H. Brinton. The doctor sat up immediately.

"Sorry to awaken you, Doctor," the sentry said, "but General Smith has something urgent to show General Grant."

"I wasn't asleep, Corporal. I was up only a minute or two ago stoking the fire. Hello, General."

"Glad to see you, Doctor," Smith nodded, removing his hat and gloves.

Dr. Brinton rose from the couch and said, "I'll go awaken General Grant."

The sentry went back outside, closing the door behind him. Smith removed his overcoat and hung it on a clothes tree next to the door. Then reaching inside his uniform coat, he pulled out a sealed white envelope and held it in his hand while edging up to the pot-bellied stove. Warming his backside, he waited for General Grant to appear.

Presently, a sleepy-eyed Ulysses S. Grant entered the room, followed by his physician. Tousle-haired, Grant was in his boots and trousers, a pair of wide suspenders looped over his shoulders. The upper half of his body was covered only by his long-johns. Blinking and scratching his beard, he looked at Smith and said, "I hope this is good news."

"The best, sir!" Smith replied, smiling broadly and extending the envelope toward him. "See for yourself."

Brinton turned a lantern to full flame as Grant moved toward it and sat in a straight-backed chair beside a small table. Yawning, he ripped the envelope open, pulled out the folded sheet of paper, and angled it toward the flame.

"Why don't you read it aloud, sir?" suggested Smith. "That way Dr. Brinton can learn of it right away, too."

Grant eyed Smith. "I see it's from General Buckner, but it was sealed. How do you know its contents?"

"The Rebel lieutenant who delivered it under a white flag told me its contents, sir."

Grant nodded, then read the message aloud:

Headquarters, Fort Donelson
February 16, 1862

General Ulysses S. Grant, Sir:

In consideration of all the circumstances governing the present situation of affairs at this station, I propose to the Commanding Officer of the Federal forces the appointment of Commissioners to agree upon terms of capitulation of the forces and fort under my command, and in that view, suggest an armistice until 12 o'clock today.

I am, sir, very respectfully,

Your obedient servant,

S.B. Buckner

Brigadier General, C.S.A.

When he had finished reading the message, Grant sat silently, reading it over again. Smith and Brinton exchanged glances, but said nothing. Both men knew that Grant and Buckner had gone through West Point together, and after graduation had served together in the Regular U.S. Army. They had great respect for each other and had become good friends.

When Grant looked up, General Smith said, "This has to be difficult for you, sir. I mean, seeing that you and General Buckner are friends."

"Better than you even know," Grant replied solemnly. He thought briefly of the money Buckner had loaned him when he was in desperate need following a business failure.

"So, what are you going to do?" Dr. Brinton asked.

Grant thoughtfully stroked his beard for a long moment, then replied, "I can't let sentiment warp my thinking, here. This is war. The Confederates broke the law by seceding from the Union. They're traitors, and therefore so is General Buckner. He wants to come to terms for his surrender, but this cannot be allowed." His face crimsoned. "No terms with traitors!"

General Grant went to his valise and produced paper, pencil, and envelope. Sitting down at the small table again, he dashed off his reply:

Headquarters Army in the Field
Camp near Donelson
February 16, 1862
Brigadier General S.B. Buckner
Confederate Army
Sir: Yours of this date, proposing armistice and appointment of Commissioners to settle terms of capitulation, is just received. No terms except an unconditional and immediate surrender can be accepted. I propose to move immediately upon your works.
I am, sir, very respectfully,
Your obedient servant,
U.S. Grant
Brigadier General, U.S.A.

Grant folded the paper, placed it in the envelope, and sealed it. Handing it to Smith, he said, "Have this delivered to General Buckner immediately."

Under a westering moon, Colonel Nathan B. Forrest was preparing to lead his cavalry unit out of Fort Donelson, along with some four thousand footmen who had chosen to take their chances of making it to Nashville rather than surrender.

General Buckner had sent Lieutenant John Carmody on horseback to the Union camp with his surrender proposal an hour earlier, and was expecting him back with General Grant's reply momentarily. In the meantime, Buckner watched as some four hundred wounded men were being crammed into thirty-two large wagons.

Captain Britt Claiborne had volunteered to take the most seriously wounded men to the hospital at Clarksville, Tennessee. General Buckner had expressed his hope that General Grant would allow those who surrendered to remain at the fort until the weather warmed up. He would even ask in the terms of surrender that medical help be given those wounded men who stayed. He thanked Claiborne for being willing to take the most seriously wounded on to

Clarksville, for they needed the help only a hospital could give. If they didn't get medical attention soon, most of them would die. Claiborne planned to drive one wagon himself, and his two brothers, Corporal Lanny Perkins, and other volunteers would drive the other wagons.

Generals Floyd and Pillow were ready to ride with Forrest to Nashville. They looked on as Captain Claiborne studied a map of Tennessee spread out on General Buckner's desk. By lantern light, Claiborne showed Buckner that his wagons would head southward with Colonel Forrest, skirt around Dover, and follow the west bank of the Cumberland River as it curved southeast to Bear Spring, about nine miles south of Fort Donelson. The river widened out at Bear Spring, making the water shallow enough to drive the wagons across. Colonel Forrest and those who followed him would go on southeast toward Nashville.

Once the wagons crossed the Cumberland, it was twenty-eight miles northeast to Clarksville. General Buckner's haggard face and tired eyes showed the strain he was under. He looked at Claiborne and said, "I wish there were more wagons and horses so you could take all the wounded men to the hospital, Captain."

"I do too, sir."

Buckner rubbed the back of his neck. "When you first came to me about this venture, Captain, I warned you that if Grant has scouts in the area, you could be in real trouble. I don't know but what he might send troops to run you down. If he does, you're doomed."

"My men and I realize the risk we're taking, sir," Claiborne replied evenly. "Grant's scouts might not realize that we're transporting wounded men, and even if they do, I'm not so sure Grant would hold back, even then. He might consider it a feather in his cap to wipe out four hundred of us in one sweep. I know what we're up against, sir, but my volunteers and I are determined to get these wounded men to Clarksville."

"All right, Captain, I wish you the best." Buckner paused, then asked, "You're not planning to take your men on to Nashville afterward, are you? Not in this cold weather?"

"I figure to, sir," Claiborne nodded. "We'll report in to General Floyd there."

"I think it'd be wise just to hole up in Clarksville till the weather warms up. It's a long way from Clarksville to Nashville."

General Floyd spoke up. "Captain Claiborne, as your commanding officer, I'll give you an order."

"Yes sir?"

"The way things were shaping up in central Tennessee when I left there, I really don't think General Johnston will be in Nashville long. A number of our troops are being marched down to Corinth, Mississippi. I believe that's the direction General Johnston will eventually take the troops that are in Nashville. Looks like there may end up being a major battle somewhere near Corinth. So when you've delivered the wounded men to the hospital at Clarksville, take your men and the wagons straight south to Corinth."

"Is that an order, sir?" Claiborne asked.

"It is. I'll take full responsibility for sending you down there."

"I'd like to ask that you put the orders in writing, General, just in case something happened to you."

"Of course. I'll do that right now."

At 2:30 A.M., General Buckner stood at the main gate of the fort and watched Generals Floyd and Pillow ride away with Colonel Forrest. Directly behind them were the wagons loaded with wounded soldiers, and behind them were some four thousand footmen. He breathed a prayer that they would make it without being detected by Union scouts. Remaining with Buckner were nearly twelve thousand men who preferred to take their chances with the Federal army rather than strike out for Nashville.

The long line had barely passed from view when Lieutenant Carmody came riding in with General Grant's reply. When Buckner read it, anger welled up within him. He sat down and penned his reply.

Headquarters, Fort Donelson
February 16, 1862
General Ulysses S. Grant, Sir:
The distribution of the forces under my command,
incident to an unexpected change of commanders, and
the overwhelming force under your command, compel
me, notwithstanding the brilliant success of the
Confederate arms yesterday, to accept the ungenerous
and unchivalrous terms which you propose.
I am, sir,
Your very obedient servant,
S.B. Buckner
Brigadier General, C.S.A.

Carmody was given the letter to deliver to Grant, and rode away while Buckner stood at the gate and watched. When Carmody was out of sight, Buckner sighed and returned to his quarters. Once again, he breathed a prayer that Claiborne and his men would make it safely to Clarksville.

By the time the sun was up, General Buckner and his men were in enemy hands. Within an hour, they were being herded northward toward Camp Douglas, a Union prison camp near Chicago.

General Grant, upon occupying Fort Donelson, realized that a great number of Confederate troops had left the fort some time earlier. He sent out several dozen patrols to scour the countryside and hunt down as many escapees as possible.

Northern newspapers picked up on the surrender, reporting Grant's harsh approach to the Rebels at Fort Donelson. They made a play on his initials, dubbing him *U*nconditional *S*urrender Grant. They reported over nine hundred Confederates killed in the two-day battle, and nearly fifteen hundred wounded. With regret, they also reported over one thousand Federals killed and twenty-one hundred wounded.

The Federal victory at Fort Donelson touched off exuberant celebrations all over the North. When President Lincoln received word of the victory, he immediately issued orders that Grant be promoted to major-general. Lincoln sent a wire, congratulating Grant on the victory and informing him of his promotion.

Word of the defeat reached General Johnston in Nashville by midmorning. In turn, he wired General Beauregard, who was in Alabama on the Tennessee River, awaiting orders. Johnston advised Beauregard of the Confederate defeat, then ordered him to take his troops to Corinth, Mississippi. Johnston explained he had word that Union General Don Carlos Buell was marching his forty-five-thousand-man army toward Nashville from Bowling Green. This would give Johnston only five or six days to evacuate his troops. He would meet Beauregard in Corinth.

After breakfast on February 17, Wayne Gordon shared a time of Bible reading and prayer with the women of the house. Gordon's dizzy spells had stopped, and his strength was quickly returning. Since he was feeling better, he decided it was time for a bath and shave. When Gordon had finished, he carried the bath water outside, dumped it in the yard, then hung the galvanized tub in its place on the back porch. He found the women busy in the sewing room.

Leaning on the door frame, he folded his arms and said, "Well, ladies, you'll be able to stand my presence easier now, I'm sure."

Hannah Rose looked up from her sewing, smiled and said, "The house smells better already."

Gordon gave her a sly grin as everyone laughed.

"Did you have any trouble washing around the bandage?" Hannah Rose asked.

Placing fingertips to the bandage, he replied, "A little. Got it wet along the edge while I was washing my face and neck. I'll be glad when I can wash my hair."

"A few more days," she said.

"You ladies do a lot of sewing?"

"Oh, I guess we haven't told you," Hannah Rose said, holding up the half-finished dress in her hands. "We make dresses for a clothing shop in Dover. This is how we've been making our living since the war started and there's been no one to work the farm."

"I see. Tell you what…I'm feeling like I need a little exercise. Any work I can do for you?"

"Are you sure you're up to it?"

"Well, I couldn't do real heavy work yet, but something light would be good for me."

"We haven't pitched hay down from the hayloft to the horses yet. Think you could climb into the loft and do that?"

"Sure."

"How about working the lever on the water pump?"

"No problem. I can even clean the barn for you, if it needs it."

"Let's not get carried away, Captain," Hannah Rose said. "If you do well with the feeding and watering today, we'll see about more work tomorrow. Oh, the horses will need some oats, too. I'll come out and show you the feed bin."

"No need," he said, throwing up his palms. "I'll find it. How much should I give them?"

"You'll find a hand scoop in the bin. Two of those for each horse, including yours."

"Okay, I'll get to it. See you ladies later."

Going to his room, Gordon donned his overcoat and hat, then strapped on his gunbelt. He pulled the .45 caliber revolver from its holster, broke it open, and checked the loads. Smiling, he said to himself, "Well, you've definitely worn a handgun. Checked the loads almost without thinking."

He moved out into the frosty air and went to the barn. It took him only ten minutes to complete the assigned chores. However, in pitching the hay, he found that the head of the pitchfork was loose. A little searching brought him to a small tool room within the barn, and he spent some twenty minutes repairing the loose handle.

He was about to take the pitchfork back up to the loft when he heard the barn door open and close. He noted with some amusement and curiosity that his hand went instinctively to his revolver. He moved through the door of the tool room and saw Hannah Rose looking about.

"Ah, there you are," she said, smiling. "I was getting worried about you."

"Oh. Well, while I was pitching hay, I noticed the pitchfork needed some repair. I was just going to take it back up to the loft." He reentered the tool room, came out with the pitchfork, and headed for the ladder that led to the loft.

While he was climbing the ladder, Hannah Rose said, "I'm sorry about the fork. Club usually fixes things like that."

Halting halfway up, he looked down and asked, "Who's Club?"

"A neighbor. Big as a mountain. He's been doing whatever heavy labor and repair work we've needed done around here since my brothers entered the war. Seems he overlooked the pitchfork."

"His name is *Club?*"

"Well, it's actually Clarence Clubson. As a kid growing up, he was always bigger than boys three and four years older than him. Sometimes, I guess, he got kidded about his size, and often beat up the kidders. 'Club' sort of naturally became his nickname. He...ah...he's got a powerful crush on Linda Lee, but she wants nothing to do with him. Club has the idea no other man ought to come near her, and he's been rough on some who've shown an interest in her."

"Seems to me if she's not interested in him, he ought to let her be."

"I know, but getting that across to Club is like trying to reason with a grizzly bear. In fact we had a problem over this not long ago, and come to think of it, Club hasn't come by to do any work since."

Climbing on to the top, he leaned the fork against the wall of the loft, then started back down the ladder. "Well, for a while, at least, you've got ol' whatzizname here to do the work for you. And I do mean *whatzizname.*"

As he reached the floor, Hannah Rose said, "I appreciate your willingness to do the work, Captain, but you mustn't overdo it."

"I'll pace myself, but I must also earn my keep around here."

"Just so you don't push yourself too hard and have a relapse. I'd feel terribly guilty if that happened."

Wayne Gordon felt his heart reaching for Hannah Rose. Before he realized it, he was saying, "You have the most beautiful eyes I've ever seen, Hannah Rose. They're like shining emeralds."

Hannah Rose was battling her own heart. This man stirred things within her she had never felt before. She wished he would take her in his arms and kiss her. Fighting off the feeling, she said, "Now, Captain, how can you possibly say mine are the most beautiful eyes you've ever seen? You can't *remember* all the eyes you've ever seen."

"Well, I *forgot* that I can't remember all the eyes I've ever seen. But I can tell you something for sure."

"What's that?"

"Even though I can't remember them, I still know yours are the most beautiful. Don't ask me how…just take my word that it's so."

Hannah Rose looked down at the barn floor. "Thank you," she said softly. Then slowly raising her eyes to meet his, she said, "Captain, I think it would be good if you came back into the house to rest. I'm afraid if you push yourself too hard too soon, you might have a relapse. Concussions aren't something to toy with."

"All right," he said, grinning. "I'll do that."

They entered the house, and Hannah Rose walked down the hall with him. When they reached the sewing room, she turned into it and said she would check on him later.

He entered his room, hung up his overcoat and hat, and glanced at the stranger in the dresser mirror. Then he laid down on the bed. He was tired, but thankful there had been no more dizzy spells. Hannah Rose was right. He shouldn't push himself too hard, or they could come back.

Hannah Rose. What a lovely name for such a lovely young woman. He scolded himself for what he had said about her eyes. If he had a wife...

It was almost an hour later when Wayne Gordon was awakened by the sound of male voices coming from the front part of the house. One was more predominant than the others, but none were friendly. Tiptoeing to his door, he turned the knob as quietly as possible and peered into the hallway. There was no one in his line of sight. Everyone was in the parlor. The predominant voice said, "Whether you like it or not, ma'am, we are going to search this house."

Hannah Rose half-screamed, "You Yankees have no right to come in here and search through our house! We're not harboring any Confederate soldiers! Now, Sergeant, take your two privates and get out!"

"Like I told you, ma'am," the sergeant boomed, "Fort Donelson is now in our hands. We are part of a patrol sent out by General Grant to track down Rebel soldiers. I have my orders, and I will obey them! Now, you ladies stay right here. Don't move. Okay, fellas, you search the second floor. I'll take this one."

Wayne Gordon could hear the two privates thundering up the stairs and closet doors being opened and closed on the first floor. It was only a matter of time till the sergeant entered the guest bedroom. Closing the door, Gordon hurriedly stuffed his overcoat and hat into a bureau drawer, along with his shaving mug and razor. He could hear the heavy footsteps overhead as he squeezed into the closet, along with some old coats. He slid down in the corner and pulled out his revolver, earing back the hammer. He was well-hidden, but if the Yankee decided to probe deep, he would find more than he bargained for.

Gordon sat there with mixed emotions. If only he knew which army he belonged to. If they found him, they would take him for a Rebel captain, and he would have no choice but to shoot his way out. His greater fear was that if there was gunplay, the women could get hit.

There was still rummaging going on overhead when the door of the guest bedroom came open, followed by the sound of heavy boots. Gordon tensed, aimed the .45 toward the closet door, and held his breath. His heart drummed his ribs as the door jerked open. A meaty hand pushed the clothes on the hangers back and forth impatiently, then the thudding footsteps left the room and faded up the hall.

Gordon squeezed out of the closet, dashed to the open door, and eased up to the frame, listening. He could hear the other two Yankees coming down the stairs, announcing that the second floor was unoccupied.

"Same down here," the sergeant said. Then Gordon heard him say, "Grandma, I want you to go upstairs and find something to do. The boys and I want to get a little better acquainted with these lovely young things."

Myrtle Crisp's voice cut the air sharply. "Oh, no you don't, you filthy pigs! You're not about to touch these girls!"

Gordon heard the sergeant swear at the elderly woman, followed by a loud pop. Something hit the floor. Gordon knew the man had slapped Aunt Myrtle and knocked her down. All four of the young women were screaming at him.

Gordon knew he had to intervene before the situation got any worse. He had hoped the Yankees would just quietly leave, but the women were too much of a temptation for them.

Gun-in-hand, Gordon ran down the hall and into the parlor, surprising the Yankees. Hannah Rose and her sister were bending over Aunt Myrtle. Donna Mae and Sally Marie were backing away from the two privates, moving close to the other women. Holding his gun cocked and aimed at the sergeant's head, Gordon spat, "All three of you! Play statue!"

"Don't move, boys. He'll blow my head off," the sergeant said.

"You got that exactly right, big boy!" huffed Gordon. "Now, you ladies go back to the kitchen and close the door. I'll handle this."

Suddenly a wave of dizziness washed over him, followed by another. The Yankees did not recognize it, but Hannah Rose did. She tensed. The threat of violence hung like a thick cloud over the room. Gordon blinked, shook his head, and the dizziness was gone. "Hurry, ladies."

It took the women a full thirty seconds to move out of the parlor, pass through the large dining room, and enter the kitchen. When the door clicked shut, Gordon glowered at the sergeant and hissed, "You know what I think of a man who hits a woman? I think he ought to have his nose shot off."

The sergeant's head bobbed and his face went dead-white. This Rebel captain just might be angry enough to do what he was thinking.

All three Yankees had leaned their carbines against the wall by the front door. None of them wore sidearms. The Rebel had them cold. The sergeant kept his fearful eyes on the muzzle of Gordon's .45, while the two privates looked at each other, wondering what to do.

Gordon nodded toward the front door and said, "Outside."

"Now, wait a minute!" the sergeant gasped. "War is one thing, Captain. Murder is something else."

"What do you call slapping an old woman? Is that your idea of war? Or how about what you had planned for the other women? Is that war?"

The sergeant swallowed hard and said nothing.

Gordon knew the only thing he could do was send them on their way. It wasn't in him to just shoot them down, and there was no Confederate installation to take them to. He thought about tying them up in the barn, but when they didn't report to their unit leader, there would be more Yankees coming around looking for them. All he could do was make them get on their horses and ride. He knew if he did, they would be back with more troops. But what choice did he have?

Through a front window, Gordon could see the three Union horses. Motioning toward the door with his chin, he said, "Let's go. When you get on the porch, I want one of you at a time to get on his horse and ride. I'll say who goes when."

The Yankees looked at him as if they couldn't believe their ears. "You…you mean you're just gonna let us ride away?" one of the privates gasped.

"That's right. What's your name, Private?"

"Helms. Elbert Helms."

"Well, Private Helms, I want you to mount up first." Looking at the other private, he asked, "What's your name?"

"Bob Finch."

"You'll go second, Finch. But only when I tell you."

Fear was still on the sergeant's face. "Don't believe him, fellas. He's gonna shoot us in the back."

"I'll blow your nose off right now if you don't get out that door!" Gordon shouted.

Licking his lips nervously, the sergeant opened the door and led the way. Helms and Finch were on his heels. The man in the Confederate uniform followed them onto the porch, holding his gun on the sergeant.

Gordon felt dizziness coming on as he said, "All right, Helms, you first. Get on your…horse and…ride."

The sergeant heard the waver in Gordon's voice and looked at him over his shoulder. Gordon was fighting the swirling of his brain. The sergeant had wondered how extensive the head wound was. When he saw a glaze come over Gordon's eyes, he lunged for him.

But Gordon's instincts were still honed sharp. The sergeant was making a mistake that would be his last. The hammer of the .45 slammed down and the gun roared. The sergeant took the slug in his heart, and was dead before he fell over the edge of the porch.

Helms grabbed Gordon's wrist with one hand and the revolver with the other, but the man in gray fought back. Finch made a lunge for the gun, also, but he was a second too late. Gordon had already broken Helms's hold and had the revolver free. Swinging almost blindly, Gordon caught Helms on the temple. Helms's knees buckled. He staggered helplessly and fell down the porch steps, sprawling on the ground.

Now Finch was on Gordon, wrestling for control of the gun. Breathing heavily, they went round and round on the porch. Gordon gallantly battled two enemies—the dizziness and Bob Finch.

While the life-and-death struggle continued on the porch, Helms staggered to his horse where a spare carbine rested in its boot. A stream of blood ran down his face from the gash on his temple.

Gordon and Finch stumbled off the porch, hit the ground, and continued to wrestle for control of the gun. The fall made Gordon's dizziness momentarily worse, giving his opponent the advantage. Finch was not able to wrest the weapon from Gordon's grasp, but he carcd back the hammer and began twisting the muzzle around to bring it to bear on Gordon's face.

Both men grunted and hissed through their teeth, knowing that one of them was going to die. Their hands quivered, meeting strength for strength.

Helms moved unsteadily toward the combatants, working the lever of the carbine. One clear opportunity and he would end the fight.

Unexpectedly, Gordon's dizziness began to vanish, and a fresh surge of strength rushed through his body. Unaware that Helms was trying to get a clear shot at him, he surprised Finch by reversing the direction of the muzzle.

Finch's eyes bulged with terror as Gordon turned the black bore of the .45 toward his forehead. The hammer snapped down, the gun fired, and Private Bob Finch was in eternity. Just as Finch's lifeless body hit the ground, Wayne Gordon jerked and staggered as the sound of an army carbine being fired assaulted his ears.

FIFTEEN

Wayne Gordon steadied himself as he saw Private Elbert Helms land on his back. The weapon fell from his fingers and clattered to the frozen ground. Looking the other way, Gordon was shocked to see Hannah Rose Claiborne standing on the porch with a smoking carbine in her hands. She had used one of the Yankees' guns to save his life.

Her lower lip was quivering as she stammered, "He…he w-was going to shoot you. I…I had t-to stop him."

Gordon took one quick look at Helms to make sure he was dead. Turning back, he holstered his .45 and opened his arms. The emotion of the moment was too much. Hannah Rose dropped the carbine, bounded off the porch, and they were in each other's arms.

Hannah Rose was weeping as Wayne held her tight, whispering, "You saved my life, little gal! You saved my life."

Suddenly the other women poured out the front door of the house and gathered around the couple. Warily they eyed the lifeless forms of the three Yankees and praised Wayne Gordon for protecting them.

"I did my best, ladies," Gordon said. "But if it weren't for

Hannah Rose's courage and fast thinking—not to mention straight-shooting—I'd be dead."

A wagon came rolling into the yard and squeaked to a halt. The elderly man who held the reins was alone. Looking around at the corpses, he said, "I was headin' toward town and heard the shootin'. What's goin' on here?"

"It's kind of a long story, Mr. Manning," Linda Lee replied. "You probably know that Fort Donelson has fallen into Union hands."

"No, I didn't know."

Gently pulling free of Gordon's arms, Hannah Rose led him by the hand to the wagon, and said, "Mr. Manning, this is Captain Wayne Gordon. Captain Gordon, this is our neighbor to the south, Walter Manning."

Wayne extended his hand and said, "Glad to meet you, sir."

"Same here," grinned Manning, gripping Gordon's hand solidly. "You took out these scummy blue-bellies all by yourself?"

"Not exactly, sir. Miss Hannah Rose saved my life by taking out this one over here. He was about to shoot me in the back."

"Well I declare, Miss Hannah," Manning said. "I didn't know you were such a crack shot."

"I'm not really, and I hope never to have to use a gun like that again. But I think we're going to need your help, Mr. Manning. Something will have to be done with these bodies." Hannah Rose quickly explained Captain Gordon's situation and what had happened with the Yankees.

Manning grinned at Gordon and said, "I appreciate you tyin' into them no-good blue-bellies, Captain. Took courage for one man to take on three."

"Had to be done, sir," Gordon replied. He noted that Hannah Rose had wisely left out the fact of his amnesia. If Manning thought he might be a Yankee, it would only complicate things.

The old man wrapped the reins around the brake handle and

climbed down. "The best thing for us to do is take these Union horses into the woods a good distance and turn 'em loose," he said to Gordon. "If you'll help me load these Yankees into the wagon, I'll get a couple of neighbors to help me bury 'em someplace where the Federals can't find 'em."

After they loaded the corpses into the wagon, Manning said, "You're lookin' a little peaked, Captain. Best you go in and lie down for a while. You catch some shrapnel in your head?"

"No, sir. A bullet grazed the left side. If I'd zigged instead of zagged, I'd be dead."

"Close one, eh? Well, let's tie these horses to the back of the wagon, and I'll take 'em a few miles and let 'em loose somewhere."

When it was done, Manning climbed up into the seat, took the reins in hand, and said, "Good luck to you, Captain. Get back in the war as soon as you can and help whip the tar outta those blue-bellies!"

"Yes, sir," Gordon nodded. He watched the wagon pull out of the yard, then worked quickly to cover the blood spots on the snow-glazed ground. More Yankees would be around looking for their missing comrades. They must not find evidence of the shootout.

When Gordon returned to the house, Hannah Rose was waiting for him in the parlor. "You're pale, Captain. Time for another rest. I'll come get you at lunch time."

Gordon's knees were watery. He didn't argue.

Lying on the bed alone, his mind replayed the moment he held Hannah Rose in his arms. It felt so right. If he had a wife, could he feel this way about Hannah Rose? How could anyone answer such a question?

The kitchen smelled of cornbread as the women prepared lunch. Only one subject occupied their conversation: the fall of Fort Donelson. Had their men been killed? Wounded? Captured? If they were alive but in a Yankee prison camp somewhere up north, how would they ever know where they were?

Linda Lee, like the others, was concerned about her brothers, but also voiced her concern for Corporal Lanny Perkins. The women agreed that all they could do was trust the Lord to take care of their men.

Donna Mae was working at the counter in front of the window that offered a view of the back yard, corral, and outbuildings. Suddenly her eye caught movement between the barn and a small storage shed. She stared at the spot where she was sure something had moved. There was movement again, but this time she saw a man—then another…and another.

Donna Mae sucked in a deep breath and held it. The other women looked at her and saw her staring out the window with her mouth wide open. "What is it, Donna Mae?" asked Linda Lee.

"It's them!" she cried and dashed for the back door.

"It's who?" Hannah Rose called, hurrying after her, with the others following.

"Britt, William, and Robert!" Donna Mae shouted as she sprang off the porch and into Britt's arms.

Tears flowed as the happy reunion began. When Linda Lee left the porch, her eyes fell on young Lanny Perkins. She screamed his name and dashed into his arms. There were hugs and kisses all around. Finally, Britt told the women that Yankee patrols were all over the area. They needed to get inside and out of sight.

Everyone hurried into the house, and the four tired men sat around the kitchen table while the women added to what was cooking on the stove so there would be plenty for all. The women wanted to know all that had happened, so Britt began the story of Fort Donelson's fall, and the other three put in their bits and pieces. They were describing taking the wounded men to the Clarksville hospital when the amnesia victim appeared at the door that led from the kitchen to the hallway.

All conversation stopped, and the four soldiers rose to their feet. "Who's this?" Britt asked.

Hannah Rose moved to her guest and said, "Britt, William,

Robert, I want you to meet Captain Wayne Gordon. Captain Gordon, these are my brothers. And this man over here is Corporal Lanny Perkins."

It was evident that Britt did not know him, but as they shook hands, Gordon watched the eyes of the other three men to catch any hint that they might recognize him. There was nothing.

Gordon was offered a chair next to Britt, and as he sat down, Hannah Rose stood behind him and said, "I have quite a story to tell about the captain, here. Let's get the food on the table, and I'll tell it while we eat. That is, after we hear the full story from our men, whom the Lord has brought back to us safely."

When the meal was ready and everyone was seated around the table, Britt gave thanks for the food and for bringing them safely back together.

As they began to eat, Britt continued on with their story. He explained that General Floyd had ordered the thirty-two wagon drivers to go to Corinth, Mississippi, where a great part of General Albert Sidney Johnston's troops were already gathering. Britt had put a lieutenant in charge of the wagons and sent them on to Corinth, advising the lieutenant that he, his brothers, and Corporal Perkins were going to make a quick trip home to let their family know they were all right, and where they were going.

They had stashed their wagons and horses in the barns of a couple of farmers near the Cumberland River. The farmers were old friends of the Claiborne family, and were glad to help. Britt told the farmers that he, his brothers, and Lanny Perkins would hole up at the Claiborne place for a few days until the Union patrols tired of searching for Rebel escapees, then they would pick up the wagons and head for Corinth.

Linda Lee looked at Lanny and said, "I'll be so glad when this horrible war is over, and we can all get back to living normal lives."

"Yeah, me too," agreed Perkins. Then turning to Hannah Rose, he said, "Before you tell us Captain Gordon's story, I think I should tell you about Jim Lynch."

Hannah Rose knew by the tone of his voice that the news was bad. Meeting Lanny's gaze, she said cautiously, "Oh, no. Don't tell me…"

"Yes, ma'am. I came across his body on the battlefield. We got separated during the fighting, and when I was heading back to the fort, I found him." Tears surfaced. "I sure will miss him."

"I'm so sorry," Hannah Rose said quietly. "He certainly was a fine man. A dedicated Christian, too. Thank the Lord we know Jim's with Him."

Everyone was quiet for a few minutes, then Hannah Rose said, "Well, let me tell you about our friend, Captain Gordon." As she told her part of the story, Wayne Gordon filled in the gaps. He told about coming to on the battlefield with his memory gone and taking the uniform and horse from the dead Confederate captain.

The men asked pointed questions, and soon understood that Gordon had no idea who he was, where he was from, whether he was married or not, and what he had done for a living before the war.

Linda Lee then told the men about the three Yankee soldiers who had come to the house that morning, and how Gordon had protected the women from them.

Britt smiled at Gordon and said, "I want you to know, my friend, how much I appreciate what you did." The other men expressed their appreciation, also.

"I just did what any man would do in such a situation," Gordon said.

"Any decent man, that is," Britt added.

"Well, thank you…and you're welcome. But can you appreciate the dilemma I'm in? I don't know which army I belong to, or even what to do to find out."

"Something in my heart tells me you're a Confederate, Captain," Hannah Rose said.

Gordon smiled at her. "I hope so." Then he said to Britt, "Dr. Stutz said whenever you showed up, as an officer, you could advise me what to do."

Britt carefully chewed his bite, laid his fork down, and wiped his mouth with his napkin. Finally, he said, "From what I've heard here, it sounds to me like you're an officer, whichever army you belong to. If so, and your memory will cooperate, you might be able to quote portions of the army manual. As an officer, I know the Confederate manual by heart. I've also seen the Union manual, and it is quite a bit different. If you can quote even a portion of the manual you learned, we'll know whether you're Rebel or Yankee. What do you think? Is it worth a try?"

"Yes, of course." Wayne Gordon's fingertips were at his temples as he concentrated. A smile broke across his face. "I think I can quote it!"

"All right, lets' hear it."

There was tension around the table as Gordon closed his eyes and began quoting from his army manual. By the time he had quoted most of Section One, Britt smiled and said, "Welcome back, sir! You're definitely a Confederate officer."

Hannah Rose jumped up from her chair and flung her arms around Gordon's neck. Suddenly she realized what she was doing, and backed away. "Oh, I'm sorry. I...I'm just so glad to know you're not a Yankee."

Gordon stood up and took her hand. "Don't be sorry, Miss Hannah Rose."

"We're all glad you're not a Yankee!" said Linda Lee, clapping her hands. Her action spurred the rest of them, and they all broke into applause. Wayne and Hannah Rose smiled at each other, then they both sat down.

"All right, Captain Claiborne, now that we know I'm a Confederate officer, what shall I do?"

"Do you think you'll be up to some travel in a day or two?"

"I'm sure I will."

"All right. We'll take you with us to Corinth. General Floyd gave me written orders to take my men and report in down there. He was certain that General Johnston—Are these names familiar to you?"

"Floyd's name isn't, but the name of General Albert Sidney Johnston sure is. He's the big gun in the western theater, isn't he?"

"Sure is. Anyway, General Floyd is certain that General Johnston will find it necessary to abandon Nashville and regroup all of his western Tennessee forces in Corinth. Since we were under General Buckner's command, and he's now a prisoner of war, we'll be assigned to existing units there in Corinth. We'll present you to whoever is in charge, tell him about your amnesia…and go from there. If General Johnston isn't there yet, it'll probably be General Beauregard."

Gordon's eyes lit up. "Beauregard! Yes, the Little Creole! I remember him all right!"

"Good!" laughed Britt. "Maybe you'll begin to remember more as time passes. What did Dr. Stutz say about it?"

"Well, he admitted that medical science knows very little about amnesia. He said my memory could come back a little at a time, all at once, or not at all. It's in the Lord's hands, and I'll have to leave it there. He allowed this to happen to me for a reason. That's what Romans 8:28 says, so I'll have to let Him work it all out."

"And God doesn't always hurry, does He?" piped up Robert.

Gordon smiled. "No, He doesn't. Unless it's to save a lost soul."

"We've been praying that the Lord will give him his memory back," Sally Marie said. "I'm sure He will in His own time."

"Well, at least we'll get you back into service at Corinth," Britt said. "Who knows? Maybe there'll be somebody amongst all those troops down there who'll know you."

Things were quiet for a few minutes as they finished their meal, then Robert said, "Britt, I've been thinking about those murders at the fort. If the killer is amongst those men who headed for Nashville with Colonel Forrest—and if they all end up at Corinth—we could have more officers getting murdered down there."

"Murders?" Donna Mae gasped. "What murders?"

Robert told how several Confederate officers had been murdered by some unknown assassin. As Robert talked, Hannah Rose noticed the rapt attention Wayne Gordon was giving him.

When a break came in the conversation, Hannah Rose said, "Captain, I couldn't help but notice your keen interest in this story. Are you getting some kind of memory flashbacks?"

Gordon nodded slowly and said, "There's definitely something, ma'am. The mention of these officers being murdered triggered something in the back of my mind, but I can't identify it."

"Well, you found yourself on that battlefield at Fort Donelson," Robert said. "You may have been among the newest reinforcements, and were told of the murders when you got there. Perhaps you're remembering being told about them."

"You're probably right, Robert," Gordon said.

"But wouldn't you men have seen Captain Gordon at the fort if he'd been part of the reinforcements?" Donna Mae asked.

"Not necessarily," Britt said. "You have to bear in mind, honey, that there were seventeen thousand men at the fort just before the battle. There were hundreds of men who never saw each other."

"Oh, I hadn't realized there were so many men there."

The meal was finished, and while the women cleaned up, the men sat in the parlor discussing the war. Frequently, one of them went to a window to see if any Union patrols were in sight. They knew the possibility was good that a search party would be looking for the three Yankees who had been killed in front of the Claiborne house that morning.

After a while, Britt and William wanted to spend time with their wives, and Lanny sat in the kitchen talking with Linda Lee. Gordon went to his room to rest, and Hannah Rose and Aunt Myrtle busied themselves in the sewing room.

The afternoon passed without any sign of patrols. After supper that evening, they all sat in the parlor enjoying the warmth of the fireplace and talked together of the war and how it was going for the South. After awhile, Aunt Myrtle announced that she was going up to bed, and shortly thereafter, the married couples retired to their rooms. Lanny was assigned a room, Robert went to his, and Linda Lee went to hers.

Wayne and Hannah Rose wanted to stay up and talk, so he threw more logs on the fire, and they sat on the floor in front of the fireplace, leaning back against the front of the couch.

They both sat and stared at the dancing flames for a few minutes, then Wayne said, "A penny for your thoughts."

When she didn't turn toward him, he leaned forward so he could see her face and saw tears in her eyes.

"What is it?" he asked.

She looked away, then down at her hands. "It's just that…you'll be leaving in a couple of days, and…and I may never see you again."

"Now, that's just not so. As soon as possible, I'll be back."

Hannah Rose sniffed and brushed a tear from her cheek. "Not if you get to Corinth and meet someone who knows you. If that happens, the first thing you'll do—which is natural—is go home. And…if you have a wife there, you'll have no reason to ever come back here."

He took hold of her hand and said, "But I may not be married, Miss Hannah Rose."

Looking him directly in the eye through her tears, she said, "I hope with all my heart that you aren't."

He swallowed hard, bit his lower lip, and choked out the words, "I hope with all my heart I'm not either, because…"

There was yearning visible in Hannah Rose's eyes. "Because why?"

Gordon struggled with his feelings. He knew he shouldn't tell her, but he was like an overloaded dam, attempting to hold back a force too great. The words gushed out. "Because I love you!"

Tears streaming down her cheeks, Hannah Rose said, "I realize we've known each other such a short time, but…is love a captive of time? Can't love be real and genuine in spite of shortness of time? It has to be so, for I've fallen in love with you, too!"

Suddenly they were in each other's arms, enjoying a sweet velvet kiss. When their lips parted, he held her close for a long moment, and neither one spoke. Finally, he eased back, looked into her eyes, and said, "I don't know what to do. My thinking is that if I have a wife, the Lord wouldn't let me fall for you like this…but I just don't know."

Hannah Rose looked at him in the firelight with adoring eyes. She reached above the bandage that encircled his head and stroked his thick locks. "You're such a good man, Capt—Wayne—oh, I don't know what to call you. You're such a good man, *darling*. I guess I should tell you I'm sorry to complicate your life like this, but I'm not. If I can have your love only for a few days, I will accept it."

He kissed her again, then said, "Even with my shadowed memories, Hannah Rose Claiborne, I know one thing for sure. There has never been a woman so sweet and wonderful as you. It's just impossible for me to believe that I have a wife out there somewhere. How could I feel so much love for you, if—Oh, Hannah Rose, this has to be the hardest thing I've ever faced."

"You have such a true and honest heart," she whispered. "If it should turn out that you are married, you and I both know the only right thing before the Lord will be for you to return to your wife."

He closed his eyes and held Hannah Rose tight. Throat constricted, he choked, "The only right thing for me to do, Hannah Rose, is to get out of your life so you can forget me quicker."

"Forget you? How can I forget you? I know my heart. I will always love you. I know for now we mustn't let things get any stronger between us, but until you have to leave, please let me at least have you near me."

Wayne blew out the lantern in his room a little while later and settled his head on the pillow. He knew what Hannah Rose had said was right. They must not allow what they felt for each other to grow any stronger. They would keep proper distance until and unless they learned that he did not have a wife. He stared into the darkness and prayed that he would find out soon.

SIXTEEN

The next day, Hannah Rose and Linda Lee drove into town to deliver four new dresses to the clothing store and to pick up some groceries. When they returned, they pulled the wagon up to the back porch, and the men started out the door to carry in the groceries. Linda Lee waved them back in, saying in a hushed voice, "Stay inside! We just saw a Yankee patrol!"

When Hannah Rose and Linda Lee entered the kitchen with the first load of groceries, everyone gathered around.

"They're about a mile north of here," Hannah Rose said. "They passed within a hundred yards of us. They looked our direction, watched us for about half a minute, then went on."

"I hope they keep going," Myrtle said.

"Oh, and Aunt Myrtle," said Linda Lee, "we were told in town that General Grant has left the area. I hope you still have a house."

"Well, ol' Useless S. Grant promised they wouldn't do any damage, but who can believe anything a stinkin' Yankee says?"

"We'll go with you and check it out," Hannah Rose said.

"'Tain't necessary," said the oldster, shaking her head. "I'll drive on home after lunch. If there's any problem, I'll be back."

"We'd be glad to go with you," said Donna Mae.

"You just stay here with your husband, dearie," said Myrtle, patting her arm. "He'll be leavin' soon enough. You two need all the time you can get."

"If it weren't for the possibility of running into a patrol, us fellas would take you, Aunt Myrtle," William said. "I just don't like the thought of you driving home by yourself."

"Hey, boy," Myrtle chuckled, "I've been drivin' myself around for a long time. If I run into one of them Yankee patrols, they ain't gonna mistake me for a Rebel soldier, are they?"

"Well, no, but—"

"It's settled, then. I'll head for home right after lunch. Like I told you, if my house ain't livable, I'll be back. If you don't see me in a couple of hours, you'll know everything's okay."

Hannah Rose turned to the amnesia victim and said, "Captain, I saw Dr. Stutz on the street. He asked if you could come into town tomorrow and let him check your wound and change the bandage. He suggested you borrow some civilian clothes from Britt—since you're about the same size—and ride in with a couple of us girls. If a Yankee patrol stops us, you're a friend of the family who's been injured, and we're taking you to the doctor."

"Guess that'd work," nodded Gordon. "And I'm sure it's best that Dr. Stutz checks this wound. I don't need blood-poisoning, along with everything else."

When Aunt Myrtle had not returned by mid-afternoon, Hannah Rose decided she would not rest until she knew everything was all right. When she announced that she was going to drive over to check on Aunt Myrtle, Linda Lee volunteered to go with her.

The sun was lowering in the western sky when Hannah Rose and Linda Lee started for home. They had found Aunt Myrtle cleaning her house, which General Grant had not harmed in any way. The wagon swung onto the road that led to Dover, and headed for the Claiborne farm, about two miles in the distance. At the same time, they saw Club Clubson coming from town on horseback. He stood up in the stirrups and waved his hat.

"Brace yourself, honey," Hannah Rose said. "Here comes Romeo."

"Well, I'm not Juliet," Linda Lee sighed.

It took Club only a few seconds to trot his horse up beside the wagon. "Hello, Linda Lee…Miss Hannah Rose," he said, smiling.

Both women nodded a greeting.

Hannah Rose held the reins and kept the wagon moving. Keeping pace, Club asked, "Where ya been?"

"Aunt Myrtle's," Hannah Rose answered.

"Goin' home, now, huh?"

"Yes." Again it was the older sister who spoke.

"Cat got your tongue, Linda Lee?" asked Club.

"No," she said, looking up at him, "but Hannah Rose is capable of answering your questions."

"I s'pose you heard about the Yankees takin' Fort Donelson."

"Yes," replied Linda Lee. "Our brothers escaped. They're at the house right now."

"Oh. So you don't need me doin' any work while they're there, huh?"

"No."

Club was thoughtfully quiet for a moment, then said, "One good thing about the fort bein' captured by the Yankees."

"What could be good about that?" Linda Lee asked.

"There ain't no soldiers gonna come around your house wantin' to court you."

"Even if they did, it wouldn't be any of your business."

"Linda Lee, when are you gonna quit talkin' that way? Of course it's my business. I'm plannin' to marry you some day. Just as soon as you figger out—"

"Clarence! I've tried to be nice to you, but you won't listen to reason. I'll court whoever I want, and you can't do anything about it."

"Well, I *can* do somethin' about it! I can crack the skull of every man who shows up on your doorstep! And I will, too! You belong to me, Linda Lee. The sooner you figger that out, the better it's gonna be for both of us!"

With that, Club gouged the sides of his horse and galloped away. Looking back twice, he burned Linda Lee with blazing eyes.

"Oh, sis, when am I going to be rid of him?"

"Like we've said all along—not until you meet the right man and marry him. That man will have to make Club understand he's to leave you alone."

"I have met the right man, sis," Linda Lee said, turning toward her on the seat. "I know Lanny and I will have to wait till this dumb war is over before we can get serious about marriage, but he's in love with me, and wants to marry me. He said so."

"Well, if he's the Lord's choice for you, honey, it'll all work out."

"Yes, I suppose you're right," Linda Lee sighed as they drew near the Claiborne house.

That evening, Hannah Rose and Wayne Gordon were careful not to be alone together. When the rest of the family decided it was time to call it a day, they went to their respective rooms. No one in the house knew it, but both lay in their beds, staring into the darkness, wishing they could be together.

The next morning, Gordon put on Britt's civilian clothes and hitched the horses to the wagon. He helped the Claiborne sisters aboard, then drove toward town. Purposely, they arranged for Linda Lee to sit between Wayne and Hannah Rose.

They saw no Union patrols while driving into town, for which they were thankful. As they turned onto Main Street and headed for Dr. Stutz's office, they were not aware that Club Clubson happened to see them through the barbershop window. He focused on the stranger who was driving and noted that Linda Lee was sitting next to him.

Wrath boiled up inside him. *Who's this new man Linda Lee has attached herself to? She's gone and dug herself up some dandy wearing a wide-brimmed hat cocked sideways.* Cursing under his breath, Club paid the barber and stepped onto the boardwalk. He moved into the street so he could see where Linda Lee and Hannah Rose were going with Linda Lee's new suitor. When the wagon pulled up in front of the blacksmith shop, he rolled his massive shoulders, set his jaw, and headed that direction.

There was no place to park in front of the doctor's office, so Wayne parked across the street in front of the blacksmith shop. He set the brake, then hopped down. Looking past Linda Lee, he said, "I'll help her down first, Hannah Rose, then I'll come around that side and help you."

Linda Lee was wearing a new pair of low-cut shoes, and the soles were slick. She placed her right foot on the metal step on the side of the wagon, then let Wayne support part of her weight with his hands as she lifted her other foot over the side. Suddenly her right foot slipped, and she fell straight down, raking her ankle on the metal step.

"Oh!" she gasped as Wayne caught her in his arms. He backed a couple of steps from the wagon and eased her onto her feet "I'm sorry," he said. "Are you all right?"

Hannah Rose climbed down from the wagon and hurried toward them.

"It wasn't your fault, Captain," Linda Lee said. "The soles on these shoes are just too slick. I...I scraped my ankle."

Hannah Rose bent over and lifted her sister's skirt high enough to assess the damage. "Oh, dear," she said, "you really scraped it bad, honey. Can you walk okay?"

Linda Lee took a step and winced, sucking air through her teeth. "It hurts pretty bad, but I can make it to Doc's office."

"No need for that," said Wayne. "I'll carry you."

"That's kind of you, Captain, but I can—" Even as she spoke, he bent over and swept her off her feet.

Just then, Hannah Rose looked up the street and saw Club Clubson coming on the run.

"Oh-oh," she said. "We've got trouble."

Wayne and Linda Lee, who had her arms around his neck, turned to see the huge man bearing down on them.

"What's his problem?" Gordon asked.

"That's Club Clubson," Hannah Rose said. "I told you about him."

"Oh, the guy who has a crush on little sister here."

"And doesn't want any other man to come near her."

"He'll want to fight you, Wayne," Linda Lee said with a quiver in her voice. "Don't let him push you into it. He's dangerous."

Club drew up with rage bulging his eyes. "Put her down, mister!"

Wayne Gordon could remember nothing about his past, but Club's insolence stirred within him some primal, bred-in-the-bone desire to resist. He found no trace of fear for the man who was much bigger than he. He met Club's gaze with icy eyes and asked, "Why should I?"

Clarence Clubson was not used to being defied. Men had always cowered in his presence. The bold impudence of the smaller man fired his temper even more. His cheeks went darker, and he seemed to swell in size. "I told you to put her down!"

A crowd was gathering. The people of Dover had seen Club in temper tantrums before.

Ignoring him, Gordon said to Hannah Rose, "Let's get her to the doctor," and he started across the street.

Club leaped in front of Gordon, barring his way, and bellowed, "Put Linda Lee down! She's my woman!"

Hannah Rose stepped between them, facing the giant, and said in a calm voice, "Club, Linda Lee hurt herself climbing down from the wagon. This man is carrying her because she's in pain. He's taking her to Dr. Stutz."

"She was sittin' next to him in the wagon! I saw it!" Looking past Hannah Rose, Club growled, "If you don't put her down, I'll beat you to a pulp!"

Purposely blocking Club's path, Hannah Rose said over her

shoulder, "Go on, Wayne. Get her into the office."

Club cursed and slammed Hannah Rose aside with his massive arm. The crowd gasped when she tumbled to the street. Two men dashed from the side of the street to help her up.

Gordon regarded Club with eyes of venom and said through clenched teeth, "You wait right there."

Club knew he had the fight he wanted. Any man who rivaled him for Linda Lee's affection had to be disposed of. This wouldn't take long.

Still carrying Linda Lee in his arms, Gordon went to Hannah Rose and asked, "Are you hurt?"

Her hair was disheveled and there was dust on her face and dress, but she assured him she was all right.

"He's going to pay for that," Gordon said. "But first, let's get sis into the doctor's office."

Both sisters begged Wayne not to fight Club, but their words fell on angry, deaf ears. He carried Linda Lee to the door of the office where he found Dr. Stutz waiting.

Setting her down, Gordon said, "Take care of her, Doc. I'll let you check me and change my bandage later."

"Don't do it, son," Stutz pleaded. "With your concussion, it could be very dangerous."

Hannah Rose had fear in her eyes. "Doc's right, Wayne. Club's vicious! He'll—"

"That sorry excuse for a man knocked you down, and I won't stand for it. I don't care how big or vicious he is."

Leaving those words to hang in the air, Wayne Gordon set his gaze on the yellow-haired giant. Removing Britt Claiborne's wide-brimmed hat and coat, he handed them to the nearest man and said, "Hold these for me, please."

"Sure," the man nodded, wondering if this tall, slender stranger with the bandage encircling his head would ever need the coat and hat again.

Club felt better already with Linda Lee out of the man's arms.

He flexed his bull-like shoulders and massive arms, pleased that a large crowd was looking on. He heard a woman ask her husband to get the town constable. A man standing near said, "Somebody already thought of that, Mrs. Jenkins. Constable Herrick is out of town."

Club laughed within. Constable Dale Herrick had given him trouble in the past for beating up men in his town. There would be no interference this time.

Gordon halted six feet from Club and regarded him with contempt. "Man who roughs up a woman is the lowest form of man there is."

"She got in the way. If you'd put Linda Lee down the first time I told ya, it wouldn't have happened."

Gordon's instincts told him to get in the first lick. He took a quick step forward, aiming a fist at Club's jaw. Club tried to dodge it, but he was too slow. The punch landed solidly and his head snapped back. On the rebound, Gordon popped him with a stiff left jab, then followed quickly with another right to the jaw. Club staggered sideways. Before he could stabilize himself, Gordon gave him a hard shove with his foot. Club stumbled and fell on his face.

The crowd cheered and applauded, which made Club angrier than ever. He was cursing a blue streak as he raised up on his hands and knees. He was just about to stand when Gordon planted his boot on his backside and shoved him again. All balance gone, Club went face-down, reduced to a clumsy, scrabbling buffoon. Swearing more than ever, he came up in a crouching position and pivoted so he could see his opponent. The curse that left his lips was a low, strangled growl.

Humiliated as the crowd continued to cheer, Club rose to his feet, breathing heavily, more from anger than exertion. Gordon was making a fool of him. This was too much. Club would kill the man right here in front of everybody.

Ejecting a beastly growl, Club went after Gordon. Gordon caught him with a glancing blow, but Club slammed him with a meaty fist flush on the jaw. The impact sent a shower of stars through Gordon's head, and a name seemed to echo against the walls of his brain. He felt his feet leave the ground. The brilliant midday sun blinded him for a second, then he rolled over in the dust and started to get up. Club kicked him in the ribs. The breath gushed from his lungs, and a fiery streamer of pain shot through his body. A wave of dizziness washed over him, and he felt a touch of gloom. If he went dizzy now, he was done for. There was murder in Club's eyes, and Gordon doubted that anyone would try to stop the man if he went for the kill. Hannah Rose might, but what could she do?

Club attempted to kick him again, but Gordon dodged the hissing foot, grabbed the man by the ankle, and gave a savage twist. Club howled and landed on the wagon-rutted street with a heavy thump.

Gordon leaped to his feet, ignoring the pain in his ribs. He waited for Club to get up, then charged him, landing four quick punches to Club's face. Club staggered, but came back strong, though he limped on the injured ankle and his lip was split.

The brassy taste of blood fueled Club's fire. He moved in and landed a glancing haymaker to Gordon's temple, enough to send more stars rushing through his head and let him hear the name he had heard earlier.

Gordon was sure the blows to his head were giving him some kind of flashback. It was a blow to the head that robbed him of his memory, and now some powerful blows had made a name echo through his mind. He tried to focus on it, but there wasn't time.

He noticed his bandage was loose. He knew if the wound opened up, he was in deep trouble. Countering quickly, he landed a hard punch to Club's wide nose. It made the big man blink and filled his eyes with tears. Gordon smashed the nose two more times, then felt a dizzy spell coming on. He staggered, swaying, and took a hard blow to the left cheekbone. He felt as if he were falling through an endless black hole, but was aware of the crowd shouting for him to finish Clubson off.

The name came again: *Julie*. It echoed through his mind over and over. He rolled to his feet, and became aware that they were now fighting at the wide doorway of the blacksmith shop.

The dizziness was subsiding again as Club came at Gordon. He took a couple of backward steps and bumped against the door frame. He could feel a trickle of blood flowing down his face from beneath the loosened bandages. Club closed in and threw a right jab that Wayne ducked in the nick of time.

Club's fist banged against the solid wood. He howled in agony, grabbing the fist with his other hand. His wide face was now smeared with blood from his mouth and nose.

Jerry Spaulding, the blacksmith, had deserted his shop and joined the crowd as they pressed into the middle of the street, not wanting to miss the finish, whenever it came. Inside the shop, two draft horses that were there being fitted for shoes were becoming increasingly nervous with the combatants fighting so close behind them. They whinnied, fought their bits, and struggled against the leathers that kept them tied to the posts.

Gordon got in another good punch, popping Club's head back, then the giant blindly swung his wounded right fist. Gordon ducked as before, and the big doors rattled with the impact. Club let out a wild howl.

Club threw his weight against Gordon, knocking him off balance. Suddenly the Confederate officer found himself wrapped in a vise from behind. His feet were off the ground. Club had broken his right hand and could no longer punch with it, but he had Gordon in a deadly bear hug, bearing down with all his might.

Gordon felt the breath leave his lungs. His already damaged ribs ached as Club did his best to crush him. Gordon caught a glimpse of Hannah Rose in the crowd. Her disheveled hair reminded him of what Club had done to her. His fury grew like a prairie fire in a high wind. Gritting his teeth, he threw both hands back and jabbed his thumbs in Club's eyes.

Screaming wildly, Club whirled and threw Gordon fifteen feet through the air. Gordon rolled toward the two horses, striking his head on the side of the firepit. He was barely aware that the massive animals were whinnying and kicking blindly behind them. The deathly hooves of the closest horse missed his head only by a couple of feet.

The jolt of striking the firepit sent another meteor shower through Gordon's head, but immediately upon the heels of the shower, he saw the image of a young woman and heard the name *Julie* come from his lips.

Suddenly he saw Club shuffling toward him, wielding a five-foot steel bar he had found leaning against the wall of the shop. Spaulding was silhouetted against the stark sunlight in the wide door, shouting at Club to stop. Those outside stood wide-eyed.

But Club paid no attention to the blacksmith. He was coming for the kill, and Wayne Gordon knew it. Scrambling to his feet, he met Club head-on, gripping the steel bar. With his brute strength, Club swung Gordon around toward the door, breaking his hold on the bar. Gordon staggered backward. Club gripped the bar at one end and rushed at his opponent, swinging the deadly thing wildly. Gordon's back was against the door frame again, and he ducked the hissing bar as it came at his head. The horses, eyes bulging, were neighing with fear and dancing about, still fighting the leathers that held them to the posts.

The bar struck the door frame with a deafening bang, showering splinters in every direction. The sound echoed down the street like the crack of a rifle. Catching Club off balance, Gordon planted his feet and landed a solid blow to his jaw. Club staggered, but did not go down. Nor did he let go of the bar.

Club swung the bar wildly and missed, throwing himself off balance. His ponderous body went full-circle, plummeting him toward the terrified horses. Club's feet tangled, and he fell forward, slamming into the rumps of both animals. Suddenly the powerful hooves were up and kicking blindly at the object that had bumped them. Two hooves found Club's head, caving in his skull. When he fell dead, the terrified animals continued to whinny and kick the lifeless body.

Wayne Gordon, still fighting dizziness, staggered toward the door and collapsed. Still conscious, he was carried by two men into Dr. Stutz's office and laid on the examining table. While Hannah Rose stood close by, the kindly physician checked the head wound and found, surprisingly, that it had not been severely damaged. He cleaned it up, dressed it good, and put on a new bandage. There were no serious injuries. Hannah Rose embraced him, relieved that he had not been maimed or killed.

Linda Lee's ankle had been bandaged up, and according to Stutz, would heal without any further complications. Together, the weary amnesia victim and the two women boarded the wagon and headed for home.

Linda Lee and Hannah Rose thanked Gordon for standing up to Club. Though Club had been a pest in her life, Linda Lee was sorry he was dead. She told herself if only he had listened to her, he would still be alive.

SEVENTEEN

A week passed, and Wayne Gordon was back to full strength. Twice during that time he had been checked by Dr. Stutz, and the second time, the bandage came off. There were no more sightings of Union patrols, and on Tuesday, February 25, Britt Claiborne announced it was time to leave for Corinth. They would head south at sunrise the next morning.

When supper was over on Tuesday night, the married couples bundled up and took a walk in the light of a half-moon, as did Lanny and Linda Lee. Robert, Hannah Rose, and Wayne Gordon were in the parlor, sitting in front of the fireplace. The flickering shadows from the fire danced on their faces. Wayne and Hannah Rose sat at opposite ends of the couch, and Robert was between them on the floor. The conversation centered on the war and the departure of the men in the morning. Hannah Rose was having trouble disguising her feelings of dread.

Robert knew his sister well. Looking up at her, he said, "Sis, you and Wayne are making a good try at it, but it's obvious you're losing the battle."

"What are you talking about?" asked Hannah Rose.

Robert grinned from ear to ear, glanced up at Wayne, then

looked at his sister and replied, "Come on. We've all talked about it when you two weren't around. You're so much in love, a blind man would know it."

Wayne and Hannah Rose exchanged quick glances.

"We all understand," said Robert, rising to his feet and looking down at them. "Wayne may have a wife and children somewhere. You two have faced the possibility, and are doing your best to keep from getting any more attached to each other. Am I hitting the proverbial nail right on the head?"

Wayne stood up, shoved his hands in his pockets, and said, "I didn't realize we were so obvious. But you're right, Robert. Even though we've only known each other a short while, your sister and I have fallen head-over-heels in love."

"So when we pull out of here in the morning, you both know it could be the last time you ever see each other."

"It'll have to be, if I get to Corinth and find someone who knows me…and that leads me to a wife. No matter how I feel about Hannah Rose, the only right thing is to go back to my wife."

"It's hard for me even to imagine what you're going through," Robert said with compassion in his voice. "But…well, we've talked about Romans 8:28. The Lord certainly could have prevented that bullet from taking away your memory. He didn't, so this has to work out for your good. It has to be part of His plan and purpose for you."

"You're right," Hannah Rose said, rising from the couch. Embracing Robert, she said, "I love you, big brother. Thank you for caring. Wayne and I need a lot of prayer right now."

Robert gave his sister a tight squeeze and said, "You also need a little time together. Morning will come all too soon." With that, he turned and left the room.

Wayne and Hannah Rose stood looking at each other by the light of the fire. A long moment passed, then he said, "I guess I better go to my room."

Hannah Rose was fighting tears. Lips quivering, she nodded, "You need to get a good night's rest."

Wayne had not told Hannah Rose about the flashbacks that had come to him while fighting Club Clubson. Even as he stood there, he could clearly picture the face of the young woman named Julie. Who was she? An old girlfriend? A fiancée? His wife?

Hannah Rose was fighting her own battle. She had fallen in love with this man the very day he entered her life—the man without a name, the man who very possibly belonged to another woman. This man was going to ride away tomorrow and maybe never return.

Wayne told himself he would rather be on the front line of battle facing enemy guns than the torment ripping at his insides. When he saw the tears trail down Hannah Rose's cheeks, it was more than he could bear.

Through her tears, Hannah Rose half-whispered, "I love you so much."

The barrier they had tried so hard to erect suddenly crumbled. They rushed to each other and embraced.

"The thought of never seeing you again is driving me wild!" Wayne said, choking on the words,

Hannah Rose broke into heart-wrenching sobs and hung on to him as if her very life depended on his presence.

When their emotions had settled, they sat together on the couch, holding hands and staring into the fire.

Soon the other couples returned. Lanny and Linda Lee announced they had become engaged and would marry as soon as the war was over. Everyone rejoiced with the young couple and congratulated them. No one said anything about the dilemma Wayne and Hannah Rose faced, though everyone wondered how the announcement of the engagement affected them.

Soon the heartsick couple found themselves alone once again. They sat together on the couch, staring silently into the dying embers. Holding Hannah Rose's hand, Wayne looked into her emerald eyes and said, "I know we both need to get some sleep. I was just thinking of what the Bible says in Proverbs 3:5 and 6. It really fits our situation."

Hannah Rose squeezed his hand and nodded. "I know the verses well."

"Let's pray and ask the Lord to help us to do our part—to trust Him—so He can direct our paths," Wayne said.

Hannah Rose was fighting tears again as together they knelt beside the couch, clasping hands. Wayne poured out his heart, saying, "Lord, both of us want to do what is right. If I have a wife waiting for me somewhere, then please help me find her somehow. Lord, You've allowed all of this to happen for a purpose. Help us both to acknowledge You in all our ways, and not to lean to our own feeble understanding. As You direct our paths, please help us to accept Your will as You reveal it to us. And…if it isn't Your will for us to have a life together, please give this wonderful woman the man You have for her."

He was about to close when Hannah Rose said, "Lord Jesus, You know my heart better than I do, but I know it well enough to say for sure that if this man I'm holding onto is not to come back to me, I can never love another man. Give me the grace, then, to face the future as I trust in You with all my heart. Amen."

Wayne was overwhelmed. Tears filmed his eyes as he helped Hannah Rose to her feet and folded her in his arms. Then he walked her to her room, kissed her goodnight, and waited till she closed the door. He went downstairs to his room and spent a restless night.

The next morning, Wayne Gordon donned his Confederate uniform and saddled his horse. He would walk with the other men, leading the horse, until they reached the farms where they had stashed the wagons and teams. Then he would ride with them south for Corinth.

Tears were shed as the Claiborne women told their men goodbye. Hannah Rose promised Wayne she would pray for him every day. He promised the same, adding that with the uncertainty of the war, there was no way he could say when she might hear from him or see him again. They would have to leave it in the Lord's hands.

When all the good-byes had been said, Wayne kissed Hannah Rose in front of everyone, told her he loved her, and joined the other men.

The women stood in front of the big white house and watched their men until they vanished from sight, then turned and went inside.

The surrender of Fort Donelson was an unmitigated disaster for the Confederacy. Morale was low when Brigadiers John Floyd and Gideon Pillow arrived in Nashville with Colonel Nathan Forrest and their four thousand troops. They found Confederate commander General Albert Sidney Johnston packing up his troops, ready to abandon the city and head for Corinth, Mississippi.

Johnston—happy to see that so many men had escaped the fort—explained that thirty-five thousand Union troops were headed for Nashville from Bowling Green, Kentucky, under the leadership of General Don Carlos Buell. Nashville was doomed to fall into Federal hands.

Forrest told Johnston his men needed to rest before striking out on the long journey to Corinth. Since it would still be several days before Buell and his army arrived, Forrest advised Johnston to take his troops and start south. Forrest and his men would follow within a couple of days.

With the month of March came heavy rains, but Johnston's troops and thousands of Confederates commanded by General Pierre G.T. Beauregard braved the weather and headed for Corinth.

Johnston had chosen Corinth because it was a strategic rail junction for the Mobile & Ohio and Memphis & Charleston Railroads. If Corinth fell to the Union, Memphis would be cut off from its supply lines on the Atlantic coast, and Mobile—which was vital for supplies coming in from the Gulf of Mexico—would lose its communication link into the vastly important Tennessee valley.

By the time the prisoners from Fort Donelson arrived at Camp Douglas, Illinois, Union commander General Henry Halleck had received important news at his headquarters in St. Louis. Federal spies within the Confederate army were reporting that General Johnston was planning to move nearly his entire force to Corinth.

Halleck went to work and drew up a plan. He would send a massive force to Corinth, wipe out the Rebels, and take the strategic railroad junction for the Union. This would cripple the Confederate cause in the western theater and help bring an end to the war.

In his plan, Halleck would let General Buell, commander of the Union Army of the Ohio, capture Nashville, then take four of his divisions to Corinth, leaving two to hold the city. He would also send General Ulysses S. Grant and his Union Army of the Tennessee and all six of his divisions to join forces with Buell. This would give the Federals an approximate strength of sixty-seven thousand men. From what Halleck knew of Johnston's army, all four corps could not total more than about forty thousand.

Halleck figured to have his troops near Corinth and ready to attack the Confederate stronghold by early April.

General Johnston knew that sooner or later, the Union military leaders would make the rail center at Corinth an objective for capture. With Nashville in Federal hands, it would probably be sooner. What better place than Corinth for Johnston to mass his troops and be ready to launch a devastating counterattack against the boldly aggressive Yankees?

Confederate troops streamed into Corinth from every direction. Among the converging Rebels were five thousand men of First Division, I Corps under Major General Leonidas Polk, who marched from Columbus, Kentucky. Under General Johnston's orders, Polk had sent the five thousand men of Second Division to defend Island

Number Ten, a fortified piece of real estate that blocked the Mississippi River near New Madrid, Missouri. The Confederacy could not afford to leave Island Number Ten unprotected.

Also among those streaming into Corinth were fifteen thousand men of II Corps under Major General Braxton Bragg. Bragg and his Second Division commander, Brigadier General Jones M. Withers, came with ten thousand from Pensacola, Florida, and First Division under Brigadier General Daniel Ruggles came with five thousand from New Orleans.

The Claiborne brothers, Corporal Lanny Perkins, and the man who called himself Wayne Gordon arrived at the Confederate army camp on Saturday, March 8. They had spotted two Union patrols along the banks of the Cumberland River just before they reached the first farm where they had stashed horses and wagons. They had holed up for a few days to make sure travel was safe, and heavy rains had also slowed them. They were immediately assigned to II Corps, Army of the Mississippi, commanded by General Bragg. Bragg placed them in First Division under General Ruggles.

The Claiborne brothers and Perkins were pleased to see a number of men they knew from Fort Donelson, including John Carmody, who had carried the messages between Buckner and Grant at the time of Fort Donelson's surrender. Carmody told them that when he returned to Fort Donelson with Grant's message demanding unconditional surrender, he took advantage of the opportunity to escape, and rode hard to catch up with Colonel Forrest and his troops. He was glad he did, since General Buckner and the nearly twelve thousand men who stayed were now in a Yankee prison camp.

While the Claibornes and Perkins greeted men they knew, Wayne Gordon watched to see if anyone recognized him. There was no sign that anyone did.

Captain Britt Claiborne then introduced Captain Wayne Gordon to General Bragg and told him they needed to talk with him and General Ruggles about a serious problem. Bragg, who was a soldier's soldier, said that whatever the problem was, it needed to be dealt with. He called for General Ruggles to appear at once. In Bragg's large tent, the generals listened to Gordon's story with keen interest. Gordon also showed the generals that he could quote the Confederate army manual almost perfectly, and Britt vouched for Gordon's integrity and ability to handle himself in threatening situations.

Thinking on it for a few moments, General Bragg decided the amnesia victim would come in as a captain and remain Wayne Gordon, since the real Wayne Gordon was dead and not known in the Army of the Mississippi. Gordon would be in Ruggles's First Division, along with Captain Claiborne. Bragg thought it best that Gordon not try to hide his amnesia, but to let the men in the camp find out as occasion dictated. Bragg would put Captain Claiborne in command of a company, and let Gordon work closely with him until he had proven himself in battle. Once Bragg received a satisfactory report, Gordon would be given a company of his own.

That night at supper, the Claibornes, Gordon, and Perkins learned from Captain Waldon McGuire that First Division II Corps had some two thousand men in it who had been at Fort Donelson and had followed Colonel Forrest to Nashville.

When the meal was over and they sat around their chosen fire drinking coffee, Britt eyed McGuire in the orange light between them and said, "Captain, I hate to ask this, but have there been any more officers murdered?"

"No, thank God. Many of the Fort Donelson men and I have talked about that since we arrived here. It looks like the assassin was either killed in the Fort Donelson battle or allowed himself to be captured and taken to the Union prison camp. If he was, as we suspect, a Union plant, it won't be hard to get himself out of the camp."

"Well, if I could vote on it," William Claiborne said, "I'd vote him killed in the battle and say good riddance."

Sergeants Cliff Nolan and Randall Weathers had been standing nearby and now joined them.

"Excuse us, gentlemen," Nolan said, "but Randall and I couldn't help but overhear your discussion."

"Sit down," gestured McGuire, adjusting his position to allow room for one man to sit next to him. The others followed suit, and the two sergeants sat down.

"Randall and I have talked about this with many of the men from Donelson," said Nolan, "and like Sergeant Claiborne here, we all hope the bloody fiend is dead."

Weathers slid his cap to the back of his head and spoke to McGuire. "Captain, we only got in on part of the conversation. Did you explain to these men that General Johnston has already advised the commanding officers to spread the word throughout the camp about what happened at Donelson?"

"I hadn't gotten that far," McGuire replied, pulling at his droopy mustache. Running his gaze over the faces of the new arrivals, he said, "Everybody is being warned that the killer could be amongst us and simply biding his time. There's been no move to institute the bodyguard program we had at Donelson as yet."

"Probably because General Johnston deep down believes the killer is dead," Weathers said. "We had a lot of men killed at Donelson. He sure could've been one of them."

Britt had been watching Gordon since the conversation about Donelson's assassin started. Gordon showed definite interest, but at times seemed preoccupied. Britt was about to question him about it when Nolan spoke to Gordon and said, "I saw you with these men earlier today, Captain, but didn't get to meet you." Extending his hand, he said, "I'm Sergeant Cliff Nolan."

"Wayne Gordon," smiled the amnesia victim, giving Nolan a firm grip.

Weathers introduced himself and shook Gordon's hand. "I don't remember seeing you at Donelson, Captain. I assume since you came in with these men that you were there."

Wayne glanced at Britt, then looked at Nolan and said, "I was there, Sergeant. Took a head wound in the battle. Of course, with some seventeen thousand troops there, no doubt a lot of us never got a real look at each other."

"What division were you in?" Weathers asked.

"I don't know, Sergeant."

"You don't know?"

Gordon removed his campaign hat, exposing the scar that ridged the left side of his head. "As you can see, I missed death by a fraction. However, the bullet jolted my head so hard, it stole away my memory."

"Amnesia?" Nolan asked.

Gordon nodded.

"I've heard of amnesia, but I've never met a person who had it." Nolan said.

Gordon knew he might as well tell his story. He took a half hour, giving every important detail, including his stay at the Claiborne farm. He left out the part about falling in love with Hannah Rose.

When it was time to turn in, Britt and Wayne found that they shared a tent. Lying in the darkness after putting out the lantern, Britt said, "Wayne?"

"Yes?"

"I noticed again your rapt attention when we were talking tonight about the Donelson assassin—like it meant something to you. Were you remembering something?"

"I...I don't think you could call it that. I wasn't getting any mental pictures. But the subject of an assassin killing Confederate officers seems familiar."

"That's all?"

"That's all."

"Well, maybe it'll come clearer as time passes. You know, like Doc Stutz told you. Maybe your memory will come back a little at a time."

"I hope so," Wayne responded, feeling a sharp pain in his heart. He thought of Hannah Rose and wondered if he would ever see her again.

As March went into its second week, General Johnston continued building up his forces at Corinth. Since the railroad was so vital, it would be patrolled and protected along the eighty-five-mile stretch all the way west to Memphis, and the sixty-five-mile stretch east to Florence, Alabama. General Ruggles's II Corps First Division shared with other units in patrolling the section to the west.

As soon as the patrolling started, small units of Federal troops began harassing the patrols. There were skirmishes every day.

On Friday, March 14, Captain Claiborne and his company of three hundred men were assigned a fifteen-mile stretch to patrol. Claiborne had ridden along the tracks that morning as he distributed his troops, assigning sections of track to patrol. Gordon rode with him.

Claiborne and Gordon stayed at the extreme western end of their assigned section until mid-afternoon, then headed back toward Corinth. There had been no sign of Yankees all day, for which Britt was thankful. They had been in a skirmish once a day for the past three days, and Gordon had shown himself quite adept. He was deadly accurate with both revolver and rifle.

The sun was throwing long shadows when Claiborne and Gordon neared the eastern end of their section. Both of them noticed a group of their men collected at the edge of the woods some thirty yards from the railroad track. They were standing in a circle and looking at something on the ground.

"I've got a feeling something's wrong," Britt said.

Both men put their horses to a gallop and quickly closed in. When the soldiers saw them coming, they broke the circle, revealing a man in an officer's uniform lying amid the long shadows of the trees.

Lieutenant Shawn O'Leary, face devoid of color, hurried to Claiborne as he was dismounting and said with shaky voice, "It's John Carmody, sir. He's been murdered!"

Without a word, Claiborne dashed to where Carmody lay face-down, a ten-inch knife protruding from his back.

"We haven't touched him, sir," O'Leary said. "I wanted you to see him just as we found him."

Claiborne felt the loss of Carmody deeply. Looking around at the men, he said in a tight voice, "This knife came from the cook shack at camp. The Fort Donelson assassin is still with us."

EIGHTEEN

When Lieutenant Carmody's body was brought in draped over his saddle, word of his murder spread rapidly throughout the camp. The men who had been at Fort Donelson were sick at heart to learn that the killer had only been lying low.

Captain Claiborne questioned the men of Carmody's unit, but not one of them had seen anything that could give a clue as to whether the assassin was even a part of their unit. Since the murder had taken place at the edge of the woods, the killer could have been any one of a number of men-in-gray who were moving about the area.

That night, General Johnston gathered the troops and instructed the unit commanders to begin the bodyguard plan that had been used at Fort Donelson. Johnston ordered each officer present to choose two bodyguards. Since all the officers shared tents at night, they agreed to choose their bodyguards in the morning. The bodyguards would stick as close as possible to the officers from sunup to bedtime every day.

The meeting broke up, and the men prepared to retire for the night. Captain Thomas Sundeen of Second Division II Corps shared a tent with Lieutenant Billy John Axel. Sundeen visited one of the latrines at the edge of the camp, then threaded his way amongst milling men, tents, and campfires to his own tent. Carrying his lantern inside, he pulled off his boots, removed his uniform, and slid into his bedroll. Soon things were quiet, and Sundeen knew that just about everybody except the sentries had retired for the night. No more voices could be heard.

Where was Billy John Axel?

Sundeen waited another five minutes, and when Axel still had not appeared, he left the bedroll, pushed the flap aside, and stuck his head out. Campfires all around were dwindling to embers. He could vaguely make out sentries patrolling the edge of the area. But there was no sign of the young lieutenant.

Worry scratched at the back of his mind as Sundeen put his clothes on and left the tent. He was hoping to find a cluster of men in conversation somewhere, but there were no men to be seen but the sentries. He approached the sentries one by one, asking if they had seen Lieutenant Axel. None had.

He decided if Axel was not at the tent by now, he would report him missing to Colonel Aaron White, commander of their regiment. When Sundeen arrived at the tent, Axel had not shown up. He picked up his lantern and went to the colonel's tent. White was disturbed at the news and ordered an immediate search.

All the men of Second Division were rousted from their tents, and began searching about in small groups. Men of other units soon joined the search. After nearly a half hour, Sergeant Ralph Ederly and Corporal Donald Yockey approached a gurgling brook swollen from the recent rains. The brook was a few yards from the edge of the woods that encircled the camp, winding its way amid the trees. Several men had already entered the woods at other places and were moving along the banks of the stream.

Suddenly Yockey pointed through the trees. "Look, Sergeant!"

Hastening together, the two soldiers came upon Axel's lifeless form. He was face-down on the bank, his head submerged in the water.

Ederly and Yockey shouted to the other searchers and were

soon surrounded. Standing over the body, which was well-illuminated by lanterns, Colonel White pointed out the signs of struggle on the bank. A canteen lay nearby. Apparently the young lieutenant had gone to fill his canteen before going to bed and was followed by the assassin. He was attacked from behind and overpowered by the killer, who forced his head under the water until he had drowned.

By the time Axel's body was carried into the camp, all the officers were up, including every one of the generals. General Johnston swore that when the killer was caught, he would be sorry he had ever been born.

Before the officers returned to their tents, a number of enlisted men sought them out and offered their services as bodyguards. The officers said they would make their choices in the morning.

Wayne Gordon lay in his tent, listening to Britt Claiborne's even breathing and wondering why the assassin's deeds picked at his brain. There was something familiar about the situation, but it just wouldn't surface. Soon his thoughts turned to Hannah Rose, and he recalled an old saying: *Absence makes the heart grow fonder*. He could vouch for that. He missed her greatly, and the love in his heart was growing.

He was about to drop off to sleep when he remembered the face of a beautiful young woman, whose name apparently was Julie. He could still picture her features clearly, but he could not recall who she was nor how she fit into his life.

Bringing his thoughts back to Hannah Rose, he finally drifted off to sleep.

Dawn came at the Claiborne farm on Saturday morning, March 15. Hannah Rose awakened and found that the man she loved was on her mind. This was the way it had been since Wayne Gordon had left. He was on her mind continuously through every day. Tears spilled down the sides of her face as she lay on her back, raised her eyes heavenward, and said, "Dear Lord, I need Your help. Please strengthen me. You know all about Wayne and his past. If...if it turns out that he has a wife, I'm going to need Your grace to see me through the heartache."

After breakfast on Saturday morning, March 15, the officers in the Confederate camp at Corinth, Mississippi, chose the men they wanted as bodyguards. Captain Claiborne picked out two men he knew well and trusted—Sergeant Weathers and a corporal named Derek Wilson. Captain Gordon chose Sergeant Nolan and a private who had impressed him during one of the skirmishes. The private was a young man from Dayton, Tennessee, named Saul Hendley.

Around seven o'clock that morning, Captain Claiborne and his company of three hundred reached the starting point of their assigned fifteen-mile section. A third of the men were left at that point, and the others moved on west. When they reached the ten-mile point, the second hundred fanned out along the track, and the remainder moved on with the two captains.

Claiborne and Gordon rode slowly allowing the footmen to keep pace. As they rounded a bend, Gordon looked north and saw black smoke billowing up above a stand of trees some eight or nine hundred yards in the distance. "Looks like we've got a train coming our way."

"Supply train from Memphis," Claiborne said casually. "General Bragg said something yesterday about one due in sometime soon."

They kept moving north, watching for sight of the train on the tracks. Soon the smokestack appeared, belching black smoke, then the rest of the engine came into view, and the sound of its chugging reached their ears. Four boxcars followed the coal car. When the train was within a hundred yards of them, it started to slow down.

Gordon glanced at Claiborne and asked, "Why would they be stopping?"

"I don't know. Has to be some reason."

Motioning for his men to halt, Claiborne pushed his horse ahead of the troops to talk to the engineer when the train stopped. Gordon stayed right beside him. Clouds of steam boiled from the sides of the engine as the big steel wheels began to squeal against the tracks.

Suddenly, Gordon saw the barrel of a rifle flash in the sun, followed by another. "Look out!" he shouted, leaping from his horse and knocking Claiborne out of the saddle. They had not hit the ground yet when the air seemed to explode with gunfire.

The four cars were loaded with Yankees. Some were firing from the train, while others piled out and fired from the ground.

Claiborne's men quickly returned fire, though several had gone down in the first volley. Britt looked around amid the bedlam, looking for a place to lead his men. If they stayed where they were, they were easy targets.

Off to the west was a deep gully, lined with naked-limbed bushes. The gully would offer some protection. Shouting above the roar of battle, Claiborne commanded his troops to head for the gully.

Just as Claiborne issued his order, Gordon put a bullet into the man who had commandeered the big engine. The Yankee grabbed his chest and tumbled to the ground.

The first volley of return fire had driven most of the Yankees back into the cars, or under them. This gave the Confederates a slight reprieve, and they darted to the gully for cover. Once over the edge, they began firing back through the bushes.

Yankee bullets hissed through the bushes, and Rebel bullets chewed into railroad cars and ricocheted off the engine. Both sides took numerous hits.

The battle area soon was enveloped in drifting clouds of smoke and dust. Claiborne told Gordon and his two bodyguards to remain where they were. He was going to take Weathers and Wilson and move a few yards to the left. Three Rebels who had been fighting from that spot now lay dead. Just as they raised up to shift positions, a Yankee slug tore into Corporal Wilson. He went down and lay still.

There was no time to check on him. Bullets buzzed over the edge of the gully like angry hornets.

Claiborne and Weathers reached the spot and continued firing toward the train. Off to Gordon's right, another gap formed in the line when two Rebels went down. Quickly, Gordon commanded Nolan and Hendley to fill the gap. They were reluctant to leave him, but knew they must obey. Soon they were firing from that position. Gordon could barely see them through the thick pall of dust and smoke.

Gordon felt the breath of a bullet as it hummed by his left cheek. He returned fire, taking out another Yankee, who was firing from the coal car. Gordon ducked down to reload, but as he did, a Yankee private, wild-eyed and screeching, charged at him through the brush, bayonet poised for the kill. Gordon dodged the deadly blade. The Yankee stumbled past him, slid to his rump, then whirled about, ready to charge again.

Gordon had no time to load his revolver. He threw it at the Yankee's face as hard as he could. It struck him square between the eyes, knocking him backward down the slope. Gordon hastened after him, grabbed the rifle from his loosened grip, and plunged the bayonet into his heart.

Gordon wheeled and picked up his empty revolver. There was a deep gouge in the bank of the gully three steps away. He dived into it for cover and reloaded his gun.

Claiborne and Weathers were still fighting side-by-side several yards to Gordon's left, and now, quite a ways above him. Weathers dropped down to shove another cartridge into his carbine. When the cartridge was in place, Weathers looked both ways along the gully. The men to his left were some distance away, hidden by smoke and dust. He looked quickly to the right and saw no one where Gordon and his bodyguards had been. His eye caught sight of Wilson's crumpled form on the dusty slope, but the dust and smoke further along the gully completely hid Nolan and Hendley from his view.

Weathers smiled to himself. The perfect moment had come.

He would aim his carbine at Claiborne's head, then call out to him. When the captain turned, Weathers would squeeze the trigger. He would then rush to the men off to his left and tell them the captain had taken a Yankee bullet in the face.

Down the slope, Gordon snapped the cylinder shut, cocked the hammer, and raised up to climb back to the crest of the gully. Just as his head came up, the smoke cleared, and he looked toward the spot where Claiborne was firing away. For a second, he couldn't believe his eyes. Sergeant Weathers was flanking Claiborne and aiming his carbine at his head.

There was no time for anything but action. Gordon took aim and fired. The slug tore through Weathers's head at an upward angle, splattering Claiborne with blood. The impact of the slug threw the carbine's muzzle off target just enough to miss Claiborne's head when it discharged. Weathers went down like a brain-shot steer.

Claiborne turned and saw Gordon and the smoking revolver in his hand. Then he looked to the would-be assassin who lay at his feet. His ears were ringing.

There was a sudden whoop of elation from his men along the line. All firing stopped at the train, and when Claiborne turned to see what was happening, a smile broke across his face. The men he left at the ten-mile point had heard the gunfire and had come on the run. They were now closing in, guns ready for action, but the reduced unit of Yankees had lost their will to fight. They were throwing down their guns and raising their hands in surrender.

Claiborne took another look at the dead man at his feet and said to Gordon, "I owe you for my life twice today."

"Just doing my duty," Gordon grinned.

The captains hurried through the bushes together, and Britt Claiborne led in the capture of a hundred and fifty-nine Yankees, forty-four of whom were wounded. Thirty-one were dead.

A quick tally showed thirty-nine Rebels dead and thirty-five wounded. Claiborne found a man amongst those who had just come to the rescue that knew how to run the engine. They loaded the dead in the last car, the unscathed prisoners into the third car under guard, and all the wounded in the first and second cars. The train moved off toward Corinth, and the remainder stayed to patrol what stretch of the track they could reasonably cover.

While the men stood in a circle around them, Claiborne and Gordon discussed the shooting of Sergeant Weathers. Everyone was shocked, but none more than Claiborne. "Randall was one of the men I chose to be my bodyguard," he said. "I trusted the man with my life."

Blanchard and Ederly, who had been close companions to Weathers, assured Claiborne they were in a state of shock also. They never dreamed Weathers could be a Union plant.

"No offense to Corporal Wilson, sir, but I'm surprised you didn't ask for your brothers to be your bodyguards," one of the men said.

"Well, as you know, William and Robert have been assigned to another company. I suppose I could've requested that they be reassigned so they could play bodyguard for me, but I had no reason to distrust Wilson or Weathers. Well, at least there won't have to be any bodyguards anymore, thanks to Captain Gordon here." The men whistled and applauded.

"Just doing my duty," Gordon said with embarrassment.

There was elation throughout the camp that evening when the news of the assassin's death was announced. Now everyone could concentrate on the upcoming battle with the Union army.

That night Gordon lay awake for some time, his emotions stirred, as he thought of the two times he had saved Britt Claiborne's life. He was amazed that he had reacted so naturally, especially when he had but a second or two to make the decision to shoot Weathers. There seemed to be absolute confidence that he would do it successfully. Wondering once again what he had been before the war, he soon fell into slumber.

He found himself standing in a large yard, surrounded by towering trees, bushes, and flower gardens. A young woman was running toward him, arms open and smiling. It was the same face he had seen in the flashback. Julie. She was in brilliant sunlight with a large white, two-story house in the background.

Julie was coming closer and her features growing plainer. She was about to wrap her arms around him when he woke up.

Gordon sat bolt upright in the dark, breathing hard. His heart was pounding. He could hear Claiborne's soft, even breathing beside him in the tent. Cold sweat beaded his brow. The dream had been so real, so incredibly real.

Lying back down, he stared into the darkness and relived the dream over and over again. Julie. Beautiful woman. My wife? Or maybe just a girlfriend? Fiancée? My sister? No, the look in her eyes was not sisterly.

The big white house. The yard. Familiar? Yes.

Gordon strained to make the picture broaden and give him more. But no matter how many times he went over it in his mind, there was always the large yard, surrounded by tall trees, thick with branches and heavy with green leaves. Cottonwoods. Yes! And oaks. And the bushes were…lilacs! Flower gardens. Small and beautiful, placed in strategic spots of the yard. Julie, coming toward him off the porch of the big white house. The house. He tried to picture what it looked like inside—upstairs, downstairs, the kitchen, the parlor. But nothing would come. What he could see was plain and clear. He had lived that scene in his life, possibly many times.

Yes. Julie had bounded off the porch many times and run toward him, smiling, open-armed, with lovelight in her eyes. This was not just a dream. These were memories.

But there was nothing more. Nothing for him to cling to but brief, haunting, shadowed memories.

There were continual skirmishes along the railroad line until the beginning of the fourth week of March. Suddenly no more Yankee troops were seen in the forests or fields that skirted the tracks. The Federals, who knew that General Johnston was gathering troops by the thousands at Corinth, were moving that direction for a giant assault. General Grant had directed the establishment of a Union camp at Pittsburgh Landing, Tennessee, a transfer point for goods and supplies shipped from the Tennessee River to Corinth, twenty-two miles to the southwest. In command at the Pittsburgh Landing camp was Brigadier General William Tecumseh Sherman, a close friend of Grant.

When Grant arrived on the scene on Thursday, March 27, he established his headquarters at Savannah, Tennessee, a river town eight miles north of Pittsburgh Landing. Grant moved into a large southern mansion, forcing the family to go elsewhere.

The next morning, Grant steamed down the river in his command boat, the *Tigress*, and met with Sherman. Grant looked the area over and liked the terrain. Sherman had bivouacked his army on a rough plateau that rolled westward from the high bluffs overlooking the Tennessee River. The encampment was protected, not only by the Tennessee, but by its tributaries, Owl and Snake Creeks in the north, and Lick Creek to the south, all of them in flood stage and twenty-five feet deep in places.

The terrain was heavily forested, dotted with farmland and orchards, and slashed by deep, narrow ravines.

Sherman had set up his headquarters on a wooded hillside a short distance away in a one-room log building known as "Shiloh Church." It had been erected long before by the Methodists, but was seldom used. A small settlement nearby had been named Shiloh, taking its name from the church.

Little did Grant and Sherman realize the irony of the place they chose to establish the Union camp. The Confederates were thought to be demoralized after the Fort Donelson defeat, and neither man expected to be attacked by them. Their plan was to establish the camp within a day's march of Corinth and launch an attack on the disheartened Confederates. Surprisingly, the Confederates were the ones to carry the battle to the Federals at their encampment. One of the bloodiest battles of the Civil War would take place at Shiloh, "the place of peace."

NINETEEN

At Corinth, Generals Albert Sidney Johnston and Pierre G.T. Beauregard were working feverishly to shape the incoming troops into a working army. There was little time to spare. Johnston had roughly forty thousand men. He was fully aware that General Don Carlos Buell was on his way to Shiloh with somewhere around thirty-five thousand troops. Scouts reported that Buell and his army were delayed by bad weather, but were expected to arrive at Shiloh on Sunday, April 6.

Johnston knew Grant had about forty thousand troops at Shiloh, and once Buell arrived, the Confederates would be outnumbered two to one. Johnston and Beauregard knew what their strategy had to be: *strike Grant before Buell reaches Shiloh.*

Since Beauregard had proven his skill at military organization, Johnston assigned him to assemble the Army of the Mississippi into four corps, each with two or more divisions. The officers appointed as corps commanders were distinguished men. Major General John C. Breckinridge, who headed a corps of sixty-four hundred men, had been vice-president of the United States under James Buchanan. Major General Leonidas Polk, an Episcopal bishop and a graduate of West Point, commanded a corps of ninety-one hundred men.

Major General William J. Hardee, whose corps had sixty-eight hundred men, was a capable military tactician who had served as commandant of cadets at West Point. The fourth commander was the rough-and-ready Major General Braxton Bragg, a West Pointer who had served with distinction in the Mexican War. Bragg led the largest corps, a crack unit of just under eighteen thousand men. On March 31, Captain Wayne Gordon was given command of a company of three hundred men, under Bragg. Captain Britt Claiborne, given troops to replace those killed during the railroad skirmishes, also commanded a company of three hundred.

Late in the third week of March, General Johnston had sent for Major General Earl Van Dorn, who had been given command of the Confederate forces in northern Arkansas on March 3. Van Dorn had led his troops into battle against the Federal forces at Pea Ridge, Arkansas, on March 7 and 8. The Yankees outmaneuvered them, and on the second day of battle, Van Dorn found it necessary to withdraw and head south. The Federals did not pursue them, and Van Dorn led his troops to a spot east of Little Rock to regroup.

The rider who had carried Johnston's message to Van Dorn returned to say that Van Dorn would begin the march the next day. In his message to Johnston, he estimated their arrival at Corinth on April 1 or 2.

At Shiloh, Grant was still complacent about the enemy forces camped just twenty-two miles away. This was reflected in the haphazard arrangements of the army's campsites. Five of the six divisions were located in the narrow plateau-like triangle of land between the creeks which extended southwest from Pittsburgh Landing.

These five divisions were commanded by intelligent and well-seasoned men: Major General John A. McClernand, Brigadier General W.H.L. Wallace, Brigadier General Stephen A. Hurlbut, Brigadier General William T. Sherman, and Brigadier General

Benjamin A. Prentiss. The remaining division, commanded by Major General Lew Wallace, was posted five miles north of Shiloh at Crump's Landing.

(Lew Wallace was a practicing attorney before entering the U.S. Army to fight in the Mexican War. He also was a poet, a playwright, and an author, and was known to be an unbeliever and skeptic. He often spoke against the Bible and took a humanistic approach to life. After the Civil War, he returned to Indianapolis and resumed his law practice. Shortly thereafter, Wallace met a preacher on a train and maligned him for his "blind faith" in the Bible and for believing that Jesus Christ was virgin born. The preacher gave Wallace a Bible, daring him to read it. Wallace took the dare, and within a matter of weeks, wrote to the preacher, telling him that he had put his faith in Jesus Christ for salvation. The lawyer-soldier-writer had successfully published historical novels in the past. While governor of New Mexico [1878-1881], Wallace wrote a biblical novel on the earthly life and crucifixion of Jesus Christ, titled *Ben Hur*.)

General Grant had employed no system in arranging his camps. The divisions of Sherman and Prentiss, made up of the rawest recruits, occupied the most vulnerable positions. Sherman's camp constituted the right flank of the advanced line and covered the main approach to Pittsburgh Landing from Corinth. Prentiss's division—so raw they had just drawn their muskets—was situated to Sherman's left, the most exposed if an attack came.

Neither Grant nor any of his generals expected an attack, however. Camp Shiloh was not fortified at all. Some young recruit suggested to his commanding officer that they dig trenches for protection just in case. He was disdained for such thinking. Early in the Civil War, entrenching for battle was considered cowardly. The Union generals at Shiloh were in one accord with Grant—entrenching would ruin the morale of their men and convey an impression of weakness to the enemy.

At Corinth on the evening of April 2, General Johnston paced the sod floor of his command tent. General Van Dorn had not arrived with his sixteen thousand men, and he couldn't wait much longer to launch the attack. Word had come that day that Buell's troops had cleared the worst obstacles caused by the heavy rains and were marching rapidly to join Grant.

Johnston wondered if it was raining heavily in eastern Arkansas.

He heard footsteps outside his tent, then Beauregard's voice. "General Johnston, sir!"

Moving to the flap, Johnston pulled it open and saw General Bragg with Beauregard. He stepped aside to allow them entrance. "Come in, gentlemen," Johnston said. "I know why you're here."

"Good, sir," said Beauregard. "General Bragg and I have been talking. We're going to have to move toward Shiloh at dawn, whether Van Dorn and his troops are here or not. Buell could put his men to a trot and get to Grant early. We must strike *now*."

Johnston nodded and rubbed his chin. "I'd sure love to have those extra sixteen thousand men, but I was about to call for the two of you. We must hit Grant at dawn day after tomorrow."

Orders to corps commanders were drafted by Johnston immediately. They were to be ready to march at dawn. One day's march would put them in position to attack the Union camp at Shiloh at dawn on April 4.

Beauregard had devised the plan of attack. He called the other three corps commanders to join Bragg and himself in his tent. Beauregard did not take the time to write out the orders. While Breckinridge, Polk, Hardee, and Bragg stood before him by lantern light, Beauregard explained an intricate pattern of march to accommodate the heavy traffic of infantry, artillery, cavalry, and supply wagons on the two roads that led to Shiloh. The infantry and artillery would take the road on the west; the cavalry and supply wagons the one on the east. The roads converged seven miles from Camp Shiloh at a crossroads known as Mickey's, named after a house that stood there. The army was to rendezvous at the crossroads, then move up under the direction of the corps leaders and form battle lines.

Beauregard's scheme was for three corps to attack the Union camp in three successive lines, each spread evenly across a three-mile front. Hardee's corps would attack first, followed by Bragg and Polk. Breckinridge's corps would remain in reserve for service wherever they were needed most once the battle was under way.

The next day, when the Confederate army was converging at Mickey's crossroads, Hardee's corps of sixty-eight hundred were not there. The army was stalled. Beauregard was told that Hardee had refused to move his men from Corinth because the army manual stated that orders for an attack must be given in writing. He would not move toward Shiloh until he had written orders from Beauregard.

Angry at Hardee's obstinacy, Beauregard quickly wrote out the orders and sent them back to Corinth with a rider. The sun was setting by the time Hardee's corps arrived. There was not enough time to move the rest of the way and set up for the attack at dawn. Beauregard pushed back the attack date to April 5. The forty thousand men, their animals and equipment, spent the night bivouacked in farmers' fields.

A cold rain began to fall in torrents and continued heavily all the next day. The roads became vast pools of water and pockets of mud. The attack would have to be delayed yet another day.

The skies cleared during the night, and on the morning of April 5, the sun shafted its cheerful light over the soggy fields where the Rebels huddled under wagons and trees, anywhere they could find shelter. The sun's cheer failed to reach the men-in-gray, who were soaked to the skin and chilled to the bone.

After a breakfast of cold rations, the corps leaders made preparations to move out. Though it was only seven miles to where they would make ready to launch the attack the next morning, they knew the going would be slow. Cannons and wagons sank to their hubs in the mire, and infantry units, trying to help out, became separated, resulting in commands intermixing.

By the time the Confederates reached the staging area, the sun was setting. Weary as they were, General Johnston knew they dare not wait. The attack would be launched at dawn the next morning, Sunday April 6, 1862.

Strict silence was the code in the Confederate camp that night. All talking must be done in low tones. Captain Wayne Gordon lay on a damp, grassy mound, glad for some rest. Since his company had been positioned next to Britt Claiborne's company, the two captains lay side-by-side on the mound. Next to Britt were his brothers, who had been assigned to his company.

While the stars twinkled overhead, Britt said softly, "Wayne, this is going to be a huge battle. If you make it through and I don't...will you get a message to Donna Mae for me?"

"Don't talk like that, Britt. You're going to make it."

"But if the Lord sees fit to take me..."

"If He does, what would you like me to tell her?"

"Just that I love her."

"But she already knows that."

"Tell her anyway, okay?"

"Okay."

From Britt's other side, William spoke up. "Wayne?"

"Yeah, I'll tell Sally Marie that you love her," Gordon said in a kidding manner. Without lifting his head, he said, "Robert, who should I tell for you?"

"Just my sisters and sisters-in-law."

All was silent for a few moments, then Britt said, "Wayne?"

"Yeah?"

"Just in case it would be you who didn't make it...any messages?"

"Yes, one."

"Hannah Rose?"

"Who else? Tell her I died with her on my mind…and in my heart."

"I will," Britt whispered, and fell silent.

In the middle of the night, Gordon sat up on the mound, his breath coming in short spurts. He had experienced the same dream again. The big yard, towering trees, flower gardens, the white house…and Julie running toward him, eyes full of love, smiling, arms outstretched. Again he had awakened just before they touched.

Lying back down, he told himself Julie was only an old flame and not his wife. He hoped it was true. He was in love with Hannah Rose, and he wanted to live through the war and spend the rest of his life as her husband.

Lying under a mulberry bush, General Beauregard was about to drift off to sleep when he heard the sound of a harmonica nearby. Sitting up, he swore under his breath. Beauregard whispered to his aide, "Corporal, find that man and tell him to shut that thing off. And bring his name to me!"

"Yes, sir," Jimmy Watts said, and hurried away toward the sound.

The general waited, and the harmonica kept playing. It was still playing when Watts returned.

"Didn't you tell him to shut up?" Beauregard hissed.

"No, sir. I'd have to go into enemy territory to do it, sir."

"What? What are you talking about?"

"The man playing the harmonica is in a Union camp just across that shallow gully over there, sir."

The general was stunned. He had no idea the two armies lay so close together.

Incredibly, the southernmost Union camp did not know that forty thousand enemy soldiers were lying on the cool, damp ground just beyond their picket line.

The surprise attack never happened.

At 3:00 A.M. on Sunday, April 6, Union Colonel Everett Peabody was awakened by Major James Powell of the Twenty-fifth Missouri Brigade. Peabody was a thirty-one-year-old Harvard graduate who commanded a brigade in General Benjamin Prentiss's division. With Powell was Lieutenant Frederick Klinger, also of the Twenty-fifth Missouri.

Klinger, a young German with pale blue eyes, had been awakened ten minutes earlier by a youthful private who had decided to desert. The private had slipped out of camp just after midnight, and losing his sense of direction, had gone south instead of north. When he had passed the southernmost Union camp, he came upon the great mass of men spread out in the fields. He could make out the Confederate flag on a staff attached to a supply wagon.

Suddenly he couldn't find it in himself to desert. He returned to the camp and awakened Klinger.

Peabody asked in anger who the soldier was, but Klinger had had to promise the soldier anonymity before he would tell why he had awakened him. Klinger felt the Colonel should honor his promise in light of the news he was bringing.

Peabody wasn't sure he believed the anonymous private. He wanted word that he knew was reliable. Powell volunteered to make a reconnaissance mission and see for himself. Peabody approved it, but told him to take three hundred men with him. Just before dawn, Powell, Klinger, and the three hundred men drew near the Confederate camp.

The Rebels were already up, preparing to launch their surprise attack, and the Yankees ran into Major Aaron Hardcastle's Third Mississippi Infantry Battalion, the advance guard of General Hardee's Third Brigade. Hardcastle's troops opened fire and fell back. The Federals answered with a volley of their own and moved forward. A long line of Rebels kneeling on bushy high ground just ahead opened fire on the advancing Yankees, and Lieutenant Klinger went down, the first man to die in the battle of Shiloh.

Powell and his men took cover and began to fight back. It was the beginning of what General Sherman would call "the devil's own day."

Hearing heavy firing, the Yankees in the adjacent camp scrambled for their weapons. Farther back, Peabody ordered the long drum roll, calling the Union soldiers to get out of their bedrolls, grab their weapons, and form a battle line. By the time they reached the front, the whole Confederate line was moving, thousands upon thousands of men advancing at once. The Federals fell back, sounding the alarm to their sleeping comrades in nearby camps.

General Johnston commanded Beauregard to stay in the rear and direct men and supplies as needed, unwittingly relinquishing control of the battle to Beauregard. Johnston rode forward amongst his troops, shouting, "Onward, men! We'll water our horses in the Tennessee River tonight!" The long day of battle was under way.

Around Johnston, long lines of grim, silent men marched through a heavy gray mist that hovered at the tops of the trees. Soon the sun began to burn off the mist and a perfect Tennessee spring day was in the offing.

Grant heard at his headquarters the dull roar of cannon. He cut short his breakfast to steam down the Tennessee River on the *Tigress*. On his way, he stopped at Crump's Landing and ordered General Wallace to hold his division in readiness. Grant, who had been so sure the Rebels would not attack, was still not sure he had a battle on his hands. Wallace told Grant his men were ready now. Grant told him to sit tight.

It was just before 9:00 A.M. when Grant got his horse ashore and put it in a trot toward the sounds of battle. As he reached the front, he found Prentiss's line on the verge of collapse. A Confederate bayonet charge, sent in by General Beauregard, swept across three hundred yards of open field and pushed Prentiss's Sixth Division back to their camp. Peabody, bleeding from four wounds, rode his horse in a gallop among the tents, attempting to rally the battered Yankees for another stand. A swarm of Rebels attacked from the nearby woods, and a bullet struck Peabody in the head, killing him instantly. Prentiss's division held briefly in the camp as the Rebels came on, then broke and scattered.

Fresh Union troops moving up encountered the men of Sixth Division as they scattered. Prentiss's men, wild-eyed, were screaming, "The Rebels are coming! They'll cut you to pieces! Run! The Rebels are coming!"

The panicked troops clogged the road and infuriated the troops trying to advance. The newcomers shouted at the fleeing soldiers, calling them cowards and traitors, but nothing could stop them from running for Pittsburgh Landing. The number of Yankees hiding at the river's edge grew all morning, running into the hundreds.

The Shiloh battlefield soon stretched over a line three miles in length. Along the Confederate artillery lines, officers shouted "Shrapnel! Canister!" to the loaders and gunners. Deep-throated cannons thundered and howitzers roared as the morning breeze carried thick clouds of blue-white smoke over the bloody, body-strewn fields.

When the Yankees wheeled in their artillery to fight back, the cry was heard along the Rebel lines, "Double shrapnel! Double canister!" The Confederate cannons fired with such rapidity that the separate discharges were blended into one continuous roar.

On an adjacent open field, opposing infantrymen moved toward each other in tight phalanxes, their gunfire sending forth a sheet of flame and leaden hail that elicited curses, shrieks, groans, and shouts. Men and mere boys dropped like flies, some dead before they fell, others dying within seconds. Still others lay in pain and agony, mortally wounded.

By 9:30, all of General Breckinridge's Rebel reserves had been called into action. Every Confederate man on the field was engaged in the battle. Johnston and Beauregard were still looking for Van Dorn's troops to show up.

Except for Wallace and his division, who were still at Crump's Landing some five miles north, Grant had every Yankee soldier in the battle. He was unhappy the way the battle was going, but expected to see Buell and his men coming in from the north at any time.

The horrid work of death was underway in the fields and thickets and along the creek banks that surrounded the little settlement called Shiloh.

As the sun moved slowly upward, the din of battle carried across the rolling hills. There was the steady *pum-pum* of the big guns, the roar of the howitzers, the shrieking of the shells, and the thunder of their explosions. Punctuating all of this ear-splitting noise was the steady rattle of musketry, the shouting of soldiers, and the cries of the wounded and dying. Great masses of men hurled death into each other's faces, lost in the blaze, the thunder, the excitement, the frenzy of combat.

In the midst of the battle, Gordon noticed a farmhouse some three hundred yards down the road. He could see the farmer, his wife, and young son standing on the porch, clinging to each other as they beheld the fire, smoke, and carnage of battle. A few minutes later, a half-dozen Yankees broke from the battle area and ran toward the farmhouse. Gordon knew the farmer and his family were in trouble. The Yankees would hole up in the house and use it as a fort.

"You two stay here and keep shooting!" Gordon shouted to Sergeants Ederly and Blanchard, who were on either side of him.

"Where you going?" asked Ederly, ducking as a Yankee slug chewed into a rail above his head and whined away angrily.

"Some Yankees heading for that farmhouse over there! I saw the family on the porch a few minutes ago. I'll pick up some men along the line so as not to leave a gap anywhere."

With that, Gordon crawled for several yards, then leaped to his feet and, bending low, tapped men on the shoulder as he ran along the line.

At the farmhouse, Eldon Coffman shoved his wife Mary and eight-year-old son Danny into the parlor closet. "Get down on the floor! Be quiet and don't move, no matter what!" he told them.

Mary's lips trembled and fear filled her eyes as she cried, "Eldon, they'll kill you!"

"Maybe not, honey. Maybe they'll take what they want and leave. Please, don't move or make any sounds." He started to close the door, checked himself, and said, "Danny, you hold your mother's hand. Take care of her. Okay?"

"Yes, sir," nodded the frightened boy.

Coffman thought of the handgun he kept in the desk drawer in the parlor, but he knew he was no match for the six Yankees running across the field toward his house. He could only hope they would take what they wanted and move on.

He moved to the front door and stepped out on the porch. The sounds of battle rolled across the fields as the soldiers ran onto the porch, gasping for breath.

"What do you want?" Coffman asked, running his gaze over their young faces. They were all under twenty and without rank.

The one who seemed to be their leader said, "We want your house, and we're takin' it."

"What for?" Coffman asked.

The leader looked toward the door. "Your family inside?"

"No. They're away visiting relatives."

"Let's go see," he said gruffly, shoving the farmer toward the door.

When they entered the parlor, one of the soldiers said, "You look healthy enough to me, fella. How come you ain't in a gray uniform?"

"Farmer exemption," replied Coffman, irritated. "Somebody has to provide food for the army."

The leader, Kent Frye, barked an order for the others to search the house. As they scattered through the one-story frame structure, Frye looked Coffman in the eye and said, "I sure hope you didn't lie to me, mister. If we find anyone else in the house, you die!"

The sounds of soldiers stomping into room after room, opening and slamming doors, filled the house. Coffman trembled inside and hoped they would overlook the closet in the parlor.

Soon the five searchers were back. "Guess he's tellin' the truth, Kent. Nobody here," one of them said.

"Better check the outbuildings. We just don't need any surprises."

Coffman's heart pounded like a mad thing in his chest. They wouldn't find anyone in the barn, sheds, or privy, but if they took over the house, they would find his wife and son sooner or later. His only hope was to admit he had hid them, and ask the Yankees to let the three of them go. They could have the house.

Drawing a shuddering breath, he said, "No need to search the outbuildings, private. My family is here. I hope you…can understand that a man's natural duty is to protect his family."

Frye's angry eyes bored into the farmer. "You lied to me, southern man."

"I just didn't want my family harmed!"

"Where are they?" Frye demanded.

"You can have the house, private," Coffman said. "Just let me take my family and leave. Okay?"

"Where are they?"

"You haven't answered my question."

Frye's face reddened. "You die!"

"No-o-o!" Mary Coffman cried as she flung open the closet door and burst into the room. She had covered Danny with clothes and told him to lie still.

All eyes followed Mary as she dashed to her husband, flung her arms around him, and screamed at the enemy soldiers, "Leave him alone! He's no threat to you! Like he said, you can have the house! Just let us go!"

"We know that, lady," Frye said, looking her up and down, "but he lied to me, and I told him he'd die if he did. I ain't goin' back on my word."

Frye pulled an officer's pistol from under his belt and said, "Grab her, Alex."

Coffman's arms were around his wife. Jerking her from Alex's reach, he blared, "Don't you touch her!"

Frye's eyes blazed as he cocked the pistol, placed the muzzle against the farmer's temple, and barked, "Let go of her!"

Reluctantly, Coffman released Mary from his arms. She was shaking all over and her lips were quivering as Alex took hold of an arm and pulled her aside.

Frye grinned malevolently, backed up several steps, and leveled the gun on Coffman's chest. The farmer said shakily, "You have no reason to kill me. If I was in a gray uniform it would be different, but I'm no threat to you. What kind of man are you?"

"Shut up, you stinkin' Tennessee plowboy! You lied to me." Narrowing his eyes, Frye said, "Besides, you said *family*—where's the rest of them?"

"There aren't any others. That's just my way of referring to my wife." Even as the words left his mouth, Coffman knew he had made a grave mistake. The soldiers had been in Danny's room. They knew at least one boy lived in the house.

"He's lyin' again!" one of them said. "There's a boy's bedroom back there."

Frye cursed Coffman and raised his revolver. Just before he fired, Coffman ducked, and the bullet struck him in the upper left shoulder. The impact turned him halfway around before he fell to the floor. Mary screamed, jerked loose from Alex, and threw herself at Frye, raking his eyes with her fingernails. He howled and yelled for the others to get her off him. Five Yankees converged on Mary, trying to pull her loose, but she was fighting like a wildcat.

Suddenly the front door burst open and Wayne Gordon bellowed, "That's enough. Leave the woman alone."

The Yankees looked around to see the room filling with gray uniforms. Alex also had an officer's revolver under his belt, and he jerked it out and brought it to bear on Gordon. Rebel guns boomed, and Alex went down.

At the same time Alex was going for his gun, Frye cursed at the gray blur before his wounded eyes and raised his revolver, cocking the hammer. Gordon's pistol roared, drilling Frye through the heart. He was dead before his body slumped to the floor.

The other four Yankees threw their guns down and raised their hands, begging the Rebels not to shoot.

Gordon motioned toward them and said to his men, "Get them out of here!"

Mary was kneeling beside her bleeding husband, checking his wound. A trembling voice came from the closet, "Mama!"

Mary looked around. The Rebel captain was standing over her, and the prisoners were being ushered outside with their hands in the air. Frye and the one called Alex lay dead on the floor.

Calling toward the closet, Mary said, "You can come out, Danny!"

Quickly the boy dashed from the closet, eyes wild with fear, and knelt beside his mother. She wrapped an arm around him, pulled him close, and half-whispered, "It's all right, honey. The Yankees won't hurt us now."

Danny looked at the two dead men-in-blue, then at his father.

"Papa's all right, son," the farmer assured him.

Danny looked to his mother for assurance. "It's only a shoulder wound, honey," she said softly. "Papa will be all right."

"Will you need some medical help, ma'am?" Gordon asked.

"I don't think so, Captain, thank you," she replied, looking up at him and trying to smile. "The bullet appears to have gone through cleanly, and there's not a lot of bleeding. I have some medical training and some supplies here in the house. I'll take care of my husband. He'll be fine."

Nodding, Gordon looked around at the few men who remained in the room and said, "All right, men. Get these bodies out of here. We'll bury them later. Let's get back to the battle."

SHADOWED MEMORIES

555

TWENTY

The battle raged as the morning wore on. The ear-piercing Rebel yell and the defiant shouts of the men in blue rose and fell with the tide of battle. Soldiers made a mad rush in tight-knit lines across the fields, firing muskets and carbines. Cannons laid down a raking storm of shrapnel and canister, littering each field with the dead and dying. All through the long morning hours, this dance of death went on…and continued as the sun reached its apex and started westward.

A fierce battle raged about a mile due east of Shiloh Church. Some five thousand Federals had established themselves in a ten acre thicket, dense with brush and tall oak. It was a natural bastion, with a sunken road running along one side, the crest of a low hill on another, and wide open fields forming the other two approaches. Confederates coming across those fields faced heavy artillery.

General Braxton Bragg discussed the Union fortress with Johnston and Beauregard, and asked for permission to pull some seven thousand of his men from other fields and launch an attack. Permission was given, and the Yankees soon faced an onslaught of yelling Rebels.

Captains Britt Claiborne and Wayne Gordon and their men,

along with many other companies, were sent to attack the Union stronghold from the side that skirted the hill. Bragg sent another unit against the position along the sunken road. He sent two entire brigades across the open fields. As the Rebels reached the 150-yard range, the Federal guns opened up, raking them with canister in a crossfire, right and left. The long lines rippled like tall grass in the wind as the shot cut through. Many went down, but still the swarm came on.

Soon, Bragg's troops surrounded the Yankee position and began to infiltrate. In some places, they were fighting hand-to-hand. In desperation, the Federals wheeled their cannons around and began firing into the woods behind them, sometimes killing and wounding their own men.

In spite of the artillery fire, the Confederates were undaunted, and the fighting continued heavy into the afternoon. Everywhere, wounded men cried and whimpered. Bodies lay in piles.

At about two o'clock, a Confederate soldier came stumbling out, needing ammunition. He approached a Confederate ammunition wagon and said to the men, "It's a hornet's nest in there!" From that moment, the bloody area was known as the Hornet's Nest.

While the Confederate soldier was unwittingly naming what would become a famous part of the Shiloh battle, deep in the Hornet's Nest, Captain Gordon's company was battling it out with the Yankees. Many of Gordon's men had been killed, and others lay wounded. Others had gotten separated from their comrades amid the smoke of battle.

Gordon had just shot a Yankee who came at him with a bayonet when he realized that he was alone. Only moments before, Sergeants Ben Blanchard, Cliff Nolan, and Ralph Ederly had been fighting next to him, along with a number of other men in his unit. Now they were somewhere out there amid the clamor and roar and smoke of the battle.

Gordon saw two Yankees rushing his way and ducked behind a bush. A few feet away, he saw a Confederate captain down on one knee, aiming his revolver through the brush. The revolver roared once, then again, and both men-in-blue fell dead on a bed of dried leaves.

"Good shooting, Captain!" Gordon said.

"Thank you," the man nodded, breaking his revolver open to reload. Neither man had looked closely at the other.

Gordon peered through the brush for sign of more Yankees. "Looks like you got separated from your company like I did."

"Yeah, you're right."

When the other man snapped his cylinder shut, Gordon looked back at him, and their eyes met.

The man's eyes widened. "Cliff Barrett, is that *you?*"

Gordon blinked at him, nonplused.

"Don't you know me?" the man asked. "We were roommates at West Point. Certainly you haven't forgotten your ol' pal, Mark Haverly!"

Wayne Gordon's heart quickened pace at the captain's words. Cold little needles pricked his spine, running its length. Reaching blankly into his memory, he echoed, "Mark Haverly."

Hearing his name on his old friend's lips, Haverly thought his former roommate recognized him. "Sure is good to see you, Cliff! We haven't seen each other since the day after graduation when you went home to Richmond to marry Julie. I still can't believe I came down sick with influenza and couldn't be your best man. Remember?"

Gordon was speechless, trying to think of a way to explain.

Haverly studied him quizzically and asked, "So how's Julie? I bet you've got a passel of kids by now! How many boys and how many girls? I sure hope the girls look like their mother. What a beauty!"

Gordon's mind was spinning. He was about to blurt out his predicament when three Yankees materialized from the smoke a few yards away, saw them, and raised their muskets to fire. Gordon brought his revolver up and fired. His bullet struck the lead one in the chest. The other two fired into the bush, and one of the slugs hummed by his ear. Gordon shot a second one, and before the third one could bring his bayonet to bear and charge, Gordon put a bullet through his heart. All three lay dead.

Whipping around, Gordon found Haverly with a bullet through his forehead. His heart sank. Here in the midst of battle, he had found a close friend from his past, a man who could give him some answers and… Wait, he had!

Haverly had told him he was a graduate of West Point, that his name was Cliff Barrett, that he was from Richmond, and that…he had married a girl named Julie.

Julie. So his flashbacks and his dreams were accurate. The name that had echoed through his head was correct. Cliff Barrett had married Julie *somebody*. He closed his eyes and saw her once again, as in his dreams, running toward him with love in her eyes, arms outstretched to embrace him.

Suddenly his thoughts turned to Hannah Rose. His insides were churning. "Hannah Rose," he breathed shakily, "this can't be happening! I love you! I don't want to lose you!"

"Captain!" came a loud voice from behind him. "You all right?"

Pivoting, the man who now knew his name was Cliff Barrett focused on the face of Sergeant Ederly. Blinking, he replied, "Yes. Yes, I'm okay." Dropping his gaze to the dead man at his feet, he said, "This was Captain Mark Haverly."

"We missed you, sir," Ederly said. "The bulk of our company is over here a ways."

As Cliff Barrett started to leave, he paused a few seconds and looked at Haverly's face again. They had to have been close friends. Mark was to have been the best man in his wedding.

Thank you, my friend. If I live through this war, I can go to Richmond and find out all about Cliff Barrett. God bless your memory.

* * *

It was nearly 3:00 o'clock when General Johnston's attention focused on a peach orchard just to the south of the Hornet's Nest. The orchard was in full bloom, a glory of pink petals that came down like snow as flying shrapnel and bullets slashed the trees. The rear of the orchard was on the sunken road that ran past the Hornet's Nest, and Federal troops held a line toward its front. Johnston was determined to break that line. He ordered a charge into the orchard by a single brigade of General Breckinridge's corps, and told Breckinridge he would lead it.

Johnston's aide in the Shiloh battle was Tennessee's governor, Isham G. Harris. He had left Nashville with Johnston and accompanied him to Corinth. When the general-in-chief was about to leave Corinth for Shiloh, Harris volunteered to go along as his aide. Honored, Johnston gave him a horse and took him north for the attack on the Union camps.

Leaving Harris in a safe place, Johnston led the charge with Breckinridge at his side. The Yankees offered stiff resistance for about twenty minutes, but the wild charge finally sent them scattering back through the orchard to the safety of the sunken road, where the sounds of fierce battle could still be heard coming from the Hornet's Nest.

Returning to Governor Harris, Johnston said from the saddle, "Governor, they came very near putting me out of the fight in that charge. Look at my boot."

Harris looked down and saw that the general's left boot sole had been sliced off by a bullet and was dangling from the toe. Eyeing it closely for blood, Harris asked, "Are you in pain, sir?"

"No," Johnston said, shaking his head. "Bullet came plenty close, though, didn't it?"

"I'd say so," nodded the governor, noting a couple of places where Johnston's uniform had been nicked. "Any pain there, sir?" he asked, pointing them out.

The general hadn't noticed. Looking down, he rubbed a hand over them and said, "Guess there were a couple of close calls here, too." Johnston's hand went to his forehead, and he seemed to sway in the saddle.

"General, are you sure you're all right?" Harris asked.

Johnston looked down at his right leg, which was opposite from where the governor stood. "Oh, no," he gasped.

Harris, worry etched on his face, hurried around to the horse's right side. It was then that he saw the bullet wound in the bend of Johnston's right knee. The pantleg was soaked with blood, and it was running down into his boot.

"Yes, and I fear right seriously," replied Johnston, about to topple from the horse's back.

Harris reached up as the general started to fall, and eased him to the ground. He called for help, and some nearby soldiers aided him in carrying the wounded general to a tree, where they sat him down so he could lean against it.

Harris told a soldier to run and find a surgeon. But before the surgeon could be found, Albert Sidney Johnston was dead. When the surgeon arrived shortly thereafter and removed the boot, it was full of blood. The bullet had severed an artery and somehow numbed the knee and leg. Johnston had bled to death, not knowing he was hit.

General Beauregard immediately assumed command of the Confederate Army of the Mississippi and ordered that Johnston's body be shrouded for secrecy and that the bad news be suppressed lest it demoralize the troops.

He then turned his full attention to the Hornet's Nest, where the fiercest fighting was going on.

Beauregard found General Bragg riding back and forth along the Hornet's Nest, shouting commands. Beauregard thought it only right that Bragg be informed of General Johnston's death. The bad news infuriated Bragg, putting more drive in him to finish the job at the Hornet's Nest. He conferred briefly with his new commander, then went back to the battle. Within another hour, the end was in sight for the defenders of the Nest. Union withdrawals on their left and right had exposed their flanks, and the furious Rebel infantry charges had hammered their flanks backward until their battle line was in the shape of a horseshoe. With the renewed thrust to Bragg's attack, the Federals were breaking up and pulling out of the open end of the horseshoe.

The battle looked bad for the Union. Grant had sent for Wallace in the early afternoon, but the sun was setting, and the Crump's Landing division had not yet appeared. The Hornet's Nest had crumbled, and all its able-bodied soldiers had made a run for the safety of Pittsburgh Landing.

As the sun dipped below the western horizon, the fields and woods were so full of smoke that hardly anything could be seen. Artillery batteries still pounded away, but most of the cannons were Southern. A struggling Union army, still firing but disheartened at the way the day had gone, moved back toward the landing.

Beauregard pushed his troops in a final effort to drive the Yankees all the way into the Tennessee River. Then suddenly he called for cease fire and ordered his army to fall back quickly. By dusk's faint light, the general had caught sight of Buell's Army of the Ohio marching down the west bank of the Tennessee River.

Darkness fell, and with it came the cries of the wounded from the Hornet's Nest, the surrounding woods, and the open fields. The Federal troops had left their wounded behind with their dead.

Weary and hungry Confederate soldiers denied their own needs until they had carried their wounded into the camp. There were thousands, and very few medics to help them. Acting as angels of mercy, the unscathed Rebels carried water to their wounded comrades.

After the troops were finally able to eat, they sat around the campfires and talked about the battle, wondering what would happen on the morrow. Van Dorn had not arrived with his men, but Buell was at Pittsburgh Landing, adding his sizable force to Grant's otherwise whipped army.

At one campfire, the man who had been called Wayne Gordon sat with the Claiborne brothers, Lanny Perkins, and Sergeants Blanchard, Nolan, and Ederly. The wide-eyed men listened as Gordon told them of meeting Mark Haverly and what he had learned before Haverly was killed.

To Captain Cliff Barrett's friends, the facts were in. He was married to a woman named Julie, and she was most likely waiting for him in Richmond. But all agreed that Cliff wouldn't know for sure until he could get to Richmond and find out for himself.

There was jubilation at Pittsburgh Landing. Don Carlos Buell had arrived with a fresh army of thirty-five thousand, and Lew Wallace and his troops had shown up at 7:00 P.M. Wallace had been delayed because of a mix-up in orders which sent him down the wrong road. Regardless of the delay, Grant was glad to see them. Things would go differently tomorrow.

General Beauregard set up his battle lines the best he could at dawn on Monday, April 7. By eight o'clock, the conflict was once again under way on battlefields already strewn with so many bodies it was difficult for both infantries to maneuver.

With his great numbers, General Grant formed a powerful counterattack, and almost immediately the tide turned for the Union. In spite of the overwhelming odds against them, the Confederates fought back valiantly.

Late in the afternoon, Captain Cliff Barrett's company—now down to 203 men—was fighting in a wooded area near Shiloh Church. Some thirty yards to his left, in the same woods, Captain Britt Claiborne and his company of 197 men were battling it out with a greater number of Union troops coming at them from two sides. The Yankees were in the open fields, inching their infantry steadily closer.

There was heavy brush in the woods, especially along the edges, where the Rebels were doing their fighting. Captain Claiborne was hunkered in thick brush, firing across the open field with his revolver. Flanking him were Nolan and Ederly and two corporals, one of them Lanny Perkins. William and Robert Claiborne had been sent deeper into the woods to carry a wounded lieutenant to a safer place.

A sergeant of Claiborne's company came dashing up, saying he needed help further down the line. Claiborne asked how many men he needed, and the sergeant said at least five. Britt ordered Nolan and Perkins to go with the sergeant, and told them the names of three other men to pick up on the way back down the line.

Claiborne turned back to the battle at hand and found his revolver empty. Dropping low to reload, he broke the gun open and punched out the shells. As he slid the last cartridge into the cylinder, he saw Ederly move away from him a few feet and bring his cocked rifle to bear on him.

Claiborne looked at the rifle, then at Ederly. "What's this?" he asked.

"The last few seconds of your life, Captain," Ederly sneered. "You southern fools thought there was only one killer at Donelson. I'll just tell 'em the Yankees got you, and they'll still think Weathers was the only assassin."

"Drop it, Ederly, or your dead!" boomed William Claiborne, who stood among the trees, his carbine trained on Ederly's head. Beside him was Robert, who also had him covered.

Ederly grimaced and let his weapon drop to the ground. They tied him up with his own belt and shirt, and Britt told his brothers what Ederly had told him.

Ederly was kept flat on the ground while the battle continued. Captains Claiborne and Barrett moved up and down the line periodically, encouraging their men to keep fighting. The Confederates stayed in the battle despite the overwhelming odds. General Beauregard's tactics proved efficient once again. However, as the sun was going down, it was evident that the Federals were taking control. Morning could bring a bloody defeat of the Rebel army.

The weary Federals withdrew to Pittsburgh Landing, and word was passed along the Confederate lines for everyone to sit tight. The generals would send word shortly about their plans to the division and company leaders. If the decision was to abandon the fight, they would pull out under cover of darkness. The men had not been told of General Johnston's death.

The sky was still light in the west when the Confederates in the woods collected into small groups and made themselves comfortable for the night. They didn't bother to regroup into companies, since they had fought in mixtures all day.

Captain Claiborne collected with his brothers and Lanny Perkins in a private spot. Perkins was shocked to learn about Ralph Ederly, who was still tied hand and foot, sitting on the ground. Soon Ben Blanchard appeared, carrying his carbine and wearing an officer's gunbelt. He had a second revolver jammed under his pants belt.

William Claiborne eyed the handguns and said, "Collect some souvenirs, Ben?"

"Might say that," Blanchard nodded, leaning his carbine against a tree. "Took 'em off a couple dead Yankees. Figured they didn't need 'em no more."

At that instant, Blanchard noticed Ederly. "What's this?" he asked.

Britt Claiborne gave a quick explanation of what had happened earlier.

"I'm shocked, Captain," Blanchard said, glaring at Ederly. "Man doesn't know who he can trust any more, does he?"

"That's for sure."

"What are you going to do with him?" Blanchard asked.

"I'll turn him over to General Bragg once he and the other generals are through with their conference. The general will most likely stand him before a firing squad here, or wherever we are by sunrise."

The group decided it was time to eat supper, such as it was.

They had a few rations between them, but not enough.

"Guess it would be all right to go lift some rations off the dead ones, wouldn't it?" asked Robert Claiborne.

"I don't see why not," Britt said. "Let's all go, and we can collect enough real quick."

"What about your prisoner here?" Blanchard asked. "He might just work his way loose while we're gone."

"I think he's pretty secure," Britt said.

"Well, I'll feel better if he's watched," Blanchard said. "I'll just stay here and keep an eye on him."

"Suit yourself," said Britt, hunching his shoulders and turning away.

Ben Blanchard could not afford to wait any longer. Though they were in a private spot in the woods, someone could come along any minute. As soon as the backs of the four men were turned, he whipped out both revolvers, snapped back the hammers, and said, "You can stop right there! Throw your guns down!"

The Claiborne brothers and Perkins halted and turned around, eyeing Blanchard with puzzlement .

"Ben, what're you doing?" Britt asked.

"Takin' you as my prisoners," Blanchard replied coldly. "I said throw those guns down."

When each man's gun was on the ground, Blanchard jerked his head at Robert Claiborne and said, "Untie my partner."

Britt's eyes widened. "Ben, what th—"

"You're smart, Britt. C'mon, now. Figure it out."

Robert stooped to untie Ederly, who was grinning from ear to ear.

"*Three* Union plants?" Britt asked.

"Yep. And it's time for Ralph and me to get back with our own kind. We're takin' you boys to Pittsburgh Landing. That'll make U.S. Grant happy. He'll get us back safely and pick him up a hotshot Rebel captain to boot. These others will just be puddin' to go under the cherry."

"So you two and Weathers were all doing the killing at Donelson."

"Yep. At Corinth, too. And it was me who took out Colonel Parker and his little group of escorts. Some shootin', eh?"

Ederly sprang to his feet, picked up Britt Claiborne's revolver, and said, "Okay, Ben, let's get going before somebody comes along."

"You were fighting against your own men in these battles," Britt said. "You could've taken Yankee bullets at any time. Weren't you taking an awful chance?"

"Sure, but no more'n if we were on the other side of the fight. War's always a gamble. But we've done away with a whole bunch of Rebel officers, and while you plowboys weren't lookin', we've been feedin' information to our military leaders."

Stalling for time, Britt said, "So when you guys were in these battles, you were making sure you missed when you shot at the Yankees."

Blanchard grinned evilly. "See, I said you were smart, didn't I?"

"C'mon, Ben," Ederly said nervously, "let's get outta here!"

"Nobody's going anywhere!" came a sharp voice from the shadows. "Drop those guns!"

Startled, both Union men pivoted to fire in the direction of the voice. A shot rang out and Blanchard went down dead. Ederly's gun fired, but a second shot from the shadows put a slug in his heart, and his bullet went wild.

Every eye was fastened on the figure that emerged from the shadows. It was Cliff Barrett. As the group scrambled to pick up their guns, Barrett broke his revolver open to reload it and said, "I decided to let Blanchard shoot off his mouth as much as possible before I moved in. Looks like this clears up the whole thing."

Word came before midnight from General Beauregard that the Confederate army was going to withdraw and head for Corinth. They would pull out two hours before dawn. Since the fighting was over, Beauregard released the bad news that General Johnston was dead.

The weary Rebels laid down to get what rest they could, relieved that they wouldn't have to go up against the Union's much larger numbers in another day of battle. All over the camp, words of sorrow were spoken over their beloved leader's death.

When Beauregard's message reached the Claiborne and Barrett companies, Cliff said to Britt, "Captain, since we're backtracking to Corinth, I'm going to see if General Bragg will let me have some time to go to Hannah Rose and tell her what I know about myself, then make tracks for Richmond. If he'll permit it, I can clear up this awful blank in my life."

"Well, let's go see what the man says," said Britt, laying a hand on his shoulder. "If there's any chance I can have you as my brother-in-law, I'd sure like to see it happen."

Barrett and Claiborne sought out General Bragg. When they found him, Cliff told the general about learning who he was and laid out his request for time to clear up the vital matters in his life.

Bragg, a crusty old soldier, rubbed his scraggly beard and looked at Barrett. "I'm glad you found out your name, and that you're a West Point graduate, Captain. I'm sure it's good for you to know where you're from, too. But this is war. And in war, a man's personal life has to take a back seat. We've got to get this army to Corinth and make ready to fight again. Permission denied."

Cliff's heart sank. He looked at Britt, then said softly, "I understand, General. Thank you for your time."

The captains turned and walked away. They had gone some twenty yards when General Bragg's voice cut through the night air. "Captain Barrett!"

"Yes, sir?" Cliff said, halting and turning around.

"Come here a minute."

Britt waited while Cliff hurried back to the general.

As Cliff drew up, Bragg said, "Wasn't it you who killed that Donelson assassin...what was his name?"

"Randall Weathers, sir. Yes, sir."

"And you saved Captain Claiborne's life when you did it, right?"

"Yes, sir, and…well, Captain Claiborne can tell you that there were actually three assassins. I killed the other two, also."

"*Three?* You did?"

"Yes, sir."

Looking toward Britt, the general called, "Captain Claiborne! Come, please!"

Britt moved swiftly past other soldiers who were milling about. "Yes, sir?"

"Tell me about these other two assassins Captain Barrett killed."

Britt quickly told Bragg about the incident with Ederly and Blanchard, explaining how they had admitted that they and Weathers were Union plants. He flourished it good when he described how Blanchard and Ederly were going to take several of them to the Union camp, and how Captain Barrett moved in and shot them down.

Smiling, Bragg looked at Barrett and said, "Tell you what, Captain. I've changed my mind. You've earned a little time off. We won't be in another battle for a while, I'm sure. I'll write up the order. You can have three weeks, then you must report to me at Corinth."

Smiling broadly, Captain Barrett said, "Thank you, sir!"

Bragg quickly scribbled the order and put it in Barrett's hand. "See you in Corinth on April 30, Captain."

TWENTY-ONE

The Claiborne women cleaned up the kitchen after breakfast on Thursday morning, April 10, and sat down at the table to pray for their men. They had learned the day before about the bloody battle at Shiloh, Tennessee, and they knew Britt, William, Robert, Wayne, and Lanny would be in the thick of it.

Their neighbor, Walter Manning, had brought them a copy of the *Dover Sentinel* at midmorning on Wednesday. The paper had given what details were available, explaining that many hundreds had been killed and wounded on Sunday, and the battle was continuing as of Monday morning. Sunday's battle had gone decidedly well for the Confederacy.

Hannah Rose had gathered the others into the kitchen on Wednesday to thank the Lord that things had gone well on Sunday and to pray for their men.

As they sat around the table on Thursday morning, Hannah Rose laid her Bible on the table and said, "Before we pray, I want to read a passage that came to mind as I was lying in bed last night. I read it first thing this morning, and in my private time with the Lord, I claimed it for our men. It's in the Ninety-first Psalm."

The others began flipping pages in their Bibles. Hannah Rose looked around to make sure everybody had the passage before them, then she began to read:

> "He that dwelleth in the secret place of the most High shall abide under the shadow of the Almighty. I will say of the Lord, He is my refuge and my fortress: my God; in him will I trust. Surely he shall deliver thee from the snare of the fowler, and from the noisome pestilence. He shall cover thee with his feathers, and under his wings shalt thou trust: his truth shall be thy shield and buckler.

> "Thou shalt not be afraid for the terror by night; nor for the arrow that flieth by day; nor for the pestilence that walketh in darkness; nor for the destruction that wasteth at noonday. A thousand shall fall at thy side, and ten thousand at thy right hand; but it shall not come nigh thee."

"That's wonderful," Donna Mae said. "I've read this passage more times than I can count, but I'd never thought of these verses, especially five and seven, speaking about men at war. But there it is—the arrow that flieth by day. Thousands of men falling in the battle, but certain ones being protected."

Sally Marie wiped tears and said, "Oh, Hannah Rose, we must claim these verses for our men."

"Yes, I agree," Hannah Rose nodded.

With their Bibles open before them, the four women bowed their heads and prayed around the table, each asking God to protect the men they loved and to bring them back safely one day. Each one asked that the Lord give them the faith to claim the passage they had just read for their men.

They were all weeping and dabbing at their noses with hankies when the last amen was said. Suddenly there was a knock at the front door.

"I'll get it," said Linda Lee, pushing back her chair and hurrying through the house.

She opened the front door to find elderly Walter Manning with a sad look on his face, holding a folded newspaper.

"Good morning, Mr. Manning. Is there bad news?"

"'Fraid so, honey," Manning replied, handing her the morning edition of the *Sentinel*. "Looks like we got whipped at Shiloh after all. General Johnston got killed on Sunday, and after the Yankees brought in massive numbers of troops Sunday night, General Beauregard led our men to fight them anyhow on Monday. We were whipped bad, Linda Lee. What's left of our army is on its way back to Corinth. Paper says we put up a great fight, but they flat outnumbered us. They don't have any idea how many have been killed and wounded, but looks like it's gonna be up in the thousands."

At that moment the other three women appeared. "It's all there in the paper," he said, pointing at the folded newspaper in Linda Lee's hand. "Well, I gotta get home to my missus and break the bad news to her. See y'all later."

The Claiborne women went to the kitchen, and leaning over the table together, spread the newspaper before them. The headlines read:

THOUSANDS KILLED AT BLOODY SHILOH!
Army of Mississippi, Vastly
Outnumbered Puts Up Gallant
Fight. Retreats to Corinth!

Saddened by the news, the four women prayed around the table again, asking God to give them the faith to lay hold of the Scriptures they had just read and to believe that their men were still alive.

It was late morning and the women were working in the sewing room, when they heard a knock at the front door.

"I'll get it," Linda Lee said, laying down the blouse she was trimming with lace and dashing out the door.

Her jaw slacked when she opened the door and saw the familiar face of the man in the captain's uniform. "Wayne!" she gasped. Turning to call over her shoulder, she shouted, "Hannah Rose! It's Wayne! Wayne's here!"

Cliff Barrett entered the parlor just as Hannah Rose ran in with her sisters-in-law on her heels. "Wayne!" she cried, rushing into his arms.

While Hannah Rose clung to the man she loved, weeping and thanking the Lord for his safe return, the others pumped him for answers about their men.

Holding Hannah Rose close, Cliff told them that Britt, William, Robert, and Lanny had all come through the battle unscathed. The women filled the room with praises to the Lord, shedding tears of relief and thankfulness. Then they sat down and listened as the handsome young captain told them every detail of the Shiloh battle, including the shooting of the Donelson assassins. The women fired questions at him right and left, and he answered each one as accurately as he could.

When they were satisfied that their men were safely on their way to Corinth, Barrett reached inside his uniform coat and produced four battered, folded pieces of paper. "I must apologize for the awful condition of these letters, ladies," he said, smiling, "but this paper's all we had to use."

There were shrieks of joy as the captain handed each woman her letter. Robert's letter, he placed in Hannah Rose's hand.

Looking around at her sister and sisters-in-law, who clutched the letters to their breasts, Hannah Rose said, "I know you will want to read your letters in the privacy of your rooms, so let me first read Robert's to you, which is addressed to all of us."

When Robert's letter had been read, evoking more tears and "God bless hims," the three young women went to their rooms, leaving Cliff and Hannah Rose alone.

When they had embraced once more and kissed each other

soundly, Hannah Rose stroked his cheek and said, "Oh, Wayne, I'm so thankful you've come back safely. But there's one thing I don't understand."

"What's that?"

"How come you're able to be here, but my brothers are on their way to Corinth?"

"Because of you," he said, rising from the couch.

"Me?"

"Yes. General Bragg is aware of my amnesia. You see, Hannah Rose, I...I learned who I am during the Shiloh battle."

Hannah Rose sprang off the couch, gasping, "You did? You did? And you're back here? That means—"

"Not so fast," he said, raising his palms toward her. "There's a lot to tell you."

"Well, before we get into how you found out, and who you are, I have to know—are you married?"

"I don't know yet," he sighed. "Sit down, please, and let me tell it to you in some semblance of order."

While the man she loved remained on his feet, Hannah Rose eased down on the couch without taking her eyes off him. "Before you start, could I at least know your real name?" she asked.

"Of course," he said, smiling. "It's Cliff Barrett. Probably Clifford Barrett. And I'm from Richmond."

Staring at the floor, Hannah Rose tested the name on her tongue. "Clifford Barrett. Cliff...Cliff." Raising her eyes to him, she said, "Yes, that fits you better than Wayne. I like it. The last name, too."

"Thank you," he smiled.

"Now, I'll be quiet. Tell me all about it."

A bit shaky, Cliff Barrett first told Hannah Rose about the flashback he had experienced during the fight with Club Clubson. Just that much brought a cold, heavy feeling to Hannah Rose's heart.

He told her about the dreams in which he saw the yard, the big white house, the trees, the flowers, and the young woman running toward him with arms outstretched. He had been sure without a doubt that her name was Julie.

Hannah Rose's heart grew heavier.

He described his chance meeting with Mark Haverly, who identified him as Cliff Barrett, his old friend and roommate at West Point, and that Cliff had left immediately after graduation to go home to Richmond and marry a girl named Julie.

Hannah Rose was feeling a bit faint, but covered it. Inside she prayed, *Lord Jesus, give me strength. I can't face this without Your help.*

Cliff told Hannah Rose that Haverly had been killed before he could find out more, but what he had learned was a good beginning, for which he had thanked the Lord. Proceeding, he explained that General Bragg had given him a three-week leave to come see her and to make the trip to Richmond to clear up the mystery of his past.

When he finished, Hannah Rose was biting her lip and trying not to cry. "Oh, Wayne—*Cliff*, I'm scared. Scared that you'll go home and find Julie waiting for you."

Taking her hand, he helped her off the couch and folded her in his arms. He held her close and half-whispered, "I'm scared, too. Maybe *frightened* is a better word. I get cramps in my stomach just thinking about going home. But...I have no choice."

"I know. It's just that...I'm not sure I can stand it if you don't...don't come back to me."

The emotion of it all was too much for them. They clung to each other and cried. Fighting the awful ache in his heart, he said, "I have to keep telling myself that Romans 8:28 is still in the Bible. And...I keep quoting Proverbs 3:5 and 6 to myself, over and over."

"Me, too," said Hannah Rose, looking up at him.

"We don't always understand God's ways," Cliff said softly, "but this whole thing is in His hands. We must trust Him, believing that He never does wrong, He doesn't make mistakes."

Hannah Rose nodded, then laid her head against his chest.

After a long moment, he said, "If...somehow it turns out that I'm not married, I'll come back to you as fast as I can. After we marry, I'll have to report back to General Bragg at Corinth. I'm due to report in on April 30."

Hannah Rose clung to him silently.

Cliff went on, his voice choking. "If I am married…I guess all I can do is write and tell you so…and never return."

Hot tears coursed down Hannah Rose's cheeks. All she could do was nod and press her head tighter against him.

"Hannah Rose," he said past the lump in his throat, "this whole thing is so unfair to you. If it turns out that I'm married, you've wasted all the love you've poured out on me. What a horrible thing for you to—"

Her forefinger was pressed hard against his lips. "Don't," she whispered. "My love for you, Cliff Barrett, knows no bounds. I would rather have had what little time we've known together—and had your love, at least for a little while—than to have loved anyone else. I mean that, darling."

"Oh, Hannah Rose, you're the most wonderful woman God ever made. I'm so sorry you have to face—"

Again her finger was pressed to his lips. "Listen to me," she breathed softly. "I will be waiting for you…or your letter. Just remember that I love you with all my heart."

He kissed her forehead. Then silently, Cliff Barrett and Hannah Rose Claiborne walked out onto the porch together. His horse nickered at the sight of them. They held each other for a long, painful moment, and kissed fervently. Then Cliff wheeled, hurried off the porch, and swung into the saddle.

Tears streamed down Hannah Rose's cheeks as she moved to the edge of the porch and dropped down to the first step, steadying herself with the banister.

The horse danced about nervously, bobbing its head as if it felt the emotional strain in the air. Cliff looked at Hannah Rose tenderly. Her lovely chestnut hair was shining in the sun, framing her tear-stained face. He felt as though his heart was bleeding. The silence between them was excruciating, but there was nothing more to say.

He pulled the horse's head around, put the animal into a canter, and rode away.

He did not look back.

On Monday, April 14, Captain Cliff Barrett arrived in Richmond, Virginia, by rail, having brought his horse in a flat-bedded stock car. When the animal was unloaded, he saddled it and rode toward the center of town. He had decided to hunt up the town constable's office. The constable would surely know Cliff Barrett, and could tell him where to find Julie or his parents...or both.

Traffic was heavy in Richmond as Barrett rode slowly along the main thoroughfare. He saw many men-in-gray milling about, which made him feel better. His presence would not attract attention. Richmond was his hometown, according to Mark Haverly, but nothing looked familiar to him. It might as well have been a town in some foreign country.

It didn't take much effort to locate the constable's office. A sign hung over the door, freshly painted, that read:

Richmond Constable's Office
Tom Berry, Chief

Hauling up, Cliff dismounted and wrapped the reins around the hitch rail. He was vaguely aware of an older couple who had just walked passed and were looking back at him. "Sure enough, it *is* Cliff, honey," the man said.

The amnesia victim thought about hurrying after them, but decided he should talk to the constable. Crossing the boardwalk, he found the door partially open and stepped inside.

Sixty-year-old Tom Berry was at his desk, working over a stack of papers with his head bent low.

Papers. Boring papers, Cliff thought, then wondered what put such a thought in his mind.

"Chief Berry?"

Berry's head jerked up. Focusing on the tall man, he said, "Sorry, son, I didn't hear you come in."

"Interesting stuff, eh?" Cliff said, noting that the man showed no recognition of him.

Dropping the pencil in his hand, Berry said, "Boring's what it is."

Same word I used, Cliff thought. Aloud, he said, "I'm Cliff Barrett."

A smile broke on the lawman's face. Rising quickly, he extended his hand and said, "Well, I do declare! I sure have heard enough about *you*, young fellow! Folks around here think you hung the moon!" Looking him over, he added, "Uniform looks good on you. Better than what we law officers wear, eh? Some change for you, I'd say. A *good* change, I mean."

"I'm...not sure I follow you," Cliff said.

"I, uh...was comparing the clothes you wore when you had my job with those you're wearing now."

Suddenly Cliff realized why he had the instincts that had cropped up so often when he needed them. He was a lawman!

"Ah...Chief," he said, "would you have a few minutes to talk to me?"

"Sure, my boy," Berry grinned. "Be better than this paper work. It's like watching grass grow."

Both men took a seat, and Cliff told him the story of his amnesia, bringing him up to the moment. Accepting it without question, the older man explained that Cliff was Richmond's chief constable up until the war started. He had resigned to reenter the army. Another man had followed Cliff, but was killed in the line of duty just three weeks ago. Berry had come from Roanoke to take the job. He had two deputies that were out of town on errands.

"I realize you're new here, Chief," said Cliff, "but would you happen to know a woman named Julie Barrett?"

Berry pursed his lips, then shook his head. "No, can't say that I do. But come to think of it, I remember somebody telling me that your pa is Reverend Micaiah Barrett, pastor of Richmond's First Baptist Church."

Though the information brought back no memories, it did explain why he had such a thorough knowledge of the Bible.

Rising from his chair, Cliff said, "Chief Berry, you've been a great help. Just one more thing. Could you direct me to the home of Micaiah Barrett?"

"No problem. Your ma and pa live in the parsonage, which is right next to the church. I…ah…haven't been inside the church because I'm a Presbyterian, you understand."

"Well, my memory may be bad, Chief, but I don't think those Baptists would bite the nose off a Presbyterian if he visited their services."

Berry chuckled. "Probably not. I just might do it some time. I hear your pa is quite the preacher. Hurry on home now, and see those parents of yours."

"I will when you tell me where to find the church and parsonage."

"Oh, yeah! That'd help, wouldn't it? You probably noticed you're on First Street."

"Mm-hmm."

"Well you go south two blocks to Third Street, then turn left and go two blocks to Oak Street. Church is right on that corner."

Thanking the lawman for his help, Cliff Barrett rode south to Third Street, turned left, and headed east toward Oak. His stomach was in his mouth and his heart drummed his ribs. The drumming became more intense when the steeple on the church building came into view, its lofty point showing above the treetops. As he drew closer, he saw the sign in front of the glistening white building, identifying it as First Baptist Church, and Reverend Micaiah Barrett as pastor.

He was nearing the corner where the church stood when an elderly man called to him from the front porch of a house. "Hey! Cliff Barrett! Welcome home!"

Cliff lifted a hand in a friendly gesture, but said nothing.

"Tell your pa I was sick Sunday, Cliff, but I'll be back in church this Lord's Day!"

"Will do," Cliff nodded and waved.

Crossing the intersection, he veered his horse toward the church yard when the parsonage came into view, standing elegant and white in the brilliant sunshine. Giant cottonwoods towered over it, casting shade on the roof and the flower gardens that adorned the base of the front porch. Bushes and trees, interspersed with smaller flower gardens, surrounded the large yard. Though he did not remember the place from the past, he most certainly recognized it from his dreams. It was exactly as he had seen it.

The house sat back some distance from the street. Cliff's mouth was dry as a sandpit when he skirted the church building and headed for the house. He saw movement at a first-floor window, then the front door flew open and the woman he had seen in his dreams darted across the porch, down the steps, and opened her arms.

Julie.

He dismounted, and she met him with tears in her eyes, crying, "Oh, Cliff, darling! You're home! You're home!"

Cliff mechanically took Julie in his arms. How could he be a husband to a woman he didn't even know?

But he knew that he must. It was only right that he return to his role as Julie's husband and the father of his children, if he had any. It was he who had changed. Not Julie and the children. They were innocent and should not be made to do without him because of his love for Hannah Rose. And it would not be right before God.

While Julie wept and he embraced her dutifully, he saw a mental picture of Hannah Rose. But the picture was growing dim. He could feel her slipping away. He would never see her again. Never hold her again. Her sweet lips would never—

"Clifford!" a woman shrieked.

He looked up to see a lovely fiftyish woman descending the

porch steps with a man about the same age following her...a man Cliff imagined he would look like in about twenty-five years. This was his father, all right. No question about it.

Julie released Cliff so he could embrace the older couple, who were shedding tears of relief and delight to see him.

Looking down at them, Cliff smiled and said, "It's so good to see you, Mother. You too, Dad."

Both of them looked at him askance. Grace Barrett frowned and said, "Clifford, dear, you've always called us Mama and Pop. Are you all right? Is something wrong?"

Cliff nodded gravely with a haunted look on his face. "Yes, something is wrong. I have amnesia. I...don't remember you and Pop. I don't remember Julie, either."

The three people were stunned.

Laying a hand on his shoulder, Micaiah Barrett said, "Son, I...let's all go in the house. This has us rather confused."

Cliff Barrett sat in the large parlor with Julie and his parents and told them the story of his amnesia, going all the way back to that frosty night when he came to on the battlefield under the shadow of Fort Donelson. He explained about his flashbacks, how Julie's name came to his mind, and of seeing her and the house in the dreams that followed. He said nothing about his feelings for Hannah Rose.

As he spoke, he knew something was awry. His parents kept sending strange glances at Julie, and she turned pale and looked at the floor.

When Cliff finished, Julie would not meet his gaze. Micaiah Barrett stood up, wringing his hands, and said, "Clifford, we are sorry that this has happened to you. And we'll be praying that the Lord will restore your memory. But...well, I'm sure you're assuming something here that isn't true. You need to be filled in on the facts.

"Of course your mother and I remember you telling us about your good friend Mark Haverly. But since Mark was ill and couldn't come for the wedding, there was something he didn't know."

Grace Barrett pulled a hanky from her sleeve and dabbed at her eyes. Julie interlaced her fingers, squeezing hard enough to turn them white, and only stared at the floor.

Rising from the couch to meet his father's gaze, Cliff said, "Go on, Pop."

Amazed at how much he and his father resembled each other, Cliff listened intently as the godly man told him that during the weeks he was home from West Point during Christmas of 1855, he and Julie became engaged. They had gone together since high school. Cliff was to graduate the following May, and the wedding was set for the first Sunday in June. However, during those months from December to May, Julie had met a handsome, dashing army officer and let him sweep her off her feet. She had run off with him the very day Cliff had left West Point to come home.

Cliff was devastated to learn what Julie had done. He pulled himself together, however, and reported for army duty at a military installation near Winchester, Virginia. With no action, he soon found army life dull. While visiting home the following summer, he was on First Street in Richmond when a gang of five hoodlums tried to break one of their friends out of the town jail.

Cliff was in his lieutenant's uniform and wearing his service revolver. He jumped in to help the town's constable, who was facing the gang alone. In the fracas, the chief was killed after cutting down one of them, but Cliff cut down two more and captured the remaining two.

Because of the way he had handled the situation, the townspeople asked Cliff if he would resign from the army and become their chief constable. Cliff liked the idea and took them up on it.

As Richmond's chief constable, Cliff proved himself a capable lawman. He was especially good at tracking down and capturing criminals. When the Civil War broke out, Cliff re-enlisted as a lieutenant, but soon was promoted to the rank of captain.

Cliff had fought in the battle at Rich Mountain, Virginia, on July 11, 1861. During that battle, several Rebel soldiers deserted and hightailed it into the Blue Ridge Mountains to hide out. Because of

Cliff's reputation for tracking criminals, General Robert E. Lee commissioned him to go into the mountains and track them down.

Cliff missed the battle at Bull Run because he was on the trail of the deserters. He was successful in tracking them down, but had to kill a couple of them in the process. Shortly thereafter, General Lee sent him to track down nearly a hundred deserters from the Bull Run battle. He was kept busy as a tracker until late January 1862. He caught the last of them hiding in the woods just east of Charlottesville, Virginia, and turned them in to the army post at Charlottesville.

Micaiah showed his son a letter he had sent home from Charlottesville, dated February 1. It told how some inside assailant was murdering officers at Fort Donelson, Tennessee, and that because of Cliff's reputation as a proficient lawman, Lee was sending him to Fort Donelson to see if he could ferret out the killer.

The letter capped off the picture for Cliff Barrett. He had left Charlottesville upon posting the letter and headed southwest into Tennessee. He had arrived at the fort while the battle was raging, and a Yankee bullet had creased his head, knocking him down and out.

While Julie wept, Micaiah explained to his son that Julie's marriage had not been a pleasant one. She had learned the first week that she had made a grave mistake. She was still in love with Cliff. But since she had made the mistake, she told herself she would have to live with it. Julie's husband was a major in the Confederate army, serving under General Pierre G.T. Beauregard. He was killed at Bull Run.

Just six weeks ago, Julie had returned to Richmond and had come to the parsonage. Micaiah had been her pastor, and she wanted counsel from him and to talk to him and Grace about her horrible mistake.

She told them of her bad marriage, and of her husband being killed, and asked their forgiveness for jilting their son. They readily forgave her. Julie's parents had moved to Atlanta a year previously, so she asked if she could stay with the Barretts until Cliff came home, which he was bound to do sooner or later. She wanted to admit her mistake, tell him that she still loved him, and ask his forgiveness. If Cliff still loved her, things just might work out between them.

Julie sat on the chair, sniffling and dabbing at her eyes during the entire time Micaiah told her story. When Micaiah finished, he looked at his son and asked, "Can you find it in your heart to forgive this precious girl for what she did?"

Cliff Barrett's mind was awhirl. He was not married to Julie! He was free to marry Hannah Rose!

"I have no problem forgiving Julie," he managed to say.

"Wonderful!" exclaimed the preacher.

"I knew you'd forgive her, son," Grace said.

Cliff knelt before the young woman with the red, swollen eyes, and said in a tender tone, "Julie, all of us are human, and we can make some awful mistakes at times. You made a big one, I agree. But I want you to know that I forgive you."

Julie burst into sobs and lunged to embrace him. He avoided her grasp and stood up. As she rose to her feet, looking at him with puzzled eyes, he said, "Please don't misunderstand, Julie. Forgiving you doesn't mean I want you back. There is someone else in my life, now."

While Julie stood in stunned silence, Cliff turned to his parents and said, "Remember I told you about Hannah Rose Claiborne taking me in and nursing me back to health?"

"Yes, of course," his father said.

"During that time, we fell in love. We tried not to, but it happened anyway. She's waiting to hear from me. If I found out I was married, I was to write her a letter saying so, and we would never see each other again. She loves me enough to wait for me...and to marry me if I'm free to do so."

"Is she a Christian, Clifford?" asked Grace.

"Yes, Mama!" responded the happy man. "The best! Oh, praise the Lord! Romans 8:28 is still in the Book! All things do work together for good to them that love God! If that bullet hadn't given me amnesia, I would never have met my wonderful Hannah Rose!"

Julie had slipped away to her room while Cliff was telling his parents about Hannah Rose. Looking around for her, he said, "I'll talk to Julie before I leave in the morning. I'm sorry her marriage was bad, but I'm sure the Lord has someone for a young widow like her."

"Do you have to go so soon, son?" his father asked.

"Oh, yes, sir. I can't keep Hannah Rose waiting. I wish you could perform the ceremony, but I'm going to marry her, then head for Corinth to report to General Bragg. When this horrible war is over, I'll bring your wonderful daughter-in-law home for you to meet. I know you'll love her! She's the sweetest, most wonderful woman the Lord ever made!"

TWENTY-TWO

It was midmorning on a bright sunny day, and Hannah Rose Claiborne was home alone, working on dress orders. Linda Lee, Donna Mae, and Sally Marie were visiting Aunt Myrtle.

Glancing at the calendar on the wall of the sewing room, Hannah Rose sighed, "April nineteenth. It's been nine days. Oh, Cliff, what has happened?"

As each day had passed, the melancholy young woman had marked it off the calendar, and yesterday her hopes had begun to die. While no letter had come telling her Cliff was married, neither had the man she loved returned.

Sighing, Hannah Rose decided to go outside and get a breath of fresh air. It was spring in Tennessee, and the dogwood was in bloom, filling the air with its lovely aroma. She settled on the old swing, idly pushing against the porch with her foot.

She inhaled deeply of the dogwood and recalled the conversation at the breakfast table that morning. Linda Lee and her sisters-in-law had told her that she just as well face it. The war was slowing the mail, and the letter Cliff had sent would be a long time coming. Cliff Barrett was a married man, and Hannah Rose would never see him again. She might as well start looking for another man.

Clearly she recalled her reply. If she couldn't be Cliff Barrett's wife, she would be an old maid.

Hannah Rose's eye caught movement on the grassy hills to the east. A lone rider on horseback was coming her way. They were too far away for her to identify the rider, but the horse was the same color as Cliff's—the horse he was falling from the very first time she saw him.

She left the swing and made her way to the edge of the porch. She shaded her eyes with her hand and watched intently, almost not believing her eyes as the rider drew closer.

Her heart hammered in her breast, and a lump formed and lodged in her throat.

It was Cliff!

Lifting her long skirt calf-high, she flew off the porch and ran toward him, her long chestnut-colored hair flying in the breeze. When they were some twenty yards apart, Cliff slid from the saddle and ran to meet her, taking her in his arms.

"Oh, Cliff!" she cried, tears streaming down her face. "You're not married to Julie!"

"No, darling, I never was. I've never been married to anyone! There's only one woman God made for me, and I'm about to kiss her like she's never been kissed before!"

EPILOGUE

After "Bloody Shiloh," the bruised and battered Confederate Army of the Mississippi stumbled back to Corinth. Though the battle was considered a Union victory, both sides suffered horrible losses. Shiloh was the scene of the first epic bloody land battle in the West, and one of the fiercest combats in the history of American arms. It was a cruel baptism of fire for the soldiers of the West on both sides, with nearly 24,000 casualties. Of those, the *U.S. Official Records* lists 1,754 Yankees and 1, 728 Rebels killed.

The most notable casualty was General-in-Chief Albert Sidney Johnston, leader of the Army of the Mississippi. He holds the distinction of being the highest ranking officer during the entire Civil War to meet his death in battle.

Union and Confederate hospitals were jammed, and urgent calls for nurses and doctors were sent out. In addition to the nearly 3,500 killed, an estimated 16,000 men, who a few days before were hale and hearty, now faced amputations, festering wounds, and disease that would eventually account for many more deaths. Doctors reported that eight out of every ten amputations ended in death.

There were no drugs to combat tetanus and gangrene, and supplies of chloroform were quickly exhausted. Workers at every hospital had to dig huge holes to bury massive numbers of amputated limbs.

General Earl Van Dorn's long-delayed army never arrived at Shiloh. The weather and many other obstacles held them up. They finally appeared at Corinth in early May, weary, worn, and footsore.

The outcome of Shiloh pointed the way to a long and bloody conflict ahead. The situation appeared extremely grim for the Confederacy in the West. Not only had they been driven from Shiloh, but they lost Island Number Ten at the same time to the Union naval and land forces. The loss of the highly effective batteries located on the island meant the opening of the Mississippi River to Union gunboat traffic.

After the success at Shiloh, Major General Henry W. Halleck consolidated the Union's western forces into an army of 128,000 and marched them from Pittsburgh Landing toward Corinth to engage what remained of the Confederate Army of the Mississippi. However, the difficulty of assembling such a massive army and marching it even a relatively short distance, kept the Union forces from arriving at Corinth until the last of May. By that time General Pierre G.T. Beauregard's army had withdrawn from the area.

The Battle of "Bloody Shiloh" remains one of the most horrendous in Civil War history. In the days that followed, as Northern and Southern newspapers published the facts and figures, along with photographs taken of the battlefield the day after, the populace was stunned. The details of horror and bloodshed left readers appalled, especially when they read of the Hornet's Nest. Reporters wrote that the bodies of Union and Confederate soldiers were so numerous that one could walk over the entire Shiloh battlefield and never set foot on the ground.

Brigadier General James A. Garfield served in the Twentieth

Brigade, Sixth Division, Army of the Ohio, and later became the twentieth president of the United States. Although he was not present at Shiloh, he reflected on it shortly thereafter with these words: "No blaze of glory that flashes around the magnificent triumphs of war can ever atone for the unwritten and unutterable horrors of the scene of carnage."

The Battle Begins…

ISBN: 1-59052-945-6

Volume 1

A Promise Unbroken (Battle of Rich Mountain)
As the first winds of Civil War sweep across the Virginia countryside, the
wealthy Ruffin family is torn by forces that threaten their way of life and,
ultimately, their promises to one another. Mandrake and Orchid, slaves on
the Ruffin plantation, must also fight for the desire of their hearts.
Heartache and victory. Jealousy and racial hatred. From a prosperous
Virginia plantation to a grim jail cell outside of Lynchburg, follow the
dramatic story of love indestructible.

A Heart Divided (Battle of Mobile Bay)
Wounded early in the Civil War, Captain Ryan McGraw is nursed back to
health by army nurse Dixie Quade. In her tender care, love's seed is sown.
But with the sudden appearance of Victoria, the wife who once abandoned
Ryan, and the five-year-old son he never knew he had, come threats
endangering the lives of everyone involved. Between the deadly forces of
war and two loves, McGraw is caught with *a heart divided*.

The Battle Continues...

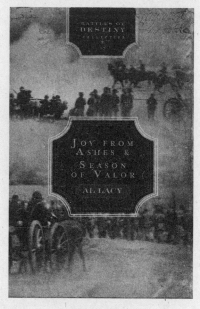

ISBN: 1-59052-947-2

Volume 3

Joy From Ashes (Battle of Fredericksburg)
While fighting to defend his home and family against Union attack, Major Layne Dalton learns that enemy soldiers have brutalized his wife. Tragically, the actions of three cruel-hearted Heglund brothers have caused not only the suffering of his bride, but also the death of Layne and Melody's unborn son. Thirsting for vengeance, the young major vows to bring judgment upon those responsible, yet surprising circumstances make Dalton—presumed dead by his wife and fellow soldiers—a prisoner of the very men he swore he would destroy.

Season of Valor (Battle of Gettysburg)
As teenagers, Shane Donovan and Ashley Kilrain promise to love each other forever. But when Ashley's parents decide to return to Ireland and take their daughter with them, the sweethearts sadly bid each other farewell and accept their fate.

After several years, both have found other loves and married. So when Ashley returns to Maine and the friendship between the two is rekindled, Shane and Ashley find that a new kind of love is needed to overcome the sprouting seeds of tragedy in their freshly intertwined lives.